EXTRAORDINAR
ANNA LEE WALDO'S
MASTERFUL BESTSELLER <u>SACAJAWEA</u>

"Anna Lee Waldo writes her story in a manner . . . akin to the slow but satisfying knitting of a colorful afghan, filling in the gaping holes in our history."
—*Spectrum* magazine

"Exceptional."
—*St. Louis Post-Dispatch*

"Engrossing."
—*Detroit News*

"A blockbuster first novel."
—*Fort Worth Star-Telegram*

"Magnificently entertaining . . . This is a novel that should be read by anyone who hasn't already done so."
—*Berkeley Gazette*

"Ms. Waldo's exhaustive research takes the reader on a fascinating, in-depth journey."
—*Daily Herald-News*

"A work of uncompromising scholarship and brilliance. It is one of the great books of this or any decade."
—*The Courier Gazette*

Also by Anna Lee Waldo

Sacajawea
Prairie

CIRCLE OF STONES

ANNA LEE WALDO

St. Martin's Paperbacks

CIRCLE OF STONES

Copyright © 1999 by Anna Lee Waldo.

All rights reserved. No part of this book may be used or reproduced in any manner whatsoever without written permission except in the case of brief quotations embodied in critical articles or reviews. For information address St. Martin's Press, 175 Fifth Avenue, New York, N.Y. 10010.

Library of Congress Catalog Card Number: 98-43611

ISBN: 0-312-97061-7

Printed in the United States of America

St. Martin's Press hardcover edition / April 1999
St. Martin's Paperbacks edition / March 2000

St. Martin's Paperbacks are published by St. Martin's Press, 175 Fifth Avenue, New York, N.Y. 10010.

10 9 8 7 6 5 4 3 2 1

Epigraphs

In the epigraphs, the reader will notice that some of the place names are archaic names for places that may have different modern-day names. Also, one may find spelling inconsistencies in some of the quoted material, especially in proper names. These variations are because the spellings of. Welsh names often differ slightly with various authors. For example: Rien is sometimes spelled Rhun; Iorwerth may be spelled Iowerth; Riyd is Rhiryd or Eiryd; David is Daffyd; Howell is Howel, Howyl, or Hywyll; Owen is Owain; Christiannt is Cristiant or Christiant; Snowdon is Snowden; Curragh is Currach; Gladys is Gwladys; Becket is Beckett; Degannwy is Deganwy or Deganway; and Dubh Linn is Dublin, etc. Each quotation uses the spelling of its particular author, and in *Circle of Stones*, I have tried to use spellings that seemed most common for the twelfth century.

For permission to reproduce the epigraphs at the beginning of each part and chapter openers, I give my heartfelt thanks to the following:

Who Discovered America? by Zella Armstrong © 1950 by The Lookout Publishing Company; *Thomas Becket* © 1986 by Frank Barlow; *Touring Guide of Wales* edited by Russell Beach © 1975 by the Automobile Association; *Letters and Notes on the Manners, Customs and Conditions of North American Indians, Volume II* by George Catlin © 1973 by Dover Publications, Inc.; "Dublin" by Maurice James Craig © 1965 by Encyclopedia Britannica, Inc.; *Guffudd ap Cynan,*

Fondly dedicated
to my husband, Bill, and
to Kloochman, who has grown into
Patricia Gwyn, our Welsh child.

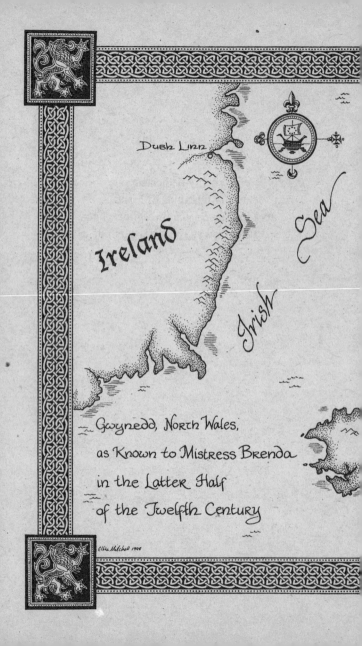

Dubh Linn

Ireland

Irish Sea

Gwynedd, North Wales,
as Known to Mistress Brenda
in the Latter Half
of the Twelfth Century

Elvia Mitchell 1998

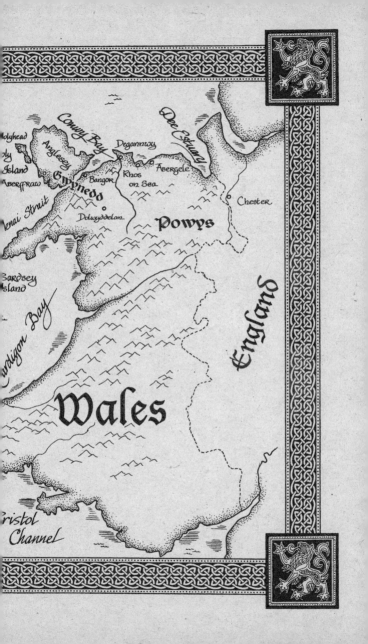

Contents

CIRCLE OF STONES

Prologue
Northern Lights

> As they penetrate the upper atmosphere, the highly energetic electrons [in the solar wind, which is an outward flow of particles from the sun] slam into oxygen and nitrogen atoms and cause them to glow. . . . The oxygen glows whitish green; the nitrogen glows pink. Those shimmering curtains of light are the auroras, which are visible from the ground [and in the northern hemisphere are called the northern lights].
>
> Eric J. Lerner, "Space Weather"

The aurora borealis pulsed extraordinarily bright under the starlit sky of Gwynedd Province, northern Wales. The exceptional sky lights flared into a green arch and spread downward like a gauzy curtain bordered in pale red.

Brenda, Prince Owain's mistress, pushed her reddish brown hair out of her dark eyes and watched the sheer, shimmering light. Then she walked away from the castle, whose shadow fell outside the bailey wall, past the guest cottages and stables. When she reached the gate guard, she gazed at the play of colors reflected from the craggy white peaks of the Snowdon Mountains. She lowered her head, as was fitting for a woman, and the guard opened the gate and clanked it behind her.

Candlelight flickered inside crofters' cottages scattered about the Nant Gwynant valley's sheep-grazing land. Stimulated by the radiance, she walked briskly to the wide heel stone that long ago had been planted outside a ring of standing stones now tumbled on their faces. Underneath powdery snow the stones were blackened with weathered lichen and half covered with earth. She brushed the heel stone, boosted herself up and warmed her hands under her arms.

What did the sky lights mean? she wondered. Were they a sign from the gods? Maybe they foretold the beginning of something good. She heard footsteps squeaking in the snow. A shadow fell across the stone, and she looked up into laughing eyes blue as summer flax; a broad-shouldered, blond Viking god.

"Owain, you heard my thoughts!" she cried, tugging on his hand. She shivered with delight when he sat close and his hand enfolded hers. "My Lord, what is the meaning of this glorious glimmering?"

For a moment he watched the lights, then said, "My beloved Brenda, I be not God, High Lord of the heavens and everything underneath, nor Lugh, ruler of the seas. Mayhap, if my youth were different, I would be a shipmaster with a dozen sails; owner of a large shipyard, watching this spectacle from a ship's prow. Next, after you, I love the feel of a rolling sea beneath me as I lie on a ship's deck boards." He put a hand against her cheek and kissed her lips.

She giggled. "Mayhap, if things were different, I would be wife to a wealthy shipbuilder," she said. "I used to have dreams of children, lots of them, here and there, running, standing and dancing. 'Twas strange; they were not small-boned, beautiful, black Welsh laddies, nay." Suddenly her voice turned husky and full of wonderment. "They were more like the ancient Vikings, blue-eyed, full of energy, spontaneous, laughing and crying."

"Sounds like the dream of an ancient druid priestess looking for a wee wood-nymph that is able to be here and there at the same time. A real traveler. Mayhap 'tis a reflection of thineself: witty, melancholy, primitive, refined, hunting for new lands. Are you studying the Old Religion?"

Brenda squinted her eyes and smiled. "Nay, I be studying the sky. 'Tis telling us something. I have a premonition of a great event. What are your thoughts?"

"I think you are full of paradoxes," he said. "Your mind is too deep for a female and would disturb most men. But you intrigue me, and I find it strange you would dream about blue-eyed children. I gave you a dark-eyed son and a green-eyed daughter. Next time dream about what your Irish father is teaching them. He might be telling them that their mother is a kelpie who loves water more than land. That is why they never see her."

"Oh, I want go to Ireland to see my babies just as soon as Lady Gladys has tried drinking nettle tea and eating muffins to keep her well," said Brenda.

"There is the proof you are a kelpie. They have great medical skill, confer the knowledge on chosen humans and heal others before thinking of themselves."

" 'Twas my dear mother who bestowed love of healing on me. She passed away before I learned half what she knew. Mayhap she was a kelpie!" She raised her eyes to the sky. "Tell me, what is the meaning of this night? What do you think?"

"Moments ago I lay on my pallet," he said, "thinking of the New Religion clergy who vow to be celibate, and I longed for you, just as those fool clerics continue to long for their favorite *Cymraes*, Welsh lady. When I was certain Gladys was asleep, I came out to breathe fresh air. Her sickness lingers on and on and tires me. I think—nay, I hope—this panorama of sky lights announces the end of my dear wife's suffering. But I know the lights have naught to do with my selfish, shallow thoughts nor hopes. In my memory sky lights have never been so unusual, like a singular beautiful, intelligent woman." He let his lips barely touch hers. "Mayhap these lights tell us that Gwynedd will shine before the world from this night forward."

"Did a druid examine your wife before winter?" asked Brenda.

"Aye, Archdruid Llieu left herbs, said she suffers from weak blood and a dry tongue, I should leave her at the Aberffraw court, where the sea air is warm during the winter, and keep her away from sweets."

"Your cousin, Christiannt, told me the god of light and the god of dark fight inside her belly. Who will win?"

Owain shrugged and lay back on the cold stone. He pulled Brenda down, held her close.

She said, "I told the gate guard that the dancing lights were like a rainbow where sunlight shines through raindrops. Moonlight shines through the high layers of fog mist to give us dancing lights at night."

He said, "That is why I be attracted to you and not the gate guard. He is not a thinker who can see rainbows in the day and sky lights in the night are related. You are far too wise for a woman. He told me the sky lights mean one more bloody battle with my brother, Cadwaladr. He reminded me that I sent half a dozen of my eldest sons, with their armies, to drive Cadwaladr into England before he takes over Gwynedd. The guard does not know my scurvy brother took two of my sons hostage to England, threatened to gouge their eyes out and put my head on a stick. My wife fears my days are numbered because soon I will go to London to bring my sons home. Pyfog's son, Howell, will go with me for protection. He will be the next prince of Gwynedd."

Brenda sat up. "Oh, Lord God, be careful. If you die I believe I will die."

"Now you are being silly like an ordinary female," he said. "Life is stronger than death. I lost three sons in the battle for Cynfale Castle. I swallowed the sadness and now sing of the richness of my Welsh life."

"I could not. Thus, I suspect I am truly an ordinary woman. If I lost a loved one such as you or one of our children, life would become thin as floss. My heart would never mend. Will Pyfog worry?"

"She is in Dubh Linn. I hardly think of her."

"How long was she with you?"

"Long enough to make a son."

She watched the dancing sky lights and refused acknowledgment of his arm drawing her closer.

"Forget Pyfog," he whispered. "Think of good times. When your father gave you permission to come to my winter court, you were so innocent. I loved you long before you knew you had brains under that crown of chestnut hair."

She looked at him through her dark lashes and said, "My darling Welsh mother was dead, and I had no one to ask about such things as brains or beauty. I believed I was simple because I could hardly wait for your answers to my questions and I thought longer and thus was slower than your other serving maids, until the day I boiled clothes and laid them on the meadow grass to bleach. My clothes were brighter than theirs and you told me I had earned my own cottage. I could not believe a maid like me could be so honored for such a small discovery. My mind was in a tangle, but I remembered to make a proper curtsy and say thank you." Her eyes shone as she thought about how that day had changed her life, and she felt an unbidden spark of pleasure.

"You smiled at me and a few days later brought fresh coals to oversee the laying of the new fire pit in my cottage," she went on. "I fed you biscuits and a beaker of mead. My stomach bubbled. You told me to take off my gown, get under the robe, and you would sing me to sleep. My heart jumped. You were the prince, the High Lord of Gwynedd, the most handsome man I had ever seen. I was a servant lass, daughter of Howyl ap Donal, lord of tiny Carno, expected to carry out your wishes. Christiannt told me she was in love with you and longed to lie under your furs. I was unsure. You pushed me toward my pallet, sang in the deep voice used for saga songs and made my heart jump into my mouth, so I kept it closed. You pushed the robe down so my shoulders were bare and moved your hand to my throbbing chest. I thought I was going to faint when you kissed my lips. Never had I tasted anything so delicious. You said I was beautiful. I was so excited I opened my mouth and your tongue touched mine. No one ever told me I could feel tingly and happy at the same time."

She saw his smile and felt his hand under her gown pressing against her back. She watched the overhead sea-green scrim unfurl and fold into restless gossamer edged in red. "I remember you took a deep breath and said you were going to couple with me. I wanted to watch you undress, but I was so shy I closed my eyes and moved to the far side of the pallet. You covered me with your body, kissed my eyes, my mouth and my breasts. You parted my legs and did it." A small grimace flickered over her face. " 'Twas a tiny torture," she whispered. "I bled. 'Twas not my time. I thought 'twas a shame on me.

"When I got up in the morning I slipped into my gown and

everything looked the same, but I was different. My back
ached. I wanted to crawl into bed, close my eyes and go back
to yesterday. I told myself I would never let anyone do that
again. Never! You opened your eyes and said I gave you the
greatest pleasure of your entire life. What had I done! Naught!
You did it. My eyes overflowed with tears. My memory became a sieve, and I forgot pain and shame and longed to have
your arms enfold me. I wanted to feel your hand in the middle
of my back. I touched your cheek. You smiled and said,
'Come inside where 'tis warm.' So I pulled off my gown and
lay between your arms. You dried my tears, kissed my face
and said, 'I be sorry I hurt you. Next time you will feel only
joy, I promise.' I said, 'I be ready for next time.' "

He cupped his hand around her breast and said, "You were
brave and beautiful, like the dancing sky lights."

She put one hand inside his cloak for warmth, felt a tingle
run down her back and lodge itself like a spark between her
legs. "The bravery was years ago in Ireland, first when I went
to my mother's funeral and second when I kissed my father
good-bye. 'Twas the time I broke away from childhood."

He took her wool bratt and folded it on the stone for a
pallet, pushed her thick hair away from her face, cradled her
shoulders, kissed her eyes with lips like butterflies and pulled
off her gown but left her boots. He covered her with his cloak,
undressed, and lay beside her. The spark between her legs
spread. "Soon you will be warm," he said. She put her arms
around his neck and pressed her wet cheek against his.

"Do you cry because of the beauty of the heavenly lights?"
he asked.

"Nay, 'tis for the girl I can never again be," she said. "Tell
me how many others have you truly loved?"

He kissed her salty eyelids. "None as I love thee. This day
and always I love thee above all others."

She felt the fever growing, let it come unheeded, and was
never happier. "I believe the skyborne glimmering foretells joy
for thee and me!" she said.

He moved as slowly as he could and when he could not
hold himself back, he thrust deeper. Her arms and legs formed

circles, keeping his body close. Their cries mingled with the crackling aurora.

Thus, under spectacular Welsh northern lights, in the year 1150 A.D., a special child was conceived over a druid heel stone. His name would be Madoc.

Part One
1151 to 1152 A.D.

Gwynedd's Prince Owain was of royal descent on both his grandmother's and his grandfather's side. "His father Gruffud was born in Dublin, in the year 1055. His [grand]father's name was Cynan ab Iago, and his [grand]mother was Rhagnell, daughter of Olaf, who had been king of Dublin. . . . One of Owain's [grandfather's] forefathers was the renowned king, Rhodri Mawr, while Rhagnell was descended from Harold Haarffager, the first Norse king to cross over from Denmark in the ninth century and invade the western island of Scotland and Ireland.

   V. Eirwen Davies, *Gruffudd ap Cynan, 1055–1137*

Listed by some authorities as a wife, or concubine of Owain, is Brenda, daughter of Howel, Lord of Carno. There is no positive contemporary evidence of this—only a certain amount of bardic hearsay—but Arthur Rhys (Historian, Chicago, 1938) names Brenda as the mother of Madoc.

   Richard Deacon, *Madoc and the Discovery of America*

In the Posidonian sources the Druids are associated with . . . learned and holy men. In Strabo three classes are 'held in special honour;' Bards (*bardo*) who are singers and poets, Vates (*ouateis*) who interpret sacrifices and study natural phenomena, and Druids who are concerned with both natural phenomena and 'moral philosophy.' Diodorus lists Bards, poets chanting both eulogies and satires, Druids, who are 'philosophers and theologians,' and *Manteis*, who divine from sacrifices and auguries. Ammianus [a fourth century historian], quoting Timagenes, has Bards again, who 'celebrate the brave deeds of their famous men in epic verse;' Druids 'are uplifted by searchings into things secret and sublime, profess the immortality of the soul and share Pythagorean beliefs;' and *Euthages* who 'strive to explain the high mysteries of nature.'

Stuart Piggott, *The Druids*

I
Story of Lug

Madoc was born near Snowden Mountain in the Valley
of Nant Gwynant in North Wales . . . the son of Owain
Gwynedd, King of North Wales . . . and . . . Brenda . . .
therefore not a son of Cristiant, Owain's second wife.
To Owain and Cristiant was born Prince David.
> Zella Armstrong, *Who Discovered America?*

In October 1150 A.D., two weeks before the birth of Brenda's
third child, Prince Owain returned from London. Brenda was
in the great hall of the winter court at Aberffraw stacking the
greasy meat platters. Everyone was gone except Owain, who
seemed to be lingering over his supper. He asked her to sit
with him at the trestle table, saying she was the one person
he dared talk to about his sick-in-the-belly feeling.

"Did the climate or food of London make you ill?" she
asked. "Mayhap you should talk to Archdruid Llieu. Druids
have a passionate pursuit of a healthy body; no disease is more
sacred than another. They are not like the Christian healers
who believe diseases are due to the position of a heavenly star
or punishment for your sins."

His eyes were ice blue and the corners of his mouth turned
down. "Nay, not that sort of ill. 'Tis in my head. There I see
the dead bodies of my twin sons."

Brenda was shocked. "Twins? In London? I did not know
you had twin sons. Lads or laddies? What happened to them?"
She sat, rested her elbows on the top of her distended midsection, cupped her chin in her hands and leaned forward.

"I had a bloody duel with Cadwaladr on the London bridge.
Howell was my surety. King Henry was both judge and Cad-

waladr's surety. Henry and my brother promised the winner possession of the hostages. We fought from noon until stars were visible, and Henry, who was dog tired, declared 'twas finished. Cadwaladr swore he had no bloody cut on his upper arm. But it dripped red for all to see. I was the winner and Cadwaladr looked me in the eye and said the hostages were waiting a short distance up the riverbank to be taken home. Henry said 'tis written in the stars that no Welsh pagan shall escape the long reach of England.

"I told him it was my goal to have a united Wales free from English rule. That I had won fair and square and was in a hurry to take my lads home. I had no heart for cutting off my brother's right hand and dragging him across the field to be hanged, as is the unwritten rule for a duel, the usual fate of the defeated."

Owain's voice was thick and he closed his eyes. "Howell and I stayed behind, on the riverbank, until I could catch my breath. Then we went for the twins, whom I had not seen in twelve years." His face was pale except for red spots in the center of his cheeks and red where his nose was peeling from the sun.

Brenda felt a chill deep in her marrow.

When he opened his eyes, they were red-rimmed. His tired voice found some unspent energy and turned black as thunder. "King Henry and my brother lied! I have fought many a bloody battle and seen many a man die, but I was unprepared for this. The lads' eyes were gouged out and their bellies ripped open, leaving a bloody feast for swarms of black flies or ravens. Twin swords and twin shields lay on a flat stone sticky with blood. A druid might have read the future in the crisscrossing of the drying red rivulets."

Brenda drew her breath inward. The baby kicked. "I pray my babe is a girl," she said, "and will never go near a battle."

"Hush," said Owain. "I touched each lad's pitiful, thin face. The skin was cold and smooth."

"Their mother," said Brenda, "pity her."

"Oriel was sister to Prince Rhys of Powys, and a harper in my court. She died when they were born. I named them Cynoric and Edwal and took them to Rhys. He mourned his sister, but was grateful to foster her weeans."

"But they were in your army, not dragons in the Powys army?" asked Brenda.

"Aye! A year ago, Rhys sent word that the lads had come to Gwynedd to join their true father's army. They wanted to meet me. I was busy and never found time to go to their camp. Surely they were brave soldiers, who now walk a road we cannot see. I squatted among the river rushes and hung my head. I can still hear Howell vomit his insides out over the wash of the river. I wept with loud keening. We must have scared all the river rats."

Brenda had never seem Owain weep. She got up from the bench, clumsy under the weight of the baby she carried, and stooped down to put her arms around him. "The Law of Howell Dada says you owe Rhys a *Recompense*."

"Please," he said, "I need only for you to understand my grief. I know the law—*Recompense* and *Reconciliation* and *Revenge*."

Brenda's fingers burrowed into the folds of her ample skirt. "I feel ill and do not want to hear more," she said. "I be angry and resentful with both Henry and Cadwaladr. I hate them as the devil hates holy water. I really do!"

Owain smiled sadly. He was used to the gracelessness and the quick emotions of his pregnant mistresses. "My legs were heavy as water-soaked logs," he said. "Howell and I wrapped the bodies in our sleeping blankets. I did not know anything about them. I closed my eyes and tried to remember when they joined my army. When I opened my eyes the sky was beginning to lighten.

"Howell had a little fire going and was roasting seabirds on a stick. I said I was not hungry.

"Howell told me it was a good idea to eat because we were going to travel without stopping until we crossed the border into Wales. I wanted to sleep. Howell said Uncle Cadwaladr might be gathering English soldiers to come back for us, and if we dallied we were certain to be caught, made hostages or—worse.

"When we were deep into the Welsh Tintern Forest, Howell

wanted to burn the bodies in an oak fire. But I thought maybe their mother was a New Religionist and so they should be buried beside a church, not in an ancient oak forest where druids carved the rocks with patterns of three connected spirals; triskeles.

"We reached Brecon and 'twas luck that Rhys was there with his hunting hounds. He had heard English soldiers were looking for us and so helped us bury his nephews' stinking corpses in the churchyard. I laid the bloody swords across their chests, and used the twin shields as grave markers."

"Is Prince Rhys a New Religionist?" asked Brenda.

"Nay, a druid. He and I made a *Reconciliation Pact* that we would fight to the death to keep our Welsh provinces from going under the rule of England. I disowned Cadwaladr, and the three of us declared that he would never become a leader in any Welsh province." Owain made a loud, discourteous sniffing sound through his nose.

"I vow I will not be quick to send future sons out for fostering nor begin their soldiering until they at least grow facial hair. Young lads need to know more about their home court and how 'tis run before sent to be soldiers or learn a trade."

"It seems to me you gave Prince Rhys an inordinate amount of sadness," said Brenda. "Aid whenever 'tis necessary to fight the English is good, but not enough. Ease his grief with something personal to show your respect and friendship."

Owain felt a weight lift from his shoulders. "I owe you my thanks," he said. "I shall find a *Recompense* for Rhys and sleep well tonight."

Brenda asked Owain if he meant that about not sending his children away for fostering until they began showing signs of puberty. He nodded and her heart sang. Her gown twitched from the baby's kicks and Owain looked perplexed. She said, "What is it? Did an oracle tell you I carry a girl?"

He was startled by her question. "The only thing I know for certes is that this baby was conceived under rivers of red and green dancing light in the northern sky," he told her. " 'Tis a rare sign and means the child will be marked in some way. Look him over carefully when he is born."

"Oh Lord God! I hope not. I want a healthy, unmarked girl-child, to love and keep close beside me for a dozen years or more before she must be fostered."

"She? Nay, I want lads who are warriors for my army." Owain laughed, feeling better.

The sun shone when the druid midwife stood back to admire Brenda and her newborn son after their washup. She asked what name was given to this babe.

"The gods of the Old Religion will send him a name," Brenda answered. "I prayed for a wee lass but carried this babe low. I ignored the laddie sign. I was foolish."

The midwife clicked her tongue, nodded and removed the bloody straw mat to the refuse pit for burning. She fastened the heavy hide door open, so that the afternoon breeze could flush away the odor of the birthing.

Brenda snuggled with her babe under a layer of coarsely woven cloths and thought of the births of her first two children, in this same cottage with its hard-packed dirt floor. Both had been with her until they were barely five. It was the Welsh tradition to foster children of royalty or wealth when they were between four and seven. Besides learning to conform to the social mores, lads learned the beginning of a trade and lasses to make a fine stitch and to speak firmly to servants.

Owain, himself, had taken Brenda's two children to Carno, knowing that Lord Howyl would give his grandchildren the best education possible. Brenda secretly hoped that her firstborn, Riryd, would never become a soldier. She thought of this newborn laddie finding some peaceful occupation that had nothing to do with warring; a stonemason, fisherman, a shipmaster, something. She prayed that Owain would remember his pledge not to foster his children away from the court until they became adolescents.

She slept the rest of the day and through the night, until she was awakened by footsteps early next morning. She propped herself up, holding the swaddled newborn in one arm so that Prince Owain could see his healthy son with hair as fine as fresh spider spin. She imagined Owain's smile and told herself she would say to him, as she had said after her two previous births, 'Twas but a tiny torture.

And he would reply, You are brave and give me great pleasure.

Instead of Owain, Llywarch, the bard of Owain's court, entered. He tucked his loose strands of gray hair into the long queue at the nape of his neck. The top of his head was bare skin, freckled and brown from the sun and wind. His beard was thin and gray. His top lip seemed to be plucked clean, like a naked chicken.

"My babe and I rejoice in your presence," she said, using the courteous words for receiving congratulations after a birth.

He frowned, cleared his throat and said he had followed Welsh courtesy by waiting one night after her parturition before visiting. Then he surprised her by lowering his bald head and muttering as though he were ashamed to speak. "Our Lord, prince of the province of Gwynedd, wishes me to bring your new babe to his wife at once."

"Whatever for?" asked Brenda. "I hoped he might come here to see his son himself, not have the babe brought to his wife! Listen to this: The midwife, a druidess with blue curlicue honor marks around her fingernails, told me that Lady Gladys dropped a boy an hour before Christiannt gave birth to her boy and then my boy came just before midnight. Three babes born under the same stars! The midwife said a triskele of boys, born of the same father, under the face of a red, full moon which is crossed by three lines of dark clouds, like triple shadows, foretells coming events. She said that the first tiny cloud quickly disappeared. Thus the baby was gone—dead at birth. The second cloud covered the moon's eyes, meaning that the second babe would embarrass his people. The third cloud was longer than the others and looked as though the moon was held fast by it, meaning that the third babe was the lad promised to the druids to lead them safely to an unknown land. The midwife put her fingers over her mouth, indicating that I was to keep my lips sealed about the importance of my newborn.

"She said 'twas an old prophecy and a secret between druids and me. Is that some pagan silliness?" asked Brenda.

Llywarch stared at the floor.

"Why does Owain want his wife to see my babe?"

He looked around to make certain they were alone. He moved from one foot to the other. "Gladys's babe never sucked air." He put his blue-tattooed fingers to his lips. "Owain fears that if his wife learns her son was born dead, she will have a fatal fainting spell." He put his hand on Brenda's head and asked her to understand the predicament he was in. "If you do not give Gladys your babe, I must drown him so that the prophecy of Lug is fulfilled."

"What!" Brenda's face turned white; her mouth went dry and her heart pounded. She hid her baby under the cover-cloth and looked at Llywarch. His blue eyes seemed cold and clear and his gentle mouth was slightly turned up at the corners. She had thought until now that the bard was a good friend. He had been someone she could count on. He had a way of making everything understandable. For instance, she had not understood why Owain bragged about Gwynedd's war victories, no matter how small. Llywarch told her that a good leader boasted, always turning a loss into something splendid, to keep up the confidence of his people. Another time she wondered why, on long or short campaigns, Owain took women, camp followers, into his war tent. Llywarch explained that Owain needed to have women around to show the enemy that he was vigorous and unbeatable. Then he blushed and said it really had nothing to do with love, but was a base emotion called lust. Men like Owain, who dealt with the violence and death of warring, possessed it.

This day Llywarch blushed again, but this time sheepishly, and he said the damn Lug-prophecy had begun two nights ago as a harmless game, as after-meal entertainment in the great hall when he noticed triple clouds crossing the full, red autumn moon and told the story of Lug and the birth of three brothers, triplets, born under a similar red autumn moon. He had no idea, no premonition, that there would be three babies born within his court grounds that very night. Lady Gladys's babe was premature and the other two could just as well have been a week or two apart. But that night the gods must have been in a trick-playing mood. "The gods, too clever by half, caused all three to be born within an hour of one another, to confound us mortals with the Lug-prophecy I so glibly retold."

"What is the prophecy?" asked Brenda. "If 'tis Irish I should have learned it as a lass."

" 'Tis a Welsh story about a druid who prophesied that he would be killed by his own grandson. When his daughter gave birth to triplet lads the grandfather ordered them all drowned. One babe, called Lug, fell out of the shawl in which the babes were wrapped. Lug was found and raised by a smith. One day he visited his grandfather and while helping him pare apples for sauce, felt faint. The grandfather grabbed him as he fell and died from a stab wound from Lug's paring knife. Lug also died from a stab wound from his grandfather's knife. On the spot where the two died there grow two hazel trees, entwined side by side.

"After I finished the story, I strummed my harp and impulsively suggested that whatever anyone in the room said before the top of the sandglass emptied would come to pass. Prince Owain stood up, gnashed his teeth, bellowed like a bull and said in jest that if he had three sons under the same moon, he would drown all but one. Everyone at the supper table nodded in agreement, knowing that three grown sons of the same age would surely fight to the death over their inherited land, because 'tis Welsh custom, especially in Gwynedd. You know, brothers battle brothers over the most trivial strip of ground. We all knew that Lady Gladys was supposed to have a wee lass according to the priest she consulted at the harvest fair, and that she was not due for another month. I stopped strumming the moment I realized that Owain spoke before the hourglass ran empty, and the room became deathly silent."

"The priest only said words that pleased Lady Gladys," said Brenda. "He does not know that women who carry an infant high means a lass and low means a lad, or that Owain sires mostly lads. Father Giff said the three of us would have lasses because we were eating sweets. Eating sweets is what everyone does at the fair! Owain would not murder his own babes, lasses or lads!" Her fists were tight balls and her lips puckered in anger. "He would not kill kin on account of words in a fantasy tale!"

"Sshh!" said Llywarch, "I wanted to bite my tongue out. I said that Owain's words were spoken after the sand ran out. I knew my words were false because my stomach pinched in on itself, and the people knew because they saw my smile was crooked. Owain proved his honesty by admitting that the top of the sandglass was not empty when his words were out in the air. He now feels honor-bound to drown Christiannt's son in order to fulfill the prophecy." His voice lowered to a mere whisper, "I believe 'tis his love for you that ruled him to save your child instead of Christiannt's."

Brenda's mouth was dry as powdered herbs. When she could speak, her voice was thick. "His love? I do not understand. Love is not bound by rules that say one child is worth more than another."

"That is your belief," he said. "Owain is bound by a strong sense of obligation to keep his word. 'Tis called *honor*." Then his face brightened. "Time is in your favor. The drowning is tonight."

She wiped her eyes on the bed cloth. "Does Christiannt know?"

"Christiannt is bilious with worry over the fate of her babe. I should cry, not you. Woe is me! Let me take your son to Lady Gladys. She will love him and believe he is her own. Owain will not harm him."

"Can I be certain?" She gave Llywarch a long, level look.

"Think of it as fostering. 'Tis even better than fostering because you will be able to watch your son grow. But remember to keep your lips sealed about his true identity. If you go along with this scheme, Owain will ask you to be nursemaid. He will plant another baby-seed in Christiannt to keep her mollified and all will be well."

"What about me?" she said. "Will I be satisfied to have Christiannt's babe drowned, to see her grieve and turn green with envy every time she looks at my babe? Will I be pacified to see my babe in the arms of Lady Gladys, a woman who suffers from fainting sickness! Nay!" She was suddenly possessed with a fierce instinct to protect her child at any cost. She looked up and saw Llywarch's eyes, as blue as glaciers.

"Gladys and Christiannt are your friends. What can you do,

Brenda?" His hand rested on her shoulder so she could see the blue honor tattoos. "Trust in your own judgment."

His hand felt like a red-hot iron. She could not let Gladys foster her son. Gladys might drop him or fall on him during a fainting spell. She bit her bottom lip and her hands were cold as ice. "If Gladys dies, what happens?"

"The baby becomes a fosterling. If he is not yet seven, you, as nursemaid, are entitled to raise him until he is ready for fostering outside the court. Owain believes in a later fostering since the death of his twins; maybe you can keep the lad until he is pubescent." Llywarch took his hand away and told her not to ask a lot of questions but to think. "Does Owain want his wife to die? Of course not! He believes that love for a babe will conquer death and Gladys will be shut of her faints."

Brenda frowned. "Infants die all the time. Gladys can face the truth. Women are stronger than men believe. Why did Owain not come and tell me all this himself? Is he afraid of what I would do?"

"The newborn exchange and the rest has to be made secretly. Owain will strangle me if his orders are not carried out. You too." He reached under the bed cloth.

Brenda held her baby close between her legs and prayed silently, Lord God, do not let me smother my own child.

Llywarch stood and said, "If you refuse, Owain orders your babe killed by holding his head in a basin of water."

"Nay! Nay! He would not!" Her words were like small explosions. "Could you give away one of your own children—if the prince ordered?"

"If I want to stay alive, I follow orders," he whispered and looked the other way. "But—if I deliberately took an innocent child's life, I could never hold my head up. To be a prince is to have a terrible power. To be a chief bard is to have an unsound mind."

"Let Christiannt give *her* babe to Gladys!" Brenda blurted and her heart beat so hard it seemed near bursting. "Tell Christiannt her son shall be raised in Gwynedd's court. His nursemaid shall be his own mother. Then say Brenda's son is cold as slab-stone. Say poor Brenda—she is wild with grief. I shall hide my babe outside Gwynedd. Mayhap Ireland." She laid down her orders and plans in words as clipped as the words of any marshal planning a campaign of warring.

Llywarch smiled, his icy eyes melted, turned watery blue, and he looked outside the door. "Aha, your mind awakes. I was waiting for you to figure this out. I have readied scones, hard cheese and a brown mare. At Degannwy there is an inn by the sea where you will stay the night. There is an old Norse saying that if a babe rides a ship before he is nine days old without becoming seasick, he shall become a shipmaster." The corners of his mouth turned up.

Brenda was not amused and said she was not interested in old Norse sayings.

"Well then, in Dubh Linn go to the *stavkirke*. The Augustinians named the church after Saint Patrick. Ask for Maude, the housekeeper. She and her brother, Gorlyn, who works in the shipyard, will arrange for you and your babe to stay in the nearby druid settlement. Dress while I tell Christiannt to prepare her babe in his whitest linens and his softest shawl. Then I shall tell Lady Gladys to be ready to receive her newborn son."

"You arranged this without asking me? I ought to have some say—" She stopped, suddenly realizing that Llywarch never intended to drown her babe.

"Yea, I sent a galloper to Degannwy yesterday to find a shipmaster going to Dubh Linn. If I had told you my scheme, you might have refused. So I counted on your logical thinking to find a way out. I counted right. Good for me! You have more heart than the other court maids."

She stared at him and held one hand to her chest, which felt as if it had been pounded by the handle of a scramasax.

"We druids know that Christiannt's son shall be raised as Lady Gladys's babe and that your son's destiny is on the knees of the gods," he said. "Your babe is the fulfillment of a secret druid prophecy that says in the year eleven fifty the prince of Gwynedd shall sire three lads during one night and one shall be a leader—a savior to the druids." He smiled and his eyes twinkled, making him look much younger.

"Please, find Owain," said Brenda. "Tell him that my babe took a chill while being bathed, inhaled his tiny lungs full of water, turned blue and still as a standing stone. An awful accident. A water sprite fell in love with him and took his spirit home with her." She took a deep breath. "I hope that he believes your bloody Lug-prophecy has come to pass and two of the three babes are dead. Christiannt's heart will be light and proud as dust motes when she hears her babe is to be raised in Gwynedd's court. Gladys will believe her son was born with a strong heart." Brenda held her mewling infant against her breast and longed to curse the gods for permitting this turn of events, but there was no time.

"I will mound the dirt a little more beside the little heap where the stillborn babe lies," said Llywarch, "and place two markers and a white quartz ring to keep the evil spirits away. Everyone will hear that I buried your babe next to Christiannt's. The young maids will have something to talk about for months, three laddies born the same night, now two dead." His face froze like a statue. "This infant intrigue is wrangly, aye, dangerous. Your secret must never leak if you wish to keep the three of us alive. When your lad is weaned, foster him with the Irish druids and come back to Gwynedd courts. 'Tis the only safe way for us."

"I shall go to my father's place in Carno and foster him there!"

"Nay—'twill be the first place Owain sends his thanes to find you."

Brenda's head felt as empty as her belly. She stood up and felt blood drain into her packing. She cast the soiled moss aside for a dry pack. She loved Wales, even its moody climate, and now had to cast the country aside as if it had turned on her. Sorrow and apprehension flooded her thoughts. She wondered if Owain would believe it was grief over a dead infant that had caused her sudden departure. She had counted him her best friend. More than once he had said he would love her always. Yesterday she had loved him with all her heart. Today she could not understand his obsession about a man's honor.

II
Maдoc

The history of the currach (a round-bottomed, keelless craft) is as old as the history of Ireland itself. Formerly covered with animal skins, usually cowhides [over wickerwork of willow twigs] the covering nowadays is of tarred canvas, over a frame of wooden laths. The currach gives easily in broken water and will survive the most violent sea.

Liam Mac Con Iomaire, *Ireland of the Proverb*

The baby whimpered. Brenda pushed the wrappings free from his face and nursed him, but it was too soon for the milk-flow. She was all thumbs as she put fresh moss inside his diaper cover. Afterward she put belly bands, shirts, diaper towels, cloth packing, and dry moss in folded bed cloths and wrapped these around her baby; a tight, fat bundle. Then she rubbed her belly, which was not as flat as she had expected, with raw, oily sheep's wool and put a clean kirtle over her nightdress. She pulled on high-topped leather boots, folded several tunics and slipped them into her rolled-up capelike cloak, called a bratt. She wrapped herself, covering all but her face, in a gray woolen blanket.

Postcontractions caused her to hunker over to ease the pain. She thought of seven-year-old Riryd and five-year-old Goeral in Carno and remembered how hard it had been to give them up. Afterward she had wallowed in self-pity for days. Her father had been glad to take them, and he had kind words to say about the prince of Gwynedd, who paid generously for his grandchildren's fostering.

Her thoughts were interrupted by the sound of a horse's

hooves. She left the cottage looking like one of the serving girls carrying a couple of blankets.

Llywarch led a gray mare saddled with a woman's low wooden saddle, which had both stirrups on the right side. He tied Brenda's clothing bundle on top of the food sack, stood close and whispered for her to leave the mare at Degannwy's Seaside Inn when she boarded the trading vessel.

She asked how she would know the trading ship and who would pay her fare. "Do not worry," he said, " 'tis my obligation to get you to the Taliesin druids. A shipmaster who understands the words 'paid by the shipbuilder' will take you to Dubh Linn and tell you how to find the stave church."

She gave the bundled babe to Llywarch and climbed onto the back of the mare. She was awkward and stiff, and her insides ached as she adjusted the blanket so that her face was nearly hidden. "How will I recognize the Irish druids?"

"They live in a camp atop a drumlin." He gave her the baby and said, "Keep your head down and the babe quiet as a slab of smoked mutton." He led the horse past the guards and out the inner bailey gate.

Brenda saw the midwife and several maids with their bratts fastened about their shoulders. They pulled hot, wet bed cloths from a cauldron, twisted out the water and spread them steaming over blackthorn and medlar bushes to dry. They looked up, but kept their faces in the warm steam and their knees close to the glowing peat under the laundry cauldron. She heard someone near the rinse vat giggle.

Between his teeth Llywarch hissed, "They think I be taking one of the maids down to the meadow grass." He laughed softly, guided the horse around the outer bailey to the front gate and whispered something to the inside castellan, who made an obscene gesture with his thumb and forefinger, pounded Llywarch on the shoulder and winked at Brenda. He whistled and told Llywarch that he was lucky to find a maid so eager, especially on a day that felt and looked like snow. He said 'twas time to leave the mountains and go back to the warm winter court by the sea.

Brenda smiled and let her blanket slowly drop to expose one shoulder.

Llywarch said she did not have to overdo the play-acting.

She pulled the blanket tight under her chin and wondered aloud how he would get back past the palisade guards without questions if he did not have the horse or the maid he took out.

"I told them I would be back late. I said I wanted to recite poetry to the wild boars. The outside castellan said I was a real *Pryddyd y Moch*, Poet of the Pigs! He said for me to leave the horse in the pasture until tomorrow morning and come in separately so that we would not look suspicious! He was being helpful about my transgression." He untied a leather pouch from his sash and gave it to Brenda. " 'Tis best to have a few coins."

She started to object, then decided he was right. She tied the pouch onto her belt and said, "I will pay you back."

"No hurry," he said. " 'Tis not exactly my money. 'Tis only in my safekeeping to be used by Old Religionists for humanitarian activities. When it comes to saving my neck, and the neck of a friend, I say 'tis humanitarian."

He led the horse away from the little valley of Nant Gwynant and into the moor that seemed to reach out to the foothills of the snow-capped Snowdon Mountains. He began to sing of the complicity of men, the ancient heroes of Gwynedd, of invading Romans, the Norse and Welsh warfare with Normans and Saxons. He made up a rhymed song full of energy and fire about Prince Owain's kin nine generations back and then about the Welsh honor code that was created three hundred years ago by Rhodri Mawr, the first king of Wales. The bard's obligation to Gwynedd's court was to keep in his mind a record of the Welsh past and impart it through song and poetry. He frowned and exaggerated facts but left no doubt that Gwynedd, in his opinion, was the greatest of the Welsh provinces.

"You might be more cheerful on this gloomy day," said Brenda.

"Like I said, 'tis not all song and dance being a household bard, even though you may think so," he said.

She swayed and put one hand on the mare's mane to steady herself. "I once believed Owain to be the most generous man on earth. I discounted the carping of the maids, thinking they were jealous and using any rumor as grist for their mill." She sniffed and wiped her nose on the blanket. " 'Tis hard to believe he would murder a newborn, especially one of his own."

"Do not do that! I cannot stand the sound of a female's sniffles. You and I know Owain is a far better province leader than most. He lives by Rhodri Mawr's honor code. He does his best for his family, his thanes, and treats his friends well. Often he disregards his own well-being while doing what is best for his people. He loves women. They love him. They may be his worst faults. Try to understand. He never mistreats them, even though he neglects them for province business. You cannot complain of mistreatment. He keeps his promise and is honorable. What more can you ask of a man, especially a province prince?"

"Umph, there be Christiannt! What kind of gesture was he giving her? Does he think making another baby would take away the hurt of losing this one?"

"He does. He likes Christiannt, even though she is a gossip with sleepy eyes that attract the court soldiers. Remember, he chose to keep your son; he loves you. And now he believes your son died, and he is devastated because he knows you grieve."

Brenda was silent, thinking that Owain's trouble was his belief in the old Rhodri Mawr code of law and punishment. She preferred Howell Dada's modified code. Marriages could be ended by common consent. A healer was liable for the death of a patient unless he had taken an *Assurance* from the patient's family beforehand. Bastards had the same rights as legitimate children.

Suddenly the mare stopped. Brenda looked down at Llywarch, puzzled.

"My dear friend, I go no farther," he said. "Find the Seaside Inn in Degannwy, even if 'tis late. Leave my little mare with Doconn, the innkeeper. Keep warm." He took her hand and brushed his lips against it. "May the Lord, highest of the gods, be with you. You and I are best friends, and destined to be united again." He put the reins in her hands, turned and walked slowly across the freezing turf toward the motte-and-bailey castle.

"May the gods send you home happy." Brenda watched

until his green cap blended with the meadow grass and the air was filled with granules of snow. She kicked a heel into the mare's side. Snow ran into her face and made her close her eyes as she rode through gorse and rowan where sheep and cattle grazed, down gentle slopes past where the rivers, Lledr and Llugwy, flowed silver under snow clouds. She crossed a swinging bridge and was in Conwy Valley. The River Conwy's banks were brown and stony.

She rode through an oak forest and pushed the fear and anger against Owain deep inside her heart, but they rose and tumbled out in front of her. She told herself that she had purposely let him use her two ways, for pleasure and as a sounding board to test his ideas of leadership. He rewarded her with flattery by saying her mind was more logical than Plato's and her body more beautiful and responsive than any woman he could name. He needed the pleasure she gave to him more than breath, and he valued her advice more than gold. She asked herself what she knew about running a province. Naught. And why did he not seek out her advice on this triple birth? She would have told him it was ignorant to believe it honorable to reenact an ancient myth and to permit a mere game to destroy an infant, any infant. He should have asked. He was stupid. For the first time in her life, she faulted him; she swore never to abet another man so readily.

It was early evening when she pulled in the reins and the horse stood still. Nearby was a shallow rock cave with a creek along one side running in riffles over ice-covered stones. Sheltered behind boulders, the closed starlike pimpernels quivered on their thin stems. I need help, she thought. In the thickening snow the path ahead was invisible. She heard the raucous caw of a raven, "Help yourself, yourself!" The baby scowled and cried lustily.

Tired and achy, Brenda climbed from the horse, held her baby against her shoulder. His warmth felt good against her cold, wet face. She tied the mare to a stout bell vine and examined the cavelike recess under the rock overhang. Seeing that the recess was dry, she spread out her bratt, laid the baby down and cuddled him under her blanket. He whimpered because her milk was not fully in. She scooped up a handful of snow, held it in her mouth, then dripped it on the baby's petal-pink lips until he licked the water and his crying stopped.

She ran around the brambles and stomped her feet until she felt them tingle with renewed circulation, then she lay down, again tucking her blanket around the baby and herself.

She woke once during the night when her breasts ached. The baby was asleep so she did not wake him to nurse until nearly daylight. Afterward she noticed that the snow was about gone. She ate a little bread, tied the baby between the food and clothing and climbed onto the mare. She made the clucking noise she had heard Llywarch make.

At the end of the day the clouds glowed faintly between the twilight arch of the horizon and the darkening vault of the night sky. The clouds were tinged with a luster of silvery blue and one star shone through.

Brenda thought about all the midwife had said. "Three babes make a hallowed number. The first boy is still as a stone statue, the second roars like an angry bear and the third, your boy, is alert with curiosity and ready to be filled with great wisdom." She remembered Llywarch's words: "Brenda, your son fulfills a secret druid prophecy and he shall be honored by men, praised by gods."

She shivered and pulled the blanket around her ears. The shimmering evening star seemed to be one more sign, a confirmation that her baby was marked for something special.

The moonlight was bright, and the mare had no trouble following the trail. Brenda found the inn on the bank of the river's estuary. It was a cottage divided into a number of empty cubicles around a central area where there was an open fire and a long wooden table.

The innkeeper's back bowed when he walked, his face was pockmarked and he was hard of hearing. In a loud voice he told his wife to show "this little mother with a newborn" a clean pallet with linen sheets, while he took her horse to the stable for food, water and a good brushing.

His wife assured Brenda that this was the Seaside Inn, wrinkled her forehead, smiled and said to the baby, "Yur papa must be an Irish Viking." She went to the fireplace to light a candle. When she came back she looked sideways at Brenda and said,

"Lucky ye are." She fussed over the baby and mentioned her own grandbabies, mostly grown.

Brenda smiled and sat on the straw-filled pallet to nurse the baby. His tiny fist opened against her breast and a finger moved in and out as he suckled. He seemed starved for the plentiful milk.

With hardly a hesitation the old woman said, "Little mother, does yur husband mistreat ye? Ye do not wear a band on yur left hand."

Brenda turned scarlet. "Oh, the wedding band! 'Tis fastened by my undergarments. I did not want a thief to take it as I traveled." She kept her eyes down so she would not have to look into probing eyes.

The old woman bent, sat on the foot of the pallet with her legs straight out and said she noticed that the clasp on Brenda's bratt was the same as the crest of Gwynedd, three lions in a circle of everlasting life. "Are ye a young sister of Prince Owain, perchance?" She stroked the baby's back and her eyes danced merrily, showing her enjoyment in fussing over the young girl and her newborn.

Brenda glanced upward to give herself a moment to choose her words. "The prince has six sisters. Which do you think I be?"

The old woman's hand went to her mouth. "Oh, mercy Anna, mother of Mary, I do know that sweet Gwenllian is on the Otherside. There is Margaret, a name that is Irish; Rhagnell and Angharad, Danish; Annest, Welsh; and—I remember!" she shouted in her raspy voice, causing the baby to jump as he slept. "Susanna is the name of Prince Owain's youngest sister. Ye be she! Mercy, Anna, ye are Lady Susanna!"

"Names are hard to recall if you do not know what the face is like," said Brenda, feeling hungry and too exhausted to play games. "I would like pancakes and warm milk."

"I shall bring ye a rasher of bacon with the pancakes. Wish I had fresh laverbread, but 'tis gathered only on the south shores." The old woman wiped her hands on her lace apron.

"I never had laverbread," confessed Brenda. "Is it made from special grains?"

"Oh nay! 'Tis a smooth, fine seaweed, gathered daily,

washed of sand, boiled five to six hours until 'tis soft, green and sinister looking. 'Tis wonderful served with vinegar to bring out the delicate flavor. My mind is not as clear as it used to be, but I seem to remember laverbread was a favorite with Prince Owain and his sisters. I could be thinking of someone else."

For a brief moment Brenda wondered what Llywarch would have her do now. She closed her eyes, too tired to disagree. The old woman went out and she could hear her whispering to her husband.

"Here ye be, Lady Susanna," said the woman, backing past the twig-and-vine bed-screen. She sat the steaming bowl of milk on the floor and the flat cakes with thick, salty bacon on the pallet.

In an instant Brenda was wide awake, savoring the delicious aroma. In a near whisper she asked, "Are you and your husband of the Old Religion? You must know Prince Owain believes some of the Old and some of the New. He gives coins to the druid *eglwys* and the Christian abbies." She breathed in four times waiting for the answer.

"Is that what people say?" said the woman, putting her hand in her apron pocket and pulling out a flat stone. On one side was a carved spiral with many rings going around each other. She spoke in a throaty voice. "Our time is midnight. 'Tis a moment like sunrise and sunset when the veil between the seen and unseen world is thin. Fairies and phantoms are sighted. Little mother, put a finger on the outer ring of the stone so that ye and the babe stay in this world." She closed her flaccid eyelids and put her index finger next to Brenda's on the outer ring. "Count the moments," she said.

Brenda counted out loud, "One, two, three, four, five."

The old woman's eyelids raised. "Praise Lugh! Ye know the five paths, five families, five signs of the *ogam* alphabet, symbols of the mystic center! I use *ogam* for divinatory purposes and to send secret messages." She called to her husband. "Lord Husband, the little mother, sister to the prince, is a druid!" She clasped Brenda's hands. "We passed the thin veil of midnight without a mishap. Eat and sleep well. Yur ship to

Dubh Linn carries a small red dragon on her prow and waits 'til morn at the wharf." She patted the baby, straightened the wattle screen and backed from the cubicle.

Brenda thought about calling the old woman back and saying she was not a druid, but on the other hand she was not Christian, so instead she ate and washed down the salty bacon with the hot milk as one nearly starved. She blew out the candle, fell asleep and dreamed of red dragons and being a druid. When she woke the sun was covered with low-hanging fog. The old woman hovered over the baby.

"What are you doing?" Brenda fought an urge to push him under the quilt.

"Lady Susanna, do ye not know? I give yur newborn the rite of five breaths, so that he has a whole life and lives to old age. Up-breath, down-breath, back-breath, out-breath and on-breath." She breathed on the baby, letting her breath out slowly.

Brenda could smell the herbs, thyme and savory, the old woman had chewed in preparation for the breathing ritual.

" 'Tis finished.. This babe will live a long and useful life. He will be an adventurer on the sea, a peacemaker, a leader, and serve his followers with great wisdom."

"I must hurry to the wharf before the dragon-prowed ship leaves," said Brenda.

" 'Twill leave when ye get there," said the old woman.

Brenda pulled up her legs and felt her midsection. It did not feel as tender as yesterday. She sat with her bare feet on the hard dirt floor and readied herself to nurse the baby. He seemed to be constantly hungry.

The old woman put a gentle hand on Brenda's shoulder and sat on the pallet beside her. "The wee one snuffles to let ye know he exists. Lucky ye have milk! I heard some gossips this morning say there are armed Welsh soldiers looking for a runaway mistress in Degannwy. The mistress is said to be crazy with grief because her child drowned in his own bath-water. The soldiers want to take her to Aberffraw so that she may be comforted by friends."

Brenda drew in her breath; her heart thundered against her ribs and she held her baby tight.

"Here, I brought a rag soaked in oak tannin—rub it over yur face and arms. Better to look more like a serving maid." The old woman's voice was husky.

The pockmarked man pushed the wattling aside, nodded but said nothing.

Brenda took the baby, now sleeping, from her breast, gave her face, hands and arms a deep tan color and handed the rag back. "I am neither Susanna nor a druid," she said.

"I knew that. Laverbread was Susanna's favorite and her mother sent south for it. I played a game to see how smart ye are. Little mother, pretend ye are the innkeepers' maid and when ye board the ship, keep yur babe quiet as dust. I be Magain, my husband is Doconn and we are druids." She held out hands that had delicate, lacelike, blue-woad tattooing around the outside of each fingernail. "What be yur son's name?"

Brenda stuttered, "Why I—I have not decided. I may choose a family name."

"Madoc! That is a family name," said Magain with glee.

"Madoc?"

"A good name. It divides into two parts, Ma-doc, like here and there. Ma- from Magain and -doc from Doconn. 'Tis a name from the Old Religion and means yur babe will be an explorer. He will study stars to find his bearing, a sailor looking for unknown lands. I be proud to give yur son a name." She chuckled, pressed one finger against the cheek of the sleeping baby and left, humming to herself.

Brenda sat still to clear her mind. She wanted to ask questions. She wanted to know why Owain had sent men to Degannwy so quickly. Did he know her baby was alive? Of course not! Why were the men armed if they only wanted to comfort a grieving mother? Had the men been looking here, at the inn? She held her lips together. Madoc was not a name she had thought of, but she liked the sound. She knew no one with that name, and it seemed right. She wanted to ask more about why the name was right for her baby, but she said nothing.

If Magain and Doconn were druids, they knew mysteries she did not understand. She noticed that Doconn had faint blue-woad tattooing around the base of his fingernails, same as Owain, the same as her father and Llywarch. Owain kept his hands covered when he was around Christians. Her mind was filled with questions. Through the druids—was that how Owain found out so quickly that she was in Degannwy? Were old Magain and Doconn trustworthy?

Magain returned with a clay beaker of warm milk and told Brenda to wrap up in her blanket rather than her bratt. "Keep that silver bratt clasp hidden in yur undergarments, like yur wedding ring. Better yet, pin up the babe's diaper towel with it. A man will undress a maid before he will touch a squealing babe's soiled towel."

Brenda drank the milk, then fumbled with the wrapping around the baby. She put clean moss between his legs and fastened the woolen towel securely with the silver clasp, a gift from Owain to hold her bratt together. When her bundles were tied, she slipped them over her shoulder, thanked Magain and Doconn, opened the door and stepped out into the sunlight.

Behind her Doconn said, "I will use the mare until the bard in the green hat comes to claim her."

"You know Llywarch well?" asked Brenda, taking little Madoc from Magain.

"Certes," said Doconn, and as they walked toward the wharf he told how he and Llywarch had been foster brothers in the druid camp. "In those old days druids lived openly. No one had to hide from Christians in a dark cave, like a mole. We exchanged knowledge and discussed the mysteries. Druids studied to be poets, astronomers, healers or lawgivers while the Christians prayed and copied songs of Solomon, Ruth and Esther." His eyes sparkled.

Brenda wanted to ask what Doconn had studied, but they were almost there. She hitched Madoc against her shoulder, reached into the leather pouch, brought out several coins and placed them in Doconn's knotted hand. He smiled and said, "I guess these came from old Llywarch. What did I tell ye? He is a good man."

Magain pointed to a dragon-prowed ship next to the wharf. "Lugh bless ye both, my dear."

Doconn waved his right hand in an arc. A man on the ship's

deck waved back. "The shipmaster knows the Irish shipbuilder who pays yur fare," he told Brenda. Then he took Magain's hand, turned and walked toward the inn.

Brenda wanted to call them back because the ship looked too small to cross the Irish Sea, and to ask how Doconn knew that the shipmaster knew the Irish shipbuilder who would pay her fare. Did they exchange secret messages, like a kind of sign language? Doconn and Magain were already far away from the wharf. She bent and picked a handful of plump greenery, smelled it and stuffed it inside her kirtle.

Gulls squawked and sailed in circles above the whitecapped estuary. The wind was damp and salty tasting. Brenda scuttled over the sandwort and ran onto the wharf.

The broad-shouldered shipmaster was waiting to take her bundles. She smiled and said, "You shall be paid by the shipbuilder in Dubh Linn."

"Babies are worse than women onboard ship," he said. "Sit in the stern with your shoes off and keep the babe quiet." He combed his fingers through his beard. "Do not exercise any divinatory powers, and for the Blessed Mary's sake do not wander about. Stay covered and do not speak to the men. The crew may not catch on that you are female. Oh Lord God, I wish I had run the ship through the smoke of a needfire to protect the crew against female witches, their curses and bloody bundles. I could have had holy water sprinkled over the mast, if there was time."

"I be not a witch and have no special powers," whispered Brenda. "I be not like murrain, an infectious disease, so needfire smoke or holy water could not purify your curragh any more than she is now."

"I be not superstitious," he said, and his voice rose. " 'Tis a known fact that women are a curse on a ship. All seamen will tell you the same. So do not ask any special favors."

"May I have a biscuit and beaker of water? I brought a handful of Scotch grass, so I will not lose my teeth, neither will I suffer from aches and pains." She reached inside her kirtle and brought out the handful of fleshy leaves she had picked at the base of the wharf.

The shipmaster's eyes crinkled at the corners. His mouth

remained a straight line. "I see you are no herb lady. Trip to Dubh Linn is no more than two days. Your gums will not rot in that short time. Did you know Gwynedd soldiers searched my ship at daybreak looking for a lone woman? I suspect she was carrying out simony."

"What?" said Brenda.

"Probably some Cornish hag looking to sell a box of pearls or other jewels mayhap stolen from the prince of Gwynedd. Believe me, they did not say they were looking for a woman with a babe. Anyway, they found nothing on my ship. No one with a babe and no one with a contagious pestilence such like putrid, bleeding gums."

"Congratulations," she said, and sat against the curved boards of the inside hull. When her heart slowed its pounding, she made a kind of tent from her blanket so that she could nurse Madoc without being seen. The other passengers had their boots off and sat far apart from one another and out of the way of the four oarsmen. She supposed they were all men.

All day the sky was overcast. The breeze was colder and damper at night. She tried to anticipate Madoc's hunger pangs and fed him before he whimpered. She waited until it was dark to upwrap his blankets and replace the moss in the diaper towel. Once she looked over the ship's gunwale and saw the sea twinkle with schools of luminescent shiners. Later the whitecapped waves increased the pitch of the ship at such sharp angles that there was a constant spray and wash on the deck. Her head spun and her stomach was queasy. She cradled Madoc and prayed that he would not cry. In the middle of the night she was surprised to see a welcome tin beaker of water and two soggy biscuits beside her blanket tent. The biscuits made her mouth taste like mildew, but the water was fresh. The wind stayed gusty, and the night was black as the inside of a cave.

She thought of Owain, who had been the most important person in her life for eight years. Now her feelings about love were snarled worse than a wind-tossed skein of yarn. She thought about the people she had loved.

Her mother, Gella, had put off teaching her embroidery, cooking, household cleaning, correct clothing and the coy

mannerisms of a proper lady. Instead she taught Brenda birds'
song, names of flowers and medicinal plants. They played
games and recited poetry. Brenda's six-year-old heart had broken when her mother took sick and died. To quell her terrible
grief, her father had delayed her fostering and taught her to
use a bow, ride horseback, read, write, figure with numbers
and to think in a straight line. She stuck to Lord Howyl like
a shadow and eventually her grief wore out.

The day she first saw Owain was as clear to her as a mountain stream. She had been thirteen and accompanied her father
to a meeting of Irish lords in Dubh Linn. At the same time
Prince Owain came to Dubh Linn to attend the funeral of his
Danish grandmother. Afterward Owain came to the meeting
seeking companionship with the Irish lords, his old friends.

Brenda had watched the lords wring their hands and listened to them complain bitterly about King Henry, who tried
his best to dictate the number of household retainers and number of soldiers to which each lord was entitled.

Weary with the arguing and hearing the men's self-pity,
Brenda had shaken her finger and whispered in an unintended
overloud voice to her father, "The lords sound like old women.
Each has the power to control the politics and economics of
his own household. Henry's dictates are no more than the
crowing of a bandy-legged rooster! He can rule the English,
but not the Irish!"

Every man had heard her whisperings. Mortified at his
daughter's brazenness, Lord Howyl groaned and bowed his
head.

Brenda covered her face with her hands. Like a heavy
woolen mantle, the silence suffocated her. When no one put
a hand on her, she breathed easier, put her hands in her lap,
and raised her eyes. There was Owain, dressed in dark velvet
princely clothes, standing before her.

Laughter bubbled up spontaneously from his throat and he
said in a loud whisper, "Amen! You spoke like a true lady!"
His breathy utterance of "a true lady" seemed loud as the roar
of a River Liffey cataract falling down black boulders. His
face drew Brenda's eyes like the face of a full moon. He an-

nounced to the entire meeting that he wanted to take her to his Gwynedd court.

She thought of the time Owain had said she was his only true sweetheart. "Neither chance nor time can ever change my love for you." They were traveling from Nant Gwynant to the seaport of Aberffraw, the winter court. They had strayed away from the caravan after supper because she was worried about her daughter, Goeral, who was ill from a bee sting. She read out loud her father's words on parchment sent by messenger. Owain took the parchment in his own hands, pointed to the date and said Goeral was probably up and about by now. "No need to worry. Lassies recover fast from mishaps." He was not overly fond of children until they were old enough to carry on a good conversation.

She had said she wanted to go to Ireland to see her father and children, especially Goeral.

Owain had said he could not spare her, could not stand her absence, even for a day. "My wife needs you to make her nettle tea. She might have a bad fainting spell and die anytime. You are the only one who can console me." That day she thought she saw into the heart of the situation, that is, that men and women react in different ways. So she asked him if he truly knew how a mother felt about her children.

He replied that Goeral was still an infant, had not yet made a large contribution to humanity and until she was older, with more experience, she was not to be fretted over or given too much devotion. "If Goeral dies, your father will let you know. Babies can be replaced." It galled him that women were so soft-brained as to carry on with tears and hysterics when a baby was stillborn, or died of coughing sickness or a sudden chill. He had said, "If only women would conserve their energy and get well, I would give them another seed to grow into a healthy soldier." He wanted his children to be sons who would become soldiers for Gwynedd. But when they competed with each other for high positions in his army, he railed against their green-eyed rivalry. He wished his sons would unite in social harmony, then go awarring to extend Gwynedd's territory and frighten the boots off the king of England.

Brenda believed that this wish of unity could never be ful-

filled because Owain's sons had different mothers. Each
mother encouraged her son to gain for himself as much ter-
ritorial wealth as possible, and hoped he might be chosen as
Gwynedd's next prince. It was said that most of Owain's sons
prayed for their father's demise. Brenda believed it was the
fault of Owain's many mistresses that kept Gwynedd ban-
jaxed, divided, in the throes of bloodshed, with brother fighting brother.

There were times when Owain had been distressed by cowardice among his progeny. Fourteen-year-old Cynan once became sick with fright and retreated from heavy warring. Owain
demanded punishment for disloyalty, so Cynan was blinded
and imprisoned. A young nephew, Canedda, was blinded and
castrated for trying to poison Owain. His mother, Edna, was
sent, in chains, back to her family in the Orkney Islands for
supplying the poisonous mushroom powder.

Owain never let himself dwell on the number of soldiers
or sons lost in battle. Instead he bragged about the bravery of
the living men and about the new territory they captured for
the future greatness of Gwynedd. He believed that staying
alive to the end of a battle established harmony among the
living and was a way to measure a man's skill.

Brenda had said to Owain, "My children will not claim
their birthright to any land in Gwynedd." Owain always found
that hard to believe. He figured himself generous in dividing
his northern Welsh territory among his offspring, legitimate
and illegitimate, male or female. When his children were sixteen, each was given a tuath, or tribe, plus the tribal land to
rule.

Brenda truly mortified him when she said her children in
Ireland would claim her father's land and not press Owain for
their land inheritance in Gwynedd. Secretly she hoped her
children would stay in Ireland and become anything but
dragon soldiers.

She tried to untangle her thoughts and understand how
Owain, the man she had loved and trusted, could order his
own infant son drowned with no remorse, but feel duty-bound
to make some inane prophecy come true.

She had been rendered blind, deaf and dumb by the intensity of Owain's charm. She was confused by her gullibility.

In the morning there were a beaker of tepid water and a damp biscuit beside her blanket. She ate slowly, sipping water with each bite. She kept the blanket over her head, even though the sun was warm out of the wind. A lump, built of sadness, grew in her throat because she was coming to her native land but dared not go home. The thought of Welsh soldiers visiting her father and discovering her sheltered here along with her living infant caused her to run to the boards to empty her bowels, which were suddenly liquified by love and fear.

Past noon, the curragh pulled into the River Liffey's estuary. Brenda raised a hand to shade her eyes against the sunlight and saw Dubh Linn's oak castle with its round tower, built by the Norse king Olaf in the 1120s with Irish slave labor. The castle sat on a massive rock ridge overlooking round huts whose framed wall panels were filled with hazel wattle; the outside was daubed with clay. The black, silent river flowing north was exactly as she remembered when she had come to Dubh Linn with her father half a dozen years before.

The curragh docked at the long wharf, where a gray-haired, unkempt man whistled to the shipmaster. She wrinkled her nose against a rancid, fishy smell as he climbed aboard. He licked a bony finger and ran it through his straggly hair. That same finger, along with a tar-stained thumb, dived into a leather pouch held from a dirty cord around his neck. He placed a tiny gold coin in the shipmaster's hand, made an unhappy growl in his chest, put four silver coins alongside it, picked up the gold coin, popped it back into his pouch and smiled blissfully. The shipmaster's eyes danced as he clasped the man's elbow in a ritualistic fashion. Nimbly the slovenly man climbed over the side of the ship and was back on the wharf and gone in less time than it took Brenda to head for the ship's side.

The shipmaster kept her bundles until she was on the wharf, then he leaned over the gunwale and casually dropped one. She caught it and laid it beside her bare feet. He laughed as she held her breath and held out her arms to catch the bundled baby.

"'You were a model passenger," he called, and nodded to two men passengers who climbed over the ship's gunwale. He held up his closed fist and said, "Paid by Gorlyn, the shipbuilder." He reached into a pocket, pulled out a couple old biscuits, tucked them into Madoc's blankets before dropping him into her arms. She looked up, smiled and said, "How do I find this Gorlyn, to thank him?"

The shipmaster said, "He knows you are grateful. Be on your way, lass, and do not let the highwayman rob you as you gawk at the yellow leaves of autumn. Set your pace and stick with it!"

She said, "In which direction is the stave church?"

He pointed and said, "Walk the rath west and turn south on the first road. You cannot miss it."

She thanked him, pulled her boots from the bundle and put them on. On a whim she called over her shoulder, "I noticed your ship had no length of bad luck with us aboard!"

"What about her steep pitch last night? You think that was only the wind?" The shipmaster roared with laughter.

III
Taliesin Druids

Dublin is a . . . seaport [that] lies on the bay of the Irish
Sea . . . at the mouth of the river Liffey, about midway
on the eastern coast of the island and sixty-four miles
west of Holyhead, Wales. . . . Dublin castle was built on
a ridge overlooking the Liffey to the north and the low
ground to the east. . . . The river Liffey divides the town
into almost equal parts, north and south Dublin. . . . Outside the walled area stands the cathedral dedicated to St.
Patrick.

Maurice James Craig, "Dublin,"
Encyclopedia Britannica

Brenda hurried through the noisy village of Dubh Linn, which
smelled of boiling tar and freshly planed pine planks. She
passed men dressed in leggings and tunics who sang as they
hammered and sawed to piece together a hull, or gunwale, or
sat cross-legged as they carved a make-believe beast on a
prow. She passed women carrying loaves of bread and calling
to barefoot children playing on the rath. Chickens pecked dried
grass seeds among bleating sheep cropping the grass. She
turned south, walked a couple dozen steps and stood in the
yard of the hundred-year-old stave church, its heavenward
spire covered with crosses. Carvings of open-mouthed dragons
spitting tongues of fire lined the area near the shingled roof.

She laid her bundles on the dried grass and sat against the
foot of a moss-encrusted Celtic stone cross. After a moment's
rest she took out the stale biscuits and ate them. Then she
peeled off the layers of bed cloths to let Madoc kick his legs
and wave his arms. She pushed up his shirt. His deep pink

color had faded and his arms and legs had filled out. Her heart swelled with love for this helpless little creature. She hoped the druid camp was not far away.

She patted a fresh puff of moss into the bottom of the towel and fastened it again with her bratt brooch. Her fingers ran over the three embossed lions on the face of the brooch. It seemed like only yesterday that Owain had given it to her for her sixteenth birthday. It was the only thing she had of his, except three children, two whom she dared not see. A surge of homesickness caused her to catch her breath as tears welled in her eyes.

Ignoring the grasshoppers that clicked in the dandelion seed mats, she dried her tears on her kirtle and sat up straight. There, I have done with it, she said to herself. I have no more time for self-pity.

Her breasts were painfully taut with milk. She unfastened one side of her tunic, held Madoc close to nurse so that he would not fuss when they called on Maude at the church. She closed her eyes until a shadow cut off the sun's warmth.

"Are ye looking for the monks or the Three Nines celebration?"

Startled, she looked up. Before her was a pretty, red-haired woman with freckles, laughing brown eyes, a fresh linen tunic and orange-colored shells around her neck.

"Oh, oh no, I look for the Augustinians' housekeeper." She pointed a thumb toward the church.

"Ye seek work as a kitchen maid at Saint Patrick's? Mayhap I can help. I be Pyfog and I know the brethern."

Brenda stared at the orange shells.

"Cockleshells," said Pyfog. "I found them on Aberffraw's beach when I was at the royal court. I like to gather pretty shells and stones."

Brenda's heart leaped. "You—at—at Aberffraw, Gwynedd's winter court?" Pyfog? Could there be more than one? She quickly fastened her tunic and cleaned the milk from the corner of Madoc's mouth with her thumb.

" 'Tis the only court in Aberffraw." Her voice dropped to a confidential tone. " 'Tis hard for me to believe, but fifteen years ago the Welsh prince gave me a son. I named him Howell after my father. The boy was fostered with Cathbad, *Bard Teulu*, the famous poet and harper, at the Prydian druid camp, not far from Aberffraw. I hear my son is a poet and one of Prince Owain's best soldiers. I wonder if Owain remembers me. Does he know where I am? I never hear from him. I hear stories from traders about his latest battles and which maid he sleeps with."

Howell's mother, here she was. She looked hard at Pyfog. Here was a woman Owain rarely thought about anymore. She was inches taller than Brenda and ten years older, but pretty as a wild rose. Brenda stood up. She was light-headed. She put out a hand to steady herself, touched the woman's arm and whispered, "A blessing to you."

Pyfog mumbled, "A blessing does not fill the belly." She picked up the bundle, put an arm around Brenda's waist and led her to a seat on the *oenach*, the assembly mound, near the graveyard.

"Keep yur head down and ye will feel better in a moment. I can see yur babe is not more than a week old. A mean-spirited man kicked ye out the minute he saw that ye were gonna spend more time with this wee thing than him? Men, pagh! They can be pigs. I be daughter of Finn, who was once lord of Howth. This yur first?"

"I be Brenda, daughter of Howyl, lord of Carno. This babe is my third."

"Yur man, yur husband, live around here?"

"He—the father of my children—lives in North Wales."

"Look at ye! Ye can hardly be past fostering age. I say ye look fourteen. Ye must have had yur field ploughed when ye were in the cradle," Pyfog chuckled in a rowdy manner. She reached out and let Madoc wrap his tiny fingers around her thumb. "Sweet lamb, what is yur name? Mayhap 'tis Howyl after yur mam's pa. So, are ye even named?"

"This babe is not named Howyl!" said Brenda. "For all you know *he* might be a *she*!" Her voice sounded peevish and she wished she had kept her mouth shut and not spilled her name to a stranger. She unwrapped Madoc and adjusted his shirt and blanket, rewrapped him and picked up her clothing bundle.

She had to get away from this Irish lass and her incessant questions.

Pyfog grabbed her arm and sputtered. "The—the clasp! On the babe's towel! Where did ye get it? Where? Look here!" She unrolled her own bratt, which was held under her arm, and began fumbling for the shoulder pin. "See! Holy toenails, they are identical!"

"I guess Owain gave you that as a gift," said Brenda. "Maybe on your birthday. He probably said that you are the most—the most—" She could not finish and sat down. Her heart thumped so hard it seemed the people on the other side of the *oenach* could hear it. "This is the craziest situation I have ever been in."

"Who are ye?" whispered Pyfog. "Oh, Lugh's lungs, are ye Gwenllian? No—I be a fool; ye are far too young for her."

Brenda wanted to say, "We have both been flummoxed by Owain!" Then she thought about saying "I be Owain's sister, Susanna," but she knew Pyfog would not buy that story. "I have no husband!" she sobbed. "I was six when my mother died. After that I went about with my father. He bartered with a Welsh prince for the bratt pin." Now I have told her something, thought Brenda. I have made up a story.

Pyfog put her hand on Brenda's shoulder. "Merciful Mary! I understand. Wait right here! I have a friend I want you to meet. She will not believe yur story if I tell her!" She ran down the grassy slope and out of sight.

And I would like Christiannt to meet you, thought Brenda. When I tell her I met one of Owain's first Irish mistresses, Pyfog, mother of Howell, her eyes will become large and bright as an unspent silver Peada coin. She sighed, stood up and found her stride. She felt weak, but she was not dizzy.

She made her way past groups of people gathering on the turf benches preparing for the celebration of Nine Nights. She knocked on the rectory door. The panel swung outward and there stood a woman built like a dumpling.

Brenda spread her feet apart so that she felt well anchored and said, "I look for someone called Maude."

"You are *Cymraes* here to find joy in our Nine-Light-Nights

Festival?" Her eyes were like currants in a round pastry. "Be I right?"

"No. Yes. I—I did not come to celebrate. I look for Maude."

The woman stepped aside and held out her hand.

Brenda thought she was asking for a coin, so she told her she had a little silver. She put down the clothing bundle, joggled the baby from one arm to the other and finally held out a silver coin from the pouch tied to her belt.

"Child, come in! Come into the warmth. At first I did not notice that you carry an infant. Forgive me. I be old Maude." She looked in Brenda's outstretched hand and said, "So he gave you a few coins and left. Men are jackals!" She held her hands up, ignored the coin, took Brenda's blanket and laid it across the back of a wooden bench in front of the fireplace. "Do not try to make excuses. He probably took his pleasures and did not like the consequences." She thumped the babe on his backside. "Women are treated like soft, fine wool at a party, but at home they are knocked about. A day will come when we will not have to submit to such. Then men will not find us so soft." She laid a chunk of dried peat on the fire. It smoldered, smoked and burst into flame. "Sit and tell old Maude your story."

"How might I find the druid camp?"

"Ha! You come to an Augustinian church seeking people of the Old Religion. That is not bright for a woman with money who just made a curragh passage from Wales."

"How do you know I came off a curragh?"

"Everything of value passes my ears and eyes."

Suddenly Brenda was overwhelmed with fatigue. "The shipbuilder paid my passage," she said, and closed her eyes.

Old Maude sat beside her, put a motherly hand on her shoulder and said that her brother, Gorlyn, was that shipbuilder. "He is druid."

Brenda opened her eyes and stood up. The hot air close to the ceiling nearly gagged her. She ran her tongue over her lips and said she had to get outdoors for a breath of air.

Maude opened the door and said, "So you are the one who has run from the North Welsh prince. Do you know he sent coins to the Augustinians here, who think him most generous?" She said she supposed Owain also gave money to the druid *eglwys*, as he was half druid and partial to them. "But he does not want to neglect the Christians. When you return to Wales you can tell him the Irish Christians have hands out for more coins."

"I be not going back soon," said Brenda.

Old Maude pressed her hand and asked what Prince Owain was to her.

"Naught," she said. "He is only a person who has lived in a certain climate for a certain period of time. I was born Irish and do not think of myself as *Cymraes*, a Welshwoman." She continued to suck draughts of cool air until she felt better.

"What a brave little person," said old Maude, standing in the doorway. "You know how to keep a secret. Aye, give your friend old Maude your coins. I will care for you and the wee thing."

Brenda ran a hand across her forehead, held Madoc closer to her breast and felt weary and stupid. She knew that old Maude could knock the baby right out of her arms and take her coins. Yet she stood there asking directions. "Please, tell me which way to go to the druid camp. My friend Llywarch said you would know."

Maude came under the door frame and spoke softly. "A druid has more knowledge in his head than a monk has in his dreams. I tell you there are druids who know more about shipbuilding than the bishop knows about prayer. If you are bent in that direction, hie yourself to their camp. Eira's there to care for you." She gave Brenda directions about counting the hills she passed and looking for the first egg-shaped drumlin with standing stones on its point.

This time Brenda put the silver coin in Maude's apron pocket, which made the old woman peer hard at her and say in a confidential tone, "I almost forgot—two soldiers were here at sunup looking for a maid grieving for an infant that died less than a week ago. I guess they were not looking for the likes of you. Your babe looks alive to me."

Brenda flashed her a look of gratitude.

*   *   *

She walked along the top of the rath, breathing the moist, salty sea breeze and counting the hills behind. When she could see five of them, she rested awhile, then followed Maude's directions from the earthworks to a well-worn wagon road of wood chips, sawdust and river pebbles, southward through scarlet-leafed oak and yellow ash. A jackdaw and several sparrows accompanied her. She laughed and sang a ditty about a brown coney that her mother used to sing.

When she came out of the woods, her weariness was back stronger than before. One of her heels stung and she suspected her boot had worn a blister that broke. She waded blindly through a creek and limped up several switchbacks on a well-worn path to the brow of a drumlin. The birds had left her. In the center of the oval summit was a low dirt fortification overgrown with tall grass and oaks. Each side of the open gate was guarded by a post with a white boar's skull on the top.

Facing into the red glob of the setting sun were several men in gray long-sleeved tunics. They stood on a flat stone half buried in the earth on the pointed end of the ellipsoid drumlin. Beyond the smooth, flat stone was a tall, rectangular slab with various lengths of notches carved along the edges. She recognized the notches as *ogam*, the old Irish alphabet. Behind the *ogam* king stone was a shorter, slimmer slab of limestone. Between the two was a middle stone, about waist high, broad and flat on top except for seven deep gouges. Each gouge was a rounded indentation about the size of the inside of a cup.

The red sun slid behind the king stone. A fiery corona blazed on either side of the stone, and in a few moments the sun was gone. The corona faded, leaving the western clouds tinted a soft pink. The men pulled their cowls over their heads to ward off the evening's sharp air. One of them, taller than the others, beckoned to her.

Inside the cowl she saw the bluest eyes and the widest grin she had ever seen. She asked the man if this was the druid camp and he answered "Aye," and put out his hand. She reached and felt his solid, steady arm. She was safe and could relax. His warm, callused hand enclosed hers. He asked her to follow him, but her tired, shaky legs were limp as day-old salmon. Her eyes closed over the twilight, which was fading fast. His voice was far away. "Hang on. I have you." A soft darkness enveloped her and she felt his strong, hard arms slip around her.

"My babe," she whispered. "Take my babe. Please."

"I have the wee one." The voice was so faint she might be dreaming, but her arms hung free. *"Diolch,"* she thanked him, and grabbed for something solid and clung to the belt at his waist. Her head lay against his broad chest and the blackness pulled her into its darkest center, and she heard nothing more.

When the blackness faded she heard water running in a fast-moving stream and saw that she was lying on the ground with her head on her clothing bundle. She sat up, looked around for Madoc and saw the man pouring water from an iron kettle into the cup gougings on one of the stones. "My babe? What did you do with my babe?"

He sat beside her and said, "Your babe is fine. Eira fusses over him."

"Eira?" she asked, trying to remember where she had heard that name.

"Aye, she was preparing supper but was more than willing to let it wait while she looked after the babe and I looked after you." He chuckled. "I think you could use a good meal and a night's rest. You have not had either since leaving Welsh shores."

She shivered and realized she was truly hungry and she managed a smile. "I have to nurse my babe, but first—may I have a sip of water?"

He took a pestle from inside his tunic and ground it, as if grinding grain in a mortar, against the sides of one of the cuplike gougings that was full of water. The water became chalky. He handed her a straw with a wide bore, pointed to the gouging and told her to drink. "So, this special, four-day-old babe nurses his mam dry."

She was surprised by his remark. She looked more closely at him. His hair was a reddish brown flame around his face. She said, "If you please, I prefer water from the kettle."

But he motioned for her to sip the water from the cup in

the top of the stone. "Cup-water is best. 'Twill put strength in your bones. The babe took his share of strength before he was born and that leaves your bones brittle. We are healers here. Ground limestone is not altogether unpleasant."

Finally she looked up and stammered, "Sire, I—I have not yet said that my babe is less than a week old. Nor that he is special and that I have traveled across the Irish Sea. Mayhap you are more than a healer, mayhap a soothsayer, a wizard."

"A messenger you met in Dubh Linn came on a blown and foundering horse with news of your coming. She said we were to have a visitor from Wales who brings the babe that the gods have promised us, but she neglected to say a beautiful visitor, before she left on a fresh horse."

"She?" Brenda's cheeks were warm.

"Aye, Pyfog came here as soon as she saw you go inside the rectory. I be surprised you did not meet her as she returned to Dubh Linn. She brings us messages once in a while and visits with her father, Archdruid Finn."

"Pyfog never once said she was a messenger, a galloper. How did she know I came here?"

"She is a druidess who lives with Maude and does the laundry for the Augustinian brotherhood. We have been looking for the babe. 'Tis foretold that he will be with us seven years."

Brenda blinked, thinking, These Irish druids have a grapevine with tendrils curling in and out and all connected to one another. She looked up and said, "You know I be Brenda, daughter of Howyl, lord of Carno. My grandfather is lord of Clochran. I have never seen my grandfather. My babe and I may go to live with him after a while." She put her hand over her mouth for speaking so boldly, but seeing the corners of his blue eyes crinkle with the finest of lines, she said, "I be sorry. I do not know why I said those last words. I have met so many new people, druids, who all know one another and all about me, so that my mind is aswirl thinking of a place to hold on to."

"Today you left Shipmaster Egan, met Gorlyn, the shipbuilder, Maude, Pyfog and me, Sein. Aye, that is a lot of new people." His voice was low and gentle.

Brenda's face showed her amazement.

He smiled so that his teeth shone in the half-light. "Gorlyn is an archdruid, a well-known astronomer and shipbuilder. He is Eira's father and my foster father. His sister, old Maude, has worked for the Augustinians since she was a girl. The monks adore her. Pyfog came back to us after Owain fostered her son, Howell, with the bard Cathbad. Maude took her in to work for the Augustinians. I know that Llywarch sent you here to save your son's life." He saw the fear in her eyes and said, "Your secret is safe."

Despite her fatigue she said, "You practice magic to know such things."

He winked an eye and made a pleasing sound deep inside his throat. "Come," he said. "Your place to rest is inside the near cottage, where there is mead and gruel." He put his arm gently around her waist and led her to the cottage, which was built of wood lath with thatch for the roof. Inside, the smell of drying herbs, and smoke from the center fire were soothingly pleasant. Sein showed her a pallet wide enough for both her and her baby and said the pallet beside hers belonged to Eira.

A blue-eyed, black-haired young woman with pale complexion came in carrying Madoc, bathed, wrapped in a clean blanket and sucking noisily on his fist. "I be Eira. Your wee lad is starving. He refused watered goat's milk."

Brenda sat on the edge of the pallet, nursed Madoc and said, "Your father is an archdruid?"

"Most of the men in the shipyards are druids. They keep their hands covered with tar and legs covered with pitch and tattered trousers so no one sees their honor marks. But 'tis not as bad for druids here as 'tis in Wales."

Sein brought Brenda a beaker of sweet, fermented honey drink and a bowl of porridge. When the baby finished nursing and Brenda's tunic was pulled straight, Sein held his arms out for Madoc, put him over his shoulder and said, "I will see you in the morning. Oh, do not worry about the wee laddie; he will be by your side when you wake. You are with friends."

When Madoc woke Brenda with his hungry whimpering, she sat up and saw that dawn had not yet come but the sky from the window and open door was filled with stars. She was startled to find that she wore a clean nightdress; her boots were laid on her folded bratt and a clean blanket at the foot of the pallet. Her blistered feet no longer stung. She lay down to feed Madoc, and the next time she woke it was daylight.

Eira was folding her own pallet. Brenda looked around and saw that the men slept on one side of the cottage and the women on the other. Eira handed her a clean, light blue tunic. "Wear this until yours is dry. I will put more salve on your feet. Are they better?"

"Aye, thank you," said Brenda. "I will know for certes when I walk in my boots." She hesitated, then said, "I would like to wash."

"Of course. You need not worry. The men never follow the women. We are druids. We have a code of rules that is not broken. Women wash in the creek behind the cottages. Men go over the brow of the drumlin far from the trail." She handed Brenda a square piece of woollen cloth.

Brenda asked what would happen if the code were broken.

"The man is stripped of his honor marks—they are tattooed out with pulverized charcoal—and he is sent away from the camp."

"Can he ever gain the honor back?"

"Of course new marks can be made on his feet, half-circles 'round his toes. But I have never seen that."

Brenda bathed herself and Madoc in the creek. He cried with the first shock of cold water, then splashed and kicked his legs, making Brenda laugh. She sat on the mossy bank to nurse him and could not remember when she had enjoyed a bubbling creek, graceful trees with scrambling squirrels and songbirds so much. She felt completely safe, except that her mind was far from peaceful.

Back at the cottage, Eira took the sleeping baby to Sein and gave Brenda a beaker with the turbid mixture of water and gritty limestone scrapings and told her to drink quickly. She said all pregnant and nursing women were given the gritty drink once a day. "When you finish, come to the table. Eat all of your porridge; you never know when the next meal will come."

"I know you tease me. No one here looks starving."

Afterward Eira washed dishes in an iron kettle and rinsed them in another.

"Let me dry and I will put the dishes away if you show me where," said Brenda.

When she finished, Eira was gone. She went outside and found Sein sitting on a wood stump. Madoc's blanket was pushed aside and he showed him off to a circle of onlookers. "I be going to foster this one who is called Madoc. Then I will teach him all that I know of natural philosophy. He will grow to be one of the *great ones*." Someone sputtered a laugh, and Sein said, "You will see, 'tis the secret prophecy."

"How do you know his name?" asked Brenda. Her mouth was drawn into a frown.

"Ah, like you said, I practice magic."

"It seems so, but I doubt it. You heard me speak it?" she said, reaching for her son and thinking that men of magic were supposed to be above the ordinary but this man held himself above no one.

"The shipmaster told Gorlyn, who told Pyfog, who told me that you crooned at night so that your babe would not fuss. You called him Madoc. There are times when advance information saves lives, so our messengers remember everything that is said and how it is said, even what the informer looks like. For instance, did you notice that the shipmaster was fussy? He wore his hair tied back, a shirt under his tunic and he had woad designs around thumbnails. Did you notice anything else?"

"Woad designs on the inside of his wrists, also," said Brenda. "But he kept them hidden for the most part. His woolen stockings were clean. Am I going to have to pay attention to details if I stay here?"

"Why not! You do much better than the average," said Sein.

She took a deep breath and said, "Could I learn about gritty stone and lotions? Could I—could I be a healer?"

"Certes. I can teach you dyes and medicinal herbs. Put Madoc on your pallet and I will show you some of our herbs."

All morning Brenda felt shy. She felt the glittering sun on

her bare arms and savored the smell of the spicy herbs Sein pointed out in the yellow grasses and dark swamps. The balm used on her sore feet was a mixture of sheep's oil, mint and thyme. She tried to remember everything he told her about the special healing plants and those used for cloth and leather dyes. She wanted to learn to make pastes, salves and infusions. She wanted Sein to be proud of her. She wondered why it was important how Sein felt about her ability to learn quickly. She could not answer the question, but she knew it was important that he approve.

When he had shown her a dozen herbs, he asked her to repeat the names and their uses. She missed only one. "Tomorrow I will show you how to use soapwort root boiled in water on a horse that has greasy skin sores."

"Aye, I do want to be useful while I be here," she said.

"*While* you are here? Are you going somewhere?"

She lowered her eyes. "I heard you say you would foster my son. When he is weaned, I have to go back to Wales. 'Tis a commitment my father made in good faith. I honor his commitment."

"You must love your father a great deal."

"Aye."

"I want you to stay and study medicine."

Brenda shuddered. If Owain found Madoc he would drown him and behead dear old Llywarch and herself, and maybe Sein for helping her. On the other hand, her father had pledged that Brenda would stay at the Gwynedd court as long as Owain wanted her.

Suddenly Sein began to sing a song about Llywarch, Brenda, Madoc and himself. In his song they were like the leaves of a lucky shamrock, held together by the stem, which was powerful druid magic. When he stopped he held her against him and rested his chin on the top of her head. She had not felt this warm and secure since she was a small child, but inside her head and heart the thoughts and poundings overlapped in turmoil. She wanted to ask if he knew Owain was Madoc's father, but she pulled herself away.

He asked, "Is the weather better in Wales than in Ireland?"

She thought of the Welsh rain that went on for days so that

the whole world seemed as bedraggled as a wet sheep. Then she thought of the clouds drifting around the blue-and-white crags of the Snowdon Mountains and the gullys and lakes in the foreground. She thought of the cattle up to their hocks in the shallow estuary and the hussocked grass of the saltings overlooked by gentle green woods. She thought of the red kite, puffin, golden eagle, the owl, the voice of the crow, the cuckoo and the goats, thousands of goats that ran wild over hillsides and meadows. She thought of the holy well, the great oaks with bunches of mistletoe on their branches, the wildflowers and slate slab tombstones and ancient standing stones. "Nay," she said, keeping her eyes down. "Ireland has most of the same things."

"And Ireland has your father and your two older children, Madoc and—me. Stay."

"What if I let you foster my son and do not stay?"

"We shall meet again. I be as certain of that taking place as I be of day being light and night being dark."

She suddenly felt that her voice was so heavy she could not bring it out of her chest to say anything more.

IV
Kinefever

> To provide protection against [disease with pustular eruptions] . . . [ancient] doctors collected the crusts from pustules of a mild case of smallpox. The powdered material was blown into the nostrils; males snorted the powder through the left nostril and females via the right side.
>
> Lois N. Magner, *A History of Medicine*

One morning Sein, with a bundle of white cloths under his arm, waited for Brenda to finish her breakfast of porridge and cup of slurried limestone. He led her to the barn to see the horse that was suffering from the grease, identified by fever and large, slippery pustules similar to cowpox in cattle. He said that if the horse survived, it would never have the disease again.

A wheezy, little work mare with glassy, sorrowful eyes lay on her side on a pile of stinky, wet hay. An eight-year-old fosterling was hunkered over with his face buried in the mare's mane, sobbing quietly.

"Ailin, have you been here all night?"

"Aye," Ailin said. "The mare is worse. I replaced her hay twice this morning. She will not leave it clean. I scold her, but she cannot help herself. She is my worst chore." He rubbed his red-rimmed eyes and then he stroked the mare's ears lovingly.

Sein rumpled Ailin's hair. "Do your best. No one asks more. Mayhap you shall be a healer. Look here, I want you to meet Brenda."

Ailin squinted at Brenda. "M'lady, two weeks I be here and

have not yet healed anything. If you wish to be a healer, learn quickly, because the little mare does not look good." His mouth puckered and he whispered, "Help me."

His dark, sad eyes melted Brenda's heart. She knelt, touched his arm and was shocked at his warmth. "Laddie, are you ill?"

He looked directly at her so she could see that his eyes were as glassy as the mare's and his round cheeks were as red as rose blossoms. "Aye, off my feed, but bound to be better by the morrow." He stood on shaky legs and to steady himself leaned against the side of the stable.

"Have you had pox?" Brenda asked.

"I do not think so, m'lady."

"Let Sein look at your tongue."

"You want me to stick out my tongue?"

"Aye, Sein can tell if you are ill by looking at the color of the coat on your tongue."

Sein mumbled, "Uhmm," when he looked inside the child's mouth.

"You can see he is ill," said Brenda. " 'Tis shameful to make him work."

"Aye," said Sein. "Lad, go find Eira and ask her for something to help you sleep. In a day or two you will feel better."

"Please look after the little mare, m'lady," said Ailin. "I will be back." Near the door he stumbled, leaned against the wall for a moment, and then he was gone.

Brenda looked Sein in the eye and said, "You are callous and unmindful to that child's suffering! He is feverish and near fainting. What sort of physician are you?"

"I try to be the honorable sort. I do not practice illusions, neither sleight of hand, nor believe in calling on spirits of the dead. I do not believe that a corpse can be undead and leave its grave at night to suck blood from sleeping persons. I have seen unburied, bloated corpses whose fingernails grow and bloody fluid collects in the mouth. That is not magic; it has an explanation. I have seen the dead jerk and gurgle when placed on a funeral pyre and heard sorcerers say they are alive, mayhap changed to vampires. I have never seen a vampire. I believe they be like unicorns, a figment of some vivid imagination. Jerks and gurgles are because of gases that build up inside a corpse. Once dead, a corpse is always dead."

"I be glad you said naught of bloated corpses in front of Ailin," said Brenda. "If one has to experience such bloody things I may change my mind about being a healer."

"Nay, I pray not! You have the eyes of a healer. You saw his flushed face and the fever shine in his eyes. You were correct to think it might be pox, which the Romans call variola. Archdruid Finn introduced Ailin to a mild form of it when he first arrived, and I promised to watch for its onset."

"An archdruid gave him pox!"

"I be saying so. When Ailin came to us two weeks ago the archdruid had him sniff powdered variola scabs. He always does that for new fosterlings. Finn and I believe 'tis right and humane to protect children from deadly variola. What do you think?"

Brenda said she thought it a dreadful, barbaric thing. "Sniff scabs! Protect from deadly pox? What are you saying? You let this Finn give Ailin the pox? Give a child a deadly, blinding disease! I have never heard of anything so barbaric!"

She snapped her mouth closed because it suddenly dawned on her that a scholarly and learned people, the druids, lived in this camp. Whatever a mere maid, like herself, thought would have no credibility.

"Our fosterlings suffer no more than two, three days from a mild variola," said Sein. " 'Tis something old Finn discovered somewhere. It still surprises me. One to three weeks after sniffing scabs the fosterlings suffer mild chills and fever, but they do not have a hard case of variola. Please do not look skeptical. Ailin will drink Eira's sleep potion and for one, mayhap two days he will sleep, then be well. I speak the truth."

Brenda took a deep breath, exhaled and thought, Aye, you can bet I will see if you speak truth. "May I see him while he sleeps?"

"Certes," said Sein, trying hard to ignore her unbidden pique by pointing to the feverish horse that lay at her feet.

She knelt to look inside the horse's mouth and was overwhelmed by the foul smell and the lesions oozing a yellowish white "grease" on the neck and belly. Its breathing was shrill and reedy, causing Brenda to think of an Irish piper. She put her hand on the mare's head and said, "Too warm, like Ailin. Can you wrap her in wet cloths?"

Sein laid cloths soaked in soaproot solution over the mare's back and belly. She raised her head, shivered but did not object.

Brenda leaned closer. "Pagh! Can a horse have a kine disease, a disease of cows? The pustules look like kinepox."

Sein's eyebrows went up and he looked pleased with her question. He told her that several years ago a fosterling wiped down with soaproot a horse suffering from the grease and then milked the cows. It was Finn who noticed that the cows became infected with variola, but the cows were not as ill as usual. He observed that the same happened time after time. Sein crouched down on his haunches, and instead of examining the mare he looked closely at Brenda.

She became flustered and said, "What is it?"

His face turned red and he whispered, "I could not help but notice that your face is as smooth as—clean beeswax. Variola leaves ugly scars. Go to old Finn, sniff the scab and avoid scarring your lovely face."

Her lips curved upward. "When I first lived at the Gwynedd court I milked kine and some days later I had a fever, then the milkmaid's rash on my chest and arms and in a few days I felt better. The rash cleared and never came back, even though I handled infected kine. Do you still think I ought to sniff scabs? The thought makes me ill."

"Nay, you are protected by having had the milkmaid's fever. Have you seen milkmaid's rash develop into greasy blisters that become crusty dry and leave pitted scars?"

"Nay," said Brenda, patting the mare's head. "I saw no blistering among Welsh milkmaids."

"Old Finn observed the same thing! You will like him. He is a wise one."

"What would he do if a child has kine blisters?" asked Brenda.

"Bathe him with cool soaproot, put him on a bed of smooth linen sheets and stay with him until his fever breaks. He would pray hard to the Lord God and all the other gods he could think of. Once he showed me a parchment written by Hildegard of Bingen. She suggests treatments based on opposites."

"Does she suggest if a child is blistered, wrap him in something smooth and blue or if a patient is hot give him something cold?" said Brenda. "I never heard of Hildegard. Is she a druid healer?"

"A mystic who hears voices no one else hears, and the first woman to put her therapies in writing. Her parchments are called *Book of Simple Medicine*."

"A salve, to keep the crusty sores soft, seems better to me," said Brenda. "Are you writing a book of your own cures? What do you do with milk from infected kine? Is the cheese blighted and does it cause a murrainlike pox?"

"You ask more questions than any woman I have yet met," Sein said. "Neither old Finn nor I know anything that prevents scarring. Salves do not work. And nay, I keep nothing written. Parchment or vellum is easily destroyed and knowledge is lost. Information stays in my head, ready to pass on to other healers and students, who keep it in their heads, ready to use. 'Tis the druidic way."

Brenda felt a tingle float from the pit of her stomach to her throat. She was puzzled how this man's words could make her so furious and moments later leave her wanting to hear more.

All afternoon she held the mare's head on her lap to ease its breathing. She rubbed its ears, sang softly, dripped water on its tongue and hoped some of the drips fell down its throat. She stayed through the night, left only to feed Madoc and replace the moss in his diaper towel. Once she looked at Ailin, smoothed his tangled hair and whispered, "Get well, little laddie."

In the morning a young, yellow-haired, violet-eyed woman came into the barn. "I be Vivian," she said. "Wee Madoc is crying for his mam."

Brenda thought, What kind of mother forgets her own son? "Lugh, my breasts are full to exploding," she said. "Sit with the little mare for a few minutes. I will not be gone long."

She shifted the mare's head to Vivian's lap. "Keep its head way up so it can breathe."

Vivian raised her knees and shifted her hands so the head was elevated.

"Good lass," said Brenda.

"Sein says you are a born healer," said Vivian.

Brenda did not answer because she heard Madoc's frantic cry as soon as she opened the barn door. She ran to the cottage, sat on the edge of the pallet and spoke to Madoc in the same soothing, hushed tones she had used on the mare. When he was full and asleep she laid him on her pallet with a light covering, and went to the kitchen for breakfast.

She found Eira shelling peas. "There must be some way to feed Madoc when I be with the mare," said Brenda. "I could save my milk, but I have seen saved mother's milk make an infant colicky."

Eira nodded and said, "Mayhap he will take watery goat's milk mixed with a bit of honey. I have seen infants suck on a piece of wool that is soaked with honey milk. Oh, something more—Ailin woke and asked if you looked after the mare. I told him aye, and put him back to sleep. Tomorrow he will feel well. His father brought him to us because he lost his mam six months ago. He still grieves. It helps if you talk to him."

Ailin's red flush had faded to milk white. Brenda felt his forehead and thought his fever gone. She began to believe Sein was right about Ailin's short illness and wondered what made Finn first decide to have fosterlings sniff scab dust to prevent kinepox. How had he known what to do or what to try or how to start?

Ailin opened his eyes. "I saw you in the cave," he said. "You sat on my flat stone and looked into the water."

" 'Twas a dream," she said. "I have never been inside a cave with water. I was here with you and before that with the little mare, who sleeps."

He smiled and said he liked her voice. It settled his stomach. His hand brushed hers and he said, "Thanks. You are my healer." His eyes closed against the glare of the flickering lamp on the floor beside his pallet.

She ran her fingers through his hair and marveled at the beauty of his dark lashes against his pale cheeks. "I be your friend, laddie," she said.

She took an apple for the little mare and on the way to the barn she wondered what the boy meant about a cave.

Vivian lifted the mare's heavy head, wrenched herself out from under it like a frantic kitten in snug quarters. "This raggy little mare could be a wonderful workhorse," said Vivian, "if she were well."

The day was near gone when Brenda noticed the mare's sorrowful eyes no longer rolled up to look at her. She held out the apple. There was no blinking, only a dull stare. "Take a tiny bite," she whispered. "Come on, fight for your life! Ailin needs you. Fight!"

Its legs thrashed and she thought it was going to stand. Her heart soared and she tried to help it up. "Aye, you heard me! Fight!" she cried.

The mare's eyes filled with fear and she fell with one leg folded underneath itself. A dry rattling sound came from her throat.

"Hang on," said Brenda.

Suddenly it was quiet and Brenda heard no wheezing, gasping breath and saw thick, slimy mucus running from its mouth.

She talked to the mare as she poured the last of the soapwort over the cloths. She gritted her teeth and blew hard into the nostrils, then grimaced as she wiped the mucus from her mouth. She wiped her hand on her skirt and for a moment nausea rose from her stomach to the back of her throat. She pounded the mare's chest with both fists. "Come on! I am telling you to live! Live for Ailin. Come on, little mare. Breathe! I be with you!" She stood, threw the apple hard against the stable's boards. It broke, spraying juice and tiny pieces. "Why did you die? Lugh's lungs, Ailin is a wee lad who expected you to live!"

She heard voices, the sound of men and women joking and making bets on who was asleep, the mare or Brenda. She heard Sein's laughter. She was angry and wanted to shout that he was too late. Instead she took a deep breath, willing her gorge to stay down, and bowed her head in shame.

Sein took her in his arms and walked her into the cool evening air. She pulled herself away. "I left the mare, went to see Madoc and Ailin, and when I came back—oh Lugh, I was gone too long. The little mare died; I failed Ailin's trust!"

Vivian put her hand on Brenda's arm. "Do not blame yourself," she said. "The poor thing was half dead when I was with her."

Brenda's eyes flared and she said, "The mare rallied and tried to stand. She was better. Moments later she—she gave up and died. I know not why. I know only that I be no healer!"

"Mayhap preparing infusions, solutions, salves and unguents is more to your liking," said Vivian. " 'Tis more to mine. I cringe at the sight and smells of sick animals or people."

Eira put an arm around Brenda's shoulder and said, "Every healer faces death. 'Tis always hard. You never get used to it. But you learn something each time and you grow stronger."

"I be Finn," said an old man with a long, thin, white beard, "and I say none could have done better, m'lady. The gods smiled on you this evening. They took one fine little horse and left us one fine lad, named Ailin. I say we got the better deal."

After he spoke, Brenda knew she was not a failure in anyone's eyes but her own. Maybe Eira was right and death was a step forward in the understanding and growth of a healer.

She turned her face toward Finn. "Thank you. As soon as I be rested I want to hear more about your kind of healing."

Sein whispered, "However long the road there comes a turning."

She went to her pallet, pulled off her boots and curled herself around her sleeping babe.

"Where the turning takes one is the true mystery," she answered, and slept.

When she woke she saw Ailin sitting on his pallet on the other side of the room. She smoothed her hair and went barefoot to sit beside him.

"I think of the mare as mine," he said. "When it is well, I shall ride her. Do you think the mare will be all right?"

Brenda asked how he felt.

He looked at her, surprised she did not answer his question.

He swung his arms above his head to show that he was much better and there was no need to worry about him. "How is my little mare?"

Brenda asked if he knew why he had been ill.

He knew, he said, because the old man had made him inhale the powder that made him sneeze. Finn told him that in precisely two weeks he would be ill, and the illness would protect him from the dreaded kinefever so that he could work among horses or cattle the rest of his life. An impish grin spread across his face. "I fooled old Finn. I was ill in twelve days, not fourteen. While I was ill I rode the mare and named her Orla, the golden lady. 'Twas my mam's name."

" 'Twas another dream," said Brenda. "While you slept I held the little mare's head in my lap."

"Orla is better?" He grabbed her hand and put it against his face. It was smooth and felt good.

She raised her eyes and looked at him. "I sang and talked to Orla, who could not throw off her sickness as you did. Although Orla tried, kicked and made terrible sounds to frighten Death, when Orla's breath stopped Death took over. I tried to make Orla breathe by pushing air into her nose, but she never felt my breath."

"Orla died of kinefever?" He sobbed and Brenda held him close. "My mam died of kinefever. Are you going to die?"

"Nay," she said. "I had milkmaid's fever and Sein told me that was good. 'Twas a fever like yours. I hear a laddie crying. Come with me." She took his hand and led him to her pallet.

"Does the babe cry because a little mare died?"

"Nay," said Brenda. "He is hungry. Sit and hold him. His name is Madoc."

"I hope the old man put powder up his nose. He looks kind of puny and his tongue has a furry coat."

"Puny and furry?" Brenda was both amused and taken aback by the child's words.

"Is he ill?" asked Ailin.

"He is not puny, only small because he is a baby," said Brenda. Her mind swirled with the child's question. Her logic told her that Madoc had not been near the mare so he could not be ill. Could he?

*   *   *

For the next few days, when Ailin was not studying, going to classes or doing chores, he was at Brenda's side. He hummed to Madoc when he whimpered. Brenda thought he probably hummed the songs his own mother had sung. Otherwise the lad had become silent the last few days. She took him to the meadow to hunt wild herbs. She showed him how to peel bark so it would not harm the tree, to dig roots but never take all the plants. His silence did not concern her. She was sure he would talk to her all of a sudden one day and the silence would be over.

One day Brenda remembered that Llywarch wore a green bratt and cap and asked Eira if there were druidic laws about using certain colors. Eira said colors were a personal choice, but some druid orders preferred white or dark robes and others preferred belts or sashes of a certain color to designate First, Second or Third Order.

"Orders?" asked Brenda.

Eira said that ages ago the druids had divided themselves. First were the bards, who were singers, poets, harpers and keepers of history.

Second Order druids were the lawgivers, and the Third Order was composed of natural scientists and healers. "This is a Third Order camp." She said that when Brenda had memorized enough material about diseases and herbs she would eventually become a Third Order druid. "Sein will like that."

"I may not wish to be a druid," said Brenda. "I may leave soon." The mere mention of Sein caused her blood to race and she felt uncomfortable, yet it was somehow pleasant. She told herself she did not have to face Owain until Madoc was weaned. To think beyond the time of weaning, going back to Wales or staying in Ireland, brought a squeamishness to her throat. Could she go to Wales and actually leave Madoc behind? It was a quandary. She lowered her eyes and said to Eira, "What do Sein's 'likes' have to do with me?"

"Well, in the first place he is my cousin and foster brother, and as kin I can sense in my blood how he feels. He loves a student who is a fast learner, like yourself. In the second place, when you were no more than a skinny tadpole, you spoke at a meeting of lords in Dubh Linn. You were a wild creature with eyes that observed the minutest detail. Behind those eyes a quick mind assimilated and judged. Sein was fifteen. He said you were gallant. He dreamed you would be a future healer, one of the best. He asked around and found your father had called you Brenda for Saint Brendan, the Irish seafaring monk. Your father so loved the sea he wanted his only child to sail. If Prince Owain had not desired you, you would have been fostered to a sailor."

"There be no such thing as a lady sailor, not even an Irish word for one," said Brenda with great whoops of laughter.

"After you went to Wales to live with Prince Owain, Sein spoke of you as that chestnut-haired, feisty lassie. When Llywarch came to visit, Sein asked about you."

"Llywarch came here?" said Brenda. "And told Sein about me?" It had to be true, why else had Sein been looking for her the day she came above the brow of the drumlin? He had not seemed surprised that she had had a baby with her. There was a Welsh druid camp outside Aberffraw that Llywarch also visited and she said to herself that Welsh and Irish druids must all know one another and have a special way of communicating. She could not imagine how they delivered a bit of knowledge or a message so fast. 'Tis the druid magic, she thought, remembering that Sein had said that druid magic was really only using known natural energies to effect needed changes, such as improving a person's attitude or improving the place in which that person lived. She thought, If Sein understands those natural energies, he is certainly more knowledgeable than most ordinary people, like myself.

"Sein brings us word from the Welsh druids on the growing intensity of the Christian terror and sends messages to Archdruid Llieu about his latest healing methods. Listen, I predict that more Welsh druids, for their own safety, will come to Ireland. Do you know any Welsh druids besides Llywarch and Llieu?"

"Gwalchmai, a harper," said Brenda, admitting that she had never even seen the druid camp in Aberffraw. She had not thought much about druids and their beliefs until now. She had left her father before mores appeared important, and

Owain had never discussed his religion with her, although she knew that he was friends with people of both the New and Old Religions. He was tattooed with druid honor marks. She wondered why she had not asked him their meaning.

Brenda and Eira ate together at the long, bog-oak trestle table in the kitchen cottage. The table reminded Brenda of the one in the great hall in Owain's winter court at Aberffraw. When she finished her meal she excused herself and got up to go to the sleeping cottage. Sein met her at the door and said he had something to show her.

"Can it wait? Madoc is surely fussing for his supper."

"Ailin is with him. This will take only a moment. I made something for wee Madoc." From behind him he pulled out a truckle bed, made of plaited straw held together by wooden nails. "See, the edge is scalloped."

"You made this?" Brenda was mystified about where he found time to do such intricate work.

"Aye. I got up early and it came to my mind that this is what I should do."

"I—we thank you." Her face became red. "What can I— how can I repay you?" She was nearly tongue-tied. It was the loveliest baby bed she had seen.

"Shag it," said Sein, grinning. "Naught to repay. 'Tis a gift."

Eira came over and admired the truckle bed. She said she saw Sein making it and thought it looked like a tiny coracle or boat.

"If you feel the need to do something in return," said Sein, "you can decide to stay, learn all there is to know of our medicinals and become one of us, a master healer, a druid Wise Woman."

Eira looked sharply at Sein and said, "Cousin, one day your tongue is going to fall clean out! Where is your tact? Brenda does not know what she will do. Let her decide in her own time. She is not yet used to us!" She looked about, lowered her voice and said, "He worries. I do also. May I show the bed to the kitchen maids? Excuse me, there is something I should have told you. There is word that Prince Owain is scouting Dubh Linn and Carno for you."

"Prince Owain is known not only as a fearless ruler, but also as a peerless lover," Sein blurted. "He has more than a dozen sons by as many women. You are not going back to him!"

"What?" said Brenda. "You have no right to tell me what I be or be not going to do!"

Sein exploded. His mouth was beyond governing, and he named all the sons of Owain and their various mothers. There were nineteen boys divided among ten mothers or mistresses, including Brenda.

"And what other things do you know about the prince of Gwynedd?" said Brenda, flinging the words out and not sure why she defended Owain. "And why not name Owain's daughters? They are rare, but he has a few, like Goeral, who is mine. There is Gwenllian and at least one more. Girls count, you know!"

Sein put his hand on Brenda's arm. She yanked it away as if it were a hot iron. "Leave it!" he said. "You are upset and I be not blaming you."

"I be not—not in the least upset!" sputtered Brenda. Her face was dark. Sein was rude and had no business telling her anything about Owain. She knew more about Owain than any of these druids. Who did they think they were? A man could have as many sons or daughters as he wanted. His land would be divided among all of them at his death. Owain knew who would get what. It was all planned. He was meticulous and mannerly.

"I cannot accept the truckle bed. 'Tis an improper gift to a woman you hardly know and whose babe is another man's, whom you also do not know."

"I meant only the best for you," said Sein. "I want you to understand what kind of man you put on a pedestal. 'Tis a waste of time. He will marry his cousin, Christiannt, when Lady Gladys dies. Do you know that he still has his sister Angharad's five-year-old son in the oak tower of the winter court at Aberffraw? He will keep him there until Angharad pays tax on the mountain sheep and black cattle he gave her. His son Rein died when he was fourteen serving as a soldier in his father's army, and he was one of Owain's favorite sons.

Llyelyn died by drowning a few days after birth. Cadell and Eunid died before either was twelve as boy-soldiers in a battle between Owain and his brother, Cadwaladr." He took a deep breath, "Please do not go back to Gwynedd. There, as in all of Britain, life has become spying and murder, father jealous of sons, sons jealous of father, brothers jealous of brothers and intrigue among the women, and on top of that the beheadings by Christians. Stay here. When Madoc is weaned, I will foster him."

Brenda put her hands over her ears and cried, "Stop! You will not foster my son and I do not want to hear more! A couple of weeks ago I knew nothing of intrigue nor jealousy in Owain's court. Prince Owain told me naught of it. I knew he was sad, from his head to his toes, over the death of his twin lads, Cynoric and Edwal. I saw him teary-eyed, broken-hearted. How do I know what you say is true? Mayhap you are taunting me with untruths. Mayhap you will laugh among your friends about the way Brenda lost her temper. Well, I do not give a fig about what you say! Do you hear? I do not care! I need time to think! So if you do not mind I will just go to my pallet!" She left, pipping.

Eira came from the kitchen with the baby bed and looked crosswise at Sein. "What did you say to her? You could have waited until she knew you better. Not long ago she loved Owain and now she does not know whom to trust. Lugh, now you look like you lost your last friend."

"I feel like the sky has fallen and the sea is about to drown me," said Sein. "I wanted to tell her that I dreamed of building her a cottage so she would not have to sleep with the others. 'Twould be easier for her to get up in the middle of the night to tend her babe if she had a place of her own."

"I see in the back of your head that the dream cottage is for the three of you. Maybe four of you. Did you include Ailin? He too loves her," said Eira.

Sein's words crawled around in Brenda's head like spiders. She did not want Ailin to see that she was upset, so she kept her back to him. She picked up Madoc. He was warm, too warm. His eyes were big and glassy. There was a rash behind his ears, on his neck and chest. Without thinking she turned to Ailin. "Young man," she said, "did you give your fever to Madoc?"

Ailin looked up at her with a puzzled smile. He opened his mouth as if he was trying to find words even though he had not spoken since the day the mare died. He exhaled a great volume of air, inhaled a little and said slow and plain as summer rain, "I be so sorry, ma'am."

Brenda momentarily forgot her tiff with Sein. She bent to hug Ailin, to praise him for finding his voice. She looked at him gently, and he looked back with panic in his eyes. He darted away before she could muster words to call him back.

V
Ailín

> The truckle or trundle bed was usually of straw rope or plait, formed like a mat and held flat by spicks [long wooden spikes] thrust through the plait. The edge was finished with two or three raised rows, kept upright by shorter spicks thrust down into the mat below. This edge kept off the draught and held in the bedclothes.
>
> Dorothy Hartley, *Lost Country Life*

Eira folded a piece of linen for the bottom of the truckle bed and asked Brenda if she could lay Madoc inside. "Just to see how he looks?"

Brenda kept her eyes lowered, removed Madoc's coverings and pulled up his little shirt to expose his rash. She watched Eira draw in her breath, sit on the edge of the pallet and examine the red welts. "Tell me true," Brenda whispered, "should I worry about my babe's illness?"

Eira's face was a controlled mask. "Nay. Brenda, you know as well as I that worry is worthless, even if 'tis kinefever. Together we will see him good as new."

Deep inside Brenda's skull there was a nagging uncertainty; kinefever was a harbinger of death. But Madoc was to have wisdom and be honored by men, therefore he would get well. She closed her eyes to send a silent prayer to the gods, to any god who would listen. Please help. I promise to honor you, sing praises of your wonderful powers and understand more of your wisdom. I will become a druid.

She opened her eyes and glanced toward Ailín's empty pallet. Suddenly her feeling of peaceful appeal was turned inside out. Some terrible thing was going to happen. She feared what-

ever it was and made a codicil to her prayer. Send Ailin back
and I shall become a healer. Aloud she said, "Eira, there is
something wrong, something for worry. Ailin is gone."

Eira held a damp linen cloth against Madoc's forehead.
"My da says a boy comes home when he is hungry," she said.

"But does your father know about Ailin? I hurt his feelings
and he ran out in the cold. Where did he go? Does he know
his way or will he become lost?"

"Oh prut! Brenda, get a basin of water and bathe your wee
one's face and arms. Between bathings try to get some sleep.
In the morning Ailin will be here. You worry overmuch! Da
says a light heart lives long."

"Your father paid my passage from Degannwy to Dubh
Linn!"

"Och, that is what Da does. He builds ships and spends his
pay to bring druids from Wales to Ireland when they are har-
ried by New Religionists."

"I be not a druid."

Eira smiled. "You will be. Now go to sleep."

"I cannot sleep. Madoc refuses to nurse."

"Try. First thing in the morning ask Sein and Finn to look
at Madoc," said Eira. "Vivian has something to soothe his
throat. He looks precious in the truckle—like a darling rabbit
curled up in a basket. Stop worrying."

Brenda wanted to shout that she could not help but worry;
a little boy was missing, probably freezing to death in the night
air, and her babe was ill with kinefever. She looked down at
Madoc's puffy, red, blistery face. He looked more like a
plucked chicken with a bad case of nettles than a darling rabbit. Perhaps Eira did not see people just right.

She did not sleep the whole night, but listened to Madoc's
every breath, kept one eye on his hot little body. The other
eye she kept on Ailin's empty pallet, and prayed to gods who
seemed deaf.

Sometime before morning light she got up and sat shivering
on Eira's pallet.

"Want me to hold Madoc for a while so you can sleep?"
asked Eira.

"Nay," said Brenda. " 'Tis Ailin. He is not home. Do you

feel anything strange when you look at his empty bed?"

Eira clicked her tongue and said, " 'Tis cold for a laddie to be away from the homefire. He has few places to go from here. 'Tis too far to Dubh Linn, but he might be with the herder Seth and his wife, Dornoll. They have a baby girl and lambs and goat kids. You know how gentle Ailin was with the little mare, and how he has been with Madoc."

"Where does this herder live?" asked Brenda. Her teeth chattered, and she rubbed the gooseflesh on her arms.

"Up the creek a ways. 'Tis a tough trail over boulders and rock cliffs. The lad never should go alone."

By now other women were awake and asking what was so important to talk about in the middle of the night. They buzzed with hushed voices like women gossiping at a quilting bee. None of them remembered seeing Ailin the day before. Brenda repeated her story several times because she was the last to see him. When their buzzing awoke the men, Sein called for Brenda to tell her story once more and not leave out a thing.

At the end of her recitation she said, "After the little mare died Ailin has not spoken, but I heard him speak clear as a willow warbler when I pointed out Madoc had kinefever."

Sein asked Brenda why she had not told him about Madoc's illness and Ailin's departure. "Did you think I was blind?"

The question made her feel as if she were staring at the point of a sword. She told herself that he need not browbeat her. Sudden tears ran down her cheeks and she stuttered, "Well—wellaway! I—I hoped Ailin would be here to sup yesterday. I—I—it is my fault he ran away. I—I made him think he caused Madoc's illness!"

Sein pulled on his trousers and a clean linen shirt. He bent, blew out the candle flame, slipped on his brogues and pulled the lacing tight.

The room, now flooded with gray daylight, became silent as a sacred well, except for the howling of the wind.

"Finn and I shall look for Ailin upstream as far as the herdsman's hovel," said Sein. "Others will walk all the animal trails to see if Ailin walked away with no great purpose or went toward Dubh Linn." He turned to Brenda. "First I will bring you something for the babe."

He returned shortly and went directly to the truckle bed. Gently he pried Madoc's lips apart and from a small ivory spoon let a single drop of oily liquid fall into the little mouth. He gave Brenda the vial of medicine, saying to use only a drop at a time. "More than that might cause convulsions."

She ran her fingers over the vial, held it up to the window, smelled it and then tucked it in the bottom of the truckle bed.

Sein put on his cap and woolen bratt, held the door open for Finn, who was fastening his bratt close around his neck. Other men, already bundled and anxious to begin their search for Ailin, pushed past Finn. A flurry of snow blew inside and melted on the floor.

Brenda sat on Ailin's pallet and pulled his blanket against her breast. She smelled the lad's perspiration mixed with earth and decaying leaves. The wind whistled. She felt dizzy and cold, as if her blood had drained away.

When Madoc awakened, Brenda bathed him in warm water one limb at a time, then his encrusted chest, belly, back and face. She wrapped him in her underskirt and held him against her full breast. His scab-crusted lips were like little bristles against her skin, but he was cooler to the touch and he nursed with vigor. After he drifted off, she went to the kitchen cottage and asked Vivian about nearby caves.

"Aye, there is one on the other side of the drumlin, opposite the standing stones. When the stream dries in summer we take water from a well inside."

"Has Ailin been there?"

"Maybe, with Eira. He cried a lot when he first came, and she took him on her chores."

"If I go, will you watch Madoc?"

"Aye, but be careful. The water is icy cold and takes a lot of warming for tea or bathing."

She put on her boots and a blanket over her head and shoulders, covering her bratt. She asked Eira, who was paring squash, if she would take a short walk before preparing the noon meal. "We shall not be gone long."

Eira pursed her lips. "If Ailin is lost," she said, "you will be blamed. 'Tis good you want to look for him."

The crisp air ran down their throats like cold spring water. They walked into the circle of nine standing stones. Eira stopped in the center and held her face toward the heavens and closed her eyes to pray.

Brenda blew on her hands, frowned and looked across the clearing toward gray stones covered with age-old, brown lichen at the brow of the drumlin. "I will race you there." She pointed. "Mayhap Ailin sits behind the stones."

Eira sprinted forward and called, "Ailin! Ailin!"

The red berries of the rowan were covered with a thin layer of snow, like white icing. The gray skeletons of birch trees held their branches up, like arms, toward the gray sky.

Brenda caught up to Eira and said, "I be responsible for Ailin, who has neither a blood mother nor a blood father. I pray to the gods; perhaps one of them will aid in our search."

"Aye, can we truly influence the gods? Or is it an illusion?" asked Eira as she searched behind boulders and inside clumps of juniper. She walked to a ledge of rock that slanted downward to the half-lit mouth of a shallow limestone cave. She pointed, and Brenda hunched to go inside.

Suddenly Brenda felt a prickly coldness move up her spine, an instinctive fear of dark places. From the corner of her eye she saw a buzzard soaring in wide circles over the trees on the drumlin, a fine sight.

"'Tis said if a buzzard does not dart down on an unsuspecting prey 'twill bring luck," said Eira. "Go into the cave before it circles lower and darts down."

"Will a buzzard truly bring us luck?"

"Since becoming a druid I believe those old sayings less and less." Eira hid her hands inside her blanket.

"Druids hide their hands," said Brenda. "If you have honor marks, you might be proud and let them be seen, admired."

"We have to be careful," said Eira, "not to show off honor marks when we are with strangers."

It was pleasant inside the cave, out of the wind. Standing on the edge of a huge rock, Brenda looked down into a natural well. There was enough light on the water to reflect her face. She could see dozens of ampullae and water jugs partly buried in mud, and asked Eira about them.

" 'Tis sacred water," said Eira, "thought to be more pure than creek water. If the rope around the neck of the jug is not secure, the water witch takes it." She giggled lightheartedly then said, "For truth, the shears that cut the holy mistletoe and sacred garments are washed here. Once Sein dropped his shears and Finn told him to leave them for the water witch, who probably plucked them from his hands. Of course he laughed. A spring feeds the well and creates a whirlpool in the center that grabs onto things and pulls them down, down." She stopped talking when she saw that Brenda was not listening, but holding her breath and studying the rocky ledge close to the water.

"You can see the whole pool from here," said Brenda. She wanted to climb down, but she was afraid the limestone was sharp and steep.

"Last person I saw sit like that was Ailin," said Eira. "I told him something that my mother once told me. When you look into a sacred pool you see your second self that lives under the water. Your second self wears the same kind of clothes you do. No one knows if the second self has a home, but some say it lives under the stones or in the mud. But everyone knows if you look long enough the second self will pull you down. It wants company."

"What is that?" Brenda pointed to the water. "Looks like a box, a wooden box—my God, 'tis a brogue—a boot!"

"I see naught," said Eira. "You are imagining. Come, let us go back to the kitchen."

"Look—on the ledge. Something moved! 'Tis—'tis a leg! Ailin! Is that you? Ailin?" She pulled off her blanket and bratt, lay down on the ledge and searched with one foot for something to stand on so she could inch her way down the lip of the precipice. The fear was gone and in its place a small tingling moved slowly up her back. She did not flinch when she slipped on loose stones.

"What are you doing?"

Brenda's foot caught in her skirt. She shifted around, came back to the top and took off her skirt, letting it fall beside the blanket and bratt. "When I call, throw down my kirtle."

"Are you crazy?" said Eira. "You will catch your death."

Brenda backed down the ledge and, shoving her boots tight against the rock pockets, slid her hands to a narrow ledge and felt with one foot for another place large enough to stand firm. At first she shivered, but after a few minutes she was perspiring, and her hands were slick with sweat.

When her feet were secure she called, "Ailin? 'Tis Brenda here." She heard the water gurgle. She moved one foot back and forth until she found another pocket, closer to the sacred pool. She looked down but could only see rock, not even her feet, which were now tucked underneath the overhang. "I be down but I cannot turn around!" she called up to Eira.

"Come back!" called Eira. "The well can swallow you! Your second self will grab you!"

Brenda said, "Prut, that is all ancient nonsense!" She looked up and could only see Eira's breath puff and fade away, puff and fade. She lowered herself down another notch and bent her head so that she could see under her arm. Both of her feet were so close to the water that if she took another step she would be swimming. One foot was already wet and cold. She bent ever so slowly and felt along the bottom ledge. Her hand bumped something wet and coarse. She willed herself to let go of the rock and bend lower. She felt along the wet thing. It was solid. Once she thought it twitched. "Oh God, what have I here?" she said out loud. She wished she could see.

"Is it Ailin!" Eira called. "Shall I throw your stuff down?"

"I cannot see! Wait!"

"Mayhap the men are back! I will get someone!"

"Listen! Wait! I have to go into the water because this ledge is too narrow for me."

"Nay!" screamed Eira. " 'Tis freezing. You will drown! Brenda, please! Listen to me!"

Close to the water the stone was freezing cold. Brenda's hands were no longer sweaty and she was not sure she could hold on if they were much colder. She bent over as far as she could and saw Ailin's large eyes looking up at her. She did not feel her hands slip from the stone, but she knew she was falling. She expected to feel icy water. Instead her knees hit solid rock.

She let her breath go in long hoarse pants and opened her

eyes. Barely two yards from her right side was Ailin, lying on his back with one foot in the water. She had a cramp in her left shoulder and her legs throbbed something fierce, but she could feel the stone, and knelt on it.

She swung around, reached into the water and pushed Ailin's leg up onto the rock ledge. It slid off and moved with the water's gentle eddy, slowly out, then back. She talked to Ailin. He did not move and there was no room for her to stretch far enough to tell if warm breath escaped from his open mouth. She saw no vapor cloud, not even a tiny one. She leaned her head against the stone and from the corner of her eye she saw him blink. Could that be, or was it a reflection off the pool where the shadows played along the stone? She did not see him blink again.

She did not think about what she had to do. Some unnamed primitive instinct slid her off the narrow ledge into the water. The water closed over her shoulders, washed over her face. She kicked her feet to keep her head in the air, but her heavy leather boots pulled her down into the whirlpool. Her lungs burned and she thought she would never draw another breath of air. She reached out for the stone ledge and her arm bumped Ailin's boot, which moved with the current. She clung to his leg and paddled to the ledge. Ailin continued to stare at her out of his blue, blue eyes. "Laddie, I be here," she croaked. The scuffed leather of his brogue was soaked through. His knee was bent at a strange angle and kept slipping back into the water. She put her cheek close to his mouth. Aye, there was breath, but so faint it was barely detectable. She held fast to the ledge, pushed Ailin's hair back and tried to move his head. She was sure that his lips turned up into a tiny smile. A blue bruise was on his cheek and she knew he had fallen. She edged along the rock ledge and found a place wide enough for her to sit if she could pull herself up. The cold air scorched her lungs whenever she took a deep breath.

The dragging current pulled her under once and she thought of the water witch. No figment of some ancient's primitive imagination was going to get her. Finally she got her bruised knees up on the ledge and pulled herself out of the water. Her breathing was hard and it was colder on the ledge than in the water. Her teeth chattered, causing her head to ache, but she was too exhausted to stop. She put her hand on Ailin's face, and her hand was too numb to feel his breath again.

She turned her face upward and shouted, "Now!" hoping Eira was still there. "Now!"

Her skirt came tumbling in a wad down the ledge, hit the water and spread open like a fishnet and swirled with the current around and around then disappeared in the vortex. Her blanket and bratt slid across the rocks side by side and stopped on the ledge directly above. She forced herself to stand, to reach up for them. She was too short.

"Run!" she yelled. "Be quick! Ailin needs help!"

Her shivering was so strong that she could hardly get her boots off. She removed Ailin's bratt, folded it and laid it on her boots. She stood on top of the pile, touched the ledge, pulled herself onto her tiptoes. For a moment she was dizzy and clung to the rock, then she jerked herself upward and her benumbed fingers touched the blanket and bratt enough to pull them off the ledge. She held out her arms and caught them before they fell into the water. Her arms and chest ached with the effort, and she leaned against the rock wall. When she looked up she could not see Eira's breath in the air. She closed her eyes and in her mind she saw her friend running over the snow to the cottage shouting for someone to help. "Go! Go!" she yelled, until a coughing spasm overtook her.

She let the blanket and bratt slip to her feet, then sat on the ledge, and took off Ailin's brogues and clothes. His right shoulder was purple and yellow-blue. She thought how he must have fallen on it and how it must have hurt when he hit the rocks. When did he fall? How long had he been here? Was it dark when he fell or was it right after he left her? He had enormous courage to climb out of the water and onto the ledge by himself. She bundled him in the blanket, took off her wet clothes, and had started to wrap the bratt around her shoulders when she noticed something. A skirt, no, Eira's underskirt, was folded inside the bratt. Dear Eira, my friend, she thought, pulling the bratt's folds apart and wrapping the underskirt around Ailin's legs. Then she wrapped herself in the dry bratt.

She leaned against the wall with Ailin in her lap and closed her eyes.

"I knew you would find me," Ailin whispered, his cold little hand finding hers.

"My laddie, I be sorry you were scared. Of course I came to find you. Help is coming. Keep your legs still."

His voice bubbled. "Mam?"

"Aye, you can call me Mam."

Ailin held his chest and gasped for the next shallow breath. "Rest now," she said.

His shoulders slumped against her chest. She tucked the blanket tighter and held him close. "Lugh," she prayed aloud to the water god, "let my warmth flow into the lad. See how snow white he is? You soaked all the sun-brown color out of his skin. For shame!"

She closed her eyes, thinking of the warm fire in the kitchen cottage. She drifted off and dreamed that Ailin spoke to her. He asked if they were their other selves and she assured him they were their own selves, out of the water. He told her he had waited for her to come. He said that Madoc was ill because he got up in the middle of the night and put his face against the babe's so he could sing to him without waking anyone. "Madoc and me were lonely, and I let him suck on my finger. But remember, you petted and nuzzled my little mare, Orla, and then you petted and kissed Madoc. Did he suck on your fingers? Babies suck anything. So mayhap 'twas both you and me who gave Madoc kinefever."

In her dream Brenda suspected that she had known all along that she had given her son the dreaded disease. She told Ailin she had loved him from the first time they met, and she would never stop. He was not to blame himself for Madoc's illness, and she was sorry that she had said words that caused him to be so frightened that he ran to the cave. He said he loved her and was glad he could call her mam. Then in the dream she heard him say clear as a sunny sky, "Mam, 'tis up to you to help Madoc grow into a shining man. Do not fret. I be getting out of here by myself."

As if it were part of her dream, she felt a warm breath blow across her forehead and strong arms lace a leather rope under her arms. The arms pulled her upright and a husky voice said, "Watch your knees. Reach up and hang on."

"Take Ailin first!" she said. "Take him where 'tis warm." Her lips had no feeling and her voice sounded strange.

"We have him. Lean against me. All right, now. Here we go." Strong arms went about her waist and she felt herself lifted up. Hard, muscular legs under her pushed her away from the rocks and they swung together as they moved up. Then she felt the top of the rocky cliff press against her feet. "Thank the gods you are all right," the voice said in her ear. "Dearest Brenda, I would die if something happened to you."

She heard Finn's raspy voice say, "For Lugh's liver! Get the rope off, the blankets around her before she stops breathing altogether. She has been in the cold too long. I can hardly feel her heartbeat!"

"Nay! Nay!" she said, pushing away from the wide chest with arms weak as watered soup. " 'Tis Ailin! He needs the blankets."

"I have him."

"Thank the gods," she said. "Take him home."

"He is there."

She sighed and let her arms relax. Everything was all right. The last thing she heard was Eira saying, "Vivian says your babe be stronger." She slid down against the sturdy, wide chest that smelled of heather, into comforting darkness and never knew that Sein wrapped her in a blanket and carried her to her pallet.

Brenda opened her eyes to find that she was nearly smothered in sheets and quilts and wool blankets.

Eira slipped a hot stone wrapped in strips of wool beside her feet. "Hallelujah! Brenda wakes from her two-day sleep."

Madoc cried lustily and Vivian, holding him, sat on the floor beside Brenda's pallet. "As soon as you drink some soup, hold him. He knows I be not his mam and he tells me about it each mealtime."

Eira held out a beaker of barley soup. Brenda clearly saw curling blue lines, like vines and tiny leaflets, around the bases of Eira's nails. On the inside of her right wrist was a little flower nestled among bent lines that looked like wild grasses. The marks were not hidden and Brenda knew she was no longer a stranger, but a friend. "The purple mossy flower is the earliest to bloom and shows that I be a healer," said Eira.

Brenda took the beaker, sipped once and asked if Finn had come to see her. Her throat hurt when she spoke. She put the beaker on the floor, tried to cough, but coughing hurt more.

"Twice a day. None of us have had much sleep, except you."

"Should I be sorry?" asked Brenda in a creaky voice.

"What you should be is grateful to Sein. He is the one who devised the ropes that brought you back up the cliff. He saved your life. If you were in the cold much longer you would have died."

"Sein?"

"Aye," said Eira. "I swear by Lugh's lungs that he would do anything for you. He—"

Madoc did not wait for Eira to finish, but screwed up his face and howled like a banshee. Vivian pushed him into Brenda's arms. "See, his lungs are just fine, and he is going to be an ugly duckling until all those scabs slough off." She helped Brenda pull up her nightshirt so Madoc could nurse.

Brenda saw that Madoc's face was smooth, with hardly a pitted red scar, and only a few black scabs, and knew that Vivian was teasing her, trying to get her to smile. Madoc was demanding and impatient. Suddenly he stopped nursing and howled.

"Mayhap your milk is frozen solid," said Vivian.

"Stop that bawling," chided Eira. "Your poor mam is trying to drink her soup and feed you at the same time, you little mewly-drooly thing."

Brenda did not know whether to laugh or cry. She did not have enough milk to satisfy this hungry babe, and these women, her friends, were teasing her. She moved Madoc to her other breast. With satisfaction, she felt the strong suction of his mouth draw out her milk. When Madoc was drowsily gratified she said, "And Ailin? Can I see him?"

Both Eira and Vivian looked down at the floor. Eira began,

"He, well—Finn brought him back and . . ." and tears filled her eyes.

Vivian swallowed. "Brenda, he died while in your arms."

"No! No! He lives. I held him to keep him warm."

"His lungs were filled with water," said Vivian.

"I held him close. My body warmed him."

Vivian put her arms around Brenda. "Finn said he could not have lived."

"Ailin and I talked," insisted Brenda.

"His ribs punctured his lungs," said Eira. "Finn does not understand how you got him out of the water."

"He—he got out by himself. He waited for me. Aye, there is some mistake. He is not dead. 'Tis shameful to make a ghoulish joke about a brave, precious laddie. Where is he?"

" 'Tis no joke," said Eira, taking Brenda's hands in her own. "Some may blame you for his death."

Brenda blinked, tensed and pulled her hands back. "I—I wanted him to live. I prayed. He held my hand so tight."

"Aye, like the two of you were frozen together," said Vivian. "Sein pried him loose."

"Ailin said he knew I would come," whispered Brenda. "He waited for me. He said I was meant to care for Madoc, who would be a shining man. He said for me not to fret because he would get out by himself. Oh, Lord God! That is what he did. He got out by himself!"

VI
Gwynedd Soldiers

The mediaeval road was not made *for* transport and
travel, but *by* transport and travel. . . . All these "roadways" had to pass near water [vital for horse or ox] and
many tracks lay beside guiding streams. . . . It was only
in towns and cities that the typical cobbled street existed,
made of local stone, rounded river stones, or close-
packed sea-beach pebbles, frequently with a gutter down
the centre. Near shipbuilding yards, sawdust and pitch
would be used.

Dorothy Hartley, *Lost Country Life*

The hills were covered with snow. The grasses that poked
above the white mantle were rimed. There were slivers of ice
along the banks of the stream.

Brenda stayed on her pallet for most of a week.

She felt stiff and sluggish and wondered if she would ever
be warm again. A whole day would go by without her hearing
or speaking a word. She hovered between living and nonliving. The fire in the sleeping cottage burned day and night.

One night, when she thought everyone was asleep, she
dared herself to look at Ailin's empty pallet and remembered
his love for the little mare and the sadness in his eyes when
he learned the mare had died. She recalled the gentleness in
his boyish voice as he helped care for Madoc, and the affection
in his eyes when he looked at her. She had given him friendship and security, and he had given her trust and love. He was
willing to do anything for her, and she rewarded him by breaking his heart with the thoughtless, false accusation that he had

caused Madoc's illness. It was her fault that he was gone, and
she wanted to tell him she was sorry.

Near morning she roused herself from the dreamy detach-
ment, looked through the gray light to the dark ceiling beams
and let her breath warm the cold air around her face. Madoc
cried and she cuddled him under her bed cloths, closed her
eyes and waited for full dawn to come. When she awoke she
saw Eira, fully dressed, lying on the foot of her pallet, as if
she had been there awhile. Brenda's whole body felt like one
large ache. She was stiff as a cornstalk. She forced herself to
sit up and brushed her hand over Eira's thick, dark hair. Eira
opened her eyes.

"No need to worry about me." Brenda's voice was hoarse
and her tongue was thick.

Eira raised her head. "Mayhap you think I be the only one
who worries about thee. Well, the whole camp is concerned
because you seem to have given up on living. I want you to
know we cannot stand still waiting for you to decide which
path you will take, life or death. We have lives that are full
and meaningful."

"You do not have to stay here with me," said Brenda. "I
like to be alone."

Eira stood and took a deep breath. "I came to say that I be
going to ask Finn to talk to you," she said softly.

"No! No! I do not want to talk to anyone."

Eira knelt beside the pallet; her eyes fixed on Brenda.

Brenda saw that Eira's mouth was set in a straight line and
knew that she was stubborn when her mind was made up about
something. "Why are you doing this?" Brenda whispered.

"You are like a sister to me. I be going to save your mind,
your judgment, whether you help me or not. If you do not
care about yourself, think about your infant son. Think about
us, about Sein, a man who would do anything, no matter the
circumstances. He risked his life for you. 'Tis time to get up
and live."

Brenda held back the tears. "I once loved a man and he
me," she said, "but now he would kill me and my babe. I
loved Ailin and would have given my life for him, but I killed
him. I do not believe 'tis possible for a person, under all cir-

cumstances, to give everything, including life, for another."

"You are so pigheaded!" shouted Eira. "If you cannot think of us"—she pointed to Madoc, then to herself—"think about what you are doing to yourself. I have changed my mind; I will not ask Finn to talk to you. But when you have figured out your problem, tell me what you are going to do about it." She got up, walked out the door, letting it slam shut.

At dawn, four days later, with barely enough milk to satisfy her son's hunger, Brenda sat up on her pallet and waited for Eira to awaken. She had decided to ask if she might supplement Madoc's nursing with feedings of watery gruel.

Eira was thrilled to hear Brenda's question and to see her sitting upright with her eyes open. "A wonderful idea," she said, crawling out of the bed cloths. "I shall bring you gruel and a small spoon. Nay, nay, do not get up."

After Brenda had fed Madoc and eaten the leftover gruel herself, Eira bathed her and wrapped a quilt around her shoulders. Eira took a long time to brush out Brenda's tangled hair, braid it, and pin it up in a loop behind each ear. Brenda asked for a pan of water so she could bathe Madoc.

Eira came back to take away the spent bathwater and admire Madoc. She waved her hand toward the doorway. "You have visitors," she said.

People came in, stamping their snowy feet. Brenda lay back against her pillow to accept their cool kisses. She thanked them for taking time to see her, and her head swirled with their names and faces. None mentioned Ailin, but Brenda saw the accusation in their eyes. They believed it was her fault the lad was dead. When someone whispered that she would have plenty of time to atone for her misconduct, the room spun and their words ran together into a steady "Umm."

Finn used his walking stick to herd them out of the doorway. "There is bread and clobbered milk in the kitchen," he said. "Time to eat." He bent and ran his gnarled fingers through Madoc's fine blond hair. "I believe 'twill be curls one day," he whispered close to Brenda's ear. "He lives for something special."

She caught his hand in hers. "Ailin could have been something special, only he is gone. 'Twas my fault. Everyone knows it."

"Posh! 'Twas fate. People influence people, no matter what age they live in. 'Tis not healthy to blame, but 'tis something people—druids are no exception—do until they have more wisdom."

Nine was a sacred number to the druids, and nine days after his death, Ailin's body was wrapped tight in a linen sheet and cremated outdoors, in an oak fire, in the druid way, while the moon was at its apex.

At first light Finn took Ailin's ashes, in a two-handled jar, deep inside the nearby cromlech.

Brenda was awake before he left and timidly asked if she could carry the amphora, but Finn forbade it, saying she was not strong enough to walk half a league in the cold air.

He does not want me up and about where I must be seen with him, she thought, and was consumed with tears of self-pity.

Sein returned with sheep oil–lotion from the herder. It was to keep Madoc's last and largest scabs soft so that the concave pink skin underneath would fill in and fade to a healthy color.

"You have cried enough," said Sein. "Any more tears are useless. Tell me, what do you cry for?"

He sat on her pallet and waited quietly. Finally she told him that she had tried to speak with Ailin's spirit after the cremation, at the peak of the night, when the veil between living and dead was weakest. "I heard not a word. Do you believe Ailin did not go to the Otherside?"

"I believe his spirit is there, mayhap telling others about your heroism."

His words made her sit up straight as a hazel stick and dry her eyes. "Nay, I be no heroine," she said. "You cannot believe that. Some say I be a source of bad luck. Think of the happy time before I came to your camp. You had a beautiful little mare and a wonderful boy named Ailin. I came and both died. I have a bad influence over people and animals. 'Tis best I leave."

"My dear, you did naught wrong. You could not possibly hurt any living thing."

She shook her head.

He said, "Tell me what you are thinking. Sometimes it helps to put thoughts in words, especially when a man's short life is snuffed out quickly as a candle flame in a strong puff of air."

"Ailin was not a man; he was a lad," she said. "A lad who would have been a fine man. His life was not snuffed out quickly. It took him a long time to die lying on a cold stone ledge by an icy pool of water. He was in terrible pain, and he waited for me to find him." A lump in her throat grew to the size of a hazelnut.

"We do not always have control over life. 'Tis in the hands of the gods and called fate."

"Mayhap nay, mayhap aye. I have thought about it over and over every night for fourteen days, and I know why Madoc had kinefever and why Ailin died. 'Twas my fault. Honest, it first came to me clear as a beaker of water while I held Ailin on that icy, cold ledge. Then for days afterwards I doubted and was not certain of my own thoughts. On that cold ledge, I told Ailin I was sorry and I did not blame him for Madoc's illness. I think he heard and understood. He called me mam and told me 'twas more my fault than his. I gave Madoc kinefever from the little horse. 'Twas my fault."

"Nay, nay!" said Sein, "You are wrong. You probably dreamed that Ailin breathed out a few words. His chest was hurt and he could not have spoken. Your thinking is wooly."

"I am thinking clearly! Hear me. I brought kinefever to my son on my hands. A mother's hands. You see, I petted the little mare, talked to her, nuzzled her and dabbed her with soaproot. I handled my son, fed him and nuzzled him. It was the same as feeding him powdered scab three, four times a day, only it was not scab, it was the muck from the fresh sores. That is how milkmaids get kinefever. Do you see? 'Twas my doing. I started all of it. Madoc's sickness, then Ailin's death!" She shivered under the woolen nightshirt.

Sein straightened, recognized that the nightshirt belonged to Finn and wished he had thought of giving her one of his.

He thought she was the loveliest creature he had ever seen, no matter that her eyes were red-rimmed and her cheeks blotched with red. Her mind was logical and wondrous. "Have you told Finn?"

"Och! I be not telling another soul. I be going to Carno to be near my father and two other children. 'Tis best. I cause only havoc and grief here."

"I heard weeks ago that Prince Owain looked for one of his mistresses in Carno. What will happen if he finds you with a babe that is supposed to be drowned?"

"You would not tell Owain that my babe lives. 'Tis a druid secret," she said with a quirky smile. "Madoc and I leave on the morrow. I do not mind being on my own. Some in the camp will be glad to have me gone." She slid down inside the bed cloths and felt every muscle in her body relax.

The first morning of spring, before the others awoke, Sein, who could not sleep for thinking of ways to keep Brenda from leaving, was out to release the camp's cattle into a little pasture enclosed by a wall of field stone. The sky was overcast, but the icy wind was gone. Soggy snowflakes fluttered heavily to the ground. When he opened the gate so the cattle could wander to the creek for water, he saw a horsebacker moving uphill.

The horsebacker was a woman wearing sheepskin trousers, a sheepskin vest and a fur cap. The horse slowed and came to a halt, and she dismounted.

Her mouth fell into a straight line, her words became ritualistic, something she was expected to say. "Is this the camp of the Taliesin Third Order druids?" Her freckled face shone with snowmelt. Her brown eyes darted from Sein to the two large cottages, now barely visible as snow fell faster. She took off a glove and held out her right hand in a ceremonial manner so that Sein could see her honor markings: dark blue fretting around the base of her fingernails and a soaring falcon on the inside of her right wrist.

"You know I be Sein, the chief of the Taliesin camp, foster son of Archdruid Gorlyn, who is related to Lug."

"And you know I be Pyfog, daughter of Finn, sent from Dubh Linn by Archdruid Gorlyn, the shipbuilder, to tell you of another curragh that arrived this morning from Degannwy, Wales."

Sein completed the ceremony by putting out his hand so that Pyfog could see his honor marks.

"Come inside," he said, "where there is a fire and something to drink. One of our boys will take your horse to the barn and give it a good rub."

Inside the kitchen cottage Pyfog took off her cap and vest, laid them on a bench in front of the fire to dry and eagerly took the horn of hot mead that was offered. "Your foster father paid well to bring you this information," she said. " 'Tis time to listen to the message. The Welsh prince, Owain Fawr, again has sent half a dozen troops to Ireland, in a curragh, to look for a Mistress Brenda."

"Why is Prince Owain so interested in Brenda, who is an Irish lady?" asked Sein guardedly.

"Pah! You know the lass and her royal story. She recently lived in Owain's Gwynedd court, gave birth to a son, who died in a pan of bathwater. Bloody weather to take a bath, especially a newborn. The rest of the story is a royal secret. Prince Owain's wife, Lady Gladys, gave premature birth to a stillborn. A third lad was born to Owain's cousin. The cousin's babe was given to Lady Gladys, who believes he is her own and named him Dafydd. Lady Gladys believes her husband's two mistresses lost their babes, and she feels guilty for having the only live birth. 'Tis hard for men to understand women. Some women do not know enough to be happy with what they get—they have to make it something to mope about. In contrast there is Brenda. That lass has courage. Methinks she could be a druid."

Sein shook his head, certain he did not understand women but knowing Brenda was in trouble. "Aye, and what has Brenda's plight got to do with us?" he asked.

Pyfog moved her chair away from the fireplace and said, "Back in Gwynedd, Lady Gladys refuses to see anyone; stays in bed suckling her babe. The prince is afraid her days are numbered unless he can find a way to break her dark mood. He says his wife is terribly fond of this Irish lass, Brenda, who took time to chat and make her laugh. He thinks that if the two women could be together again, his wife would be comforted." Pyfog wiped the perspiration from her face with the back of one hand. "Where is she?"

Sein did not answer. His mind was aswirl with things he might say to throw the Welsh troops off track if they should come to his camp.

"Actually, I understand your puzzlement," said Pyfog. Why would Gwynedd soldiers come to a druid camp tucked away in the hills? Do they know the Welsh druids sent her here? Or are they just following orders? Prince Owain has druid honor marks. He must know something. I pray he does not know the babe did not drown. But if you ask me, I think that Prince Owain wants Brenda back for himself. I remember what she looks like; even nursing a babe, she is a real bonny lass. I think she is a favorite with Prince Owain. What do you think?"

Sein's backbone stiffened. "Why does it take six soldiers to pick up one helpless lass?"

"Six soldiers show Owain's power."

Sein scratched his head. "Ireland and Wales are on friendly terms. Maybe the secret story about the ill wife is false. The Welsh might be slowly sending army troops into Ireland while the Irish sit around and ignore them." Sein poured more mead for himself and Pyfog. "Welsh soldiers on Irish soil are themselves cause for alarm." He could hardly swallow the sweet, fermented honey because of the tightness in his chest.

Pyfog stood up, put on her vest and cap. "Do not feed yourself wet hay. Keep the babe, but let her go. She is trouble." She opened a shuttered window, saw a young lad watering her horse, pointed to a streak of blue sky. "Enough blue to make a lass's kirtle—a sign of good weather. Snow shower is over." She went to the door and asked the lad if the horse was fed. The lad smiled, nodded, and she turned to Sein. "If Gorlyn hears of more soldiers, he will tell me and I will tell you. What will you do— spread the news among the local herders, hide an Irish army in these hills to protect Ireland, or to protect the lass and her child? Be sensible. Let Prince Owain have his mistress. He will not harm her. She will be safe with more luxury than she has here. Foster her child, whom, we suppose, Owain believes dead. Hear me, there is talk among the Old Religionists in the shipyard that the child is special, destined for leadership when grown. Have you not heard?"

Sein was afraid to acknowledge what he knew and said nothing, but he wished Pyfog would hurry off.

"I have seen the wonder-child," said Pyfog. "He is like any other babe, drooling, mewling, suckling and eliminating. I mean he did not have a glory mark, his face did not shine from a halo of light 'round about his head. Brenda loves him. Would she leave him with you to save his life?"

Sein stood next to the door. "Like most mothers, I suppose she would do what is necessary to save her babe. But, my friend, I will not fight Welsh soldiers. Warring solves no grievance. It only causes death and destruction. Man is a thinker. He talks and finds ways to work out his problems. Old Religionists, like us, use both ancient and modern knowledge."

Pyfog said, "My friend, the Welsh soldiers are armed. You know man has fought ever since he has been in this world. You think you can change his nature?"

"Appeal to his higher sense. Teach him to love, not hate. Love is harder to overcome, even though hate is easier to learn. We Taliesins are not impractical dreamers. We are realistic."

"Teach the child the ways of peace and druid philosophy. But teach grown men to use a battle-ax. That is power an enemy understands."

"Power is not well used by most men," persisted Sein, following her outside.

"I hear your thoughts and find your thinking straight, yet we differ on the nature of man. My horse is as ready as I for our return to Dubh Linn." She let Sein take the reins.

He led the horse to the edge of the drumlin. "Aye, please ride so as not to cause alarm among the Welsh soldiers that may be on the path," he said, handing the reins to Pyfog.

She raised her hand and trotted off in a spray of slush.

For several minutes Sein stood with his hands at his sides. Then he walked around the encampment, burst into the sleeping cottage and announced an immediate council meeting in the center of the stone circle.

*   *   *

Standing in the center of the nine other council members, Sein said, "If we keep Brenda, the Welsh soldiers will find her sooner or later. They will discover that her child is not dead. How can we save both of them without a thought of war?"

A freckled man said that Brenda was a woman who brought bad luck, a sorceress. He wanted to send her to a camp of druids in the kingdom of Munster. Another man suggested sending her to a druid named Connacht, who would move her from one farm family to another.

"She cannot run here and there," said Vivian. "If she is such a troublemaker, put her on a ship going to the green country where Erik the Redhair was banished. If she is not a troublemaker, treat her like a real person."

"If she goes to Gwynedd, the prince will treat her well. Owain is known to be just," said a man wearing brass-studded gloves.

"Aye, that is it," said a young woman called Ebrill. "Let her go to Owain. Then if she is trouble, we will have none of it. 'Twas her sharp words that cut the life from the laddie, Ailin. She and her babe are better gone."

"What about her babe? He is not yet fully weaned," said Eira.

"How about sending the baby to the herder's wife, Dornoll, in the hazel grove beyond the next hill?" said Sein reluctantly. "She has a child who is not yet weaned. Mayhap there is milk enough for two."

"Let Brenda decide," said Finn.

Brenda, wrapped in several quilts, was brought to the council. She stood alone in the center of the circle.

Sein explained the problem.

She could not believe what she heard. Some said she had an evil eye, she was an enchantress, a sorceress and a troublemaker with a tongue sharp enough to cut the thread of life from a filly and an innocent laddie. She bit her lip and said she was going to Carno. Choosing to leave and being forced to leave were two different things. Who could think of separating her from Madoc? First Owain had turned on her, now

Sein. Who would be next? Eira? Finn? Llywarch?

Eira stepped forward and put her arm across Brenda's shoulders. "Carno is the next place the Welsh soldiers will look. 'Tis not safe for you, nor Madoc, to go there. What will happen if Owain learns Madoc is alive?"

Brenda tried to put on a bold face. "He will kill Madoc and me and—mayhap you for keeping us." Her voice turned into a whisper. "I cannot be responsible for more deaths."

Finn pointed out that if she left Madoc with the herdsman and his wife, they would say the babe was theirs. He would be safe until Brenda could claim him later, and she would be safer if she were not caught hiding.

Vivian's violet eyes flashed as she said that Brenda might seek out the Welsh soldiers and let them invite her back to Gwynedd. "That way you will be an invited guest of the prince and not harmed."

Finn suggested that Brenda go to Wales and stay until Owain's wife was out of her present mood, then come back to Ireland to visit her father and other children and decide where to send Madoc for further fostering.

"Who shall pay for his fostering?" asked Ebrill.

"I will pay if Brenda agrees," said Sein. "The herdsman's wife will nurse him."

"And feed him gruel and pottage. Surely I will be back in time to continue nursing my son! I can hire out as a wet nurse for a while. Babies are not weaned until they are two or three," said Brenda. "Owain's wife is ill. Everyone says she will not live long. Lord God bless her!"

" 'Tis best not to return too soon," said Eira softly, so only Brenda heard. "When the bad feelings about the death of the little mare and Ailin have faded, then 'twill be safe to come back."

"My son becomes more precious every day," said Brenda. "I cannot part with him, even though I prefer him raised by Old Religionists instead of New Religionists. I do not know what to do! Och!" She lowered her head and covered her face with both hands.

"You have to make a firm decision," said Sein.

Brenda looked up. Her face was contorted with anguish.

She left the circle of people, walked past the standing stones, past the flats and into the thicket called the bosket. She stood alone among the pine trees.

Eira held Sein's arm. "Do not follow. Let her work her way out."

Brenda did not know how long she wandered, except twice she felt milk spill from her breasts. She was trapped, like a caged bear. She was surrounded by people who had ideas of what she might do and where she might go, but she did not know what she wished to do. She could not believe her every move was watched by Prince Owain. How dare he do this to her? Finally, she leaned against the rough bark of a pine and her thoughts began to untangle.

Owain cannot know that Madoc lives. He has compassion and wants me at the court to help Lady Gladys, she thought. She felt the harsh bark against her face and sat on an exposed root. Owain believes I be overcome with grief because of my babe's death. In troth I grieve because I do not want to leave this camp. I love Eira, and Vivian and old Finn and—and I would do most anything to prove my worth.

Her breasts engorged a third time and she pressed her arms against them to relieve the pain. The front of her shirt was sticky wet. She knew she had to go peaceably to Wales and that Madoc had to be left in a safe place. "I cannot cause this camp more distress," she said aloud and to herself added, "How can I possibly leave him behind?"

She thought of Britain's *Law of Distress*, which was the universal method of solving this kind of dispute. The Welsh soldier would complain to the local Irish Lord that a certain druid *eglwys*, or camp, held his prince's mistress. The druids would be forced to give up not only Brenda, but their land, buildings and livestock. If the druids evaded seizure, the debt would be doubled with a fine of five *seds*, large silver coins. When there was no property or coins to seize, the debtors could be taken and made to work as slaves until the debt was paid. This was the old Brehon Law, first encoded by Irish druids more than nine generations ago. No Irishman would dare fight the Brehon Law.

She heard an eerie cry and thought of *gwyllion*, the Welsh pale ghost. Instead she saw a green woodpecker, its crown crimson, its rump yellow. It was an Irish sign of happy times. "Shoo, fly away!" she said, flapping her kirtle. "Naught here is happiness!"

She walked past the scrub gorse and headed for the openness, the callows, in front of the camp's cottages, where, to her surprise, there seemed to be another outdoor council. The camp's inhabitants were circled around two strange horsebackers. Brenda stepped behind a thick clump of gorse and saw that the men had three golden lions in a red circle embroidered on the backs of their heavy gray tunics; soldiers from Gwynedd.

They wore no armor. They were armed with long spears and battle-axes tucked into their bronze chain belts. There was a bronze oblong shield tied to each saddle pack.

Brenda saw the two soldiers dismount and go through the cottages, the barn and the outbuildings. She scooted farther back inside the gorse when they were at the outer edge of the crowd, looking here and there.

Eira must have seen the bushes move because she looked hard in Brenda's direction, then came slowly toward the gorse, walking backward, facing the crowd.

Brenda called out in a loud whisper, "Eira, what is going on?"

Eira ducked behind the gorse. She was startled to see that the quilt over Brenda's shoulders was torn and full of briars, that her hair was full of brambles and bits of dried leaves. "The Welsh soldiers come for *you!*" she said.

"Where is my babe?"

"Floating in the creek below the hill."

Brenda made an anguished cry in her throat and stepped toward Eira, who hissed "Ssshhh!" and pushed her back. Then Eira hunkered beside her and whispered, "Sein made a coracle from the truckle and Finn sewed a greased sheepskin on the outside. Madoc was made fast asleep by an herb. Pray the herder's wife finds him."

"Goder-heal, he is a wolf's supper!"

Eira clasped her hand over Brenda's mouth so that she

would not cry out again. "Sein rubbed the coracle with skunk oil. Now you go past the shallow fortification and act as if you have just climbed the drumlin by walking out into the callow and looking around. Pretend to be lost." Eira stood up and slowly, with her head down, kicked at clods of wet earth and went back to the crowd.

Brenda sat on a pile of wet oak leaves and thought, Pray. Picture your babe in the loving arms of the herder's wife. She nurses him. When things are right, Sein will contact me to come back. She licked her dry lips and thought, I do not remember the name of the herder's wife. How can I go with these soldiers?

She forced herself to think of a kindly-faced herder and his wife with a smile on her face as she carried an infant up an imagined narrow pathway to their tiny wattle-and-daub hut.

She brushed the tattered quilt and folded it neatly across her shoulders, wishing she had told Eira to bring her underwear, stockings, a skirt and tunic. She was wearing her boots against bare feet and Finn's long woolen nightshirt, her bratt and a quilt. She fussed with her matted hair so that the part was in the middle. She looked through the gorse toward the woods and hunkered so that her head could not be seen above the brush. Her heart pounded as she pushed between the pines and toward the oaks, whose leathery brown leaves were falling with each gust of wind.

When she was well into the bosket she straightened, clumped through wet snow and leaf mold, and between boulders to the break in the dirt fortification. It occurred to her that she could see the creek from the clearing, and she might have a glimpse of her babe in the coracle. Her foot landed on a loose stone that sent several other stones rolling down a cutbank. She managed to pull herself up by grabbing handfuls of spineless knapweed, and she looked far down to the dark silent creek. She saw nothing unusual. Sein said Madoc would be in his care for seven years, she thought. Humpf! I guess he is not really a farseerer. She wiped her eyes on the quilt's edge, realized there was mud on her hands and boots and looked for a handful of slushy snow for a wash.

With no warning, she felt a huge, rough hand pull her

around and she was face-to-face with a black-bearded soldier. His tunic was embroidered with the red-and-gold emblem of Gwynedd. He wore a bright brass helmet decorated with multicolored scrolls and spirals. *"Pwy dach chi?"* he asked in Welsh. "Who are ye?"

"Daughter of the lord of Carno, *ydw i.*" Her mouth went dry. She looked at her muddy feet. "I have walked all night thinking I was on the Carno road," she said. "Be I near the village? Is this the Carno hill? I be so tired. *Os gwelwch chi'n dda,* please—let me sit."

"I can see ye have walked a long way. These huts belong to paltry, pagan kineherders. 'Tis not Carno. We have come for ye. *Dewch ymlaen.* Come here. We know ye be Mistress Brenda, daughter of Howyl, lord of Carno. Ye will ride in the cart waiting on the road."

"Dydw i ddim yn deall," said Brenda, telling the soldier in Welsh that she did not understand. "I be on my way to Carno. You came for me?"

"Byddwch yn dawel," said the other soldier, whose hair was cut short and showed that the top half of his right ear was missing. "Be quiet and come along. Yur father, in Carno, is not expecting ye. Ye can rest in the cart." They led her across the little clearing. She stumbled once and Half-Ear took her arm.

He said he had heard of the loss of her child and he was sympathetic. "Prince Owain has spared no expense to bring ye back to the heart of Gwynedd."

"He wants me back?" said Brenda. "I cannot believe it. He wants me even though his baby son died?" She bit her tongue so that she would not say more.

"Byddwch yn dawel. Be quiet," said Half-Ear. "Prince Owain is going to a lot of trouble." Under his breath he said, "I know not why. Ye look like the devil, worse even than this seedy tribe of Irish peasants."

Brenda gave no indication that she heard his slur. She walked meekly at his side with her head lowered so that she saw only her muddied brogues. The soldiers took her past the milling crowd at the druid camp. She did not look up. Someone brushed against her arm. She knew instantly it was Sein

because of the powerful skunk odor. The gesture told her that
he would think of her; watch after Madoc. Tears spilled from
her eyes.

Brenda crossed the Irish Sea in a kind of half-sleep. She
dreamed of Madoc, laughing and cooing as his small coracle
bobbed along the high-banked creek. She was conscious only
when her breasts became engorged and ached. She pressed her
hands against them for relief. She was surprised at her own
hunger. The soldiers shared a leather pouch full of apples with
her the evening they were anchored offshore from Holyhead.

   In the morning the wind was with them so that they made the
bay at Degannwy in less than a day. They did not go near the
Seaside Inn, but the four soldiers took her directly to the Degannwy royal court, where they were fed well in the great hall.
Brenda was given a clean, whitewashed hut for a bedchamber.

   The maid, called Brigid, told Brenda that the lady of the
court was gone for a day or two to bring back another fosterling. Lord Iorwerth and his lady had a handful of fosterlings
whom they cared for and tutored. So far they had no children
of their own. The lord of the court was hunting boar near
Londontown but was due back any day. Brigid offered to wash
Brenda's nightshirt, bratt and quilt while she rested. She was
glad to be rid of Finn's nightshirt, which was stiff and sour-
smelling from dried milk. Brigid gave her a small bath using
a cloth and a basin of water, then combed cornmeal through
her hair to clean it of dust, oil, leaves and twigs.

   In the morning Brenda felt much better, and when she told
Brigid good-bye was even looking forward to riding a royal
horse down the broad vale of the Conwy River and finally
seeing the green valley of Nant Gwynant.

   She did not look forward to seeing Owain, even though not
many months before she had thought she was head-over-heels
in love with him. The pain he had put in her heart simmered
like a fire under a bed of peat that would never burn out.
Llywarch was the person she was anxious to see. She hoped
that the old bard had word, through the druid line of communication, about Madoc. She felt like an empty hull without
baby Madoc in her arms.

Part Two
1152 to 1164 A.D.

Into this land of magical allure the Christians came, but they never altogether traduced it. . . . For many centuries the [Christian] Cross and [druid] Magic cohabited in Wales, and the faith of the people was a rich palimpset, one belief layered upon another.

Jan Morris, *The Matter of Wales*

Children were expected to participate in the adult world as soon as they were old enough to be free of their nurses and mothers, usually at the age of seven or eight. . . . Throughout the Middle Ages it was customary to send sons and daughters to the home of other noblemen or churchmen to be educated. [This custom was known as fostering.]

Joseph R. Strayer, editor in-chief,
Dictionary of the Middle Ages

VII
Sein's Song

Records suggest Owain had as many as nineteen or twenty-seven children. Apart from one legitimate daughter, Angharad (whose mother was Gladys), who married Morgan ab Seissyl, some authorities refer to two other daughters . . . Gwenllian and Goeral. . . . Various opinions have been expressed on the sons: "Rhodri, Hywell [Howell], Dafydd and Madoc were the most distinguished," wrote Meiron (an eighteenth-century bard), and he acclaimed Howell as a poet of some distinction, eight of whose odes have been preserved, adding that Howell's mother was a native of Ireland, a statement which is also borne out by other sources, notably *Brut y Tywysogion*, which describes her as "an Irish nobleman's daughter," whom the *Dictionary of National Biography* names as Pyvog. There was considerable disagreement as to which of Owain's children were legitimate, and the D.N.B. curtly states that "few of his children are regarded as legitimate." It is certain, however, that Owain had only two wives, though doubtless a large number of mistresses.

Richard Deacon, *Madoc and the Discovery of America*

Brenda arrived quietly at Nant Gwynant Court on horseback, accompanied by six Gwynedd soldiers. She went directly to her cottage as though she had never left, and became Lady Gladys's handmaiden.

Llywarch was first to come see her. "You had to return to Gwynedd; 'tis written in the stars," he said. "The gods have given you a long life. There are things for you to do here, and you have not seen the last of your Irish friends, nor your last-born son."

If Owain was enraged because she had run away to Ireland, it was well concealed. After welcoming her back, he was quiet and generally distracted with provincial duties or filing arrow-heads from sheets of English sword-steel to use on hunting trips.

She could not understand the fascination men had with the hunt, walking deep into the woods, often becoming lost, to sit motionless on a stump, freezing in the dark before dawn to wait for deer, grouse or boar to come by and to take their well-aimed arrow. Afterward they talked over their hunts with the same enthusiasm and boasting they gave to warring ex-ploits.

She was home hardly a month before Owain surprised her. He came to her while she was feeding Gladys at suppertime and asked her opinion on a problem with court servants, who did not always do as he expected.

There was a long silence before she replied. "You might meet us here in the great hall," she said. "Tell us exactly what you want us to do." She paused to steady her voice. "If the first meeting ends with good feelings, have more meetings from time to time. Let us talk about our problems; listen, an-swer questions, make suggestions, and make it clear that we need not fear reprisal if we speak out."

"Aye!" he cried. "I knew you had the answer. Without fear of reprisal! Thank you."

He did not call a meeting or speak to her again until after the court moved to the warm seashore at Aberffraw. Then he called maids and male servants together, and asked them to talk freely about their concerns about running the court in an efficient and orderly fashion. He admitted that generally this would be the concern of Lady Gladys, who was not well. After that he had periodic meetings, which raised the morale and loyalty of his retainers and the thanes who were permitted to live and work Owain's land, as long as they served in his military. He was pleased when several of the heads of other provinces asked how he kept his people so content, with few runaways and defections. Prince Rhys of Powys came to one of his informal meetings, and was surprised to hear the maids and menservants speak freely and unafraid. It was something unheard of. Owain never said it was his mistress's idea. He smiled; enjoyed the praise.

One evening in mid-February when most everybody had gone from the supper table, Llywarch hung his harp's strap over his shoulder and followed Brenda out the door. He stayed so close that she could hear him draw in his breath before he spoke. "I have news that your lastborn is safe with an Irish herder's family."

She stopped and wrapped the fingers of her hand tight around his. "Is that all?" she said, hoping that there was more, maybe the name of the herder's wife.

He smiled, causing the skin at the corners of his eyes to wrinkle. "Sein sends this message: 'With flaxen hair and blue eyes the baby is a sharp contrast to his dark, earthbound foster family, who adore him. He gurgles when Dornoll sings, watches Seth like a hawk and coos and grabs onto two-year-old Wyn's dark hair.' "

The names of the foster family made Brenda's heart pound, and in her excitement to hear more, her voice rose. "Dornoll, Seth and Wyn!" In response to a warning squeeze from Llywarch, her voice fell. "Thank the gods and the Irish druids." They were both quiet a moment with their own thoughts, then she whispered, "His name—his name is *Madoc*." The hesitation in her voice betrayed her emotion.

"Aye," he said, and let go her hand. "Sein sends word that Madoc has his mam's sensitivity and whimpers in sympathy whenever his foster sister cries. He has your stubbornness, does little complaining, and his smile is sweet and quick. He prefers being outdoors near the winding creek. The water sings to him as it rolls over and around the rocks."

Brenda touched Llywarch's arm, made a tiny sound in her throat and ran to her cottage. Llywarch blinked and made a gentle croak through his nose.

For months afterward there was no other word about her lastborn, even though she frequently visited Llywarch's cottage and asked if he had heard anything. "Has Sein sent word about Madoc?"

"The lad is fine," said Llywarch each time. "If not, we would hear."

Once she was quite brash, went to his cottage and said, "My father is able to send word by bards and traders about my two children in Ireland. They progress well with their studies, making him quite proud. Riryd is like me, with dark eyes and hair. Goeral is fair, like Owain. Why does Sein not send me a word?"

"I hear, in your voice, that you are happy to have good fostering for your older children. Have you told Owain how well they do?" asked Llywarch.

"He does not wish to be bothered unless 'tis a provincial problem. Weeks ago I told him that I long to visit my father and two children. He said my duty was to care for his wife and if I attempt to leave again, he will treat me as a traitor; lock me in the tower. I said, 'Unfair!' and he said I was property and he would do with me as he saw fit. I said I had a right to have my problems aired without reprisal same as any other servant. He got my point, saw my disappointment and said to tell him about my longings and our children another time, when he did not have so much on his mind. What can I do? I do not want to wait. It might take years and the children will be grown and I will be old before I see them. I be impatient. Mayhap I should just go."

The light from the wall-torch made Llywarch's hair look like fine silver; his eyes held tiny golden sparks as he patted her cheek. "You dare not," he said. "Gwynedd's court would send a watcher and sooner or later Owain would find out about—"

His warning brought Brenda to herself. "I long to see my older children, but the youngest most of all," she said. "I know I cannot talk about him, except in secret with you."

"Thank the gods he is happy," said Llywarch. He opened his door, and she knew he had said all he had to say.

Lady Gladys was infinitely delighted to have Christiannt, a friend she knew and trusted, as her baby's nursemaid. She let Christiannt name him Dafydd and never discovered that the child, who called her Mam, was not her own, but Christiannt's.

Dafydd was a fussy baby, angry with the world from the moment he was born. Christiannt rocked him day and night to stop his squalliness. Exhausted, she gave him to Brenda, who wrapped him tight in a linen sheet to keep his arms and legs from thrusting here and there in wrath. She sang to soothe him out of his indignant furies, but bestowed no other affection, as if hugging or kissing him would in some way be a betrayal of Madoc.

When Dafydd learned to walk, Brenda took him out of doors, rain or snow. Gradually she took more and more comfort from the lad.

He astonished Brenda, when he was four, by saying the moon became thin when it had nothing to eat, but round and fat when he fed it supper scraps. Not long after that he said, "The morning sun appears the moment I be out of bed. If I awaken late or stay abed too long, the sun hides behind clouds."

"You are sure 'tis you who controls the moon and sun?" Brenda asked.

"Aye, but my mam knows naught about my power."

"Why not?" she asked.

"She would say pish-posh and roll her eyes."

Brenda chuckled softly and said to be patient with his mother. She taught him to speak concise Welsh, granted few of his sneering commands. Christiannt tried to teach him that for every privilege there was a responsibility, but she caved in and let him have his own way.

When he was five he said to Brenda, "Do not stare at me, and when you do look, always show the highest respect."

"Why?" she asked. "What did you do to earn that high privilege?"

His green eyes squinted and his brow furrowed. "Because I have wonderful powers. I run toward a bird, tell it to fly and it does. I run among the sheep, tell them to bleat and they do."

"You must not think like that," she said. "Anyone can do those things. You know you are lazy, rude and evade the truth. When you conquer your bad habits, I will believe you have power."

"How can I do that?"

"It always surprises me how my mind can straighten out a problem if I think calmly and quietly about it," she said. "Some say that is when the gods take over and straighten out our tangled thoughts." Her eyes twinkled.

"Do the gods like us or do they think they are much better and we are mere chaff?"

"If they look after us, they like us. I believe it is kind of the way your mother and Christiannt think you are so wonderful."

"My father—does he think I be wonderful?" His eyes glittered.

She knew that he used guile and deceit to win approval, but suddenly realized that he especially wanted a favorable attitude from his father. She put her arms around him and said, "He loves you, Dafydd, but he is disappointed that you pretend things be troth, when not. He sees through shams. You see only what your heart desires. Open your eyes, see beyond your nose, dear lad. Be honest and your father will believe in you and be pleased."

Dafydd, flushed with anger, reached out, pinched her lips together and said, "You are an ugly, jealous toad! Mayhap there are no gods at all. You have never seen one!" He twisted, turned and pulled away from her arms, kicked her knee and ran off.

Gladys told Dafydd that he held the strings to her heart in his darling hands. She felt the sun rose and set with him. Holding him on her lap was her greatest pleasure. She rocked him, watched him at play, let him know she adored his capricious chatter and tolerated his temper tantrums. She sat in the room when he was tutored, and chuckled behind her hand at his saucy, incorrect answers. She anticipated his every need and desire. Behind her back, he ridiculed her.

As he grew older he wrapped both Gladys and Christiannt around his little finger. Neither woman taught him self-restraint. Brenda tried, but was never sure he took her words to heart.

During this period, Dafydd threw away any semblance of

orderly conduct, pulled out of the submission-to-authority harness, and became unfettered and entirely self-centered. He roamed the court freely and lived by no rules but his own, which were few.

Owain, who might have disciplined him, was gone most of the time.

One spring morning, Brenda tied up her hair with a strip of cloth and made preparations to give ailing Lady Gladys a bath. She gathered an armload of linen towels, pushed aside her leather door-flap and heard shouting and tramping outside.

There was Owain in the center of the courtyard, dressed in tight-fitting trousers, a long-sleeved shirt, a short tunic, boots and leather gloves. He bellowed out military drills to two dozen barefoot recruits. No Welshman wanted to wear body armor, which they claimed weighed them down so they could not move.

Brenda smiled when she saw six-year-old Dafydd strutting with cocky self-assurance behind Owain. He carried an iron pot lid like a shield and wore a short, narrow-bladed, wooden dagger hanging from his rope belt.

Owain stopped marching and gave the signal for a trial battle. The young recruits chose sides. Opponents parried sword thrusts but never nicked another's flesh. When a recruit fell or was tapped by an opponent's sword, he was carried off the field to watch the finish of the mock battle. Owain did not enter into the fray, but closely watched each retainer's dexterity.

Dafydd, nose freckled, cheeks red, mouth open, stood on the sidelines watching. He scrunched his green eyes to mere slits, thrust his wooden dagger at an invisible foe, and warded off imagined blows with an imagined shield. His feet moved in an erratic dance, stirring up dust.

"Might I be a horsebacker?" asked Dafydd, in his thin child's voice. "I could throw a straight javelin while galloping."

Owain laughed out loud. "My small son, you need years of practice. You cannot yet plant your feet properly to throw a stone at the back side of the great hall."

The lad's mouth turned down; he kicked his father's shin and said, "You mule, I be a real horsebacker! I shall steal a horse and show you!" He thrust the wooden dagger at his father's midsection.

Brenda thought Owain would thrash the boy in front of everyone, but he did not.

Suddenly she thought of Madoc following behind the herder mimicking his footsteps. She thanked the gods that Madoc was with the herder and not playing war games. She dropped her door-flap, walked across the courtyard, through the great hall and to the royal chamber.

She knocked, then opened the door. Gladys pulled a shell comb through her wispy brown hair and nodded toward the empty beaker on her bedside table. Gladys was thin, almost skeletal, and her incongruous but strong, magpie-like voice said, "I fancy a beaker of chamomile tea."

Brenda got hot water, chamomile flowers and linden leaves from the kitchen. As Gladys watched, she crumbled the dried herbs into the beaker.

Gladys noticed that some dried material fell to the hard-packed dirt floor. She fumed and cawed about Brenda's clumsiness. "Next I expect you will spill red wine on my best white chemise."

Brenda picked up the dried stuff, put it in her pocket and said, "I will bathe you quickly so that you might rest a while, before Dafydd bursts in to tell you how good he has become at sword play. I watched him march behind Owain like a regular soldier this morn." She poured water from a bucket against the wall into a basin beside Gladys's bed.

"He practices not to be a soldier, but to be king," said Gladys, relaxing as Brenda bathed her. "Each day I encourage the laddie to think of himself as king of Gwynedd."

"Aye," said Brenda, "but none of us knows when Owain will announce his successor. 'Tis unfair to throw dust into the eyes of a wee lad."

"I do no such a thing," said Gladys. "Do you realize Dafydd can control natural events? 'Twould bode well for the future to advise Owain about the lad's talents. Owain relies on your advice." Her voice was prickly.

"Actually, Owain asks my opinion of very few things. In the end he does what he thinks best. Whatever I might say is really of little consequence."

"Well, 'twould behoove you to speak to Owain about the future King Dafydd. My son knows so much for his age. He has a special gift of intelligence." Gladys sat up to sip her tea and looked straight ahead as Brenda washed her front and back. Brenda draped a linen towel around Gladys's shoulders to keep the draft away while her legs were rinsed off and dried with another towel.

"Changing the title from prince to king of Gwynedd is something Owain, as well as Henry, might find objectionable," said Brenda. "Owain is prince. Henry is king, head chief of all Britain. You are poking fun and not truly ordering me to ask Owain to groom a six-year-old to be *king* of Gwynedd, so that his title and office be equal to King Henry's—are you?"

"I be ordering you," said Gladys, sitting up and smacking her lips.

Brenda took a deep breath and said, "Much as I be fond of you, I cannot do such a foolish thing, m'lady. Dafydd is a dear lad, your pet, but not a leader. He is an overindulged child who makes up stories to fit his skewed logic. Even if we give him another dozen years, he will not know enough to be an intelligent leader because of the crooked path he is on. He will never know more about being king of this province than a twisted willow stick."

Gladys gave Brenda a long, sharp look and said, "Well, of course Owain shall train him in provincial affairs, same as he trains him to be a good soldier."

"Gladys, I love you, and so I be telling you to use your brain. There is Howell or Iorwerth to take Owain's place. Owain would not permit a mischief-maker to be Gwynedd's next leader."

Gladys leaned closer and slapped Brenda's jaw, making a loud smacking sound. "Speak to me with respect. I be Owain's wife!"

Brenda stood, struggled to gain composure, kept her eyes down and turned to fold the bath towels. She heard Gladys struggling for breath, saw that her eyes bulged and her face was red. Brenda grabbed her arms and held them up to open the air passage to the lungs. Gladys twisted her neck, and her face became darker. Brenda put a fist in Gladys's chest and pushed her down hard on the pallet. Gladys coughed, sputtered and brought up slimy chamomile flowers and linden leaves.

"You were not supposed to inhale the beaker's dregs," said Brenda, with a sigh of relief. "Here, let me clean you up and you will sleep."

"I—I drew in a breath and forgot the leaves in my mouth. I was sucking out flavor and you made me gasp. I could have choked to death!"

"Nay, I would not let that happen," said Brenda. She went outside to empty the basin of bathwater, came back to gather up the soiled towels.

"Wait!" said Gladys. "You are not to speak of this."

"I be ordered not to speak to Owain about Dafydd and his talents?"

"Aye, do not say a word to Owain, nor to anyone. There be another who will do as I ask, without coming at me with a lot of questions and pish-posh that can choke me to death."

"Are you thinking of getting Christiannt mixed up in your scheme?"

"That is not your business! Go! I be tired."

Brenda went outside and blinked in the sunlight. She decided to take her time walking across the courtyard to the laundry hut.

She saw the recruits leaving and talking among themselves. Owain appeared to be explaining something to Dafydd, who scuffed his toes in the dust and turned his body from side to side. Dafydd waved to Brenda and swirled his dagger around his head.

She waved back. You little show-off, she thought and smiled. "*Bore da*, good morning," she said, walked around them, and when her back was turned, she heard Dafydd scream. Owain crouched on the ground beside the shrieking lad, who was doubled up in a bright red pool. A small dagger lay beside him.

She knelt beside Owain, who pulled away the red, soggy stocking that was slashed the length of a hand. Blood gushed with Dafydd's every heartbeat. Owain grabbed a towel from the tumbled heap on the ground and pressed it over the wound. Dafydd continued to scream.

Brenda remembered the crushed herbs in her pocket and put a large pinch of them in the lad's mouth. His wide eyes squeezed shut, he slobbered and gagged.

"No matter," she said and gave him another, held his mouth closed; the screaming stopped and his eyes opened. Gently she told him to chew and swallow the watery paste. "'Twill be bitter, but you are brave."

Owain's face was white as quartz and he whispered, "Thank the gods the bloody screeching is over. The lad's caterwauling cuts through me." He called loudly to the last retreating recruit to get mead and a physician. The recruit hollered that he would find a priest and trotted toward the gate.

Owain had seen enough battle wounds in his day and watched the druids dress wounds and heal them so that he knew what had to be done. He did not like the idea of a priest working on his laddie, but he knew Gladys would. She had become a New Religionist because it was fashionable these days for a court to keep a priest instead of a druid as the royal healer. Gladys called druids pagans, and said they were not only uncouth but stupid to believe that there were many gods working with the chief Lord God, who was all-powerful and could do anything by himself. She said druids practiced magic and tattooed their skin with dirty blue woad.

Owain discarded the bloody towel and tied another, like a tight bandage, over the gaping wound, which still welled up red. "I wish I had mead for the lad while we wait. 'Twould dull the pain and make him sleep."

Owain hoped he could talk the priest out of bleeding the lad. There had been enough bleeding already. Dafydd's face was white as a ghost's and the pulse in his neck was rapid. Owain wished the priest would hurry. He wished he had something to pull the flesh together. He could sew the wound closed if he had boar's gut and a fine bone needle. He had seen it done often enough and had even done it a couple times himself when there were more wounded than a druid physician could care for on the field of battle.

He turned back to his son and used a damp towel to wipe his face and told him to stay still.

"He needs help now, not tomorrow," said Brenda. "Where is that priest?"

Owain looked at her, then back at the boy. He felt impatient himself but said nothing.

Brenda said, "You carry him." She lifted Dafydd against her shoulder and gave him to Owain. "Ah, good. Hang on." She headed toward the gatehouse.

Owain gasped, "Where are you going, woman? Stop!" He stepped backward and scattered a group of chickens that had come to investigate the black runnels of blood seeping into the ground.

She walked backward looking at him and said, "Keep one hand pressed on the towel and follow me."

Owain was dumfounded to see Brenda, a woman he thought he knew well, ignore his orders and order him about.

The outer gate guard asked Owain if he wanted a cart.

Brenda said, " 'Twould take too long to hitch up a horse. We go to the druid camp and have no time to spare."

Dafydd lay stiff-backed in his father's arms. His tunic and hands were spattered with drying blood. "Will there be a scar on my leg?" he asked. His eyes looked dreamy, as if he were looking at something far away.

"Probably," said Brenda.

His mouth made a broad, crooked smile. "I want a soldier's scar," he said mulishly.

They came near the Church-with-the-White-Porch, but as yet had met no priest. "I will get him," said Owain, running ahead. He stopped short when he saw the recruit and the priest sitting on the porch having tea. He turned back and told Brenda they would go on to the druid camp.

"Tell the druids to leave a scar," Dafydd mumbled.

"I have nothing to do with it," Owain said. "The druids push the wound together so the scar is as small as possible. That is the soldier's mark of having a good healer."

Dafydd's eyes closed and he went limp.

"He fainted," said Owain.

" 'Tis a good sign," said Brenda, rubbing her free hand

across the lad's white cheek and feeling his strong breaths on her wrist. "How did the accident happen? I never saw a thing until I heard Dafydd howling."

"After I dismissed the retainers, the bantling whined around until I caved in and sparred with him. It was just for a moment so he would not pester me all day about it. You know he is spoiled rotten." Right away Owain looked embarrassed and said, "My words were uncalled for. He is the only thing that keeps Gladys alive. She adores him."

" 'Tis all right. He is a blessing for Lady Gladys. Mayhap, soon you shall foster him with someone known for discipline." Brenda lowered her head. She was in no position to tell the prince of Gwynedd how to raise his son. She had given enough advice for one day. Shyly she asked again about the accident.

"He stubbed his toe, and fell before I moved my sword out of the way. Blood spouted like a geyser. He screamed when he saw he was in the middle of a warm, red pool and screamed again. He thinks he cut himself with his puny dagger, else he would have called me a bloody bear or a dirty dog. Gladys will call me something worse." His voice lowered and he looked sheepish. "You will not say anything to Archdruid Llieu, will you? He and I were foster brothers for a short time."

"I will say 'twas an accident," said Brenda. An unbidden gladness filled her heart because he had confided in her.

They skirted a small patch of nettles with white flowers, hurried to the shade of a crofter's apple trees. Owain looked at her and said, "I noticed how clear-headed you were today after the accident. With such strong nerves, you would make a fine soldier."

"What I would like is to be a healer," she said.

"A healer?" He was walking fast.

"Would I not make a fine healer?" She had to run to catch up.

"Really, Brenda, only druids have women healers," he said. "You are not a druid."

"Druids also have wisdom," she said, and her lips turned up a little more. "I shall ask Archdruid Llieu about women healers, who are called Wise Women."

"You surprise me. I suppose that is why you are my favorite lady. If you were younger, I might be persuaded to ask
your father to foster you to some druid camp to learn to be
my personal healer, but look at you"—he laughed—"a grown
woman now."

"I may be past fostering, but not past learning."

"We are about there," he said and pointed with his chin.

On the right side of the trail was a raised circle of earth.
Inside the circle a ring of sticks enclosed a number of thatched,
wattle-and-daub cottages. In front of the gate two wooden
posts supported carved heads with faces front and back, to
guard both sides of the gate. Brenda looked through the spaces
between the sticks and saw other posts supporting white skulls.
Sein's druid camp in Ireland had nothing like that.

Owain saw her gawking and said, "Those are boars' skulls.
Druids eat boars same as you and I. They believe the boar
protects them from starvation and honor it. 'Tis well, for it
indeed deserves to be honored."

"I do not know much about druids. I know you have their
honor marks, though you keep them covered when you leave
your chamber." She did not have to look at his arms or hairy
legs to remember that they were tattooed with the exquisite
drawings of birds and sea animals. Her face became warm and
she wished she had more control over her tongue and mayhap
her eyes.

"Ha—so, you kept your eyes open when we coupled," he
said.

She pretended she had not heard his last words. "You never
talked much about being one of them. I thought, since Gladys
is a follower of the New Religion, you gave up the Old."

" 'Twould take more than a woman to make me cast off
the Old. My friend Thomas of London agrees with me that
druids are far ahead of Christians in honor and wisdom. He is
a man who might have been a famous archdruid, but his early
training took the wrong trail, so now he walks with his Church
and King Henry, and meets trouble at every turn. He thinks
with a druid's logic and I love him for that."

Brenda did not have time to ponder Owain's friendship
with the archbishop of Canterbury because a gray-haired druid

met them in a gray work-gown with a multicolored sash similar to the one Llywarch wore. He wore a wide gold bracelet on his right upper arm, a string of amber beads around his neck to signify his high office. The druid and Owain exchanged nonchalant nods, but when their eyes met, Brenda was certain they were old, old friends. She thought they would have embraced if Owain had not been carrying Dafydd.

"Llieu—Archdruid Llieu, this is my wife's handmaid, Brenda."

"Oh *ydy*, yes," said Llieu with a wide grin for Brenda.

"By accident, my son suffers a sword wound," said Owain. "We came right away."

Archdruid Llieu indicated, with a slight motion of his head, for them to bring the lad into the first cottage. There were a table and a chair near the center fire ring and a pallet against the whitewashed wall opposite the door. The clean, white wall on the left was lined with spicy-smelling drying roots, twigs, berries, flowers and leaves. The right wall was made of woven withies, held tight by a weaving of thick linen twine. Fastened on it were diagrams drawn on large linen squares. To Brenda they looked like roadways in red and narrower trails in yellow. She drew in her breath when the druid rolled up the wall and fastened it to the ceiling. Now there was as much light inside as outside.

"My friend, put the lad on the table," Llieu said.

"Where are the others?" asked Owain.

"Teaching the fosterlings. Surely you have heard that Henry's soldiers have come across the Chester border to take land from our brother crofters. To keep them from harm, crofters are fostering their children with us."

Llieu had Brenda put her hand firmly on Dafydd's wound. She wanted to ask about the colored markings on the linen.

Llieu smiled at her as he tied a leather thong high on Dafydd's leg. The thong was so tight it seemed to embed itself in the boy's flesh. Now she wanted to ask if the thong should be loosened, but Llieu said, "Take your hand away; the wound will not bleed." He took away the bloody bandages. "You are a healer?"

She saw he was right about the bleeding. She stepped closer

to see the gaping wound. "Nay, but I think about it." She looked up and smiled.

"The diagrams on the wall are blood vessels," he said. "Red lines leave the heart, yellow go back to it. My students find the drawings helpful, because they have not seen what is inside a person as many times as I."

"So the midportion that looked like a lopsided ball is the heart?" she said.

"Aye, about the size of my fist."

Owain wiped his forehead and sat on the edge of the pallet. He avoided looking at his son's wound and spoke in a peevish voice to Llieu. "The lad needs help. He is my wife's lastborn. He is her heart, the morning sun, the evening star." He took a deep breath. "The wound—'tis like a deep well with red sides and a bloody bottom. I have seen men with legs cut off, with their insides strewn on the battleground, making the snow crimson; lads twice his age, with eyes gouged out and cold as stone, and today I cannot look at this laddie, who is pale as watered milk and suffering awful pain."

"Owain, the lad does not feel a thing. He is asleep," said Llieu in a good-natured tone. "I smell chamomile on his breath."

"Nay, he has had nothing, no tea," said Owain.

Brenda put her hand over her pocket and her face turned red.

"Brenda, do you have something in your apron pocket?" asked Llieu.

"Aye, chamomile and linden. I gave it to Dafydd to chew and swallow. I hoped 'twould make him drowsy and ease his pain."

"Aye, no one could do better."

Brenda tried to suppress her grin, but could not.

Owain scowled. "I would have used mead."

Llieu examined the wound, poured warm boiled water over it and let some dribble inside. Next he poured a little greenish solution in the wound, and washed it out with more warm water. "An extract of thyme and sweet clover heads," he said. "Keeps the wound clean so no rottenness forms."

He cleaned and dried the outside of the wound with a piece

of unbleached linen. Then he showed Brenda how to dip two linen scraps in the greenish antiseptic and hold the wound together, so he could stitch it with a fine bone needle and thread made of softened boar's gut. Then he bound it tight. "There, 'tis done. Keep the lad quiet with chamomile. Sweeten it with honey and he will take it readily. I will see him back here in nine days and we shall see how the cut is healing. I will let you remove the boar's gut when the wound is healed. Keep the lad in bed five days, even if you have to get Llywarch to sing nonsense songs or do impersonations to entertain him."

"What if I smell the rottenness in the wound?" asked Brenda.

"Bring him here right away." He looked at both Brenda and Owain to make certain they understood. "Tell Lady Gladys that Brenda will care for the lad until the tissue grows and holds the flesh together."

"Scar tissue!" hollered Owain. "There will be a scar!"

"Of course there will, but 'twill be small and the lad will be happy with it. You know lads and battle scars. Remember your first one?"

"Of course! But I was not six years old!"

"See, that is what I mean. 'Twill be something special for the laddie. Tell your wife not to fuss. The boy will be fine." He turned to Brenda. "What do you think?"

"I hardly know what to say, except I hope Dafydd's accident does not hinder his running. A lad needs to run."

Llieu looked at her in a pleased way. "Lugh, I should have thought of that! So—you would like to be a healer. I suggest you move his legs and his arms each day while he is bedridden. Have him push against your hands, for exercise. When the lad is up and running again, could you arrange to come here two afternoons a week?"

Brenda's heart hammered and she looked at Owain, wondering if he would permit such a thing.

Owain answered, "If the lad recovers, you may come."

"Then she will come," said Llieu. "Bringing your lad here saved him from bleeding to death, but she saved him much pain. You owe her something, my brother."

"Umph," said Owain. The sound came from deep inside his chest. "I dislike being beholden to anyone, especially a woman."

"I will ask Lady Gladys if I might have time for myself. She sleeps most afternoons and may not miss me. But what will Christiannt think?"

"If Christiannt gets wind of where you are, she will think you are studying to be a druid," said Llieu. "That is something for the maids to talk about." His brown eyes gleamed.

Owain laughed as if it were a great joke; as if Brenda could not possibly become a druid.

On the seventh anniversary of Brenda's leaving the Irish druid camp, Llywarch waited by the door of the great hall when she came to supper. He sat close and when everyone was busy chewing and slurping, he whispered congratulations to her for cleansing the wounds of several of Owain's soldiers with warm water.

She told him that when there were many puncture wounds, she could not always find the opening to an embedded arrow to pull it out with thumb and forefinger, so then she made the soldier eat boiled leeks. "Llieu did not tell me this little trick. 'Twas something I figured out myself."

Later Llieu told Llywarch that she was one of his brilliant pupils. "I be admitting that I have a female student who is better than most of my male students. Some would say 'tis not natural. But 'tis a true fact," he said. "I like Brenda."

"You thinking of making her a druid?" asked Llywarch.

"Aye, if that is what she wants," said Llieu. "But do not say a word about it to her, yet. Just tell her what we learned about young Madoc."

The next time Llywarch saw Brenda he was effusive in his congratulations for using the strong smell of leeks to lead her to the hidden entrance of the wound. "Such a simple thing, but I never thought of it and I bet my best wool cap that even Sein does not know about your technique." Then in a low whisper he said she should come to his place to hear a poem about the journeying boy.

Her heart leaped and she could not eat. She did not know

if she should be happy about his praise or sad, because he mentioned Sein, which made her think of her third child. What did he mean, "journeying boy?" Had Madoc run away from the herder and his wife? Where was he? She left the great hall and went to her cottage, and put on her best clothes, a blue skirt, white bodice and leather tunic.

She tapped on Llywarch's door.

First she noticed that he wore his multicolored sash and the fire pit was swept clean of ashes with the outer stones in a perfect circle. Then she saw that fresh green rush fronds, with small green-yellow mistletoe flowers poking their heads here and there, covered his dirt floor. She wished she had taken off her scuffed brogues before coming inside.

A pottery pitcher of mead sat on his table with two beakers beside it. He filled the beakers and handed one to Brenda.

She sipped, grinned and sat on the floor.

Llywarch grinned, picked up his harp and sat cross-legged in front of her, looking like a bard prepared to sing before the royal court. "I asked you here so that you would not feel ashamed to weep when I recite a poem brought to me by a female horsebacker before sunrise."

"Female horsebacker?" said Brenda.

"Pyfog. Remember her father, old Finn, in the Irish camp? He made pottery beakers and bowls for Degannwy's Seaside Inn and sent his daughter on a trader's curragh to deliver them. She rode all the way from there and brought these beakers to me." He took a long drink. "Doconn sent her on my old horse. We decided 'twas best if she did not seek you out, but she asked that you remember her. I sent her to find a ship or a raft to take her across the Irish Sea at Holyhead. One of Llieu's fosterlings rode with her and will bring back my old horse. I told the fosterling to stay clear of robbers and he could ride my horse again."

"I remember Pyfog, Howell's mam. She warned Sein about the Gwynedd soldiers who had orders to hunt all of Ireland until they found me. If I shed tears over a song or poem from Pyfog, I hope they are for joy."

Llywarch said, " 'Tis Sein's poem, dear child." He covered her hand with his and squeezed it, and she knew he meant there was no need to keep her emotions inside. He strummed softly, hummed, then sang so that the sounds reminded her of a redpoll trilling while in flight. The words brought to her mind the smell of the Taliesin druid camp, seeds, roots, leaves, herbs, a tiny baby, a little horse and a small lad.

> Yesterday a royal child was brought to the druid, Sein, for fostering.
> The lad believed he was the true son of a herder.
> Sein believes
> He is a son of the mighty whirlwind,
> He is a son of the roar of the sea,
> He is a son of the delicate dewdrop.
> Today the lad weeps because his world washed away in a flood.
> The lad learned of his royal lineage, and the troth repels him.
> Sein believes
> The lad is a son of the dry peat that carries seeds that blossom with rain and sun.
> He is a lad who carries an intelligence that will flower into wisdom with education and experience.
> Tomorrow the lad shall discard his name, Brawd, for his true name, Madoc.

Brenda's mind's eye saw a sturdy, smiling blond laddie with eyes as blue as the summer sky. Her heart thumped, tears welled in her eyes and spilled against her will.

Llywarch stopped, put his hand on the harp strings to hold them silent and looked at Brenda. Softly he said, "Sein sends you greetings. He sends health to go with your long life."

Brenda thought, Dear Lord God in Heaven, Sein has my baby to love and educate! But she said, "Is that all?"

"What is it, lass? What more do you want?"

"I, I, Sein—there be naught."

Llywarch sipped his mead and teased her. "Where the tongue slips, it speaks the truth."

"I be surprised that Sein is fostering Madoc. Why is the child *repelled* by truth? Where is the herder and his family?"

"The herder, his wife and wee daughter were drowned in the fast-flooding creek."

"And Madoc was spared? No wonder—'tis heartbreak he suffers." Brenda's eyes were large. "Details? Do you know?"

"Only that Madoc was with Sein and the druids when the rains came and made the stream a torrent. The laddie wants naught to do with his true father. He is repelled by the idea that he is of royal blood and strangers are his true parents."

"Why did Sein tell Madoc now that he was the son of Prince Owain?"

"Perhaps 'twas the right time, so he would not grieve overly much for his dead foster parents."

"And did Sein tell him his mam was but a lowly maidservant?"

"Not so lowly, my dear," said Llywarch. "You will one day be a well-known healer, a member of the druids. Your children will be proud to call you Mam. Sein knows you are a healer. I believe he would send you a kiss, but he does not trust me, an old man, to give it to you proper."

"How you talk! Me a druid, ppft!" Brenda felt her face tingle and her heart thump. It was so good to know that Madoc was safe with a man who would educate him, discipline him and, and aye, love him. A man with shining red hair and the bluest eyes the gods ever gave a human. Suddenly the smells of woodsmoke and steaming mead were underlaid by the scent of heather and meadow flowers. She sang, "*Diolch*, thank you," over and over. When she got up to leave, Llywarch said, "I know you were pleased with Sein's song. Now forget you heard me sing it. I told you long ago the lad was all right."

"Aye, and can you tell me when I will see him?"

"Madoc or Sein?"

She had her hand on the door latch and was tempted to say "Both." But she bit her tongue and said, "Madoc, of course. I be his mam."

"When the time is right you will see him. He is your secret," he whispered.

VIII
Dafydd

Owain's second wife, Chrisiant, is not included in some records on the ground that this marriage was disallowed by the church, but Professor Barbier and others who have delved deeply into the history of this period refer to her as Owain's second wife, and it is now generally accepted that she was the mother of Dafydd.

Richard Deacon, *Madoc and the Discovery of America*

In the fall of 1158, Christiannt gave birth to a fat baby boy, whom she named Rhodri.

Eight-year-old Dafydd could not believe that his nursemaid, Christiannt, would want a squalling baby to care for when she already had himself. He was puzzled about how the baby got to the nursery without him knowing about it, so he asked his father.

Owain said the baby grew inside Christiannt and when the time was right pushed himself out.

Dafydd frowned and said, " 'Tis hard to believe."

Owain was dismayed that Dafydd, who played with the court's dogs and cats, could not link them to human procreation. He told him that animals and humans were exactly the same when it came to making babies.

"I know about dogs and cats, even horses, but a man walking on his hands and feet and mounting a woman, who is walking on her hands and feet," said Dafydd. " 'Tis ridiculous. I be not that gullible!"

Owain cleared his throat and said, "Believe me, son, strange things happen between men and women."

"Mam said that she found me as tiny as a green worm,

under a cabbage leaf." Dafydd squinted his eyes to slits. "I looked. There are no teeny babes under cabbage leaves. Brenda said 'twas *you* who put the wee babe inside Christiannt to grow until it pushed itself out. Tell the truth, how do you put a babe, no bigger than the tiniest worm, inside a woman?" Dafydd's eyes were intent on his father's.

Owain nodded. "Aye, 'tis no trouble." He looked at his son a moment, appalled at his belief in the fanciful and disbelief in the truth. He wondered what sort of logic the lad's tutor, a white-haired, white-robed monk chosen by Gladys, taught. The more he thought about it, the more he decided it was the women who influenced Dafydd's thinking on procreation, not the monk.

He pledged to forbid Gladys, Christiannt and Brenda to sugarcoat the truth of anything for Dafydd. A lad needed facts. How else could he make rational decisions when he was mature?

Christiannt was so wrapped up in caring for Rhodri that she ignored Owain and Dafydd. Each one pretended he did not mind.

Owain believed that Gladys lived because of Dafydd, therefore he tolerated the lad being tutored in the home court. Owain considered Dafydd a nuisance, too young to think logically and to carry on a good conversation. The home castle was now turned into a nursery, where the striplings held sway. When Owain was younger he had sworn this would not happen. But with the brutal gutting of his twin sons on the bank of the Thames, he had begun to believe that his children had been fostered much too young. He also believed that by letting Gladys keep Dafydd, he kept peace.

Often he absented himself from that home court because he did not relish being near the devilkin Dafydd. He hunted with lords and princes of Powys and Deheubarth, attended defense meetings, then moved his army to push the Normans and English away from Gwynedd's borders. To pacify King Henry he promised again and again not to use the title "king." Title made no difference to Prince Owain as long as his people were well fed and none of Gwynedd's borders were obfuscated.

The Nant Gwynant court was a series of wattle-and-daub buildings held close together in a rigid framework of posts and struts. The inner bailey held the great hall, kitchen and laundry and a scattering of wattled buildings. At this time Owain realized that he would need more than that for defense if the English came as far inland as the Snowdons, or if the New Religionists became well organized and went after druids.

For a long time he dreamed of having an oak-trussed castle with large, rounded oak towers made of wooden beams, posts, lintels and rafters. He found the ideal limestone outcrop close by Nant Gwynant, in the tiny Dolwyddelan Valley nestled in the southern foothills of Moel Siabod, the solitary, snow-capped, mountain peak near the Lledr River.

During the summer of 1159 Owain recruited quarrymen, mortar makers, carriers, diggers and carpenters for the construction of the Dolwyddellan castle.

He wanted the outer gatehouse flanked by a system of bridges, gates and limestone barriers. He wanted his chamber, his wife's chamber, several guest chambers, a chapel, a couple of small offices and a dungeon built in the towers of the inner wall. Other residents of the castle would live and work in ordinary thatch-roofed, wattle-and-daub buildings in the inner bailey. The great hall and the kitchen would be built of wooden slabs fitted against the inside of the inner stone wall. On the right side of the inner gatehouse Owain used Brenda's idea to dig the well, so that the castle's water supply could not be poisoned by an outside enemy.

Gladys was delighted that Owain was busy outside the castle and that Christiannt was occupied with Rhodri. That gave her Dafydd all to herself. No matter how obstreperous the lad became, she forbade anyone to lay a hand on him.

In the spring of 1159, Owain announced that the royal family would remain in the Aberffraw castle until the Dolwyddelan castle was finished.

Going on outings from the castle to the village in a covered cart, Gladys seemed easily excited by unfamiliar scenery, street vendors, a short rainfall or the giggling of her maids. When overly excited, she fainted, which terrified young Dafydd. He became moody and sullen, but spoke to no one about the anguish that worry over his mother's sanity caused him.

He was a different child around the household servants. For attention he laughed, cavorted and mimicked his doddering mother. He charmed the servants whenever it was to his benefit. Except when he was with Brenda, he was like a ship without a rudder, blown here and there with nothing to guide him.

On Rhodri's second birthday, work on the Dolwyddelan castle was stopped because of cold weather. Aberffraw's early morning sky had a heavy coat of dark gray clouds.

Brenda gathered eggs in the lap of her apron so that the kitchen maids might make Rhodri a birthday pudding. She took the eggs to the kitchen, and as she passed the fireplace the great kettle gurgled and water splashed over its sides. She looked inside the kettle and saw Rhodri waving his chubby fists, eyes closed, half crying, half gurgling with water up to his dimpled chin. She took him, dripping and shivering, to the kitchen, where the maids' tongues clicked over his blue lips and mottled skin. Their questions and suppositions flew back and forth like black gnats. Someone said that Dafydd had been in the great hall moments before Brenda. He had sat in his father's chair near the fireplace with his feet perched on a pile of fresh-chopped wood, as if he ruled the roost.

Mention of Dafydd so upset Brenda that she almost forgot to thank the gods that the water in the kettle had been stone cold. She wrapped Rhodri in linen towels and comforted him against her shoulder.

She hied herself to Dafydd's chamber. She did not knock or call out, but barged into the middle of the room.

Dafydd was a good pretender and looked asleep on his pallet.

She saw his eyes open and shut and prodded his side with her foot. "Get up! Now!" she shouted.

He rubbed his eyes, blinked away the feigned sleep, pointed to the sniffling baby and said, "My God, Brenda, what is that?"

"You gomeral, you simpleton, you need not ask, you know 'tis a precious, wee life!"

"Life? 'Life is nothing more than a constant struggle that,

in the end, is lost to rot.' 'Tis a quote from my ignoble tutor," he added, pulling on his britches.

"Tell me why you put this babe in the kettle."

"To see him parboiled," he said, and smirked.

"Boiled? A babe?"

He shrugged and said, "A sacrificial gift to God. Mam says God takes a human sacrifice to grant a favor."

"You do not really believe that?" Brenda gave him a clout on the jaw that sprawled him back on his pallet.

"Hey!" Dafydd gawped at Brenda from the middle of his rumpled bed. "The babe's cries kept me awake—they got on my nerves. So I figured his life is shorter than anyone's in the castle. He has done nothing to advance humanity, so as far as lives I counted around here, his was the least value. I asked God to grant me the favor of peaceful sleep. In return I gave Him a crybaby. After all, he is unfinished. Babes his age walk and talk. He crawls and babbles."

"You are an insolent beast," she said. "A bully, an enemy to society, uncivilized, disgusting and malicious!"

Dafydd's greenish amber eyes were glassy-hard. His petulant lower lip thrust out momentarily, then pulled in, and his mouth turned up at the corners, as if he was amused by her tirade.

She waited until her breathing calmed and said, "Life is beauty or shame, as you make it. You live with *your* deeds, with *your* thoughts and with *your* feelings. You can make what you will of your own destination. The gods see your deviousness."

One corner of Dafydd's mouth twitched. "The gods are deaf, dumb and blind. They care naught for what I do."

"You should care about what I be going to do," she said sharply. Her dark eyes were big and bright. She laid the swaddled baby on the floor at the end of the pallet and grabbed Dafydd by the neck of his nightshirt. She sat on a chair, laid Dafydd, belly first, across her firm knees. He yelped, squirmed and kicked. She swung her hand, palm down, hard until it was stinging red.

He yelled, "Help! Murder!" until his throat was raw, then, in a voice that sounded like a croaking bullfrog, begged her to stop. She gave him a couple more swats for good measure, stood him on his feet and said, "Are you sorry for what you did to an innocent babe?"

He snorted, "Nay!"

She pushed him onto the pallet on his back and with her knee firm against his windpipe, stared at his distorted, angry face, waited for her hammering heart to calm, and then said, "You discomforted a wee babe. What if an older brother treated you in such a miserable manner?"

She moved her knee ever so slightly and he said, "I have the power to frighten him to death. I change forms; sometimes I be a bear with great strength in my legs, sometimes I be a buzzard, using my arms for wings and my sharp teeth to rip apart flesh! I can shrink you to a worm, and put you into the belly of a witch and in nine months you will come out a warty, squally toad. Mam says I have the power of a true enchanter."

"Is that so? Then you know Lady Gladys believes most anything, true or not. She believes Father Giff's gold ring has magical powers." She felt his fingers twitch. "Real power is based on personal loyalty, of which you have little. You cannot even see the loyalty your poor ill mother has for you. You are a demon."

His face was dark, but he said nothing.

She let go of him, picked up Rhodri and before Dafydd could catch his breath, was gone.

She found Christiannt in the kitchen, nearly hysterical, surrounded by maids murmuring endearments interspersed with words like "water," "baby," "drown," "murder."

Brenda pushed her way to Christiannt and said in a loud voice that the baby was not drowned, not murdered, not harmed. She shoved Rhodri into Christiannt's outstretched arms and said that she had punished Dafydd for his prank. "He is a lonely recalcitrant lad, who, right now, is feeling sorry for himself. Take Rhodri and go to your cottage where 'tis quiet."

On Rhodri's third birthday, before cockcrow, Christiannt found him sitting in the hen clutch. " 'Tis a miracle the hen did not peck his eyes out," she told Brenda. "He might have left the clutch and toddled off anywhere."

" 'Tis hard to think of him toddling anywhere on those short, chubby legs. You carry him everywhere, Christiannt— like a precious fat white dumpling."

"What?" asked Christiannt, laughing.

"I wonder how he got into the hen house," said Brenda.

"Daffyth," said Rhodri, tilting his head and drooling on his thick chest.

Later in the same week, Dafydd filled Rhodri's diaper cloth with stones and told him to walk. The child could not move with all that weight. Dafydd chortled and called him Pork-Bottom. Christiannt watched a few moments and let her anger rise. She demanded that Dafydd take out the stones and told him that he must begin to put aside childish actions and fill his mind with proper thoughts. She followed Brenda's advice and whipped him hard with the broad side of a straw broom. Her anger melted when he cried. She knelt to hold him close against her breast, murmured endearments used for babies and tearfully told him that he would never understand how much he meant to her. Giggling and drooling, Rhodri went around and around the two of them before either noticed he was walking by himself.

Three years later Christiannt found Dafydd trying to smother Rhodri in his feather bed.

Brenda said thirteen-year-old Dafydd should be fostered before causing real harm.

"I talked to Owain and he wants to wait until Gladys is well," said Christiannt. " 'Think of Gladys,' he said. Holy Mary, I tried. The more I think the more I hope she will die!"

Brenda gasped a dry laugh and said, "Keep that thought to yourself. How about Father Giff? You two seem to be friends."

"I talked to him," said Christiannt. "He will not foster the lad, but said Owain can send him to a monastery in the south. He said Dafydd is a child of God and we should pray for his well-being. Ummph! Prayer is no answer. You are the only person left that I can talk to. I need someone to tell me a true answer."

"I have told you fostering and the final answer to that comes from Owain, who is the sovereign authority," said Brenda, with frustration in her voice.

Christiannt wiped a hand across her forehead, pushing her thick yellow hair back under her cap. "My poor, precious Dafydd."

Brenda noted that she said "My Dafydd," and knew she was at the end of her rope. "Talk to Owain again. He is wiser by far than me."

"I told you what Owain will say. 'The two of you are close. I suppose you are conspiring to be rid of Dafydd so that he cannot be on the royal throne of Gwynedd!' "

That fall the seacoast weather was unusually warm. Fishermen continued to gather oysters from the sandy bottoms close to shore. The court supped on Caernarfon Bay oysters, packed in kelp and furze to keep them fresh for several days. One evening Owain ate the week's remaining oysters for his supper, and in the middle of the night was ill.

In the morning Brenda made him fennel tea to relieve the nausea.

Dafydd chose that time to attract attention and annoy a lot of people, by running through the Aberffraw castle like a maniac, howling at the top of his lungs whenever six-year-old Rhodri cried, which seemed to be constantly.

At noon Owain shouted to Brenda as if she were deaf. "The lad drives me barmy! Stop the bloody caterwauling!"

Feeling better by evening, Owain went to the great hall to hear Llywarch play the harp. He sat next to Brenda, leaned close and said, "I shall foster both Dafydd and Rhodri as soon as someone will take them."

Brenda smiled. " 'Tis time. What will happen when you tell Lady Gladys?"

He shrugged and reached for the mead pitcher. "She will make a fuss, become speechless and faint. 'Twill be hard on her and harder on me to see her upset."

"If I be permitted to make a suggestion, arrange for your

wife to visit Dafydd once in a while," she said. "Perhaps you can foster both lads close by."

Owain did not answer.

She said, "You might want to think about letting your oldest son, Iorwerth, foster Dafydd and Rhodri."

"I talked with Iorwerth about Dafydd months ago. He fosters only children whose both parents are Old Religionists. Gladys and Christiannt follow the doctrine according to Father Giff." Owain lifted his beaker, drank, drew in his breath and said, "For a long time, I could not admit that I had made a mistake. I pitied my wife because she was ill, and believed Dafydd's presence would heal her. Lugh's lungs! I was mistaken! My pity made Dafydd a small barbarian, filled with boasting and deceit. The same will happen to wee Rhodri if Christiannt hangs on to him. Father Giff wants the two lads to become Christian, one of them to take my place, and Gwynedd be the first Christian province in Wales. I have been generous, beyond fault, with coins to his church, so he does not say a word to me against druids, but he eschews my views and is jealous of my knowledge. He, like other New Religionists, is under the thumb of King Henry, and we know what Henry believes."

Brenda silently thanked the gods for bad oysters. She wanted to praise Owain for coming to his senses, but instead she said, "Father Giff's thinking may be twisted, and so is Dafydd's, but both are intelligent. There lies your challenge." She looked at Owain's contrite face from the corner of her eye, half afraid that he would be angry because she agreed with him.

Instead he nodded and his voice was full of determination. "With the gods' help, I shall foster Dafydd before the week's end!" He reached out, touched her cheek ever so lightly and excused himself.

The following evening the people in Aberffraw castle, including Owain, supped on boiled cabbage flavored with chunks of mutton and sweet clover, not oysters. Afterward Owain asked Brenda to sit a moment beside the warm fireplace. He said he had given more thought to his wife's feelings and was not going to discuss the idea of fostering with her.

Instead he was going to make fostering so enticing to Dafydd that he, himself, would talk his mother into acceptance. "The lad has admired Archdruid Llieu ever since he sewed up his sword cut. Llieu will foster him, if I ask." Then he lowered his voice and sounded conspiratorial. "Brenda, Dafydd listens to you, so I be asking you to tell my son some interesting things about the wise Old Religionists."

After breakfast several days later, Brenda spotted Dafydd sitting with his back against the outside wall of the great hall. He said he had left his tutor for a moment to sit in the sun away from Rhodri.

"That baby is such an annoyance I want to throw him down the nearest garderobe or privy." He said he wished Christiannt would get another tutor for wee Rhodri. "Why must I study in front of a baby, and wait for him to sing a wee song before my lesson resumes?"

She saw a bloody bandage on the ground, then saw that the old scar on his thigh was scabby, swollen and oozing yellow matter. There were red streaks radiating from it. "How did you hurt yourself?" she asked.

He opened his fist to show her a sharp-edged stone. "It hurts, but I be sucking up nerve to cut more of the flesh apart. I widen the scar a little each day so that in the end 'twill look like a large, wonderful, glory mark."

"Is that so?" Brenda nodded, understanding his need to feel important. A big, livid red scar would be something to brag about. "You know Archdruid Llieu is known throughout Gwynedd for his healing. He made your original wound heal so fast that it left very little scarring. I suppose you did not know that is another kind of glory mark. If you say that you were healed by the famous physician Archdruid Llieu, people's eyes light up. You can tell your friends how deep into your thigh the dagger went, clear to the bone, and the blood gushed out like a fountain, and then show them a white-line scar. Your friends will be truly impressed." She looked at his thigh and saw that the old narrow white line was gone. She picked up the soiled bandage and asked if she could rewrap the wound he had made.

" 'Tis my leg and I will do what I want with it," he said, puckering his mouth and putting his nose in the air.

"What will your mother say when she sees it?"

"Druids are shabby healers."

Brenda leaned closer. "There are the signs that your leg is rotting and mayhap will have to be cut off to save your life. Have you ever seen a one-legged soldier?"

Dafydd put his head down, picked at the putrid dried blood that had oozed from the broken flesh. Finally he scowled and said, "I think my wound is warm and I can see 'tis black as dried raw meat. It does hurt something fierce."

"Let me rewrap it, then come with me to the druid camp. Llieu has an ointment to ease pain, heal and cool hot flesh."

"Mayhap you have something?" he said, with his brows still drawn together. "I do not want my leg cut off."

She wrapped his leg in the soiled bandage as tightly as possible. "I do not have the antipain salve that is made from fish oil. Together we shall ask Llieu for the recipe. He is the wisest man I know, and he may have something to wash a putrefying leg so that it does not have to be sawed off."

"I heard druids use dung and flue soot on a festering sore," said Dafydd, hanging back.

"I heard that they use maggots," said Brenda.

Brenda told the tutor that Dafydd was feeling a bit bilious and was leaving for the rest of the afternoon. Dafydd stuck his tongue out and made a retching sound for Rhodri, who wanted to leave with him.

Dafydd complained that his leg ached and pointed to shade under a large apple tree. They rested a moment and Brenda told herself this was the perfect time to talk to him about the advantages he would have if he lived with druids. "You can ask them questions anytime. Every druid is a teacher. If you live with them, your mother will come to see you. You will learn to recite poems about your famous ancestors nine generations back and play the harp. You will not be followed day and night by a six-year-old brother who, in troth, adores you."

"Babies do not adore anything. They are dumb. So, if I go with the druids—will I learn to use a regular-size sword? Da said he admires a soldier who has a swift sword and rides a horse well." He bent to pick up a pebble, pulled a sling from the waistband of his trousers. He shot the pebble into the dense tree foliage, causing a large apple, still green, to fall. He bit into it with a crunching, sucking sound.

Brenda saw him grimace and his eyes water. "You may learn the art of fencing with a saber and to ride a horse, and"— she looked out of the corner of her eye—"not to take things that are not yours, such as unripe fruit from another man's croft." She pointed to the house on a little rise, barely visible from the road because it was surrounded by apple trees planted in neat rows. She guessed there were probably a barn and more trees behind the house.

"Ho! My da is prince. This is his province. He takes anything he wants. I be his son, therefore I can take whatever, whenever I please!" Brenda sighed, grabbed his hand and started walking.

At the camp Llieu looked at the wound, clicked his teeth and washed it with a slimy-looking liquid that made the sharp, throbbing pain a dull ache. Llieu told Brenda to hold the lad's hands and talk to him. With a small, sharpened wooden probe he cleaned out dead tissue and pus. Brenda was so interested in what he was doing that she forgot to talk.

Llieu tapped her elbow and said, "Hold the lad tight!"

She wrapped her arms tight around Dafydd and whispered in his ear, "Grit your teeth. This is it!"

Llieu poured scalding water into the wound, followed quickly by a stream of cool water. Dafydd screamed, pulled away and jumped around like a madman. Llieu told him to stop jumping like a baby and act like a man. "Lie quietly on the pallet against the wall with naught a thing touching the wound. You are in luck. Tomorrow I would have had to cut your leg clean away and let maggots eat the rest of your putrefied flesh."

Brenda held a beaker under Dafydd's nose. He sniffed, hiccupped and turned his tear-stained face away, saying under his breath that it smelled like rotten cabbage and his leg hurt like hell's fire.

"The tea will ease the pain and put you to sleep," she said. "Drink it like a man."

When Dafydd opened his eyes again, he did not feel the burning pain in his leg. He sat up on the pallet and asked Llieu if he had a horse.

"Several," said Llieu. "I like to ride."

"Would you foster me?"

He said he had been thinking of fostering a lad who would go out on the moors to gather certain water-loving plants, go to the crags with tarns to gather leeches, and go out on the grasslands to gather the eggs of certain birds. He sat on the foot of Dafydd's pallet and was quiet for a while. Finally he said that Dafydd might be the lad he was looking for.

"What about riding a horse on the grasslands and using a sling to scare birds from their nest?" said Dafydd.

"Certes," said Llieu, wrapping a piece of clean linen that was smudged with a gob of black, fishy-smelling salve tight around Dafydd's thigh. "After the required memory work there will be plenty of time to learn to be a horsebacker who gathers plants and leeches, and a sling-shooter that hunts birds and eggs."

"What if I decide not to stay? Can I go back to the court?"

"Well, of course—you are not held prisoner. But I shall be your foster father for no less than five years. Let Brenda change the dressing on that wound in a few days. I showed her how to make the salve. Do not get your leg wet."

Dafydd touched the bandage, grimaced because the pressure of his fingers made his wound hurt. He said, "Friends? Can I have friends?" He looked at Brenda.

"Certes, Brenda may visit you. Your mam and da may visit. I have four other foster sons. You boys will be close, eat together, study together, wash together and sleep together—on separate pallets. You will be foster brothers."

Dafydd looked like he had been slapped in the face and said he thought he would be Llieu's sole fosterling. "I do not want brothers, no half-brothers, no foster brothers. I hate brothers more than anything." He let out his pent-up breath, his shoulders sagged, his face flushed. "My da said I would learn to be a soldier and like it here. He lied. My mam said I would abhor every minute here. She was right. She told me exactly what you said: Druids remove their clothes and wash together. Washing is for women! Soldiers have no time for a wash. My da lied! I cannot learn to be a good soldier here." He sputtered, "I—I hate my da! I hate druids!" He thumbed his nose at Llieu, called him a pus-faced lassie and stormed for the door. He turned back and said he would kill his da. He pointed to Brenda and said, "I shall remember how you tricked me into coming here. You shall regret I ever crossed your path!" He limped to the castle by himself, full of his own importance, resentment and bad temper and with a throbbing thigh.

That winter Dafydd ignored Brenda, except on the days she changed his bandage and smeared his thigh with the black salve that smelled like rotten fish. He mimicked her behind her back, because she continued to go to the druid camp twice a week for healing studies. He begged his father for a horse, saying he knew how to ride faster than wind.

Owain refused, saying he had not yet shown any responsibility and, therefore, could break his neck riding fast.

Dafydd cried, saying he was old enough for a horse and if he broke his neck he would never blame his father.

Early on a breezy spring morning in Aberffraw, Brenda folded linen in the laundry cottage, looked out of the open door toward the western sky and saw cloud-islands streaked with orange that melted into pink and faded into pale yellow. She imagined Madoc up early, doing chores, looking at the same sky. "My son," she whispered, "do you think of me as often as I think of thee?" A tap-tap on the walk startled her out of daydreaming.

"Sorry, ma'am," said a wide-shouldered, hard-bitten man in a gray uniform. Brenda recognized him as the castle's outer gatekeeper. He raised his voice, as was his habit when speaking to females, whom he deemed were all born half deaf. "Master Dafydd came to the outer gate with a message for ye. He said to go directly to the druid camp with linen strips, acorns and dried kelp."

"Dafydd? What was he doing outside the castle's ward? Is someone hurt?"

"He was either hiding from that bulky laddie, Rhodri, who sticks to him like a sand burr, or he went to see the fire at the Fardd place. I saw the smoke when I came to my post at first light. Ye know the place with the apple trees ye pass on the way to the druids' camp? Master Dafydd said naught about anyone hurt, but mentioned that Eben Fardd's house and barn burned, saying 'twas because Fardd was a bloody pagan." The guard turned to hurry back to his post.

Brenda picked up a sack of acorns and one of kelp, which hung drying on the kitchen's fireplace wall, then stopped at her cottage for a clean but worn pallet cover. She tapped on Christiannt's door but she was not there, so she stopped at Llywarch's cottage, told him about the fire and where she was going. "I do not know when I shall return, so ask Christiannt to look after Lady Gladys."

Small groups of folk walked down the road, coughing and talking excitedly in hushed tones. They pointed ahead to knots of people huddled together opposite the rise where the Fardd cottage stood.

Brenda went past the big apple tree. The cottage's center fire stones were still in a ring. The oak cruck that was the cottage's center beam lay across a couple of the fire stones smoldering red, then silver, like a living thing. It looked like a thin dragon breathing fire. Men with water buckets pushed her aside. They doused what had once been mud-daubed, wattled walls, causing them to hiss and crackle and send billows of white steam over the blackened fire stones.

A shout came from the bottom of the rise. The men with buckets ran behind where the house had once stood. Brenda followed.

The far end of a large barn was burning with long, licking, orange flames pushed by the wind. Brenda saw hay on the ground and guessed that it had been in the loft and had fallen when the back wall collapsed along with half of the sod roof. Suddenly the air cleared and she saw two men standing together next to a row of apple trees.

She uncovered her nose and asked one of the men what had happened to the folks living in the cottage.

He wiped his sleeve over his eyes, pointed to the man standing beside him, who held a big gnarled hand over his nose and mouth, and said, "This be Jack—he saw the young lad from the castle lead Fardd's wife and his five wee uns to the druid camp. Some of the young uns' hands was black with pitiful burns and their mam was cryin'. Ye be a friend o' theirs?"

"I have talked with Molly in the marketplace," she said. "Where is her husband?"

"Only the gods know, missus. None o' us has seen Eben all morn. His horses, cows and goats were not in his barn and 'tis too hot to look for him there now." He licked his dry lips and pointed to the burning, roofless mess that no longer looked like a barn.

Brenda said, "Mayhap Eben went to find a safe place for his animals. In that case, he will be back soon."

"Aye, no sorrow like the loss of a friend," said the man behind his hand.

Brenda put the end of the pallet cover over her mouth and nose and slowly made her way through the smoke, along the sandy path back to the top of the rise. Now, for the first time, she noticed that the apple tree between the cottage and road where Dafydd had shot down a green apple was a scorched skeleton. Apples on the ground were black dried nuggets or black mushy balls. She wondered if the tree had burned first and the wind sent sparks to the roof of the cottage and then sent the cottage's sparks to the barn.

Llieu's door was held partially open against the wind by a large stone. He was kneeling beside a little girl on a pallet. One side of the child's face was puckered with smoke-blackened skin, as was her forehead. She had no eyebrows or lashes.

Molly Fardd, with her thatch of coppery hair tucked under a blue kerchief, was beside Llieu dabbing the child's blistered neck with a cloth soaked in a pale yellow liquid. Molly did not look up when Llieu motioned for Brenda to enter.

He stood, squeezed Brenda's arm, relieved to see her, and in a low voice said that moments before, a runner brought him a message that Eben was found holding a small goat in the barn's ashes. "Both were charred worse than sausage cooked over hot coals. Eben's horses are gone."

"Why, oh why, did Eben stay in a burning barn?" said Brenda.

"I suppose he chased the large animals out and came back for the stubborn goat and was surrounded by fire with no way out."

"I stopped and looked at the barn," said Brenda. "One end was still in flames. Ash was so thick I could hardly see, let alone breathe. I should have stayed longer. Mayhap I could have found what happened."

"Nay, nay! I need you here," said Llieu.

"Does Molly know—about Eben?" whispered Brenda.

"Aye, but she does not believe it. She brought the five children out of the burning cottage. Jen is the worst." He nodded toward the little girl. "The others have burns on their cheeks and hands from trying to put the fire out. Molly's hands and arms are burned, but she says it does not hurt. Tonight she will be in agony. I thank the gods you came."

"But I thought, Master Dafydd—was he sent to fetch me?"

"Aye. 'Twas he that had the good sense to bring Molly and the children here. When I thanked him and sent him to bring you, he was pale as skim milk and shaking like a leaf. Give the lad credit for doing something right."

"What was he doing out before dawn?"

"He did not say."

"The castle gate guard sent him to bed and gave me the message himself. He saw the smoke."

Llieu nodded. "Smoke in the air woke me."

"There is nothing left at the croft but the garden and apple trees. The big tree by the road is a black scrag." She scratched her head and said again, "Why?"

"Who knows?"

Brenda looked around the room and saw the table and chair were moved to make a place for pallets. Four other chin-dimpled children, with hands and faces wrapped in damp bandages, were sleeping.

"When they wake, give them drink," said Llieu. "Burns take water from the body. They like chamomile with honey. Jen and her mam refused to drink. Mayhap the hot smoke seared their throats. We will know if they cough by morning. Wet the rags on their hands and face with the yellow datura to keep the burn area cool. Comfort Molly."

Molly's blue eyes were sunken into deep, gray hollows. Brenda knelt and showed her the sack of dried kelp, added water to the sack, kneaded it like dough, then added more water until it became thick soup. "Kelp holds moisture and promotes healing," she said and showed Molly how to pat the soup on Jen's face and neck.

Molly nodded, looked about the room like a frightened animal. "Eben? Where is Eben?"

"His spirit is on the path to the Otherside," said Brenda gently. "He saved all his animals, except a little goat."

"Exactly what Llieu told us. 'Tis hard to believe. Why?"

Aye, the question we all want answered, thought Brenda.

After the evening meal Brenda asked the eldest, eight-year-old Cian, if he had seen anyone around their place who looked suspicious, someone who did not belong.

"Only Master Dafydd," he said. "Da said Master Dafydd came to see me because he was bored with court life. He is not one of us."

"Did he come to play often?" asked Brenda.

"Well, after the first time he came every day," said Cian. "He showed me how to shoot his sling. When I shot the settin' hen Da told me to tell him to take his sling and go home."

"Dafydd wanted to play soldier and ride a horse," said seven-year-old Brian. "Da did not like him sitting on our horses. He said he could ride one of his own."

"Nay," said Cian. "Dafydd told me that his da would not let him have a horse. I think he did not take good care of animals."

"He broke a branch on Da's special tree and said he could make apples ripen before their time," said Brian. "I knew he was blowing in the wind. The apples are still green."

Suddenly Cian said, "Master Dafydd had naught to do with the burning, did he?"

"I hope not," said Brenda. "Go back to sleep."

In the morning Jen's fever was gone. Llieu was impressed with Brenda's healing skills and said so. She told him what the Fardd children had said about Dafydd.

Llieu frowned and said he would send for Dafydd and question him about the fire.

"If he will come," said Brenda. She stayed the week to care for Molly, little Jen and the other four. During the morning of her last day, she and Molly were measuring the children so that they could alter the clothing that village folk had brought them.

Molly asked Brenda if she had a sweetheart.

Brenda flushed. "You know I be a maid mostly for Lady Gladys. I was once a mistress to Owain but he has other things on his mind lately. 'Tis no secret I have a boy and a girl fathered by Owain and fostered by my father in Ireland. I miss them terribly. My father sends word of their progress two or three times a year. 'Tis not near enough to satisfy a mother's wonderings."

"Aye, you need a young man who likes children and will take care of you," said Molly. "Someone kind and loving, like Eben was to me." Her eyes brimmed with tears.

In her mind's eye Brenda saw Sein's broad smile and his deep blue eyes crinkling at the corners. His red hair was sunlit and shone like a torch around his head. She bit her tongue and put her hands in her skirt pockets.

Molly saw that Brenda was embarrassed and turned to the children, who were huddled around a pile of clothing, trying to decide who would have what. When she turned back to Brenda, she whispered that her Eben was the most beautiful man she knew. "When he came into the house after working with the trees he took my breath away. His eyes were dark, nearly black. His nose was thin and his mouth was wide— long, curved upwards as if he knew some sweet secret. His face and hands were bronze and the rest of him an even tan, the color of well-preserved hide. God, I love that man! He will

never be gone. I shall keep him alive in my thoughts forever!"
She looked up and saw Llieu standing in the doorway. She
blushed.

His eyes twinkled and he said he had felt the same when
his wife died. He asked Molly to finish measuring the children.
"I need Brenda for a while."

Master Dafydd had chosen this morning to show up. He
had not knocked but had stalked inside thinking he was asked
to come to be honored for his good deed of leading Molly
Fardd and her five children to the druid camp. On the way to
meet Dafydd, Llieu told Brenda that he wanted her there as a
witness to hear what the lad had to say. "He is the son of the
prince of Gwynedd, so I must do this right."

Brenda nodded to Dafydd. He looked the other way. She
poured warm mead for Llieu while he talked to Dafydd about
the health of his mother, Lady Gladys.

Dafydd turned toward Brenda and scowled. She smiled and
half filled another beaker with hot water, added mead and gave
it to him.

His face brightened and his yellow-green eyes glistened as
he shifted the beaker from one hand to the other and sniffed
his hot drink.

"Why were you in the neighborhood of Fardd's a week ago
when it was not yet light?" asked Llieu.

Dafydd was so startled that he burned his tongue on the
first sip of mead. "Well, I—I walk about at night when I cannot sleep. I test my sling on voles and night owls."

"Ah—you are skilled at using a sling. Did you bring it with
you?"

"Nay."

"Well, you are a clever lad to get past the night guard."

"He sleeps against the wall and I know about a broken stake
in the palisade. I crawl through and be on my way." Dafydd
smirked.

Llieu studied the lad, who was getting more bull-necked
the older he became. "I suppose 'tis a thing a lad living inside
a court is bound to do."

"Aye, the court is boring. I told you my mother is ill and
stays abed. My father is gone and will not permit me to be

one of his soldiers, not even an ordinary dragon, nor ride his
horses. My tutor is dull." He dared himself to look at Brenda
for a moment and went on. "I be scolded if I look cross-eyed
at my drooly half-brother, Rhodri. Lads like me need excitement."

"So you played with the Fardd children?"

"Aye, that was some excitement. I ate supper with them,
rode their horses and shot down apples and birds and things
while they watched. Then one day for naught, the old wind-
bag, Fardd, told me if I set foot on his place again he would
take a cudgel to my backside. I be only a lad, and I said he
could not do that. I said my da would have his croft and he
laughed."

"So a week ago in the middle of the night you walked to
the Fardd place?" asked Llieu.

"Aye. And I remember seeing something just before the
fire. Fardd was arguing with one of Da's dragons in front of
the barn door. Fardd punched the dragon in the jaw, went
inside the barn and next I saw horses and cows barge out and
trample the dragon into the ground." His eyes grew large and
his hands became animated. "Then—"

"You went into the yard to see this?"

"Of course not! I stayed on the road."

"You did not go to the barn, maybe to look at the horses?
Maybe to see if Eben was all right?"

"Nay! I would have ridden one of his horses if I had a
mind to, but I was only prowling for cats that night. Do you
know cats' eyes are pinpoints of fire in the dark? I aim a stone
right between the two fires. Zing!"

Llieu nodded and thanked Dafydd for coming. "You have
told me quite a lot. Greet your da and mam for me. I wish
them well."

"Hey, you have not heard me out! There were other dragons
skulking around the house. I think they were after Fardd because he is—was a druid."

"A druid, like me?" asked Llieu, holding up one hand.
"How do you know? Did you look at his hands?"

"At sup I saw blue tattoos around his fingernails, like
yours." He looked at Llieu's hands, which were covered with

skin-tight hide gloves, and his face became red.

"Are you certain?" asked Brenda.

Dafydd looked at her with contempt. "Do you misbelieve me?"

"Lad, your story sounds made up," said Llieu, giving his beaker to Brenda. " 'Tis not yet clear why you were there the night after Eben told you to stay away. You cannot see the barn from the road. Why did I, a physician, not hear of a soldier trampled by cows and horses? You brought Molly and the children to me when they needed help. Why not bring the soldier to me if he was hurt and needed help?"

"I swear I saw the barn's blaze from the road. The flames were high against the sky. And the trampled man was burned to naught but a ghostlike gray ash."

"Do the Fardds have cats?" asked Brenda.

"Aye, they had cats in the barn. Everyone does."

"So you went in the barn and shot at the cats."

"Well, so—I—I bè only a lad and can get things mixed." His eyes were on the floor. "You cannot accuse me. I be of royal blood." He raised his head.

"Like I said, thank you for coming," said Llieu. "You may go now."

"I be also going back to the home-court," said Brenda. "Will you walk to the castle with me?"

"I do not have to walk with anyone," said Dafydd. He stuck his tongue out, turned and stomped out of the cottage. From the doorway they watched him bolt through the gate and run, with a slight limp, down the road. His feet made little clouds of dust rise high in the air behind him.

Neither Brenda nor Llieu knew what to make of the story of soldiers lurking around the Fardd place. Were Owain's retainers becoming so bold? It was hard to believe. There were always rumors, but until now there had been no evidence of violence against druids around Aberffraw.

Two weeks after the burning of the Fardd place, most of Gwynedd's court remained in Aberffraw while Owain went to Dolwyddelan to oversee the building of the new summer castle.

Young Dafydd prowled around Aberffraw like a lost hound

that had no master and nowhere to go. He was morose and blamed his father for not taking him to Dolwyddelan. He wanted to have a hand in building the new castle.

Christiannt and Gladys were closer than ever. Gladys watched over Rhodri when Christiannt wanted to spend time with Dafydd. The two women laughed and said they had traded laddies.

Brenda blamed herself for Eben Fardd's death. She talked to Llywarch about how she had failed to get Dafydd to stay with Archdruid Llieu at the Prydian druid camp. " 'Twas my one chance to help the lad and I failed. Because of my meddling, Dafydd set fire to Fardd's house and barn. I have no proof but I am sure of it. Owain does not want to believe his son is capable of such beastly acts, and he does not stay in the home court long enough to see what is happening. I have word that Christiannt hid Dafydd directly after the fire. That is why I could not find her the morning I was called to bring kelp and acorns to the druid camp. Dafydd told me he went straight to her and said he needed to be away from the court for a few days. She asked the lad naught—she is afraid to know what he has done—but took him to a soldier she knows—one of Owain's men!"

"I thought she would come to you for help," said Llywarch.

"She is angry that I blamed her for Dafydd's miserable behavior."

"Work through Owain," suggested Llywarch. "He respects your judgment. He asks for your advice, so give it to him."

"But," she said, "Owain is the prince of Gwynedd; he will do what he wants. He has the last word."

"Aye," said Llywarch with a crooked smile. "Now hear me. Owain expects to hear flattery and sweet nothings from his women. He needs that. You and I know 'tis only honeyed talk."

" 'Tis funny," she said, "but when around Owain, most women believe he is Adonis. He charms *them* with his sweet talk."

"On the other hand, you are not most women." Llywarch's eyes danced. "You listen to him and let him talk politics and province business. You have a mind of your own; mayhap that is what he loves about you. He respects your answers to his problems, even though he has never known quite what to make of you. My advice is to tell him how just he is—then tell him the court and the whole village of Aberffraw would be better served if he sent Dafydd somewhere far away—anywhere, fostered or not."

Soon after Owain returned to court, Brenda found him one evening lingering over his supper. He sat in his hide-covered chair next to the fireplace sipping a beaker of mead. She sat on the hearth and looked up at him, then at the dying embers. She had thought of what to say ever since talking to Llywarch, but still she was uncertain how to bring up the subject of Dafydd. Finally she said, "I do not sleep well—my mind is in a whirl." She caught her bottom lip between her teeth.

Owain looked at her for a count of nine breaths and told her she had the best mind, was the most beautiful, albeit the most stubborn, of all his mistresses.

Brenda blushed and thanked him, then said that he could one day change his mind about her beauty and brains but he was not wrong about her being obstinate. "My father told me about this fault many times when I was a child." She wove her fingers and then cupped them together to hold them still and said how pleased she was with his friendship. "Are you back in court to prepare us for the trip to the new summer castle in the mountains? Rumors are that you know exactly how to get the best out of your stonemasons and woodworkers. I can imagine how lovely it is."

He said that was exactly why he was in Aberffraw. He had left his oldest son with his men to work the last details on the Dolwyddelan castle. "Iorwerth told me he loved the view of the Snowdons and would like to have Dolwyddelan deeded to him. He dreams of having a son of his own stay at Dolwyddelan and rule over Gwynedd. We talked of the way the pale, moist air heightens and dramatizes everything near the mountains. Even though 'tis not true, the Dolwyddelan towers appear much higher than Degannwy's tower and the new oak crucks seem larger and richer than others I have seen."

"I cannot wait to see it," Brenda said. "Mayhap Gladys will have flowers planted by the front palisade."

"Aye, talk to her about it," said Owain. " 'Twould do her good to have a garden of her own. Now what is on your mind?"

Brenda rubbed her moist hands on her skirt and stammered. "I—I wonder if Dafydd would be more settled if he had more responsibility. The lad is closeted with his mother, who is not well and does not need the challenges of raising a half-grown child. For instance, could he work at the slate mines?" Brenda swallowed and held her hands tight together. She wanted to say more about Dafydd, who she figured was planning another disaster to draw the attention of the court and the village away from himself and the Fardd fire, but Owain beat her to it.

"I talked to Dafydd," he said. "He has a mind I do not fathom. The only true facts I know is that he is my son and gives my sick wife comfort."

" 'Twould be so easy to take him to the quarries of Penmaenmawr as our cavalcade goes on to Dolwyddelan," said Brenda. "He might find cutting out roofing tiles or ax-heads will keep him busy."

"Aye, 'tis something to ponder," said Owain. "I bid you a good night." He left the table and headed for his chamber. Brenda poured herself a beaker of mead.

A week later, Brenda put clean linen on the court's pallets and swept the cobwebs from corners of the chambers and cottages. In Dafydd's small chamber she found a quilt jammed in a corner behind the chair. When she pulled on the quilt, dozens of fat apples rolled out. Some had cloudy white stripes, others were pale yellow, most were green. The quilt was soiled with dirt, twigs and leaves.

With the soiled quilt over her arm, she interrupted the tutor and said she needed to talk to Dafydd. She took him to his chamber, pushed the quilt into his arms, asked him to explain where the apples on the floor came from and watched him closely.

His face paled as he stared at the floor. He licked his lips and swallowed. "Do you suppose one of those soldiers I saw did this? He might have seen how good I was with my sling and tried to make it look like I shot down all these apples." His hands shook. "I have a special power to make them red and sweet. You want to see?"

"Nay. I want to know if you can tell your da who took the apples."

"Aye, and he will put that dragon in the donjon," said Dafydd with a snigger, "then you will leave me alone." He looked at her a moment, threw down the quilt and went out the door.

Brenda picked up the quilt and followed him, saying that Owain was in the great hall drinking mead and listening to Llywarch sing about his ancestors.

Owain had raised his eyes to the soot-coated ceiling when he saw Dafydd come in followed by a stern-faced Brenda. He dismissed Llywarch and motioned for them to sit at the table. When the silence became overpowering, Brenda nudged Dafydd and reminded him to tell his father about the quilt filled with apples. After Dafydd's story, Owain asked if he could identify one of the soldiers he saw on the Fardd place. Dafydd wiped his eyes, bit his bottom lip, went outside and pointed to the first soldier he saw walking across the inner ward.

When questioned, the soldier flared and said he had been on a two-day march with Prince Owain himself. "Remember, I was the one who kept my brogues dry by sloshing barefoot through the wet moor?" The young man looked from Owain to Dafydd. He was puzzled and angry at being accused of something he knew nothing about.

Owain remained silent.

Dafydd looked cunning as a fox with wide, innocent eyes. "Da, I told you he is a New Religionist after druids and guilty as sin."

Owain sent Dafydd back to his tutor and placed the soldier in the donjon until he asked Brenda why there was a fuss over apples. "Do you still think Dafydd is guilty of killing Eben Fardd?"

"I do," said Brenda.

" 'Tis hard for me to believe that Dafydd pointed his finger at an innocent soldier. The morning of Eben Fardd's death that soldier was, in troth, on a practice march with me and fifteen other retainers." Owain studied his boots, causing the slack skin of his neck to fold over his Adam's apple. "The lad belongs in the donjon."

"You have done worse to other kin for lesser crimes," said Brenda.

Owain looked tired.

"A man with honor marks on his hands, same as your own, has died. A man who wanted only to propagate apple trees that fare well in the Aberffraw climate is dead. Your people believe in your strength. Can you afford to be weak when dealing with a problem such as a mere lad?"

Owain was quiet. Brenda thought he was thinking of dropping her in the donjon. She tensed when he spoke. " 'Tis my place to say what is to be done with the lad, not yours," he said, then whispered, "If you bring the gossip about the Fardd fire to Gladys's attention, 'twill kill her for certes and you shall sleep on fetid hay. Remember I promised to foster him as soon as I find someone who will have him. I shall release my innocent soldier, with an apology."

Brenda shoved the dirty quilt into Owain's hands and said, "Master Dafydd is guilty of murder."

The evening of June 1, 1163, just before the move from Aberffraw's seaside to the newly built stronghold in Snowdon's heartland, Owain waited for Brenda to finish supper, then he sat beside her. His eyes were red-rimmed and the corners of his mouth turned down. He looked like an old man near the end of his rope. "I wish to heaven that Dafydd was not mine. The lad is constant trouble and now he has disappeared— gone."

"Gone? Where?"

Owain's mouth turned down and his eyes were a dull gray. "I know not. He is not at the Penmaenmawr quarries. He has not been with his tutor for a week, and Lady Gladys has not seen him for seven days. She is sick with worry. I have soldiers combing the fells and becks. I thought I was above the law. I acted above the gods. I was wrong. Whatever he does, I am responsible. Goder-heal! I should have held him in the donjon. This son is my retribution, my Nemesis." Then his eyes became more green than blue and he said, "Mayhap the lad is waiting for us at Dolwyddelan."

The royal family took two weeks to settle into the Dolwyddelan court, and Dafydd was still missing.

Llywarch told Brenda he thought the boy had run away to avoid working in the slate fields or sitting in the donjon, and was possibly traveling with one of Owain's army patrols. One patrol covered the coastal regions and the other the mountainous areas to keep them clear of English soldiers and land-hungry Northmen. Which would Dafydd choose?

"My soldiers will continue their search," said Owain. "By and by the lad will show up demanding something impossible from me. You can bet on it. I am surely blessed that I do not have three sons the same age, with the same impudence." He closed his eyes as if remembering the night Llywarch told the old Welsh tale of the birth of triplet boys ordered drowned because it was prophesied that one would live to kill his grandfather and himself accidentally.

"Aye, the old 'Lug prophesy,' " whispered Brenda.

IX
King Henry II

On 1 July 1163, Henry, following his military expedition into south Wales, on which he had captured the rebel Rhys ap Gruffydd, held his court at Woodstock, near Oxford (England), one of his favourite hunting lodges. ... At Woodstock he turned his attention to the general land tax, danegeld, an unpopular levy.... The argument got out of hand. Henry, swearing as usual *par les olz Deu*, by the eyes of God, ordered that these sums should be entered as shrieval debts on the Pipe Rolls. Thomas declared by those very same eyes that not a penny should be paid from his estates or church lands. Thomas carried the day, presumably because the king received little support from the other courtiers present; and Henry was furious.

Frank Barlow, Thomas Becket

Brenda opened her door-flap and was shocked to find Owain standing there. For several moments she did not ask him to come inside. It was the first time he had visited her cottage since she had returned from Ireland, more than a dozen years ago. She asked him to sit on her willow chair and she sat on her pallet. His blond eyebrows and lashes were actually white. His yellow hair was streaked with white. She had not dreamed that Owain would ever grow old, although thinking back, she had seen the signs. A lock of hair like a coiled rope of flax fell over his forehead. His gloved hands hung relaxed at his sides.

"Two weeks ago," he said, "I received a brief from King

Henry inviting me to Woodstock for an important meeting on the first of July."

He looked at Brenda's open mouth, chuckled low in his chest and said, "My dear, the prince of Gwynedd is important, but he is not the only important man Henry invited to this meeting. The English messenger told me that invitations were sent to Thomas à Becket, the archbishop of Canterbury, and to the bishops of London and Lincoln. I expect various barons and other officials of Britain were invited. Henry signed the invitations "Sovereign," which makes us mere attendants, rather than councilors as prescribed by English law. You understand that I must go to see what is going on. My friend Rhys, prince of Powys, is a prisoner at Woodstock."

"You will plead for Rhys's release?" Brenda felt that was what he had on his mind to tell her.

Owain was always astonished when Brenda spoke up in an impulsive, fearless manner. He stared at her and wondered if he actually could bring Rhys back to Welsh soil.

" 'Twould be the right thing," she said.

"I have had that thought," he said. "But I cannot tell my wife, nor the *uchelwyr*, my noblemen, nor my army officers, where I be going. They would insist on coming with me. In England I do not want to look hostile with a retinue of soldiers." His voice vibrated deep within his chest. "While I be gone I want you to keep your ear to the ground for any hint of the whereabouts of Dafydd. I want no trouble from him while I be gone."

She said, "If I find Dafydd, I will tell you the instant you return. But if I were he, I would not reveal myself to anyone, not my mother, not the maids, and not the gate guards. I would stay away from people who pry me with questions."

"You are logical; Dafydd is not! So I say use your feminine intuition. Does it tell you that Dafydd already knows about Henry's call for a council meeting? Does it tell you that he is planning to let me know I cannot hamper his wiles? Think like Dafydd!" He smiled, showing even, white teeth.

Brenda shrank back, blushed and felt the heat rise from the soles of her feet to the top of her head. He asked the impossible. No one could think like Dafydd. She wondered if he

were testing her and she felt angry. After a moment she said,
"People in the village trace a cross in the air, the sign against
evil, before they speak of Dafydd. I will watch for any sign
of Dafydd's pranks with an eagle eye, not because you treat
me like I do not know chalk from cheese, tell me what to do
and how to think, but because we are friends. I be not certain
of my intuition. I cannot think like Dafydd, and never know
what he will do before he does it." Her heart pounded. "This
I know: Dafydd is a frightened laddie. He knows he killed a
man the night of the Fardd fire. The knowing eats him. He
cannot sleep. He needs someone he can trust, someone like a
father."

Owain stared straight ahead and left only silence between
them. Finally he nodded and rose.

Suddenly she knew what it was that had attracted her to
him years ago. He was self-confident, always right. She had
wanted to be in control of her feelings the way he was. She
had studied him and tried, but seldom could she control what
she felt. Today proved it. She could not control her anger, her
hurt feelings, or her tenderheartedness, no matter how hard
she tried. For years she had thought Owain respected her because she worked at being logical, not sentimental. Sentimen-
tality had to do with intuition. It was influenced more by
emotion than reason. Now he had asked her to use her intuition, and she feared she could not know something without
the conscious use of study, reasoning and experience. Then
she remembered the strange, indefinable feeling she had had
before she knew that Ailin was in the cave dying. "If Dafydd
shows up, I shall use what intuition I have to keep him here
until you return."

He stood in the open doorway, his wide, strong back toward
her. "That is what I want."

Brenda watched him mount his horse and ride toward Dolwyddelan's gate. She looked up and saw the snow-capped *Er-
yri*, Snowdons. She thought no view could be better than the
one she had now. The corners of her mouth pulled up and she
remembered all the aches and yearnings, tears and laughter
that Owain had created in her younger self. The first time he
had coupled with her she was filled with a constant longing

for his touch. She could not keep her hands off him whenever they met by chance or arrangement. She would touch his hand, his arm, his jaw, and wanted to touch other places under his clothing. The wanting was so strong that it had made her dizzy-sick. She had told herself the feeling was pagan and wild and something to be controlled. He seldom touched her, even in those early days. He had coupled with her only enough to give her three children. When they were together he had talked for hours about his life as a child in Ireland, his life as leader of Gwynedd, and his dreams.

In the last dozen years, when he detained her at the long table after supper, he talked little about battles lost and won, but mostly about what he wanted for the people of Gwynedd. She still believed him the most talented and totally disciplined leader Britain had ever known, and, in her mind, there was no doubt that he would accomplish what he wanted: to keep Gwynedd together as one province. He would be counted as a great leader nine times nine generations hence.

Recently, he had begun to question her and ask her opinion about what he had done or was about to do in connection with governing. She was flattered beyond description. But advising him gave her no inner joy. She told no one, called him a wonderful friend in her own mind and remembered that he had a dark, forbidding side. His dark side drove him to kill in the heat of battle, to murder or mutilate kin in anger and to destroy babies in the name of honor. She felt a surge of loneliness that lay deep at the bottom of her heart.

After Owain left for Woodstock, Christiannt told Brenda she would no longer come to supper in the great hall until Dafydd was found. Brenda tried to talk some sense into her but failed. Christiannt refused to eat anything but hot posset, milk curdled with wine, and nursery food, gruel and pudding. Once she said, "Owain's refusal to stay and hunt for poor Dafydd is slowly crucifying both Gladys and me. I tell you, Brenda, 'tis more agonizing than what was done to our dear Christ on the Rood, the holy Cross."

Brenda was dismayed at Christiannt's spiteful words, how-

ever, she could not bring herself to say that she was sorry
Dafydd was not at the royal court.

Two days later Brenda had no warning, no special intuition,
but remembered Owain's words that Dafydd might be planning another disaster. In the afternoon, black clouds of birds
swirled and swooped over the castle. Curious, she followed
flocks of crows along with their larger cousins, hawks and
ravens, to the outer gate. There, on palisade stakes around the
castle's outer ward, the birds fought over half a dozen bloody
rams' heads. Six headless, maggoty carcasses lay in the dry
moat.

The guards assured Brenda that they had not seen anyone
suspicious around the palisade. 'Twas a riddle who had beheaded the rams.

Brenda recalled once answering Dafydd's question about
druids. "They put skulls of boars on their gateposts because
they want to believe that the animals' spirits protect them,"
she had said.

"Ram-skull spirits could protect us in the royal court," Dafydd had said. "If I put ram skulls on either side of the outer
gate and on the palisade stakes, Da would have the priests
bless me and the bards sing a praise song for me. What do
you think?"

"I think your imagination runs like a wild fire," she had
told him, then laughed and forgotten about it until now.

On the third day of birds, Brenda fixed a tray with tea and
wholemeal bread and went to see Gladys, who was abed staring at the ceiling. She eschewed the food and drink Brenda
had brought and said she was weeping over the disappearance
of Dafydd. Her eyes were dry and her lips curved upward.

On the fourth day the birds were gone, and Gladys continued to refuse food and drink. The rams' skulls and skeletons
were pecked bare. Seeing Gladys smile, Brenda wondered if
Dafydd, up to his old tricks, had come to tell his mother he
was well. She asked Gladys if she had heard from Dafydd,
but Gladys kept her lips sealed.

Brenda asked the kitchen maids who had beheaded the
rams, and Dafydd's name rose to the top like cream on milk.

She gave the maids an enigmatic smile and said, "Three clear days predatory birds flew over the castle. If 'tis in troth the work of Master Dafydd, he is staying quiet while he draws a herring across his trail. If perchance you see or hear of him, let me know."

The day Owain returned from Woodstock, Brenda sent word to him that Gladys was starving herself.

That evening Gladys surprised everyone and came to the great hall for a supper of salted mackerel and fresh barley bread. Everyone told her how beautiful she looked and she smiled.

Owain stood, looked smug and confident. He announced that he and other British heads of provinces had just attended a meeting with King Henry. "The outcome of the visit relieves anyone in Gwynedd of paying taxes to England." The applause was loud and long.

During the evening someone asked Owain if he knew about the flocks of birds that had stayed for three days to eat the flesh from the rams' heads at the outer gate. He said that he had heard talk among the English at Woodstock that his Dol-wyddelan summer castle resembled a druid encampment. Owain sang a song about the jealousy of English lords, who had no ram skulls to protect their castles. "I suggest the English adorn their castle doors with rabbit skulls. 'Twould go with their timid, hoppity nature."

Everyone laughed, and Brenda thought he was more like the old Owain she had known when he was young.

Gladys's eyes closed, her head bobbed, her eyes popped open and she motioned to Brenda that she was ready for bed.

When Brenda returned from Gladys's chamber, she noticed that there was pride in Owain's voice as he told his court that the ram skulls would be permanently fixed on special posts at the outer ward's entrance. "If there is a protector spirit, we shall benefit; if not, they will frighten the boots off English soldiers." He looked sideways at Brenda and she guessed that he wanted to talk to her after the others had gone. Perhaps he would scold her for not intuitively knowing who had beheaded the rams.

When everyone had left, Owain moved to a bench on the

semicircle of gray tiles in front of the fireplace, where Brenda
joined him. "I have something I want to share with you while
'tis fresh in my mind," he said. "I be going to tell you something I will not tell the others. Dafydd is no good, but I love
him. Archbishop Becket told me the lad would be the death
of me." In the flickering candlelight Owain looked like an old
man.

"Nay," said Brenda. Her lips turned up and she shook her
head doubtfully. "Not Dafydd, 'twill be a woman!"

"Mayhap some woman and Dafydd together," he said and
rolled his eyes. "Like the Christians say, it takes a mother and
son to murder a good husband."

"You have heard from Dafydd?" she asked.

"Aye and nay, I have had reports of him being around the
castle. So I know he is safe but keeps out of sight, just as you
said he would."

"I heard a story of Dafydd riding off on one of your war
horses," said Brenda. "I deemed the story was castle gossip
until I heard that several broadswords were missing. Without
intuition, that sounds like Dafydd joined a band of dragons."

"That is my hope," said Owain, with a broad smile. "Best
thing in the world for all of us." He took Brenda's right hand
and shook it as if she were a man. Then he said, " 'Tis more
than a dozen years since you returned to me from Ireland. I
be glad you are back."

"I did not return to you; I was brought to you," said Brenda.
She did not say it in an accusing way. She wanted Owain to
speak the truth about her.

"These days I marvel how you think," he said. "I want you
to know I appreciate your keen mind and I wonder why I never
realized how useful 'tis before you ran away."

Brenda smiled, pulled back her hand and with a lilt in her
voice said, "You were young and did not believe that a woman
needed to be wise."

He leaned forward. "I be smarter now. If I tell you about
King Henry and Thomas of London, you will know more than
most. And then, if I ask, you can advise me better on matters
pertaining to either one. Listen." He did not touch her, but she
could feel his warm sweet-mead breath on her face.

She was flattered by his attention and his wanting to honor her with his story. No other woman would have the privilege of hearing firsthand about the Woodstock meeting, or even be interested in the hearing. Her head bent toward his wide shoulder and she was ready to be totally absorbed in the drama he was about to unfold.

On the first day everyone in the great Woodstock hall was quiet as Henry rose, stood on his tiptoes to make himself look taller and complained that Thomas of London was skimming off parishioners' money for church coffers and not sending the full amount to England's treasury. Henry looked directly at Thomas and said, "By God's eyes, I be being fleeced by you rapacious, ecclesiastical officials. Therefore, I am ordering *all* British landowners to pay a supplementary tax into the royal treasury."

Thomas at first was taken aback and quiet. Then, angered by the accusation, he stood and with an aristocratic manner shook his finger at Henry while speaking slowly as he tried to avoid his usual stammer. "Your Highness," he said, "your accusations are unfounded. I do not fleece nor rape, nor order such activities. Once a year, as required by law, my chaplain sends the English royal court ten p-percent of alms and other offertories. By God's eyes, not a p-penny shall be p-paid from my estates nor from church lands and I shall encourage p-parishioners to ignore your supplementary tax as unfair and exorbitant!" Though he had stuttered, he spoke with conviction about standards that he would not modify. He clasped his hands together, remained standing with his tonsured head held high. He appeared almost regal in a light blue full-length robe, except that a white wool pallium with pendants of lambskins enveloped the shoulders of his round torso like the final covering on a fluffed-up, rotund featherbed.

Owain smiled at Thomas, glared at Henry, pulled his royal-blue linen bratt straight across his shoulders, shook his white-blond head and shouted, "Thomas is right! Henry, you are a money-grubbing blackguard and shall receive no supplementary tax from North Wales!"

Malcolm the Fourth, king of Scots, and some of the other

courtiers nodded their agreement with Owain, whose eyes glistened.

Thomas could not hide the satisfaction their support gave him. The corners of his mouth tilted upward and his eyes twinkled.

Henry's face turned purple, his nostrils flared, he snorted and unfastened the top hooks of his ermine robe. He was so furious that he could not speak for several minutes. He looked like someone on the brink of a seizure. He cut the meeting short and refused to let the dissenters, led by Thomas and Owain, view his hounds and hawks. They were not invited to sample the afternoon refreshment of beer served from a spigot in an iron-hooped wooden cask. The snub was not appreciated.

Owain told Thomas he was ready to go home. Thomas said that the next day's council's agenda held the fate of Owain's notorious friend and kinsman on his father's side: Prince Rhys ap Gruffydd of Powys.

The previous spring Rhys had fought against Henry's retainers, who came into Powys to confiscate Welsh crofts, claiming falsely that they were on English soil. Those same English retainers had skulked into North Wales, were chased out and fled through Powys, where they took Rhys hostage. He was now confined to the donjon of Woodstock's small stone castle.

Owain stayed to see Rhys and hear the charges set against him the second morning of the meeting.

Henry, in a black mood, asked Rhys if he had destroyed bridges and roads, ambushed and used cudgels on English soldiers who removed Welsh crofters from illegal farmland around Chester.

"Aye!" shouted Rhys, "and I would do it again!" He pounded the table, called Henry a bloody *celwyddgi*, prevaricator, and explained to the court that those bloody English soldiers were nearer Hawarden, well within the Welsh border, not Chester. "Your Highness," he said, "Welsh crofters do not farm English land. None of your armed soldiers lost their life, but six unarmed druid crofters, and two children, were brutally murdered. You deliberately distort the facts to make your soldiers appear as law-abiding angels while they gut and behead unarmed druids' children!"

Rhys slammed his gloved fist harder against the table and declared war against all New Religionists for confiscating land and slaying Old Religionists. He had the guts to point his finger at Henry and declare him his chief enemy for ordering headhunting exploits on innocent druids. Then he threw off one leather glove, pulled up his sleeve, proudly showed his woad honor marks and admitted that he exhorted fellow druids, who are pacifists, to do what was right to save themselves and their families from extinction. Not once did he mention the vicious murder of his sister's twin lads. Though Owain thought he could have.

Rhys said the druids must fight with what they had, fists, clubs, stones and, better yet, their hunting weapons. They must stop the well-armed English, who pillaged lawful Welsh crofts, raped Welshwomen, murdered Welshmen. He said, "Pagh!" and asked how the English soldiers could look at themselves and say they were the New Religious. "Does the New Religion condone rape and murder? If so," said Rhys, " 'tis something created by the devil, not the Lord God!" He looked some moments at Thomas sitting bug-eyed with the bishops and said, "My lords, you know 'tis a fact that some of your New Religious intend to expunge all of us Old Religious, no matter that we both believe in the omniscient Lord of Gods." Then, turning back to that cullion, Henry, he asked, "Your Highness, why is it that the New Religious close their ears to words of peace, yet they expound the words of Christ, who was a teacher of peace? Have you infatuated the Christians with the power of warring?" His voice reverberated through the men in the hall like thunder. "Why exterminate druids, who have not lifted a finger against you? Through past ages druids were highly respected. They were first to heal Christians' diseases, to tend their battle wounds and to educate their children. 'Tis druids who wrote and executed your British laws with justice and honor. In troth, I believe some of you have become as spoiled children, demanding your way with no thought nor consideration beyond yourself. Responsibility has become unbeknownst to you. 'Tis a new age ruled by selfishness and greed."

The court was silent, awestuck. Henry was like a statue.

Owain thought of his son Dafydd and stood in the shine of Rhys's wide, grinning face; stood up in his hunting boots, leather tunic, trews and tooled gloves and shouted, "Amen!"

The room was charged with tension like dry air before a storm. Owain remained standing for at least two times nine heartbeats. Then, with every eye on him, he became bold, and talked of the folly of pitting Britains against Britains over religious beliefs. He reminded Henry that murders were unlawful and punishable by death. He suggested that Rhys be released with an agreement from both Christians and druids pledging no further violence against one another. He told Henry that under English common law a monarch's leadership was supposed to be under the Lord God and the law of the land. "Henry," Owain said, "you have put yourself above both the chief God and law! For that you are due for a great fall."

While Owain spoke, Thomas set aside his white pallium and box of government seals. Symbolically that gesture suspended him from his English government functions. When Owain sat, Thomas stood.

His head was bowed in prayer. Then he looked up, waved his arms for order, tried his best to avoid stuttering with careful inflections and suggested that the king of England subscribe to Prince Owain's suggestion to release Prince Rhys. "As a human being I have great empathy for Rhys's rebellion. He knows right from wrong, good from evil." Thomas pointed to his government seals, which lay on the floor. "As a Christian and an ordinary English citizen, with no connection to government, I know 'tis wrong to pillage, rape and murder in the name of Christ. I find druids intelligent, honorable and wise. Many of them are my good friends. They teach peace between men. They carry no arms, only tools for hunting and butchering. For centuries, battling Britains have depended upon and protected druid healers, who give aid to their injured troops. There is an unwritten law that says, 'Without prejudice or rancor, the same kind of aid received by thee shall be given to thine enemy.' Can you, as king of Britain, punish a man by holding him hostage for wanting to protect his family, protect his people from illegal murderers and molesters? Remember the fifth commandment: 'Thou shalt not kill.' "

Malcolm, the king of Scots, who was set stout upon his legs, shuffled his feet, got up beside Thomas and surprised everyone because his voice was a prissy chirp, which he detested. "I agree," he said, "with everything in that magnificent speech by Thomas of London."

His words made Henry squirm. His mouth trembled; he told Malcolm to shut up or leave and Owain and Thomas to sit down. He said that the king of Scots, the prince of Gwynedd, and the archbishop accepted his generous invitation to meet with him to solve a few political problems, but now the three of them conspired against him. He said enough codswallop had gone on; his patience had run out. He ordered Rhys back in the donjon to be beheaded anon.

Rhys looked from Henry to Thomas, to Owain, to Malcolm, and made a funny sound in his throat. Thomas signed a cross in the air and glared at Henry.

Owain stood. His legs shook like pudding. As calmly as possible, he said that it was only fair to wait until morning, to have the execution at sunrise.

Rhys made another little squeak in his throat, Thomas wheezed, Malcolm clapped his hands and the other courtiers stomped their feet. The sound was startling and made the welkin ring.

Henry saw that he had lost and grudgingly indicated agreement by a stiff nod of his head and adjourned the famous Woodstock Meeting.

Malcolm, with no word of thanks to his host, left Woodstock immediately with his entourage.

Owain waited for the noon meal. Afterward he changed his tunic and trews to the linens he wore for traveling. He and Thomas found other participants who were leaving instead of waiting for morning. Owain wished them God's speed home and Thomas blessed them. Then the two of them quietly settled their retinues under cover of vines and trees at the crossroad outside Woodstock's gate. They talked, made plans and walked around the fenced forest where Henry kept lions, camels and even porcupines. It was twilight when they sat on a rotting log to visit, in a friendly manner, with the gate guard.

After a while, the guard felt comfortable enough to admire Thomas's wool pallium and Owain's waterproof hunting boots. He said he would give anything to have such finery; the boots for himself and the pallium, a cape, for his wife.

"This is your lucky time. They are yours," said Owain, pulling off his boots.

Thomas held the pallium close to his breast and told the guard it was made of the finest lambskins and warmest wool in the world. Then he asked the guard what he would, in troth, give for the gifts.

"Like I said, anything I can. Ye want one of the king's falcons? I can put the bird in a single-handled box. 'Twill look like ye carry naught more than bed-gowns."

" 'Tis said that if the Welsh hostage dies," said Owain, "you will bury him behind the hunting lodge. Give him to us before he dies."

The guard's eyes widened. He said that Henry had sent orders for him to place the hostage in front of the practice target at sunrise so that Henry could test the flight of his arrows against a pagan target.

Thomas pointed to the boots and pallium lying on the ground near a clump of flowers and said, "Your new finery appears to be a gift the wee folk left among the gillyflowers. Forget you ever saw us and we shall disappear among oak and maple as if evanescent. God's blessings."

The guard studied the shadows made by the setting sun for a long moment and then left carrying his gifts under his arm. When he returned, twilight was fading, and his arm was around Rhys.

"The prisoner is clever," the guard said in a whisper. "He escaped from the donjon and through the gate like vapor in night air. I felt a chill, but heard naught and saw naught." He winked, pushed Rhys through the gate. Then he grabbed Owain's bratt. "Henry has word," he said, "that the north Wales summer castle is surrounded with rams' heads sitting atop posts. 'Tis odd, but he believes 'tis something to do with warring."

"Nay," said Owain hastily. "A ram's spirit resides in its skull. Whenever it smells the blood of an Englishman its skull rattles, thus warning the Welsh."

The guard turned white as a bed cloth and ran back to the gate.

Owain and Thomas took Rhys deep into the woods before permitting him to say a word. By then he was so overwhelmed with gratitude that he grabbed Owain by the arm and said that he would combine his armies with Owain's to fight the English whenever it was necessary. Thomas shaved Rhys's beard and mustache using a blade, slippery elm and holy water from a small flask hidden in the pocket of his cloak. Owain swapped trousers and tunics with Rhys so that he would not be easily recognized as he traveled to Wales as one of Owain's cart drivers. Rhys kept saying he owed them his life and that meant he owed them any favors they asked. Owain could think of nothing except that he had paid him *Recompense* for the lives of his sister's twin lads. He wanted nothing more than to go back to his summer castle.

Before leaving, Owain said, "Henry is sore as a boil with us for upsetting his Woodstock Meeting, and you can bet he will foam worse than his English beer when he finds Rhys escaped. Henry cannot be trusted."

Thomas took Owain's hand, looked him in the eye for a few moments. "Henry has not b-been a friend to you nor to me for quite a while." His eyes danced. "I say what is got b-badly, goes b-badly and a p-plague upon him! When that tyrant discovers his hostage is gone, he will explode like a hot wine b-bottle! We should leave him a couple boars' heads to protect his gate."

"Rams are far easier to catch," said Owain. "Henry would not know the difference!" He could not explain why, but unexpectedly Dafydd took over his thoughts even though his mind had been clear of him for three days.

Thomas said he looked like he had seen a ghost.

"The ghosts of rams rattling their skulls," Owain said.

Suddenly they both doubled over in a fit of laughter that felt good because by the morrow they both faced home tasks. Owain would face Dafydd, squarely.

Rhys was perturbed by their laughing. "Gentlemen, I beg
you save your hilarity until I be across the border in Powys
and out of sight of England," he said.

Brenda looked at Owain and said, "Who sent a messenger to
England to tell Henry about the rams' heads?"

"Use your intuition," said Owain. "And tell me about it."

Brenda needed only a moment before answering her own
question.

X
Royal Caravan

> We feel their [the druids'] presence constantly, for all
> over Wales they have their monuments: crumbled stone
> villages and turf-covered hill-forts, queer circles of boul-
> ders on isolated moors, astronomically aligned perhaps,
> or ritually conceived.
>
> Jan Morris, *The Matter of Wales*

At daybreak Owain assembled his noblemen to tell them he
would call on all of his lords throughout Gwynedd and forbid
them to collect levies for the benefit of bloody King Henry.

Next he went to Christiannt's cottage to say he was taking
Master Rhodri south to Barmouth, where there was a small
camp of druids who would foster him.

Christiannt begged him to let the boy stay at the castle for
another year at least. Owain ignored her, put Rhodri's bundle
of belongings under his arm and took him by the hand to the
stable. The groom put Rhodri in front of Owain on the saddled
horse, smiled as Owain sang and put his arm around the laughing boy. They were gone in a swirl of dust.

Christiannt went straightaway to Brenda's cottage. "Damn
that pigheaded Owain! He took Rhodri away before I could
give my baby a hug and tell him to be a good boy. If I were
one of those oiled, bare-breasted, muscle-bound female soldiers I hear Owain has added to his dragons, I would wear a
tiny battle apron around my waist, strap a metal shield to my
arm, and run my sword through Owain again and again!" She
jabbed here and there with her woman's meat-knife. Her
breath came in huffs that grew louder the closer she came to
Brenda.

"Are you barmy?" Brenda forced a smile, pointed to the willow chair and moved closer to the doorway.

"Ever since you started studying with Llieu, you think you are better than I," said Christiannt. "So mayhap it was you who told Owain to take Rhodri away. What bloody else are you plotting? Someone has to stop you!" Her blue eyes rolled upward, staring. She closed the door and stood stiff as a statue. Flashes of bright light pulsed behind her eyeballs, making a pounding sound like the surf against black rocks.

"Whatever you say," said Brenda, "is all right by me. Put the knife away." She slowly reopened the door and realized she had left her woman's knife and scissors in the laundry room. "Put your knife down. You want to talk about Owain's pigheadedness?"

Christiannt closed her eyes and the flashes became hot liquid that had to be poured out. She opened her mouth to release them, let out a piercing scream and lunged for Brenda's throat with her meat-knife. She missed, stumbled and leaned, puffing, against the doorjamb.

Brenda looked about frantically for someone to help, but there was no one.

Christiannt straightened and glared. "Do not move nor yell, or I will really run you through." She waved the knife near Brenda's midsection, then opened her mouth and felt the colored lights dribble down her chin as her words poured out. "Why is Owain not collecting levies to send to England for the armies? He has to do that! Henry is going to take over Gwynedd and Owain's soldiers will be in the English army. We are close to being English." Her eyes rolled wildly, like beads in a bottle. "Owain must collect taxes for King Henry. Why cannot Owain see that?" She pressed the cold knife blade against Brenda's throat.

Brenda could smell her own fear in the pungent odor of perspiration. "Owain sees it," she whispered, "but he is Welsh and stubborn. He will never give in to someone as cheeky as Henry. How can you favor being New Religion and English?"

"I should let my knife slice your throat and your blood spill," Christiannt growled. "We destroy pagans." Her eyes were sightless. She did not see Brenda held in a corner by her knife. She did not feel the smooth bone handle of the knife. She heard only a rushing, like wind, in her head.

Brenda took a deep breath. "Christiannt, the oldest of Welsh legends predicts that the *Angle-Ish* will attempt to swallow *Y Cymry*, the Welsh, and will gag in the process," she said.

Christiannt was startled when she realized Brenda was talking to her. At first she saw only a pale, indistinct shadow. She held the knife tight under Brenda's chin. She blinked as the blood pounded at her temples and behind her eyes. When her sight was near restored, she watched Brenda like a hawk watching a small rabbit.

Brenda spoke louder. She prayed that Christiannt was listening, not playing deaf. "Would you step on the fairies, the wee people? Of course not. You would scratch the eyes out of anyone who did. You would be like a lioness protecting her cubs. The Welsh have vowed on their honor to protect the wee people forever, just as a mother protects her young. I saw you protecting Rhodri from Dafydd's pranks. You were a loving mother." Brenda's eyes did not stray from Christiannt's hawkish gaze. She wanted to take the knife. She did not want to die. She had so much she wanted to do. She longed to hold her children against her breast and tell them she thought of them every day. She wanted to see Sein. She wanted to be a healer, to do some lasting good in the world before leaving it. She hummed in a low tone, " 'Twas you who protected your handsome laddies. You are a good mother."

Christiannt's face was so close to Brenda's that she stared at the parted red lips and saw a tongue moving in the dark cave behind white teeth. She saw a flash of bright metal below the moving lips, blinked again and heard a clatter. The noise startled her. She rubbed her hands together, looked down, and saw the meat-knife on the floor.

Brenda stopped humming, put her arms around Christiannt and held her close.

Christiannt patted her and said in a small voice, "Aye, I be a good mother. All my sons have given proof to that. Owain once said I would be known far and wide for the kind of treatment I gave my sons." She rubbed her temples, smoothed her tunic. "I be terribly thirsty. Come, be friendly and pour the mead."

Brenda poured two beakers of sweet mead from a clay jar. Her hands shook. She waited for Christiannt to empty her beaker, then offered her a second.

The fermented honey spread its warmth through Christiannt's midsection, then to her arms and legs like the summer sun warms the blood of a lizard dozing on a rock. Slowly she remembered why she had come to Brenda. "Owain did not ask me if I wanted Rhodri fostered this year or next, nor where. The not-asking fermented inside my skull and made my head ache. I had my heart set on Rhodri going to Bardsey Abbey."

"You wanted Rhodri to be fostered by his brother Cadwallon?"

"Aye, Cadwallon has taken the Augustinian vows. He is a real monk and Bardsey is a place to brag about. 'Tis a holy place where *Myrddin*, Merlin, the seer, is buried alongside twenty thousand saints. I know the island is surrounded by racing tides and furious western storms but 'tis so well known. Who has heard of the pagans at Barmouth by the Bay? I prefer my baby to be fostered in a famous abbey. Pagans know too much, think too much and believe God, who is already omnipotent, needs lesser gods to help Him care for all mankind's problems."

"I suspect Owain left the Barmouth druids a large handful of coins," said Brenda. "Your laddie will be well cared for. 'Tis far easier for you to visit Barmouth than the Isle of Twenty-Thousand Saints."

"Well, I admit 'tis better than taking the laddie to my second son, Maelgwyn, who has his own army and wars against his half-brothers. Did you know that I put Maelgwyn out of my mind long ago, and just in the last few weeks have thought of him over and over? Do you think he is all right?"

"If something happened to him, Owain would tell you," said Brenda, sinking down onto her pallet. She felt exhausted and her eyes burned as if she had faced the wind all day.

"When Rhodri is older, he can be a soldier; maybe a chariot driver hurling javelins, with plenty of courage."

Brenda kept her eyes on the knife on the floor. "No one knows what the future brings. We try to have our heart's desire, but things happen that we forget were unresolved, and they affect our future."

"Brenda, I swear you talk like a druid ever since you started studying with them. Listen, did I tell you bards shall sing my praises for bringing forth such beautiful, brave sons?" She kissed Brenda's cheek, giggled, went to the door and whispered, "I be still angry with wart-faced Owain. He better bring me a gift from Barmouth to chase my lonely megrims; mayhap a silver hair clip. If not, Owain will be surprised when I ask him for another babe to fill my empty arms!"

On the twenty-ninth day of September, which the New Religionists celebrated as Michaelmas, Owain was home and asked Llywarch to sing a song about young Rhodri after sup. Owain let everyone know the lad was well and properly fostered. Next Llywarch surprised everyone by singing praises for Dafydd, who, Brenda had learned from Archdruid Llieu, was soldiering in the army of his half-brother, Lord Howell.

The hall was quiet as a tern on a warm summer evening as the people listened to every word:

Master Dafydd hied himself
To a suitable occupation.
He is a sling-shooter,
A regular risk-taker
And the best of Howell's dragons.

When Llywarch ended there were smiles of satisfaction. Only Gladys gave a fluttery cry. Then she looked up at her husband for confirmation.

Owain patted her milk-white hand and stood. "Dafydd is with Howell stalking Danes around the seacoast," he said.

Christiannt shouted, "Praise God for the dear lad!" and let tears slide unchecked down her cheeks; the next moment she was bent over with laughter.

Brenda looked beyond Gladys and said, "Christiannt, if you long for fresh air I will accompany you."

"Nay, if I want company I will look for the most handsome man in the hall." She straightened up and gave Owain a wink. "I be so happy Dafydd is safe. I could fly like a gull."

The great hall drew in a collective breath when Gladys stood, nervous as a tree sparrow, and in a tremulous voice announced that she praised God in Heaven for taking care of her son Dafydd. She looked up at her husband, whose face was expressionless, and said that she truly loved the magnificent new court at Dolwyddelan and gave thanks to Owain. " 'Tis a place filled with good luck. And now, while my last-born's star is in the ascendant, I wish to leave Dolwyddelan before the earnest snow covers the ground and freezes my bones. Remember the wild roses I had planted by the castle gate? Without looking I can see their pink summer petals and their red winter berries."

At first there was silence and kind smiles, then polite murmurings about the beauty of wild roses. Someone shouted, "Thank you, Prince Owain, for Dolwyddelan!" and the hall broke into a thunderous ovation.

Owain nodded, waved both hands, and was pleased that Gladys, close to sliding to the Otherside, had enough strength to stand up and give her thanks before the whole court. He flashed her a wide smile.

She gazed around the long supper table and twisted a ribbon on the yoke of her dress. "On the way to the warm Aberffraw coast, the prince and I shall visit our first son, Lord Iorwerth, at Degannwy. I long to ask why Iorwerth's wife is not yet carrying a son."

People nodded, their eyes brightened and corners of their mouths turned up. They understood a woman wanting grandchildren to fuss over and give back to the parents without a thought of recrimination. The role of a grandmother was to be indulgent.

Owain asked Brenda to take his wife to her chamber and ready her for bed.

Gladys was still full of talk, even when Brenda bathed her. She said she wanted to examine the stitching of the wall tapestries that King Louis of France had sent to Iorwerth when he married. For the dozenth time she told about the fine stitching she put into a linen bed-quilt she had sent to Louis as a comforting gift after his first wife, Lady Eleanor, left him for his arch enemy, King Henry. "Despite Louis's feelings, I like Henry and Eleanor. I shall send them a wedding gift. What is appropriate?"

Brenda said, "Mayhap blown-glass goblets."

Gladys nodded, changed the subject, and talked about the Samhain census. If the Aberffraw count ended with an odd number, it meant that someone would die to keep the count even.

"Who shall die?" asked Gladys.

Owain rode his gray stallion at the head of the royal caravan as it left Dolwydellan for Degannwy. Before him the royal flag-bearer carried the house-arms banner, three golden lions sewn onto a red field flapping in the breeze. Jingling bells were tied to the colored ribbons plaited in the horses' manes and tails. A dozen thanes rode with the caravan's red, blue and green horse-drawn carts for protection against marauding English soldiers or land-hungry Danes. Yellow silk streamers fluttered from the green canopy of the first cart, which carried Lady Gladys and her handmaidens. Gladys's eyes moved back and forth like those of a cornered frightened animal. She said that she knew that all her handmaidens were devirginated, and that the census would end in an uneven number. "Father Giff told me that if there was an eclipse of the sun, before Samhain the most influential man in Gwynedd shall die, but if there was an eclipse of the moon, the life of someone close to him shall be snuffed out like a candle light."

As Gladys's fainting sickness became worse, she found a hidden meaning in nearly every mundane thing. She believed that priests were able to control star movement, read eclipses and spread spells to block a death that was about to take place.

The caravan stopped at noon and Brenda's young dark-haired maid, Mona, boiled water over a peat fire for tea. Gladys fidgeted with her beaker and finally said, "Who do you think is the most influential royal person in Gwynedd?"

"I think 'tis Prince Owain," said Mona.

" 'Tis King Henry," said Gladys. "Next is his wife,

Eleanor." She giggled nervously and said, "Mona, honey, ask Llywarch to do his wizardry. If the Samhain count is uneven, Owain must not look at the full moon, to block the Samhain death. You know, I could not bear to have Owain go to the Otherside. I feel in my bones that 'twill be a *geis*, a prohibited thing, if a member of the royal family looks at the moon on Samhain this year. I pray Llywarch might use some pagan magic to hide the moon so that death cannot see us."

Brenda held out her beaker for more tea. "Do not be silly," she said. "Llywarch is not a priest and certainly no wizard. But I myself will speak with him. No one is going to die— not yet awhile."

"Brenda, go speak to Llywarch at once," ordered Gladys, "or I shall tell him that you often follow him into the oak forest and listen as he recites poetry to the wild boars. I shall say 'tis you who call him *Pryddyd y Moch*, Poet of the Pigs!"

The other handmaidens giggled. Brenda's face turned red as the sunset. She did not want to bother Llywarch with foolishness. Stinging from embarrassment, she went to look for him.

He said that the whole thing was a superstitious weakness that sometimes showed up in women. "I promise to talk to Lady Gladys, if you will promise that the superstition-weakness does not overtake you, my dear."

Brenda smiled her thanks and forgot about Gladys's wish to block an upcoming death.

Owain and the men slept wrapped in woolen blankets, on open ground or under the carts. The women slept in multi-colored linen tents with banners and streamers on their door-flaps.

Degannwy court stood on a palisaded hill. The great hall and single tower were built with oak trusses. The stairways and outside walls were made from rough oak planks.

First thing, Gladys, like an uncertain child, took Brenda's hand and told her she wanted to go into the lord and lady's chamber. There, bold as a bumblebee, she turned over the heavy French tapestry and examined its fine weave and stitching. She found nothing to complain about and was quiet for several moments. Then she said that the dyes were so vivid the colors hurt her eyes. Brenda took her to the guest chamber and suggested that she look at the fine stitching on the white pallet cover as she rested.

Owain spoke to his eldest son, Iorwerth, about the land-seeking Danes who sailed from Holyhead along the southwest coast to Caernarfon.

"If Marared and I have our own son, I would like him to live in a court like Dolwydellan," said Iorwerth. "From what you have said, 'tis perfect in the fastness of the mountains."

" 'Tis done," said Owain. *"Drwyndwn,* Crooked Nose, I promise to deed my new court to your firstborn son." Owain's eyes twinkled because he had used the name Iorwerth acquired when he was born.

Iorwerth asked his father if he had made up his mind who would be the next prince of Gwynedd. "I hear that Maelgwyn and Dafydd are vying for your position."

Owain put his arm around his son's shoulder and was quick with his answer. "Of all the sons I have, there be no other but you who is fit to take my place. I damn the *Welsh Law of Defects* that states a person with a physical defect cannot hold any title higher than lord, and wish with all my heart you could be called prince of Gwynedd, or mayhap high lord of all Gwynedd. But I must choose another and I choose Howell, but I have not yet told him."

"The last I heard of Howell, he was still with the poet and harper Cathbad," said Iorwerth with a chuckle.

Owain told him Howell had been fostered with Cathbad for nine years; after that he joined the Gwynedd army as a runner. "No one on Anglesey was his equal in tourneys, jousts and feats of arms. But when he did not advance to messenger, his temper flared and he left, with some of my soldiers, to form his own dragon army. Listen, when my death comes, the moment when the raven casts its shadow over me, Howell is to take my place as prince of Gwynedd. Do not let anyone do differently."

*　　*　　*

During supper, dark-haired, blue-eyed Marared whispered to Brenda that Lady Gladys looked poorly. "When the time comes, I hope Owain will not take a second wife in haste. In truth, I hope Owain marries you." She touched Brenda's cheek. "We are friends. You are more level-headed than—" She nodded toward Christiannt.

Brenda no longer harbored the girlish desire to become Owain's wife. Owain would marry his cousin Christiannt. Sein had said that long ago. "Owain is my friend, and I be his, but he will not marry me." She savored the sweet taste of mead.

"You and I will see each other again," said Marared. "Right now tell me the best herbs for croup. I have a new fosterling who is croupy whenever the weather changes."

"Put half a handful of bruised anise seeds in a pitcher with two beakers of boiling water, steep, cool, strain and make it tasteful with honey," said Brenda. "Hold the child on your lap and give him a teaspoon four times a day. Keep his room moist with a pot of boiling water day and night. He will breathe easier."

The caravan headed along the shoreline of Conwy Bay toward the Menai Strait. Owain wore a red cloak but no cap nor crown. He thought of ways to keep the English from taking over Gwynedd and destroying all of Wales in one great bloody battle. Power-hungry Henry was enough to drive a man over the edge of the Earth, he thought. The village of Aberffraw seemed defenseless without the fastness of the mountains that gave Dolwyddelan security.

Lady Gladys's cart, with yellow streamers, traveled behind Owain. Lady Gladys sat between neat-waisted Brenda and plump Christiannt. Younger maidservants sat behind them.

Brenda said little the morning the caravan ferried across the strait at Caernarfon. She watched the frothing white breakers wash high on the beach, leaving curving lines of foam on the sand. The gulls walked through the shrinking bubbles and followed the waves back to the water's edge. The sea met the sky in a line so misty she could not tell where one began and the other ended. She wondered if there was another land that existed past the Irish mist. If I were a man, she thought, I would sail through the mist and see what was there. She felt a restlessness, a yearning that she could not name.

Later Christiannt leaned out of the cart to see Owain better, said she would like to give his hair a wash and rinse with chamomile tea to make it soft and shiny. She winked at Gladys, leaned against the cushions and said, "Owain looks worried. Is he concerned that one day his warring sons will claim this island? He need not. Dafydd awaits the opportunity to be king."

Gladys nodded and said, "Aye, if my laddie does not become king of Gwynedd, I shall tell Owain that you grow teeth in your vagina and 'twould be dangerous to couple with you."

Christiannt's face turned red, but she laughed.

Brenda grimaced at the crude way Gladys had begun to talk and told her to hush.

A ripple of laughter came from Mona and her friend Annesta, who brushed Christiannt's curls.

Christiannt braced her feet against the floor of the swaying cart. After a while she looked at Gladys again. She found her asleep, leaned over and whispered to Brenda, "Owain received a parchment, written by Cadwallon, right after Beltaine. The lad makes finer letters than Owain, and he is only nineteen. I close my eyes and imagine him with a quill spewing out ink on parchment like a squid skidding ink across the bottom of the sea. It depresses me that Cadwallon knows nothing of his mam beyond his fifth year. The Black Canons, bloody Augustinians, told him Prince Owain was his father, but they said naught about me."

"I guess that is how 'tis with monks," said Brenda. "Being celibate, they do not think of women."

"You do not know how 'tis with monks!" said Christiannt. "If they do not recognize the mother exists, if she is not the *wife* of the father, how do they think the boy came to be? I have a notion to tell them right out that I had my field ploughed early. They know about plowing." She clicked her tongue and asked Brenda if she had heard from her son in Ireland.

The question startled Brenda, then she realized that Christiannt was asking about her firstborn, Riryd, and admitted she had not heard a word since he became lord of Clochran. She hoped Owain would permit her a trip to Ireland to see him and her fair-haired daughter, Goeral. "I really want to go before Goeral is old enough for a husband."

Christiannt asked if Riryd was a black Irish retainer who planned to come to Wales, use his sword and take his father's place.

Gladys opened her eyes, pushed her mouth into a thin line and said, "Forsooth, the only difference between the devil and Owain's Irish sons is that their tails are in front." Then she closed her eyes and continued her nap.

Brenda assured Christiannt that no one had to worry about Riryd taking his father's place or his land. He was not a warrior and had no ambition to rule Gwynedd. Then she reminded Christiannt that there was a rumor that even little Rhodri, who was barely six, was boldly plotting to usurp his father's lands.

Christiannt smiled at the silliness of that gossip. "A bostoon like your Riryd, fostered in Ireland, lacks know-how to start a war, but it would be meet, fitting, for Riryd to come to Wales to kiss his father's feet," she said. "On the other hand, I believe that Dafydd is ready to take over the kingdom of Gwynedd the minute his father dies. I know that Dafydd would serve better than Rhodri, who is still a child, or my firstborn, Maelgwyn, whom I have not seen since he was seven and wore a crown of laurel to show he was of royal blood. I hear he has an army of dragons who take land away from Old Religionists."

"What a pity," said Brenda. "A mother needs to know more than that about her children." She bit her lip, thinking how little she really knew of her own. "Have you heard the rumors that Owain grooms Pyfog's son, the war leader and jouster-poet Howell, to oversee Gwynedd?"

"I heard Howell made a name for himself by leaping a fourteen-foot drainage channel near the big house at *Abernodwydd, Pas Bwyn*. His power is in his legs. What kind of ruler would that be? Pfftt! Dafydd joined the army and by now knows all of Howell's tricks. Like your Riryd, Howell is naught more than a fly in Gwynedd's soup."

Brenda glared and put her hand over her mouth to keep

from sputtering. She saw that the caravan was near the Prydian druids' camp. A raised circle of earth ringed the palisade that enclosed the thatched wattle-and-daub cottages. Through spaces in the palisade she saw the wooden posts with tops carved into heads with faces on both sides guarding both sides of the gate. On several of the posts were white skulls.

Christiannt shook her blond curls, shivered and pointed out that centuries ago druids beheaded lawbreakers, leaving their heads for buzzards to clean and the sun to bleach. It reminded her of Owain's ritual hall with shelves of white enemy skulls, and Dafydd's rams' skulls at Dolwyddelan's castle gate. "Behavior is the same in any age. The difference is the people involved in that behavior."

Brenda said, "Those are boars' heads on the posts and they are thought to hold a protector spirit, same as you believe in protection by the Holy Spirit or a cross. Druids eat the boar meat, same as we." Brenda felt a sudden trepidation for the druids. Her hands quivered like aspen leaves.

Christiannt asked if she was feeling ill. "Verily, you look white as bleached bone and twitchy as a drunken warrior."

"I be a bit drouthy, as if something unexpected is about to happen." She turned and looked at the horizon. "When we arrive at the court I will be ravenous for cold ox tongue and a drink of watered milk."

"I crave watered milk only when I be carrying an unborn babe. On Mary's honor, after all these years, are you—?" Christiannt looked for the swell of Brenda's belly.

"Of course not!" said Brenda.

Thirteen-year-old Annesta, Llywarch's granddaughter and Christiannt's maid, leaned forward and said that Brenda had asked for cotton rags yesterday because her flow had caught her by surprise.

Christiannt turned and looked directly at Annesta. "You would lie for Brenda anytime of day!"

Annesta waved the hairbrush in the air and blushed. "I do not lie. Mona opened a new roll of linen strips to give to Brenda yesterday morning. I saw one of the caravan guards get the roll for her from a pouch strapped to a packhorse."

Mona giggled and said, "Annesta, you wished you had an excuse to flirt with the guard."

Annesta stiffened and said, "I be loath to flirt. I have not found a man to interest me." Suddenly her face and neck turned dark as red coral. She stared at two lads on the road, one fair, the other dark, carrying a willow sling that held a wounded companion. She pointed to the blond and under her breath she gasped, "There is the most handsome lad I have ever seen."

Christiannt leaned out the window, boldy waved at the lads, and two soldiers from the rear galloped up to stop them for Owain's interrogation.

"Look at Fair-Hair's red cheeks. His eyes are like a clear sky. He enjoys the out-of-doors," said Christiannt, who thought herself an expert on men. "Mayhap he is a Dane. He looks no more than fourteen. I could show him a few things."

"See the thin gold circlet on each lad's upper right arm? That tells you they are studying with the druids," said Brenda. "Each knows more sagas and poetry than you or I together."

"Dark-Hair is surely Welsh or Irish," said Christiannt. "And the wounded lad—he is no Dane, see his limed hair? He is a Welsh dragon." She leaned out still farther. "His face is so swollen that the freckles have grown to huge dots. I cannot make out the house-sign on his shield 'cause 'tis under him." She pointed to Fair-Hair and said, "I wonder if he uses a rinse of chamomile to bleach and shine his hair?"

"Listen to what they say," said Brenda, looking intently at Fair-Hair. His eyes never wavered from Owain's face while he said that they gave aid to the wounded man, who had done battle with a band of Northmen. "You, with a caravan carrying women," he said and glanced over his shoulder at the near cart, "are lucky you missed the Northmen."

"Danes are armed and ravage any women in their path," said Dark-Hair.

Owain pointed to Dark-Hair's shoulder wound.

Fair-Hair pointed to the man on the litter. "This *Cymro* tried to kill us with his spear. He knew we were druid fosterlings, unarmed."

"How old are you?" asked Owain.

"Sixteen, almost seventeen," said Dark-Hair.

"If the *Cymro* was wounded and insensible, how could he go after you lads with a spear?" asked Owain.

" 'Twas before the *Cymro* was wounded senseless," said Fair-Hair. "What would you do, sire, if a spear had already wounded your friend's shoulder and now was coming down on your head?"

"Well—I—I—"

"Exactly," he said. "I moved out of the way and the soldier fell on his own spear. He is lucky that my friend is one of the most gifted students of healing arts. If I had been alone, I would have thrown him into the sea. Medicine is not my subject."

Dark-Hair smiled broadly.

Brenda wondered why she had not seen either lad since she had begun to study healing with Archdruid Llieu. They must have been newly fostered during the summer while she was in Dolwydellan.

Owain scowled at Fair-Hair, made certain the wounded man breathed and said, "So the sea is your destiny."

"Aye. A man's destiny is a powerful thing."

Brenda felt herself drawn to the blond lad. She looked closely and for an instant could not breathe. Like Owain, the fair-haired lad emphasized his talk with his hands. She found herself staring at a space between his top front teeth, exactly like Owain's. Then she noticed a scar near his left ear. It was round, like—like a pox-mark. Kinepox! Her heart rose to her throat.

"Please, sire," said Dark-Hair. "You are not interested in my friend's destiny, however the destiny of your countryman is prime. If you live around here you know of the noted physician, Archdruid Llieu, who will be honored to treat a wounded soldier from the House of Gwynedd. Pardon us— we hurry before sensibility is regained and the patient hollers with pain."

"From the House of Gwynedd?" asked Owain with a scowl. "Did you not notice the flag-bearer carrying my banner, three golden lions on a red field? Is the archdruid getting so lax that he is not teaching observation to his fosterlings? I be the prince of Gwynedd." He bent, looked at the wounded man again and shook his head. "I do not recognize him with his poor face as fat and mottled like a green and yellow squash. If he is my soldier, let me carry him in one of my carts."

"Your Highness, forgive me," said Fair-Hair, turning red as a sunburn. "We are in a state of hurry-up to get to the physician. Archdruid Llieu taught us observation, but above all else, he taught us to make every effort to save a life."

"Your Majesty, jiggling in a cart is bad for this dragon," said Dark-Hair. "We did not expect to meet Gwynedd's prince this day, but we thank you, and you can see we do not have far to go."

Fair-Hair reached up to pet the nose of Owain's horse and said, "You might say a prayer. The archdruid will practice his healing art, have your soldier on his feet in a few weeks, and you are welcome to visit him while he recovers." He pointed to the dagger and double-bladed ax hanging on Owain's belt. "Come unarmed. The trappings of war offend druids."

Owain snorted, thinking how brash young men were these days. He said his thanks, snapped his fingers and motioned for the caravan to move on.

Fair-Hair turned to watch the caravan and Brenda could not shake the thought of his uncanny resemblance to Owain. She reasoned that it was only a coincidence that Fair-Hair looked to be near the age of her lastborn, who was surely hidden in Ireland. She continued to gaze back even after the youths disappeared behind their dust. She felt her heart palpitate and held her trembling hands in her lap so Christiannt would not notice.

That evening, halfway through the meal Prince Owain stood and said, "I had forgotten how cold the warm air off the sea could be in Aberffraw. Tomorrow is Samhain Eve and there will be storytelling, acrobats, harpers and pipers if you can stand their noise." His smile made deep creases around his eyes. "We will have apples and hazelnuts with supper, as well as hot mead. There are more poets in Gwynedd than all of Britain, and two or three of our own will recite while you eat. Marriage divinations will be read for those of you not married. Beware of the danger of seeing a coffin instead of the face of your future partner on Samhain's Eve. Death lurks between the boundaries of the living and the dead, the male and female, one man's property and another's, between the present and the future."

Brenda forgot about being tired. Tingles went down her spine. Owain had a magical power in his talking. He looked around the hall and finished by saying, "New Religion priests from the local church will be tomorrow's guests. I myself cannot see much difference between the New and the Old Religion as long as each acknowledges a force that is on a higher plane than man. I cannot see what matters if we call the force Wonderful, Zeus Councilor, Lord God, Odin, Teacher or Cysgod. Lady Gladys and I retire now, for we expect to get up before early to see the sunrise."

As Owain passed Brenda, he held his left hand down by his side so she could see that he had two fingers extended. She drew in her breath. That was their sign. Two together. He had indicated he wanted to see her this night!

XI
Aberffraw

Aberffraw is a grey, somnolent Anglesey village which has little to show of its historic past. Between the 7th and 13thc it was the capital of the Kingdom of Gwynedd. Llywelyn [ap Iorwerth] the Great (1194–1240) held court here . . . but no trace remains of the palace. It was probably of wooden construction. Mountainous sand dunes hide the sea, but at high tide the water rushes down towards the village's historic hump-backed bridge. Accessible at low tide on a rocky islet near by is the church of St. Cwyfan, restored in 1893.

Russell Beach, ed., *AA Touring Guide of Wales*

After Owain and his wife left the great hall, the bards, Gwalchmai and Llywarch, straightened their gray gowns and multicolored sashes and held up their crwths, instruments much like lutes that hung on straps around their necks.

To attract everyone's attention, Gwalchmai looked beyond his aquiline nose, opened his expressive mouth and said, "Remember when Saint Cwyfan's was built? We called it the Church-with-the-White-Porch." He sang about the church that was the first and only one in all of Britain with a porch. Lime and lard held well on its oakwood, to give it a white patina that could be seen from all corners of the village. He announced that Prince Owain would give a silver chalice to the church.

The people stamped, clapped, and the bards' colored sashes bobbed back and forth as they strummed their crwths. Then Llywarth sang of Owain's generosity and his first battle with Lord Hywel of Powys, when he was but a boy foot soldier almost fifty years ago. Gwalchmai sang about the Battle of 1123, when Owain and his brother, Cadwallon, took the Powys cantref, Meirionnydd, from two uncles, both of whom Cadwallon slew a year later.

Brenda could hardly stay seated. She wondered if she ought to go to her cottage, change her dress and comb her hair. She wondered if she was expected go to Owain's chamber, or did he mean he would come to her? Finally, she whispered to Christiannt, who was smiling and batting her eyes toward the bards, "There is too much slaying. Why must harpers sing of it? I wish people could settle differences in a civilized fashion and harpers would sing songs of love."

"Hush," said Christiannt, holding a finger to her lips. "Gwalchmai sings of bravery. If you listen, you will hear there is rapture in a just murder. Killing is necessary to show who has power. The New Religionists do not object to just killing. In no wise do the bards offend me. In troth, the druid foster- lings we met on the road probably had a hand in some bloody battle. Lads enjoy fighting, you know. 'Tis their nature." Her face was flushed; her eyes shone in the lamplight.

"That is what I be talking about," whispered Brenda. "Rel- atives killing relatives, and no one measures heartache. There is pain with each death. Think of those left living. Think of the wives and children, tears and broken hearts. Do not bring in religion, just murder, or innocent druid fosterlings. Just think grief! What can we do to lessen it?"

"Hush!" repeated Christiannt in a whisper. "I do not need to think. I know that one day, after a period of bloodshed that is necessary to teach the Welsh who is in charge of this prov- ince, Dafydd will bring peace to our land, even if he has to stop the breath of all the free-thinking Old Religionists. You wait, the bards will sing the praises of King Dafydd."

"What sort of peace would that be? With Dafydd?"

"Listen, Lady Know-It-All, Howell cannot be leader. Ru- mor says he was the wounded soldier whom the druid lads carried. His tongue was cut so badly that he must learn to talk again. His half-brother, Caded, was found dead and buried by those pagan lads we saw. I bet my best bed-gown that the lads killed Caded and buried him hoping no one found out. Dafydd will be the next leader of Gwynedd. Only the two of us and old Llywarch, who has probably forgotten, know whose true son Dafydd is, and Dafydd will never know." Christiannt smiled and looked smug. " 'Tis our secret."

Brenda bit her tongue, saw Christiannt's hands tremble like harebells in a breeze and hoped this battle talk did not send her off into a fit of brooding. But not for a minute did she believe those druid lads had anything to do with killing or purposely wounding the man who might or might not be Lord Howell.

Gwalchmai sang about Owain and his warring brother, Cadwaladr, who was blinded by the Danes. The army of Cadwaladr burned Norman crops, cottages and castles and was cut to half size with all that warring. The few remaining soldiers of Cadwaladr brought home a cart loaded with gold goblets, stones of ruby, amber, amethyst and pearl.

Owain's army brought home no loaded cart of rewards, but each man brought home something more valuable: his life.

During the Deheubarth battle, Owain's sister Gwenllian, who once had been an English hostage, married a Christian, Owain Cyfeiliog, and the next day she took a bold notion to lead a vengeful attack against the English in Kidwelly.

"That is what I be talking about," said Brenda, unable to keep quiet. "Where is the notion of peace? Cadwaladr slaughters Normans and half his army pays for the battle. Gwenllian, a New Religion–woman, leads an army. 'Tis unthinkable. And next to come will be Dafydd head of this province? Impossible! Owain will never allow it."

"You talk too much!" Christiannt sniffed and turned her face away to listen to the bards' songs.

"Gwynedd," sang Gwalchmai, "reaches as far as the River Clwyd in the east to the borders of Deheubarth in the south, where men are ribald, impulsive and mystic. Women are fresh and pretty as ripe apples."

Brenda looked from one end of the timbered hall to the other. The left side held two chambers, with two rooms apiece, sometimes used by members of the household, such as the servants, but usually by guests of the court. The right side held two chambers, one for Owain and one for his wife. Brenda did not want to go to Owain's chamber. She would have to make herself really bold to walk to that door. She whispered to Christiannt that she was tired, excused herself and went to her own cottage. She thought maybe she had been foolish and read Owain's sign wrong. Perhaps there had been no sign at all.

Mona waited in Brenda's cottage with scented water to bathe her. She had a habit of flipping her short dark hair out of her eyes as she tidied the room. Brenda gave her a small bone comb to hold her hair in place. Mona was delighted and smiled as she dressed Brenda in a brocade tunic over her night-clothes. Her dark eyes lit up when she heard someone tap and scratch the thick hide door-cover.

Owain ducked his head to enter and walked to Brenda's desk in front of the only window.

Mona winked at Owain, touched his arm, and bid him a good night. When she was gone, he folded his bratt over the back of the chair, laid down several sheets of vellum and a thin-lambskin parchment. "I want to establish an ambassador-ship with Louis le Jeune, king of France," he said. "The time is right."

"I cannot see where I be useful in this matter," said Brenda, who was still peeved about the songs of war. "I do not know the king of France. I only have heard stories and most are about warring."

"My dear, your mind is unencumbered by rote learning. I came here because I expect quiet so that I might compose a brief, and I expect your straight answer to solving a simple problem that the bards answer in songs and riddles. I believe you will tell me something I have not thought about, some-thing fresh."

Brenda smiled and felt better. Certainly this was the natural thing to do. Owain had discussed Gwynedd's policies with her before and she had freely told him her thoughts. So why not now?

"If Louis and I set up ambassadorships between Gwynedd and France, we strengthen both of our armies so Henry will think twice about moving his army onto Welsh or French ter-

ritory. My problem is: Who will take my message to Louis?"
He stepped closer to her and took her hand.

"I be pleased you have chosen diplomacy over warfare, my
lord," said Brenda. "Death and destruction bring no man
honor. A man with a gift of words can accomplish more with
less heartache and hard feelings."

Her logic always pleased him, and this night he was spe-
cially delighted to be with an intelligent woman whose beauty
did not fade with age.

"Both willingness for battle and diplomacy are indispen-
sable to keep a land in peace," he said. "Would you give
Gwynedd to the ferocious Danes or England's pip-squeak,
Henry the Second?"

"Nay, never," she said. " 'Tis fine to be prepared, but only
give your people a war after all other settlements are discarded
and exhausted."

"You understand 'tis mandatory that my soldiers are forever
ready to fight," he said. "Otherwise, God forbid, men of ambition will believe I be weak and will not listen to any amount
of oratory or persuasion. They will call all my truths lies. Of
necessity, I must have the best swords to keep peace." Owain
pushed the chair back and left the desk. He stood against the
wall, waved his hands and said, "I study battles of my father,
and those of Rhodri Mawr, and as far back as the Spartans,
who were the finest soldiers the world has seen." He closed
his mouth and held his arms across his chest.

"*Eisteddwch*, sit down," she said. "There is quill and ink
in the cupboard above the desk. I shall be quiet as an oyster
while you write."

He sat down, licked his lips, picked up the quill and put
his hand on a thin sheet of vellum. "Thank you. I think better
here than in my chamber, where I can hear the voices of the
servants as they come and go to see Gladys, who now has
taken to moaning in the middle of the night."

She thought, The weather changes, people fight wars, win,
lose, make up, and Lady Gladys's health rallies and sinks with
the seasons.

As Owain wrote, his shoulders drooped; suddenly he
looked up and said, "I wish old Sack was here. He, too, had

a way of looking though complicated matters. Like you, he concentrated on the heart of a problem."

Years before, Brenda had asked him if monks had taught him to write. He had laughed and said, "My father believed monks narrow-minded and sent me to an Irish druid called *Sach*, Sack, because of the way he wore his gray work tunic."

Brenda smiled. "You told me Sack went to live on the Otherside. He is dead. Owain, concentrate on the problem of sending an agent with a special mission to France. That cannot be so hard. Whom dost thou trust to carry thy message?"

"My dear, the choosing of an emissary is complicated. He must understand what is going on between Henry and myself." Owain laid down the quill and ran a hand across his forehead. "Peace between Gwynedd and England is fragile, which is why I seek to align Gwynedd and other Welsh provinces with some powerful ally. Louis's army is strong and no one better understands King Henry's cruel streak and Queen Eleanor's ruthlessness."

"I remember when Eleanor was married to the French king, Louis, and gave him only daughters," said Brenda. "Louis wanted sons and had the marriage annulled, so Eleanor laughed in her sleeve and quickly married her fourth cousin, nineteen-year-old pimply-faced Henry. He became count of Anjou before he was king of England. Word is that today Henry is careless about his appearance and Eleanor is silly about fashion. They profane English and speak French. Eleanor corrects Henry's syntax, pretending to be fashionable. She is eleven years his senior. For God's sake, does Henry need a mam?"

"Forsooth, my dear, Lady Eleanor laughed in her sleeve because she married Henry out of spite. Not so long ago the two of them dared to ask for a visit to my new Dolwyddelan court, saying they wished to wrangle with me for the fine timber of Gwynedd. I put them off, saying my wife was ill."

"Louis is lucky to be rid of her," said Brenda.

"That is the exact opinion of my friend, Thomas of London," said Owain. " 'Twas Thomas who persuaded the French clergy to annul Louis's fifteen-year marriage to Eleanor on the basis of consanguinity. Thomas told me that Henry had the nerve to send him to Paris to settle the terms of the marriage contract between Henry and Eleanor. At Woodstock, Henry boasted that he had asked Louis's new bride, Constance of Castile, to consent to a marriage between his eldest son, Henry, and Constance's firstborn daughter. He talked as though the whelps already ruled half of Britain. 'Twould be a cradle-marriage, a foul mix, like moldy nine-day-old porridge and sour milk! Henry had the nerve to ask us to do homage to nine-year-old Henry the Third, titular overlord of Britain! God's eyren! Thomas said out loud that it was unseemly to do homage to a beardless cub. Henry swore and threatened to take the milk-toothed scamp away from Thomas's tutelage. Can you guess what Thomas said to that? He said he had fostered the lad for seven years and the lad was a boor with uncouth manners. Henry published orders for Thomas to leave England. I made Thomas welcome to stay in Gwynedd as long as he likes. At my insistence, he went to the village of Bangor, where Saint David's is bishopless.

"Thomas and I are disgusted with Henry, and I suppose that is why we became close friends at Woodstock. He even showed me his signet ring, a ruby with a carving on its face of a man standing against a pillar. Around the silver frame are the words *Sigillum Tome Lund*, seal of Thomas of London. He said he got it from a druid in Bologna and swore me to secrecy, because if his clerics found that his seal originated with druids, they would slice off his head."

"I shan't tell," said Brenda. Her eyes sparkled.

Owain cleared his throat, dipped the quill into the ink and said, "When Thomas traveled with Rhys and me back into Wales, he told us things that he dare not say to his Catholic brethren. For instance, he told us that he had had a dream in which he and I would be murdered a year apart. He said I would go first, poisoned by one I cherish, and he by an ax in the hand of one of four men he trusts."

Brenda made a little gasp. "Oh, no! 'Tis only the idle thought of a man with an active imagination. I do not like Thomas. He cannot know those things."

"But Brenda, you would like him," said Owain. "He has a keen sense of smell and sharp ears, and he can memorize everything. He is a free thinker, reads and writes Latin, speaks German and French besides English and recites poetry more eloquently than Gwalchmai. He would have made a splendid druid if he had become interested in the Old Religion before he heard of the Roman popes. He wears a black stole day and night. The same stole. 'Tis never washed."

"Oh my, I thought he had a keen sense of smell!" Brenda put her elbows on her knees and her chin in her cupped hands. "What about King Louis? Does he like Thomas?"

"Certes. Thomas once suggested that there be ambassador-ships from the major countries to the Vatican." Owain bent over the vellum, scratched a couple of lines with the quill, rubbed his forehead and looked at the words he had written. "My fear is that Louis will think Gwynedd is too small to exchange ambassadors or share armies. There are complica-tions. My proposition to Louis must be diplomatic and secret so as not to incite the wrath of Henry and bring the English army storming into Gwynedd." He waved the dry quill over the vellum several times before he dipped it again. " 'Tis hard to be secret in this court." He let his fingers dance on the desk a few moments, then said, "I want to say that we count on Louis for help in case England attacks Gwynedd or any other Welsh province. French soldiers may be enough to make Henry think twice about a Welsh invasion. On the other hand, if Henry attacks France, the Welsh provinces must supply sol-diers, and even food and ammunition, to help protect her." He pressed his lips together and scratched more lines on the vel-lum.

Brenda was pleased that Owain had discovered the use of communication, instead of war, to get his way. She thought that he, too, secretly hated fighting and violence, but in no manner could he say so. She watched the push and pull of the small muscles in his hand and found herself listening to the beating of her heart. She remembered the feel of his hands pulling firm against the small of her back. He used to pull her so close in an embrace that she felt secure from any catastro-phe. But since coming back from Ireland she had lived rather like a hostage. On purpose, she had not rebelled against being confined to Gwynedd's courts. By not causing trouble, she found it easy to keep secret that her lastborn was alive. She found no fault in Owain's actions toward her. She was honored that he came to her cottage to write his brief to King Louis the Seventh of France.

He put down the quill, sprinkled sand on the parchment. "Now, tell me who might deliver my brief?"

She sat on her pallet and tried to think of someone who had integrity. "You have a trusted retainer?"

"I fear even a trusted retainer might read what I have written and divulge the message before it gets to Louis. I would not hesitate to match arrows with any man who would permit Henry to get wind of this. You know I seek someone who understands politics between Gwynedd, England and France and is trustworthy. I am asking you, because I know you are wise when dealing with people."

Surprising herself, Brenda said, "Druids understand the politics of the day. They are taught to memorize, to think independently, to respect mankind. A druid's word is sacred. Remember the blond, blue-eyed lad you met on the road near the druid camp? He was mannerly, appeared intelligent and willing to work. Maybe it seems a foolish choice, but I believe the lad would welcome the challenge and be an ideal emissary. He would die before betraying your mission to the English. Choose him and there would be no gossip nor jealousy among your retainers."

Owain stood and bent to kiss the top of Brenda's head. "I should have thought of a druid youth myself. You do not have to lecture me on the honor of the Old Religionists. I know better than you what they are taught and the acuity of their memory through unmerciful training. I knew you would have a perfect solution. On the morrow I be going to the druid camp to check firsthand on that wounded soldier's well-being. I have word that he is my son Howell. He wore the crest of the House of Gwynedd on his shield. While at the camp I will ask Llieu about the blond lad." Owain bent over the vellum. "My son Caded is dead—buried by those lads. I will ask much about each of them."

Brenda said, "But those lads had naught to do with Caded's death. I would bet my soul on it. For troth, I took a fancy to the way the blond youth looked because he reminded me of you. His face was like an open scroll. I be certain he is honorable."

Owain looked up. "What is his name?"

"I do not know," said Brenda, pressing her fingertips against her brow as if to remember something. "He reminded me of our dead babe who would be about his age, thirteen, fourteen. The lad had self-confidence and a way with words. Aye, he did remind me of you. The way you were when I first met you. I hoped our babe would be like that." She bent, picked up the fur robe that lay on top of her pallet and laid it across her lap.

Owain tugged at the lacing on his tunic. " 'Tis warm in here."

"I shall open the shutter," she said.

"Nay, pour two beakers of cool mead," he said.

The spicy aroma tingled Brenda's nostrils and she sneezed.

"Ah, see, there is a draft even without opening a shutter." He put the fur robe around her shoulders.

"Truly, I sneezed because of anticipation. You forgot that I enjoy the tingling of mead. Even when 'tis cold, it warms me from the inside out. It makes my arms and legs feel as though I am standing close to a roaring fire," she said.

"I hope it does the same for the fingers of my right hand. They are stiff with writing." Owain flexed his hand several times.

"I know the cure for stiff fingers. Catch some long-legged field spiders and roast them. Rub your fingers with the ashes. That will make your fingers as agile as the spiders' legs." Brenda giggled and put her hands on his. Instantly she felt a prickling along her arms and in her chest. The feeling was pleasing and she did not pull her hands away. "Tomorrow is Samhain," she whispered. "Do you believe in ghosts?"

"Nay," he said, "I have talked with too many druids. I find that ghosts live only in imagination. However, I believe there are certain women who are witches. You may be one. Whatever you do with your fingers on the backs of my hands, hardly touching my skin as they slide up and down, no other woman I know can do that." He sat on the edge of the pallet and pulled her close to him.

He brushed his lips over her sun-tanned chin, not closing his eyes but looking at her long lashes closed against her rounded cheeks. She opened her eyes. He loved their dark color, like the depths of a woodland spring. He did not think of his ill wife, and he felt no guilt as he had years ago when he and Gladys were first married and he dallied with interesting women.

"Aye, I be a Samhain witch come to put a spell on thee," she teased. "I would have you believe that I be the only woman in your life and I be your chief adviser. Thus, the young druid fosterling shall be your emissary to France."

"Ah, my dear Brenda. You have borne two of my children and you still make me feel shy, like a boy."

"Three children, two boys and a girl," she corrected, and her voice trembled.

"One babe died," he said, and he put his hands together so that she could continue her magic rubbing.

Her knees tingled. Suddenly she wanted more than anything to know how he had felt. "Did you mourn his death?" she asked in a whisper.

He saw sparks, like flecks of gold, in her eyes and wondered at them. "I was more grieved about you and your behavior. I was concerned that grief would affect your mind or you would die of sadness. I never suspected you to find more comfort in Eire than in my court. Here anything you want is yours." His voice was husky.

She put her hand against his lips. Her voice was low in her chest. "What if—what if the babe had lived? Would you have destroyed him—our son?" She held her tongue between her teeth and wondered what was causing her boldness now, of all times. These were questions she had kept pushed to the darkest corner of her mind for nearly fifteen years. Suddenly they were not hidden but out in the light, and they needed an answer. She exhaled slowly and waited. Her hands perspired.

Owain pushed her hands away. He watched the candlelight flicker, picking up the reddish highlights in her hair. He made a low guttural sound; almost feral. "Aye, I would have destroyed our child as a farmer puts a stone in a sack of unwanted kittens."

She sat up straight. "Why? You do not really mean that!" She rubbed the fur robe nervously. "Would you not be overjoyed to find that you had a son who was strong, healthy, and mayhap studying Welsh law or healing arts with the druids?"

"You, above all of my women, know the answer. Already I have sons who vie with each other for cantrefs and tuaths. Christiannt's Rhodri and Maelgwyn, Gladys's Dafydd scheme behind my back for the rule of Anglesey. Lugh's lungs! Sweet Anna! If I found out the lad you had a dozen plus three years ago was living today, I would feel betrayed and disown him. If you withheld information from me, I could not trust you again. I would deal with your dishonesty the same as I deal with any man who is a traitor. I would have you and your son hung on Samhain, you as a witch and him as an intruder. Now do you understand me?" A faint mawkish smile formed on his wide mouth. "Why do you plague me for an answer that displeases you? Your babe died; stop asking all these damn questions about what would have happened if he had lived."

Brenda felt as if a knife had stabbed her heart. This night became different from any other. After she and Owain talked quietly, she wanted it to end quickly before it turned into something she could not control.

Owain cleared his throat, lay back and pulled her beside him. He smelled the scent of roses in her hair as he lay against her and stroked her thigh. His large hand was warm. The hollow of his throat lay close by her face. It was tanned like fine leather. His chin whiskers were long and wiry, not silky like the blond curls on his head that reminded her of the root hairs of the parsnip-like plant called likeness-of-a-man. She thought of the time Sein showed her where to find the roots on Dubh Linn's limestone bluffs. He said they were an aphrodisiac and a heart adaptagen: If the heart needed stimulating it would work; if the heart needed calming it would work.

Owain fumbled with her brocade tunic. When it was laid aside he fumbled at the ribbon enclosing the neck of her gown.

She shivered, put her hand over his. "No," she said a little breathless. "You are not obligated. I be your adviser, no longer a mistress."

"You are not like other mistresses. I gave you Mona, a maid of your own, even though you continue to be a handmaid to my wife and wherever you are needed. Thus, 'tis right and proper that you are also my adviser." He pulled the ribbon so the gown fell. Quickly he released the plaiting of her hair so it fell thick and crimped to her waist.

Her nipples rose hard as pebbles the moment the cooler air struck them.

She pushed her nightgown up against her throat and pulled away with all her strength.

He smiled, and the center space between his gleaming upper front teeth was a little upside-down black V. His eyes were heavy-lidded, half closed, making him look like a half-asleep wolf. His powerful hands were warm and pleasant when he cupped her breasts for an instant. "You used to like it," he said. "Have you missed it?"

She glared at him and did not know if the question was rhetorical or something he had thought about for some time. "Uhmm," she said. When she had first come back from Ireland, she was glad he had left her alone. She became busy helping Christiannt care for Lady Gladys and studying medicine, and had no time to dwell on their past intimacies. They were friends and that was sufficient. She was uncomfortable when he reminded her of their long-past joys.

"I have neglected you. And be reminded that you are shy like a lassie. 'Tis part of your charm." He ran his fingers through her hair and let his arm rest lightly around her shoulder.

"I do not intend to charm thee," she said, moving away. "I will advise thee and that is the end of it. We are good friends. Let it remain thus, my lord. I be a grown woman now."

He moved against her, kissed her hard, pushed his tongue over and under hers, so she could feel its roughness and say naught but make a moan in her throat.

She tried to pull away, but he drew her closer. She was rattled and blamed herself for letting things go so far. She had felt the nagging fear earlier and chosen to ignore it. He was the prince, the powerful head of Gwynedd. He could do what he wanted. She was cared for under his roof, in his court. She could not complain against him no matter what he did. She moaned again.

He pushed her away, got up and moved to the window, breathing the cold air that found its way inside through the ill-fitting casement and shutters. "If you were not the kind of woman you are, I would not be so easily aroused," he said, and chuckled to himself. "I told you long ago that I love thee, and 'tis still true. I love thee more than all other women."

Her cheeks were hot and she could still feel the touch of his tongue; her face flushed from the unfamiliar tingling caused by his beard and mustache. She snorted and pointed to the pen and vellum on her desk. "Will you finish the brief this evening?"

Owain nodded, took more deep breaths of the cold air, and claimed he was in the mood for talk before he completed his writing. To prove this, his voice was deep and loud. "There is Pyfog's son, Howell. He is intelligent, cunning, and he has his own thanes. What with speeches and coaxings, he so beguiled me that I trusted him with weapons and advice. He keeps his men hungry for battle by fighting the small bands of marauding Danes. I thanked him for that, but I know he has thoughts of usurping my power when he thinks my back is turned. He has already sent emissaries into the armies of his half-brothers to cause discontent and woo their soldiers to his side. Now I hear he lies wounded in the druid camp." Owain came back to the pallet and put his arm around Brenda's shoulders. "You have to put yourself in my place and understand my feelings. 'Tis no good to have many sons. Better to have daughters to marry the sons of the men I wish to make strong allies. But fate dealt me a different set of game stones. I be cursed with sons." He lay his head on Brenda's shoulder.

She sat perfectly still. "My lord, did you forget I gave you a beautiful daughter who may one day marry the son of an important lord in Ireland? Our son Riryd is not the least interested in squabbling with half-brothers over Gwynedd's land. He is content with what he has in Ireland. If I had another living son, I would foster him with druids to improve his mind, to make him curious about nature. I loathe fighting. 'Tis you who might try to understand me." Her tongue ran over the small swelling where she had bitten her lip.

"Oh, my love, I try. Honest, I do try," he whispered. "But women are a mystery."

Brenda's back stiffened.

He sensed her tenseness and grasped her small hands within his large ones and said, "I have to ask you something."

"What?"

"Dost thou remember a maid called Brigid?"

"I do," she said, puzzled. "She gave me clean clothes when I was brought back to Gwynedd from Eire by your Cymreig soldiers. She was at the Degannwy court."

"Aye. Brigid told me your breasts were not dry, yet your child had died months before. Why?"

"Oh—oh, why?" She pushed her hair out of her face, rubbed her moist hands together, sat on the pallet and held the edge of the robe to keep her hands quiet. She began a made-up story that grew with the telling.

"Owain, I was so filled with grief. You cannot imagine how bleak my world seemed. I—I hired myself out as a wet nurse in Dubh Linn and thereabout. How else was I to save a few coins, have a roof over my head and a crust to eat? I longed to hold an infant. I pretended those babes were mine as a wet nurse is wont to do. To see a weean grow and be healthy because I gave it nourishment gave me a reason to live. Try to understand what went on in my mind."

He sat next to her. "The moment I believe with certes that I know what is going on in a woman's mind, I find I be in the wrong camp. Women to me are an enigma. And you, my lovely witch, are the biggest riddle. You have the analytical mind of a man and the volatile emotions of a woman. 'Tis a most powerful combination."

She folded her hands in her lap and twisted a long strand of her hair.

He caressed her shoulder, slipped the white gown lower and lower until the cleavage between her breasts was a shadowy hollow. That dark hollow sent a glow as warm as mead radiating from the center of his belly. The question of what

Brenda had done for many months in Ireland had been logically answered. He forgot he used to lie awake nights wondering about it.

Brenda sighed with relief and closed her lips. She felt certain that for the time being Owain believed her story and
would not ask again about what she did in Ireland. The next
moment she was enfolded in his embrace. Her face burned
and she closed her eyes so he would not see her chagrin. If
she told him she no longer was attracted to his advances, he
could easily snuff out her life with one deadly blow to her
head with his powerful fist; he could strangle her with his
viselike fingers; he could pluck out her eyes.

"Aye," he said, "take off my boots and let me soak my feet
in a basin of scented water while you run your fingers from
my ankles to my thighs. There is a glowing ember in the pit
of my belly that can be brought into a flame that will make
my sigh hotter than sun in a cloudless sky." He removed his
tunic and shirt.

Her eyes flew open and she noticed that high on his left
arm were tattooed an eagle and a boar, tattoos she had not
seen before. The eagle showed that he had stayed above a
battle, negotiated his way to a peaceful settlement. The boar
signified great hunting skills. "My lord, for some time I have
been troubled." Her voice was low and trembly. " 'Tis about
the recent killings and those druid youths hurrying to take the
Gwynedd soldier who may be your son Howell to Llieu for
healing. Who were the soldiers warring? Were they Danes or
their own kind? Gwyneddmen against Gwyneddmen? How
can Welshmen hold life so cheaply, when 'tis the dearest thing
we have?"

"Sshh! The trouble is too much talk." He sounded like
Christiannt.

Brenda felt ill. There was naught for her to do but to finish
what was started this night.

Slowly she pulled off Owain's boots and put his sweaty
feet in a basin of cold water. The sudden coldness made him
pull up his feet. His mouth became a round circle and he drew
in his breath. She pushed his feet back into the water and held
them there for several seconds. He shivered and said, "What

are you doing? Is this the cold-water cure? Are you seeing someone else? One of my soldiers?"

"No, my lord. I be not interested in your soldiers." She patted his feet dry on a linen towel from the cupboard and remembered that Christiannt was interested in his soldiers. She knelt in front of him and gently rubbed warmth into his feet and ankles. "Why do you ask ridiculous questions?" She could not look into his face because she was wondering what Sein would think if he knew what she was doing. Would he care? Mayhap he was married and never thought of her. Why should she think of him?

" 'Tis you who began this ridiculous questioning. Women are wont to change attitudes and ask strange things when they have no interest in lovemaking."

"My lord, 'tis your imagination and the effect of the coming Samhain. Unseen things are in the air that affect us all." Brenda moved her hands deftly over his instep and around his ankles, trying to think of some way to distract him from the fire in his midsection. "Do you think the king of France will read your letter in a favorable light? I have an idea. I could read it and tell you what I think. I will pretend to be Louis le Jeune."

He stood, removed his trousers and undergarments and said, "I would never, not even in pretense, lie naked on a couch with the king of France. Brenda, heart of my body, my sweet soul, I want you, I need you. You have built an enormous fire at the top of my legs. I cannot hold the conflagration. Your skin feels more wonderful than I can say. Let me put my hand under your nightgown. *Plis.*" He motioned for her to join him on the pallet.

She was still kneeling and pretending she did not see him naked or understand his words or his hand signal. Her inner conflict was so overwhelming that she began to massage his feet furiously. She was hurt by the anger that he could hold against her and their lastborn baby. She was torn apart by her desire to see Madoc and her own infidelity of not ever being able to say that he was alive and living with druids in Ireland. She was forever grateful that Sein was fostering Madoc. Sein would never, in her worst dreams, embarrass or degrade her the way Owain could do. At the same time she knew, in her heart, that Owain still cared for her. He said she was his best friend and he loved her. She continued to massage his feet.

"I said my desire is fierce," said Owain. He pulled his feet away from her rough handling so she would look at his fully raised manhood. "When our fire is gone, when our wild embrace and delicious coupling is over and we have rested, you can sit in the chair at the desk, read my brief and pretend to be king of France."

Brenda looked into the face of the man she had once loved. If she wanted to live, it was best to let him press his body against hers.

He reached down, grabbed the hem of her nightgown, slowly pulled it away and pushed it onto the floor. He watched the candlelight play over her small breasts. The areolae were wide and pink-bronze. Under his hands the nipples again became hard as beach pebbles. He traced the line of her jaw and let his lips gently caress her turgid nipples.

She licked her lips and ran her hands through his hair and down his shoulders. The fur robe was soft and warm to her bare skin.

He slid downward and kissed the insides of her thighs. At first she felt nothing, but the fire in her belly grew. 'Tis a small thing, she told herself. I can endure by thinking of something else. Owain will never know my thoughts.

The delicate scratchiness of his beard caused her to gasp and arch her back in fierce physical desire in spite of herself.

She closed her eyes and imagined Sein's magnificent body full naked on top of her, even though she had never seen him naked. His tattooed hands were entwined in her long hair and they moved sensuously, slowly downward to cup her behind. Her hands slid through Sein's red hair and down his shoulders to his narrow waist. His knee spread her legs and she brought them full apart to encircle his buttocks tightly as his manpart slipped deep inside her. She moved in perfect rhythm with his motions until together they let out a rapturous, deep guttural involuntary moan.

After a while Owain slid to her side and cradled her in his arms. They slept.

Before dawn Brenda awoke and lay on the far side of the pallet with her eyes wide open, thinking of Sein collecting herbs and hunting game. Near dawn she laid more sticks on the fireplace embers, put a fresh candle in the clay holder on her desk. She bathed with cold water from a clay pitcher, put on a fresh gown and slipped the brocade tunic over her head. She sat at the desk, looked at the half-unrolled brief and started to read Owain's bold handwriting. She heard footsteps outside the cottage.

"Lady Brenda!" the call was anxious. "*Agorwch y drws*, open the door."

Brenda recognized Mona's voice. She unbolted the door and said, "*Dewch i mewn*, come in. Pray, what is it?"

The young maid looked past Brenda to the prince, who was wrapped only with the short fur robe. "'Tis—Lady Gladys! Come quickly." Then her voice dropped so that it was barely audible. "Best to get him up and dressed. His wife has had a bad fainting spell. She wheezes to bring in air and cannot be roused."

XII
Lady Gladys

Little is known of Owain's first wife, Gwladys, daughter
of Llywarch ap Trahaiarn, except that she died in 1162
and is generally accepted as the mother of Iorwerth.
　Richard Deacon, *Madoc and the Discovery of America*

"Gladys, you are breathing. I see your breath on the silver,"
said Brenda. She sat on a pile of rushes close to Lady Gladys's
pallet and held a palm-sized piece of polished silver.

Owain barged into the chamber without knocking. Mona
came behind, holding his bratt. He looked at his wife for several moments and asked how long she would remain unconscious. When Brenda shook her head and said she could not
tell, he said, "Months ago Gladys began seeing Father Giff
instead of Archdruid Llieu. Giff does not know an asshole
from a knothole and I can do no good in a sickroom—in this
room."

Owain frowned and Brenda's face turned red when Mona
giggled about in whose room she thought Owain could do
good. Owain reminded Mona about a maid's place in the
Welsh court.

Mona bowed her head but her brown eyes twinkled.

Brenda whispered to her that if she wanted her supper for
the next month she had better mind her own business.

Owain looked dour, turned to the doorway and said, "I be
going to the druid camp for Llieu."

"You stay with her," said Brenda. "When she awakes she
will want you. I can go for the archdruid."

Owain looked at her with a hard face, which softened as

he realized she was trying to do him a favor. "Nay, you stay, because you know more medicine than I."

"I will go," said Annesta, who had been standing unnoticed in the doorway. "I be fast on horseback." Her auburn braids lay in a halo around her head with a silver clip above each ear. Her brown eyes were large and velvet looking, her long lashes brushed her tanned cheeks and freckles sprinkled her pert nose.

Owain usually said something about Annesta's good looks, but this time he said, "On horseback I be faster than the wind," and he left.

Mona ran after him, holding out his bratt.

Gladys moved, causing the sheets on her pallet to rustle. Brenda and Annesta held their breath. Finally Brenda said, "My lady, are you awake? You had a long faint."

Gladys rubbed her eyes and said she was hungry, but she ate only a dab of porridge and a crumb of bread. She asked for Owain. Brenda told her he had gone to the druid camp to bring a healer. She puckered her mouth and spat on the floor. "I do not want to see that pagan healer, old Llieu. I have known him too long." Her voice changed to a growl. "I want him beheaded because he told me that he did not have a name for my illness, and predicted I would never have my health again. Father Giff says I have polymorbus. He says 'tis caused by foul spirits that swim in my blood and nibble in my stomach like rats. He says the spirits will leave when they possess the rainbow so they can cross to the Otherside on it, or when I leave a large gift of silver to the Church-with-the-White-Porch."

Tired by her long monologue, Gladys closed her eyes and slept until Owain returned with Llieu.

Owain and Llieu spoke in hoarse whispers. Gladys awoke, waved her hands, and cried, "Off with your heads! You pagan cowards will make desirable sacrifices to the Lord God in Heaven! Brenda, bring me a carving knife!"

"Lady Gladys, calm yourself," Brenda said, "You know that human sacrifices are an act of cruelty, whether you are pagan or Christian."

"Father Giff says that when druids die their spirits feed the

Lord God," said Gladys. "God is propitiated by a druid's death; 'tis a sacrificial gift." Her thin lips stretched across her teeth and her sunken eyes shone. "Christian retainers who come here to see me say 'tis so."

Brenda was appalled, but neither Llieu nor Owain paid any attention. Standing where Gladys could not see, Llieu gave Brenda a packet of herbs and told her to make a tea for Gladys.

When the tea was done, Gladys sat up, drank half a beaker, smiled, thanked Brenda and said she had never felt better.

Llieu told her how good she looked with some pink in her cheeks. She smiled again and he sat on her pallet, patted her hands and told her that she must eat only the most appetizing food and stay calm. He rubbed her bony forearms, looked at her eyes and tongue, looked at Owain, shook his head and under his breath said, "Hummmmm." Louder he said, "Your lady's eyes shine like flaxflowers after a rain." Her hands fluttered around her throat and she asked if he was going to bleed her.

"Nay."

"Well then, I feel good enough to go to the Samhain festivities this evening. Will you come with the prince and me as an old friend?"

"I be honored, but we druids have the sacred ritual of the full yellow-faced moon to perform tonight," said Llieu.

"Eclipse?" said Gladys. "Father Giff said—"

"Nay," said Llieu. "A big harvest moon."

Gladys's eyes grew large when he told her about Lord Howell, whose tongue was accidentally cut by his own sword. "That poor dolfirt is hungry as a horse but can hardly swallow. I cannot stay because I have to feed him."

"Is he healing?" asked Owain.

Llieu cleared his throat. "You were in such a foam to get back here that I forgot to tell you or even let you see him. 'Tis a difficult wound to heal. His tongue is swollen too big for his mouth and 'tis painful. No need to fuss and fume; one of my newest fosterlings is coming to tell you all about the accident."

"Please send that fair-haired, blue-eyed lad," said Brenda.

"Child, you are too bold," said Llieu.

"I remember the lad's demeanor; intelligent and self-assured, he was," said Annesta. Her cheeks were deep pink. "Brenda said the same."

Llieu's eyes twinkled. "I be outflanked. So to keep these shameless ladies happy, I shall send the lad who is a copy of a typical Viking shipmaster."

Annesta whispered to Brenda that her grandfather was having a game on the *tawlbwrdd* in the maids' cottage.

Brenda nodded, letting her leave.

Owain said, "I heard through the rumor mill, which moves faster than any water-driven mill, that my son Caded was with Howell, but was left under a dog rose, and now he is missing. When I was a druid fosterling, I was under oath to deliver all men to their platoon if they were left behind after a battle. So where is Caded? Lugh's lungs! Today's fosterlings are not like we used to be."

"Whoever told you about Caded is a blind fool," said Llieu. "The lad's body was buried under the dog rose."

Owain, with a snap in his voice, said, "If you are my friend, you shall tell me how Caded died and who bloody well buried him."

"My friend, where is thine patience? I told you the blond fosterling, whom you have already met, is coming to tell you everything you want to know. Ask what you want. He will tell truthfully what he saw and what he did."

Watching Owain from the corner of his eye, Llieu said, "Perhaps the jugglers and harpers can come to Lady Gladys's chamber this evening."

Owain agreed that he could arrange it.

Gladys's eyes popped open. She shook her finger at both men, cleared her throat and said the dressmaker had made new clothes for her. "I have never missed a Samhain. The future is foreshadowed at midnight by a voice crying the names of those who will die during the rest of the year. So far the voice has been quiet to my ears. This year—who can tell? A full moon tonight." She suddenly remembered that the moon was a portent and cried, "I must keep my eyes closed. 'Tis *geis* to look at a full moon—*puca!*"

Llieu made a wry face, but he did not tell Gladys to stay

abed and not look at the moon. Before leaving for his camp, he told both Owain and Brenda to stay close to her. "She is not as well as she imagines," he said. He motioned for Brenda to come with him outside. "Dear lady, tonight look among the supper crowd carefully. Llywarch shall have my newest blond fosterling as his guest and, if the opportunity is right, he will introduce you to him. Please, do not cry out. Remain calm and know that the lad will be as surprised and pleased as you to renew this unexpected acquaintance."

There were no meat forks or knives at the table this night because it was Samhain Eve, the death of the old year. It was an old Celtic or pagan custom that after a death no one used sharp instruments, lest the ghost of the deceased be wounded. Gladys pushed a piece of mutton around on her wooden plate and licked her fingers. Brenda pulled the meat apart and fed Gladys a few strips as if she were a child.

The meat, spiced with herbs, smelled delicious, but Brenda did not take any. She took a piece of bread and broke off tiny chunks and ate them slowly between sips of mead. She kept looking for Llywarch. Finally she could stand the suspense no longer and bent toward Owain on the other side of Gladys and said, "Have you seen Llywarch?"

"Nay," he said, standing to announce the name of a bagpipe player from Ireland who was ready to perform. Some people clapped, others cried, "Oh nay, nay, none of the Kilkenny cats!" or "Not that racket!"

Next came a fellow with several sleight-of-hand tricks. Everyone clapped and called for more when he was finished.

Then came the royal household bard, Gwalchmai, who recited some new songs about Owain's greatness. "Prince Owain will neither cringe from his enemies, nor will he hoard up wealth from his relatives."

A bard from France recited poems in French. The servants could not tell if he praised or damned Owain.

Llywarch, with his harp under his arm, climbed on top of the long table. Brenda looked for the blond-headed stranger. Gladys rocked back and forth on the bench. Brenda told her to sit still. Gladys whispered that she wanted Brenda to go to the garderobe with her. Christiannt jumped up and went with them.

The garderobe was reached by a narrow stairway. It was lighted by an open window during the day and a candle in a recessed wall-sconce at night. The seat was a slab of wood or stone with a round hole, held onto an outer wall by supporting timbers. On the ground, directly under the garderobe was a cesspit, which was cleaned regularly.

When Gladys was inside the inner-curtain garderobe, Christiannt pulled on Brenda's hand and whispered, "I have to tell you something dismal, but you have to promise to keep your counsel, never breathe a word." Brenda nodded and Christiannt said, "I be with child."

"Why are you unhappy?" asked Brenda. "I thought after Rhodri's fostering you wanted another *baban*."

Christiannt looked to make certain Gladys was still sitting down and no one else was nearby. "I told Sir Lloyd, my lover, that I could pretend the babe is Owain's and all will be well. But he is unhappy."

"Why are you telling me?"

"I want you to know, so you do not harangue me about food, which makes me nauseous, except dry bread. Do you know how to rid a woman of this problem? Druid medicine must have an answer."

"When was the last time you lay with Owain?"

Christiannt looked in to see if Gladys wanted help putting her clothes in order. "Keep your voice down!" she told Brenda. "It has been ages. Owain lost interest in coupling a long time ago. You know me, I never will. I will be coupling when I be shriveled and gray-haired. Coupling calms me. I feel renewed and needed."

Brenda wished Christiannt would take care of her own affairs. "If you are going to say the child is Owain's, for Lugh's legs, lie with him! Give him a good time so that he remembers when you were with him. He would love to have a daughter. Hope and pray you carry a lass."

"Aye, Owain sires mostly lads."

"I be ready," called Gladys, pushing the heavy tapestry curtain aside to show that this garderobe was now unoccupied.

Back in the hall Brenda saw Llywarch, still standing on the table, point the handle of his harp to someone in an oversized hooded tunic. The stranger sat with his elbows on the table and his face nearly hidden by the cowl. Brenda wondered if he kept his face hidden because it was hard to look at, misshapen.

In a high-pitched, birdlike voice Lady Gladys asked about the night's divinations. "How will I know who lives for another year?" It was a ritual she went through every year.

"Dear lady, there are two ways," said Llywarch. "One, throw your quartz crystal in the bonfire. Pray that you find it clear in the morning, meaning you shall live. Two, stand on the freshly limed porch of the church and wait. Eventually you will hear a spirit voice naming who will die during the year." Llywarch followed with his ritual of gasps and put his hand over his heart. "Beware, my lady, you run the risk of hearing my name, the name of your loved ones—and—your own among those doomed." His voice was low and unearthly deep. "The census has been taken. The number of people in Aberffraw, which includes this court, is five hundred and sixty-seven." There were whisperings about the number being uneven. "We are all powerless in the hands of unseen spirits, in the darkness of night, and the gray chill of the new year," said Llywarch. " 'Tis fate."

His performance made Brenda shiver. She felt an uneasy pall move through the hall. She fastened Gladys's bratt. It was traditional that the royal wife lead the women once around the perimeter of the hall and out the open double door. She looked for Christiannt to help and saw her talking to a handsome, dark-eyed court retainer who pounded his open palm with his fist. Christiannt said something in his ear and pointed to Brenda. He stared at Brenda, smiled, nodded and joined a group of soldiers.

Gladys let Brenda take her arm as she walked around the room and led the women outdoors. Owain followed, leading the men.

When Christiannt finally came to help support Lady Gladys, Brenda asked why the retainer had pounded his fist and stared.

"I told Lloyd not to have a convulsion, that you were a healer and knew about herbs," said Christiannt. "I told him you can bring a woman's bloody flux back."

All of a sudden Gladys stopped shuffling one foot ahead of the other, looked at Christiannt and said, "You silly goose, rejoice! Never ask for it when 'tis gone! The flux is the devil's curse on womenkind."

Christiannt laughed and said, "My lady, 'tis easy for you to say."

Brenda moved close to Christiannt and whispered, "Mayhap you miscounted."

"That is what I said. I will wait another full moon. If naught then, Lloyd will come to you with coins to buy the herbs." Christiannt spoke behind her hand. "He does not want Owain to know."

"About your condition?"

"About us, me and him."

There was a sudden hush over the crowd exiting the castle. Each person hoped to catch a glimpse of some specter that he or she might recognize as a deceased friend or relative. This was the evening when the deceased spirits were said to return to earth to see how the living fared. The people stood still as statues and looked at the sky. Thin clouds spread over the face of the full yellow moon.

There was a soft sighing, like the rustling of leaves in a gentle breeze. In hushed voices the people asked each other what the spirits were saying. The yellow moon soon turned to a silver globe. It was so bright the faces close by were easily seen.

Gladys, as breathless as if she had been running uphill, said slowly, "Father Giff sang me a song about the face of a Samhain moon fading from yellow to silver as it glided across the sky. As surely as the cock crows at dawn's first light, 'tis a sign as great as a lunar eclipse that someone shall die. Mark my words! The moon faded from warm yellow to cold, naked silver. Eeii!"

Christiannt bent her head behind Gladys's back, nudged Brenda and whispered, "She is not herself, mayhap there is a devil loose in her head. Lord God, forbid that I become old and doddering." She rolled her eyes toward the moon.

Brenda said, "Hush. I see it."

Outside the bailey on the rocky spit in front of the church, there was a roaring bonfire encircled by townspeople chanting odes to the spirits of their dead kinsmen.

Most everyone carried a white quartz stone to the bonfire. The facets on each were memorized by its owner. The stones were tossed into the fire's dying embers. Next morning they were raked out in a heap of ash. Each person hunted for his or her own stone. The stones that turned black indicated that something dreadful would happen to the owner during the coming winter.

Somebody pushed hard against Brenda as she tried to move closer to the porch. Brenda turned and saw that it was the mysterious visitor, who hid inside his cowl. He pushed the cowl to one side to see better where he was going and said he was awfully sorry. "I was watching this night's full moon, m'lady. 'Tis the earth's shadow that falls on the moon, making it smaller, then the shadow falls away and the moon becomes larger. You have noticed the shadow is always round? Therefore, the earth is round."

Brenda remembered Llieu's warning and drew in her breath. Her heart pounded and she could not take her eyes off the handsome lad and finally blurted out, "Oh my, you are one of the lads the royal caravan met near the druid camp. And you are so observant."

"I be told 'tis a gift my mam gave me." He looked directly at her with clear blue eyes that sparkled like the ocean in sunlight, and his wide mouth turned up into a dazzling smile.

"Your—your mam?" she said.

"A-are you my m—Are you B-Brenda?" he stuttered.

She thought, The lad is as nervous as I, and met his blue eyes with her brown ones. Her dark lashes did not flutter when she reassuringly put her hand on his arm.

"I be Madoc ap Owain," he said softly.

She thought her heart would jump out of her throat.

Christiannt pulled on her arm.

She waved Christiannt away and said, in a voice too loud,

that she would be along in a moment. She could not move. She did not want to move.

Just then, Llywarch squeezed between the two of them, pulled the lad's cowl into place and whispered in Brenda's ear. " 'Tis Madoc, your son."

With trembly fingers, she lifted back the cowl a little, put her hand against his blond hair, and shivers of joy ran down her backbone. Her heart fluttered like a cloud of butterflies.

"A few days ago," he said, "I saw you in the carriage and thought you more beautiful than the others."

"I knew 'twas you," she said, "but would not believe my eyes." She could see his lips quiver and moved her hand to his face and saw there were tears in his eyes.

She grasped one of his hands in hers and, so that only he could hear, said, "You are just as I imagined. Oh, sweet Madoc! My beloved son!"

Lady Gladys called from the edge of the porch for Brenda to come stand beside her.

Llywarch muffled a sigh and, from between his teeth, said, "Brenda, do not speak of what you see. Madoc is only a friend of mine, a visitor. Do you understand?"

Brenda ignored Llywarch, who stood behind her. She could not help herself. "Oh, my son!" She put her arms around Madoc again and pulled him close. "We must meet again. There is so much to say."

"I shall arrange a meeting," promised Llywarch. His head bobbed up and down. "Now, for the sake of old Lugh, go back to Lady Gladys before someone comes after you and sees you crying." He pulled Madoc away and stood with him behind the crowd that was pressed around the white porch. "I be a clumsy old fool," he whispered.

Brenda trembled as she put her arm around Gladys and watched Owain, holding a silver chalice, walk onto the church's porch. He was bare to the waist.

His purple bratt, trimmed with an edging of ermine, was thrown off his shoulders and hung regally down his back. His skin, covered with lampblack mixed in oil, shone like polished jet. Every eye was fastened on him.

Brenda had never seen him display his body in public and

wondered why he would do so now, with his skin blackened, at an ordinary Samhain celebration.

There was a hush on the porch as a black-robed priest accepted the chalice.

Gladys nudged Brenda and said, "See how handsome Father Giff is! A man looks civilized in a black robe, not in black body paint! Och, methinks Owain hides his pagan tattoos, which are not popular with Christians."

Brenda thought Owain looked more dignified and powerful than the pale priest, but said nothing. Her mind was in a whirl. *My son sees his true father in black paint! Lugh, what is the lad thinking? I never thought this day would come, though I prayed it would. Now 'tis here and I do not know what to make of it.*

Owain led the crowd to the bonfire, which was now a bed of hot coals. He threw the first quartz stone among the coals, pulled his bratt over his shoulders and arms and motioned for Brenda to bring Gladys closer to the coals so that she could drop her stone. The crowd threw their stones, and the sound was like a small hail storm. A dog barked and another answered, then they were quiet. When the stones were spent, nothing could be heard except the water lapping against the rocks in the narrow bay and the wind gusting. Brenda thought of Sein and forgot to throw her stone. She wondered if he knew Madoc was in Aberffraw. She wanted to ask Madoc about Sein. Her hands fluttered like aspen leaves in the wind. She felt cold and hot at the same time. Her feet rocked to and fro like half-parched peas on a hot stone.

Then without warning, the wind changed directions and whined around the corner of the church. Gladys looked up in time to see the silver moon slide away from a patch of thin, gauzy clouds. Brenda felt Gladys's body grow taut as she raised her head and gave an ear-piercing cry, followed by a high-pitched cry. "I saw the naked moon! The census is uneven! The breath of sorrow speaks my name! My name! If my name is rubbed out, the census is again even. It must be so for balance!"

The crowd gasped and rustled. Brenda drew Gladys close and tried to hush her. " 'Tis all right. Only the wind groans, my lady." She looked for Christiannt but could not find her. Panic rose up her backbone. She had forgotten to throw her stone and wondered if that would make the count even.

The crowd parted as Owain moved around the bed of coals and laid his bearded cheek against his wife's soft white one. He whispered to her in a fierce voice, "Be strong, my beloved." He lifted her in his arms and carried her to the court gate. Brenda followed, finding it hard to shake off the terror in Lady Gladys's voice.

"Do you believe Lady Gladys heard her name on the wind?" asked Annesta, catching up to Brenda.

"I think she heard something," said Brenda.

"But she is ill and does not think straight," said Annesta. "I heard naught but the wind and the dogs bark." She tugged on Brenda's bratt and said, "You saw him, Grandfather's friend, the yellow-haired lad who stood on the road opposite the druid camp. Is he the handsomest lad you have ever seen? I think he looks like Owain. Christiannt said he is probably one of Owain's many forgotten spawn, not much account, the way he huddles inside that ugly cowl. I loved his blue eyes and thought they showed determination and kindness. I saw Grandfather introduce you. So what do you think?"

Brenda was flustered and did not know what to say. "I—I thought his eyes showed intelligence and his mouth showed stubbornness." She wondered why she had mentioned stubbornness. Maybe it was true; after all, she herself was stubborn. "Aye, lass, he is handsome, in the rugged way the Vikings are."

"After Christiannt is settled in her bedclothes I be going to visit Grandfather," said Annesta. "I will have a good look at the stubborn stranger."

"Please, help me with Lady Gladys first," said Brenda, watching Annesta's shoulders droop. "We will fix Gladys the tea Archdruid Llieu left, then we will wash and dress her for bed. Afterwards Mona can comb her hair and you may go to Llywarch's cottage. Pray that Gladys sleeps quiet as a rock and the gods are willing to see her feeling better tomorrow."

* * *

The next morning Brenda awoke and found the sun beginning to peek above the horizon. She heard footsteps and Owain's voice, "Brenda! Wake up! Help me!" She was up in a moment, slipped her bratt over her shoulders, and opened her door.

Owain came inside, out of breath and in a dither. "I cannot rouse my wife. Last night before I went to bed I looked in on her. She talked of her parents as if they were in the same room. In troth, they have been long dead. I went to my chamber and tried to sleep, but I could not. I thought of Caded, a son I do not know, buried underneath the dog rose, and how he must have a proper burial in the courtyard. Near dawn I went for a walk. I wondered if Northmen or druid fosterlings killed Caded. I became angry with myself because I could not remember the face of Caded's mother. I remembered only an Irish lass who said the name Caded was close to her heart. Was that his mother? When I came back from my walk, I stopped to ask Gladys what she remembered about Caded or his mam. She would not talk. She would not open her eyes. She would not draw in air!" His eyes were wet. "I saw the full moon gliding down to the western horizon. Gladys believed a full silver moon had some meaning. Father Giff filled her head with half-truths. She is gullible as a child."

"She is not well," said Brenda. She took her linen bag of healing supplies off the shelf and went outside barefoot. She and Owain hurried toward the great hall and Lady Gladys's chamber.

Gladys lay on her pallet as if still asleep. Her skin was cold as the floor stones. Her lips were pale. Brenda found no sign of breath on a piece of polished silver.

Owain knelt beside the pallet holding his wife's hands to warm them. He pushed the covers aside and held her shoulders against his breast. "Her spirit has truly gone to the Otherside," he said with tears in his eyes. "She smells like she soiled herself." He rubbed his hands together and let them hang loose at his sides. His face was pale and glistened with perspiration. He looked like a drowned man.

Brenda covered Owain's cold hands with her warm ones. She whispered close to his ear, "I shall get one of the young maids to help me make her ready for viewing. I shall go for

Father Giff and have Llywarch strum his harp to inform people of the court that they may pay their respects."

Owain whispered, "My soul is steeped in misery and my heart bleeds."

" 'Tis all right, even for thee, a prince, to weep."

From the hall a tentative voice said, "Your Highness." Llywarch, standing beside Madoc, cleared his throat and said, "I beg your pardon, but when the two of you went into the great hall, we followed to see if there was something we could do."

He put a hand on Owain's arm and said, "I be sorry for your loss."

"Thank you," said Owain, clearing his throat. "I be glad you came." He sounded half asleep. "I knew death was near and believed I was prepared, but truthfully I be lost. I do not know what to do first. Is a priest necessary? I be supposed to bury Caded in the courtyard today." Owain looked like an aging, gray-faced crofter who was not certain if he should first plow the land or cut a tree for firewood.

"You need not worry," Llywarch said. "Gwalchmai and I will take care of Caded's burial. You may send word of his death to his Irish mother, Semios, with a druid fisherman."

"Aha, Semios," whispered Owain. "She was a good-hearted lass."

Brenda made her voice soft as it passed the lump in her throat. "Lady Gladys regularly went to mass. She espoused the New Religion." She placed her hand on Madoc's shoulder, felt its firmness and said, "Find Father Giff and send him here. Then return to Llywarch's cottage. He and Owain will be praying for the lady's spirit to find a safe journey to the Otherside. When they finish, tell the prince what he wants to know about Caded, who was a brave soldier."

Madoc left without a word, wondering if it was proper to talk with Owain about the soldiers Caded and Howell this day. Death made everything so complicated.

Brenda wondered what was going through her son's mind. It never occurred to her that he would think that his real mother was the first woman, outside the Irish druid camp, he had seen who gave orders to men as though it was a natural thing.

He promised himself to ask Llywarch how she, a royal maid and one of Owain's mistresses, had acquired so much power that Owain, a prince, would do as she suggested. Then he chuckled deep inside his chest and said, "I like her! I cannot wait to tell Sein that she is bossy, but in a gentle way."

Brenda went to the maids' cottage, which was buzzing about Lady Gladys's death. She suspected that Llywarch had spread the news and told the maids to go about their regular business until Prince Owain or herself told them something different. She asked Annesta and Mona to help her prepare Gladys's body for the court's visitation.

Annesta nodded. Mona tugged at the lacing on her gown and said she had not washed a dead body before. Brenda said it was not in the least distasteful. The girls were quiet on the way to Gladys's chamber. Brenda showed them how to place tightly rolled strips of linen so that there would be no soiling or wetting as the body's muscles relaxed. The girls kept looking at one another as they cleaned Gladys. Finally Brenda asked what was going on.

Annesta spoke in a hushed whisper as if she was afraid Gladys could hear. "Christiannt joined us to watch the sunrise and said that if Lady Gladys's spirit was with the Samhain spirits, she would see the court's seamstress this very morn."

Mona's tongue loosened and she said, "Aye! No one could believe what we heard."

"So I asked her whatever for would she need a seamstress," said Annesta.

"She said, 'To have my wedding gown made,' " said Mona. "Has Christiannt gone witless?"

"No one thought to ask her about the bridegroom," said Annesta.

"Llywarch told us Lady Gladys died in her sleep," said Mona.

"I was a real griffin and asked Grandfather how the moon knew 'twas Gladys's time to die," said Annesta. "He looked at me as if I was still a child and said, ' 'Tis hard to avoid the gods' plan. They wait, with their arrows, behind a cloud.' "

Both girls giggled nervously.

Brenda stamped her foot and said, "Keep your mouths straight and look sad on the day our lady's spirit travels to the Otherside." She watched them for a moment and then suggested that Annesta take beakers and a kettle of mead from the main kitchen to her grandfather's cottage, where Owain and Llywarch prayed to keep Lady Gladys on the wide path to the Otherworld. "Be quiet as a sleeping cat. Pour more mead when their beakers run dry."

She asked Mona to find Gwalchmai and tell him to work with Llywarch to bury the soldier, Caded, in royal ground as soon as the retainers brought the body in. "After you talk to Gwalchmai, come back and help me finish making Gladys beautiful."

Brenda dressed Gladys in her new Samhain clothes and her blue slippers. She fixed her mouth into a smile and propped her up with embroidered pillows on the pallet. Mona returned to sprinkle Gladys's clean, fine, yellowed white hair with powdered charcoal to make it black, the way it used to be. She painted the cold blue lips with a mixture of red cinnabar in a little mutton grease, which gave the corpse an illusion of life. She sprinkled perfume on the coverlet.

Brenda left the door open so that people would know it was all right to come in and pay their respects.

XIII
Death

Such was Owain's prowess that outside his own lands
and in England he was known as the "King of Wales."
Indeed, even much farther afield, he was called by this
title, and Barbier's description of him as "a sagacious
diplomat" is not overdrawn when one considers that this
Welsh chieftain, remote in his mountainous domains
from the seats of power in Europe, was nevertheless able
to negotiate an alliance with the French King Louis VII
against King Henry. Louis le Jeune had in 1152 repu-
diated his marriage of Eleanor of Aquitaine, who had
not only since married Henry II of England, but brought
with her as dowry some of the richest possessions in the
south-west of France, not to mention a less important
but equally delightful attribute, her personal patronage
of the code of courtly love. Not unnaturally Louis was
bitter towards England and welcomed any ally who
would be in a position to cause his English adversary
embarrassment.

Richard Deacon, *Madoc and the Discovery of America*

Brenda held Gladys's cold white hands and softly said her
farewell. She heard a muffled sound, turned and saw Father
Giff: cadaverous face and skeletal body dressed in a black
gown with a large silver cross hung on a tasseled waistband.
He asked if the pagan lad who brought him was one of the
two who were rumored to have caused the death of Owain's
dragon-son and sliced off Lord Howell's tongue.

"The lad is a fosterling," said Brenda, "and peaceful as a
newly laid egg."

"From what I hear, the two fosterlings were leagues away from peace. They were out hunting Christians!"

Brenda's hands balled into tight fists, but as calmly as possible she said, "Father, you must be mistaken. I saw those two laddies and neither is old enough to hunt anything but frogs and maybe a *cwningen*, rabbit. I pray that you do not spread falsehoods about them. You do not want Prince Owain to doubt your intelligence nor integrity, do you?"

"Nay, nay. I do not! I be sorry. I only repeated what I heard from my rectory maid. What does she know?" He laughed, looked sheepish and pulled out a dozen small candles. He lit one from the wall-sconce, let a little of the wax drip on the head of the pallet and held the candle there until it was tight. He set four along each side of the body and the last one at Gladys's feet and mumbled something about candles set around a laid-out corpse being a sensible precaution to prevent premature burial during coma. "Also useful," he said a little louder, "because the lady is laid out with gold clasps on her robe and rings on her fingers. I recognize Prince Owain's gold cross at her breast. It would not do to have the corpse robbed by servants." He looked crosswise at Brenda.

"Lady Gladys looks asleep," said Brenda, "but she is not going to awaken. You can be certes no castle servant will touch her jewels. But I fear your candles will set fire to the bedclothes and burn her to a crisp." Brenda looked crosswise at Father Giff, who clenched his teeth, making a grating sound. There was something about him that made her draw in her breath and say more. "Your rectory maid knows only rumors she hears from the soldiers she meets after dark." She bit her tongue and wished she had kept quiet.

He looked at her as if trying to see if she carried pagans' blue tattoos on her hands or neck, and it made her uneasy. He turned his head and spat outside the chamber door, directly on the hall floor. "The maid is a *neidr*, a snake!" His eyes were dark. "Had I known the lass was not tending a sick mother when she went out, I would not have treated her like *y Forwyn Fair*, the Virgin Mary!"

Brenda surveyed Father Giff with some speculation, and could think of nothing to say except "Thank you for coming."

She moved closer to the pallet where Gladys, propped against lace pillows, was quite beautiful in candlelight. She looked Father Giff in the eye and spoke softly about the Lady Gladys she knew when she first came to Gwynedd's court. "She loved the holy festivals and giving bountiful feasts for visiting heads of Welsh provinces. In those days she was known as proud and kind, dignified and courteous. During her last days she became thin as a stick and leaned on all of us."

Father Giff blinked and reminded her that he came to pray for Lady Gladys's soul.

Brenda touched Gladys's cheek lightly. "Fare thee well," she said, then put on her bratt. "Please, to avoid a cremation take your candles when you leave." Father Giff had his head bowed over his pipkin of holy water. She hoped that Gladys's spirit heard his prayers and they gave her solace for the long journey to the Otherside. She remembered that Owain and Llywarch were saying druidic prayers for Lady Gladys. She smiled and asked herself if the journey was, in troth, long. Maybe, she thought, 'tis short as a blink of an eye.

She did not want to be alone, so she went to Llywarch's cottage. Annesta was already there, warming the mead kettle. Madoc had his cowl drawn close around his face.

In a quiet voice, she told them that Father Giff was with Gladys and she thought the maids would be paying their last visit as soon as he opened the chamber door.

Owain was on the floor opposite Madoc with his back against the wall, his eyes closed. "We shall have a Christian funeral in three days," he whispered. "I expect Father Giff will tell his parishoners that Gladys wanted to be buried in his churchyard."

"I suppose so," said Llywarch, "but first he will tell everyone a pagan lad visits Gwynedd castle."

"Giff does not dare denigrate anyone I choose to meet within my court, because if he does, he knows the extra coins from my coffer will dry up." Owain's mouth twisted wryly; he gulped the last of his mead, coughed and held his beaker so Annesta could fill it again.

Brenda drew in her breath and motioned for Llywarch to come outside. She asked, "Did M—the fosterling speak to

Owain about . . . you know, what happened to Howell and Caded?"

"Aye."

"Listen," she whispered, "I have been thinking—Owain gives Father Giff extra coins. Are they used for operating the church or does Father Giff use them for something else? He is a New Religionist and against pagans. Something is in the air. Do you feel it? I felt it when I was with Father Giff—an uneasiness."

"You are talking about Death!" said Llywarch, giving her a long, appraising look and shaking his head. "That man looks like Death. Owain understands him and tries to confound him. I do not see much respect between the two men, although they behave civilly toward one another."

"I worry about Madoc," said Brenda.

"Brenda, hear me! Madoc is a nice lad from the druid camp. Llieu sent him to talk with Owain. Naught more. Pull yourself together, act not like a mother and forget making up thoughts of conspiracy and machination. Owain likes this new fosterling of Llieu's. They had a good talk, druid to fosterling. Owain even talked about the time the lad would become an initiated druid. He does not even know his given name and calls him *Brawd*, Brother."

"I tell you there are rumors that Madoc killed Caded and wounded Howell," said Brenda. "If Owain believes the rumors, he can give *Justifiable Retribution*. Can you say something to Owain to strengthen his belief in a lad he does not know and has not seen before this day?"

"Brenda, Madoc left Father Giff at the castle and came here, had a sip of mead, then the three of us did a moon chant to commemorate the full moon. After that Madoc told Owain his story of finding Caded dead by the hands of Northmen. He and his friend Conlaf buried Caded to keep preying animals from the body and they brought Lord Howell to the best physician in Wales. Llieu is mentor to the lads, their foster father. At this moment Owain is exhausted from grief and lack of sleep. Has he said he disbelieved Madoc's story? Nay! Woman, where is thy patience?" Llywarch had a hard time keeping his voice low.

"A mother's patience is short when it comes to the life of her child." Brenda bit her lip. "You should know that."

Llywarch smiled at her and said in a whisper, "Madoc will be fine. If we must do something, we will do it when the time is right." He looked over his shoulder, saw Owain coming from the cottage, and in a louder whisper said, "I be glad that Lady Gladys is dressed and looking elegant for her farewell."

Brenda was surprised when Owain took her hand in his and said softly, "My dear, no one looks good dead. I thank you for what you have done for my wife this day and before. Earlier I wished Archdruid Llieu were here to fill in what Llywarch and I forgot in the moon-chant ritual. 'Twould be nice if that Irish lad might hear the whole of it. The lad has a way with words and quickly memorized our chant. I wish you could have heard him. He makes one believe his story is troth. Lugh's lungs! He should take off his moldy cowl; makes him look like he is wearing a hangman's hood. Say, where is Christiannt?"

Brenda swallowed and said in a small voice, "My lord, do you need Christiannt? How can she, a maid, corroborate the lad's story of Northmen fighting Welshmen?"

Owain's red-rimmed eyes, sunken as a dry bog, flashed and he said in a hoarse whisper, "I seek Christiannt for a question far more important to my court than some stripling's story of how he and a friend carted away dead and wounded soldiers from a battlefield. Now, where is Christiannt keeping herself?"

Brenda could not say that she had heard Christiannt was going to marry someone and had gone to the seamstress. "She is so sad that she walks around the bailey tear-blind."

"I shall find her, ask her the question, then I shall sit with my wife for the rest of the day, and welcome those who come to pay their respects."

"Question?" asked Brenda. "What question?"

"Will she marry me and move into the royal chamber?" he said and bowed, unaware that Brenda's mouth was open and she had lost her voice. He left, slowly shuffling one foot ahead of the other toward the castle.

When Brenda found her voice, she lashed out at Llywarch. "You should have stopped him. I wanted to talk to him about

Madoc's story. I wanted to say that the druid fosterlings are truthful and know naught of vengeance and warring. And now Owain is going to marry his cousin. Ha!"

"Would you marry him?"

"Nay, I would not!"

"Then do not look disappointed. Owain knows about Madoc's truthfulness. On the other hand, he needs to be close to Christiannt's prevarications, to know her comings and goings. She is not to be trusted; you are. To him she is an enemy, a disciple of King Henry. Most of all he loves Gwynedd and will do anything, even marry a traitor, to keep his province out of the hands of the English."

"Marrying for knowledge of enemy moves? Mayhap he is losing control."

"Mayhap 'tis you losing control. Now, come back inside."

Brenda let out an exasperated breath. She was able to take care of things. Llywarch was wrong and most likely had not heard the latest false rumor that the two pagan fosterlings had killed Caded and wounded Lord Howell. She drew in her breath sharply. Maybe Christiannt was the source of that rumor!

Bristling, Brenda followed Llywarch inside. She meant to have Madoc tell again of his innocence, but when she saw him sitting on the pallet close to Annesta, she froze. She could not believe what her eyes told her.

Llywarch said, "Whoa! What goes on?" and the corners of his mouth turned up in a knowing smile.

Annesta turned crimson. Madoc stood up like he was struck with an arrow and stammered, "I, well, we—a, Annesta was crying. I tried to comfort—I told her that death comes to everyone. 'Tis a part of living to lose friends and kin."

Llywarch seemed amused to see his granddaughter seek solace in Madoc's sun-browned arms.

Brenda did not know what to say. She was fond of Annesta, but she wanted to shake her and scold. She wanted to say, "Get out! Leave my son alone. I hardly know him and look at you, taking his affection without even consulting me. I be his mother! He is my heart and soul. I love him. Let him love me before you plant yourself between us with girlish infatuation." She went to the shelf for a beaker and then to the mead kettle. She gulped one swallow after another until the beaker was empty and then deliberately took Madoc's place next to Annesta.

Annesta pointed to Madoc and said, "Brenda, I told this fosterling how you treated Lady Gladys with kindness, even when she became wretched. I said you were a great believer in learning, even for women. He said he truly wants to know you—to be your friend."

Brenda felt a flutter in her breast.

Madoc forgot his billowing tunic, took a tentative, barefoot step toward Llywarch, stepped on the hem and could not move. "Lugh's liver!" He swore and pulled the gown from his feet, bloused it up at the waist, retied the narrow sash, folded his legs and sat down.

Brenda smiled in spite of herself.

Annesta giggled, her rosy red face shone and she whispered to Brenda, "See, I told you, he is so beautiful. But I do not think he has been around lasses much. We unhinge him."

"Push off the cowl so you can see where you are going," said Brenda.

Madoc grunted deep in his chest and left the cowl over his head. He thanked Llywarch for his hospitality and said he would bring the borrowed gray gown back as soon as he had something else besides the old Augustinian robe to wear.

Brenda said that she would look forward to his next visit and noticed that Annesta was again misty-eyed.

Madoc kissed one of Annesta's hands and said, "I thank the gods for Welsh friends." Then he kissed Brenda on the cheek and asked, "Do you think that the wind has a voice?"

"Of course, but not a voice like yours and mine. Wind is not a thinking person. You must know that, if you have been with Llieu," said Brenda.

"Do you think the full moon foretold a death?"

"That is an ancient belief. We learn more about our world all the time and even though many ancients were full of intuition, they did not have the truth for all things. We modify our beliefs as we learn."

"Father Giff said Lady Gladys died because she looked at

the moon's face. I believe portents are accidental. When the
priest said Lady Gladys found herself in a situation where she
could not avoid breaking a *geis*, he only makes a natural oc-
currence sound mystical." He smiled, squeezed her hands and
made her heart jump with love and worry for him. "This morn
I told Prince Owain that I will not back away from a fight,
but I will do all I can to avoid warring. Anger and vengeance
do more harm than good, in my opinion," said Madoc.

She freed her hands, put them on the sides of Madoc's face
and kissed his forehead.

He flushed and drew the cowl up tight so that only his eyes
showed.

She fingered the small purse tied to her belt, a part of every
woman's costume, which held a knife no larger than the palm
of a woman's hand to be used for self-protection, scissors and
sewing things, and said she had an idea. "Come sit here by
the candlelight. No one in the court but the three of us has
seen you without a head covering. I be going to cut your hair
so no one will notice how close you resemble a ruthless,
bloody Viking whenever you remove that moldy cowl."

Annesta's eyes shone. "My lady," she said, "you know 'tis
against custom to use a cutting tool for four days after a death.
Did you not put your sewing scissors in the leather collection
bag last night?"

"Someone forgot to collect mine, or I left before the collection began." Brenda put her hand around the smooth metal
of her scissors.

Madoc looked puzzled and Llywarch explained, "The bard,
who is head of the household, pours nine barrels of water over
all the sharp instruments. Water washes away violence so that
the forks and various cutting tools, swords, knives and scissors, will not be used as weapons against any person."

Madoc was flabbergasted at such a custom. "Is this a Christian or an old druidic superstition?"

Llywarch's lips parted, showing teeth the color of walrus
ivory. " 'Tis an Old Religionist ritual handed down from the
Celts, who, tired of warring, wanted peace in the land. Welsh
druids do not practice every ancient rite, and the Irish druids
are known to forget most of them, so 'tis no wonder there are

some you are unfamiliar with. Did you notice that none of the servants swept up bits of food that fell from the table last night? The morsels were left for the lonely souls that have no living relations or friends to leave food to feed them on that special night. Only when we finish the meal will the servants sweep. Then they sweep the lonely souls out of the hall, saying, 'Dear ones, you have had your fill. Good-bye, good-bye.' "

Brenda took out her small scissors and said, "I give thanks to the gods that my scissors were not collected."

Annesta pushed the cowl off Madoc's head and combed his hair so that it hung over his ears. She was ready to be an accessory to Brenda's breaking an ancient rule.

Madoc said, "Tell me about Dafydd and Maelgwyn—are they soldiers in Prince Owain's army?"

Llywarch answered. "Nay, they were once, but now each man has his own army. And then there is Rhodri, who is little more than half your age, and looking for recruits of his own."

"Rhodri is ten years old," whispered Annesta, waving her comb in the air.

"These lads are barely yet men, but are always at each other's throats and vying for each other's land," said Llywarch. "Dafydd brags that he will become king of Gwynedd, trade with England and unite the Welsh armies with the English. He blows his own trumpet. No true Welshman wishes to have the Welsh and English armies under one leader, especially an English leader. Dafydd is so jealous of his father that his eyes are green as pickled sandworts."

"I came to Wales to study navigation," said Madoc. "I want to sail, to own a ship, mayhap be a trader one day."

"Prince Owain used to dream of sailing ships," said Brenda. "If I were a lad, I would not sleep until I had become a shipmaster." She snipped away the yellow curls and thought about Madoc as a sailor. Finally she looked at one side of his face then the other to be certain the hair was cut even. On the floor was a pile of silken yellow curls.

"How do I look?" Madoc asked Annesta.

"Like the stubble field behind the village," she said, and

then giggled. "Your face looks bigger and your eyes look larger."

Llywarch held his sides and stifled his laughter. "Methinks Madoc's head looks white as a plucked goose. No one will mistake him for a land seeker; instead they will think he is a poor crofter's son whose da overused his sheep shears. I should have thought of a haircut! We cannot leave any clue that the ancient ban on sharp tools has been broken. Hee hee, tee hee! That is it, Annesta, sweep up those butter-colored curls, put them inside a trash heap and bring back dry rushes to cover the hair clippings beside my bed."

Brenda looked up with a sudden wave of relief. Her whole body seemed lighter and unfettered. She put her scissors away and put her hand on Madoc's arm. "If Owain plans it, would you go to France as a Welsh emissary?" She held her breath waiting for his answer.

"What?" He brushed hair-snippets from his face. "He would not!"

Brenda's words came in a rush. "Aye, he would." She looked sideways at Annesta.

"I do not know what an emissary does!" He frowned then said, "For Lugh's sake! I must go back to the druid camp."

Llywarch said, "Owain asked me to tell you he will have a private audience with you nine days after the funeral."

"Me?" said Madoc. "He wants to see me again? Why?"

"He wishes to strengthen his court against the English," said Llywarch. "He does not like the English, especially King Henry. His son Dafydd likes Henry. That is a constant worry to him. He wants someone he trusts to take a message to France's King Louis, who also dislikes the English. He believes the Welsh and the French should join forces against Henry's soldiers. I mentioned the integrity of druids and he recalled that Brenda said something about a druid fosterling. I told him that the fosterling was you."

Madoc stepped away from the pallet so that Annesta could scatter fresh rushes over the old to hide any forgotten snippets of golden curls. When she sat down he sat on the pallet beside her and looked at Llywarch. "You did that? For me? For someone you did not know until yesterday? You think 'tis right for me to do this?"

" 'Tis not for me to say," Llywarch said softly, "Fate brought you to this point and you have to make your own decision. But I can say your life is going to change."

Brenda sucked up a mouthful of air.

Llywarch looked at her sharply and said, "My lady, Madoc's haircut has wiped away most of his good looks. Look at him! The shortness and the white scalp are so startling that no one will notice his refined nose and mouth. Truthfully, at first glance, I still say he looks like a dumb son-of-a-herdsman."

"What a monstrous thing to say!" said Brenda. "Of course, the thing to do is to keep the appointment. I shall find the right moment and remind Owain that this lad is his emissary."

Llywarch stamped both feet and said, "Woman, if you want to make the gods laugh, tell Owain what he should think." His voice was stern and his face dark.

Brenda felt like a chastised child. She followed Madoc out the door.

Madoc reached out, touched her cheek and said in a whisper, "Please, do not say a word on my behalf to Prince Owain. You and the bard inside saved my life long ago by doing something far more dangerous than telling the gods your future plans. I will do my best to balance the score by being honorable. I know not how, but it will come to me."

Brenda was filled with pride for her son and felt ashamed of her earlier peevishness. She nodded, went back inside, sat on the pallet and put her arm around Annesta. She sighed, relaxed and knew the mead loosened her tongue and let her speak true.

Gallopers were sent out to invite Owain's grown sons and other relatives and friends to a short service in the village church held three days after Gladys's death. Gladys was buried in the cemetery. Brenda saw Dafydd whisper with his father for half a dozen heartbeats, then disappear like smoke on a windy day. She looked for Madoc and bumped into Llieu. She said, "Excuse me," and Llieu said, "You look like you lost a precious friend. Do not worry. Madoc is very busy memorizing the accomplishments of Prince Owain before he goes to see him."

She smiled, denied that she was worried and then whispered briefly with Lord Iorwerth and his wife, Marared, who had come in a caravan from Degannwy. They were gone the next morning before Brenda could bid them good-bye or ask Marared about her small fosterlings and their health. She wondered why they had left so soon, and asked Llywarch.

"They think it wise not to aggravate kin who are New Religionists, like Dafydd and Christiannt," he said.

Brenda knew what he meant, but had so many things to attend to that she could not think too long on the problem.

Owain's sons Rhodri, Maelgwyn, Cadell, Phylip and Edwal camped inside the outer bailey with their own military retinue. Christiannt was not with the female maidservants during or after the funeral, but hung fast to Owain's right arm like a young falcon to its fleece ball. Christiannt dabbed at her eyes, coquettishly tipping her chin up and smiling whenever Owain spoke to someone. The arrangement perplexed Brenda and she sought out Llywarch, who said, " 'Tis what I predicted. 'Tis Owain's way of announcing that he will soon marry his cousin, Mistress Christiannt. I told you, he chose well, in order to keep an eye on her. She has two agendas, one, to promote Dafydd to king of Gwynedd, and two, to annihilate all druids, wipe out every vestige of the Old Religion and give the country away, like a gift-head on a silver platter, to King Henry. She is a spy for the English king and queen."

Everyone in the castle had heard the many broad hints for the first agenda. Even Gladys had promoted the idea of Dafydd being king of Gwynedd. And it was true that Christiannt had been seen talking with royal retainers who were known Christians about decapitating druids. Suddenly Brenda recognized the wisdom of sending Lord Iorwerth and Lady Marared, both druids, back to the safety of Degannwy. She could not help but smile when she thought of Christiannt's pregnancy and future marriage to Owain. The more she thought, the more intertwined and convoluted Owain's life seemed to become with both the Old and New Religionists.

*   *   *

On the ninth day after Gladys's funeral, Brenda looked forward to seeing Madoc again. She hoped he would stay the night with Llywarch and they might visit after supper. As the day progressed and she did not see or hear that he was in the castle or courtyard, she became nervous. She was not certain what she wanted Madoc to do: keep his appointment with Owain or stay in the druid camp. She knew only that she would not be satisfied until something happened. She did not like waiting.

Neither Owain nor Llywarch nor Madoc appeared at supper that gray wet evening. On the way back to her cottage, Brenda saw Llywarch coming through the icy rain like an apparition. His boots squished through puddles and his bony hand held his bratt over his head. She felt a shiver run up her back and was half afraid of the news he was bringing.

"So you were expecting me and holding the door wide open." He chuckled and took off his bratt and brogues and laid them on the warm stones around the small fire in the center of the floor. She offered him a small, flat sweet cake and a beaker of water after she smoothed her pallet so that he might sit there.

He sighed and said, "I do not know who has had Owain's ear, perhaps Father Giff. But now he suspects that Madoc and Conlaf murdered Caded and tried to kill Howell. He suspects that Dafydd or one of his men put Madoc up to this deviltry." He patted her hand and in a low voice told her that Madoc had come, retold his story to Owain about the dead and wounded Gwyneddmen. "The lad sounds credible to me."

She pulled her hand away as though it was scalded and her mouth became dry as grain dust. What she was afraid of had happened. The rain clouds had brought ill luck.

Llywarch shook his head and continued. "Owain asked Madoc to identify himself. He said he was the son of Seth, an Irish herder who drowned, so he dwelt with Irish druids. When his learning showed he had an interest in sailing, he was sent to the Welsh druids to study navigation, tides and astronomy. Owain became sarcastic because the dark-haired lad, Conlaf, had not come with Madoc to exonerate himself, and they exchanged angry words. It was agreed that if Madoc could prove his innocence with a sword, then his life would be spared. Welsh law states that the accuser shall claim support for his accusation with his sword. The accused will be given an opportunity, in a fortnight, to defend himself with his own sword. There was an alternative: Madoc could be Owain's hostage until the archbishop of Canterbury saw fit to come to Aberffraw and hear Madoc's story. Madoc chose the sword, knowing that the archbishop of Canterbury would never come to Anglesey Island to hear a story from a pitiful druid fosterling. Madoc will stay with me until the duel takes place."

Brenda could not speak. Madoc did not believe in warring or fighting. Could he even use a sword?

"In a way Owain will keep him hostage until he has learned to use a long sword," said Llywarch. "Illtud, the swordmaster who schools Owain's soldiers, will teach him. Do not look so down in the mouth. Illtud is a druid. Trust the gods. Show that you have confidence in your son."

When Llywarch was gone Brenda lay on her pallet listening to the rain. She could not sleep. She built up her fire with dry turf and thought of a driftwood fire that would crack, snap and burn with streaks of red, blue, green and yellow within the great orange mother flames. Sein had told her that the many colors came from the burning of the various minerals imbedded in the dried wood. She tried to imagine what Sein would say to help Madoc. The words *Believe in your son* popped into her head.

She let held-back tears spill down her cheeks. Her mind, released from tension, replayed a hundred times her meeting of Madoc on Samhain Eve. She was forever grateful to Sein for forming Madoc's thoughts and behavior. Oh, dear Sein, if you only knew what is about to happen, you could tell me if the lad is prepared for such an ordeal.

Finally she slept and dreamed that she wrote *Madoc* on the wet sand. Her life's purpose sang through her mind. The song was happy no matter what sacrifice she had to endure. Her purpose was to make certain her lastborn would fulfill his destiny of being a great leader on a glorious mission. The mission waited for the right time to reveal its true form. She must be patient. Madoc was her gift for the people she admired—the druids. What better gift than a special son?

The next morning Brenda was up early to bathe, braid her hair, dress and then she was off to the maids' cottage. She sat on Annesta's pallet before the work chores began and said, "How do you feel?"

Annesta was tired and hollow-eyed. She bowed her head so that she would not have to look at Brenda when she answered in a whisper, "I be sad. I—I try to remember Gladys as a wonderful lady, a good mother and wife, but I remember her cranky and hard to please."

Brenda smiled, wiped Annesta's eyes with her own petticoat and said, " 'Twas illness that changed her happy personality to that of a—a grouchy witch. 'Tis a pity you worry about that."

Annesta knew she could not fool Brenda. "I confess, my sadness does not dwell on Lady Gladys, but on the future. I want the duel to be over, and at the same time, I never want it to take place."

A shiver skipped down Brenda's backbone. "I know exactly how you feel," she said.

XIV
The Duel

March brought roaring winds and spasmodic storms. Inside the great hall turf fires burned brightly. When the air became soft with the promise of spring, nesting birds called to one another and gulls dotted the sky. All the while Illtud instructed Madoc in the art of dueling, and rumors flew about that the pagan fosterlings had deliberately killed Caded and wounded Howell. By month's end decrees had gone forth to Lord Dafydd to act as Owain's surety; to Conlaf as Madoc's; and to Father Giff, at Dafydd's behest, to judge the upcoming duel.

At the first opportunity Brenda waylaid Owain after supper and asked why he had chosen Dafydd as his surety. "Did you forget the lad is responsible for the death of an innocent man, Eben Fardd, one of your subjects?"

"It was never proven who was responsible for Fardd's death," said Owain. "Dafydd is my son, head of his own army and knows something about dueling. 'Tis time to trust him."

"And Father Giff? Do you trust him to be judge?"

"These days 'tis the thing to do. Province leaders hire priests rather than druids to oversee special royal household activities."

"That makes priests more powerful," said Brenda. "Father Giff is known to be manipulative and underhanded. How many untruths did he tell Gladys to bind her to the New Religion?"

"Safety of my people is my chief duty," said Owain. " 'Tis up to me to be watchful, to counteract anything unlawful, devious or underhanded. Rhodri brings me stories about the two fosterlings and their unusual hunger for warring. Are you against me sparring with that young *hogyn* in a public event to prove or disprove his honor?"

She again protested the warlike nature of the fosterlings. "Talk to them. They abhor violence. One is studying medicine with Llieu, the other is learning to duel to prove that his honor is clear. Your Highness, 'tis going to be a one-sided duel unless you bring in someone, like Archdruid Llieu, as co-judge to remind the people of your honesty and fairness. Clean hands do not defame."

"I will win the duel easily, but the presence of Llieu will certes make the spectacle honorable in people's minds," said Owain.

For the dueling feast, a long double-trestle table was illuminated by candles, which gave more light than the usual torches set in wall-sconces. The maidservants were seated at smaller tables close to the walls. Colorful banners hung from the ceiling of the great hall and fresh reeds covered the floor to commemorate tomorrow's duel.

Brenda came to supper with Mona and saw Owain in a dark linen tunic embroidered with silver thread. He sat on the raised dais at the head of the table, with Dafydd on his right and Father Giff on his left. They were flanked by war officers and retainers. On the other side of Father Giff sat Master Rhodri, whispering in Giff's ear. Their faces were flushed with excitement and hot mead.

Annesta sat with her mistress, Christiannt, on the right of Owain's retainers. Sir Lloyd, the tall, dark retainer, sat next to Christiannt. Ah, Brenda thought, the pair of them seem shed of worries. So Owain will wed Christiannt as soon as courtesy dictates. She wished Christiannt a good evening and whispered to Owain that she hoped he was able to control any contumacy during the duel, which made him laugh. She barely nodded toward Dafydd and smiled at Annesta. Then she and Mona sat at a table near the wall opposite the doorway.

Only a few heads turned when Madoc entered dressed in a druid's brown gown. But when he pushed the cowl back and removed the gown, there was a loud gasp, a short silence, then everyone spoke at once about his oiled bald head and shiny leather tunic, which reflected the golden beams of candlelight.

Brenda noted that Owain had ordered the use of the best and largest kitchen trenchers for the dried figs, raisins, fresh apples and pomegranates. Silver bowls, part of his war booty taken from the province of Powys during the great battle of Welshpool, held boiled grains. Silver wine goblets were from Rome and flowered clay beakers had once belonged to Northmen. Spanish red bowls with a glossy surface, decorated with stamped designs, crosses or running leopards, held mutton and roast boar.

Madoc could not sit still. He passed the trenchers and urged everyone to eat, for "who knows what tomorrow may bring?" He laughed and juggled apples before losing them to the feasters.

His actions put Brenda's nerves on edge and the fine feast turned dry as meal in her throat.

Gwalchmai, chief bard from the Dolwyddelan court, who preferred to spend his winters in Aberffraw, stood on the long

table, adjusted his crwth, a lute that hung around his neck, and
sang:

> Two men, one young, one old, accuse each other of
>   lies, murder and horrible deeds;
> Each man is loved, each man is stubborn, which
>   brings them to duel on the neutral island sands of
>   Anglesey.
> Oh Lugh, protect the youth,
> Lord in Heaven wrap your arms around our prince.
> Make time for each man to dream of peace.

Afterward there was tremendous applause. People shouted
"Owain! Owain!" Gwalchmai turned to Madoc and sang:

> Madoc kindly apportioned gifts of fruit;
> He did more to please than offend me.

There was a short applause for the unknown druid fosterling who was to duel their popular prince. A few men mouthed
profanities aimed at Madoc, whose face turned red. His lips
formed a straight line and he did not bow his smooth, shiny
head but held it high like a man with nothing to hide.

Musicians, acrobats and jugglers provided more entertainment.

Brenda excused herself, got up from her table during the
acrobats' act and left.

Madoc slipped into his gown and excused himself while
everyone was busy watching a team of tumblers.

Brenda left her door open. The candles in the wall-sconces
were lit and the coals in the center fire glowed.

Madoc stood in the doorway, acted witless by scraping his
feet and rubbing his oily head.

Brenda told him to come in and sit. "There will come a
time when Owain is no longer able to rule and the sibling
warring will put another man in power. Some say the man will
be Dafydd, others say 'twill be Howell or young Rhodri. Of
the three, Howell has the intellect. But 'tis wisdom that counts,
my son."

His wits came back and he lifted his head so that he looked directly at Brenda's face as she talked. He was fascinated. Never before had he heard a woman speak about intellect and wisdom. Lugh, this thinking woman, this beautiful woman, is my true mother! No wonder Sein raved about her like a man drunk on love.

"Ages ago Owain's ancestors were more interested in the sea than in their own land," said Brenda. "Owain himself loves the sea and would have made a fine trader, if the gods had not seen fit to make him head of a province. He always wanted a son interested in the sea. I thank the gods that Owain's scrappy sons have not shown an interest in sea warfare." Brenda sighed and her breath smelled of honey from the mead served at sup.

"Mother, I be the son with an interest in the sea," he said.

"You? Ie, I know."

"I would travel the Western Sea to unproved lands, if I had a ship," said Madoc. "I would fain set up a colony where Gwyneddmen could farm or herd in peace, without worry that the land is confiscated, or the animals taxed or killed by a neighboring tuath." He saw his mother tremble as if skittery field mice ran through her muscles.

"Your ancient grandfather Harold Haarffager was the first Norse king to sail across from Denmark to Ireland." In a small voice she said, "Old Magain also said you were the son who loves the sea."

"Old Magain?"

"Fifteen years ago, I fled the Gwynedd royal court with my newborn. Before taking a curragh to Ireland, I stayed at Degannwy's Seaside Inn run by an old woman and her husband. She gave my baby a druid blessing, predicted he would be a leader of men, sail the sea as a peacemaker, and named him Madoc, a combination of Magain and her husband's name, Doconn."

"Sein never told me how I was named." Madoc's voice was strong. "King Harold had ships with keels that rode less than an ell below the waterline. That is why they could travel up rivers and easily land on beaches. I could design a craft that can withstand many days at sea, through every kind of storm."

"It seems to me you are far too young to design ships," she

said. "There is so much to learn about you." Her eyes were moist when she said, "Start from the beginning and tell me about yourself." She pointed to a place next to her on the pallet. "Sit here."

"I would like to talk all night, but the duel is uppermost in my mind. When 'tis over I shall talk with you as long as you like." His throat constricted. He feared that after tomorrow he would never again talk with his mother, or anyone else. He imagined the cold finger of Death pressing on his backbone. He did not want to leave so soon, so he sat on the pallet.

Brenda put her arms around him and said, "I want you to wear my scarf for luck. Think of it as protection." She took a flimsy silk scarf from around her neck and tied it around Madoc's neck. " 'Twas once a dull yellow until Annesta suggested that I tie it in knots and dip it in madder when I was dying yarn one day. See how beautiful it is with red, yellow and orange swirls? Owain will never know 'tis the same one he gave me when I came back from Ireland."

"Did you—did you give my father a good-luck charm?" As soon as the words were out he wished he could suck them back within his chest.

Brenda's soft laughter greeted his jeer. "Son, you have no need to be jealous of your father. I do not love him as I once did, never as I love you. He has fought other duels. 'Tis your life I worry about."

" 'Tis against the rules of the duel to wear a charm. But I shall let Conlaf hold it. I thank thee. To tell you true, I do not want to kill anyone—not my father!" Madoc's voice broke. He jabbed his fists into his eyes.

Brenda gave a little cry, like a bird caught in a thornbush. "What can you do?"

Madoc slammed his hand hard on the pallet, making a little hollow in the goose down. "If my father is such a great leader of men, why does he not believe me?" Madoc's tongue was thick and cold as stone.

Brenda saw the agony in his eyes and her breath grated in her throat. "Your father does not know the truth of Caded's death, or Howell's wounds, because Rhodri and Dafydd, as if to cover up their own actions, spread rumors about you and

Conlaf. Howell's swollen tongue is so painful that Llieu gives him poppy-seed tea to make him sleep. He cannot tell Owain what happened. Owain believes Rhodri's and Dafydd's twattle and ignores their faults, while he grieves for his beloved wife."

"Did he love her? His wife?"

"Aye, as much as he is capable of loving any woman. In his way he also loves Christiannt and—and—me. Your father is a man who needs the comfort of a woman." Brenda ran her hands over Madoc's cheeks, noticing the soft pubescent fuzz on his upper lip and the space between his upper front teeth.

"Why do you stay?"

"After I came back from Ireland knowing you were safe, he and I made a pact. If I left again he would send soldiers looking for me. If I was found, the soldiers would not bring me back alive. I have asked him more than once to let me go to Ireland to visit my father and your brother, Riryd, and your sister, Goeral, accompanied by him or two of his soldiers. He will not permit me to leave, saying any leave-taking breaks our pact. The pact was made in good faith by us both."

Madoc stared at her bowed head, trying to understand. "Sein sends a message: He misses you."

She looked up. "Did he tell you I was learning to be a healer in Ireland; that a fosterling drowned in a sacred well? The drowning was my fault, therefore some in the camp were glad I left." She was surprised that Ailin could still make her eyes water. "When Owain sent soldiers for me, 'twas my opportunity to leave. Here I be asked for by villagers and crofters to supply cough medicine and birthing help, to lance boils, ease the passing of stones, kill a fever, set a bone or cure a rash."

"Do people pay you?"

"Of course. They pay me in friendship, with a chicken or two, or a sack of grain, a pot of honey. I give the food to others who have a need or I take it to the court's kitchen, where 'tis appreciated. In that way I pay for my food and shelter."

"Sein said I would not have survived kinepox if it had not been for you."

" 'Twas the gods who willed that you become strong and

healthy and full of smiles. My son, what I be going to say is not going to sit well with you. I gave you kinepox. I had to see that you lived beyond it, and Sein helped me. You are destined to be a leader, someone special. You were conceived under a sky of rare dancing lights."

"Mam, I be not a leader. My friend Conlaf is the leader." Madoc was thoughtful for a moment, then said, "Why is Annesta a handmaiden to Christiannt? You and she are such good friends. 'Twould be a better arrangement if she were your maid."

"Nay, 'tis better the way 'tis. Annesta can tell me gossip from Christiannt's chamber that I would never hear with another arrangement. Annesta is a true friend, and the only person, besides Llywarch and Mona, in whom I can confide."

"How can you be sure that your maid, Mona, does not take tales to Mistress Christiannt?"

"Mona's mother's tongue was cut out so that she would not carry tales when she was a Northman's slave in Dubh Linn. My father thought the woman was beautiful, bought her, but he did not know what to do with someone who could not talk. She and I became fast friends. We conversed through writing and certain head nods and hand signs. She told me that she had a daughter, Mona, by the same Northman, who was sold to an Irish family. When she died, I was with Owain, and heartbroken. Owain surprised me by going to Ireland and buying Mona. He knew her mother's fate. Some soldier will marry Mona and they will have a half-dozen children. That is the fate of all our beautiful handmaidens."

"Nay!" said Madoc, clamping a hand over his mouth so that he would say no more.

"My son, what do you mean, nay?" She looked at him curiously, "So, you noticed that Mona is beautiful and intelligent?"

"Well, aye, but . . ." he whispered. "But Annesta—she and I—you know—I would like to be her friend. A close friend . . . you know." His face glowed with the perspiration of hope and fear.

Brenda ran her hand across the blond stubble on his head. The sensation was pleasant and she did not stop.

He grabbed her other hand and said, "Mother, my life takes an unknown path on the morrow. I shall do my utmost to make you proud, no matter what the outcome." He pushed her scarf halfway into his pocket and fumbled with the door's latch.

"Old Magain was right; you shall live to be a leader and meet your full brother, Riryd, who is Celtic-dark like my family, and your sister, Goeral, who is blue-eyed and Viking-blond like you. Go and sleep well. 'Twas fear that gave birth to the gods," said Brenda. Her eyes were wet.

"I thank thee." Madoc was utterly miserable, thinking what if those gods abandoned him?

Neither Brenda nor Madoc slept that night. Brenda sat outside her cottage and counted the stars. She thought about the creatures that swam and drifted in the sea, such as fish with two legs like man and some with four legs like a dog. She wondered if mermaids were real and if the crystal columns that floated the north seas were truly there.

Madoc walked around the courtyard, looked at the stars and listened to the whooshing of the tide as it came in. He talked to the gods in a friendly way and told them he was going to do what he could to save both himself and his father from the sword. He could not tell them what he had in mind, because there was no plan in his mind.

Toward morning Conlaf massaged Madoc with sweet, herbal oils until he relaxed and slept a few hours. Before noon he pulled the short leather tunic over his loincloth. He remained barefoot, to be quick on his feet.

Early in the morning Brenda bathed and washed her hair. She put on a loose gown and sat in front of her cottage in the sun. When her hair was dry, she circled the braids around her head and fastened them in the back with tortoiseshell pins. She put on clean underclothes, a skirt, an embroidered blue tunic, and went to the great hall before noon.

The sun rode a cloudless sky and the day was warm. Hundreds of seabirds nested in the cliffs near the sea, kittiwakes, shags and guillemots. After washing down half a biscuit with cottage tea, Brenda stopped at the maids' cottage for Mona, and the two of them went to the dueling grounds behind the castle. Red campion shone in the grass.

Brenda greeted Christiannt, who was already there with her lover, Lloyd, and Annesta. She greeted Father Giff, who wore his black robe with a silk cord around the middle, on which hung his silver crucifix. He carried a wooden staff with a silver cross painted on its head.

On the far side of the grounds Madoc, in only his loincloth, stood barefoot, shiny with oil. A thin gold circlet was on his upper right arm to show he had been a druid fosterling for at least twelve years. On one side of him was Llywarch, who wore his gray gown with the multicolored sash. On the other side stood Conlaf, who wore a sleeveless brown linen tunic and a gold circlet. He was also barefoot.

Brenda and Mona stood on Madoc's side of the field. Madoc did not acknowledge them, but Llywarch smiled.

Owain came dressed in a scarlet bratt and carried a scepter that was decorated with red and gold ribbons that fluttered like butterflies as he walked. His feet were clad in leather sandals with lacings around his ankles. His legs and arms were blackened with charcoal mixed in sheep tallow.

Behind him limped his surety, Dafydd, wearing a ragged black bratt and dusty, worn boots. His hair was blackened with sooty lard and it hung in greasy strings against his thick, muscular neck. His yellow, catlike eyes looked around with disdain.

Behind Dafydd came half a dozen soldiers carrying sheathed swords at their waists and oblong, hard-leather shields painted with three golden lions on a red field, Gwynedd's coat of arms. The soldiers sang a roundelay depicting Madoc as a loutish pagan who had goaded a grief-stricken prince to challenge him to a duel. Behind them came the court's servants and a crowd of villagers booing and chanting that the young pagan was sure to lose.

Brenda worried that they might cast a spell so that this would be the last day Madoc saw the sun shine. Suddenly she was aware that these thoughts were foppery, a way of laying blame to some superstition she had no control over, in case Madoc lost the duel. She recognized several people from the

druid camp, especially red-haired Molly Fardd, who moved to
Madoc's side of the field and elbowed her way toward Brenda.

"Look at that poor laddie," said Molly. "Had his head
shaved, and not a very good job either."

Brenda looked at her crosswise.

"Well, ye can see he is pretending to be a big man, with
all that shine. But I know the laddie's insides are in knots.
Cian told me he is a real decent sort, not out to harm a bumblebee. Speaks to everyone, without his nose in the air. I told
Cian ye would be standing on his side of the field in case he
is sword-stuck, ye being a healer. Ye stand up for the disad-
vantaged so I thought I better come to stand beside ye. The
children send their love. They are healthy and getting along."

Brenda shook like a leaf in a winter gale. She clasped
Molly's hand to steady herself and smiled.

Molly said, "Life shrinks and expands in proportion to
one's courage."

Archdruid Llieu walked across the field to Madoc's side.
He carried a bleached boar's skull on a wooden staff. Owain's
crowd hissed and stamped their feet.

Brenda kept her eyes on Madoc, whose shoulders and back
were being massaged by Conlaf, who wore her scarf tied
around his waist. Conlaf helped Madoc back into his leather
tunic and slipped a leather shield over his shoulder.

Prince Owain shuffled onto the field flanked by Rhodri and
two war officers. With one hand he shaded his eyes to look
at the large crowd forming on his side of the grounds. They
roared "Hallelujah!" and Gwalchmai sang songs of his prowess.

Dafydd followed with his dark, stringy hair dangling past
his thick neck and brushing his bare chest. He took Owain's
scepter and bratt.

Brenda said, "He looks like a barbarian."

Molly shivered as if the air had turned cold and whispered,
" 'Tis the hellhound Dafydd." She shook her fists in the air
and said, "I thought I had forgiven him, but seeing him makes
me want to pound the life out of his arrogant body. Lugh,
forgive me!"

"Lord Dafydd is Prince Owain's Nemesis," said Brenda.

Owain stripped down to leather breeches but left his sandals on. Dafydd dabbed more blackened tallow on Owain's arms, back and chest and gave him last-minute instructions by lunging here and there. Owain made an irritated slashing motion to tell Dafydd he did not need instructions, and straightened the shield strap on his shoulder.

The co-judges walked to the center of the dueling ground. Llieu put the boar's-skull staff in the sandy soil against Father Giff's already planted staff with the painted silver cross. Owain ran his hand impatiently across his face and paced in a tight circle, waiting for Madoc to come onto the field.

Madoc hesitated as though he wanted to bid farewell to his small crowd of friends. He glanced to the other side, and Brenda knew he was searching for Annesta. He smiled when he spied her. Halfway to Owain, he stopped and faced his swordmaster, Illtud, who stood with Owain's other retainers. For a moment Illtud stared back, then said, "Just keep your feet moving and your eyes open."

Madoc nodded, looked ahead where the judges' staffs were now planted on either side of the dueling grounds next to where each surety and judge would stand. He went to the circle drawn in the sandy dust where Owain waited.

Llywarch stated the offical rules of a judicial duel. Then Father Giff asked each man to swear on his silver crucifix that his case was just, that each believed his own testimony true and that each had no concealed weapons and "no stone nor herb of virtue, no charm, experiment nor other enchantment by which the word of the Lord God might be diminished and the devil's power increased."

Each contender said, "I do swear," and Archdruid Llieu asked them to shake hands and step back quickly to their places. The crowd was still; not even a whiff of air moved. The only sound was a brief swishing of feet in the sand.

When the sun was directly overhead, the priest and archdruid held their hands in the air simultaneously, turned and walked to the side of their staffs; the signal to begin.

At that moment Brenda had an intuitive understanding and wondered why she had worried so much. Owain was so aggrieved over losing his wife that his own life had shrunk and he was ready to give up living and go to the Otherside. Madoc was predestined at birth to be a leader and man of peace. He had just begun to live; his life was expanding. In the next few moments the lives of these two would be out of the hands of men and in the hands of the gods. Brenda raised her eyes. "So be it," she whispered.

Madoc rubbed his hands on his tunic.

Owain stepped forward and threw down the gauntlet, a large leather glove with long fringe on the cuff.

Dafydd held out Owain's sword. Owain squinted and placed his hand on the hilt.

Brenda imagined the smooth coldness of the sword that Conlaf held out to Madoc. She expected to see Madoc's thumb find the hilt's ring and grip into it, but he never reached for his sword, never took his eyes off Owain's face and right hand.

Owain's mouth twisted. He turned his head to the side, out of the direct sunlight. His eyes were the color of moss in a frozen pond.

Llywarch's words that only priests, women and the ill could claim exemption from this type of trial went through Brenda's mind. The loser's right hand would be cut off and he would be dragged by his heels off the field. If he was still alive, he would be hanged. A defender who resisted deep wounds until the stars shone won his case.

Madoc moved one foot forward. He still ignored the sword Conlaf held out to him. He moved the other foot forward, carrying him closer to the glove on the ground. One more step and Madoc's foot was on the glove. The crowd did not move or utter a sound. The tension was invisible but thick as fog. Madoc was face-to-face with Owain, whose pressed lips were colorless. Madoc licked his lips and looked over at Conlaf, who nodded. He glanced to the other side and saw Lord Dafydd bent forward in anticipation, his upper lip curled. It was time for Madoc to take his sword and pick up the glove. Madoc opened his mouth and made a sound: "Ahagh—" then he sucked in air and said, "My lord! 'Tis indeed a pleasure to be here before the great prince of Gwynedd. All my life I have heard wonderful tales of your skill on the battlefield and of your kindness to your people. I have heard you are fair and honest and that you believe in the old *Laws of Hywel Dda*."

Owain frowned; his hand on the sword hilt remained tense.

"Sire, there is no law that says the participants in a judicial duel cannot talk to one another before both swords are drawn."

Owain nodded and let out his breath.

"I want to ask thee two questions. One, you have sworn that you have no concealed weapons and that you have taken no mineral nor herb. Yet I see your eyes squint in sunlight and in shade they are wide open. The pupils are unusually large. Did you take something just before noon that would give you strength for this duel?"

The crowd was stunned. Brenda could not believe her ears. She looked closer. Madoc was right! She, a healer, should have been suspicious when Owain walked with a shuffle, when his eyes squinted in the sunlight and the pupils enlarged when he turned his head aside. Owain turned scarlet from the back of his neck to his forehead and said, "Well, I turned down a wooden tub filled with hot peat moss sent to me by my friend Archdruid Llieu. It was tempting and would loosen my muscles, but I turned it down, thinking that taking something from the other side would be unseemly."

"Aye," said Madoc, squinting at Conlaf, who had a hand over his mouth to suppress his laughter. "So you are saying you have taken no mineral nor herb?"

"Och! Instead, I—I took a simple glass of red wine handed me by Mistress Christiannt. There is no law against that. Verily, she told me it would dull the pain in case I suffered a sword scratch. I turned down the tub of hot water and moss. I tell the truth."

Many a head in the crowd nodded.

"I believe you," said Madoc. "Was anything added to the simple wine?"

"I do not know for troth," said Owain.

There was laughter with frowns.

"Second question: What did Rhodri tell you about the death of Caded?"

"Usually I do not put much stock in the words of that young *hogyn*," said Owain. "They have naught to do with this duel."

"They have everything to do with this duel, which is about

my honesty, my honor! Were you going to check my words against what you will hear from Lord Howell? Or are you relying on hearsay? Court gossip runs faster than water flows downhill, so I be certes you heard what Lord Dafydd wished he had done to Lord Howell? A missing tongue prevents a man from speaking."

Owain scowled and wiped his hand across his face.

"Why, you dirty, druid pagan!" shouted Dafydd.

Frowning faces turned on Dafydd.

Father Giff put a hand to his mouth to remind Dafydd that he must be quiet or he could be severely punished, even put to death.

Dafydd ignored the priest. "Father, do something about this impertinent whoreson! He soldiers in nobody's army! He asks questions that are not his business. In my opinion, Lord Howell is no better than this pagan. He wanted me to unite my army with his. He saw the whole battle. If he says I killed Caded, he deserves to have his tongue cut clean out." Dafydd moved onto the dueling ground. "Flesh the pagan, run him through! He killed Caded and buried him under the dog rose."

Owain looked embarrassed. "Close your maw," he said between clenched teeth. "Under *Dda Law*, anyone, except combatants, who speaks before the gauntlet is held can be lashed to death. I heard Caded joined Howell's army to war against you, Dafydd."

"Your Highness," said Madoc, "if that is what you know, so be it." Madoc's foot was still on the glove.

Owain had turned white as sea salt. "Dafydd, 'tis common knowledge you coveted the taxes Caded collected from the wealthy herders around Lake Coron. Did you kill him thinking you would collect the taxes?"

"Nay! Absolutely not! I be incapable of killing anyone by throwing a lance through their breastbone then pulling it out on the other side. 'Tis a brutal, gory action!"

Owain's mouth twisted to one side as though he tasted something bad. Yesterday, while feasting, Llieu had told Owain that there was no weapon found near Caded. Llieu said he had not told anyone but Owain that from the fosterling's description of the wound, he was sure it was caused by a war lance pulled through from front to back. "Wellaway!" said Owain. "You forgot the two fosterlings were unarmed, but you carried a war lance." He motioned for two of his war officers to bring Dafydd back to the surety's position and hold him there.

Dafydd's voice was startlingly loud. "Father, order your men to unhand me! Call off your officers!"

The officers stepped away from Dafydd but were close enough to grab him if Owain ordered.

"Listen, I told Rhodri naught except that the pagan has a lust for blood," said Dafydd. "On my honor, I swear 'twas the pagan who killed Caded with a lance to the breastbone! Rhodri thinks the same. Ask him."

Each person stood in place, frozen like a statue. Nothing like this had ever happened.

For a long, silent moment Owain looked at Rhodri, who shook like clabbered milk in a storm, then his eyes went back to Dafydd. "You make up stories to fit your purpose. You are thine worst enemy. You know not truth from falsehood. To ease my grief, I sought revenge for the death of Caded by having a perfectly legal, judicial duel with a stranger, a fosterling of Archdruid Llieu. Now I have no heart to parry sword blows with this innocent lad. Judges, as prince of Gwynedd, I say you call the duel a no-contest! There is other punishment to mete out."

Brenda kept her eyes on Madoc, who stood with his back and shoulders straight. She tried to remain calm and put her thoughts in order, but her head was in a whirl.

The sigh from the crowd swelled to a murmur, like a distant hum, a great wind, moving closer and closer. The hum grew to a rumble like thunder.

Madoc spoke as clear as a bell above it. "The prince of Gwynedd admitted he partook of wine," he said, projecting his voice from the pit of his stomach so that everyone could hear. "Mayhap it had a painkiller added to it. You heard Prince Owain's confession and you heard the confession of the one who killed Caded. Your prince has more heart than most. I take my sword from my surety and give it to the swordmaster, who taught me more than I ever expected to know about dueling." He took the sheathed sword from Conlaf and handed it to Illtud, who grinned from ear to ear. "I leave the final decision of this meet to the judges."

Father Giff and Archdruid Llieu stepped close and talked mouth to ear. When they stepped apart Father Giff's face was dark; he pointed his staff at Dafydd and his mouth moved but no words came forth.

"The duel is ended!" shouted Llieu, laying his staff on the ground. "There be no deaths this day!"

The crowd turned wild. Strident voices demanded punishment for Lord Dafydd.

Brenda's eyes were wet. She felt someone brush her hand.

"Why do you weep?" asked Madoc.

" 'Tis for thanksgiving," she whispered.

"Thank you from the middle of my heart." He grinned and handed her the scarf that Conlaf had worn.

"Keep it for luck," she said.

XV
Emissaries

Willem [a thirteenth-century Dutch troubadour] tells of
Madoc's fame as a sailor, which was explained by his
grandfather being "half a Viking," and how he went to
the Court of Louis VII of France, disguised as a monk
as an envoy of his race. This would certainly seem to
identify Willem's Madoc as being a son of Owain Gwynedd, for Owain sent two Welsh monks with letters to
the French king, offering his support against Henry II.
  Richard Deacon, *Madoc and the Discovery of America*

A crowd had gathered at the center of the dueling ground.

Dafydd's bratt and shirt lay on the grass. He wore only
leather britches and brogues, and was laid across a board supported by trestle-type legs. His hands shook like banners in a
wind. His face was tear-tracked and smudged from the ashy
grease in his hair. He cried in a high-pitched voice, " 'Tis the
bloody pagan's fault! He never took his sword! Why do this
to me? 'Tis a bitter pill!"

"You will learn to follow the rules of dueling and to find
wisdom," said Llieu and closed his mouth before he spat out
more.

Owain held up his hands for silence and announced that he
himself would deliver two times nine lashes with a knotted
whip to his surety, Dafydd ap Owain.

Christiannt fell at his feet and pleaded with Owain to let
Dafydd go.

Owain pushed her away and silently thanked his lucky stars
that Gladys was not here to see this. He reminded the crowd
that Dafydd had broken the code of silence during an official

duel and either public whipping, loss of a limb or death was lawful justice. One of the war officers handed Owain a whip, its end weighted with a stone the size of a plum. Small, sharpened sheep bones were tied between knots. He flexed the whip, cracked it in the air above his head and made everyone jump.

Madoc looked grim, as if he wanted to get the thing finished. There were scattered shouts saying that the pagan lad was the hero of the day. Others cried out that Owain could have won before the sun started its downward path to the horizon. One man said the duel ended because the pagan had a way with words. Another yelled, "The pagan has courage. I like him." Still another said, "Prince Owain, 'tis time to flay your notorious outlaw son's hide to a fare-thee-well!"

Molly shouted, "Aye! Ye cannot be soft!" She moved as near to Owain as she dared and said, "Lord Dafydd deserves naught less than to be burned alive in a basket!"

Owain recognized the outspoken woman as Fardd's wife, and answered her gently. "I agree, my lad deserves more than a whipping, but to take his life will not bring back the dead. Because I be prince, 'tis I who names the punishment. My sympathies to you over the loss of a good husband."

Suddenly Dafydd lifted his head and shouted, "I swear, on my honor, one day I shall break my father's neck, at the very least kill him!"

Someone shouted back, "Your honor is not worth piping about!"

Owain delivered nine lashes to Dafydd's bare back, then stopped to rest. Dafydd cried like a baby before each lash and howled like a werewolf after each one. A woman sobbed that nine lashes were enough, any more would surely tear apart the poor lad's back.

Owain delivered nine more lashes, directing every other one to Dafydd's leather breeches. He was sweat-drenched when it was over.

Dafydd lay so still that some said he was dead.

Christiannt asked to take Dafydd to her cottage, where she could attend to him.

Owain said Dafydd should be taken to Llywarch's cottage, where a healer would wrap the wounds.

Christiannt said, "The last thing he needs is tending inside a pagan's bloody cottage."

Owain opened his mouth to speak, but he was worn out and slow. Conlaf stepped up to Christiannt and promised that Master Dafydd would not die. He said he could dress wounds outdoors as well as in the bard's cottage with the help of a healer's ungents. Christiannt took one look at handsome, assertive Conlaf and said, "Physician, be a hero. Show me what thou canst do." She smiled and tilted her head so that the sunlight glinted off of her white teeth.

He was not gulled by Christiannt's smile and grinned knowingly at her flirty ways.

Brenda watched him put his hand on Christiannt's shoulder and heard him say close to her ear, "A female with child who is prone to fainting ought not be in a crowd, in the hot sun, nor in the middle of bloody things, like duels, lashings or hangings."

Christiannt's tongue was honeyed. "Physician, thou art too young and too knowledgeable for thine own good." She gave him a fawning smile.

Conlaf's face turned red; he backed away and bumped into Brenda. He asked her for a black ichthyic salve that he knew she carried.

Christiannt scowled and said Dafydd would smell like rotten fish and she had changed her mind. He could go to Llywarch's cottage.

"Take the lad," said Conlaf, "He needs a gentle touch. But do not wet the linen wrapping for nine days, a magic number for good healing. After that you may wash him."

Christiannt's eyes blazed; she jabbed a finger into Conlaf's side and turned to face Brenda. "You and this—this pagan pup! If I did not know better I would swear you and he are in partnership!"

Conlaf said, "Aye, any good healer going to a duel prepares a specific for sword cuts and welts." He winked at Brenda and the others beside her and left to look for Madoc.

The soldiers lifted Dafydd and followed Christiannt, whose face was as bright pink as wild penstemon.

Owain shook hands with Madoc. "Is it true Lord Howell's tongue will heal so he can talk?"

Madoc wanted to say "I told you the tongue heals." Instead he stood straight and smiled foolishly.

Owain remembered what Madoc had said about Howell's tongue healing. Suddenly he thought, This lad reminds me of my younger self. He is not a blusterer, but believes in honor and justice. He bested me and I like him. He would make a good emissary. I too can do the right thing. He cleared his throat. "Will you accept the position as Gwynedd's emissary to France? Take my brief to King Louis and speak to him on my behalf?"

People close enough to hear Owain clapped their hands with approval.

Conlaf nudged Madoc and said he wished he were going to France, where there were exotic diseases, for instance leprosy, that he had never seen. His dream was to learn about all the diseases that plagued mankind. In a fit of enthusiasm he said, "There are hospices in France that do nothing else but care for lepers."

To have a friend at his side in a foreign country would be a great comfort to Madoc because the fifteen-year-old lad was as fearful of meeting King Louis as he had been of dueling with his father. "Your Highness," he said, "I believe two Gwyneddmen together, with four eyes to see what is going on in the French court, are twice as good as one Gwyneddman. Two men will impress the king of France that you, the prince of Gwynedd, are sincere. You can be sure that whatever I miss seeing, my friend Conlaf will see. What I miss hearing, Conlaf will hear. What I miss keeping in my mind, Conlaf will remember." He put his hands together so they would not shake, held his breath and looked at Owain.

"You are saying that if I send two emissaries instead of one, my message will appear twice as important?"

Madoc let go of his breath and gulped in a lungful of air. "Aye, sire, ah—a—Your Highness."

"Then I say you shall meet with King Louis and my co-emissary, Conlaf, shall meet with the chancellor, Hugh de Soissons, who is a major figure in French diplomacy." Owain placed a hand on Madoc's shoulder. Madoc imagined a burning sensation where his father's large hand lay.

The dislike that previously had filled Madoc's heart was replaced by an impetuous camaraderie, a filial devotion, a bold, new feeling. Owain held up the hands of the two druid fosterlings and announced that they would leave as soon as a trading ship stopped in Aberffraw that would take on passengers, and if they were not prepared to leave on that particular day, they were insane and should resign immediately. Archdruids Llieu and Llywarch were the first to shout, "Hear, hear! Amen!" and clapped their hands in agreement.

Conlaf grabbed Madoc and said, "If you be seasick on the way to France, I could help."

"Help me be seasick?" said Madoc, with dancing eyes. "Listen, my friend, I rode in coracles and curraghs all my life, in all kinds of weather. All *you* do is push bones together, rub on salves, and make people drink vile concoctions. You do not know a thing about sailing."

Brenda sat with Llywarch at the supper table and asked what he was thinking. He thought Madoc and Conlaf ought to travel to France not as druid fosterlings, but disguised as Augustinian canons. "That way they shall be quite safe from the private armies that roam the French countryside looking for pagans. And they can keep a diary, even though druids are not in the habit of writing things down on parchment. If the court scribes embellished the vellum with colored dragons, unicorns, half-moons, the leaves would appear biblical. They can jot down prayers and read them from their diary. People will put coins in their hands," said Llywarch.

"They will remember the prayers. They have learned to memorize anything, no matter how difficult or how long, but reading from the diary is good. They will appear to carry holy books," said Brenda, overjoyed with Llywarch's idea. "Oh Lugh, I shall miss him."

"Me too," said Annesta, sliding down the bench to sit beside Brenda. Tears filled her eyes.

For a moment Brenda thought, Annesta, you have no right to my son, to miss him or look at him with calf-eyes. Then she silently chided herself as a selfish old woman and gave Annesta a hug and told her about Llywarch's good idea.

The royal court was moved from Aberffraw to Dolwyddelan three weeks after the duel.

Owain and Christiannt were married on the longest day of the year, June 21. It was Owain's idea to marry during summer solstice for good fortune.

Christiannt told the household maids that Owain was getting paganish because he wanted the wedding to take place in the flank of the windy summit of the mountain called *Yr Eifl*, The Forks, because of its triple peaks. Near the mountain's pinnacle was a small group of empty circular stone huts sheltered by a rampart of loosely piled stones, in front of a lichen-covered stone wall that undulated through short green grass to the summit. From a tall stone cairn in the center of this pre-historic settlement called *Tre'r Ceiri*, Town of Giants, one could see the sea on a clear day. Owain thought it the most · beautiful sight in the world.

Molly told Brenda she thought Owain planned to couple with Christiannt next to the great stone cairn soon after they were married. Thus he would be assured that the babe conceived on their wedding day would be a great leader of large stature. Brenda smiled knowingly but said nothing.

Father Giff refused to marry them. " 'Tis a sin to marry your first cousin, milady," he said. "The children such a marriage begets will be imbeciles." Apparently he never thought of. the children Christiannt and Owain had already produced.

Owain was angry as a stirred hive of bees that Father Giff would not break a small Church law to keep Christiannt happy and said he would never step inside the church again and Father Giff need not expect any further donations from the royal court.

Archdruid Llieu performed the ceremony on the summit of Yr Eifl with poems of love and songs of fidelity. Afterward he led the guests down to the center of the stone huts for refreshments. His eyes sparkled when he told the guests to look for Owain and Christiannt to come down to eat a little later.

Brenda asked Llywarch why Gwalchmai stayed away.

" 'Tis a secret that he stayed behind to entertain, with some aged mead, Christiannt's paramour, Sir Lloyd, who threatened to choke Owain if he married his precious treasure," said Llywarch. "Gwalchmai explained to Lloyd the consequences of that action and promised him some aged mead was better than the swish-swash the Gwynedd army provided. Gwalchmai promised that by the time the wedding party started down the mountain, Lloyd would be blind to the world."

By fall, when the court was back in Aberffraw, Christiannt could not keep her pregnancy a secret. Owain dreamed of monumental plans for this newest child he thought he had fathered.

Madoc spent his free afternoons at the wharf along with other folk to hear the news and look over the passing ships. Harvest was done and crofters stayed inside next to their fires. The royal court closed their heavy wooden doors and window shutters to keep out the icy mists and damp, penetrating wind that made the air bitter cold.

Annesta met Madoc at the wharf some afternoons when the wind was calm and the sun was bright on the snow. But no ship sailing for France docked.

Once Annesta told Brenda she wanted to help at the druid camp.

Brenda smiled and asked, "What would your mistress say to that? Did you forget that Christiannt finds it difficult to get around now that she is big with child? And what if a ship bound for France comes while you are gone? You would miss telling Madoc good-bye."

"Pshaw! No ship sails for France in winter storms! Madoc knows that truth and does not go to the wharf anymore. He is in the camp studying, waiting for spring."

Christiannt flew into a tirade when Brenda asked if she was willing to let Annesta go to the druid camp twice a week to help with the ill. "You think I do not need her?" she asked. "I cannot get around by myself. I need her to fetch water, dress me, comb my hair, a hundred things. Druids are a bad influence on a lass her age! They will stuff her head with so many thoughts and ideas that she will go mad or her head will burst open."

"I be not going mad," said Brenda.

"Humpf! You have no sense!"

Druids observed winter solstice, when the sun is farthest south of the earth's center. Madoc learned about Paris and French trading ships. Conlaf studied the spongy gums, pox and nose-bleeds that afflicted sailors.

Brenda was midwife for Christiannt, who, after a prolonged labor, gave birth to a baby boy whose head was large as a grown man's. With his long nose and small chin, he reminded Brenda of a goat. The newborn gave one lusty cry and from then on remained quiet. Christiannt named him Morgan and held her tongue in her cheek when she told everyone that Morgan came two months early. "His wee body had no time to catch up with his head."

On the fourth day after Morgan's birth Brenda stood outside Christiannt's chamber and heard someone speaking in hushed tones. She tapped on the door. "I be nursing," said Christiannt.

Brenda laughed and said, " 'Tis me, Brenda," and went in. Then she understood the hushed voice. Christiannt had been talking to her infant as he cuddled in her arms and nursed. Her face was tear-stained, but she smiled and nodded to the edge of the pallet so that Brenda sat down. The baby made small sucking sounds.

"I be blessed with a good infant," said Christiannt. "He never cries. I was telling him about his brothers, especially about Rhodri, who walked and learned to hold his head up later than most but is a fine soldier now."

Brenda nodded and said she always told her infants things she could not tell anyone else. "I used to talk to my babes before they were born."

"This babe in my arms is not at all what I imagined," said Christiannt. "He dawdles. Look how he nurses, as if he does not know if he is hungry or not. My other babies were rav-enous little coneys." She rocked back and forth, tears slid down her cheeks and the baby's head fell against her arm. He was fast asleep.

"Every woman cries easily after giving birth. 'Tis natural," said Brenda. "You had in mind one kind of babe and you got another. In another day or so, you will love this one as much— no, more than the one you dreamed about."

"The babe in my arms killed the dream that grew under my heart," said Christiannt. "I cannot love him. Not now."

"Do not say that! All mothers love their children."

"What about fathers?"

"Men? They look at their sons or daughters and all they see is something that looks like a hairless worm and is as helpless as a newborn kitten. They try to imagine what the babe might be in a few years. Owain thinks of his sons as potential soldiers and in terms of the glory they will bring to Gwynedd. But a mother knows the heartache of warring, and weeps."

" 'Tis not warring makes me weep," said Christiannt. " 'Tis the power a child can abuse when he becomes an adult. Life is strife and contention, anger and jealousy. Dafydd understands life."

"Where are love and humility?" asked Brenda, running her hand over the silky hair on the baby's head.

"Gone, a spent dream."

When Owain finally came to see Morgan and looked at his overlarge head, he thought it big as a bull's and wondered if the babe might grow into a giant. That would be some warrior! Then he noticed that Morgan's body was puny and he was listless as a damp rag. The nursemaid took Owain aside and told him there was nothing wrong. "Just look at that baby's head of black hair, thick eyebrows, long lashes, long fingernails."

When Owain told her he thought the baby was a mopus, she said, "Your Highness, believe me, Morgan shall be walking by next year's Christ's Mass."

The soft rains came. Then the sun shone warm and yellow, turning the earth into a deep green with the growth of new grass. The oyster catchers brooded their eggs in the rocky shingle of the beach. Squared peats, stacked like hunks of black bread along ditched gashes in the earth, dried in the hot sun. The Aberffraw surf was like thousands of tiny prisms refracting the light into one large multicolored spectrum, dazzling and brilliant. Wildflowers blossomed as a never-ending sea of precious jewels.

Baby Morgan fleshed out with fat arms and legs, smiled and cooed, but he did not roll over or hold his head up. Christiannt said that he was too interested in twisting his tongue and making cooing sounds to be sitting up.

"Give him time," said Brenda, who massaged his arms and legs, bent and straightened his knees, bent and straightened his elbows.

Christiannt told her to stop. "Hold him and sing. He likes that. See him smile? He is such a good babe. He does not need all your fussing with his arms and legs. Father Giff said, 'He shall crawl when God says the time is right.' But he would not sprinkle him with holy water, so I did it myself. Water is water."

The Gwynedd court did not leave Aberffraw for the summer because Christiannt said the trip to Dolwyddelan would be too hard on Morgan.

At the end of sup one evening, Owain left his chair to sit beside Brenda, who was reciting nonsense poems to giggling Annesta and Mona.

He dispensed with any preliminary small talk and said, "I be glad we have not left for Dolwyddelan because a ship, the *Morlo*, is beached on log rollers near the wharf. 'Tis leaving for the Bay of the Seine on the morrow with my two emissaries aboard."

Annesta's words came in a rush. "Are you talking about the ship that Madoc and Conlaf are to take?"

"Aye." Owain turned back to Brenda and said, "Did Llywarch give you the robes and the shoes as I instructed?"

Brenda wiped the palms of her hands on her tunic and swallowed hard. "He gave me two black woolen robes from the rectory in the village and the druids made the lads untanned leather brogues, which they wear already."

"I shall be busy with my troops in the morning," he said. "They must be ready in case English soldiers slip into Gwynedd. You understand, I do not trust Henry. Take the robes to the Aberffraw dock at sunup. Speak the lads' names as you give them their robes. Everyone likes to hear his name spoken in a language he understands best. They are going to a foreign land."

"I will tell them God's speed in Irish and say their names in *Gwyddeleg*." She was glad he had asked her to carry the robes to the lads. Still, she thought it odd that he did not see the lads off himself. For a brief moment she wondered if he knew she was Madoc's mother and was being especially kind to her. But a second thought dispelled that notion. A heaviness filled her breast. Had she not been the one who asked Owain to make Madoc an emissary from Gwynedd to France? How had it come to pass that she wished Madoc would not leave? She looked back at Owain, and her lips pressed together so that none of her concerned words would fly out. " 'Twill be good. The lads will learn patience and responsibility."

"Lugh knows I be taking a chance," Owain said with no smile curling the corners of his mouth. "Young men are prone to let their thoughts be ruled by the fever of their loins instead of the wisdom of their minds."

"Your Highness, your thoughts are wrong," said Annesta quickly. "These lads are reliable. They shall not disappoint you."

"And what do you know about lads?" asked Brenda, perturbed because Annesta had been impolite. It was the older woman's place to speak.

Annesta's face flamed and she hung her head. "I know by their actions that they are honorable," she said.

Owain chuckled deep inside his belly and said, "Lass, you have a tender heart for one of my co-emissaries. I be not wrong about that."

In the first pink of dawn, Brenda stood on the wharf with two black monks' gowns laid neatly side by side over one arm. She was proud that Madoc did not show his excitement by chattering and moving about in a nervous dance like a child. She pulled a gown over his head, letting her hands glide slowly over his damp hair and cool cheeks. "I love you," she whispered, pulling him close so that she heard the crackle of the parchment briefs that were in his tunic pocket.

His face and neck became crimson and he said, "Do not let the sailors onboard see you. They will think I be a sissy to let a women dress me here in front of everyone and whisper in my ear. Where is Prince Owain? He should bring the robes. We are his emissaries."

"He could not come," she said, and turned before he could see the tears spill down her cheeks.

Right away he was sorry he had said anything about his father, who probably had important things to do. "Mona and Annesta will keep you company until we return," he said.

She pulled the other gown over Conlaf's head. He thanked her and smoothed down the sides. "God be with you, milady," he said. "Do you want to say a prayer before we leave?"

Madoc frowned and jabbed Conlaf in the ribs.

Brenda held a hand of each lad and knew by their nervousness that they were excited and apprehensive. She bowed her head and said, "Lord God keep both of these fine lads from harm and Lord Lugh send them across the water and back safely."

"Amen," said Conlaf.

Brenda's breath caught and she said, "Go now and act like monks, or else I shall kiss thee both farewell like small lads leaving their mam for the first time."

Conlaf and Madoc blushed and backed away. "We shall return soon as 'tis possible," promised Madoc, swallowing a lump as large as a hickory nut in his throat.

A smallish, pockmarked man, not the shipmaster, welcomed the monks aboard the *Morlo*, which he said meant sea lion or seal. He pointed to a ladder, told them to go on up and then said, "Hey, no brogues are worn on a ship's deck!"

Brenda watched the crew load sacks of grain, bales of wool, bags of dried plants used for dyes, small-breed Welsh horses bound for Lundy and half a dozen crates of white chickens to be divided between Bardsey and Lundy Islands. The ship was then pushed along log rollers into the water. Half a dozen sailors carried the rollers to the wharf and loaded them onto the ship, then they they jumped aboard just as the *Morlo*'s oarsmen dipped their oars into the water.

The *Morlo* sat low and rocked from side to side. Her planking above the waterline was fastened by wooden nails to naturally bent oak branches called knees. These were fixed to the crossbeams with iron rivets. The rowlocks were fastened with wooden pegs, trenails. She carried a mast and sail, which lay in a groove in the deck.

Madoc's curiosity about the trading ship was so overwhelming that he did not look back at the receding shoreline of the little village of Aberffraw. If he had looked back he would have seen his mother wave.

Her face shone with tears but a smile crept out and bowed her mouth. Her son was alive and not afraid of the adventure that lay ahead.

XVI
Morgan

> The ancients did not see any reason for a strict separation between natural and supernatural diseases. . . . Remedies fortified by spells were said to open and close the bowels, induce vomiting, expel worms and demons, cure fevers, rheumatism, cough, bloody urine, and a plethora of other diseases. Hemorrhages and wounds could be dressed with a mixture of oil, honey, and roasted barley, and covered with fresh meat . . . dung, human urine, natron [sodium carbonate decihydrate] and ostrich eggs."
>
> Lois N. Magner, *A History of Medicine*

Winter and summer passed quietly in Gwynedd's royal courts. At the autumn equinox Christiannt abandoned her motherly chores and let Mona care for Morgan full time. His back bent like a crescent, his arms hung at his sides and he could not stand alone. To give Mona a little time for herself, Brenda worked with the child several afternoons a week. During Samhain festivities, Brenda asked Christiannt to visit the nursery to see his progress. Christiannt refused.

That fall Brenda lanced boils and treated skin infections with poultices of roasted onion or turnip. She treated bleeding gums, which she knew were caused from a steady diet of salted meat and bread, with a rose-hip tea and fresh onions. Some of the ailments she could not cure, such as the swelling usually found in women in the lower front of their neck. These women ate a diet of mutton and boiled grains. Brenda tried medicinal teas made from the flowers of chamomile, elderflower or clover. When that did not diminish the goiter, she tried powdered minerals in wine, and sometimes that helped.

When muddy roads froze and snow hid footpaths, Brenda stayed at the druid camp and reread the Welsh translation of the writings by the German woman Hildegard.

Llieu carefully kept the vellum scrolls hidden from all eyes but druid. Brenda was the one exception, because Llieu knew she would eventually be one of them.

In the Hildegard writings Brenda found that shrimp baked in seaweed was beneficial in decreasing neck swellings. By trial and error and the aid of the little birds that pecked around the edge of a salt-swamp, Brenda found that sea salt dissolved in creek water arrested certain neck-growths and in many cases the swelling subsided. She wished she could discuss her treatment with Hildegard from Bingen. She fancied they were sisters in the art of healing, and even though they did not speak the same language, they would understand one another through signs, drawings, and the handling of herbs and other curative substances.

A dozen times Llieu said the vellum rolls held the first words written by a female healer, who, like Brenda, had a boundless curiosity about natural history. " 'Tis known only by you and trusted druid healers that I have these precious translations, given to me for safekeeping by my father," Llieu said. "Hildegard comes from a tribe of *Teutones* who came to *Cymru* to raise goats, praise the gods and study the heavens, the earth and the seas in peace. New Religionists would destroy the scrolls. 'Twould be good if you would commit them to memory."

Brenda was honored and smiled to herself the rest of the day.

With the Church's movement against druids, it was becoming more and more common for priests to treat the sick, even though they had no formal training in healing and did not know much about what caused diseases. Father Giff was known to sell sick persons amulets, such as an eyetooth he said was from St. James, the younger brother of Jesus, to be worn in a little linen case around the neck to frighten away the devil and bad spirits. He had a clay jar nearly full of eyeteeth from St. James. He told his patients each tooth was ready to bite the hand of the devil who bestowed evil diseases or temptations. For one or two coins he gave his patients tiny ampullae he said contained tears of certain saints. He promised that if the ampullae were worn around a patient's neck, whatever their affliction, it would disappear. He encouraged people with certain illnesses to swallow their own tears or other body fluids to restore their health.

The cold weather moderated, and mothers from nearby crofts waited at the royal gate for Brenda to come out and prescribe herbs and salves for themselves and their ailing children. She was paid in chickens, mutton and flat bread, and found good use for all of it. Often she stopped at Molly's cottage. They talked about everything, from herbs to local customs. Once they argued dandelions versus apple bark to cure the persistent warts on a young male patient. Another time they discussed the intricate details of grafting apple trees to produce sweet red fruit with few worms.

Molly sold her apples in the village, sometimes door to door. She told Brenda that three or four of Owain's soldiers were seen living in the little cottage beside the big oak. "Villagers hope this is Owain's way of stationing retainers among them as a kind of secret lookout. They want protection from the increased attacks from Dafydd's dragons, who look for lone druids to behead." She warned Brenda not to stay in the village after dark, then lowered her voice to a whisper and said, "I sold apples day before yesterday and tapped on the door of the little cottage. I heard voices and thought to sell a full basket to the soldiers inside. When no one answered, I pushed the door open a bit. There in the middle of the day, Lady Christiannt and Sir Lloyd, pink naked as newborn mice, were tangled in bed cloths! Their faces were red as my apples."

"Did Christiannt say anything?" asked Brenda.

Molly chuckled. "Nay, except for me to get out or I would lose my head. Listen, we cannot tell anyone about this because there would be no end to the gossip. Prince Owain would put ye, me and Christiannt in the donjon."

*   *   *

A week later Molly appeared at Brenda's cottage before break-fast. It was warm, and Molly was glad to lay a cloth bag of bark peeled from pruned apple branches on the floor, wipe her face with her skirt and drink a beakerful of water. "Here 'tis, my best cure for warts," she announced. "Tie the inside of the bark against pared-down warts and they disappear overnight."

Brenda hugged her, put the bark on a shelf and took her to the great hall to break fast with cornmeal mush topped with sour cream. They sat at the end of the table, where they would be away from the hot sunshine coming through the open door. After eating, they sipped cottage tea, hot water laced with cream. Molly talked about her children. Then she asked if the two lads who went to France three years ago might have hit the end of the earth, been wrecked and drowned, or decided to live the rest of their lives in France.

"Mercy, put those thoughts out of your head!" said Brenda. "The lads are having an adventure that you and I cannot imag-ine. The gods protect young, enthusiastic lads who are not vain nor selfish. One day we shall hear about it. But if you want something to worry about, have a look at Morgan."

"I heard that the royal laddie cannot stand. He is water-logged," said Molly, tucking a strand of orange-red hair under her kerchief. "When folks talk of him, they click their tongue against their teeth in a sympathetic way. What do ye want me to see?"

"Fat legs that are limp as wilted dandelion stems. No amount of special gruels nor mossy baths strengthen them. I know you well enough so that I can say my mind. This babe has grown so chubby-faced it hides his previous goatish nose. He looks like a bladder of lard with pudgy arms and legs. His back curves like the blade of a sickle and his head lolls from one shoulder to the other."

"Are ye saying that he is a changeling?" asked Molly.

"Of course not!" said Brenda. She laughed so that the cor-ners of her eyes were crinkled with tiny lines. "We have seen babes with mushy muscles. Remember Rhodri was slow to walk, but now he is a dragon soldier. So should I fret over Morgan?"

"Does this laddie who changes from a billy goat to a bladder of lard have a nurse?" asked Molly.

"Mona and I look after him. He is no trouble except he grows heavier each day. He makes soft whimperings and lies quietly in my arms, not moving his head a tum but staring upward. He smiles, drools and coos, with his tongue resting between his lips. When his front teeth came he did not bite, but sucked gentle, same as a newborn." Brenda's brow furrowed. "I stand him on his fat pink feet and his ankles turn in and he topples facedown to his belly. Then his arms and legs wave, like a bug on its belly in water. He does not crawl like ordinary children. He pulls himself forward by his arms, not up on his hands and knees. Christiannt told Mona to put him over the garderobe so that his bedclothes stay halfway clean. The poor thing has no idea what to do at the garderobe. I believe Christiannt hides her true thoughts about this laddie. She pretends he is smarter than all her other sons, but she does not come to the nursery to hold him."

"Mothers do that," said Molly. "What do ye think is wrong with Morgan? Is he an ogre? Or a troll?"

"I do not know," said Brenda, shrugging her shoulders and wiping the perspiration from her face. "I have never seen an ogre nor a troll. But since he was born, he has not cried out loud but once. Mayhap one cry was all that the gods stored in his wee breast. Although he has lots of feeble mewlings. That is not normal. Healthy babies cry."

"Does Owain visit the nursery and say anything about this laddie being a leader? Ye know, like the bragging he did before Morgan was born."

"He has not visited Morgan for months. Last year Owain told me Morgan was either a throwback to some lumpish Celt on Christiannt's side or—and he made a crooked face when he said this: 'I know Christiannt well enough to wonder if Morgan is related to one of my low-bred soldiers.' Even Owain is not so blind that he cannot or will not see that Morgan resembles none of his other offspring."

"But then Rhodri never looked like Owain," said Molly, looking out of the corner of one eye at Brenda.

Brenda looked around to make sure no one was near

enough to hear their words, took a deep breath and said, "Owain would kill Lloyd if he found Morgan was his."

Molly twisted a strand of her hair and leaned closer to Brenda. "Christiannt wears breeks, a shirt under her tunic, like a soldier. She shares a tent with other women who dress the same and follow Lord Howell's troops on practice maneuvers to Llyn Coron. From those visits, she learns where and when Lord Howell's army will be awarring. When she comes back, she talks with Lord Dafydd. I know, because I heard her talking with one of Dafydd's soldiers outside the bailey." Molly's voice dropped so low Brenda barely heard her ask, "Is he a curse?"

"You know Lord Dafydd is a curse."

"I mean Morgan. I mean a living curse for both Christiannt and Owain. The gods vent their mischief in the rifts of human relationships," said Molly, drawing her brows together. "'Twas mischief against Owain when Christiannt married him."

Molly had just given voice to the terrible conclusion that Brenda had thought of many times but had kept hidden in the bottom of her soul. She had put into words the dark fear that Brenda had never talked about, even with a trusted friend, until today. Underneath her breastbone lodged the fear that Morgan could, in some terrible way, turn Owain's court upside down.

"When Mona sits with Morgan on a blanket in the morning sunlight, Owain walks by," said Brenda. "The look on Owain's face would shatter your heart. I wish I could do something for the laddie."

"Ye mean something for Owain," said Molly with a smile. She put her hand on Brenda's arm. "I see what ye are thinking plain as daylight. If ye can heal the laddie, ye think Owain will be grateful and grant ye the favor of a trip to Ireland to see yer children and father. Tell me I be wrong!"

Brenda felt foolish. She looked at Molly for a long moment until their eyes met and then she thought, Of course Molly is right. If she can read my face, what do I have to say? 'Twould be nice to visit my two children and my father. And Sein— do I long to see him? Mayhap! But I cannot go. I must wait

until Madoc returns. I have to know the lad is safe. Then—
mayhap.

The following winter, winds brought snow that piled deep
around the Aberffraw castle walls. It nearly covered the low
cottages in the bailey. Brenda kept a path swept from her door
to Llywarch's and to the great hall. At night she watched the
aurora borealis stream in green and yellow luminous bands.
Sometimes a plum-colored curtain lay across the dark sky and
she thought of the time when she was young and in love with
Prince Owain. During the days she and Archdruid Llieu
treated crofters and their families who were wounded by
dragon soldiers. A wife of one of the decapitated crofters told
Brenda a grisly story.

With tears in her eyes, she said, "Mistress, I love Gwynedd,
with her tall grasses and purple thistles, where the marbled
white butterfly resides, and her short grasses with wildflowers,
where the spider orchid grows. But when the snow melts I
cannot look closely into the beautiful grassland, the gorse
groves, the thick heather hedges and timberland of my homeland, because there will be headless skeletons hidden in all
those places. Our sacred wells are defiled with the heads of
our dead men. The water is unfit for the living to drink."

Brenda wondered if the woundings and killings were done
equally by Dafydd and his dragons, and Father Giff and his
New Religionists. No one seemed to know exactly where to
place the blame.

The crofters, fearing reprisal from the Church, were closed-
mouthed. Owain traveled from village to village in Gwynedd
to announce that it was unlawful for any of his soldiers to
maim or kill crofters or their families, whether they had druidic honor marks or not. If a Gwynedd soldier disobeyed,
Owain promised that both the soldier's hands would be cut
off at the elbow. Howell's soldiers joined with Owain's and
camped in the Aberffraw outer bailey, where the troops drilled
together. Their pipers' sounds echoed back and forth during
the day. When Owain heard several reports that Dafydd had
been seeing Father Giff and now they openly aligned them-

selves with King Henry the Second, he and Howell prepared their troops for an English invasion of Gwynedd.

Morgan was four years old and no longer let himself be held. He was like a soldier compelled to perfect his drill. He drove himself to use his legs, to walk, to run, to jump. Christiannt was astonished when she saw him and told Mona to let him wander through the castle, or out into the bailey.

"I should go with him," said Mona.

"Morgan is like a pet dog. He will be back when he is hungry," said Christiannt.

Each day Mona watched him get up early and go to the outer bailey, where he was close to the creak of the pipers' bags and could see the drones exposed behind the pipers' arms. He called the pipes *wyn*, which made Mona smile, because they actually did look like some small struggling animal, a lamb, under the pipers' arms. By grunts and hand signs he showed her he loved their music and wanted to be a piper.

One warm day outside the great hall, the knight, Sir Lloyd, saw Brenda working with Morgan on his vocabulary and came over to say a few words. He stared at Morgan and said he had never heard the laddie speak before. Another time he remarked about the thickness of Morgan's shoulders. Brenda smiled and said he exercised to be fit as a piper. Lloyd asked Brenda's permission to teach him to throw small sticks and stones on target.

"He is more interested in becoming a piper than a stone-thrower," she said.

Lloyd put his hands over his ears at the word *piper*, said he hated the squeaky sounds and bent down to ask Morgan if he would like to throw stones at the center of a target.

Clear as a bubbling brook, Morgan said, "Aye, also blow pipes."

Brenda asked Christiannt what she thought about Lloyd teaching Morgan to throw.

" 'Twill give the laddie something to do, something to look forward to," said Christiannt. "Frankly, 'tis better than a squealing pipe."

" 'Tis a thing lads learn without a teacher, and has to be curbed in most cases," said Brenda.

Another day Lloyd was blunt and told Brenda that he planned to wean Morgan from the castle, foster him when he was seven and take him out on practice army skirmishes. He gave Morgan three spearlike sticks to show Brenda how good he was at throwing. "He is a born soldier." Lloyd bragged about the force and precision Morgan had in his arms. "The enemy, whoever 'tis, will be surprised by the powerful hurlings from one wee, hunchbacked laddie."

"This laddie wants to be a piper," said Brenda.

"Naw," said Lloyd. "He does not know yet what he wants. He is my way to a higher rank." Lloyd told Brenda how pretty she looked early in the morning, when most maids were dull with sleep.

Brenda wondered how Christiannt could stand this man who thought of his small son as nothing more than a warring tool, like a javelin or battle-ax.

That evening Owain sat on the bench beside Brenda after supper, saying he wanted her to listen to his ideas. "I have seen my wife talking with Sir Lloyd and Father Giff on more than one occasion. 'Tis said they both come from Chester and are Englishmen. If I verify their English ties, I shall have Lloyd dismissed and ban Giff from coming to the castle on the grounds that they are English spies."

Brenda sat perfectly still and said she could not argue with that idea.

"Now comes the big idea I want you to hear," Owain said. "I saw Morgan throwing stones at a battered shield. I was amazed at the accuracy of his aim. So I spoke with him and said he would make a fine soldier. He did not remember me and mumbled gibberish. I thought he was unable to speak, but Mona had him rhyme words and said you taught him."

Brenda smiled, held her back stiff, and waited for Owain to tell her his "big idea."

"For days I have been thinking what Morgan, hunched over like an old man, could do with a sword," he said. "With such strong shoulders, he surely would have a powerful thrust. By the time the lad is ten or twelve, he might truly be an unusual swordsman. I want you to teach him to speak well. You are one of the best healers in Gwynedd, according to Archdruid Llieu. When the lad is seven, I will foster him to a swordsman and in another couple of years Gwynedd will have an army with a surprise weapon, an unbelievable fighter: a hunch-backed laddie."

"What did Christiannt say about this?" asked Brenda.

"She wants to send him to a priest in Holyhead; someone Father Giff suggested, who is a mystic and able to put words in people's mouths. I told her I would never leave my son with a New Religionist. She surprised me by saying that Sir Lloyd wanted to foster him." Owain let out a little explosion of air through his mouth. "If I forbid my wife to send Morgan to a mystic-priest in Holyhead, you can be sure as rain that I will never let that Anglophile Sir Lloyd get his hands on him."

"Of course not!" said Brenda, feeling her blood boil. "This mystic performs the stunt of speaking from the belly, throwing out his voice so it seems a baby or even a chair can speak well."

"I inquired about Giff's recent activities myself," said Owain. "He organized a group of New Religionists to destroy Old Religionists. He believes in purifying the land for New Religionists. 'Tis barbaric! We have to watch that man."

Brenda made a funny noise in her throat.

"Do not get tied in a frenzy," he said. "Just tell me if you can teach Morgan to speak clearly."

For years both Lloyd and Owain had shunned Morgan. Now that the laddie could throw stones in a straight line, they were both interested. Brenda drew in her breath, held it for nine heartbeats, then let it out. "So you would take a lad who wants more than anything to be a piper and make him a soldier in your army?" She stared at Owain, who glowered back. Suddenly she loathed the smell of him, the unwashed sweat and the leather breeches. She scowled, closed her eyes and wondered if she could control her rage.

"I order you to be Morgan's tutor before I let my sword-master friend on Holyhead foster him," said Owain calmly. "Keep Morgan out of the hands of Lloyd and Giff."

His voice piqued her. She was not going to trot tame as a trained hound when Owain signaled the order. "Morgan is as stubborn as you." She snorted. "He takes his own time to learn. It took so long to work strength into his arms and legs that Christiannt forgot she had given me permission. When she remembered, she thought mayhap I used sorcery. If Morgan learns to talk, will you forget that it was both he and I who struggled with the learning? Like misted breath in winter air, I bet your memories vanish and you will claim Morgan's good speech was learned from you." The words came out easy but raspy like dull knives, and they were not what she wanted to say at all. Her fiery rage had cooled and her blood seemed ice-cold.

"Nonsense." Owain cracked his knuckles. "I know you do not pursue private heavens. When you reason, you use the cause-and-effect relations of nature. You heal with known, natural laws. You do not need mumbo jumbo nor magic charms. I know you. You can give knowledge through language to the laddie. Do it for me."

"What would Christiannt say?" Brenda puckered her lips.

"She believes you are jealous because I married her," said Owain.

"She still comes to me with whiny problems," said Brenda. "Would she truly like her laddie trained to hunt and kill pagans? The laddie wants to be a piper."

"Morgan is too young to know what he wants," said Owain, putting an arm around her shoulder. "My wife knows you did her a favor when you put strength into Morgan's arms and legs."

"Milord! I did that for Morgan!" Brenda pushed him away.

"When I wish, I shall take Morgan, who belongs to me, to do with as I see fit. If my wife interferes, I shall have our marriage annulled. Because of our marriage I be excommunicated from the Church by Archbishop Becket! Lady Christiannt, daughter of Goronwy ap Owain ap Edwina, cannot forget that we are cousins in a marriage that is illegal; thought unnatural by some, incestuous by Church law." Owain raised his fist.

Brenda thought he was about to strike her and moved with

her head tucked between hunched shoulders. When nothing happened she looked up, but there was no blame, no ill will or desire to harm her in his eyes. He looked at her for several moments, then said, "Christiannt does not care about me nor Morgan. Take the laddie under your wing, teach him to talk, to communicate and think logically. Afterwards I shall take you to Ireland to see your—our two children and your father."

Brenda's mouth gaped. This was what she had wanted for so long. This was a true gift. Was it? She should thank him. She said nothing.

He grunted and walked away.

It was true what he had said, Brenda mused. Christiannt would be glad to see either Owain or Morgan go.

For four years Christiannt had pretended, in Owain's presence, to love the lad. Then this very afternoon, before supper and Brenda's talk with Owain, she had shown the absolute depth of her feeling. "Morgan is a swag-bellied, hunchbacked dwarf," she had said to Brenda. "I hate him. Lloyd has told me a bloody, rotten story that I cannot repeat to Father Giff, but I have to tell someone or I will burst. Lloyd said I ought to know about his *brawd*, brother, who is like Morgan. His brother learned to walk and talk later than most. His mother kept him in Lloyd's bed closet. At night he was tied to the pallet with leather straps because he had powerful tantrums. When he was five, he was strong enough to smash furniture and faces. They called him *Demon*. Lloyd was afraid to sleep beside his brother, so he joined Gwynedd's army."

Brenda's stomach pinched and she had to sit down. She wondered how a mother could name her child Demon.

"After that I looked at Morgan with different eyes," Christiannt had said. "I thought both Owain and Lloyd offered me a wonderful gift, in the form of an opportunity to get rid of him. However, I did not want either man to know that worry and fear about Morgan made me brittle. I was sorely tempted to let one of them teach him soldiering, even if his future shall be death by the sword. Morgan is a disgusting child. He is not normal. To be rid of him would be a great pleasure."

"Morgan could be a piper," Brenda said. "He is not some

monster. You could find someone to teach him. Pipers join
the army, but they do not use swords."

Christiannt's head shook. "No matter. In the end, one of
his fathers, Sir Lloyd or Prince Owain, who both hate pipers,
would take him away to be a child-soldier, a warring-hurler.
Mayhap Morgan could be happy to be the best stone-thrower
in all of Wales." In a whisper she added, "If he just goes away,
I shall be happy."

XVII
Mystery

The castle's many toilets, called garderobes, were located in the curtain wall and were reached by narrow passages. Each garderobe was lit by a small window or arrow loop. The seat was simply a slab of stone with a round hole cut in it. Along the outer curtain the seat was supported on corbels and projected out beyond the face of the wall. The garderobes of the inner curtain were often grouped together over vertical shafts either within the wall or built against it. These led to a cesspit at the foot of the wall which had to be periodically cleaned out.

David Macaulay, *Castle*

On a Sunday morning Brenda went to the nursery. Before opening the door she overheard Mona and Christiannt talking loudly inside.

"Milady," said Mona, "I cannot find the laddie. I looked for him hiding behind the cupboards and such. But he is not there. He has disappeared like sea mist. Poof!"

"Never mind!" thundered Christiannt. "He is hiding somewhere, laughing at us. He crawled out from the quilt you wrapped him in and left this. *Edrych!* Look! Poor laddie must be cold on the bottom end without his diaper cloth. Mona, what good are you? You saw he was asleep when you came from the great hall last night. You giggled. Said you and Brenda had a little mead during sup."

Mona sniffed. "Milady, Brenda had naught."

"I would say you had more than a little! I expect you to

watch my laddie, to keep your eyes open, hang on to him, and not let him wander."

"Milady, I do my best, but he is stronger now, you know. He goes where he wants. You said he could roam the castle. He—he refuses to use the night-pot and climbs to the garderobe alone."

Brenda went into the nursery.

Mona cowered in a corner holding Morgan's diaper cloth. Her face was wet with tears and her lips trembled.

"What is the trouble?" asked Brenda.

Christiannt pointed her finger. "Mona slept beside Morgan and now he is gone."

"Did you look in the garderobes?" asked Brenda.

Christiannt grabbed Brenda's arm. Her throat turned pink and a light flush spread across her cheeks, but her watery blue eyes looked straight at Brenda's. "Not yet. We—ah, Mona just discovered him gone—missing."

They walked single file up the narrow steps inside the thick stone curtain-wall until they stood inside the well-used garderobe above the nursery. The morning light came through the small window and lit their faces with a silvery glow.

"Naught here," said Christiannt. She reached for the diaper cloth that Mona held against her breast, glanced up, and saw Brenda watching. She pulled her hand back, dropped her eyes, and flushed deeply. A small bunch of wilted meadow flowers lay on the cold, stone slab.

"He gathered 'em yesterday next to the bailey wall. I took him for a walk," said Christiannt. "Later he cried when he lost 'em." She choked back tears and waved the diaper cloth in front of Mona's nose and whispered, " 'Tis clean. The laddie never wet it. The last time he ran away—you remember—I found him here, in the garderobe. This time where did he go? To the bailey wall for more flowers?"

They left the garderobe, went down the dark, narrow stairs back to the nursery. Christiannt made a noise in her throat and said, "Brenda, you are the wizard who does not need to be in the same room to make someone or something talk. Mayhap you can make someone disappear."

"Fie! You know I be not a wizard," said Brenda.

Mona lay down on the pallet to show how she slept with her arm over the child huddled inside the rolled-up quilt.

Christiannt looked behind the washstand and shook her head. "Not here." She looked at the little bunch of flowers in her hand. Then with no warning her face became white with rage. She crumbled the pitiful flowers and threw them into the washbasin.

Mona sat up, took off her apron, and offered it to Christiannt to wipe the flower stains off her hands.

"Mona, I could choke you with your own apron," cried Christiannt. "Surely for the sake of the Lord God, Holy Mary and the Infant Jesus you could have done something!"

"I loved the laddie like he was my own wee brother," said Mona, her eyes red and teary. "See there, when I woke I found the empty quilt rolled around his diaper cloth. I be not a sound sleeper. I should know if he slipped out. I know naught!" She flung her arms out.

"You said you had a mead-sleep," said Christiannt. Her icy eyes met Mona's with a question. "If you had too much mead how could you know what happened?"

Mona flushed as though she had been slapped and tears ran down her cheeks. "I would know. That is the way 'tis."

Brenda watched Christiannt shrug her shoulders. There was something wrong, but she could not put her finger on it. She looked at the empty pallet where the lad had slept and wondered if either Lloyd or Owain had taken him. She looked from Mona, whose shoulders shook with sobbing, to Christiannt, whose hands shook but whose eyes were dry. Christiannt's child was missing and she was dry-eyed. Why? Was she in shock and acting in a contrary manner? Or did she know something that she did not tell?

Mona held out the diaper cloth and said in a sad voice, "This is all we have. Was he carried off by spirits? It can happen. A woman in the village had a laddie who was carried off by a big bird. She never saw him again. Never."

The castle was turned upside down and inside out as everyone searched for Morgan; in the meadows, in the barns, on the hillsides among the sheep, near the sacred wells, streams and lakes. The royal caravan did not go to Dolwyddelan for the summer so that everyone might look for Morgan around Aberffraw.

Christiannt continued to accuse Mona of being careless and letting the lad wander alone at night. Next Christiannt blamed Brenda, who had taught Morgan to do the impossible: to walk and to talk.

Brenda said it was something she had to do and wondered how his talking had anything to do with his disappearance. She suspected that Christiannt had bragged to Lloyd how well the lad could talk, and she told herself there was a simple explanation for the lad's disappearance. But what was it? Mona was heartbroken and innocent and prayed the lad was being cared for wherever he was.

Brenda talked to Owain and a handful of his soldiers about searching for Morgan throughout the inner and outer baileys. "Look for breaks in the wall. See if a small child could squeeze outside. Talk to the guards, crofters and traders. Mona and I will talk to the villagers."

Owain went to Father Giff and asked him to have his parishioners look in their barns and sheep pens. He told Archdruid Llieu to have crofters watch for a wee, bent-over lad in their fields. No sign of the child was found and Owain, with a long face, admitted defeat.

When Christiannt blamed Mona once too often for Morgan's disappearance, Owain told her to hold her tongue. Christiannt said Mona had to be punished. "I say cut both her hands off for not holding on to our precious laddie," she said.

Certain that Mona was innocent, Owain sent her to resume being Brenda's handmaiden.

Lloyd organized soldiers with rakes to search the cesspits. Christiannt complained that the sight of rakes scraping around in the cesspits made her ill. She told Lloyd that a child like Morgan would never go out of his way to a garderobe. "He only used the one above the nursery."

Brenda missed the pudgy hunchbacked lad and was reminded over and over of her frantic, hollow feeling when wee Ailin had disappeared. She knew how true it was that a laddie might disappear with no one seeing him. She slept fitfully while pieces of her life buzzed around in her mind.

A month after Morgan disappeared, Owain had word that English troops gathered outside of Chester ready to invade Wales. Owain and Howell prepared their combined armies to leave for Hawarden, next to the Welsh-English border, to drill.

Brenda asked Owain if he was going to send word to the king of France to help Wales against the coming English invasion.

"With English troops gathering at the Welsh border, traders are less wont to come to Welsh towns and seaports," Owain said. "I hope that Louis already has the word about what is happening on the border. Every day I pray he hates the English as much as I think he does. Mayhap my emissaries are on their way home and they bring some word from Louis. One thing I remember is that he has a troublesome habit of putting off unpleasant actions until some future date."

Christiannt moped around, blaming Mona less and Brenda more for the disappearance of her lastborn. Once, standing by the outer bailey fence to watch a flock of birds pass over, she told Brenda that she'd had a dream. "In my dream you took Morgan close to the sea. The sand was warm and you let him wade out where the water was cool. The waves closed over him and he could not touch the bottom. The sun was gone and it was dark. You left him and looked for the shore. Next morning I found him on the sand. He was white as a water lily. His back was straight. His legs were slim and his lips were pale as the quarter moon. Red worms crawled out of his eyes." She screamed like a crazy person, "Oh God! You let him die!" and reached for Brenda's face with her long fingernails.

Brenda held tight onto Christiannt's hands and told her to pray. "Listen, God will tell you I know not what happened to your son. You must leave the past and find yourself facing the morrow."

"Nay, Father Giff tells me that Death is not only at the end of life, Death hangs around pulling and squeezing. Do you feel it? I do and I be tired of Death's embrace."

Brenda let go of Christiannt's hands and told her to go to

her chamber. "Sleep. No one will disturb you until you are ready to awake to a fresh morrow."

Summer was done. The grass was gold and the weather was windy, cold and rainy. One day the rain became snow. The next day the snow melted and the sandy road through Aberffraw was a small rivulet of brown water mixed with fallen orange-colored rowan berries. Red and yellow leaves floated on top of the rushing water.

Brenda put on high-top brogues and went to see Llieu. She said that Owain was spending too much time away from his home court. "He needs to spend more time with Christiannt. There is something strange and brooding about her. She talks incessantly about the many ways she grieves for her lost laddie. Her eyes are clear, not red-rimmed from crying. Is her sadness genuine, or is it attention-getting? Is she pretending to drown her sadness in mead until she is squiffy as a piper?"

"Owain has a duty to protect not only his province but also the rest of Wales from the anticipated English incursion," said Llieu. "You of all people must know that Wales comes first with him. Reassure Christiannt that she is loved. She is the wife of a prince and so has a duty to the people. Make her feel important. But never close your eyes, nor your ears. Listen to her sniffling and she may tell you something."

Brenda nodded, then said that Owain seemed preoccupied or forgetful. "Before he went to Hawarden, he searched for days for Morgan and could not remember the laddie's name."

Her words made Llieu laugh and say, "My dear, how many sons does the man have? Two dozen, more or less? And he is getting older. We are all destined to take the road's last turn one day and become forgetful. 'Tis one of the most unexpected things to happen to a man. 'Tis not a crime, but 'tis incurable."

"I never think of him as old," said Brenda. "Although I have seen his hair go from gold to silver. If I thought of him as old, I would have to think of myself as aging. Actually, I came to trade you some dried figs for camphor balls."

"I have no more camphor balls," said Llieu, laughing. "I had patients with coughs when the weather turned cold. With no camphor, I told them to put a clove of garlic in a silver or pewter locket around their neck and take a tiny nip once or twice a day. Garlic wards off coughing." ·

It was Brenda's turn to laugh. "Garlic in a locket? 'Tis strange how people believe in charms. The locket works as well as the garlic. I too have seen such cures."

"My dear, did you forget what I told you long ago?" said Llieu. His eyes sparkled with amusement. "Nature heals more things than we give her credit for. Give a patient with catarrh nothing and usually he is well in two weeks. Give him a charm and he credits you with the healing in fourteen days. Thus you have made a follower of your healing. Honestly, garlic helps."

On the way back to the castle Brenda stopped at the cottage of a silversmith to inquire about a small locket to hold a clove of garlic. The smith gave her a locket and promised to make her two more if she would cure his wife of snoring. Brenda said she would try, but could promise no lasting cure.

When she came out of the cottage, she bent into the wind, which promised rain or sleet. She shuddered with the cold and found herself still looking here and there for a small, hunched child—for Morgan. The yellow leaves, fallen days ago from the cottonwoods, were blowing about in little swirls on the wet, sandy ground. The day became dark early this time of year, but now it was darker than usual because of the heavy clouds. She hurried to reach the castle gate before dark.

That night at sup she gave Christiannt a silver pomander-locket containing garlic. "This is to keep you from becoming consumptive," she said. "Your cough can lead to another sickness, then another. Each is worse than the first. Stop worrying about things that are out of your hands. If Morgan is nearby, he will be found."

Christiannt was touched by the gift and wondered what Brenda wanted from her. "For troth, I worry more about Owain," she said. "Suppose there is a war with the English?"

"See, that is what I mean. If there is a war, we will do what has to be done. Until we know something, 'tis best to take care of our health and enjoy the days that are sent us."

"This is the worst of days," said Christiannt, coughing. "God is angry. I feel His cold, wet blast every time the wind blows. If Owain were here he would fain fix my window. The shutters are loose and snow may blow in by morning."

"You ask one of the menservants to fix your window," said Brenda. "You are the Mistress of Gwynedd, Prince Owain's wife."

Owain surprised them and came home in a cold rain while sup was served. He stood close to the fireplace in the great hall and announced between coughs that an English invasion of Hawarden had been nipped in the bud. "The English planned more than a cattle raid, but when they saw the number of our Welsh troops along the border they hightailed it for home." He went directly to his chamber without sup, and without seeing anyone.

Christiannt followed him, but a short time later returned to the great hall with her eyes swollen and red.

"Look at Christiannt," said Llywarch, who sat next to Brenda. "She finally found the tears to mourn the loss of her laddie."

"She went to see Owain," said Brenda. "He said something that upset her. Mayhap he told her to stop moaning over Morgan's disappearance. He is tired of her whining and so be I."

"You begin to see people in their true light," said Llywarch. "Watch her. See, she sits down. Look how she holds her head and how her shoulders move. She is tense and glances at Owain's empty chair. She wishes he was supping. She would like the maids she sits with to think she is enjoying herself by giving them the pleasure of her company." He lowered his voice to a whisper. "I have to tell you that I saw Christiannt and Morgan, clear as two peas in watery soup, walking close to the wall when I left sup the evening he disappeared. 'Twas twilight and I saw the laddie picking flowers. Christiannt says the laddie was asleep at that time. You and I know Christiannt can make up a lie when the truth sounds better. Now look. She squirms, gets up and sits again. She is up. She is uncomfortable. She looks at you. Be careful."

"Christiannt told us she put Morgan to bed. Mona said she lay down with her arm around the bundled quilt believing him there," said Brenda.

"Aye, but it may be that only Morgan's dry diaper towel was rolled in the quilt."

Brenda raised her eyebrows and felt a dryness in her throat. "You think Morgan was gone before Mona came back from her sup?"

"That is what I think," said Llywarch.

"Christiannt knows something she is not telling," said Brenda. "What about Owain?"

Llywarch reached out and touched her hand. "Owain is a pragmatist and never had much hope for the laddie, except mayhap as a stone-thrower in his army. He wanted the baby's life snuffed out at birth."

"What about Sir Lloyd?"

"He seems to know naught."

"Morgan was learning to put words together," said Brenda. "He could have amounted to something. Is it my fault? I told Owain that Morgan said a few words but I did not want him to get too excited about the lad's accomplishments."

"Not your fault and do not think that way. Christiannt was half afraid of the laddie." Llywarch's eyes closed. "Because he was so unlike other children."

Brenda nodded and suddenly thought of Lloyd's brother lying bound to his pallet.

"What do you think is happening in her mind?" said Llywarch.

Brenda told Llywarch about Christiannt's dream where the red worms crawled out of Morgan's eyes. "I do not believe he lives on this side," she said. "He has lived on the Otherside for several months."

"Uumm." Llywarch's mouth was set in a firm line. "Can you see there is a hardness in her face?"

Brenda looked at Christiannt, who was talking overloud, waving her hands and laughing when no one else laughed. She was not certain about the hardness.

Llywarch sighed and excused himself. "Come with me and I will show you something ironic."

Brenda nodded, got up and went out into the blustery rain with him. On the way she heard footsteps running behind her. She turned and through the grayness saw Annesta wave.

When Annesta caught up, she was bubbly and full of news. "Guess what? Owain will not have Christiannt in his bed!"

"Granddaughter! Is that a sad rumor?" asked Llywarch, blowing on his fingers for warmth.

"Nay, 'tis for troth," said Annesta. "Christiannt asked him for another child to take Morgan's place." Annesta's teeth chattered and she was nearly out of breath. "She told us maids she promised Owain the next son would be as wise as Dafydd. Owain blew up and said she has had all she deserves. And just because she thought Dafydd was wise did not mean that he, Owain, thought the same. She said that Brenda did not like her and must have planted a dislike for Dafydd in Owain's mind. And I spoke up and said 'twas not true. I said, 'Christiannt, you are Dafydd's mam and you certainly can remember the dastardly deeds that came from Lord Dafydd when he was a lad.' Christiannt said Brenda kept Dafydd's childish antics alive by reminding people about them. She said Brenda was jealous of her being the wife of Prince Owain. She showed us a garlicky silver pomander on a chain and said it was a charm to put a death spell on her, and you gave it to her."

"I did," said Brenda, "but 'twas a gift to ward off a cough. I told her to take small bites of the garlic inside. She suffers from catarrh. She needs rest."

Llywarch paced back and forth, muttering about women standing in the rain.

"But you must listen to this," said Annesta. "Christiannt said Brenda wants Owain to think that Morgan is not his child, so mayhap she did something—put a spell on Morgan that made him disappear."

Brenda looked at Llywarch, who shrugged and looked back at Annesta. "Why does Christiannt torment me with falsehoods?" Brenda's lips quivered.

Llywarch said, "I told you, Christiannt knows something, but she is not ready to tell it. We shall wait, but not in this cold rain."

In his cottage he wiped his face and head with a linen cloth, handed it to Brenda, who used it and handed it to Annesta. He told Annesta to put her apron by the fire to dry and to get his latest carving. Then he sat in his chair, folded his hands in his lap and said words that Brenda could not understand. She supposed they were ancient Celtic and had something to do with what he was going to show her.

Annesta brought out a little whistle made from a willow branch. It was tied to a braided flax thong so it could be worn around the neck. There were lines and curlicues carved on it around the three holes. Annesta put it around her neck and lifted it to her lips. She blew and made three loud notes. The notes were shrill but pleasant. She thought they could be heard all over the castle and through the baileys. She smiled, blew and tried to make a tiny tune with three notes.

" 'Twas a birthday gift for Morgan," said Llywarch. "He wandered in and out of the castle rooms and I thought 'twould make Mona feel easier if he would give a blow when he needed to find his way back to the nursery. His blankets are cold, the dry diaper towel lost his smell and in my mind's eye I never saw him blowing my whistle. 'Tis irony. The gods gave him no chance to see if he could play a tune, and they laugh at our seriousness. The joke is on us, who believed he was safe from destiny."

"Destiny?" asked Annesta.

"Aye, you know destiny is something that each person— you, Morgan or me—creates. One destiny may be intertwined with another, such as a mother and son, or lovers. It may be preordained from a force we do not understand. 'Tis a mystery."

XVIII
Consanguinity

Owain's second spouse ... was the cause of much dis-
unity in the ranks of Gwynedd as well as the disapproval
of the Church. Chrisiant, daughter of Goronwy ab
Owain ab Edwina, was Owain's first cousin, so the marriage was in fact illegal and regarded by the Church in
those days as incestuous. Owain's defiance of the
Church's ban on such a union resulted in his excom-
munication by Thomas à Beckett, Archbishop of Canterbury.

Richard Deacon, *Madoc and the Discovery of America*

The rain stopped for the week of Samhain, which inaugurated
winter. It was the return of chaos, meaning bad weather, in
the air, on the land and on the sea. Much of the uncanniness
of Samhain Eve, when man was powerless in the hands of
fate, would prevail until spring. It was a *puca* time when the
spirits escaped from the burial mounds so that the dead were
abroad in a more real sense than at regular times.

On the morning of Samhain Eve, Owain had a white heifer
slaughtered and roasted over an open pit. The pieces were
passed out to those who gathered around.

Christiannt left Owain's side and spoke to Llywarch, saying
that she could not remember Morgan ever eating roasted
heifer, or asking for it. "I do not believe he ever saw a white
heifer. You pagans keep everything to yourselves." She
seemed to make it the bard's fault that Morgan had missed so
much in his short lifetime. "I say 'tis a crime. And if pagans
are not going to share their knowledge with the rest of us they
are not fit to live."

"My lady," said Llywarch, struggling with his words. "You cannot mean what you say."

"What are you saying, Christiannt?" asked Brenda, who was with Mona and Annesta. "Llywarch is your favorite harper. Remember how he played everything you wanted at your wedding?"

"I be saying New Religionists are correct in striking the death knell on Old Religionists. I be coaxing Owain to make Father Giff his adviser instead of Gwalchmai or Llywarch. Father Giff can read the stars."

Owain heard her and his face turned dark. "Giff is a gull for King Henry! Wife, do not speak of ignorant treachery. It does not become you. You understand as well as anyone that druids are not pagans. They are peaceable and share their knowledge, if asked. The peace and knowledge of the world is lessened each time a druid dies."

Christiannt looked at her husband, drew a deep breath and let it out slowly. "Ppfftt!" She stalked away with Owain following her.

"Lady Christiannt grows more potty each day," whispered Mona. "She prowls around the garderobes like she is hunting treasures."

"Hunting?" asked Brenda.

"Aye," said Mona. "Annesta and I found her with a mortar-maker's hoe poking into the cesspit at the back of the castle—you know, above the nursery. She hid the hoe in the pit and acted like she was on a walk hunting wildflowers near the bailey wall. I cannot imagine what she intended."

"How sickening! And shameless!" said Brenda.

"The cesspits were cleaned months ago," said Llywarch.

Brenda wondered about Christiannt's mind. Was it buzzing with hidden guilt, or was it stinging from the whisperings of her odd behavior?

After the feast, Llieu touched Brenda's shoulder and whispered, "We druids want you to be one of us. Molly is a novice. She is studying druid philosophy and I told her I would ask you to study with her."

"I do not know what to say. I would like to, if the time is right," she said.

" 'Tis prophesied that my fosterlings, the emissaries, will soon wear honor marks," whispered Llieu. "And there is Sein in Ireland, who has been given new marks for keeping everyone well and alive last winter in his camp."

"How long have you known this?"

"All summer, and now 'tis time for you to know," said Llieu.

"If the emissaries are to become druids, then logic tells me they will return well and safe," whispered Brenda. "Thank you for that."

The following day Brenda was summoned to the great hall, where Owain awaited her. "I have a message from my friend Thomas of London," he said. "The brief was written two months ago and I cannot think straight because of the tangled consequences. I need you to hear my thoughts."

She nodded, sat by the fire and waited for him to continue.

"You know that I be excommunicated from the Church because I married a first cousin. I cannot attend the church in Aberffraw, or anywhere else, but that is of no consequence to me. The Old Religion is more satisfying. However, I have been disturbed that I cannot be entombed beside my father in Saint Dafydd's Cathedral in Bangor. When I told Christiannt, she was furious and, unbeknownst to me, she sent a messenger to Thomas in Canterbury saying that I have every right to be interred next to my father. In nine days Thomas is coming to Aberffraw to make it as clear as his tongue can make it that when I die my body can be preserved on Bangor's holy grounds, *only if*"—he hesitated—"only if, at the time of interment I be not married to my cousin. What do I tell Christiannt?"

"Do you wish to remain her spouse?"

"It is not a matter of my wish. I must not let her be out of my sight nor hearing. She is more dangerous to Gwynedd than King Henry."

"M'lord, surely you exaggerate. Christiannt is just Christiannt; we all know her. Thomas of London is still a true friend?"

"The truest."

"Then my thought would be to trust him," said Brenda. "He will say the right thing in this delicate situation."

Owain sighed, told her thank you and as an afterthought he said, "Since I have told you much about Thomas, I would fain have you be hostess at the banquet I give for him. You dare not refuse. 'Tis my order."

Brenda blurted, "Christiannt will be angry!"

"I have explained to her that she is not invited to this banquet because she sent a messenger to Thomas without my knowledge. She understands 'tis better to stay in her chamber than the donjon. She asked me to tell you Thomas will grant me a burial place in the Bangor cathedral next to my father, if you tell him 'tis the right thing to do." Owain left Brenda sitting with her mouth open.

Archbishop Thomas Becket was given the guest chamber. Most of his entourage stayed in tents in the inner courtyard, near the doors of the great hall, where they were assured plenty of water. Their horses were fed, watered and brushed in the barn.

Brenda had the ceiling beams of the great hall cleaned of soot and bat dung, and all of the wall-sconces polished and filled with fresh candles. The smell of pine resin burning in the fireplace was sharp and invigorating.

The afternoon before the banquet, Brenda went to Christiannt's chamber. Christiannt said she did not mind that Owain had asked Brenda to be hostess for the archbishop's banquet. She was in a state of doldrums and had no energy. Brenda asked why she was listless.

"Owain found me with Sir Lloyd near the Aberffraw wharf," she said. "I be innocent of Owain's base accusations. In the twilight, we watched the herons fishing. Owain would not let me explain. He said that Lloyd was an English spy and I was mixed up in a sordid business. What a terrible thing to say about a Welsh knight. Later Owain ordered Lloyd to leave the province. Lloyd said he was going home and would not

set foot in Gwynedd again. We said our sad good-byes and I
came back to my chamber. And now he is gone."

Brenda saw that Christiannt was not having a flood of tears,
even though her voice sounded weepy. "To be separated from
Lloyd and the spying business is probably best," she said.

"Nay, the separation will be the death of me," said Christiannt.

" 'Tis hard to believe now, but you will get over him," said
Brenda. "It seems to me that men wait by the castle gate for
thee."

"Brenda, do not make jest of this. Love is like war, easy
to begin but hard to stop. Lloyd taught me all that Owain kept
hidden from me. I pray Owain did not strike Lloyd dead, because if he did, I be in great trouble and may be next on his
list."

"Christiannt, you exaggerate." Brenda said that Annesta
would bring her dinner and left. She believed that Christiannt
was not in trouble even though 'twas common knowledge that
she gave Gwynedd's military information to Lord Dafydd and
Lloyd gave information to Father Giff. Both sent gallopers to
Chester or London so that King Henry always knew what
Owain's army was planning. Brenda supposed Owain had
come face-to-face with Lloyd for leaking information to King
Henry. 'Tis Father Giff Owain should face, instead of his wife,
she said to herself. Then it occurred to her that Father Giff,
Lord Dafydd and the New Religionists would protect Chris-
tiannt. Thinking of the myriad of terrible consequences the
New Religionists could cause Owain and the druids made her
shiver.

Banners of the various provinces were hung inside by the high
windows in the great hall on the night of the banquet.

Brenda wore a blue velvet gown with tucks and lace across
the bodice and on the puffed sleeves. Her chestnut hair was
piled in curls on top of her head and fastened with pearl-
studded combs at the sides. She sat at the left of Owain on
the dais. He was dressed in his best black velvet tunic embroidered with gold thread.

Among the invited guests were: Prince Rhys of Powys;

princes of Ceredigion and Deheubarth; lords of Rhos, Rhufoniog and Maelor; lords of Gwynedd, Howell, Maelgwyn, Rhodri and Dafydd; Archdruid Llieu and Father Giff. Owain had reluctantly sent Lord Dafydd an invitation. He came with a swagger and was dressed in a lace-edged shirt, black stockings, green velvet breeches and shoes. His hair was tied back with a ribbon.

The archbishop arrived with his chaplain. Brenda was astonished to see that Thomas matched the description Owain had given her. His head of brown hair was tonsured and his clothing was layered so that he was actually round as the huge ball young boys rolled with a stick. He wore a lambskin pallium over a dark full-length robe. He sat on the right of Owain with his chaplain beside him and smiled at all the guests sitting at the high end of the table, which was marked by a row of saltcellars, then he bowed and smiled at those folks beyond the saltcellars, who were villagers and servants seated at the lower end.

Earlier Brenda had noticed that the kitchen had several casks with Thomas's mark burned into their side. Inside each cask was Augustinian tart red wine, a gift to the prince of Gwynedd. She thanked Thomas as beakers of wine were passed around.

With little stuttering he told Brenda that his physicians advised him that water was particularly harmful to his stomach, which had a cold complexion. He said he drank cider, but rarely, and good wine in moderation.

Owain raised his beaker, nodded to Thomas and said, "I be pleased to welcome our friend Thomas of London to our sup."

Brenda was appalled to see that Owain's shirt was wrinkled and gray, the lace on the cuffs frayed. His hair fell over his eyes. When he pushed it back, Brenda noticed the smell of stale sweat and his unclean fingernails.

She was embarrassed that Owain had not washed for this occasion. She made her lips tight and asked herself when had Owain grown careless. Why had Christiannt not had his clothing mended and cleaned and have him bathe before this important sup? What was happening? She vowed to herself to mend and clean Owain's clothes herself and hint to Christiannt that he needed to bathe regularly.

Thomas's chaplain, dressed in a black mantle, stood, bowed his head and said a long blessing in Latin.

Maidservants, freshly washed, with crisp white aprons and caps, served steaming leek soup and hunks of oat bread with salt. Next, menservants, freshly scrubbed, hair combed and tied in back with black yarn, brought in two boars on huge platters, followed by smaller platters of venison, pheasant, chicken and lamb. The maids cut generous portions of meat, then left additional servings up to the participants. With the meat was served pottage of chopped kale leaves and parsnip leaves stewed to a pulp and added to oatmeal. Boiled beans and cabbage were flavored with fennel. Green peas were flavored with butter and basil. Then came seed cakes, jams and cheese, apples, hazelnuts and more red wine. The flickering wall-sconces and table candles gave a golden glow to the great hall.

During the sup Llywarch and Gwalchmai played their harps quietly with no singing, jokes or storytelling. Their soft music filled the air with tranquillity. People felt at ease; their mood was happy and dreamy.

Thomas leaned close to Owain and said, in a stuttery whisper, that he had failed to work out a deal with the pope. " 'Tis a ruling straight from Rome. I corresponded with your wife and asked her to have your marriage annulled and carry on as you have b-been. She said, 'Never.' As the wife of the p-prince of Gwynedd, she forbade me to appoint a b-bishop to Saint Dafydd's Church in B-Bangor. She sides with the king of England, and has vowed to destroy all p-pagans and p-pagan things. King Henry's goal is to make Wales p-pure for the English, who intend to take over all of it."

Brenda saw Owain stiffen and stare, without really seeing, down the center of the long table. He had lost his appetite. He seethed. She prayed that he would not call in Christiannt and blast her in front of everyone.

He sat quietly, and Brenda guessed he was imagining a calm, soothing place, which was the druidic method of controlling anger.

Finally Thomas made the sign of the cross in the air between himself and Owain and whispered, "My dear friend, are you aware that your wife is p-power hungry? She can eat you, along with North and South Wales."

Owain's face became red; he was silent for several moments. Then he said, "*A fo ben, bid bont*. He who is chief, let him be a bridge. A bridge to peace and civility."

"My good friend, I pledge my help wherever I can find it," said Thomas.

The symbolism of bridges was purely ancient Welsh. It was on bridges that agreements were made between lovers, husband and wife, between heads of provinces. Bridges linked life and death, the known and the unknown. Brenda thought it was up to Owain to bridge the chasm between himself and his wife and to keep the English out of North and South Wales by closing those bridges until a peaceful agreement could be worked out.

Thomas said right out to Owain that he was vexed with Christiannt for not compromising to keep peace between herself and her husband. "As a matter of fact, I much p-prefer your hostess," he said. " 'Tis shameful that you felt forced to marry a traitor and a shrew instead of Mistress B-Brenda." He winked, leaned toward Brenda and said, "Have you heard the tale of the Devil's B-Bridge, my dear?"

Brenda flushed and admitted she had not.

Thomas stood and said, "I wish to thank my host, P-Prince Owain, for a more than satisfying meal. 'Twas more b-bountiful than I needed, b-but I see there is not much left and everyone looks well satisfied, so I declare it a genuine success."

There were several fast arpeggios on Gwalchmai's harp and more applause. The maidservants came around with mead. Thomas took a sip and patted his mouth on his napkin. The hall became quiet to hear what more the archbishop would say.

"As it is customary for your guest of honor to make a little speech after sup, I have chosen to tell the tale of the Devil's B-Bridge, with appropriate accompaniment from the harpers.

"So listen, please, to what I have to say, and let me tell my tale as best I may. A maid stands beside the flooded gulley of the Mynach River, in Dyfed, wondering how to reach her goat stranded on the other bank." The smiling harpers played several bars of a melancholy dirge. " 'May I help you?' says an enchanting voice, and the maid turns to see a cowled black monk, with his rosary in one hand, standing behind her.

" 'How can you help me?' said the maid. 'Can you get me over the river to that goat?'

" 'For certes,' said the monk. 'I can easily span a bridge across the chasm.'

" 'Well,' said the maid, 'that would be a kindness, but how am I to pay you?'

" 'Ah, let me have for myself the first living thing that crosses the bridge when I have built it.'

" '*Da iwan*, all right,' said the maid.

"But the *merch*, the lass, did not like the smooth sound of the monk's voice. She was no fool.

"In a very short time the monk finished the bridge and called the maid from her cottage to get her goat. She brought a loaf of bread with her and a small black dog. She rolled the loaf across the bridge and watched the dog, the first living creature to cross the bridge, scamper eagerly after it." The harpers played a short, jolly tune.

"The monk swore an unmonkly oath, and with a fizz and a strong smell of sulfur, disappeared. The maid recovered her goat and the bridge is still to be seen spanning the dark gulley of the river."

Most of the listeners, including Owain, understood the point of the tale right away. Beware of schemes sounding too good to be true. Think wisely to counter such propositions.

Amid the applause Owain stood and put an arm around Thomas. "Thank you, my friend," he said.

"I warn you," whispered Thomas. "King Henry is going to do his best to annihilate his enemies, the Old Religionists, you and I. He will separate us from the people we love, your wife, your sons, my bishops, my chaplain."

Owain nodded, and felt a little dizzy. The warning was nothing he did not know, but it was sickening to have his own knowledge confirmed by an archbishop and a good friend.

"I was amazed you spoke with no stuttering," said Brenda, shaking his moist hand.

"Ah," said Thomas. "When I tell a favorite tale, it glides without a stop like water flowing downhill."

She had a feeling that Thomas was one of those men who enjoyed life. She truly liked him.

Thomas leaned close to Owain and told him once again of his recurring dream, which began on the eleventh day of the eleventh month when he was canon of St. Paul's in London a year and a day after he returned the Great Seal to Henry the Second and surrendered his chancellorship. He dreamed he saw Owain holding his hands to his throat. In the dream, a year later, four of his own knights murdered him. " 'Tis a warning," he said. "My friend, you shall be murdered by one of your sons one year before my own demise."

Owain's mouth was dry as a dusty summer road, and his voice sounded high and sharp as he tried to make a joke of Thomas's dream. "Well, if 'tis troth, 'tis up to me to welcome you when you move to the Otherside."

Before Thomas's caravan left, Owain gave him a gift of the finest pelisse lined with the whitest lamb's wool that he could find, because Thomas had mentioned that he was cold in the damp confines of the Bangor cathedral and got a stitch in his side when he walked too fast. Owain also found half a dozen men among his landowners who were loyal to him and thus would be loyal as bodyguards for Thomas. With these gifts Owain hoped that Thomas's dream of an untimely death by four knights would be thwarted.

Brenda thought of warning Thomas about Sir Lloyd. Then she thought better of it. Sir Lloyd was Owain's problem, not Thomas's.

Christiannt did not leave her chamber for several days after the banquet.

Well, she thought, no wonder I be partial to King Henry. On the other hand, Thomas of London, even though a New Religionist, opposes, with a passion, King Henry's policy against the druids. She sighed and was not able to figure that out. So she thought of something else. She thought of a scheme to make peace between Prince Owain and King Henry that she thought was certain to please everyone. As a consequence the archbishop would permit her husband to be buried inside Bangor's cathedral and then she, Lady Christiannt, Prince Owain's wife, could be buried there next to her husband. What a pox on Rome's bloody law forbidding cousins to marry! The rotund archbishop of Canterbury would owe her a bloody apology! The thought was so delicious she licked her lips.

Later Christiannt told Brenda that she had had several dreams about King Henry's desirable half-sister, Emma of Anjou. She had never met Emma, but she liked her name. She said it was a wonder that Emma was not married. "I be going to tell Lord Dafydd about Emma and urge him to marry her. 'Tis time he married. An English wife will settle him so that he shall be known as the perfect future king of Gwynedd."

Brenda was so surprised that she snorted and her mouth fell open as Christiannt went on. "If Henry's half-sister is married into the royal family of Gwynedd, there shall be no warring between the English and Welsh and all will be paradise in North Wales. Everyone will know that it was my idea, and sing hosannas to me. The archbishop will permit both Owain and me to be buried inside the Bangor cathedral. Father Giff will bless me. Owain will kiss me."

When Owain found out about his wife's scheme, he did his best to discourage Dafydd, but it was too late. Dafydd was stubborn and said he had already made wedding plans and immediately left for England to woo a young lass he did not know, but whom the English knew as buck-toothed, fishy-eyed Emma.

Lord Dafydd met with King Henry and received permission to marry his half-sister, Emma. After the wedding he felt so important that he took his English bride to Bangor, Wales, for their first month of marriage. While there, Dafydd met with Archbishop Becket and demanded crypt space for himself and his new bride inside the cathedral. "I be the next king of Gwynedd, and thus my wife and I deserve a space inside the church where my grandfather, Gruffudd ap Cynan, is buried," he said.

Remembering his promise to Owain and guessing that Owain's wife, Christiannt, had put Dafydd and Emma up to this absurd scheme, Thomas refused on the grounds that Dafydd's kingship was not at all certain. "Not only that, there are rumors you are the spawn of your father's cousin, Mistress Christiannt, long b-before their marriage. Therefore, b-by canon law, you are not allowed to b-be b-buried inside the B-Bangor church."

Dafydd flushed and he said in a loud voice that Lady Gladys was his mother and Lady Christiannt only his nursemaid.

When Christiannt learned of this from Dafydd, she was livid. She had never told him about his birth and thought Thomas had no business mixing himself into her affairs. Suddenly she thought that Brenda, the hostess at the grand Gwynedd banquet, must have told Thomas. Brenda had acted like Queen Mab, fulfilling everyone's dreams of a lavish feed last month when the archbishop visited. I will show her! Christiannt thought. So she warned Lord Dafydd and his bride that Brenda was a witch aligned with pagans. "By using pagan medical treatments, she entices patients from Father Giff and damns him with faint praise. Your father should have skinned her alive years ago. He is too soft for a province leader. King Henry would never tolerate a witch in his royal retinue!" She smiled, knowing she had planted a seed of mistrust against Brenda and more doubt against Owain's judgment as head of a province.

The roiling, low clouds brought snow during the *cel-ddyddiau*, Omen Days, the twelve days before Christ's Mass. It was said that those who died during this time went to heaven without having to face Purgatory and Judgment.

From old habit, Brenda was up before most were awake. She braced herself against the raw Welsh wind as she went from her cottage to the great hall's kitchen the day before Christ's Mass. Owain had purchased a supply of expensive mead. Before the kitchen servants drank it, she wanted each harper to have a pitcherful of the fine metheglin flavored with herbs and spices.

She was surprised to see Gwalchmai up so early. He followed her into the empty kitchen and began rifling through dried fish hung on a ladder thrust out an open window. "I came to find something to quell the hungries in the middle of the night," he explained, smoothing his wind-tangled, white hair and long beard with bony fingers.

"Will this do?" Brenda said, pointing to the mead, "Everyone loves your beautiful harp music, especially me." She dipped out a large pitcherful and pushed it toward him. He hesitated until she said, " 'Tis all right. 'Tis my gift to you, for being a skillful harper."

His eyes sparkled warm as blue columbines and he said he would repay her with news that had perhaps not yet reached her ears.

Brenda nodded and stood against the wall.

"Have you heard what happened to that soldier deserter, what is his name? He bragged that he was knighted by Prince Owain and King Henry, both. He had to leave Owain's army." Gwalchmai took several swallows of mead.

"Are you talking about Sir Lloyd?" asked Brenda.

"Aye and, pshaw, the man was no knight. Owain never knighted him and I doubt Henry has ever seen him. I saw him hanging around the castle on Samhain Eve."

"Probably he came back to see Lady Christiannt," said Brenda.

"Aye," said Gwalchmai. "Everyone knows the two of them carry messages through Father Giff and Lord Dafydd to Henry's soldiers in Chester. With Christiannt's help, Dafydd has wolfed up Howell's lands and set himself up as chief lord collecting the *gwerin*'s taxes. The *gwerin* have those little black huts with no windows so they escape the higher taxes levied on cottages with windows. After Lord Dafydd collected the farm folks' taxes, Christiannt enticed him to make the folks put in windows and pay more taxes or move from their farms to villages, where the stone houses have windows."

"Windows only let in more cold air!" said Brenda. "And village life is not for the *gwerin*! The Welsh farm folks have lived in dispersed crofts or farmlands for ages." She was appalled at the boldness of Christiannt. "What is the matter with Lady Christiannt's thinking?"

Gwalchmai licked his lips and said, "Lord Howell helped the *gwerin* move back to their crofts and patch up the windows with shutters or daubs of mud. He pleaded with Owain to censure Lord Dafydd and put him in the Dolwyddelan donjon. Instead, Owain soothed Howell's fury by reminding him that he would be his successor."

"That is Owain's wish," said Brenda. "Did Owain order Sir Lloyd out of Gwynedd, like Christiannt says? I hope Howell can deal with traitors who lie about their knighthood, desert their army and consort with their father's wife."

"Well, you have come to the point. Here is something to ponder: Sir Lloyd made an appointment to talk with Owain the day we took Thomas to the druid camp. Said he had important personal information. On the day he was to see Owain, a day of ill omen, he had a strange accident with his crossbow. Fishermen found his body floating belly-down in the water under the Aberffraw wharf. An arrow went through the heart. His right hand held his bow," Gwalchmai dipped his thumb into the mead, sucked on it a moment, and watched Brenda.

She drew her brows together and thought, How could a soldier who was a knight, even though there was some doubt, accidentally shoot himself in the heart? And Christiannt said naught about Lloyd's accident. "Are you certain the dead man was Sir Lloyd?"

"I be."

Then Brenda remembered something. "Christiannt told me that Sir Lloyd went home."

"Exactly. Owain had one of his retainers take Lloyd's body home on the back of an army horse."

Brenda took a deep breath. "I do not believe Lloyd shot himself with an arrow."

"I agree," said Gwalchmai. "What did Lloyd want to tell Owain? Is this intrigue about power?"

"I do not know," said Brenda. She leaned against the wall because her legs went limp as calves' liver.

Gwalchmai shrugged and backed out of the kitchen with

one arm around the pitcher of mead and the other hand holding
a stack of dry, smoked fish fillets.

Careful not to spill the mead she carried, Brenda tapped lightly
on Llywarch's door. Her head swirled with questions. There
was no answer to her tapping and she pulled at the latch with
one finger. She set the pitcher on the table and called, " 'Tis
me, Brenda."

Her eyes widened when she spied a beaker holding grasses
and dried flowers. She picked it up and held it in the flickering
firelight. Wild weeds, just like Morgan loved to hold in his
chubby hand. "Holy Macha! Morgan? Are you here, wee laddie?" Her eyes examined the floor, under the table and then
halfway toward the pallet she saw a pile of clothes, men's
clothes. There were dirty woolen stockings, well-worn breeks
stiff with salt water and a black gown; a monk's gown. Some
curate had come through briars, brambles and marsh to bring
news of Morgan. She moved her eyes to the pallet, hoping
against hope to see the child. The pallet was empty. She lifted
the breeks and sniffed. Her nose wrinkled. "This has not seen
a wash for years," she said aloud.

"Four years," said a deep voice.

She looked up and saw a grown man standing in an iron
washtub at the far end of the room. His wet, blond hair was
slicked back from his face. He held a linen towel across his
middle and what she could see of his slim, muscular body
shone with water in the lamplight. His blue eyes glistened, and
his mouth smiled from ear to ear, showing a space between
his top front teeth.

"You have Madoc's blue eyes, and the gap between his
front teeth—" A tingle went up her spine. "These clothes smell
like a sailor who forgot there was land and fresh water."

"Mam," said Madoc, "I do not think it proper for you to
see me naked. So please hand me another one of the towels
that Annesta left by the fire's warming stones. You like my
flowers?"

"Your flowers?" Brenda's voice was little more than a
whisper.

"Annesta brought me flowers. She dried them and saved

them. I really missed the flowers, especially in Iceland, where I saw only heather."

"Iceland? I thought—I thought you went to France. Oh, glory be! Annesta here? She saw you?" Her hand shook when she handed him the warm towel. "I saw no trading ship. No one said a thing about one coming into the bay. I was with Gwalchmai and he said naught about a ship."

With the towels tied around his waist, he stepped from the tub and put his arms around her. "We came in during the middle of the night and went to the druid camp."

She could hardly catch her breath. This was not how she had pictured herself greeting Madoc on his return. "My dearest heart!" was all she could say, yet she had rehearsed much more.

"Oh my, you, you are thinner, handsomer and taller than I remember." She marveled that this tall, comely, bewhiskered man was truly the young, spraddle-footed lad who was sent to Paris.

She held on to his arm and feasted her eyes. She hugged him again and this time failed to hold back tears of happiness, which spilled onto his shoulder. "Glory to the gods, I found you while thinking I might find Christiannt's missing laddie, Morgan. Tell me everything. Paris—were you truly there? Iceland—why? Your friend Conlaf, where is he? What took you so long?" She bit her bottom lip, thinking her words were jumbled and foolish.

"We had to find a trading ship coming to Wales and that ship went to Iceland first. Conlaf could not wait to tell Llieu of a sickness, called leprosy, that is spreading in France. We brought back a friend, Troyes, who is to become a physician. I came here to get clean clothes before I see Prince Owain to say that we are back with signed briefs and full logbooks. Conlaf is going to meet me in the great hall before we see Owain."

"The other friend, Troyes?"

"We met him in the Paris prison."

"You—and Conlaf in prison?"

"Aye. Do not worry, Mam, we are home. Hand me Llywarch's trousers and tunic. I have naught else to wear until my other things are washed." He slipped on the trousers, let the towel fall to his feet and pulled the clean but worn tunic over his head.

Brenda said she would wash his soiled gown, breeks and stockings and all of a sudden noticed snips of blond curls lying between the reeds on the floor. "Who cut your hair?" she asked.

"Annesta," he said, running his hand over the golden stubble and lifting the tunic's cowl around his head.

He reached into a worn hemp bag and brought out a scarf of lavender wool. " 'Tis for thee—made in France."

Brenda held the scarf to her face and smelled heather and seaweed. " 'Tis as soft as Welsh wool and fine enough to be drawn through a wedding ring. Thank you." She started to put her arms around him again, but he pulled away, grinned, pushed at the doorskin and said, "Where does Llywarch want this scummy bathwater?"

Brenda dropped his bundle of soiled clothing on the floor, laid the scarf on the table beside the pitcher of mead and helped him turn the tub upside down behind the cottage, thinking that it was better than waiting for the maids, Mona or Annesta. Annesta had already done too much, seeing Madoc before his mother even knew he was back from Paris—and Iceland.

He said, "I shall stand in the cold air for a moment and collect my thoughts before I take the briefs and log to Owain."

She said, "Lately Owain seems to be short-winded and cranky. Here, wear this old bratt of Llywarch's. He will not mind. 'Tis beginning to snow."

"I be not a lad. I be used to all kinds of weather. I be a man now."

A flush crept up Brenda's cheeks. "I will look for you in the hall at sup." She wanted to kiss him, but instead she studied him. His eyes were blue as flaxflowers, his face was weathered to an even brown like tanned cowhide and his hands callused from heavy work. He was taller than she.

He opened the door, reached for the bratt she held and said, "Thanks, Mam. 'Tis good to be home."

As soon as the door closed Brenda clutched the lavender

scarf to her breast, leaned against the wall and let the tears run down her face. Madoc was safe and grown and fine looking. She wondered about the experiences he had had. What about his time in the prison? What had he done? She promised herself that she would bide her time and hear the answers soon enough. She wanted to savor Madoc's homecoming, and resented the nagging thought of Lloyd's death. It would be wise to talk to Christiannt, who was probably devastated with the news.

She pulled her bratt over her head, held it tight against her throat and hurried to Christiannt's chamber. The wind had become fierce and the snow fell thick and fast.

Her knocking went unanswered. She went to the maids' cottage. No one had seen Christiannt since early morning.

The snow stopped and the temperature dropped. Water that stood in the buckets behind the kitchen froze solid under a cap of snow. Later the sun came out and made the snow sparkle like small quartz crystals, but did little warming.

Brenda tried to think where Christiannt might go and suddenly remembered the little cottage. She told herself the walk would do her good and she would be back long before sup. She took her linen medicine bag and added a jar of salve, several bandages and a packet of dried herbs.

The gate guard said she should not go far because the air was cold enough to freeze a pig's squeal.

"Did Lady Christiannt go out today?" she asked.

"She came through before daybreak, dressed like a soldier, in boots and breeks," the guard said, beating his wrapped hands against his thighs. "I told her astrologers say only the reckless should undertake business of any consequence today. Prince Owain came through shortly afterwards, and was back moments ago. When he left I told him the storm would not last long but the cold snap would be in place two clear days. He told me to mind my own business. He was in a better mood when he returned, singing a song about sailors on a calm sea."

"Did they leave in the same direction?"

"Aye, toward Aberffraw. The prince on horseback, m'lady on shank's mare. Mayhap they went to the village to celebrate

the Omen Days. Lady Christiannt looked like she was dressed
for some buffoonery."

Brenda hurried to Aberffraw. The cold sucked at her breath.
She walked briskly to keep warm. She avoided the vendors
with warming fires. Smoke rose out of a hole in the thatch of
the little cottage. The moisture from her mouth froze on her
new scarf. She had to use two hands to draw aside the stiff,
heavy hide door. Inside there was the dank smell of animals.
Two sheep huddled on a pile of straw in the far corner. Half-
burned sticks mixed with foul-smelling straw smoldered on
the center fire. Beside the fire pit stones were clean bones,
probably left from a meal.

Bed cloths were rumpled in the bed closet. The shelf was
bare except for a round candle holder or a belt buckle. Brenda
held the cloths to her nose and smelled a man's dried sweat,
days old, and chamomile. Her mind gave her a picture of
Christiannt's blond head snuggled next to Lloyd's bare chest.
The dirt floor in front of the closet was scraped, and a pair of
fire-sticks lay outside the bed closet. Who had started the fire?
Christiannt? Where had she gone? To the druid camp? Back
to the castle? Was she even here?

She put snow on the fire and threw the half-burned sticks
outside on the frozen ground. It crossed her mind that maybe
someone left the fire going, hoping that a strong gust of wind
would blow down through the roof and cause the whole place
to catch afire. That was silly; no one would leave the sheep
inside if they planned to burn the cottage. Would they? She
pulled the hide cover over the doorway and looked at the shed
in back. It was empty except for a small pile of dry gorse
twigs and a half-used tallow candle in a tin plate. There were
no footprints in the snow but her own.

She quickened her pace to the druid camp. Molly was glad
to see her. " 'Tis so cold I did not expect you to come for
druidic study today," Molly said, putting cheese, bread and
warm mead on the table. They talked about natural philosophy, which Llieu was teaching them, until Brenda asked if
Molly had seen Christiannt. "Nay," she said, "but Owain came
to see Llieu. I heated mead for Llieu. Owain likes his cold
and heard him say Dafydd planned an attack on the castle.

Owain looked terrible, face drawn and sallow, like he had fought with the *fiana*, Sid-folk from the Otherside. Then he said something about if a man wanted something done, 'tis best to do it himself. He left without taking off his gloves or drinking a sip of mead."

"Is that all?" asked Brenda. "Just talk of Dafydd?"

"Llieu told Owain that arrangement of the Omen Days' mistletoe boughs and the white bull's innards indicate no warring on the royal court for at least nine times nine days after Christ's Mass. Owain said not to worry, his army was prepared." Molly shook her head. "I do not like talk of war."

"Owain and Howell have been prepared for weeks," said Brenda, wrapping a piece of cheese in a hunk of bread. She put it in her tunic pocket, saying that she was going to have to hurry to meet Christiannt, who had probably taken a short-cut through the village on her way back to the castle.

Outdoors, Brenda was blinded by snow that swirled in fierce gusts of wind and grabbed at her breath. She pulled her lavender scarf over her ears. All of a sudden she said out loud, "I have to go back!"

Brenda hurried to the dark little cottage, fastened the hide door open and felt on the bed closet ledge until she found the round metal piece and held it in her bare hand. It was a silver bratt brooch with the Gwynedd arms, three lions with their tails curled over their backs. "Christiannt, you were here," she whispered. "Where are you now?"

XIX
Christiannt

David made himself unpopular by his marriage to
Emma, half sister of King Henry II of England. Many
Welshmen felt that David, by this alliance with the ruling family of England, betrayed them into the hands of
their ancient enemies. The fears of the nation were jus-
tified when soon after the marriage David sent a thousand men to serve under King Henry in Normandy and
a little later went to Oxford to enter Parliament and
swear allegiance to the King of England. The dissatis-
faction among Prince David's people because of the
marriage may have been a contributing cause of the
ready enlistment of men and women under Madoc for
his expeditions.

Zella Armstrong, *Who Discovered America?*

Brenda had a feeling of urgency as she approached the village.
At the same time she felt worn out and longed to rest. Thinking of death and war saps a person's strength, she told herself.
The cold wind carried the revelers' merry voices. She half
hoped that Christiannt had gone on to her chamber in the royal
court. Then she saw a lone lass standing alongside the road.
She clutched the bratt brooch in her pocket, ran, waved and
stopped. The lass was not blond or stocky like Christiannt, but
dark-haired and wiry thin. A lassie, like Annesta. Annesta?

"Annesta!" called Brenda.

"Have you seen Madoc and Conlaf?"

"Nay," said Brenda. "Christiannt? Have you seen Christiannt?"

"Aye, here," said Annesta, pointing. "Do you know something about this?"

"This?" Brenda looked down at what seemed like a pile of old blankets thrown into the ditch. Her heart pumped as she recognized the rawhide boots stained with mud and the leather trousers above the boot tops. She stepped into the ditch and lifted the corner of a blanket. She brushed the blond hair from the pale face and said, "Christiannt! Oh, Lord God, Christiannt!" She looked up toward Annesta and asked, "How? What happened?"

"I thought—I hoped you knew," said Annesta. "We found her here—like this. Madoc and Conlaf are bringing a cart to carry her to the druids."

Brenda could not believe her eyes. How could this happen? She knelt, raised Christiannt slowly by the shoulders, and the head rolled from one side to the other, then dropped back so she saw the blue line on the neck. It was the burn of a rope, or of some tight cordage that had shut off the windpipe. She sat in the snow holding Christiannt's head and shoulders and wept. Between sobs she whispered against Christiannt's cold ear, "Tell me, who did this to you? A *draig*? A dragon soldier? More than one? Was it O—O—?" She could not say the prince's name. "Did you see him? Oh Lugh, did he find you in the bed closet? Did you hear him come inside the dark cottage? Did he tell you Lloyd is dead? How often did I warn you that Owain would lose his temper if he found you had a lover? Did you ever listen to me? Sometimes you are so stubborn! You close your ears and do not ask for help until 'tis too late!" She pushed the yellow curls away from the wide-open eyes, closed the lids with her thumbs and sobbed, "I cannot stand to have you stare at me!" One lid slowly opened and Brenda held it shut with her thumb. "Oh, you want to give me a truly angry look because I suspect you pushed Morgan or deliberately let him fall into the cesspit. Why? Was he too much for you to care for? Lads can be a handful, but you could have had all the help you needed. You were afraid to admit it to yourself, but deep down in that secret place, you knew. I have no proof, except your insane words and actions, like raking through cesspits. Now you have no words, so the

gods will deal with you in Sid, the Otherworld. Someone took
your life. Who will make amends for that?"

Annesta watched the road, wishing Madoc and Conlaf
would hurry. The wind rose and ruffled her skirts, making a
loud flapping sound.

Brenda tried to think. Logically, who would do this to
Christiannt? Why? Owain, Molly had said, never took his
gloves off at the druid camp. Why? It was common courtesy
when speaking to a trusted friend like Llieu. Owain looked
frightful and said he did something he wanted done. Or was
it *needed* done? No one would criticize him for taking the life
of a traitor. It was known that he demanded fierce and brutal
penalties for disloyalty. That was expected. It was a province
leader's job. But the traitor was the province leader's wife!
Oh, Lord God, what was happening in Gwynedd?

"I can hear a cart coming down the road," whispered Annesta, squatting beside the ditch.

"Pray 'tis Madoc and Conlaf," said Brenda. She climbed to
the side of the road and squinted into the setting sun trying to
see, and when she could not, felt panic rise. She wanted to
take Annesta's hand and run. Run fast before they were found
with the dead body of Owain's wife. There was no need.

Madoc and Conlaf lifted Christiannt's body onto the cart
and covered it with linen bed cloths.

As the four of them walked back to the druid camp, they
ignored the squeal of the cart, the creaks of the trees in the
gusty wind. Not one of them noticed that the incoming clouds
became crimson as the sun set.

Brenda sighed and said, "Poor Christiannt. We had our differences, but I loved her more than I disliked her. Owain understood her best. He will be so aggrieved that he will forget
awarring and not think straight. 'Tis a bad time for Gwynedd."
As she spoke she questioned her own words. Possibly Owain
already knew his wife was dead. Had he gone to Dafydd's
camp at Llyn Coron and not found her there? Had he gone to
the little cottage and found her? Had he found out at the druid
camp that Dafydd was on a secret mission?

Madoc said, "Llieu is going to see Prince Owain early on
the morrow. He will tell the prince about Lady Christiannt

when he gives him a palliative for his back pains and fading eyesight. Lord Dafydd is planning a war against Prince Owain, mayhap this night."

Brenda brushed her hands in front of her face and said, "Nay, nay. Courtesy demands that I tell Owain about his wife tonight. 'Tis something I need to do."

"I found her. I will go with you," said Annesta.

Owain appeared genuinely shocked that Annesta had found his wife dead in a ditch. Brenda told him that the body was at the druid camp. He had a hard time finding his voice. After pacing back and forth and swallowing several times, he said in a whisper, as a courtesy to the dead, "You know my wife preferred Father Giff and was an adherent of the New Religion. Her body does not belong at the druid camp."

His words made Brenda wince as though she had received a blow on her head for the mistake.

"You might have brought her here to her own chamber!" He did not ask how his wife had met her death. His lips were pushed together as if he did not wish to speak and he looked weary and old.

Brenda rubbed her forehead and said, " 'Tis a terrible shame. Christiannt was garroted. Did you know?"

Owain looked at his hands and whispered, "Send Annesta away. 'Tis too hard to look at my wife's handmaiden."

When Annesta was gone Owain told Brenda to sit down on the pallet beside him. " 'Tis more of a shame that Christiannt heard voices that no one else could hear," he said. "Mayhap you noticed her thoughts and actions were peculiar. She let the spirits from Sid control her. She became a person I did not know, a complete stranger. Llieu knew no cure for her troubles. Father Giff suggested exorcism. He waved a wand, burned incense, rubbed his ring and recited incantations, but for naught; the spirit voices stayed. She carried tales of my comings and goings and movement of my troops to both Father Giff and Dafydd, who, we all know, are in league with King Henry. I was once truly fond of Christiannt, but not of what she had become. 'Twill be a far better Gwynedd without her."

Owain put a hand on Brenda's cheek and said, " 'Tis hard to lose another wife."

Suddenly there was an enormous ache in her heart and she covered her face with her hands. Her thoughts swirled and the only thing that floated to the top was the fact that Owain was a leader, who held the good of Gwynedd uppermost in all things he did. He could not tolerate anyone, no matter his relationship to that person or persons, denigrating his beloved Gwynedd. Someday there would be a confrontation between him and Lord Dafydd. It would be a terrible war. The last thought did not come in a flash, but dropped off slowly like the spent petal of a fragile flower. War was inevitable.

She took her hands down, looked Owain in the face and said, "I be so sorry. There is so much mixed up here: triumph, glory, loyalty, justice, and betrayal." Her eyes never left his. Such sorrowful eyes, she thought, quiet and deep as a frosty blue mountain lake.

"No need to be sorry." He sounded dog-tired. "I want to tell you about something I found this morning before sunup. I was on a walk around the inner bailey and saw a shovel in the cesspit near the chapel. I was about to scold someone for not putting it away, but decided to dig a little. The air was so cold there was no smell from the pit. The digging was not easy. I found a bone, but tossed it aside, then more bones and the skull of a child. My heart jumped into my throat. I put the spine together and it curved—like Morgan's. I quickly re-buried the bones in the frozen pit, except for a shinbone I kept."

Owain took Brenda's trembling hand and said, "I had heard rumors about Morgan going to the garderobe. And rumors about Christiannt and Morgan being seen by the gate guards, picking flowers along the wall the night he disappeared. Christiannt always denied that she took him for a walk or to the garderobe that night. This morning I found her in a cottage where Lloyd told me they met. She went mad when I showed her the shinbone. She told me—she pushed Morgan into the pit."

Brenda heard a deep cry and looked around before she realized it came from her own throat.

" 'Twas my duty to rid Gwynedd of a baby killer and a

traitor. My honor is known by what I do. A Roman statesman once said, 'What is fitting is honorable, and what is honorable is fitting.' I could not expect anyone else to mete out justice for the death of the wee laddie." He buried his head in his hands and sobbed. "Christiannt had become bereft of reason. I have proof my wife gave an armload of my military information to English sympathizers."

Brenda listened to his soft snuffling breath and her own breath going in and out. Finally she said, "Christiannt was not herself. She suffered from delusions, and would not seek help. If she had, I do not know if I could have helped her." She kept her eyes on her lap and did not look at Owain. She was angry and sad at the same time. She did not like Owain, yet she was his loyal mistress. From the bottom of her heart she felt sorry for him, but she was not proud of him. Why had he not punished Dafydd years ago when he burned a man's barn and took his life? Of course, that was because of Gladys and Christiannt. But still it was beyond understanding. It would take days to sort out her feelings.

Owain lifted his head. "Gwynedd's destiny is to be free from English domination," he said. "The irony is that I will not be here to give her that freedom. But she has a new shipmaster, and trade will give her economic freedom."

She looked at him and was perplexed.

His eyes misted but remained fixed on hers. Then he let his head rest on her shoulder.

She felt wetness on her shoulder and knew he wept. She kissed his wrinkled cheek and scabby brows, and raised his head. She held his face between her hands, and watched tears seep from closed, gray eyelids and disappear into his thin beard.

"You appointed a shipmaster?" she said.

"That lad, what is his name? The blond one with the space between his top front teeth. He loves the sea as much as I do!"

"You asked Madoc to be your shipmaster?" Her heart thundered. "When?" Her eyes probed his for the answer.

"This morning after he told me about his trip. 'Twas a great joy to listen to him. He has a gift with words. He and his physician friend, Conlaf, brought all my briefs back signed. I appointed Conlaf as my royal healer, sent Madoc to Afon Ganol's quay to rebuild the Viking hafskip, and repair any usable vessels perched on dry land beside the quay." The weariness left his voice.

She too forgot about being tired. "For shame, you are a poltroon! A shuffler! Those old wrecks will never sail. Gwynedd was not meant to trade by sea."

"Mistress Brenda, I beg to differ from thee. Madoc is a remarkable lad. I expect he can do it."

"Aye, you sent him to the ships' grave, and you expect him to revive the dead relics."

"He will. I see ten sails in my dream."

"My dear friend," she said, trying to control her beating heart, "to dream is a vanity. You generally choose responsibility. You let yourself suffer the consequences of being sincere with your people. Nothing else matters but honor. Is it honorable to let a lad believe he is getting something, when 'tis naught but a wooden tub with dry rot, and several coracles that are sieves?"

"Aye, he is my hireling. I pay for the repairs. He will build a hafskip that is far better than the Vikings build in Dubh Linn shipyards. 'Tis my destiny to be remembered as Gwynedd's honorable prince, and this lad will make it so." He lowered his eyes. "My time is almost gone. With bull's blood and mistletoe boughs the druids foretell my destiny. The season of my death is nigh. There will be no huge battle for the Gwynedd courts. I give thanks to the gods for that."

"What about Lord Dafydd?" said Brenda. "He is planning a war against your court!"

"He carks me! He thinks I be too ill for warring. His troops are ill prepared. The battle will be for naught." He looked into the fireplace. The flames were drawn upward by the wind. He seemed to have forgotten her and whispered to the spirits in the flames, which cracked and popped back their undecipherable answers. "That miscreant goes across the Welsh border to Britain," he mused, "instead of staying on this side to protect it. The oily-tongued rogue assembles his troops with the English! He has no understanding of war. He loves garlic and drinks red wine until all he sees is hazy. In the old days warring was not done with rage, out of jealousy or retribution, but with exhilaration, out of a sense of honor and justice." He threw up his hands and said he was thinking of taking Dafydd prisoner until he pledged to curtail the dragons' rape, plunder and murder of druids. "Murder is a foul injustice against the gods' reason." He paused, wiped his mouth, looked at Brenda and said in a firm voice, "If racked, I will not speak of my latest deed. I shall not be hanged by my neck. Instead I shall be given homage and praise for doing what I believe was just."

"You left her in the ditch," said Brenda, "hoping no one would find her. Then people would think Christiannt mysteriously disappeared, same as wee Morgan. Where was thine honor this morn?"

He excused himself to call his retainers to bring his wife's body to the castle. Without preamble, he ordered Brenda to wash and dress the body as soon as it arrived.

She could not refuse. Owain had bared his soul, told her everything. Except—except what? Lloyd? He was a spy. Owain probably killed him. There was no mystery left. Owain would never say more, would not have to. Morgan, Lloyd and Christiannt were dead, and that was that.

He reached for a polished ox horn from the shelf over his writing desk and gave it to Brenda, saying that he had inherited it and its contents when his father died, in 1137. Inside were four rare, uncirculated, triangular silver coins with a hole in their center. He said, "Lay a pair on Lady Christiannt's eyes, and when I die, lay the other pair on my eyes."

"You are not going to die soon," she said. "The times are terrible, but not the end of everything. Enjoy life while 'tis with you. Meet death only when 'tis unavoidable." She bit her tongue and said, "You have seen the death of friends and kin before." There was a pounding inside her head because she had wanted to say that he had been the *cause* of the death of friends and kin before. He was generous, but bloodthirsty. The bards sang songs and recited poems of murders, mutilations and tortures carried out at his command, especially on his kinfolk. Death was not a stranger to him.

"I hear the banshees' wail at night even when the wind is

still. I have seen enough for two men." He stared off into some vague place and time and spoke in a whisper. "Give me a druid burial and afterwards go to the place you have longed to go—Ireland. My respect for you grows each day. My love for you has never dimmed, never will dim, even if I lose my life because of it. Thomas of London was right about my future."

She caught her breath. Did he say he would die for loving her? Nay, that could not be.

Next he said in solemn tones that each of them would take what chance they found. "When you leave for *Iwerddon*, Ireland, take with you our druid friends. Old Caradoc knows the safe place." He held the door for her, but his head was turned toward the window so that she would not see the tears in his eyes.

Brenda was in bed when she heard a tap on her door.

"I want to prepare Christiannt's body," said Annesta, coming inside.

"An older woman does that," said Brenda, remembering it was something Owain had asked her to do.

"I was her handmaid."

"You would turn green as a frog!"

"Nay, I helped you prepare Lady Gladys's body, so I be not entirely uninitiated," whispered Annesta. "Together we shall lay the body out in finery fit to wear at a banquet. I am not frightened by things such as life and death."

When Annesta left, Brenda thought, I have yet to get this lass's measure.

Sometime before dawn, Llywarch tapped on Brenda's door and said softly, "Christiannt's body is in her chamber and Owain refuses to look at it dressed in boots and leather trousers and tunic. Go, prepare the body for public viewing." When it seemed to him that Brenda hesitated he added, "Go now, because 'tis a terrible thing to know a truth and not act properly."

"You know I know the truth?" Brenda said.

Through the door Llywarch said, "And the white bull's intestines know."

"I be going," she said, and went to find Annesta at the maids' cottage. They washed Christiannt and dressed her in a royal purple robe that was covered with orphrey, embroidery in gold and silver thread. Brenda used the bratt pin she had found to hold the front together. They put a silk girdle set with precious stones around her waist, and around her neck they fastened a collar of gold that was set with jewels in the same fashion as the girdle.

Mona came to hear how Christiannt was found and to wash and braid the long yellow hair into a single thick plait, pulled back from an unblemished face, which Annesta made rosy with a fine powdering of talc tinted with berry juice. Christiannt's dead berry-red lips were turned up into a smile. Her head rested on a white pillow decorated with a cross she herself had embroidered with strands of her own yellow hair. In one bejeweled hand she held a rosewood comb. In the other hand she held a silver mirror.

She was not tight faced, the way Brenda imagined a traitor. She had the self-assured face of a lovely lady, a queen. Brenda opened the ox horn, took out two silver coins with holes in their centers and looked at them closely. The circular inscription showed that they were minted during the reign of Owain's father: *Gruffudd ap Cynan—un o frenhinoedd mawr Cymru*, one of the great kings of Wales. On the reverse side was the name and town of the minter, *Halli, Caernarfon*. She laid one on each eyelid.

At noon, on the third day after Christiannt's death, her body was laid in a marble coffin. Next to the pillow Brenda placed a silver-lidded glass jar holding layers of different spices, ready for use in the next world. She saw none of Christiannt's grown children present at the funeral. " 'Tis a pity," she whispered to Annesta and thought of Morgan, who had had no proper funeral.

Archbishop Thomas Becket pushed Father Giff gently to one side, made a ritual sunwise circle around the coffin and the sign of the cross three times three to the sun at its highest

point, to pacify any ghosts or spirits that might have slipped
over the bounds to attend the service. The crowd was hushed,
straining to hear if someone dared to speak. Thomas raised his
hands and said, "What lies before us is a small matter when
compared to what lies beyond us." He pointed into the coffin.
"The lady's spirit has fled across the bounds and we shall
never know her earthly, highest hopes." He grabbed Owain's
arm and whispered, "Help me." Together they laid the marble
lid over the top, hiding Christiannt's face forever from the
sunshine that spread over the graveyard of the Church-with-
the-White-Porch.

XX
Louis VII

In 1163, when Henry II's forces again moved against
Gwynedd, the archives of Lundy Island recorded that
"an emissarie of the Prince of Gwynet landed at Lund
to seek aide against Henrie of Englande." (Devonshire
Records, Exeter, 1893)
Richard Deacon, *Madoc and the Discovery of America*

Nine days after Christiannt's funeral, the winter cold snap
moderated and Llieu called a special outdoor meeting under
the sacred oaks. All the Pyrdian druids, their fosterlings and
trusted friends came to hear Madoc's and Conlaf's explanation
of why it took them four years to bring home the signature of
the king of France.

Annesta and Mona helped Brenda lay a calf-hide on the
cold, soggy ground where they could sit. Molly and her children laid their hides close to Brenda's.

Brenda thought Owain looked as though he were balanced
on the thin edge of a sword blade and could fall off at any
moment or, worse, be sliced in half. He was thin, with dark
rings under his eyes, and his fine white beard had turned brittle
and yellow.

Llieu stood so everyone could see he was wearing a multicolored sash around the middle of his gray tunic and a string
of amber around his neck to show that he was the one who
had called the meeting. "I ask the gods to bless all of us gathered here," he said, "especially the two lads who were gone
so long that I thought they were drowned or killed by French
freebooters or that they fell off the edge of the Earth." The
words brought forth murmurs and chuckles. "Anon! Both lads

came home healthy with experiences they will never forget. Prince Owain already has had an audience with them, which he says captivated him so much he lost all track of time. 'Tis with joy that I bring you Master Madoc, who studies navigation and movement of the stars, and Master Conlaf, who studies the art of healing and natural philosophy."

Llywarch and Gwalchmai played an introduction on their harps.

Owain smiled and said in a loud voice, "I rejoice and say thank you, uh—I forgot your names—for keeping my signed briefs in a waterproof sharkskin pouch and leaving those dog-eared, water-stained holy books that were your journals on my desk for me to read."

Llieu whispered in Owain's ear.

"Aye, Madoc and Conlaf," Owain said aloud. "I thank the gods that the sun shines warm today. Five, six days ago I nearly froze, was snow-blind, and I lost my way coming from Llyn Coron. I wanted to have a feast of reason with my foolish son, Dafydd. I failed, and instead I buried my wife. I be here today because, in troth, 'twould please me to hear about Paris." His bewhiskered lips curled upward and he held out shaking hands toward the speakers' station.

Brenda could not get over the sunken cheeks, the bony arms and blue-veined hands, which had not been possessed by the hearty, mature leader she remembered before Christiannt's body was found. Owain wore a brown gown with a plaited blue girdle such as a crofter might wear. He wore no cap or crown, but his yellowed chin whiskers were neatly tucked inside a leather bag and tied behind his ears. He had withered to a wizened old man almost overnight. The sight of him saddened her.

"Folks," Madoc said, "Prince Owain is used to standing before a crowd and talking about things he knows best, more so than either myself or my friend Conlaf. We have already told him about our trip, but there may be things we left out or that he would like to question. Will you permit the prince to talk with us as we talk about our four years away from Gwynedd? Conlaf will keep the stories of our travels moving. The prince will ask us questions that will lead to questions you might ask us and we will try to answer them. Be comfortable because this is the story of four years compressed to one afternoon."

People smiled and there was a tremendous applause.

Brenda felt chagrin at criticizing Owain's age. Madoc had used Owain's age and experience to a great advantage without detracting from his dignity. It seemed to be a natural ability. She was proud of him.

"I really like that lad," said Molly, noticing that Annesta could not take her eyes off of Madoc.

Owain sat against a pile of goatskins with his back to a freshly kindled fire. He tucked his feet under his thighs and motioned with trembling hands for the crowd to be seated. He listened attentively as the two young men on either side of him vied in their enthusiasm to tell about their adventures. They interrupted each other, struck each other on the chest and pushed or pounded on Owain's knees for attention.

Being the centerpiece for the zeal of the two lads, Owain felt better than he had in a long time. He moved his eyes from one to the other as if he watched a cockfight. He could not control the flow of saliva and kept a clean, white cloth in one scrawny hand to dab at his mouth from time to time. "I praise the gods," he said. "The passion to kill is not in either of you lads, so I do not have to worry when you are near me. 'Tis wearing to be head of a province these days."

Madoc raised his eyes to meet his father's and smiled faintly. He wished he knew more about this man who wore druid honor marks but was well known to take the life of a man or woman who stood in the way of peace or liberty for the people in Gwynedd. Druids believe life is sacred, a gift to be treasured. What did his father believe? Did he believe in freedom and peace?

While Owain held forth, Madoc moved to the other side of Conlaf. Instead of complaining about the true inward smart he felt because his aging father was taking up the afternoon's time, he admonished Conlaf not to talk to the prince about the more complicated political maneuverings now taking place in England and France. He whispered, "Conlaf, keep your mouth shut about how the New Religionists are mixed up in the gov-

ernment of England and France. Prince Owain is an old man
and will not understand. I think 'twould be best not to say that
King Henry holds Archbishop Becket's life in his hands.
Owain has just buried his wife and has a lot of other things
on his mind."

"Owain looks beyond tired," Molly whispered to Brenda. "I
wish he would sit still. Remember when he rode two times
nine leagues a day in sleet or rain without feeling tired? Something hangs heavy on his shoulders."

"It must be waiting for the war with Dafydd that has un-
nerved him," said Brenda. "He has fallen to his nadir."

Emphasizing her words with hands dry-brown as seaweed,
Molly said, "The Greek Euripides said old age leaves a person
'a mere shadow with a voice.' "

The harshness of Madoc's admonitions about what not to say
annoyed Conlaf. "Prince Owain," he said, "druids and friends,
can you believe the Church is mixed up with the politics of
both France and England?"

Owain cleared his throat. "I know Thomas of London has
enemies inside Henry's court, but that is naught. Caesar had
his friend, Brutus, and I have my son, Lord Dafydd. People
are anxious when they no longer know what the bounds are."
He made a twisted smile, leaned against the goatskins,
wheezed and gasped for breath with what Conlaf thought was
surely a churchyard cough.

Brenda had seen Owain smile with the onset of the pain
and heard her own heart beat. Owain relaxed and his face
brightened. She shifted her attention to Madoc.

Madoc whispered to Conlaf, "Any damn fool can see the
prince is ill."

Conlaf whispered, "I can see his cough brings up red-
speckled sputum."

Owain said, "I would give anything to change shape into a
lad like you and not wander off the main road."

Madoc took a deep breath to overcome his flusters.

The harpers sang a song, and Owain told the lads to continue.

"Thomas of London found out that King Henry kept the coronation of his eldest surviving son a secret," said Conlaf. "Thomas was so furious that he excommunicated, with papal authority, all the bishops of London and Salisbury who participated in that crowning. The coronation was Thomas's obligation; no wonder he was angry. Next Henry accused Thomas of spending wantonly when he was chancellor. That made Thomas hide somewhere in France. Now 'tis rumored that his life is in danger."

The crowd was deathly quiet; even the small children sat still.

"Thomas's life—?" Owain wiped his mouth. "Who said that?" He looked Conlaf straight in the eyes, making him uneasy.

"Who?" said Madoc. " 'Tis Conlaf who is the first to tell you what we found out from King Louis in Paris." Madoc throttled his pity and put a hand on one of Owain's bony knees. For the first time, he noticed that the brown gown was faded and stained with dried food and sputum. His blood boiled at seeing his father ill-kempt and he told himself to rebuke his mother or one of the maids for not taking care of him. "Do you know that Henry had his young son crowned by the archbishop of York, against papal prohibition, to ensure the family succession? Shamelessly in his own lifetime!" he said.

Owain shook his head. "For God's eyren and the love of Lugh! 'Tis against the natural order of things! I, the prince of Gwynedd, ought to know what is going on! I have informants to bring information, but no one brought that to me."

"That is what I say, for the love of Lugh!" said Conlaf. "A prince of Gwynedd ought to know what is going on, not leave the world upon a shelf. He should have knights or squires to bring him information!"

"I have emissaries! I sent them to Paris to bring me information. They stayed long enough to grow into men. I ask you, were my emissaries planning to stay? What made you come back? Tell me your names once again." Owain's red-rimmed eyes squinted as if the filtered sunlight was too strong. He looked confused.

Madoc looked at Conlaf. "I told you not to perplex him."

Brenda wished she could move closer to hear what the whisperings were all about.

Madoc said, "When it was time to leave, we, Gwynedd's emissaries, took the only ship coming this way. Unfortunately, the shipmaster was a trader who insisted we work for our passage. We sailed from France to Iceland, then to Aberffraw."

"Iceland!" Owain swung his head back and forth like a bear with a hornet's nest about his ears, and no other words came from his open mouth.

Madoc said, "Your Highness, remember we have much more to tell the folks."

"I wish Owain would be quiet and let the two lads tell their story," said Brenda. "Owain acts as though this is his last chance to speak and he will not let go of it."

Owain put one parchment-dry hand on Madoc's knee and with tears in his eyes said loud enough for everyone to hear, "Women! Love for one can drive a man across mountains, but usually in the end 'tis too soft. Respect is more important and it is not gained by putting an arm around some smooth-skinned female and whispering honeyed phrases into her ear." He poked Madoc with a sharp elbow, wiped his mouth and said he knew his wife had had a lover, who was the slain false knight. He rolled his eyes and said the day came when an arrow flew the wrong way from the knight's crossbow, piercing his heart. " 'Twas a terrible accident. Women keep their tongue in their pocket until they marry. Anyone who marries Henry's homely half-sister, Emma, is not fit to be a king in Wales!"

This is my children's father, thought Brenda, whose wits are unsettled, whose body disintegrates. Her heart ached.

Owain spoke in a loud voice to Madoc and Conlaf. "A strong leader cannot afford to have known enemies, especially if they be kin."

Brenda felt a tingle of fear run up the middle of her back. Her mouth went dry and her heart hammered against her chest. She wanted to tell Madoc to change the subject quickly before Owain's loose tongue said too much.

The harpers began, and before they finished Owain waved

a clawlike hand and said, "Thank you. Gwynedd has the best harpers in Britain." He stretched out his spindly legs. His worn-thin, soft-soled shoes seemed to be molded to his feet. His face relaxed; he arranged a fur on his lap and smoothed it over his knees. He touched Madoc's hand. "Do not worry about Henry," he said. "His army is unwieldy and no match for Gwynedd's soldiers in windswept, rain-soaked bogs. When Henry crossed the Berwyn Mountains in a torrential autumn rain, he had one look at me and my soldiers and ran home with his dismal tail between his legs." He laughed, wiped his mouth and said, "Lads, tell us chronologically what happened on your trip. Start at the beginning. 'Tis late, but never too late for a good story."

Madoc told about stopping at the Bardsey monastery and meeting Cadwallon, who by now was probably a full abbot. "Your son, Cadwallon, could have been a good chief or lord of a province," he said.

"Nay, my friend, you are looking at only one side of the man. You see him as easy to talk with and how quickly he understands others' feelings. To be a lord of a province, a man must be able to put all emotion away. He must do what is best for the future of his people, even it it means a war, using his own kin as hostages, or his own life. He can never cry over what is done or what is inevitable. Do the druids still make that clear to their students? If not, I shall have a talk with Llieu."

Brenda was relieved to hear Owain speak clearly and sensibly again.

"Yes," said Madoc. "The druids teach that each of us carries his own destination in his heart. It takes only courage to fulfill it. I do not believe, as some do, that whatever befalls us was preordained for us from eternity. We make our own destiny."

"I like a man who thinks for himself," said Owain, clapping his hands and standing so that the crowd applauded.

Madoc sat up a little straighter and smiled.

Brenda could see that he was beginning to like Prince Owain.

"Your Highness," interrupted Conlaf. "Lord William of

Lundy worries that the English king will build a military base on his island. William, like you, does not trust King Henry." His eyes lit up and a quirky little smile flitted across his face. "While we were at Lundy—imagine this!—Madoc and I married a lot of the couples because a man of religion had not been to their island for years."

Owain's head tilted toward Conlaf and his hand shot up to make a cup against his ear.

"Madoc, dressed as a priest, was so aroused by the mating festivities that he—"

Madoc's face turned red as a wild strawberry; he ground his teeth together and hissed, "Shhh! This is not a story to pass around like sweet cakes at Samhain." He reached his arm out and slapped Conlaf on the back, causing him to cough. " 'Tis nothing of real importance," he said, looking at Annesta, who had one hand over her mouth.

"Do you think I do not deserve to be told?" asked Owain, pointing his bony finger at Madoc. His eyes glinted in the sunlight.

"Well, nay, my lord," said Madoc. "So, 'twas this way. I talked to one of the Lundy lasses, because she understood Welsh. She explained the Lundy customs while we paddled around in a coracle, much like our own fishing vessels. She called the craft an eggshell."

Brenda saw that Madoc was embarrassed because he ran his words together with hardly a breath between.

"We went swimming and the girl took me home, where, we—you know," his face turned red again, "we *danced*. 'Tis the custom, when there is a marriage, for unrelated men and women to pair off and to *dance*. The lass, named Blackberries, knew what to do and it was—ah, nice, ah, surprising—oh Lugh! What I mean—you know what I mean!"

The men in the crowd stamped their feet and gave appreciative chuckles.

Brenda frowned.

Molly slapped her knees, saying, "That lad is too honest for his own good, and I truly love him!"

Owain raised his head so everyone could see the creases at the corners of his eyes. His mouth was turned up, and he guffawed. Afterward he said there was no reason to act as though it was something to hide. " 'Tis a natural pleasure the gods gave us. I agree with you, lad. The first time a man *dances* with a lass is a nice surprise. 'Tis good for him. I bet my silver bratt-pin that Conlaf was jealous." He laughed and winked at Conlaf, who blushed.

Brenda, Annesta and Molly looked at one another. Molly could not suppress her giggles and said, "I told you he was a good lad, truthful, and knowledgeable. The best kind to know."

Annesta hid her red face.

Brenda giggled. "I be learning more about this trip than I thought I would."

Conlaf pushed his hair from his eyes, sat straight and told Owain about the time they were abducted as spies and taken to the royal prison in a two-wheeled cart that smelled like it had hauled human waste. "Christ's eyes! Madoc was scared we would be tried and judged by the king's men and lose our heads. King Louis knew we were innocent, but he acted capricious and did not prevent our imprisonment nor give us a pardon. Luckily he had already signed your brief. Your Highness, he may be your good friend, but we were lucky to meet an Algerian trader. He got us and one of the prison guards out of prison and onto a ship, where we became messmates, deck-swabs and, in a rare instance, pilots to pay our passage to Aberffraw."

Madoc changed the subject and said, "Did you notice that King Louis sent you a treaty written not on vellum, but on an eastern medium he calls *papier*? 'Tis made from rags and gelatin. Louis stamped the brief with a fleur-de-lis, his coat of arms. He says it shows his devotion to the Trinity. If you cannot read French, I can, or Conlaf, who is even better than I."

Owain searched the furs for his cloth and stood up. His thin, mottled hands shook when he broke the wax seal. He turned, held the paper to the firelight and scratched off some of the gelatin. "I studied with druids, same as you," he said. "I can read French—and Latin, too." He read the words and raised his face to the sky. "Hallelujah! Lord Lugh and the Lord

God are good! My dearest wish has come true. I be not the only ruler who feels Henry is treacherous. Louis writes that he has proof the English king talks from both sides of his face. No one who reads this can say I will die alone in a fight against that weasel Henry." The hollows in his cheeks were dark. He wiped the spittle from the corners of his mouth and read on, "Conan the Fourth, Duke of Brittany, is pushing his daughter, Constance, to marry King Henry's son Geoffrey. I would like to warn her that Geoffrey is a bloody tomcat. Anyone can see that Conan is trying to unite France and England, but, according to my reliable friends, having his daughter marry King Henry's son is not the way."

"We talked about a lot of things, but Louis never told us about trouble with Conan of Brittany," said Madoc.

"Louis is unable to say boo to a goose," said Owain, "but he has manners and is well born. He is more like an honest man than a criminal. I believe he will not break a pledge nor a treaty with Gwynedd. Louis falsely believes a king commands incessantly whether he wins obedience or not. He falsely believes everything will be the same a century hence. He lets grass grow under his feet, is dreamy and dull with reminiscings. I can die happy! France is on our side against England." He sank back into the pile of goatskins.

"Do not speak of dying," whispered Madoc. "It does not appear seemly. When you feel ill, Conlaf will help you beat the bounds."

The audience stood on their feet and clapped heartedly. Some examined the *papier* and compared its light weight with vellum.

Brenda stood on her tiptoes, saw Madoc rise to his haunches and put his hand on his father's shoulder. She thought he looked like he really wanted to call Owain "Father." She had an almost irresistible desire to call out, "Owain! He is your son. The son that loves the sea!"

Owain spoke in a loud voice so that Madoc and Conlaf could hear above the applause. "Listen and remember. Thomas of London told me long ago about a recurring dream. He sees me gasping for breath and looking into the face of one of my dragon sons, who smiles and looks down into my dead eyes.

And in the same dream, Thomas sees himself, a year to the day after my death, dying at the hands of one of his most trusted men, his chaplain. Thomas says there will be a celestial phenomenon, such as an eclipse, comet or falling star, announcing our deaths. He insists we both will die of unnatural causes."

"Do not dwell on superstitious signs," said Madoc.

"Well, hear this: My mistress, Brenda, told my fortune by runes last week and in four casts the messages were black. In the first cast the rune naut, which is a warning, fell in the lagu section, which means all my plans will fail; then the rune of thorn fell in the earth quadrant, showing there was anger in my future and someone would rebel against me. The rune oss fell outside the circle so I can be sure there will be some miscalculation or some accident. When skjabene fell outside the circle, I knew, before Brenda told me, that it meant *my* death, not hers."

The applause stopped and Brenda moved closer. Her eyes met Madoc's. He blinked, then moved closer to Owain. "I have seen the archdruids play with stones on which three sets of eight runes are chiseled," he said. "They make a game of the castings and do not put too much emphasis on their troth. The game pieces are only stones with carvings and can just as easily land inside as well as outside the circle. Please, look at the pledges that your son, Cadwallon, from Bardsey and Lord William of Lundy sent you. Believe me, they respect and honor you and the time left in your future. I want you to have a long life."

Madoc's words brought a lump to Brenda's throat. When she looked up she saw that Owain's eyes had misted and Madoc was holding his hand. She wanted to tell Owain to fight for life because Gwynedd needed him. Oh, how she wished Owain would put his arm around Madoc and call him "son." The thoughts were foolish, and she hid her face in her hands.

Madoc pulled his hand away, gave his father both Cadwallon's and Lord William's briefs and waited quietly while Owain read. He did not look at Brenda.

Owain's pale face brightened and his droopy blue eyes seemed to shine against the yellowed whites. He read on several minutes, then looked from Madoc to Conlaf and said, "I regret that Henry tried to be cunning and send a make-believe abbot to run the Bardsey monastery. I be sorry Lord William had to put a viper, that same abbot, in his prison pit for safe-keeping. For every act there is a reaction." He paused and said, "It just occurred to me that while my son Cadwallon is looking after things on Bardsey and Lord William is in charge of Lundy, a Welsh trading ship ought to stop at both islands with the goods they need. Bardsey can trade grass mats for Welsh flour and honey; Lundy can trade baskets and dyes for Welsh chickens."

"Your Majesty," said Madoc, "I would like to be that trader for Gwynedd. I shall go to Bardsey and Lundy to trade and at the same time keep you informed—as your ambassador. I dream of adding high sides and high ends to one of those ships you have given to me, to better ride the heavy seas. I will have raised and covered platforms fore and aft to keep precious papers and some of the crew out of bad weather. Most will sleep in leather pouches on the deck. I shall build Gwynedd's sea trade. Can unproved land be so very different from what we already know? Wherever there is unclaimed habitable land, I shall claim it for Gwynedd." Madoc let the words slip from his tongue, not holding anything back.

Madoc is as impulsive as his father, thought Brenda. This will change the course of his life. Is trading by sea his destiny?

"Will you indeed?" Owain's piercing ice-blue eyes seemed to look through to Madoc's soul. "Would you go like that?" He pointed to Madoc's black gown. "As an Augustinian? Would you take your friend, who sits here gaping like a hun-gry baby bird?"

"If that is your wish," said Madoc. His blue eyes sparkled. He grabbed Owain's hands and said, "To tell the truth, my friend would like to know more about leprosy, which deadens rotting limbs so there is no feeling of pain. In France some healers believe those with leprosy should be isolated to keep it from spreading. If leprosy comes to Gwynedd, Conlaf and I will encourage you to build spitals along every wayside."

Brenda's breath caught in her throat. Her lastborn was a bold lad, telling the prince of Gwynedd what to do as if he were an architect talking to a province planner.

Conlaf's eyes widened but he was silent.

"Is that so?" said Owain, running a sleeve over his eyes. "First answer this: Will you work for me?" Above Owain's beard was a small pink rose in the center of each cheek.

"Aye, as a shipmaster."

Brenda hardly breathed. The flames behind the speakers' station flared once, then died among the red coals.

Madoc put his arms across his chest.

Brenda imagined that he was trying to keep the sound of his heartbeats quiet. She fancied that he longed to tell Owain that he was his son who loved the sea much less for warring and much more for exploring.

She looked at Owain and thought she would never forget his probing blue eyes looking into Madoc's as if seeing into his very soul. She recalled that Owain's hair used to be golden as beeswax and how robust he used to look sitting astride his horse. She imagined him as a horsebacker in battle regalia with a bronze cap on his head, dressed in a leather tunic and a sword and buckler at his side. He led his dragons to quell a quarrelsome band, brandishing his sword and speaking words of wisdom, such as "I be the ruler; you are the ruled. Remember: The ruler rules; the ruled obey." It was said that Owain loved to ride till dawn grew pale and he slept as little as a nightingale.

Brenda stared at Owain and saw a great leader sitting among his furs, shriveled to a driveling old man warming his back against a dying fire. She used to believe he ruled with decorum, firmly and wisely, according to his time. But now his time was changing. The crofters and villagers loved the prince and he relied on that love and took constant care not to cause his people to hate him. Today she remembered events in his life that had led him to be ruthless but reliable. These traits made Owain loved by many and feared by a few. She felt no regret that she no longer loved this man who was the father of her children. Nevertheless, her heart fell to the floor and she wanted to weep because truth was a painful thing; but she could not weep, because regret would have been far worse.

* * *

Owain gathered a second wind and said, " 'Tis known I fa-
vored druids most of my life. Therefore, 'twould not be
strange if I asked one who will soon become a druid to be
shipmaster and another soon-to-become-a-druid to be ship
physician for a fleet of trading vessels. I know four men who
have been living in a small abbey looking after my old ships.
I owe them an honorarium. Take it to them." He dug into his
trouser pocket and came up with a handful of coins, which he
dropped into Madoc's hands.

Madoc said, "Your coins are safe with me."

Owain nodded. "My father, Gruffudd, predicted that I
would have a shipmaster who was equipped with powerful
devices that could tell directions."

"I have a lodestone that causes an iron needle to point
north," said Madoc. "I have seen an astrolabe and an Iceland
sun-stone that tells where the sun is located on a cloudy day."
His eyes met Owain's and for a brief moment they locked in
a chasm of introspection.

Owain looked away first. "So, Shipmaster," he said. "Go,
look over the large hafskip at Afon Ganol. The dowels in the
skip's planks are rotted. I bartered her from a Norseman by
giving him Cellan, my father's chief harper. Cellan was blind
and did not mind where he ate or slept after my father died,
as long as he could play his harp. The truth is, I got no bargain.
That decaying skip and some others lie in the tidal creek, not
far from the great rock called the Great Orme's Head. 'Tis
near a small village called Abergwili, some say Abergele.
Look for four men at the small Llandrillo Abbey, by a stone
quayside called Aber Cerrig Gwynion. Afon Ganol flows into
the quay." He scratched his head and thought of something.
"I think 'twould be better if you stayed Augustinian, even if
you are given honor marks. If you have one enemy, you meet
him everywhere. If you have a dozen friends, you have none
to spare. I prayed that one of my older sons would sail the
skip, but those days are past. Those lads never loved the sea,
not as I do." Owain momentarily lapsed into a reverie, then
said, "A man learns he is related to all men when struck with
intolerable suffering that grows worse each moment, like an
impending storm at sea."

Madoc was so overcome by his good fortune he did not hear the talk of Owain's suffering. "Oh, I love the sea!" he heard himself babble. "I always wanted a ship of my own. From the inside of my heart I thank you! Your four friends can help me repair the ships. They will not ask excessive fees for their work. The omens are good near Beltaine, first day of summer, best time for marriage. 'Tis a new beginning. So, if Conlaf and I will be druids, 'twill please us to be called pagans, same as you."

Owain winced and sat up. "Where there is good, there is the opposite, evil. Keep your eyes open"—he gasped for air. Spittle ran through his beard. "Lean toward the light, son. . . ." His words turned to mumbled undertones as the crowd in the sacred oak bower stood and sang out a praise to the Lord God, chief of all gods: "Hosanna!"

Brenda wondered again if this was the big task Madoc was destined to do. She was so overwhelmed with pride for her youngest son that she could barely think straight.

Annesta gave her a hug and whispered, "Like Molly, I love that lad."

Mona wiped her eyes and said, "Do you believe the druid fosterlings can bring the Old Religion back by trading from ships?"

"Aye," said Molly, "but never on our shores, lass."

The harpers played softly as the people filed out through the low-lintel gate and turned for home. It was the kind of a meeting to be remembered in bard-song for a long time.

Brenda did not get up right away. In her mind she heard the words over and over: Grief befalls a just ruler who loses faith in himself.

XXI
Troyes

The first navigators steered by the stars whenever they were out of sight of a familiar point of land. . . .

The first important instrument to help sailors find their way across the ocean was the compass. This is supposed to have been invented by the Chinese, and Arab trading ship captains seem to have borrowed it from them some time before the thirteenth century. Europeans learned about it during the Crusades, and the modern skipper of that day had his needle, magnetized by rubbing it on a loadstone, floating on a straw in a bowl of water and pointing miraculously north.

It is supposed that the astrolabe, an instrument which can measure the altitude of the sun, was learned from the same source at about the same time. . . . However, some unknown genius invented what was called a cross-staff, by means of which the navigator could calculate the distance between the moon and a fixed star and thereby get some rough idea of his position.

Peter Freuchen, with David Loth,
Book of the Seven Seas

The morning was cold but clear, and the wind blew dry leaves about in whirls of dust. Madoc and Conlaf came to the royal court's great hall to break fast and to talk to Owain about their ideas on sailing ships, ways to keep sailors healthy and trading. They greeted Llywarch, then Brenda, who sat mulling over a single word Owain had used yesterday: *son*. Did he have any idea what he had said, or was it only a manner of speech? She wondered if he was sending Madoc a message, the way a father tells a son he is loved without saying so in words. She was not entirely sure Owain had said "son" with a reason, nevertheless she felt a glow of satisfaction. She looked up and smiled at Madoc as he went over to sit on the other side of Owain. She noticed that Owain was perspiring and she was concerned because the hall was icy cold.

She told Llywarch and they moved closer to Owain, who sat up straight, said he thought a spirit had come through the thin veil between sunup and midmorning and sat on his chest.

"As a physician I say that was no unseen spirit, my lord," said Conlaf.

"You could see it?" asked Owain with surprise.

"Nay," said Conlaf. " 'Twas inside your chest. Your heart is tired of pushing blood back and forth from your head to your toes."

"I've never heard such a thing!" cried Owain. "I have the heart of a lion. It can stand anything. I have tested it many times and found it can be crushed, trampled and broken but it always mends. 'Tis my stomach that cramps now and then."

Brenda opened her mouth to reply.

Llywarch put his hand on her shoulder. "Let him be," he whispered.

Conlaf brought a beaker of mead for Owain to sip and sat next to Brenda to ask what she knew about the strange pains the prince was having.

Suddenly, a red-haired man wearing wool leggings and boots of deer hide and leading a small band of rowdy, grimy-faced dragons in Gwynedd's blue tunics strutted into the hall. A polecat's front claws were fastened to the outside of each boot heel to give him footing in mud or snow. Standing close to the leader was a short, stocky man with thick black hair and tangled brows.

Llywarch leaned toward Brenda and whispered, "Do you recognize them? The redhead is Lord Howell and the short one is Lord Maelgwyn."

Maelgwyn carried a long-handled spear, the blade decorated with different qualities of iron and steel wire welded together and hammered when hot. Several lengths of green, umber and blue yarn were tied below the blade, as though it was a ceremonial staff showing the colors that identified this particular dragon band. The soldiers elbowed their way past the serving maids. Some of them grinned, made the sign of the cross and asked for bread and mead, others moved their arms back and forth in front of the dying coals. All of them wore short bratts fastened on the right shoulder with elaborate brooches. The right side of the bratt was open, leaving one arm free to use the sword that hung from their leather belts.

Owain stood and nodded to the curious kitchen maids to place mead and bread on the table for the noisy newcomers.

Howell's right hand remained on his scabbard as he approached Owain. He spoke haltingly, as though he had run a long way and held a small stone in his mouth. "Father, I be heartened to see you looking so well. You can see that I be well enough to be with my soldiers. First I want you to see that my brother Maelgwyn's retainers have joined with us and he is now my staff-bearer. Second, I have come to warn you that Dafydd plans to invade your keep, rout you out like a dog and let you live however possible off the land. He is at war with us. Your late wife informed Dafydd that your health is sorely slipping, your soldiers are stationed at the English border and the stars are favorable for a military takeover of Gwynedd. I ask your permission to place retainers inside your courtyard for your protection. Other troops will camp outside of Aberffraw near the shore. I ask you to declare war on Dafydd. If you say aye, my men are prepared to call your soldiers away from Offa's Dyke and set up camp with us here."

"Do you question my ability to take care of my own court and run off an enemy, no matter who 'tis?" said Owain. "I may be old, but I tell you there is naught wrong with my brain and there is no need for one brother warring another. My own soldiers can take care of Dafydd, who, I admit, seems hell-bent on battle."

"Lord Howell looks all right," Brenda whispered to Llywarch. "Better than when I saw him at the druid camp."

"He talks funny," said Madoc.

"So would you," said Conlaf, "if your tongue had been cut off and sewn back on." He pulled his Augustinian hood around his face and nudged Madoc to do the same. Neither wanted to be recognized by Lord Howell.

"Howell, I have never asked you to take care of my problems," said Owain. "My soldiers can send Dafydd's dragons, and even yours, hightailing. Take your hand off your scabbard. 'Tis ill luck to unsheath a sword inside my castle."

"Be it as you say, Father, but mark my words; Dafydd will not heed you, and you will sorely need us in the days to come," said Howell. "If our men battle this night, the combat is not ill luck, but it becomes a divination rite because 'tis at the boundary of the sun season."

Owain laughed. "Beltaine marks an *adwy*, a gap, in the fighting season." He paused for nine heartbeats and said, "The man who flees and the man who fights are equal fools!"

Howell looked puzzled.

Owain said, "If you, or any sons of my flesh, contrive my downfall, you should remember that a man is hard to kill until his time comes."

"I come in peace!" protested Howell. " 'Tis not I who wants war."

Owain turned and pointed a thin, clawlike finger at Madoc and Conlaf. "You there sitting beneath those black cowls! Get up! Come here! Tell these numps how you are going to build my trade in the coastal waters and pick up unproved land in the name of Gwynedd, same as Saint Brendan did for Ireland. Explain how a man can turn a trading ship into a war ship using Greek-fire to fight off anyone, including King Henry's navy."

Madoc stood straight.

Brenda's heart thrummed against her chest as she saw her son trying to think what he knew about Greek-fire.

Madoc looked at Conlaf, who spread his hands and whispered, "If only he had asked me to explain leprosy!"

Madoc stuttered, " 'Tis—'tis not helpful for a trader to be known as a rogue. If *Y Cymry* had a trading fleet there would be more contact with outside peoples and Gwynedd's position would be strengthened because there would be an interest in larger trading fairs, more to think about, less time for warring it, a peaceful existence. Transactions of a good trade are twice blessed; they give benefit to both parties. If we begin small to get tuaths and provinces in *Cymru* trading with one another, they would bond in friendship."

"Your Holiness," said Howell, "if you trade by sea, what kind of ship would you use, a curragh?"

"The hafskip," said Madoc. " 'Tis shorter and draws more water than the longskip. 'Tis broader in the beam and has a higher freeboard. Its proper keep makes a tall mast possible. In strong winds 'tis a faster sail. It has a massive steering paddle that is secured to the steer-board. I would have the square sail made of linen. Leather gets heavy when wet and can break a mast."

"So what about the tackle and anchor cable?"

"Both can be made of walrus hide, on account of its great strength."

"How will you keep your cargo dry?" asked the flag-bearer, Maelgwyn.

"Store it amidship and cover it with ox hides. On top I would lash a coracle or two. I shall have a ship's tent or awning that can be rigged when conditions are favorable. I shan't have banks and banks of oars, just a few fitted fore and aft and used for getting in and out of port and for use in times of calm. I would fain like a pennon or wind-vane at the masthead."

Owain surprised him by asking, "Have you thought of the sagging and hogging on your ship?"

"The hafskip is light and flexible, and rises and falls easily on waves. My ship shall draw no more than three feet of water. As for sagging, 'twill be naught because the hafskip is short. The trick of hogging is slight, since the cargo is carried amidships. If I need more weight I can carry extra tuns of fresh water or stones. I will set a trade route from here to the Southern Isles; the Hebrides and the Sheep Islands; the Faeroes, all the way to Iceland and west to unnamed lands."

"What if your ship meets a freebooter?" asked Maelgwyn. "You monks think you know so much."

Madoc's eyes opened wide and he knew there was only one thing to say, "I would use Greek-fire."

"And pray tell what is this elusive Greek-fire?" asked Howell.

" 'Tis a mixture of certain gums," said Conlaf, smiling and winking at Madoc.

"Like sulfur, pitch and oil," said Madoc.

"And wine, horse manure and vinegar," said Conlaf, holding his head high.

"You forgot walrus vomit," said Madoc with a slight upturn to his lips.

"When set on fire 'tis almost inextinguishable," said Conlaf with a smirk.

"You seem to know something of weapons and ships," said Howell. "I wish you good fortune and a pocketful of coins to build the hafskip you described. The English brag about having a powerful navy. I hope they leave your trading ship alone. If my father likes Greek-flame and you are going to work for him, you ought not be priestly passive about using it for a little warring. Pray tell what that Greek-flame will do besides smell foul and burn like an all-night candle."

Madoc's face turned red. "If Gwynedd had one well-built ship, she could hold off two English naval vessels. Greek-fire can be a liquid and pumped at enemy ships or thrown as a solid. It depends on how much resin is used in the ingredients." He was pretending confidence, but sure as morning light he knew about early explorers and ships, and he would find out more about this Greek-fire. He took a deep breath, looked straight at Lord Howell and figured if he did not question his story, he did not know what Greek-fire was either. "Think what Greek-fire could do for a battalion of soldiers on land," he said. "Take my word. It smells and looks worse than hell's fire. A man never forgets a siege with Greek-fire. It sears his brain and becomes imbedded in his nostrils so he smells naught else for the rest of his life."

Brenda saw Owain put his hand over his mouth and nose, raise his eyes to the ceiling and quickly turn back to Howell. "You and your brother Dafydd, and any other son of mine, would do better to unite and defend our land against the English. This night marks the beginning of a whole new fleet of trading ships. Gwynedd will be known in foreign ports. One

day she will truly expand her territory in unexplored lands."
Owain moved one step at a time until he stood close to Howell. "The light fades," he said, "and 'tis time for you to be in
your camp."

" 'Tis midday," said Howell. "You speak as if you are daft!
Planning a navy or even a trading fleet with monks. Gwynedd
with a shipmaster-priest!" He shot Madoc and Conlaf a dark
look. "So be it for now. You will need us and we will be
back—you can bet on it!"

Maelgwyn and the dragon soldiers followed Howell outside. Owain closed the door behind them and wiped his mouth.
His eyes softened from steel gray to misty blue. "Your orders
are to build me a fleet of trading ships. A fleet that can be
transformed to a navy or, better yet, outfitted to explore new
territory in the name of Gwynedd. Lads, if you tell a big story
about the future, be certain that it happens!" He grinned from
ear to ear. "Lugh's lungs, you not only know ships, you have
a way with words. You are lucky I did not say *stop*! God's
teeth, I wish I had known men like you years ago. We could
have been a terrible trio! Those fine soldiers had no idea what
you were talking about. It was all Greek to them!"

Brenda's heart pounded harder than the incoming surf in a
wind storm as she watched Madoc seize Owain's hands, shake
them and say, "Your Highness, you were feistier and stronger
than most men half your age."

"Do not fret over cost, but be frugal," Owain said, waving
them toward the door. "Thanks to you, those two sons believe
I be mad! A shipmaster-priest! Unheard of! Greek-fire and a
Welsh trading fleet! A fiendish dream! Be gone! Out of my
sight! And I love you!" Before the door shut he called, "Bring
me your plans on vellum!"

Midmorning was cold and blustery. Brenda was outside stirring the boiling laundry with a bleached pole when she heard
approaching footsteps. She looked up and saw Madoc and
Conlaf grinning on either side of a great hulk of a lad clothed
in black. His unkempt hair and tangled beard were black as a
tinker's pot. With one hand he held firm to a black tricornered

hat trimmed with yellow braid so that the wind would not steal it off his head.

Madoc said, "We have come to introduce you to our good friend Troyes, our former prison guard. His da was a Lorraine druid, who tended the wounded soldiers who fought on the side of Louis the Sixth against the brigand Thomas de Marle. His da preached peace and justice but lost his life in Marle's second campaign. To honor his da, Troyes is going to study medicine and become a druid."

"When I met these lads," said Troyes, "I wore a tunic that reached my knees and iron keys on a leather belt loop. The only thing left of my French guard days is this hat." He laughed nervously and rubbed wind-blown dust from his eyes. "It honors me to meet the famous woman healer. Archdruid Llieu told me ye heal wheals, pustules and pimples overnight and ye concoct new curatives just as fast."

"Mother of God! You speak Welsh!" said Brenda.

"*Frère* Madoc and *Frère* Conlaf would let me speak naught else on the ship from Paris. I beg yur pardon for my *Français* accent and words I forget. My memory is not as good as yours."

"Oh, my," said Brenda, stretching out her hand. "I be the one honored. I be indebted to you for getting these lads out of prison. Come inside the laundry cottage, all of you—out of the wind."

Brenda noticed that Troyes dragged one foot, making him walk with a limp.

"We are on our way to the great hall to meet Llywarch and let Madoc say his good-byes. Come with us," said Conlaf.

"I leave tomorrow," said Madoc. "The weather is good to begin repairs on the old ships rotting on dry land."

She wanted to cry out that he had hardly been home long enough for her to know him. Instead she reached under a clean laundry pile, pulled out a gray woolen bratt and handed it to him. " 'Tis yours," she said. "I worked on it whenever I had an extra moment."

" 'Tis beautiful and exactly what I need," he said, smiling, and on impulse kissed her cheek.

She gave one of the other maids her laundry pole, saying

she would not be gone long. On the way to the hall she asked if Troyes was going to help repair the ships.

"*Non*," said Troyes. "I have too much to learn about Welsh healing. When I see a tongue that is dry, cold, moist or hot, I know the seat, the humor and condition of that person. But I know little of the powers of pestilences, favorable planets, digestives and nutritives. Mayhap ye will teach me."

"I too want to study with you," said Conlaf. "I be staying with the druids to treat Prince Owain."

Brenda was surprised and flattered. "Someone ought to go with Madoc!" she said. "What does he know about repairing ships?"

"I will be close to several villages, Rhos, Llandudno, and Degannwy. Surely someone there can help me," said Madoc.

"Aye, yes, go to Degannwy, to the court on the hill, and see Lord Iorwerth. He will find someone to help you," said Brenda.

Madoc gave his mother a sharp look and mumbled between clenched teeth, "I be not a wee laddie. I can look out for myself."

They found Llywarch in the hall talking with Annesta and Mona. Annesta asked the location of Afon Ganol.

Llywarch said, "Granddaughter, you know where lies the Great Orme's Head? Go from there east along the shoreline to the Little Orme's then to Rhos on Sea. 'Tis there Madoc will find his ships or ask someone where they are hidden."

Mona could not take her eyes off of Troyes's muscular arms. "I was thinking how easily you could pull back on a tight bowstring," she said, and blushed red as the coals in the fireplace.

"*Oui*, I could," Troyes said. "But weapons of war are not my goal. I threw my lot in with two scruffy Augustinians who believe one's freedom and dignity is a natural way of life. Now I cannot go back to Paris unless I want to be hanged."

Mona's eyes grew large. "Oh, no!" she squealed.

"Do not fret. I owe allegiance to no one in France. With these two, I have seen things ye would not believe. Sea monsters with eyes as big as bread plates, backs as broad and long

as a crofter's barn, mouths as big as a washtub and teeth as
big as your fist."

Mona clapped her hand over her mouth with disbelief.

Troyes laughed deep inside his thick chest. "We saw an
Icelandic father throw his newborn lassie into the sea to drown
because he had no food for an extra mouth. Most men would
not think of fishing a wee lassie out of the icy sea to bring
her aboard a trade ship. Madoc did. He named her *Seren*, Star,
and took her to Brendan's Creek on one of the Faeroes. He
gifted her to mademoiselle Freda, who was so lonely she
wanted to die. The Faeroese have probably added Madoc to
their *Faeroeinga Saga*. Living in these times is a privilege."

Brenda could not help but like Troyes. Llywarch clapped
Madoc on the back and asked how he was able to bring an
infant aboard a trading ship.

"In a box that had my clothing piled on top. 'Tis a wonder
I did not smother the weean. I fed her goat's milk from a
bottle plugged with a wad of wool. 'Twas harder to bring the
bloody goat aboard."

When the three young men were ready to leave, Annesta
asked her grandfather if she might walk as far as the druid
camp with the lads. "I want to ask more about Freda and Star
and the sea creatures they saw. I will be back before sundown."

Llywarch turned to Brenda. "What would you say?"

"I would say, 'Aye, if Mona goes.' " She touched Troyes's
hand and said, "*Merci bien!* for permitting two lads from Gwynedd to escape the Paris prison."

She caught Madoc by the sleeve. "I will say good-bye on
the morrow."

"I leave for Afon Ganol before sunup." He put one arm
around her and whispered, "Please, take care of Annesta."

Brenda hugged him and nodded. "Send us a message if you
can. We shall miss you."

Madoc saw that Llywarch was still talking with his granddaughter, so he whispered, "Will Owain ask you to marry
him?"

"If he did, I would tell him nay. If I were his wife we
would not get along. He has changed. He plots the future of

Gwynedd with the archbishop of Canterbury, who mixes the New Religion with the Old. I do not love the man he has become. He forgets to bathe. He hardly knows I be about. Shhh, that is a secret you must promise to keep." She put her arms around his neck, kissed him and whispered close to his ear, "I love you and know that your destiny is greater than any woman's love, Annesta loves you and does not burden herself with your destiny. I envy her." She gave him another hug and told him that the dusty wind and smoke from the fireplace caused her eyes to water.

Llywarch, loath to let Annesta go, held her hand. "Since Lady Christiannt's death you hang around looking for something to do," he said. "Make me a bratt as handsome as the one Brenda made for Madoc. Clean my cottage. Be my maid!"

"I be your maid, Grandfather. See how you make Madoc wait. He and I shall never catch up to the others!"

"Oh, 'tis the gods who caused me to detain you!" said Llywarch. "They know the future better than I. Go! Stay away from Lord Howell's soldiers who march along the roads. I do not want one of those soldiers telling me they saw my granddaughter looking moon-eyed at a monk or, worse, found her in an uncommmendable position with an irresponsible monk."

She gave her grandfather a black look and scurried out the door, pulling red-faced Madoc after her.

"Woe is me!" sighed Llywarch. " 'Tis frightening how two young people of the opposite sex burn to be alone, though they would swear to the contrary. 'Tis impossible to keep them apart for a moment. I know from experience the joy that young men and women have together. I can almost hear the gods laughing behind my back and saying that I be a jealous old loon who cannot tell a love song from a lament. I promise you, I can tell!"

Brenda uttered a deep sigh and told Llywarch that he was not the only one who was burdened with worry about hot-blooded youth. "Mayhap that is why destiny sends my son away. 'Twill give your granddaughter's fever time to cool."

"And time for your son to remember a druid acts with the good of others uppermost in his thoughts," said Llywarch.

"My son is not a druid," said Brenda.

"He was fostered by druids most of his life," said Llywarch with a gleam in his eye. "And Owain said he would be a druid."

" 'Tis wrong for us to bicker," said Brenda. "I love them both."

"Me too," said Llywarch. "But when your son wants something, he overwhelms with his use of words." He chuckled. "Just like his *mam*."

Brenda gave him a crooked smile and sipped her mead.

XXII
Awarring

> The Welsh recognized no allegiance to Rome [or England]. . . . By the eighth century a frontier dyke, built by King Offa of the Mercians, acknowledged the particular separateness of Wales. The dyke is still there, a bumpy ditch and earthwork which marks, in many places, the border between England and Wales. It is not a very fearsome barrier, in many stretches hardly more than a gentle heave at the edge of a meadow, and it seems to have been made by agreement between parties, not as a fortification but as a demarcation zone (though its more puzzling gaps may have been left deliberately as killing grounds). Its construction however was to have a profoundly allegorical meaning: on the eastern side of it the English rose to world supremacy, on the west the Welsh survived.
>
> Jan Morris, *The Matter of Wales*

Owain's back was stooped, his hands trembled and one corner of his mouth twitched. His brown-mottled face was as juiceless as last year's apples. He sat down at the table opposite Brenda and Llywarch, quietly sipped cottage tea until the light faded and retainers brought in candles for the table and torches for the wall-sconces. Brenda asked if he wanted his beaker refilled. He licked his lips and scolded them for not noticing that he had been waiting to be introduced to the Frenchman. "Now the lad is gone! You show me no courtesy. I stood by the wall and saw him for the first time yesterday." With milky eyes he looked from Brenda to Llywarch and back to Brenda. "You people have abandoned courtesy and lack manners and generosity toward your elders." He turned away from Brenda's stuttering sounds and fluttering hands and turned to Llywarch. "But, out of kindness, you, who are much older, might have called me over." His body moved from side to side, like an animal ready to pounce.

Llywarch was mystified by Owain's accusation. "Your Highness, we did not see you standing in the shadows. Let us help you back to your chamber where we might talk in private."

He pointed a bony finger at Brenda. "I also saw you kiss an Augustinian and there were tears in your eyes! Is he someone new? A friend of yours? What is he to you?"

"What is he to me?" Brenda did not know what to say. She could not say that the Augustinian was her son—*their* lastborn son.

"I have a notion to crush your head into pomace!" shouted Owain.

"Pomace? Pulp? You wish me dead, like Christiannt? To save my life I can not recall misbehaving with the druid fosterling, who was told by you to wear the gown of an Augustinian." Brenda's breath came in spurts. Her mind whirled as she tried to imagine what Owain might have seen. Finally she asked with as much calmness as she was able, "What foulness be I accused of that would suggest my head be used for verjuice, the juice from sour, green crab apples?"

"With my own eyren I saw you and the monk caress each other and kiss and kiss," said Owain. "Monks do not avail themselves to foreplay in my court! What is your story?"

"I was not—!" said Brenda. She felt perspiration run down her back. "The lad needed a motherly farewell. Owain, poor Owain, are you jealous of a lad—a lad whom I hardly know? He is your emissary. Is your mind so woolly that you forget you sent him to Paris? Remember, he dressed as an Augustinian for safety? This same lad leaves on the morrow to repair your wretched ships. He does not speak of a family. So my heart went out to him. I thought, what if this were our son, Riryd, who had come from Ireland and was going to work on those worm-eaten, moldy ships? I knit the lad a new bratt to wear when he goes to Afon Ganol. I suggested that he see

Lord Iorwerth for help in rebuilding the broken-down vessels
you were so generous with. So that is what I did; I gave the
lad a warm bratt and some kind advice like a mother might
do. And he gave me a goodwill blessing, like a lad might give
to a kind friend. That is my story."

Owain thought to himself, When I asked the castellan about
Brenda and the Augustinian he said the same. He had said,
"Brenda has a moral conscience and is completely trustworthy." Owain scratched his head and wondered if he could have
been so terribly wrong in suspecting Brenda, the woman he
loved more than any other. His fleeting logic told him she
would not misbehave with a monk. He asked himself if the
monk was his emissary or a fosterling and found no answer.
He blushed and fumbled with a dry cloth to wipe his slob-
bering mouth. "My friend Thomas once said, 'Women break
a man's heart, and the Lord God mends it,'" he said.

Brenda stood up, went around the table, cupped her hands
around Owain's face, kissed his cheeks and, without taking a
breath, lingered long on his soft, moist mouth.

"Do not kiss me as if I were an addled child!" said Owain,
feeling a pleasing warmth build in his midsection, which he
had not felt in a long time. "I know what I saw. You expect
me to be blind, at the same time flattered by sweet talk, and
become generous with gift giving? Christiannt tried to fool me
that way but never did. Not another woman will make a cuckold of me!"

"I would not do that!" said Brenda with a huff. "You know
in your heart of hearts that I pledged allegiance to you."

"Humpff, I know your pledge," said Owain. "But the sadness in this court is so thick it could choke a horse. We could
use some heart." He looked at her through narrowed eye slits.
"I hear my son Dafydd thinks so much of me that he plots
against my life. Rumors say he has scouts behind boulders
watching the castle. I hate him and be guilt-ridden for not
loving him."

"You cannot force love," said Brenda. "That is why we use
fostering. It gives the child foster parents who might grow to
love him."

"I do not trust anyone." Owain's voice rose to a sharp pitch.

"Recently I did battle, but it was not an honorable victory. I took a life and I could do the same to you! I want the Augustinian gone, made invisible! I order him from my castle and my sight!"

"He leaves on the morrow's sunup," said Brenda.

"Go, woman, before I order the same for you!"

Brenda's face turned ashen.

Llywarch took her elbow and steered her toward the door. "Do not answer," he said under his breath. "The prince does not realize what he is saying. He is overwrought. His grief for his wife is a terrible sickness. Best leave and forget. On the morrow he may not remember speaking those words to you."

When they were outdoors, Brenda looked Llywarch in the face and said, "You and I heard Owain confess that he killed Christiannt. 'Tis best to speak about it to no one." She scrubbed her mouth hard on her bratt.

" 'Tis locked behind my lips," said Llywarch. "The murder of his wife eats at him so that he is not the man he was. But you—you kissed him. Good God, Brenda, you were slabbered and sossed! You kindly ignored the foul stench of him, all that devilish drooling, held your breath, and went for his lips. He took pleasure in it and probably thinks about your kiss this very moment. Owain may be old and cantankerous, but he is still fond of you. You are a fine lady."

" 'Twas a filthy embrace," said Brenda. "I kissed a confused stranger to prove my allegiance to Prince Owain of Gwynedd." Brenda rubbed her mouth on the back of her hand and was surprised that she was not angry with Owain for making a fool of her with his accusation. "No one can fault a prince for being upset if he has lost his wife, but if his conscience pinches for knowing too much about that death, 'tis his problem to work out with his gods. Justice will be done."

After all these years maybe I be learning patience, she thought, and was amazed with that thought. She wondered if she was becoming a blend of her old self, her present self, and some unknown future self, the more she thought of the future self, the more she thirsted for something of the past in Ireland, her father, her two older children and Sein. Do not forget Sein! When she thought of the present, she hungered to keep things

as they were. She wondered how she could thirst and hunger
for opposite things in the same moment. She imagined the
gods were playing with her and laughing up their sleeves. She
told herself she would stay patient, keep her head clear and
sleep well. The morrow would be time enough to look at the
present and think of the future.

Brenda ate supper with Llywarch, in his cottage. Afterward
she checked the maids' cottage and found that Annesta and
Mona had not returned from the druid camp. She went back
to ask Llywarch if he thought the lasses might stay the night.
"I be sure Molly will take care of them."

With a funny little smile Llywarch said, "I be sure. I can
tell you now that Madoc and Conlaf are being awarded their
first honor marks before the morrow's daybreak. Tonight, no
one will sleep in the camp. On the morrow the two monks
shall be druids."

"Madoc never told me." Brenda felt a small hurt in the pit
of her stomach. "I did not know he wanted to become a druid
so soon."

" 'Twas secret," said Llywarch. "He studied until he was
seven with the Irish herder, then with Sein another seven years
and now with Llieu, the healer and with Caradoc, the astronomer. He learned much about foreigners and their way of
thinking in the last four years. He has the knowledge, the
quality and ability to be a civil leader. He holds life sacred."

"Will the lasses go to the honor ceremony?" asked Brenda,
wondering why she was not invited if Annesta and Mona
were. She and Molly were memorizing druid philosophy every
day and studying twice a week with Archdruid Llieu, who had
said naught. "You could have told me."

"No, the lasses will not see the ceremony. They are not
druids, but they will see the lads when 'tis done. Neither Madoc nor I could tell you until after the ceremony. Come to the
camp with me and congratulate the lads. Owain will not be
there on account of Lord Dafydd's threat of war. We will
come back when the moon is a little past its zenith, to give
Madoc time to rest before he leaves with the first light."

"Clouds and fog hide the moon," said Brenda. "I was going

with the first ray of morning sun to tell him I hope all his roads are smooth, except those he roughs up himself."

"Come now," said Llywarch. "If you wait you may miss him."

The castle guards were awake and spoke to both of them. "God be with ye as ye hurry through the village," one said. The guards at the city gate were half asleep and said nothing. Most of the cottages were dark and quiet after supper, except for barking dogs and a crying baby. A half-moon rose above the eastern horizon and was quickly covered with low clouds. A fogbank had formed over the sea near the edge of the village.

Men dressed in black tunics and stockings came out of the fogbank, and when they were close Llywarch saw that they were soldiers with slashes of red and yellow paint on their cheeks. He and Brenda moved to the opposite side of the road. More soldiers came into view, wearing black clothing and led by a man in a helmet with a wrought-iron boar crest.

" 'Tis Dafydd and his dragons," said Llywarch, and he took off his wide sash so that his gown hung loose and he resembled an itinerant monk. He told Brenda to wear the sash over her ears, like a woman's scarf. "There will be a warring this night. The castle guards asked God to be with us. They never do that. It was a warning to hurry through the village. You can bet that Owain is awake, readying his soldiers to meet Dafydd's dragons when they should try to break into the first bailey." He reminded her that Howell's men wore dark blue tunics, same as Owain's, and they shared an encampment close to the seashore. He said in a calm, matter-of-fact voice that he believed Dafydd's dragons would begin their ambush in Howell's camp.

"We should warn Howell," said Brenda.

" 'Tis not safe for a woman, even if she tries to stay hidden. If it becomes necessary, I will go," said Llywarch.

"No!" said Brenda, hanging on to his arm. "I was wrong. Think! Howell's men must know something is going on. They will warn Owain. If Dafydd's men catch you, they will not hesitate to use their swords, especially when they find you are not a priest!" Brenda walked faster.

Llywarch stopped. He smelled smoke and heard the cry of a war trumpet. He pulled Brenda into the ditch and told her to hunker down and be still. Wispy fog passed over them. The air was cold close to the ground. Time passed one heartbeat at a time. Llywarch prayed that they were not in the midst of the battleground.

Brenda saw two of Howell's dragons, swinging maces with spiked metal heads, come out of the fogbank. They walked on either side of a war cart drawn by a single white horse. A man carrying a smoking torch rode in the cart with a basket of spears and axes at his sandaled feet. On his limed head he wore a circlet of oak leaves, signifying that he was in charge.

"The man in the cart is Howell," whispered Llywarch. "He knows what is going on, like you said." There was a tremor in his voice and his hand trembled.

Suddenly a single-file line of men emerged from the mist, carrying firebrands with spiraling tails of dark smoke. There was no singing or talking. As the line came closer, Brenda saw that behind the line of horsebackers was a long line of Owain's soldiers, with Gwynedd's crest, three golden lions on a field of red, painted on the backs of their blue tunics and on their round warboards. Another line of Howell's men with limed hair carried blue leather shields with iron bosses. It was obvious that the two armies were united.

A wolf howled from the top of a dune. A fourth line of soldiers came behind the first three. These men carried no torches. They wore dark blue tunics and carried small, oval shields and a sword or curved dagger. At each man's left side hung a double-bladed ax. Their faces were painted blue and their hair stood up in stiff white peaks.

Llywarch whispered that the axes were hollow and weighted so they could be hurled.

When the soldiers were past, Brenda said, "They look more like spirit people—ghosts walking the moor."

Llywarch shook his head. "Not ghosts, but Welshmen going to kill Welshmen. Howell's dragons are quietly going behind Dafydd's lines."

"Aye, so Dafydd will find few men left in the camp and be surprised by an attack from the rear."

"Sshh!" Llywarch helped her out of the ditch to scrubby brush atop a dune so they could see better. The incoming fog had not yet hidden the tiny campfires behind the dune.

Brenda squeezed her eyes half shut so she could see the flags and banners flying above row after row of tents pitched behind dunes along Aberffraw's seashore.

It was as silent as the mouth of a dead man. She had never seen how large Howell's camp was. "Dafydd's army is coming and those in the camp are asleep. Who will warn them?" she said, fighting hard to steady her nerves. "Where is Howell now?"

"They do not sleep," said Llywarch. "Their nerves are as tight as harp strings with waiting. I saw the blade of a sword reflect some hidden firelight. Howell's four lines of men await behind that far dune." Llywarch watched the silent camp and was filled with dread, which he tried to hide from Brenda. "Dafydd intends to wipe out Howell, then approach the castle. Dafydd will be in for a surprise because he will not get to the castle. Do not move around. Are you cold?"

"Aye, and I do not like this. Dafydd's dragons do unspeakable things." She remembered what she had heard about the vicious hackings, rapes and plunderings Dafydd's soldiers had perpetrated on Welsh crofters and their families. "How do you know he will not get to the castle?"

"Dafydd will draw his men up into the traditional broad line of frontal attack. Howell's men will surprise them by coming from behind. Watch."

Dafydd's raiders fanned out under cover of a short-lived gray mist and slipped two of their lines, charioteers and horsebackers, inside Howell's camp. If it were not for the torches left burning in the camp, Brenda and Llywarch never would have seen that the charioteers were first, holding reins in one hand and long spears in the other. Their hair was stiffened to look like the high-flying manes of galloping horses. On the carts' floors were baskets of iron balls on chains and axes to be used in hand-to-hand combat.

Next came more horsebackers, with vividly painted faces

above black tunics. They held short bows, and a handful of arrows stood in leather carriers slung across their shoulders. Each man carried a torch in one hand and a dagger attached to his waistband.

Oh, Lugh's liver! thought Brenda. This is really a true battle. I knew it was coming but, as for death, I be not prepared. "God, where did one brother learn to do this to another?" she said aloud. "Sweet Anna, I pray Owain knows of this."

"For sweet Anna's paps! Keep your voice down!" warned Llywarch. "Dafydd's men are positioned all along the road. Owain has scouts and spies out there." He hunkered down behind a tangle of gorse, held Brenda's head against his breast with his hand partially covering her eyes. "The brothers learned from ancient Welsh tradition. 'Tis warring."

The third line of Dafydd's army was made up of infantry warriors. They waited outside the camp beside the drummers, trumpeters and pipers. Some of the boldest infantrymen wore only black stripes of charcoal and grease on their bare chests and backs. They also wore rings, bracelets and neck torques. They carried battle-axes and shields decorated with feathers and ribbons. These men believed chain mail hampered their efficiency. Llywarch imagined he could see their moist breath every time they exhaled.

Without warning there were drummings, loud trumpets and piercing cries. Brenda pulled Llywarch's hand away and saw the tiny fires scatter. Dafydd's charioteers slashed their hot torches in the faces of Howell's security dragons stationed behind the tents. One large ax blow and the head of a horse rolled on the ground. The rider, with blue paint on his face, held on to the reins, stunned. He was quickly beheaded.

Dafydd's raiders set fire to banners, linen awnings and sleeping pallets. The second line of raiders, horsebackers, pinned Howell's security guards and their horses to the ground. Oaken stakes were driven through the horses' bellies so they could not roll in the dirt to smother the flames when the stakes were set on fire. Frantic horses not pinned down whinnied, reared with fright and ran frantically here and there with burning manes and tails. More than one of the horses was slashed from neck to mid-belly and fell with blood and entrails gushing out on the ground.

Dafydd's charioteers raced back and forth through Howell's camp, yelling, slashing burning tents with spears and pushing Howell's diminished security force away from the seashore and closer and closer to higher ground next to the road.

Mixed with the smoke, the smell of blood and guts reached the little dune and made Brenda's stomach churn. " 'Tis not human!" she said, and gagged.

" 'Tis sibling jealousy," whispered Llywarch, lying on his belly so he could not be seen from the road. "Both Howell and Dafydd want to be Gwynedd's leader. They are blindly jealous of one another and recognize no superior leader, such as their own father. They go beyond rational thinking, but you can bet your wimple that if King Henry gets wind of this disarray in Gwynedd, he will amass his troops and overtake this divided land as soon as he can get here."

Brenda lay on her belly and Llywarch kept his arm across her back. All her instincts told her to get up and run to the druid encampment, where there was safety and sanity. She fought back another wave of nausea. "Is anyone taking care of the injured?"

"Howell's musicians are druids. You have not heard them beat their drums nor sound their trumpets because they will be tending the wounded and dead this night."

"Suppose Dafydd kills them? Where are they?"

"Hidden in coracles under the wharf, out of the fray."

"How do you know that?" asked Brenda.

"I hear them singing in time to the water that laps and sucks against the boats. Their song is one that I know, because I gave it to them. 'Tis about the sadness of war."

"I cannot hear them!" said Brenda.

"You are not yet a pagan."

Oh, Lord God, she thought, this very night Madoc is becoming a druid. In the eyes of the New Religionists a druid's life is worth less than a pig's foot. Honor marks used to mean so much and bring such pride; now they are a death warrant. What is my son doing? She felt goose bumps rise on her arms.

"The passage of time feels like Madoc is in the middle of

becoming a druid," said Llywarch. "Madoc the shipmaster," he whispered. "I pray the old portents are troth."

"Will the druids miss you?"

"Mayhap," he said, and his haggard face tightened. "But Llieu knew in advance about tonight's battle between these brothers. He has long ears. Listen—look there—by an agreed signal from Dafydd's pipers, the two armies are parting to give their men and horses a breath."

Brenda watched a soldier in black, who was slow to part, twirl the spiked head of a mace in front of a dragon in blue, then drop the mace behind the blue's shield. Blue's face and chest were torn to a bloody pulp.

She turned her face away and whispered, "Will Dafydd's dragons go through Aberffraw cutting down people in their beds, or across the moat, through the palisade and inside the royal bailey?"

"Not tonight. I told you, this battle is between Dafydd and Howell."

A small group of men scrambled up on the wharf. They carried no weapons. Llywarch nudged Brenda and she knew they were druids. They knelt by the fallen men of both sides and carried others to carts. Dafydd's warriors formed a circle where he and his charioteers and horsemen took shelter and a short rest.

"What if Dafydd's dragons start again before 'tis time?" Brenda asked.

"They will be shot full of arrows. Look on yonder dune. See the line of bowmen on horseback? Those are Howell's men."

"Can we go now?" she asked, stifling a shiver.

"Wait!" Someone pushed Howell's empty chariots together and set them on fire. A hail of arrows followed and Dafydd's drummers began a tattoo that sounded like the continuous pelting of hail on sun-dried ground.

Half rested, the armies rushed at each other and this time Dafydd's dragons were surprised by the number of Howell's combatants who moved through their lines. Howell's men came from behind the dune and used two-barbed pikes to charge and overwhelm Dafydd's uneven lines of leather-

garbed horsebackers. There were loud battle cries echoing the
beat of drums followed by a clash of battle-axes against pikes.
Many of Dafydd's men were unhorsed and their heavy axes
thrown aside. Double-barbed pikes went through leather
shields and pierced midsections. Extraction was impossible.
Horses and carts trampled everything on the ground. A line of
Howell's dragons, half hidden in the fog, made a semicircle
around the back flank of Dafydd's three broken lines and
pushed forward. Dafydd's men were driven into the sea, where
they sputtered, waved their hands and cried out to stop before
they drowned.

Dafydd, sitting atop his horse on a rise, held up a lacy cloth
in front of a flaring torch and the trumpets blared a single
sustained note that signified retreat.

Llywarch said, "*Mawr Duw!* The sign of retreat is lace! No
doubt 'tis the kerchief of Lord Dafydd's latest mistress." He
stood up, took Brenda's hand and started to lead her down the
dune and to the road.

"What will we do if we meet a soldier?"

Llywarch said, "For a soldier to slay an old man like me
is cowardice. Besides, I be a priest. See?" He smiled and
pointed to a hand-sized cross he had fashioned out of some
white sticks while lying with his belly against the cold ground.

Brenda's hands shook as she pulled long strands of wool
from her bratt, braided them into a necklace that slipped over
his head. She fastened the cross to it with more wool and was
glad that it was easy to see the white cross against his gray
gown.

"Hurry," said Llywarch, "if you want to see Madoc."

At the bottom of the dune she stopped. "Listen." A low
moan came from somewhere in front of them.

Llywarch went forward. He could not see in the dark, and
his foot struck something. He bent down and touched bare
flesh. He squatted against his heels and saw a man in a black
tunic, his black hair streaked with lime, his face turned sideways.

The man had managed to tie a leather thong around the
stump of his left arm. The bone did not show, and it was not

oozing blood. Brenda felt the binding and said that he had
saved his own life.

"He does not hear you. Hurry on," said Llywarch.

"I cannot leave. I be a healer," said Brenda. Pulling more
of her bratt apart, she tied the man's arm against his side to
protect it and keep it warm until he could reach the healers
who were still on the battleground.

The man opened his eyes and startled them by saying,
"Lord Dafydd's camp is outside the village north gate. Point
me in that direction. Lord, have mercy, I saw eyeballs explode
in fire and flayed skin lay across blackened bones like sun-
dried meat. I saw legbones, skulls, bloodied spears, war axes
and gutted horses! I be sick of death!"

Llywarch helped the soldier to his feet, took him as far as
the road and showed him the trail to the north gate. "God's
blessing," he said, and made the sign of the cross in the air in
front of the soldier.

"God bless ye," the soldier said. "I be Lord Maelgwyn and
will not forget your good deed."

When Llywarch returned, Brenda pointed. "Over here.
Come. There is another black tunic."

This man's pulse was so faint that Brenda would have
missed it if she had not made herself wait another instant. "He
needs mead," she said, and showed Llywarch an egg-sized
swelling behind the man's ear.

"I will fetch it." He put his gloved hand on the wooden
cross and hurried behind the soldier headed for Dafydd's
camp. "Keep the birds away."

Brenda caught her breath. She could not remember seeing
any birds this night, not even the flesh-eating ravens. She
wrapped the upper part of the man's body in what was left of
her ragged bratt.

He awoke, grabbed her hands and said, "Sister, 'tis war that
exhilarates a man to a passion beyond his control."

She thought he was hysterical from the blow on his head
and told him to save his breath for the mead he was soon to
have.

"Mead? Come, lie beside me until I be strong. 'Twill be
the greatest pleasure ye ever had."

The dread in her heart nearly choked her. She backed away.

He tried to rise to his feet; when he could not, he tried to crawl after her. Finally he gave up and said, "I be a born loser. Sister, I warn ye, if ye meet a dragon with his blood still up, ye will not be asked to lie down as kindly as I asked. If ye refuse, ye lose; die. The dragon gains in pleasure. That is what he wants." He closed his eyes and put his hands against his head.

She heard voices and scrambled behind a thick stand of gorse. Two of Dafydd's dragons hunkered down beside the man; he pointed in her direction and filled her with panic.

"Brenda, where are you?" a voice called.

It sounded like Llywarch, and she looked carefully to make certain.

The wounded man laughed uncontrollably.

Llywarch held up his wooden cross, looking here and there.

The dragons poured mead between the lips of their wounded companion. "Thank ye, Friar," a dragon said to Llywarch and half carried, half pushed the wounded man to the north-gate trail.

Brenda came from behind the gorse. "There is naught heroic about soldiers after a battle," she said. "They become men without dignity." She glanced at the graying sky. The fog had gone and the moon had ridden far past its zenith. "I be twice blessed, first to have you as my friend and second to have a son who is a pagan."

"Woe, dear lady! You are not the only one the gods bless. You and I shall always be friends and I have the sweetest granddaughter on earth, who is head over heels in love with that pagan son of yours. I shall hang him by his heels if he does not treat her well." Llywarch's eyes crinkled at the corners.

"Let us go on," said Brenda, taking his hand.

XXIII

Prínce Owaín

A solar eclipse is the most awesome of all astronomical phenomena if the rays of the sun are entirely blocked from the observer. As the moon slides over the disk of the sun, an unnatural darkness descends on the earth, and the birds cease their chatter. For several minutes the moon blots out the sun entirely, the temperature of the air drops, and the solar corona—the sun's outer atmosphere—appears as a pearly, shimmering halo around the moon's black shadowing disk. The brighter stars and planets become visible in the sky at this time. . . . The ancients regarded eclipses as harbingers of important events. . . .

A total eclipse can be seen at a given spot on the earth only once every 360 years. References to eclipses can be found in cuneiform inscriptions on Babylonian tablets that date back to the second millennium B.C.

Robert Jastrow and Malcolm H. Thompson,
Astronomy: Fundamentals and Frontiers

Llywarch said Madoc would bring Annesta and Mona back to the royal court before leaving for Afon Ganol. If they did not go on to the druid camp but hurried back, they might catch him.

Brenda said she did not need more excitement and would like only a calm farewell with her son.

In the morning light they saw that the castle's outer palisades and gates were protected by many guards. Inside the bailey every cottage, hut and shed had an armed retainer beside it. Owain's soldiers, holding scramasaxes with broad thrusting blades eighteen tums long, stood at intervals along the inner palisade.

Llywarch entered his cottage and called, "Thank Lugh my granddaughter is safe!"

Brenda followed and saw Madoc holding teary-eyed Annesta. His hands were bandaged. She wanted to hold his hands, comfort him, but instead she said, "I be terribly proud you have been given honor marks." In a dark hidden place in the bottom of her heart she was angry with New Religionists who taught that druids were pagans from a leftover, outdated way of life. Her lastborn was now committed to hide from murderous New Religionists like some feral animal.

Annesta pulled away from Madoc, put her arm around Brenda's waist. "When you and Grandfather did not come for the Honor Celebration, we worried."

Brenda was silent thinking how quiet it was without the snorting and whinnying of horses, without blood-curdling shouting and heart-piercing cries of fighting men.

"By now you know we were detained by a battle Lord Dafydd began and lost," said Llywarch. "Thanks to Lord Howell, Gwynedd still has Prince Owain and his royal army, and all is well." He slumped on his pallet and motioned for Madoc to sit beside him. "Now that you have become a druid, you are aware that grief, anger, love, hate and malice are the different divinities." He watched Madoc's eyes and spoke with a stern voice. "Their conflicting energies guide a person. 'Tis time to pull together the energies you value. Your life and mine are forever bound by the truth of the Old Religion, the sweetness of my granddaughter and the mutual friendship of the maid Brenda."

Madoc looked up with a grateful smile.

Annesta helped Brenda make tea from dried red-clover blossoms and took four beakers off the shelf. Shyly she showed Brenda her headband made of ribbon and tiny fresh flowers woven together.

While the tea steeped in the kettle, Brenda said, "I like the way you wove together the delicate blue flowers and bird feathers, like a marriage band."

Annesta's face turned crimson. "Aye, that is what I want

to tell you. We married ourselves. 'Tis all right. Do not frown. Neither I nor he could wait for him to rebuild ten ships. You understand. I hope Grandfather does."

Brenda suddenly wanted to walk barefoot on the edge of a beach surrounded by sand, water and breeze. She wanted to be alone to think about what Annesta had said. Instead she clasped Annesta's hands. "Thank you for telling me," she said. "The ships have been out of water for an age. Most of them must be beyond repair. Maybe from three or four Madoc can make one that is watertight."

"When Madoc comes back with drawings we shall have a formal marriage." She bit her bottom lip and said softly, "My mam baptized me Christian when I was a weean, too young to know what I would want. I want a druid wedding, even though Madoc says we already had one. Madoc does not talk about his family who drowned, and my mam is dead, so I want you to stand in the place of our mams."

"Ah, I be honored. So—so you and Madoc—ah . . ."

Annesta put her hand over her mouth for an instant to hide a little giggle, then breathed against Brenda's ear, "Aye, we did the wonderful-together-thing. It was a natural, meant-to-be coming together. I be happy to have you for a friend who knows about such. Madoc said he would tell Grandfather; a man-to-man thing."

Brenda thought what to say about the wonderful-together-thing that had been done. Mothers warned their daughters. Had Llywarch forgotten to warn his granddaughter? He had taught her to be open in her speech as she was in everything else. Brenda admired that, but she was at a loss for words when Annesta's speech strayed over into the sexual. Maidservants were by no means chaste, but there were rules about when it was appropriate to talk about it. One did not speak of sexual matters in front of males, but in the kitchen or laundry hut, where there were only maids, it was all right to sing sexy songs, tell insinuating jokes, talk knowingly of how to make a man wild with desire and what herbs to take to prevent an unwanted pregnancy. Had Sein spoken to Madoc about such things? Had Llieu? It was a natural thing—mayhap, bound to happen.

"Are you surprised?" asked Annesta.

Brenda looked at Llywarch and Madoc, who had their heads together as they talked man to man. Her face flushed. Annesta grinned.

"Aye," said Brenda and heard a singing in her ears, more like a rushing of wind or water. Of course she was surprised that it had happened now, but not really surprised that it had happened. Life was built of layers and layers of things going on. There was too much going on now, too many things to separate and think clearly about each one. The battle, which maybe signified future warring for Owain's throne; Madoc becoming a druid and leaving to work on ten sails; and now this coming-together thing between Annesta and him. She was overwhelmed, and a little envious of Annesta, who had only a blossoming sexuality and lover to think about. She liked Annesta, really loved her, but if Annesta had come to her for advice, she would have told her marriage was a serious thing and to wait until Madoc had a trade. No, to be truly honest, she would have told Annesta that it was not in the stars for Madoc to marry. She would have been tempted to tell about the northern lights in the sky when Madoc was conceived and say that he was chosen by the gods to do something extraordinary. She thought, Annesta would have giggled and said Madoc had time for being extraordinary later, if he honestly wanted that. Brenda could not have expected Madoc or Annesta to ask her permission to do what they did. In her heart she hoped their first lovemaking was a joyous, spontaneous, breathtaking, holy thing. She had hoped, no, had known, that the two would be husband and wife one day. She had daydreamed of making the wedding headband and embroidered white gown. But they were young, eager for each other, and could not wait. They had made love and declared themselves husband and wife. Suddenly she remembered how she had felt when Owain first made love to her. She was younger than Annesta. So now her lastborn's self-marriage was done and she had had no part in it. She put her arms around Annesta and kissed her on both cheeks. "I shall make thee a proper wedding gown later." She eased down to the bard's company pallet. Conversation flowed around her, her eyes drifted closed and she gave in to a sense of dreaming that she waded in cool, sandy beach water where all was quiet except for the gulls and the gentle breeze over the wash of the water.

Madoc's face was pink as the sunrise. "Annesta is more important to me than anything in the world," he said. "I be proud to be her husband."

"I be not deaf nor dumb," said Llywarch. "I knew before either of you said a word that there was more between you than a wet kiss. There is a gentleness in your eyes. My granddaughter's face glows inside her crimson aura. Besides, she wears a marriage band in her hair." He looked stern. "I expect you to hold both the Old Religion and my granddaughter sacred. Center yourself and spare me the carnal details of your recent tryst."

Brenda woke up and poured steaming tea through a thin cloth to leave the flowers behind. She passed the beakers around and said tea would soothe the nerves.

"Physical and spiritual love are the greatest gifts two people can give to one another," said Llywarch, sipping cautiously.

"I love your granddaughter," said Madoc. "We—"

"Madoc," said Llywarch, "it carks me when you try to make an excuse or apologize. I know you love her and cadged her into consummating that love. Woe is me! 'Twas bound to happen. She loved you from the first time she set eyes on you. I watched your love for her grow, as did your—my dear friend." Llywarch nodded toward Brenda, who was quiet as a clam.

She was thinking, I do not even really know this son of mine. I do not know any of my children. Do other mothers who have fostered their children feel the same? Maybe there is something wrong with our way of doing things. Druidry is not the only thing that is going to be changed. There is something more going on than fighting between brothers and King Henry's dislike of pagans. 'Tis something bigger than a lad and lass in love. We are living in a time of change. Lugh, I hope we all live to see what comes of it when 'tis settled. What I actually want is to tell Annesta I be her husband's mam.

Llywarch was talking overloud, for emphasis. "I tried to

keep the two of you apart, but you would not have it! You exasperate me, but at the same time I love you. 'Tis an enigma. Because of your bloody impulsive nature, I foresee your future destined to unheard-of things. Only the gods know in what strange way you foredoom us *Cymru* druids. 'Tis hard to believe you shall be the one to save us from annihilation."

Madoc was not certain what the bard was taking about, but he held his hand out and Llywarch clasped it, then encircled Madoc in his arms and said, "I feel a bit of pride toward you, as I would toward a grandson."

Llywarch was a good judge of character and he had a third eye, like many of the old druids who studied people and the natural wonders of the earth. He sensed what was coming. He was not as good as Caradoc in predicting when a storm was near, nor was he good at the mathematical art of predicting eclipses, like Llieu, but he knew human nature and could tell when someone was headed for disaster or joy.

He said sadly, "Owain and his grown sons are on a collision course. Out there among the dunes Brenda and I saw dragons fight to the death! Soldiers and horses made the ground crimson. Carts, tents and a whole camp were burned. In the big events of time, 'twas a futile fight. It should have been settled by communication. I predict the royal court will be attacked shortly after Dafydd asks his brother Rhodri to combine forces with him. Dafydd, like most of today's young people, has ears closed tight as an oyster's shell out of water whenever adults honor him with advice. He knows it all! He is the Lord of Warring, higher than the old Celtic God of War, Camulos! He passes flasks of wine containing rosemary leaves to his dragons before a battle. They believe the herbal wine gives them energy for the battle and wards off pain, so they can fight like berserkers."

" 'Twas terrible," said Brenda, thinking of the horse that was beheaded and gutted. "In the old days, druids were able to stop a battle. Today the gods turn their backs on war. Today, if a druid stood between two fighting forces he would be slain by both sides. Times are changing into something we know naught."

"Ppfft! The gods are used to men warring," said Llywarch.

"In the old days women were warriors fighting alongside their men and druids did not fight, but directed the battles. Today's druids hide their honor marks to avoid a beheading by New Religion warriors. Times change slowly or quickly depending on the motivation of the people involved. Mayhap future priests will lead the wars, tend the wounded and bury the dead."

"Are you talking about Father Giff beheading druids?" asked Annesta stiffly.

"Are you squeamish about that?" asked Llywarch.

"Certes!" said Annesta. "My husband is a druid!" She sat on the company pallet and did not drink her tea.

"Lord Dafydd craves power like a hungry wolf craves food. Hear me, I predict he will become chief of Gwynedd, even if it means killing his father and a brother to do so," said Llywarch. "Dafydd recently gifted the Church with silver goblets and other loot. He received the blessing of Father Giff."

Brenda refilled Llywarch's beaker. He sweetened his tea with honey and sipped.

"Will the people of Gwynedd back Dafydd?" asked Madoc.

"No, most want to continue with Prince Owain, who is truly loved—but he is old and ill." There was more sadness in Llywarch's voice.

Madoc whispered, "Last night Llieu said Owain's time will be marked by the sun's eclipse. Is that troth? You druids know when he will die? I thought he said it to confound my thoughts about the mysteries."

"Aye, most people are like you and will not believe until the time comes," said Llywarch. "I used to believe that phenomena such as eclipses, dancing skylights or falling stars were a coincidence if they occurred at some precise moment in a person's life. But I have seen these things happen and now believe 'tis another part of the mysteries we are not wise enough to solve."

Madoc said, "What happens if Owain dies and Dafydd's and Rhodri's dragons overtake Aberffraw, then rush the court's palisades? Is it true that Owain's dragons will stay with Howell's to protect the court?"

Llywarch said, "What is whiter than snow? Truth. Who

knows truth? The gods, and they do not always speak so we can hear."

Brenda saw that Annesta's cheeks were wet. She set her beaker on the earthen floor, cradled Annesta's head against her shoulder and said, "Dear child, when you miss Madoc, come see me."

Annesta dried her tears, lay back against Brenda's shoulder, looked at Madoc and listened to her grandfather.

"I expect neither Dafydd nor Howell to protect women and children," said Llywarch. "They will use them as slaves and hostages. 'Twill be worse than what we just saw."

Madoc shivered and his eyes glowed with rage. He ran a hand across his forehead, took a deep breath, and made his lips stiff.

Llywarch saw the shivers and said, "You are not to worry about Annesta and Brenda. When Owain passes on, I will take them to the safe camp. And you—you must go to your ships. 'Twill not be easy to repair them and at the same time prepare yourself to be leader of Welsh druids."

Madoc stopped pacing and sat down. "Leader?" His knees felt limp as overcooked bean pods.

" 'Tis meant to be after Prince Owain dies. He may live through the winter, or may not. This is the way. Life begins, it ends. You are chosen to save the knowledge by saving the druids."

Madoc blinked, flung his arms around Llywarch and said, "I pray the Lord God blesses both you and me. If He has me in mind as a leader, He jests, plays a frivolous game, because I tell you I have no leadership ability. I will think hard about what you have said because 'tis a mystery." He hugged Brenda and then gave Annesta a lingering farewell kiss and whispered in her ear, "Love you, my dear wife."

She took off her headband, untied the strings and pulled it in half. This act signified that her life's road was broken and she was now walking a new road. She made half into a bracelet for Madoc, the other half into a bracelet for herself.

The three left behind stood at the open door, watching Madoc go. Brenda put her arm around Annesta, who let her tears slide unchecked. Llywarch ran a sleeve across his eyes and sniffed loudly. His gray pigtail bobbed up and down as he called, "Lord God be with you until we meet again—you rascal."

When Madoc turned to wavè he saw the thin bands of gathering ragged clouds, as if a storm was building.

The picture of Brenda in the arms of a visiting monk would not leave Owain's mind. He forgot that he had accused her of kissing a strange Augustinian in the great hall. He had sent for her the night of the battle, to keep her safe inside the keep. He was disappointed that she and Llywarch were gone. He imagined that Llywarch had taken her to the druid camp and thought he would scold them both the next time he saw them. He also forgot that he had appointed one of his emissaries to be his physician and the other a shipmaster. The thought of Dafydd's battle for power provoked him. Every day his mind swirled with a mounting mixture of perplexing, half-remembered thoughts and questions. Was the strange Augustinian spying on him? Did the Augustinian know he wore druid honor marks? Was the Augustinian spying on the court druids, such as Llywarch or old Gwalchmai? Was Brenda leading the Augustinian to the druid camp? How could that be? She was the most intelligent woman he knew. No one defamed Brenda. Why did he question her motives?

On the day before the New Year of 1169, Lord Dafydd himself came into the great hall alone, with a scarlet-colored flask of wine held under his bratt. He stamped the snow off his boots and looked around, waiting for his eyes to adjust to the inside. Instead of acknowledging his father and Brenda sitting on the dais in front of the smoky fireplace, he sat next to the penteulu, the chief bard and head of the household, old Gwalchmai, who strummed his harp.

"Lord Howell tricked me and used some of my father's retainers in his army, causing a dozen of my dragons and their horses to be drowned in the sea. 'Twas a vicious, underhanded maneuver," Dafydd said in a loud voice so that Owain and Brenda might hear. "You can count on another battle. Next time I will come into this castle before you realize my dragons surround it. I will show you a real battle. When it will take place is my decision." His teeth flashed white in the sooty semidarkness. In a confidential manner he asked Gwalchmai if his father's health was improving.

Gwalchmai's look made Dafydd close his mouth and sit for a while as if enjoying the music. Finally he leaned close to Gwalchmai and said, "You are the court's best harper." When Gwalchmai would not meet his eyes, he asked, as calm as a day without a breeze, what tonic Brenda brought to Prince Owain.

Gwalchmai frowned, shrugged and said, "Mead? Mayhap red wine? I do not know. 'Tis there on the table in the clay jar beside the hawthorn wreath. Ask her. 'Tis something she concocted. Well, it looks like you used a tonic for strength. I never dreamed you would grow to be so muscular."

Dafydd's face brightened. He put his arm around the bard and spoke so low that Owain and Brenda, sitting three man-lengths away, could hear only a word now and again.

Brenda wondered why Dafydd, a known Christian, was talking to a druid harper about healing instead of following the latest fad of consulting a priest.

Owain watched Gwalchmai and Dafydd with their heads together at the end of the long table; Dafydd, thick like the trunk of an old beech tree; Gwalchmai, thin like a hazel sapling. He imagined that they plotted some grisly scheme, and grew nervous. When he could stand it no longer he thundered, "Do you think you can make a fool of me?"

Gwalchmai looked startled and confused. "Your Highness, 'twas naught. Lord Dafydd asked if you would be in the hall for sup. I told him it was up to you. He asked if the tonic Brenda brings is restoring your health. I said, 'By Lugh's lungs, I hope so.' "

"If he came to visit more often, he could see for himself that my bad spells are farther apart, so 'tis logical that one day they will be gone," said Owain.

"And you with them," murmured Dafydd with nostrils flaring and a snarl in his voice. His thin-lipped mouth was hidden by a walrus mustache. His watery gray eyes blinked, and his throat moved when he quietly added, "Take a much-needed rest. I could oversee the leadership of Gwynedd until you are well."

Owain winced. "I could throw you in the donjon. First tell me, does a trader want the raw wool he sells?"

"Of course not!"

"Because he does not want it, does he give it away without a price?"

"He wants payment. Money is utltimately the price," said Dafydd, clutching at his dagger's brass hilt. "For tending your business while you rest, you could pay me in gold or in cattle."

"But I did not tell you my price," said Owain. "When I be ready you will know how much your services are worth to me."

"When will that be, Father?"

"When *you* are ready! My son, how many times have I told you that men have desires, some greater than others, but in the end they always pay more than anticipated for realizing those desires."

Brenda watched Dafydd's mouth purse, then glanced at the open doorway to see Archdruid Llieu standing with Conlaf's friend, the student healer, Llorfa.

Llieu was dressed as an ordinary crofter, wearing a woolen tunic under his bratt and long-wristed woolen gloves.

Llorfa was a petite, dark-eyed beauty with thick black hair braided around her head like a crown. Her goal in life was to keep people well and happy. She was understanding, sensitive and sang healing songs to keep her patients calm. Her friend Conlaf was a diagnostician who knew precisely the correct medication to use for most any ailment that had a name. They made a good team.

Llieu asked Owain if there were any new problems to talk about.

Owain grimaced, stuck out his tongue and waved his hands for Llieu to sit beside him, close to the warm, smoking fire. "A physician worth his weight in salt can tell what the problem is with a man by looking at the coat on his tongue! But you did not notice, so I will tell you what my problem is! Women!"

"My friend, that is an old problem!" Llieu smiled and gave

Owain a flagon containing wine mixed with crushed poppy seeds, dandelion and bell-vine blooms.

Owain set the flagon on the table beside Brenda's jar of mead. "I feel no pain today," he said. "Brenda brought me mead and a wreath." He stabbed a finger at the circle of leaves, hawthorn twigs and berries meant to decorate his chamber.

Llorfa held up the wreath, admiring Brenda's workmanship.

Owain said, " 'Tis unlucky to bring hawthorn twigs indoors?"

Brenda sat silent for a moment and thought, His mind may be a little vague. " 'Tis an old superstition that cannot be proven," she said. "The vine sweetens the air."

"It adds ill luck to air already heavy with the portent of evil," said Owain. "Take the wreath out! You want to bring me bad luck! For shame! Take it out!"

"Aye, my lord," said Brenda, thinking, His thoughts are running backwards. She looked at Dafydd, who smirked and stood close to Owain. She turned to Llorfa, who was singing ever so softly. Brenda shrugged, trying to hide her embarrassment, and left.

Owain fussed with his backrest. When he looked up he noticed that Brenda was gone and he said in a loud voice, "Listen now, I want to tell you healers about the one woman who breaks my heart so that it festers." He bellowed flummeries about women in general, then said, "Mistress Brenda once gave me an oath of fidelity for so long as I shall live. But can I trust her? My own eyren espied her in the arms of a holy man. Hear ye! She kissed him on both cheeks and he kissed her back with a boiling passion that left tears in her eyren. Methinks the monk forgot his oath of chastity! Everyone I have spoken with says good things about Brenda and tells me not to worry. However, she brings a hawthorn wreath indoors for me. With your own eyren you saw that she wished me ill luck!"

Dafydd jumped to his feet. "It does not surprise me that Mistress Brenda would charm a monk. She is the devil's handmaiden and should be burned in a withie basket, like the lawbreakers in Julius Caesar's time!"

Owain's mouth dropped open.

Dafydd turned a little sideways so that he could see both Llieu and Gwalchmai. "I say, if other women in Gwynedd knew that Brenda paid the supreme penalty for breaking her oath of fidelity, they would dare not break theirs. Brenda is a favorite among crofters' wives. She sets them examples. Methinks her examples are not so exemplary!" His lips peeled back from his teeth and he turned to look at Owain, who looked pale as death. "She mocked you, the prince of Gwynedd! Made you a cuckold. Do not worry a scintilla; when I find her with that lecherous monk I shall give them both just punishment!" He looked at Owain with half-closed eyes, clenched one hand around his dagger and lifted it a thumb's-width from its scabbard.

Gwalchmai stood up and said, "If you harm Brenda in any way, you will have to answer to me and a lot of crofters and their families." He limped stiffly toward the door, distressed that Owain endured Dafydd's vitriolic words. Everyone knew that the one woman Owain had always loved was Brenda and she was as loyal as a pet hound. He stood silent beside the door, watching.

Llieu's eyes were shiny black and hard as obsidian. "Lord Dafydd," he said, "what are you saying? You would murder an Augustinian monk, a fellow Christian? You would murder Brenda, who took care of your mother when she was ill and you when you were a wee laddie? Would you go on naught but circumstantial evidence without letting Brenda, a member in good standing of Gwynedd's royal court, plead her case before the Council of Law? If so, you are more mad than a bull in a pasture of spring heifers."

Dafydd's neck turned red and he did not dare look at Llieu. He dropped his dagger into the scabbard and stuttered, "A-Arch-Archdruid, you just made an enemy!"

"False," said Llieu. "I have found one. Better that he is in plain sight than hidden behind the spiny furze."

Gwalchmai came back, stepped between Llieu and Dafydd and murmured that this was no time to fetch enemies. Dafydd slammed the old bard's head against the fireplace stones and shouted, "This *is* the time. And I shall make big changes around here, starting now!"

Dazed, Gwalchmai held his hands on the sides of his head and walked out of the door.

"Hold on!" said Owain, struggling to stand. "Dafydd, 'tis time to leave." He pointed a clawlike finger toward the door that closed behind Gwalchmai and breathed through his mouth as if he were running hard uphill.

Llieu whispered, "Go before you cause your father to have an attack."

Outdoors, Gwalchmai tensed and stared at the cloudless winter sky. He sucked in the cold, fresh air, but there was something wrong. He could hear no dog bark, no sheep bleat, no chicken peep. The dogs were nowhere in sight and the daylight's brightness was filtered to a peculiar dull yellow.

Holding the hawthorn wreath in one hand, Brenda stood beside him. "Owain distrusts me."

"He does not always mean what he says these days. He is exhausted, laid on the shelf. I believe he knows not what he truly sees."

She pointed skyward. "See there! The moon is covering the sun. 'Tis eating it."

" 'Tis the eclipse that has been foretold," he said. "Do not stare; the sun's fire will burn your eyes."

Together they took small peeks as the moon rode slowly across the face of the sun.

"Something dreadful is about to happen!" whispered Brenda.

They went inside the hall to tell the others and found Dafydd pacing back and forth.

Llorfa was singing softly to calm his nerves.

"Come outside," said Brenda. "See the moon swallow the sun."

Owain's brow creased with curiosity. He stood, grabbed Brenda's hand to steady himself and took a faltering step. His head wobbled as if his neck were too thin a support. From his open mouth came a wheezing sound, his chest heaved like a frightened coney, his hand fluttered away from Brenda and grappled at his chest. His eyes bulged like overripe grapes.

Brenda put her arms around him, pulled him back to his seat, his legs crumpled and he fell to the floor. He lay on his back with his arms clutching his chest. His breath came in hissing gusts. His gray-green eyes were open, glazed. "Something is squeezing his chest so tight he cannot move," Brenda said. "Did he swallow a ghost from Sid?"

She told herself to be calm, pulled the cork from the jar of mead, knelt, held Owain's head on her arm and said, "Sip. 'Twill restore your breath."

Dafydd stood up, swept his arm over the table so Llieu's flagon of wine smashed on the floor. He pushed Brenda out of his way. The mead jar fell from her hand and Owain's head hit the floor. Dafydd ignored the clatter, turned his back to everyone. In a flash of motion he took a small flask from under his bratt and poured the contents into a water goblet. He laughed and said, "I be a bit clumsy, but I too brought a special gift for my father. 'Tis red wine from Aquitaine to deaden his pain."

The wine was a beautiful clear red. Its fruity bouquet was strong. Llorfa hummed and Dafydd smiled. He squatted beside his father and said, "Smell that full aroma. Take a sip, you stubborn old *gafr*!"

Llieu said, "You are the goat! A man cannot drink with his head on the floor!"

Brenda knew she had smelled that odor before, but she could not place it. She wondered why Dafydd had not placed his gift of wine on the table right away. She could not dispel her suspicion that there was something wrong with Dafydd's wine and looked for a bit of mead in the beakers left over from the midday meal. She found one, pushed herself against Dafydd, and tried to hold Owain's head up so he could drink easily. "Help me," she said.

Dafydd did not move, but said in a high-pitched voice that his Aquitaine wine was best.

Brenda sat on the floor, put her fingers in the beaker of mead and wet Owain's lips. His eyes fluttered open for a moment, then a spasm twisted his face.

Llieu boosted Owain's head and shoulders to Brenda's lap. "Pagh to you pagans," said Dafydd. "Your mead is weak!

My wine will cleanse his system, wipe out all pain!" He snatched the mead from Brenda and slammed the beaker across the floor. He held the sweet-smelling goblet under Owain's nose and said, "Open your mouth! Drink! All of it! 'Tis all right. Quiet . . . watch . . . hush . . . listen . . ." His knees were bent and he teetered on his toes. "Your Highness," he said, "if you do not drink, I have an overwhelming desire to slit your flabby white neck and watch your bright red blood gush out and cover the obscene blue honor marks on your shoulders and behind your ears."

"Let him be!" said Brenda. "You demon! He needs air!"

"Shut up!" said Dafydd, making a noise in his throat that sounded like a startled wolf yelp. He shook his head, pressed the goblet back to Owain's lips and forced his mouth open. "I have no choice."

Brenda was outraged. "There is always a choice! Even the moment before the arrow flies, there is a choice."

Owain gasped. His chest gurgled. With a shallow sigh he pushed the wine goblet out of the way and expelled his breath in one tiny, explosive word, "Liar! 'Tis you—who broke your oath—to force your way—to the throne. You—you, not Brenda, deserve punishment! You—" His head bobbed like he wanted to sit upright. "Three babes! Gladys's—died—and no—!" He fell back, a dead weight in Brenda's lap. There was no sound in the hall except the fire's crackle and Brenda's sharp inhalation.

Dafydd raised his head and said, "Bloody liar! You do not know what you are talking about!" The words cracked like thunder against the ceiling beams. "I be Lady Gladys's babe! I be far from dead."

Brenda stared at Owain's silent face, the wide-open mouth and eyes. She blew against the eyes. They did not twitch or flutter. She felt the blood channel in his neck—no pulse—and she laid him gently on the floor with his arms at his sides.

Llorfa had stopped singing and the hall was quiet as a clam.

Dafydd, with eyes blazing, emptied the wine goblet into Owain's open mouth.

Owain's beard was stained red. Wine stained the sides of his neck, the front of his tunic and the top of his trousers.

Down on his hands and knees, Archdruid Llieu kissed Owain's cheek and whispered, " 'Tis all right to bid us farewell, Owain *Fawr*!" He took a breath, gagged from the sweet, fruity odor and was sure there was more than wine in the goblet. He drooled saliva on one glove and rubbed his lips because they had touched Owain's wine-wet face.

Owain's face was white as a fresh-peeled willow stick. His lips were blue. The tattooing on his neck and behind his ears stood out like fine filigree. His eyes stared unseeing at the banner that hung from the center ceiling beam: three golden lions on a red field.

Brenda's voice was barely audible. " 'Tis almond poison used by some to kill rats."

"You imagine things," said Dafydd.

"But I do not," said Brenda.

He stammered incoherently about how his father had gone mad and now how peaceful he looked.

Llieu sat back on his heels, put his hand on Owain's neck, blinked back tears and said, "Our dear friend walks a new trail. Death, the ultimate mystery." His voice was like the rustling of dried oak leaves.

"No! Not true! You lie!" said Dafydd, waving the empty goblet in the air. "Oh, God! I tried to help! I gave him wine, the purest of elements! Wait! You saw. The old man choked because he did not swallow. 'Twas his fault! I did not kill him! He may be alive, pretending death."

Llorfa took a polished silver piece from her tunic pocket, held it close to Owain's nostrils, and everyone saw no moisture formed. "My lord, I smelled that sweet-sick odor in your wine. 'Tis poison, not used by Welsh lords, Christians nor pagans, but by foreigners, Frenchmen. Where did you fetch it?"

Dafydd turned pale as skimmed milk and said, "My father must have a splendid funeral and afterwards the guests will witness the most spectacular crowning of a new king to ever take place in Gwynedd. I shall be crowned Lord King Dafydd!"

" 'Twas your father's wish that Lord Howell be the next

prince of Gwynedd," said Llieu, taking the goblet from Dafydd's hand.

Dafydd jumped backward as if he had been hit in the stomach.

Brenda had seen right through his skin to his heart. "You have good cause to flinch!" she said. "The gods were not deceived by your words of generous gift-giving nor concern over your father's health. They read the dark side of your heart better than I and were quick to take him to the Otherside moments before you emptied the poisoned chalice into his maw. You came here to murder!"

"Not me! I came because my father was dying under Archdruid Llieu's treatment. I came to take him to a priest in Chester who is known for using life-giving elixirs and powders. My father could have had a long, long life, but for you pagans. Ah—"

"Aagh!" Llieu growled and was about to censure him for his dishonorable audaciousness when Brenda noticed that Dafydd was having difficulty breathing. She led him outdoors to a bench beside the great hall. "Your half-brother Howell must be notified before funeral arrangements can begin. You may sleep on the pallet in the guest chamber until the funeral."

Dafydd stiffened, took a deep breath of air; his mouth turned down and his eyes held tears. "It hurts when you cut me down like that! I be not some no-account vagabond. I be the future king of Gwynedd. I deserve naught less than my father's chamber."

Brenda stared at the darkened sky. The errie yellow light was gone, but it was nearly dark as night. She told him to look up.

He sucked in the cold air.

She said, "You are a murderer."

He said her words were an atrocity. His midsection was squeezed dry, and all of a sudden he raised his head, which pounded with pain. "Nay! Nay! The day turns into night. This is as perverse as the corpse that lies inside and speaks against me. Oh God, have mercy! The day of judgment has come. Lord of all gods, wait! I be not ready!"

The air turned cold and there was a frosty silver fire flickering around the moon's black shadowing disk. Stars became visible. "Oh Lord," cried Dafydd, "tell me what to do to restore the face of the sun? Do you want a sacrifice? The head of a druid? Give me a sign."

Brenda said, "Lord Dafydd, there is no need to ask for anything. Prince Owain is dead and you are seeing a solar eclipse that was predicted ages ago."

Llieu and Lorfa, servants and guards, came into the bailey to see what had caused the night to come so quickly.

Gwalchmai said, " 'Tis altogether right that such a rare happening mark the passing of our wise leader, Owain the Great." Then he warned them that looking directly at the sun's light as it was being swallowed or disgorged by the moon could burn the eyes.

In a loud voice Dafydd said the sun disappeared from the sky the moment his father's spirit departed his body. "No one can tell me what to look at. Mine eyes glance where I will them. Frozen darkness will cover the earth from now on!" He wrapped his arms around his chest to hold in his shivering.

As if to prove his words true, the unnatural darkness deepened. For a handful of heartbeats the moon blotted out the sun entirely. And the stars shone bright.

Dafydd kept his eyes on the ring of silver fire that danced around the outer edge of the moon. Then he watched the sun shyly reveal itself as a thin crescent. How could the silver fire burn? It was not hot. Even the air had become freezing cold. He told himself that the Lord God had sent him this sign and he would never be punished for his father's death. Slowly the moon slid away from the sun and the coming daylight again became a weird yellow. He knelt on a skiff of snow and said, "Lord God, I show my innocent face to Thine sacred light!" He looked skyward until the moon went on its own course and left the sun's golden orb looking like a perfect round medallion. "Keep the sunlight whole before me, I command You!" He continued to stare at the sun for nine times nine breaths, long after the others went back inside to clean Owain's body. Afterward he bowed his head to acknowledge that God was greater than he, although the thought was form-

ing in the back of his mind that he himself had brought back
the sun when he held his innocent face to the heavens.

Other thoughts swirled to the front of his mind. He believed
that no one truly knew of the certain powder that went into
the wine he had brought to his father. He had planned to serve
the wine at the evening meal. But when his father had that
stupid attack, he wanted to finish him off before the angel of
death herself took him. Owain's death had come too soon. The
wine had had no effect. He thought of the druids washing and
dressing his father, exposed to the deadly red liquid. In a
roundabout way his father would kill the druids who dressed
his body and take them with him to the Otherside. His father
had had power and now he, Dafydd, possessed that power. He
smiled. Everything would work out in a pleasing way. His
retainers were not yet in the courtyard for his protection. He
believed that the next few hours would be a test to see if he
could stand his ground against those who would say he killed
his father. He would weave around himself a protective net, a
net of his own spinning, like a spider.

Brenda stood in front of him and told him not to stare at
the sun. He seemed not to know she was there. His ears were
closed, but he did not move his head or close his eyes. His
eyes saw the bright warm sun that he himself had restored.

The weeping servants asked Gwalchmai if they could dress
Owain's body. "As penteulu, it is my duty to prepare our
leader for his final rest," he said. "But I will need help anoint-
ing his body with oils and preparing his pallet so his feet face
the setting sun." His voice was like waves lapping against
beach sand.

"What about sacred paint?" asked a servant who believed
that the loss of the sun was a sign that even the heavens
mourned Owain's death and remembered that druids buried
their important dead with a sprinkling of red ochre pigment.
"The red earth in the dingle is damp with last night's frost."

"Aye, take an empty beaker to Llywarch. He knows where
the best pigment lies."

Llorfa sang quietly:

Our venerated leader's life is gone
In a blink,
He travels the spirit trail back
To the Great-Connecting-Link.

Llieu sniffed and thought of almonds. He went to the table
to smell the goblet and the flask. The sweetness took his breath
away. He closed his eyes to clear his head, and the goblet
slipped. It fell against a bench and left clear splinters mixed
with the clay shards of the broken wine flagon. He held his
hands up to warn the servants. "Do not pick up the splinters!
They will—they are sharp and will cut. Leave the body and
bring in Mistress Brenda as fast as you can." Like Llorfa, he
remembered that the smell was from smashed bitter almonds
Troyes had brought from France. How had it gotten into the
wine? His face was melancholy as a gib-cat's.

Someone had placed the hawthorn wreath on Owain's
chest. Lorfa asked if it ought to be removed.

"Leave it be," whispered Llieu. "Neither the wreath nor the
wine had anything to do with this death. 'Twas his time. The
pain in his heart killed him. It was forecast that he would die
at an auspicious time, by the hand of a son. Did Dafydd cause
the pain? 'Tis hard to know for certes. Did the gods stage the
eclipse for him? I cannot say for certes."

Annesta, pale as bleached linen, appeared in the hall with
her grandfather.

Llywarch bowed his head and said a prayer to the gods that
he believed would welcome his friend to the Otherside. He
told Llieu that he did not like the smell around the corpse and
that he was leaving with his granddaughter and Mona to fill a
beaker with red ochre and would be back before supper. He
took Llieu's hand and whispered, "I knew Owain was not well,
and thought I was prepared for him to go, but I be not. I would
like to see the prince given a druid funeral worthy of a king."

"Me too," whispered Llieu. "Tell Howell this evening at
supper."

Brenda held back her tears. At first she could not acknowledge Owain's death. She pretended the eclipse was the most
important happening and said she had noticed how the light

that shone between the needles of the evergreens near the castle made tiny shadows of the sun being eaten by the moon. Then she said to Llorfa, "Lord Dafydd is standing in the snow, holding his face toward the sun. He acts dazed and does not see nor hear me."

Finally she worked up enough courage to stand by the corpse.

Llorfa sang, "Avoiding Death takes too much time, and too much care/When at the very end of all, Death catches each one unaware."

Brenda opened the door to air out the hall.

"Aye!" whispered Llieu. "Remember the almond extract Troyes brought from Paris?"

Brenda could no longer hold back the flood of tears. Her voice cracked as she agreed that the smell was like the oil from crushed bitter almonds. "Troyes was very careful handling it," she said. "He used tongs to touch the soaked rag when he put it in a cage with a rat. The rat became crazy, ran in circles, jumped, twitched and died. He burned the rat and the rag."

"He wanted the druids to see what he had brought from France and left his herb and mineral display in Llieu's cottage," said Llorfa. "After Madoc's honoring ceremony Troyes told me the vial was missing. Only druids went into his cottage and I thought he had misplaced it. I do not know what the elixir was called. I do not use it."

"Before the honoring ceremony I let in a couple of crofters, who said they were afraid of Dafydd's soldiers," said Llieu. "The crofters were not druids and stayed in my cottage. They were gone when I went back after the ceremony was over. That was the night Brenda was to stay with Molly and Llywarch with me—of course, neither of you came."

"The crofters—what did they look like?" asked Brenda, wiping her eyes on her skirt.

"I barely remember," said Llieu. "I was busy with the ceremony and worrying about you and Llywarch. They were dressed in sheepskins. Their hair was tied at the napes of their necks. The fellow with a clean-shaved face and a cap on his head did all the talking. The other had a scarf around his face because of the cold wind. His eyes were small and gray. His biceps and thighs bulged big as firewood. His neck was thick. Oh Lugh!" He slapped his head with one hand. "He could have been—you know, Dafydd. That devil will do anything. Steal rat poison for murder!"

"How would he know about bitter almonds?" asked Brenda.

"The old woman in the village," said Llorfa. "She looks at your palm and tells your fortune. She asked Troyes and Conlaf about simple herbs for headaches and heavy female bleeding. Troyes might have offered her almond extract. She had plenty of rats. How will we get this sickening smell out of our nostrils?"

"As carefully as we prepare Owain's body so the people can say their farewells," said Llieu.

"Lugh's lungs, I will miss him," said Brenda.

"Troyes and I will move the body to Owain's chamber for the preparation," whispered Llieu. "Brenda and Llorfa, clean up the shattered shards and glass. Please do not touch anything. Use a heap of rags."

"Is it troth that Dafydd expects to sleep in Owain's chamber?" whispered Brenda.

"I bet my wool stockings that he will take the guest chamber when he espies Owain sitting on the pallet." Llorfa chuckled.

Part Three
1164 to 1170 A.D.

On the death of Owain Gwynedd there was immediate strife within the House of Gwynedd. The sons of Owain fought among themselves as to who should rule the land. . . . Howel, "a base sonne begotten of an Irishwoman," was the first to seize power. It was inevitable that he should provoke civil strife and a stern challenge to his authority, for in 1146 he had joined forces with the Normans temporarily against the sons of Gruffydd ap Rhys. Howel was an opportunist and prepared to change his loyalties for an offer of property or loot.

For two stormy years after Owain's death Howel precariously held the reins of power. Then he went to Ireland to claim his mother's property, and on his return found his brother Dafydd asserting his right to rule by force of arms. There are conflicting versions as to what happened to Howel after this. According to the *Myvyrian Archaiology*, he was wounded in battle, and taken to Ireland where he is said to have died. But *Annales Cambriae*, a more reliable source, states that Howel was killed by Dafydd's forces in armed conflict in 1171. . . .

Llywarch's odes frequently struck a note of foreboding. He wrote many poems on Dafydd and Rhodri and, reading between the lines, one can discern a certain wistfulness and the mournful note of one who sighed for happier days and feared to tell all. Gwalchmai, somewhat disillusioned, sought relief in love lyrics, composing some exquisite odes to his wife, Eve, rather than enter into the quarrels of the warring brothers of Gwynedd, and he, too, seems to have been torn between duty and his innermost feelings. Love was a safer subject than family vendettas.

Richard Deacon, *Madoc and the Discovery of America*

XXIV
Royal Funeral

Owain reigned for thirty-two years. He died in December, 1169, and was buried at Bangor. As he had been excommunicated by Beckett because of his illegal marriage to his cousin, controversy over his burial in consecrated ground raged for some time. Owain had continued to live with Chrisiant until her death and the ban on him was not lifted by the Church even then, as Owain had been openly defiant of the ecclesiastical authorities. When Baldwyn, Archbishop of Canterbury, came to preach at Bangor in support of the Crusades against the Saracens, he saw the tomb and charged the Bishop of Bangor to remove the body from the cathedral. The Bishop, who had his own ideas as to how a Welsh hero should be treated, made formal signs of obedience, withdrew the body from the tomb but made a passage from the vault through the south wall of the cathedral and secretly deposited Owain's remains outside, but still in consecrated ground.

Richard Deacon, *Madoc and the Discovery of America*

Llorfa hummed as she picked up the broken pieces of clay and glass with serving tongs, and put them on a large rag. She used other rags to clean the slate floor, then threw all of it, including the tongs, in the midden heap. The strong odor caused her to feel nauseous. She squinched her face and held her breath as long as possible.

Llieu stood in the open doorway. "Wash your hands," he said. "Then help Brenda clean and dress the body, wash your hands again, then go—go to the safe camp with Brenda, Annesta and Mona." He hesitated to see if she understood.

She looked puzzled, but Brenda, still there, had heard and understood. She whispered, "We wash our hands of the next event."

"The funeral?" asked Llorfa.

Llieu looked around the room and his voice became very low. "The four of you leave quickly, before the funeral; before the New Religionists decide to make you prisoners, or worse. So as not to arouse suspicion, Llywarch and a couple of us from the druid camp will stay for the funeral. All of us will meet you at the wharf in Holyhead, where Irish curraghs will be waiting. If you miss us, find your own way to Dubh Linn and the safe camp. Go quietly, mayhap as crofter women, or gypsies, whose men have become soldiers."

"Aye," said Brenda. Be I ready? she wondered. For most of my adult life I have wanted to return to Ireland. Some days I was so restless that I could hardly wait—but I did not want to go this way. Things are happening too fast, too soon. I need all of my brains, discipline and cold, clean reason to get to Ireland safely. Does Sein know we are coming? Oh, aye, he knows. He is helping us get there. God's gizzard, I be going to Dubh Linn and I be scared. A part of me does not want to leave Gwynedd. I have lost a dear, dear old friend. Owain and Gwynedd have been my life for so long that I cannot imagine being without them. I should be happy, but . . .

For a moment she lost herself in thoughts of Owain and how he had looked like a Viking god when she had first met him.

Llieu nodded wearily. "All I know is *Cymraeg*," he said. "I will miss *Cymru*. The gods have blessed us and let us breathe with New Religionists all around us. It could not last. We must not reason too much or too little, or we are lost."

Llieu was silent when Dafydd came inside the hall with a hammering in his head and a buzzing in his ears. Dafydd blinked to clear his muzzy sight and drew a cross in the air over his father's corpse. The sight did not fill him with horror, or pity. Long ago his blood had turned to ice.

Aye! My doing! he thought. No one else, not even Howell, had the guts. The old man was ready to go behind the veil and I gave him the push. I be strong as any god! Who said the wine was foul? Does that mean unclean or defiled? How could Brenda know? Because she is solid with the pagans? The stargazer-woman told me the pagans' almond paste mixes with water or wine and leaves no trace. She did not mention 'tis deadly to touch! Did I perchance filch the wrong vial at the pagan camp? He closed his eyes thinking, The sky has fallen and the sea is about to drown me. God, do not let me go under. He felt a spasm in his gut and told himself that he must not act like a scared maidservant facing the whip, shaking with fright and willing to do anything to avoid the whip's terrible bite. He opened his burning eyes, edged his way out the open door and gulped the fresh air.

Weeping servants came into the hall with a litter to take Owain's body to the solar.

Brenda saw them hesitate to lift the body with its wine-stained clothing. It was like a bad dream listening to her own voice explain to them that the prince's last drink was befouled and they should not touch his beard, the yoke of his shirt, or other wet places.

· She vowed to remember Owain, Prince of Gwynedd, with yellow curls, soft blue eyes, thick-chested, broad-shouldered, vigorous, full of life, stubborn, self-confident, quick-witted; a friend, and the most generous leader Gwynedd had known thus far.

Grim-faced Dafydd spun back inside, where his eyes took a long time to adjust to the uneven darkness. Owain's body had been taken away. Someone was wiping the floor. Aye, mop up the evidence, he told himself. I can take the credit or blame it on anyone I choose. I be king! 'Twill be pagans' word against the word of King Dafydd. He skirted the room until he was close to the knot of servants standing around Gwalchmai, rubbed his eyes to make them water so the images appeared sharper. All eyes turned his way when he spoke. "I shall sleep in the king's chamber. I be king of Gwynedd."

"My lord, Prince Owain's body will lie on the pallet in the royal chamber for the final farewell of friends and family," said Gwalchmai. " 'Twould be more fitting if you occupy the guest chamber. Much preparation has to be done. Officials from all over. Throngs of locals will pay their respects. In the meantime I suggest you consult your brother Lord Howell."

"Bloody hell with officials, respects and preparation," said Dafydd. "My father is to be oiled, dressed, and taken by sail to Saint Dafydd's Church in Bangor. 'Twas my mother's wish that his body be in a marble sarcophagus inside the cathedral." He held his naked dagger in his right hand to show his authority. "Now prepare the royal chamber!"

Dafydd could not see clearly. The thought that the sun had burned his eyes as it reappeared in the sky danced rapidly through his head and was discarded. He pounded his fists against the sides of his head and shouted, "My sudden failing eyesight is my father's parting gift. What a hateful father the gods gave me!"

Gwalchmai kept his hand on his head. Dafydd's blow had raised a throbbing lump on his head and he did not want another fuss with this puffed-up peacock. "The body will be ready to sail to Bangor soon after the morrow's first light, my lord." He tried to be dignified by keeping his head up and his back straight as he went to tell the servants to prepare the royal chamber for Lord Dafydd and to move the corpse to the guest chamber.

After Owain's body was made presentable and painted with the red ochre, Brenda led Llorfa, Annesta and Mona to the barn, where the stable-boy was not in sight. Brenda sighed with relief and told them to choose a horse.

Both of the gate guards recognized Brenda and assumed that the ladies, who wore black lace over their heads, were going to the church to pray for a safe journey for Owain's spirit to the Otherside.

"Beware," one of the guards whispered to Brenda. "Howell soldiers in Aberffraw prepare to oppose Dafydd's troops should they attack during the funeral. Rumor says Dafydd is out to·behead anyone who used to be close to the prince."

The women were close-mouthed, not wishing to draw attention to themselves, as they traveled on the road leading outside of Aberffraw. They passed the druid camp and it appeared deserted. Llorfa insisted they stop and gather *bogets*, or water bags, and a couple kettles and *points*, or leather ropes and a billhook to cut withies for shelter or cut dry sticks for fire kindling. Brenda thought it a good idea to see if they could find blankets because the nights were icy cold.

Near Llieu's cottage she noticed something that looked like a pile of blankets or clothing. "Mayhap there is someone there who would rather join us than be left alone," she said.

Annesta stared. The clothes looked familiar, like those her grandfather had worn yesterday when they had gone after the red ochre. The closer she came, the more familiar the gray clothing became. She said mayhap her grandfather had decided to wear something else to the funeral and left his other belongings here for later. She could not keep out the dread that seeped into her thoughts. The wind blew the bottom of the gray tunic back upon itself. A gray pigtail waved in the breeze. She dismounted and stood still as a statue, and her heart thundered against her ribs.

She knelt with her arms against her chest, then slowly pulled the tunic away from the shoulders. Llywarch's head was severed from the neck and lay facedown in the rocky soil. The pooled blood was still wet. He had not been dead long.

"Oh, Grandfather!" she cried. "Why have they done this to you?" She saw that his gloves were gone and plain as country shale there was her answer. The wrinkled white hands had blue tattooing as far up as the elbows. She picked up one of the cold hands, kissed it, looked around and, seeing the broken harp, she lay it in Llywarch's crooked arm. "He is himself now."

"I know the real why," whispered Mona. "Your grandfather, Llywarch, died saving us."

"What are you saying?" asked Annesta, wiping her mouth on the back of her hand.

"Two, three times while going after the red clay, he told us to stop. 'Be still,' he said. He heard something. We laughed, made fun of him. On the way back he said he heard a wolf on the prowl. I thought he was teasing. When we were close to the druids' place he told us to hurry on as fast as we could through the village, on to the court, and to stop for naught.

He said he wanted to talk to Llieu about the Irish safe camp.
I thought Llieu was at the court, but I did not question him.
We went on, giggling, thinking he was overcautious. I turned
once and he was not going to the druid camp, but looking and
listening back up the path to the ochre bed. I did not say
anything. But now I think he could have been looking for
something—someone. He wanted us to leave before—before—
Oh Lugh's legs! We might be lying headless on the ground if
he had not sent us back!"

" 'Tis New Religionists' work, for certes!" said Annesta
with tears running down her face. "Once he predicted that he
would die by the hands of those who called him a pagan."

Brenda held both Mona and Annesta close, telling them to
hush.

"We will stay here for shelter tonight, like gypsies," said
Llorfa. "No one, not even soldiers, will bother us if we stay
out of sight."

Annesta pulled away, crouched over her grandfather's body
and tried to hold the gory head in place.

When her sobbing subsided, Brenda said they would wrap
the body so they could bury it.

"Oh, no, no! He is to be cremated and the ashes left in a
container in a cromlech. That is the druid way for bards. A
body is born with life through water and leaves that life by
fire. The ashes are left in a cave or cromlech so the spirit will
not come back looking for the body."

"Pray it does not rain," said Brenda.

After dark they placed Llywarch's body in one of the old
wattled lean-tos that held wood and set fire to it. They said a
going-away prayer for the spirit of the bard. Then they spread
blankets and bratts on the floor of one of the cottages and
slept.

Clouds sat over the towering mountain peaks and hid the
jagged, rocky ridges. The rocky outcroppings were black and
shiny. It was drizzling in the pine-clad foothills and misting
along the ocean's shore. Brenda wondered about the druids.
Where were Molly and her five children? Mayhap they all
went to the court and stayed the night to bid their last farewells
to the prince. Surely Gwalchmai would feed them and give

them a place to sleep. Or had they been captured by Dafydd and his men? Nay! She could not believe that. Who could tell the druids about Llywarch? She could leave a message, but what if the druids did not come back to their camp? She sighed and told herself it was in the hands of the gods. She heard Annesta whimpering and thought of a newly orphaned child crying for the loss of a beloved grandfather. Once love binds you to another, you cannot cut the bonds. Annesta will always love Llywarch, she thought. He raised her during her childhood years. They were more like child and revered teacher. I, too, loved Llywarch as a friend I could always count on. He never deceived me, never looked down on my mistakes and always was pleased with my successes. What did I give to him? It was my trust. I will always cherish his friendship and keep it alive in the center of my heart.

In the morning the fire was spent and the ashes damp with misty rain. Annesta scooped up some of the ashes into a leather pouch and they moved on as gypsy women.

The first gray light of morning crept through the shutter in the royal chamber. There was a great row in the hall with shouting, clanking of swords, scraping of benches, crashing of an iron wall-sconce, clanging of shield rims and banging on the door.

Dafydd rubbed the sleep from his eyes; everything in the room had a dull, fuzzy cast. He opened the door and was greeted by soldiers in blue tunics and his half-brother, Howell, wearing a blue velvet tunic edged in silver brocade.

"Morning's first light is here!" said Howell. "Are you going to sleep or stand in the line to say farewell as our father's bier is boarded on a ship bound for Bangor?"

"I was not told about a ship and everything being ready," whined Dafydd, shivering in the cold, dank air that came out of the foothills. He pulled on his wool stockings, then his boots. "I fear our father threw me his poor eyesight. Since yesterday I cannot see well. Where is my bloody body servant?"

"Ha! Your bloody body servant is right!" said Howell. "He boasted, within hearing of my men, of being in the service of

the new king of Gwynedd. My men know that no one is to
be called king and that I be the new prince of Gwynedd. Your
soldiers came sneaking in to surround the court's wall last
evening. You drank enough mead to drown your own army
and retired early so you did not see your troops defeated, nor
the scuffle when your flag-bearer lost his head. Your men and
Rhodri's are my slaves, to give to anyone I want. I may give
them to Maelgwyn for choosing to be under my command."

"Maelgwyn is here? You jest!" Dafydd put his hands
against the sides of his head to hold back the confusion. His
ears rang with battering waves of panic. He hardly knew Maelgwyn. "You would do this to me, your brother?"

"Half-brother. You were there when our father named me
his successor. You saw the lords cast their votes last night.
The people chose me as Gwynedd's leader. You know brothers who speak fair to your face and do evil behind your back?
I be not one of them, but I be not sure of you, nor Rhodri."

"What will you do with me?" sobbed Dafydd, following
his brother into the great hall. Howell pointed out dark-haired
Lord Maelgwyn. Dafydd saw through a fuzzy haze that Maelgwyn's troops had formed a ring around his and Rhodri's
men, who were tied together by iron wrist-chains. "You
chained my men like dogs!" His protest sounded like the
whine of an injured pup.

"Dafydd, 'tis up to you," said Howell. "You can cooperate
and let me rule this land peaceably, or you can flee and I will
put a claim against you that follows the *Law of Distress*. You
will owe me your land, buildings and livestock if you flee. I
will announce the debt and 'twill be doubled if you evade
seizure."

Dafydd rolled his thick tongue over his scummy teeth and
did not remember filling or refilling his drinking horn with
that much mead last night. His mind and body were dull as
ditch water, but he could never admit weakness. "By Christ's
eyes, I am the better man and so should be king of Gwynedd!
Unchain my men and I swear I shall not invade your lands as
long as either you or I shall live." He stretched out his hand,
feeling for his brother's to seal the bargain.

"When you have my hand to seal a deal, you may depend

on me," said Howell, and he indicated with a slight gesture of his hands that the prisoners were to be freed. He did it to honor his father, who had put up with Dafydd, the turncoat, the black sheep in the family, for years. He did not take his brother's hand and promised nothing. He slipped in front of his highest officers, marched outside into the cold, wet, winter air, and his mouth tightened into a bitter smile.

Owain's body, wrapped in a purple linen sheet, was carried on a portable framework by four castellans stationed at the four corners, which represented the four directions. It was carried nine times around the great hall, representing the good works of nine generations behind Prince Owain. Directly behind the corpse came Howell, then a court guard carrying the banner that had hung from the hall's center beam. It was a flag on which were embroidered three life-sized golden lions, one under the other, with tails held over their backs, on a red silk field.

Next came a guard carrying a pole to which was attached a white banner with the ringed scarlet cross of Christ on a white field of purity. It was well known that Owain gave generously to the churches. Then came the penteulu, Gwalchmai, strumming a six-stringed harp to accompany the kinship experience-poems that recalled the highlights of Owain's life, including the deeds of nine generations of his ancestors in stanzas of three lines interlocked by chain rhyming. Behind him was Archdruid Llieu, chief physician for the late prince, and Conlaf, Owain's student physician; their eyes were ringed with dark circles. Behind them was Prince Rhys of Powys, then Caradoc, and other druids mixed among the lords of Gwynedd. Last came the household servants, men and women snuffling together at each ninth step. Then they made a single sound to express the strength of their grief: "Ah!" Slowly the body was carried between two lines of Howell's soldiers.

Owain's gray hair was neatly combed and hung over each shoulder in thin braids. The top of his head was scrubbed until it shone and then painted with powdered red ochre and oil. A gold circlet fit snugly on his head. His beard was combed and tied with a purple band. Triangular silver coins lay over his closed eyes. He was dressed in a white silk shirt, his finest purple velveteen tunic; black shoes and stockings covered the blue honor marks on his thighs and calves. A gold crosier lay at his side. His bare hands lay on his chest and the blue-woad curlicues around his fingernails and on the backs of his hands were clearly visible through the thin coating of red ochre. The back of his left hand was pricked with a blue picture of mysterious twisted vines and intricate leaves. The back of the right hand was pricked with the outline of a single lion, its tongue out, its right paw in the air and its tail forming an *S* over its back. This was the first time many had seen Owain's honor marks. On his right hand there was a ring with a gold cross, a gift from Archbishop Thomas Becket that symbolized their common Christian beliefs.

There were muted whispers about Prince Owain's paradoxical belief in two different philosophies. Some said he lived by the best teachings of the Old and New Religions. Others said his life was inconsistent and contradictory, such as loving women of either Welsh or Irish heritage and having sons who were either honorable or shameful.

The procession marched through the double doors of the keep to the first court gate, where the linen sheet was folded like a blanket around Owain's broad shoulders. The bier holding a white marble coffin carved to resemble a cave with curling vines where animals and fishes hid among the leaves was placed on the floor of a four-wheeled cart. The body was placed in the coffin and the cart was pulled by two white horses through the second gate, down the berm to the seashore. The road to the bay was lined with village folk, crofters, nuns, priests and clerics who wept and called out, *"Owain Fawr! Owain Mawr!"*

Llieu leaned over and said to Gwalchmai, "How long can Howell and Dafydd keep the lid on the cauldron that boils in Gwynedd?"

"How long is the tail on a falling star?" answered Gwalchmai.

Early morning fog lay over the sea and the beached Welsh curragh with its red sail and multicolored banners was barely visible until the procession was several ells away from where it was beached. Owain's soldiers formed a semicircle around the curragh as the corpse, now shrouded in the Gwynedd house banner, was placed on the curragh's deck. The circle closed and Howell's and Maelgwyn's soldiers formed another around the first. Dafydd's soldiers stood behind the circles and Dafydd stood behind Howell.

When the body was safely on the curragh, there was silence so only the lapping of the waves and the cries of gulls searching for food was heard. Some mourners made the sign of the cross in front of the ship; others faced the ship and closed their eyes to hold on to the image of Owain, their beloved leader. Suddenly the crowd chanted, *"Owain Fawr! Owain Mawr!"*

Tears ran unchecked down the faces of Archdruid Llieu and the harper Gwalchmai. Simultaneously they thought, We druids are now no more than fly specks in Gwynedd's order of things. 'Tis time to leave. They removed their bratts, scuffed their soft leather brogues with stones and rubbed their hair with sweet oil. When they passed the village gate guards, Llieu appeared to be a street beggar with long, filthy, oily hair, wearing stained garments. Gwalchmai, in a sleeveless tabard, acted as a befuddled herder who had lost his sheep to a band of dragons. The guards were glad to see them go.

Dafydd whispered to Howell, "If a man's finger is cut off, he cannot be king by Welsh law. The same goes for a tongue, even though 'tis not stated in the law."

Howell whispered, "Despite what you believe, druid physicians were wise with herbs and tongue exercises." He stuck his tongue out and his eyes flashed. "Does it look cut off? If it were, could I speak? 'Tis more whole than your eyesight."

Sweat ran down Dafydd's face. He did not wait to see the curragh pushed into the sea. He went to Rhodri and they gathered their men and quietly disappeared behind the dunes, among the trees and gorse.

Nine of Owain's soldiers somberly pushed the curragh off the shore, then stood with their hands in the air shouting, *"Ffarwel!"* The sun burned through the fog and shone yellow-bright on the curragh, making it glow like gold. There was an intake of breath throughout the crowd as hands raised simultaneously, a parting gesture to a beloved ruler. The rowers took the little ship beyond the strong tide race, where she sailed southeast toward the Menai Strait, then through the strait to Bangor.

Inconspicuously that same day, other druids left for the safe camp in Ireland. Many of them traveled in fishing craft hugging the coast toward Holy Island. Llieu, wrapped tightly in his wool bratt, stretched his legs in a coracle paddled by Troyes. "Seeds are blown by wind and carried by water to sprout anew, so are ideas and beliefs blown by necessity and carried by desire to bring forth new knowledge," said Llieu.

"Ho!" said Troyes. "The ideas and beliefs we bring to Ireland will be buried. We are but a few going to live among many. The many swallow the few, killing new knowledge."

"You are wrong, my friend!" Llieu's words were grainy from the anger and sadness sitting in his heart. "The few are chewed up and spit out. That is new knowledge. Ideas and beliefs are mixed together, and what results is something new, composed of bits and pieces of the old. You wait and see. This is but a small beginning."

XXV
Gwenllian

We cannot know just how much the mediaeval midwife learnt from observation about pre-natal influences which male astrologers attributed to the influence of the planets, but she would note that a child conceived in autumn and carried through the dark months of sparse diet when there was no meat, nor milk, nor eggs, or green food, was likely to be a poor baby at birth; but if it survived it would have the good spring and summer foods, and sunshine and warmth for its first year of growth.

A baby girl born under Venus would have:
Pretty mouth to sing a song, eyebrows delicate and long,
Bodies made for bodies' bliss, sweet smooth faces, warm to kiss,
Loving music, well can they, upon the lute or tabor play.
Swift in love and swift in quarrel, and deliciously immoral.

Dorothy Hartley, *Lost Country Life*,
from a medieval *Hausbuch*

The women tied the bottoms of their skirts around their waists, bound their shoes and wool stockings together, slung them over their shoulders. Brenda had left a note in charcoal on the wall of Llieu's cottage: *Royal bard found beheaded. Ashes with kin.* She had suggested they draw a cross with charcoal on their foreheads. " 'Tis an outward symbol that we mourn the death of Prince Owain with the same intensity we would have mourned the death of Christ," she said. "Think of our safety. No one else will do that for us."

Annesta carried the leather pouch that was gathered tight at the top by a thong. She looped the thong around her neck and hid the pouch under her tunic, close to her heart.

No soldiers followed them to the north side of Trecastell Bay, so they stopped to rest at the old haunted megalithic tomb, Barclodiad-y-Gawres. They smiled at each other's soot-stained faces, which made their eyes as round and white as hellhags'.

They rode as close as possible to the sandy shore, past the craggy black rocks, and watched for signs of dragons. The wind blew hard, dried any trace of the rain from the night before and made clouds of fine sand. When the wind died, the grass, brush, horses and riders were covered with a powder of gritty dust. Then they were hungry, so they boiled a mixed grain called mestlin. Before every swallow they ground grit between their teeth.

By late afternoon each of the four women began to feel her horse's backbone and complained of sore thighs. Finally, Brenda said it was time to make camp. They tethered the horses to a scrubby stand of yew and felt their spines tremble like withies in the breeze. Their legs were wobbly as eels when they dismounted. They were too tired to eat. Mona fussed over Brenda, rubbed her legs and back with bruised plantain leaves. Afterward Brenda told her that she no longer need act as her maid. "We are all friends."

They slept huddled together and were grateful for the huge stones that kept them sheltered from the wind. Annesta took her blanket and precious pouch of ashes to the foot of a thick, dark stone. She pulled her bratt tight around herself and buried her face in her arms.

Brenda moved her blanket close, put an arm around Annesta and said, "You have us. We will look after each other. You have Madoc. Dwell on the future. You have to go on with a new kind of life, same as the rest of us."

When Annesta finally slept, Brenda sat up, pulled her blanket tight around her shoulders and thought of springtime and warm sunshine, when seeds would sprout and bring forth a riot of wildflowers. She thought of the Welsh seasons and life and death. Cold wind blew across her tear-swollen face and it was soothing. Was it the spirit of Llywarch come to comfort them? "Aye, I, too, look forward to the time Annesta is with Madoc," she told him.

• The next day the sky was white with high snow clouds. The women put on their stockings and shoes. Lazy wet snow-flakes fell during midafternoon but stopped by dark. The next morning there was more snow. It melted on their faces, leaving dark and white streaks. Brenda felt that every muscle in her body was stiff and achy. Through puffy eyes she saw two men standing by a clump of trees. She clenched her teeth, ignored the pain and went to see who they were. No one was near the trees, only footprints.

They cleaned their hands and faces with snow that covered the red grass and dried themselves with the edges of their kilted petticoats and skirts. They ate strips of salted mutton with a handful of icy grass to dilute the bitterness of the salt.

Brenda remembered the last few months of Owain's life when he became openly suspicious of everyone close to him. Several times she had feared that he would, in some spur-of-the-moment decision, actually poison her food or see that she had some terrible accident, like Christiannt. Her heart could not bleed for his death. He was unmistakably a great leader, but he had had an ability to enslave women. Still, she did not regret having loved him. She anticipated her path in Ireland, which would lead to Goeral, Riryd and her father. She hoped the gods would lead her to renew her friendship with Sein. She smiled and told herself she would leave the future to the gods. There were other things to think about now.

The next morning was cold, but instead of snowing there was thunder, fierce flashes of lightning, rain that clung to their gowns and chilled them to the bone. They passed a large croft where the cottages and barns were recently burned. The crofters lived in makeshift alder lean-tos. Brenda waved, climbed stiffly from her horse and said, "We offer good-luck charms that may help brighten your future." She reached deep into her bratt pocket and brought out several river-smoothed quartz pieces.

A bent old man shook his head. "We are beyond the luck of Gypsy charms. Thieving dragons took our cattle, burned our places and declared this valley property of Lord Dafydd. Those bullfrogs slaughtered our sheep. What they did not eat or take for hides, they left for buzzards and flies after the wolf had his fill. They bound us, expected us to starve to death and give the wolves another feast. My woman was stronger than the dragons supposed. She clawed her binding loose and freed us. We gathered grain ahead of the fire that raced across the fields. Saved enough for winter and next spring's seed." He smirked. "We salted the mutilated mutton before the wolves and buzzards found it."

Brenda said, "We will barter genuine fortune-telling for mutton."

"How about that sack of hazelnuts?"

She untied the thin linen sack, wondering how he knew the contents.

"I can smell 'em," he said, and took the sack into one of the lean-tos.

The others thought Brenda had lost her senses to give away food, and showed their dissent by scowling and shaking their fists. An old woman with a black wool shawl over her head came out of the lean-to, thanked Brenda for the nuts and invited them to stay for a meal of boiled grain. Brenda smiled and beckoned the others to follow her. After the meal Brenda took the old woman outside and told her that the lines in her palm told her life's history. The old woman's eyes shone. "Will I outlive my old man?"

Brenda admired the knitting in the black shawl, stroked the old woman's hand, and asked her gently about her man's health. She closed her eyes, held her face toward the swirling clouds and said in a faraway voice, "You are going to outlive this unrest. You will see better times in a new cottage, with oiled linen inside the window shutters to let in the light, let out the smoke." She rubbed the old woman's palm with fragrant oil, and put a small round quartz in the center. She opened her eyes and with a touch of sadness said, "Your soul

will be called to Heaven before your husband's. I be sorry—
still you have many good years."

"Heh, heh! That is what I wanted to hear! I do not want to
live alone. I fear loneliness worse than death." The old
woman's laugh was like the cackle of the red kite bird. She
gave Brenda a sack of barley and whispered that other crofters
had told them Prince Owain was dead. "Lord Dafydd's firebrands were seen pulling a large catapult through the bed of
boulders on the shore nearest the royal court's palisades. They
will draw back that timbered monster's arm, release the pressure and fling boulders against the wooden stakes. Then they
will set them afire. When everyone in the courtyard dies or
flees, that wind-breaking Dafydd will have only his half-
brother, Prince Howell, to fight."

"What then?" asked Brenda.

From the lean-to the old man said, "Prince Howell be not
strong enough to keep Lord Dafydd off the throne." He came
out and spit on the ground. "Some from the royal court will
settle along the road outside Aberffraw's gates, to sell their
meager goods to the soldiers and villagers. After Dafydd, there
will be a new prince and some of us may be bold enough to
move back and rebuild our crofts. The population outside the
village walls will grow, more cottages will be built, even rolling mills for flour near the creek and lime vats for tanneries,
tallow-rendering huts and apiaries for wax shops. Streets will
wrap around the village wall, a village outside a village. In
time the first wall will be torn down. This is the way Gwynedd's villages will grow into towns." The old man's eyes
shone. "Good comes from evil." His head dropped as if bowed
in prayer.

"Have you the gift of foretelling?" asked Brenda.

"I have the gift of observation and deduction."

The women went past the small lakes to the ferry that crossed
at the narrowest point to Holy Island. The horses were not
allowed on the boats so the women stayed with them as they
swam across. That night they huddled around a tiny fire fueled
with bunches of twisted grasses to dry their clothing and blankets. In the morning they crossed the grassland leading to the

small village of Trearddur, beyond which, Llorfa remembered, were some cromlechs, caves flanked by upright stones. Annesta might leave her grandfather's ashes there. Annesta held the pouch against her bosom, and said she could not part with it. "I like him near."

"Wait 'til we get there and you will see 'tis a good place to leave him," said Brenda.

Near sundown they came across several horses in a pasture behind a rectangular boulder-built cottage set into the side of a hill. The roof of birch boughs thatched with heather had been recently burned. Cows grazed outside a blackened wattle barn attached to one side of the house. Not far from the barn a spring ran from a quartzite bank between two oak trees. Beside the spring was a wooden sled half loaded with bricks of turf. A mattock lay against the peats.

Before the women dismounted, a crofter with silver hair and brows and lashes the color of moonlight pushed aside the door-flap. His eyes, nose and ears were pink as the wild rose and his lips were like strawberries. He wore a wide-brimmed hat and said he had expected them sooner. They were to stay at his place, because he had word that soldiers in Holyhead were looking for a woman called Brenda who had poisoned Prince Owain. "This woman has long chestnut hair and is traveling with a younger woman with auburn hair and blue eyes."

Brenda drew in her breath. "There are four of us," she said, in a cool voice, "and we have the color and length of our hair hidden under shawls and bratts."

"Ye know a harper called Gwalchmai?" he asked, putting on a face mask and blinking his pale eyes in the last rays of sunlight.

"Prithee, a harper?" said Brenda trying to act like a gypsy.

"Of course, ye know him. Ye fair maids come from Aberffraw's court. Gwalchmai is my cousin and I used to carry messages to the pagan camp from the Irish druids. My cousin told me if things became bad at the Holyhead wharf to keep ye here, and when ye are permitted to sail, I keep yur horses. He did not know that Lord Dafydd's men would try to annihilate us."

"Lord Dafydd—his dragons did this to your roof?" asked Llorfa.

"Come hither," he said, and took off the hat and mask. "Garth will show ye." His hair was tied in a club in the back of his head. He said he was of the old ways, pushed up his sleeves and showed them his honor marks. His skin was snow white. His face crinkled into laugh lines around his rosebud eyes. The inside of the cottage was a shocking sight. The walls were blackened with soot. The earthen floor was scorched and smelled of smoke and dampness. Nothing was there, not a bed, not a cupboard, not even a chair. Garth stood, with a faraway look, by the charred door frame.

His wife was as dark as he was light. She rubbed down the horses and took them to a water tub in the pasture. She was slim and short with black hair and eyes so dark they seemed like polished hematite. Her skin was smooth and tanned as fine leather. When she came back she said her name was Hyfra. She knew they wanted to go to the safe caves near Dubh Linn. With a catch in her voice she said it was not safe to travel to Holyhead. She pointed to Llorfa and Brenda, said they were healers, put a hand on Annesta's belly and said she was with child.

"Nay!" said Annesta, "that cannot be."

Hyfra put her arm around Mona and said she had great creative talent. "Gwalchmai says yur needlework is as fine as any artist's and ye have a gift for colors. I shall teach ye to paint pictures. Stay with us until 'tis safe to travel."

Over the next few days Garth cleaned out the well the soldiers had filled in with dirt. He brought in a flat stone to use as a table. The women sang and scrubbed the inside of the cottage and rebuilt the fire pit. They dug up the hard-packed, scorched dirt floor. The loose dirt was piled and packed on the floor against two inside walls. One pile formed a low ledge for seating and the other formed a wide ledge for six pallets against the opposite wall. The dug-down floor gave more headroom and stopped any draft along the floor.

Garth disappeared for several days. He came back with a grin and a cart full of fresh wool. He told how he and several other crofters had rounded up hundreds of abandoned sheep into stone-fenced pens.

The women sang as they took turns carding and spinning the wool into long twisted strands on a "throw cock," or spindle. Then Hyfra showed them how to weave on the shuttle Garth built. Hyfra called her weave *sprang* because the warp was hung double and the front and back threads were interwoven to give a kind of elastic fabric. Mona showed Hyfra how to dye the wool bright red, green, yellow, or blue with plant materials and set the colors to make them permanent with vinegar. Garth took the finished fabric to Holyhead to sell to wool merchants. He was pleased with the coins the colored fabric brought and once or twice in Holyhead bragged about his "daughters."

Brenda asked if the seaport in Holyhead was safe.

He answered, "Not yet."

After a week with the crofters, Annesta began going outside before the first meal of the day was finished. She kept her hand over her mouth to keep the nausea down and walked with her eyes on the ground. The cool, moist air felt thick to her. She clung to the large rocks and vomited. One morning she heard footsteps behind her, turned and saw Brenda. She said, "I be having another bilious spell. I believe they come on when I think how much I miss Madoc."

"Do the spells come each morning with the smell of food?" asked Brenda.

"Aye, and other times when food is cooking and sometimes for no reason at all."

"Hyfra was right, you have a seed growing in your belly," said Brenda. " 'Tis bad luck and good luck all in one."

"I do not want to cause bad luck, but I do want a baby. Madoc will be surprised—and happy? We will see."

Mona wanted to know if it was all right for Annesta to be a horsebacker.

Llorfa said that the swoon of Annesta's belly would not be noticeable for some time. "There be no need for frets. If Annesta is not tired she has no need to rest."

"A wee new life is a natural event," said Hyfra with a wink. " 'Tis something that is hard to hide."

Garth talked about enlarging his cottage to make a special room for Annesta and her baby.

One day Brenda went by herself to the Holyhead wharf to ask about a boat going to Ireland, or a fishing curragh willing to take four people from Holyhead to Dubh Linn. She learned that Welsh fishermen were inclined to take no more than one passenger at a time. Each passenger was sworn to say he was also a local fisherman, if perchance he was questioned by dragons or court soldiers. Careful whom she asked, Brenda could find no one who wanted to risk taking them across the Irish Sea. That added to her concern about the Aberffraw druids. Had they made it safely to Dubh Linn or were they also hidden in isolated crofts waiting to find a way across?

Back at the cottage, Brenda insisted that Garth and Hyfra teach them the art of gathering crabs and cockles in the tide pools. They always stayed together when they were near the sea, saying it was for Annesta's protection. Not only because she was pregnant, but because there was strength in numbers. If Dafydd or his dragons recognized any of them, they would be burned in a withie cage, or beheaded.

Garth made money by selling the crabs and cockles they gathered and later there were winter onions to barter for bread and flour. Still when the women asked about the safety of going to Holyhead, Garth said, "Not yet."

"Can we find a curragh at some other point that will take us to Dubh Linn?" asked Brenda, spinning the last of the wool one day in the early spring. "I have not seen anyone stop by your croft in weeks. How do you know things are not safe? Mayhap you are lonely and wish to detain us forever." She could have bitten her tongue when the words were out, but it was too late. She had revealed her impatience and doubts.

"Fie upon thee!" said Garth. "Ye well know my information comes from my cousin, Gwalchmai. I do not ask how or why he sends it. 'Tis best not to know too much. Someone bumps against my side in Holyhead and says, 'Yur cousin said, watch out for dragons.' Or a shopgirl leans close and says, 'Yur cousin thinks the sea is too rough.' I have had no words saying 'tis safe to let ye take a curragh across the Irish Sea to Dubh Linn. I do not know if Gwalchmai is in Dubh

Linn. There are no ships coming from there and even fewer going to there. In troth, I have not heard from my cousin for several months. Ye have to wait until he says 'Go!' "

Brenda felt the back of her neck and her cheeks burn with shame for doubting him.

"Yesterday, while trading onions for goat's milk, I heard of bloody fighting between the soldiers of Prince Howell and Lord Dafydd at the burial chamber near Trefignath. Lord Iorwerth, the peacemaker, tried to get them to talk about their grievances and end the fighting, but they threatened to march onto his land and take his Degannwy court. Lord Iorwerth was fostered with druids at Llyn Llygeirian before he was out of diaper cloths. His crooked nose angered Prince Owain and he threatened to have the ugly infant put in a sack with a stone and drowned same as a litter of unwanted kittens. Prince Owain—gods rest his spirit—wanted everything he owned to be perfect."

"Can a man's soul rest when he says he loves his children but he murders the ones he does not want?" wondered Brenda.

"Good thing he let Iorwerth live," said Garth. "He is the best-beloved son. There are no more than a handful of people in Gwynedd who do not love and admire him. He is competent and honorable, but he can never be head of this province, nor any other, because of his crooked nose."

"I met him and his wife at Degannwy court," said Brenda.

Hyfra left the pot of soup on the coals and sat on the floor beside Brenda. "I sometimes think about moving to Degannwy, where there is peace. My mother and father were killed while living in the Bwrdd Arthur hut-circles because Christian soldiers believed they were druids. I hid in the gorse, too frightened to move, until druids, Garth being one, found me and brought me to Degannwy. We stayed with Magain and her man, Doconn. She is a kindly woman who practices the Old Magic." She looked at Brenda, who was tight-lipped, wondering what Hyfra knew about Magain and her husband, Doconn. "Daughters, you would like it there in Degannwy," said Hyfra. "Not as much fog as here. And 'tis peaceful."

All was quiet for a while, then Mona asked, "What if something happens to Gwalchmai and he cannot send you information?"

Hyfra smoothed the front of her blue tunic, feeling the yoke where Mona had cross-stitched rows of red Xs. "Go to Degannwy and pray that he remains safe in Ireland with others."

"Is he in Degannwy?" asked Mona.

"Nay, he and Molly Fardd teach the fosterlings in caves near Dubh Linn," said Hyfra, patting Mona's hand. "Brenda knows Molly."

"Aye. They are friends," said Mona, looking at Brenda, who wondered if the druids were truly in Dubh Linn. Surely they are not beggars on the roads, she thought and looked around at Garth, who was smiling at her.

"I also heard yesterday," he said, "that the druids in Ireland are molding small glass wine beakers and selling them for fancy prices. The druids have a secret formula for making especially clear glass. I bet my best milk cow that those bloody New Religionists have no idea 'tis pagans making their wineglasses."

One especially warm day Annesta and Brenda bathed in the creek. Annesta looked at Brenda's naked trim waist, then down at her own and was surprised at its broadness. Her hips had widened and her belly had swollen with a distinct roundness, like bread that has risen slowly in a warm place. Inside her round belly she felt a kick as she slid down into the cold, clear water. Her breath caught and she put her hands on her breasts. They were not as tender as they had been a few months ago, but now they seemed heavy and full. Again she looked at Brenda's slim, supple body and said, "Will I ever look like I used to? I be as big as a cow."

"You will never be quite the same, but you will slim down and be agile again. And you will be more attractive than before."

"I be glad Madoc cannot see me clumsy," she said, remembering how he had wrapped his arms around her tiny naked waist and then placed his newly tattooed hands on her breasts. She dreamed about making love. She longed for the pleasure. Before she and Madoc had made love, she had thought about it, but the idea was not persistent and she could live without the togetherness-thing. But now she sometimes felt she could not live without it. She thought about it constantly. Even with a baby growing inside her, she wanted to feel Madoc pressed hard against her flesh.

"Some men like the looks of a pregnant woman," said Brenda. "It arouses them."

Her words made Annesta blush. She finished bathing and slipped her tunic over her head before Brenda was out of the water.

Garth brought news from Holyhead that Lord Dafydd had sailed for Ramsey Island to meet with King Henry. Then Prince Howell met with Dafydd, who had forbidden anyone to leave Gwynedd except traders. Gwynedd had only one trader who traveled by sail. He was well known and called a priest because he wore an Augustinian's gown, but no one knew his name, only that he was well liked and dealt fair and square.

Brenda was certain the trader-priest was Madoc. She believed he had restored one of the rotten ships Owain had given him and was trading, while at the same time having the rest repaired. She wondered why he had never come to Holyhead for trading. She worried about Annesta, who now wanted to stay on her pallet curled into a ball. I will be glad when she delivers, Brenda thought. 'Twill be easier to travel with a wee one than with a woman made clumsy with a large belly.

Brenda also worried about the fright that spread over Gwynedd, encircling people like stale smoke. The smell of woodsmoke used to be a sign of a busy croft; now it meant a malicious fire. A fire used to mean warmth and a hearty meal. Now it was death and destruction. A stranger used to be a welcome source of new stories and songs; now he or she was shunned and looked on with suspicion. Where there used to be friendship there was distrust. Where there used to be love and family, there were anger and grief.

She had dreams about the trader-priest who could come and go as he pleased. She dreamed that he went south to Cardiff, west to Aberystwyth, north to the Isle of Man and once he sailed from Degannwy to the Irish Sea and across to Dubh Linn with herself and Mona and Llorfa standing sad-eyed at the gunwale of his ship. Degannwy? That was what Hyfra said. Go to Degannwy? She wanted to tell the others about that confusing dream, but she did not know what was important about it. She thought sailing from Degannwy made no sense. So she did not put it into words.

One night she dreamed of Sein brushing his lips tenderly across her cheek, saying, "I told you before that I would always love you, no matter what." It was so real that she woke with her body still tingling. She lay awake wondering how she, a grown woman, could be so foolish. Then she felt something soft as bog cotton brush across her face, and she sat up in a panic.

"Sshh!" whispered Llorfa. " 'Twas only a chicken feather. Come, Annesta is having contractions!"

Hyfra was heating a clay pot of water. Garth was in the barn with the horses.

"What is Garth doing there?" asked Mona, unraveling a wool petticoat into diaper cloths and a swaddling cloth.

"Praying to the gods for a healthy baby," said Hyfra, looking at Mona as if she should have known. "For such a tiny thing, you ask so many questions."

Brenda and Llorfa watched Annesta stiffen and draw her legs up. She growled deep inside her throat like some hurting animal. Her body was covered in a sheen of sweat.

Brenda pressed a hand firmly on Annesta's belly when the next contraction came and said everything was fine. When pinkish water seeped between Annesta's legs, Llorfa helped her remove her clothing and lie on a damp bed of moss near the center fire. The bed was sprinkled with water from the spring to bring lasting health to the new mother. Garth's ax was laid under the moss to make the birth easy. Annesta said the ax hurt her back. Brenda moved it to the bed's foot and Hyfra gave Annesta a soft band of leather to bite on when the pain became great. Llorfa sang a birthing song to soothe both mother and infant. She spoke softly in a singsong manner for Annesta to push but not to overwork. "There is a time for life, a time for learning, a time for loving; there is a time for death."

Annesta gasped and arched and pulled on the leather. She panted and growled, and said, "I wish Madoc were here. If a baby's father suffers the birth pangs along with the mother, the baby will have a healthy life."

"Never mind. I be here, feeling your pangs," said Brenda.

"The baby's health depends on a mother's care," said Mona. "What good would it truly do if Madoc saw you growling and shuddering? Just look at you, all red-faced, sweaty, hair tangled and crying like a she-wolf. That scares men. You saw Garth leave."

Annesta gritted her teeth, growled and arched her back. Afterward she looked at Mona and giggled.

Between contractions Llorfa scooped up the bloody moss and spread clean moss under Annesta. If the soiled moss was taken outdoors the wolves would smell the blood and come prowling. They could not afford to have the horses mauled by hungry wolves. So the sticky-wet moss was spread close to the center fire to dry and then burned. It made the room smell fetid and close.

The pains went on and on. Brenda made strong willow-bark tea for Annesta. Llorfa gave her a root to chew on that she said would bring the baby out faster. Not to be left out, Mona kept a cool, wet cloth on Annesta's forehead.

Annesta twisted, moaned and made the deep-throated growl. She took Brenda's hand and asked her to promise to take the baby if she should die. "I see Madoc's face. It may be a sign. I cannot take much more of these twisty pains. I be too tired. O-o-o, I do not want to die!"

"Sshh," comforted Brenda. "You are all right. There is a little more work to do, then 'tis over. Sing with us." And they hummed lullabies. Annesta hummed, but it was broken with deep-throated groans through gritted teeth as her muscles tightened, and she could not help but push, push until the contraction was finished.

"I be going to die!" Annesta screamed. "Blood will come like a fountain, then death! Help me make ready!"

"No! No! Do not talk like that," said Brenda, in her scolding voice. "You will be fine. Everything is all right. The first *baban* usually takes long."

There was no air; the room smelled like a charnel house and it was dark except for the red glow from the coals in the central fire.

Annesta sobbed. "I have sinned. I went against the teachings of the Church. We did the together-thing before Madoc married me the old druid way. Oh, God, I wanted him to love me. Oh, I did want it! Now I pay for my wickedness. I can see only blackness, the gods' doom. I lost Madoc's face! I hear a roaring in my ears. 'Tis the awful voices of the gods. Please, find Madoc and tell him I love him. Brenda, I love you. I be so sorry I be a wicked lass. I go now! Ohoogagh!"

When the contraction was over Brenda said, "Annesta, you went nowhere. You are not wicked. The New Religion does that—you know, to keep its people under the thumb of the Church. Guilt and fright are powerful tools. You could do nothing so terrible that the gods would take your life. This is guilt you have in your head and 'tis wrong. Priests are not all saints. Have we not all heard they become drunk on sacramental wine, lie, take bribes and lift one another's skirts in the dark? They condone the beheading of druids. Your husband is a druid, so how can you let some priest make you feel guilty? 'Twas the gods who gave men and women those instincts and tell us to be fruitful. 'Tis up to us to be responsible about the gifts the gods give us."

Brenda looked up and realized it was light outside.

"I know I can trust you to take care of my *baban*, and tell Madoc I love him with all my heart," said Annesta, breathing easier.

"You tell Madoc how much you love him," said Brenda. "He needs to hear it from you. Remember, you have not sinned any more than Madoc."

Mona wiped Annesta's forehead with the damp cloth. "Save your breath and push that *baban* out," she said.

"Amen," said Llorfa.

"Ladies, pray pardon?"

"Garth?" said Hyfra. She had been kneeling beside Annesta's pallet; now she got to her feet and raised her head. " 'Tis about done. Please, do not come in yet. Go on back. 'Twill take a little more praying. Talk to the horses. Animals understand that a birthing mother does not belong entirely to this world. This young mother lies between the world of the living and the world of the dead, and can be a source of harm to herself and us. Placate the gods on the Otherside and come back later—anon."

Garth shook his head and said that he wished it were done before this birthing daughter brought him foul luck.

Brenda felt her heart skip a beat. "What foul luck?" she whispered.

"When the infant is born you will plan a way to leave us and mayhap take the horses," said Garth. "I do not want to lose my daughters' help in the garden, collecting shellfish and spinning beautiful colored wool. I do not want to lose the horses."

"If we take a ship from Holyhead, you keep the horses," said Brenda.

"I be afraid," said Hyfra. "The birthing is taking too long. The morning star is already visible. Soon 'twill be light and the sunrise."

The air was split apart by Annesta's banshee-like cry. Her fingernails dug into the ends of the leather strap as she pulled hard. Brenda sang a song from Taliesin about women being created from fruits and flowers and water from the powerful ninth wave. She pushed on the upper part of Annesta's swollen belly, trying to coax the infant out. Llorfa held Annesta's legs apart and said she could see the head crowning, coming out slowly like a wet, bloody coney poking its head cautiously out of its hole.

Brenda felt excitement run down her spine. Tears ran down her face when she saw a wrinkled, elfish, red face emerge. She was bound to this brave girl who was her lastborn's bride and to this small, wondrous, wormlike infant. Brenda had her hands under the slippery, bloody, red infant and as soon as the folded legs and tiny toes were in view she told Llorfa to catch the coming afterbirth. She tied the cord with undyed flax thread and began to gnaw the cord from the afterbirth.

To cut the cord with a sharp blade meant either the mother's or child's life would be endangered. Some midwives believed the quivering, bloody mass of evil-looking flesh could curl over itself and turn into a full-grown troll and cause a lifetime of havoc to the newborn. The afterbirth had to be buried right away. Thinking of the silly myths made Brenda smile. She stopped gnawing the cord and snipped it quickly with the tiny sewing scissors tied to a thong at her waist. " 'Tis a darling girl," she said, and a sense of wonderment shook her.

Garth pounded on the door and shouted.

Hyfra told him not to be such a wretch, but to hush and wait a bloody moment. She opened the door a crack and peeked out. First thing she saw was the bright morning star above the horizon, then Garth. His hair was chock full of straw and his eyes were red as rose hips. "My belly growled and pinched something fierce, then I had a dream," he said. "Lugh, the god of waters, spoke to me saying that if the child is a boy he must be cleansed by passing him through smoke from a sacred oak tree, if 'tis a girl, cleanse her in water from a sacred stream. I want to know if I should chop down one of the oaks growing alongside the white spring."

"Did ye hear that?" asked Hyfra, pointing to Brenda, who was bathing the howling infant in a pot of warm water. Hyfra grabbed the infant, held her against her shoulder and fled outdoors.

Brenda spun around and yelled, "Come back here!"

"Where is she going?" asked Mona.

"To the spring where the water is ice-cold!" said Brenda.

"Go after them!" said Llorfa, packing woolen petticoat strips and moss to absorb the flow between Annesta's legs.

The old couple squatted between the two oaks on the mossy bank in front of a spring that seemed to bubble up below a huge quartzite rock. Garth held the infant close to the bubbles and she went head over heels into the dark, cold pool of water. Her shrill crying was immediately silenced and she was seized by Hyfra, who swaddled the bluish body in her shawl, patted it dry until it began to wave its thin little arms and cry again. Hyfra told the infant to hush, handed her to Brenda, smiled, looked sideways at Mona and said, "Curious daughter, do not ask the name of a *baban* born under the sign of Venus. You will soon know it to be Gwenllian, after the white rock behind this sacred spring."

"The name is up to Annesta," snapped Brenda, rocking the infant in her arms until the clear blue eyes were closed and the fine dark lashes lay upon the smooth, pale cheeks. Sitting on her haunches, she stroked the light fuzz on the infant's head and examined the tiny rose-colored hands. Her heart pounded as she held her face to the sunlit heavens and the fading morning star and whispered, "*Diolch i Chi.* I thank You." She wanted to shout her thanks from the bottom of her lungs, but she was too tired.

XXVI
Degannwy

Deganwy, Gwynedd—A pleasant suburban face distinguishes the fact that Deganwy was once an important strategic site, renowned for centuries before Conwy's battlemented towers rose on the opposite bank of the estuary. Behind the village on Verdre Hill stand the ruins of the castle of Deganwy, built on two volcanic outcrops and famous for its position in the struggle between the Welsh and the Anglo-Normans. The original castle was built in the 6th century by King Maelgwn of Gwynedd, but this was partially destroyed by lightning. In 1088 Hugh Lupus, Earl of Chester, built a castle on the same site after taking the coastal plain from the Welsh. . . . Nowadays Deganwy is a small holiday resort, and its south-facing position makes it one of the sunniest places on the north Wales coast.

Russell Beach, ed., *AA Touring Guide of Wales*

Annesta drank plenty of cow's milk in order to enrich her own. Brenda brought in meadow moss to pad thread-drawn linen diaper covers and the bottom of the baby-basket that Hyfra made from ropes of rye straw. This basket could be suspended from the ceiling by a rope Garth wove from horsetail hair. Mona made a little tunic, a cap and a woolen blanket.

"I wish your grandfather could see her," said Brenda.

"He sees," said Annesta. "His spirit is with us." She held up the little pouch of ashes.

"Going to name her Llywara after him?" asked Brenda.

"She is Gwenllian," said Annesta. "She is fair-haired. Her skin is white and smooth, like the finest lambskin. Prince

Owain had a sister with the same name, who was also born under Venus's sign." She smoothed the fine, barely visible pale fuzz on the baby's head.

The communication among druids became scarce, because most were in hiding or had already left Gwynedd. Garth heard nothing from Gwalchmai. A week after Gwenllian was born Brenda dreamed about being onboard a ship with the trader-priest. She went to Holyhead and heard that Gwynedd's trader-priest's ship was called the *Gwennan Gorn*, or *White Horn*, because of the white deer-horn pegs used to hold her planking together. There were rumors that the trader was frequently seen in Degannwy. Degannwy! Brenda could not wait to get back and tell the others of her recurring dream of going across the Irish Sea in a curragh piloted by the shipmaster-priest. "In my dream we always left from Degannwy, not Holyhead," she said.

Garth and Hyfra nodded and went outdoors with their heads close together in a private discussion. The next day they left a few coins for each of the women and went to Llanfachreth to sell a full cart of rolled fleeces Garth had gathered in Y Fali Valley.

Hyfra said she wished everyone could go to Llanfachreth, but this way, if they did not all go, she would have a reason to hurry home. She held baby Gwenllian, babbled to her sleeping face, then put her arms around each of the women and kissed them.

Garth shook their hands and told them there was not only milk but plenty of meat, bread and grain, so no one would go hungry. "Eat plenty of greens. Keeps yur teeth in yur head." He touched his own head and chuckled. He wore his hat with the cloth mask that protected his face from the sun.

He hitched all four horses to his small cart. At first Brenda thought it strange, when one horse could do the job, then she thought he wanted to show off to his town friends. When she thought more about it, she decided he took the horses because they were his to do with as he pleased when the women left for Ireland.

As soon as the couple was out of sight, Brenda said, "I

think this is our time to go. I believe Hyfra and Garth left so that if questioned they would not know when we left nor where we went. Come on, ladies! Pack your things. We go to Degannwy, on the Conwy Estuary, known for its edible mussels and dab fishing. Mayhap we will see the trader-priest."

"Who cares about mussels and dab?" said Mona. "Annesta needs to ride horseback if she has to carry the baby! You cannot mean that she is walking!"

"The soldiers looking for us know we took four horses. They expect us to be horsebackers," said Brenda.

"Annesta is able to walk," said Llorfa. "We can take turns carrying wee Gwenllian."

"We are supposed to leave from Holyhead," said Mona. "What if a curragh waits there for us? What if we run into soldiers on the way to Degannwy?"

"Why not go to Holyhead and wait? We do not know for sure that Madoc is the trader," said Annesta. "He is probably still repairing his ships."

"Annesta, think!" said Mona, putting her hands on her hips. "Holyhead is crawling with Lord Dafydd's dragons, whose eagle eyes are looking for people from the court to behead. Dafydd knows us. He told his soldiers what we look like. He tells terrible lies about Brenda." She made the last word sound like a strangled bleat and looked at Brenda.

Llorfa looked at the druidic honor marks around her thumbnails. She sniffed and held her thumbs inside her closed fists. "He does not know about Gwenllian. He may be looking for four women horsebackers, but not four women walking and carrying a baby."

"I believe Garth would have told us if there was a ship at Holyhead," said Brenda. "He heard me talk about the shipmaster-priest trading in Degannwy and he never once said we ought not go there. Remember when Hyfra said go to Degannwy? She was trying to tell us something and I was too stupid to hear."

"Listen," said Annesta, changing her tone. "Degannwy is not far from Afon Ganol. We can see Madoc there. He will take care of us. Mayhap take us to Ireland—if he can. Dragons will never believe we went to Degannwy on foot. We can hide during the day and travel at night. Brenda is right, 'tis the place to go."

They left that same evening at twilight and it was one of those spring days when the air is so clear just after the sun has set that one can count the green blades of grass, see the lichen in the fissures of the rocks and actually see the difference between bird nests and clumps of mistletoe in the trees on the far hills. The leaves shone in the silver light as if they were under water. They found a mossy stream to refill the sheepskin water bag.

The starlight made walking easy until they came to the rocky country. Annesta tired easily, stopped every few hours to nurse baby Gwenllian, and thus was constantly thirsty and looked for springs to quench her thirst. Once they slept in holes that had been the floors of circular huts. Another time they stopped at the foot of a tall *broch* or rock that had been planted by the Old Ones beside a stream.

Another time dark clouds rolled against the blue sky and brought in jagged jolts of lightning and giant rumbles of thunder that woke them. Annesta wanted to know why the god of thunder was speaking to them. " 'Tis a warning."

"A warning that rain is coming," said Llorfa, laughing.

It was raining when they came to a crossroad where they smelled woodsmoke and saw crude skips of barley straw.

In the old days hospitality was important to the Welsh. A knock on a crofter's door, and a cup of clover tea and a hunk of bread is ours, thought Brenda as she scratched on the stiff deer-hide door.

The crofters inside were frightened by the visitors and would not say, *"Dewch i mewn,"* or "Come in." Finally a round-bellied man came out and put bits of dry bread in a pot of hot water and called it *sgotyn*. The women sat under a beech tree, whose coppery leaves gave off red flashes through the rain, and waited for the water to cool before they ate. The crofter cleared his throat and said that some roaming farmers had warned him about people dressed as gypsies or tinkers seeking shelter. He thought they would claim his sheep, goats, cattle and land. " 'Tis an unlucky time for the *Cymreig*."

"We heard about things like that," said Llorfa, keeping her thumbs well hidden inside her fists. "Are you an Old or New Religionist?"

A woman, peeking from the doorway of the nearest hut, said, "New Religionists sometimes tattoo themselves to pretend they are Old just to get inside a pagan's place."

Brenda was certain she had seen woad marks on the crofter's hands when he had brought out the bread and water. She drew in her breath, ready to say the times were so bad that pagans also pretended they were something else.

The woman said, "Trust nobody."

Brenda let her breath go out, narrowed her eyes and tried to see if the woman had woad marks on her neck, which was covered with a wide band of decorative woven grasses.

The woman blushed and fingered the neckband. "A gift," she said.

Brenda pointed to Annesta holding baby Gwenllian and said the infant needed better shelter from the rain than the big beech.

The round-bellied crofter said the beech was resistant to lightning more than other trees because of its special oil.

The woman pointed to a path that she said led to *Bryn Celli Ddu*. There an ancient spiral burial chamber with *ogam* slashes was roofed by two large, flat stones and a polygonal heap of dirt. She said it was a place to rest. She smiled—slyly.

The crofter laughed, making his belly shake, and said, "Ghosts and ancient markings frighten young people today. Young wanderers like you are even afraid of work. You are only interested in filching food and shelter."

Mona said, "For all we know, you could be spies for Lord Dafydd. We, young people, do not fear ghosts nor work half as much as well-fed, fat strangers."

As they walked away they could hear the man and woman calling them names in loud voices.

Baby Gwenllian's cries echoed eerily down the chamber's inner passageway. Annesta shivered and unfastened the neck of her wet shirt so that the baby could nurse.

Brenda studied the hard-packed slanting floor. It was warm

and dry and would do for one day of sleep. The crofter and his wife had left them with uneasy feelings, so she thought it best to take turns standing watch.

When everyone was asleep, she walked around the chamber in her bare feet to feel its size and to keep herself awake in the dark. A shoulder-high shelf ringed the chamber. On it she felt bones, small pots and skulls. Once she sneezed from dust or ash. She heard the faraway bleating of sheep. It was a comforting sound, like the gurgling of a fast-flowing creek, and she thought Annesta would surely leave her grandfather's ashes in this pleasant place. She walked up to the entrance to see if the rain had stopped. It had not, but the clouds directly above had broken so that the sun gave enough light to see wide puddles of water standing close by.

For the first time she noticed markings on the stone walls of the outer chamber. Long ago she had learned to read the horizontal, vertical and angled long and short marks while sitting beside her father. He had told her that language begins with the mark. More than one mark was an attempt to make order of the forces of nature or to help the mind recall a mystical canto or poem. She ran her fingers upward over the marks in square columns depicting the names of the people buried here. The marks were cool and damp, and left her fingers tingling. She examined the opposite wall and read upward from right to left a runic warning underlined by a dirty dark line: "This is a holy place for spirits of nonliving. Living beware—if you use this place as a dwelling." She wondered if the dark line was made for emphasis. Cold air blew across her face and made the hairs on the back of her neck stand up. It was time for Llorfa to take over the watch.

Slowly feeling her way back to the inner chamber, she thought of the time she first learned to swim in a pond no bigger than one of those rain puddles. She had not sputtered, but had kicked the way she had seen dogs swim. Her father had praised her for keeping her head above water and not crying out in a panic. "Wisdom flows; it is not stagnant," he had said. "Wisdom never counsels cowardice."

The words molded her thinking. She remembered feeling compelled by some inner force to practice swimming over and over until she had mastered it. It had been that way with most everything she learned, a necessity, like breathing, until the challenge was won.

There was no light in the inner chamber. She slumped down, leaning her back against the chamber's wall. She let her eyes close against the darkness for a moment before she woke Llorfa.

The next thing she saw was light coming from under the ceiling's capstones where soil and thatch had fallen away. Then she heard a strange roar and looked through the passageway. Halfway through she saw a little stream of light on something shining, like a rolling, wet ball. The roar grew until it was like a dozen wooden cart wheels rumbling across a plank bridge. From the bottom of her lungs she moaned an awful basso sound, not her voice but an ancient aboriginal sound, a warning used in times long blown away and forgotten. Her throat vibrated, and the inside of her head cleared of every thought except getting out of this deadly trap—now!

The women scrambled to their feet. "I hear a *pistyll*, a waterfall!" screamed Brenda. "*Rhedeg*, run!" She pulled Mona to her feet and told her to gather the blankets in the baby's basket. She shook Annesta and said, "Keep the baby's head high on your shoulder!" She carried her brogues and pushed through the wall of water first, bracing her arms against the side of the inner passage, groping for Annesta's hand.

Llorfa pushed Mona against Annesta and came last, carrying the other brogues in a blanket. She shoved Mona through the rolling, rushing water. She heard the baby cry and Annesta sneeze.

Brenda knew she could not fall backward or they would all topple and drown. Suddenly it dawned on Brenda that the line under the *ogam* warning that it was not a safe place was a high-water mark. Rains caused water to rush into the chamber. She gritted her teeth, tasted muddy water and guessed that they were halfway through the spiral passage. After the first assault, the force of the water was not so powerful. Llorfa kept a steady pressure on Mona, who pushed on Annesta, who pushed Brenda.

Brenda moved slowly, surely and steadily. When she came

to the short outer passage, the water was suddenly shallow. She felt as if she were coming out on the other side of a great door. "Come on!" she shouted. "I see light!"

Outside the rain was no longer torrential, but a soft drizzle. The puddles Brenda had seen earlier were now one large pond, like a lake. She looked more carefully at the sides of the concentric stone rings, and saw what she had not seen in the rain, that the chamber was built down from the hillside so that water flowed into the walled passageways like a catch basin. When she stood at the top of the first ring, the passageways appeared level because the two huge top stones were buttressed together evenly and were smooth all the way across, but in fact they were thicker at the inner ring than at the outer ring.

"The crofters' fear of strangers was so great that they could, without a twinge of conscience, send strangers to their death," said Llorfa. "Will we end up going backward—living in tribes, hiding from one another?"

"Life is not always what it seems," said Brenda. "Dark times eventually turn bright. Life is a matter of adjusting to the unexpected."

They lost a couple of blankets, the baby's basket, clothing and food in the swirling brown water. But they were alive! They put on their brogues and sang. They walked to keep warm until the late afternoon sun came out, then they stopped to dry their clothing and blankets on the rocks along the shore of the Menai Strait.

Llorfa stood naked on a tuffet of grass, faced the west and held her hands high. On one white shoulder blade were four petaled flowers. On the other was tattooed a physician's staff with the head of a winding snake on the top. The faint blue curlicues around each of her thumbnails showed plainly in the fading daylight. She gave thanks to the gods who had lent their strength to each of them so they did not panic and their lives were not cut off this day.

Brenda watched Llorfa's slim, graceful body with a prickly tinge of envy. She wished that she had taken the druid vows and been given her own individual honor marks. After all, she knew as much medicine as Llorfa, maybe more in some areas. Then she told herself she was going to Ireland, where she had promised Sein she would take the druid vows. She stood in her underclothes and sang, "Hey, ho, ho! Death was nigh, we whimpered not, nor wrung our hands, nor wept as do women elsewhere. Ho, hey, hey! Baby Gwenllian, you will sing, you will dance, you will tell your children what brave women carried you away from the dark, rolling waters. Hey, ho ho!"

They watched screaming gulls dart hither and thither over the water in the twilight. Playfully Annesta picked up four twigs, held them out of sight and said, "Whoever takes the smallest stick shall barter a good-luck fortune or a song for food. The longest stick belongs to whomever will find transportation across the Menai to Port Dinorwic. The other two will stay, wash the mud out of blankets and clothes and make everything dry."

Mona pulled the shortest and Brenda the longest.

Brenda walked a way up the strait and found a boy sitting on a stone with a line in the water. "Can you see we need a boat to go across to Cefn Bach?" she said, pointing to the tiny settlement on the other side.

"I see one of ye singin'· without *dillad*, clothes. Better that ye swim across and get the mud off ye," he said with a crooked grin.

"I cannot swim," she lied and pointed again.

He looked disgusted and said the place she pointed to, across the water, was called Moel-y-Don and was once used by Vikings as an anchorage and fishery.

"Is there a ferry to go across?"

"Used to be," he said, "but the ferry moved to Menai, where there is more traffic. *Arglwyddes*, lady, if ye can paddle, take the coracle from the reeds in front of ye. Leave 'er on t'other side well anchored or tied to a willow. 'Tis almost dark— hurry before ye cannot see t'other side. Be careful to walk around the tarns, *mawn* pools, and peat bogs."

"Thanks," she said. "You are a saint." She poked around in the marshy reeds until she found a round withie craft, a coracle that was covered with hide and tarred until it was black inside and out. The single paddle, with a claw carved on the top of its loom, lay in the bottom.

By the time Brenda pulled the coracle back to where the

others waited, Mona had returned with a clay pot of cheese and whey. "Found it on a stoop," she said. "No one was around and it spoils if left out overlong."

"You took it from those dastardly crofters," chortled Annesta. "I love you!"

Mona giggled and ventured out to help Brenda, who was standing in the muck bringing in the coracle. They passed around the pot until it was clean, left it bobbing among the reeds, and piled into the coracle, elbow to elbow, knee to knee. Brenda began to paddle. At first they went around and around. Then she found she had to paddle on one side then the other to keep heading straight across the water.

Baby Gwenllian's crying made her nervous, but she dared not stop to see what was the trouble. Her arms ached, but she could not stop in the middle of Menai Strait. The crying stopped, she heard the booming call of bitterns, saw gray reeds and knew they had come safely across the strait. She stood in the wind and was so cold that she could not hold her lower jaw still. It was hard to move her legs to pull the coracle ashore. With each step her brogues made a sucking sound as if she were in a bog of quicksand. Finally she told everyone to climb out. They left the little round craft in the reeds with its frayed rope tied to a half-submerged log.

In starlight they climbed a muddy embankment and went through a forest of oaks. On the other side they saw a couple of burned crofts, blackened oaks and scorched earth, and their spirits fell. They stopped for water when a stream gurgled across their path.

Brenda thought that she saw footprints in the mud and made everyone stay quiet for a few moments. All was quiet. Near dawn they ran across several deer, but no humans.

Each evening they felt more weary when they woke than when they had lain down to sleep. Brenda said it was because they were hungry. They passed burned trees that had fallen onto black ruins of barns or cottages. The land looked dead. Underneath the scorched grass where once there had been families of voles and beetles now there was burning peat, and the fire spread slowly underground.

Once in the twilight they walked across stones covered with toads warming themselves from the smoldering peat underneath. They squatted by a spring to wash underclothing and sour diaper cloths. Two men with long-sleeved tunics and calf-skin gloves warmed themselves on stones above the spring. They talked softly and once in a while looked back at the women.

Brenda walked beyond the spring in order to hear what they were saying. The blond one said, "Me thinks the pagans on Mon are gone."

"Nay," said the other, who had a thin red mustache across his upper lip and made Brenda think of Sein. "There be a camp of 'em near Pas Newydd waiting to go to Ireland. We should go with 'em."

Brenda wanted to run after them, but Llorfa said, "Nay, we do not know if they are real pagans or soldiers for Lord Dafydd. Mayhap what they said was only to lure us to them. We need to be more careful. Remember the spiral chamber that was a siphon for rainwater?"

Of course she remembered. Llorfa did not have to remind her that she was the one who had led them into that disaster. She was truly sorry, but it was done and over with. She told herself that she had to think all the time and not take anything or anyone at face value. But she also had to remember that four young women wandering the moors were at risk.

They took food whenever they could find it, from abandoned cottages or an occasional root cellar not destroyed by fire, and they found wild crab apples, peppery watercress and garlic growing wild. They were a smelly, grimy lot, but the nighttime air was warmer than before, fragrant, and it filled them with happiness.

Brenda espied the Conwy Estuary and talked the other three into using one of their precious coins to stay a night in Degannwy's Seaside Inn so they could look around and ask questions about the shipmaster-priest. Annesta wrapped Gwenllian in her clean lacy petticoat so she would look nice going into an inn where Brenda said she once stayed. They arrived in the middle of the night.

The next morning they hovered over a tub of steaming water and scrubbed themselves clean for the first time in days. Brenda was combing her hair when the innkeeper knocked and said she had burgoo and oat bread. Brenda stared at the bright-eyed old innkeeper, then put her hands out to gather old Magain close to her breast and said, "Remember me? I be the runaway-girl."

"My mind is not gone—of course I remember. Ye pretended to be Prince Owain's sister, Susanna, who loved laverbread! But ye did not even know how the bread was made. Ye did not know how to tell a lie. Sweet little mother."

Magain saw Brenda's discomfort and said, "Dear child, my hair is now white, I be wrinkled, and look a *canmlwydd*, a hundred years old, and my beloved Doconn is on the Other-side. Thank the gods, he went in his sleep—not by the hand of the bloody New Religionists."

Brenda introduced Llorfa, Annesta and Mona, saying that Magain had the Gift, meaning that she was able to see in her heart bits of the future.

"Prince Howell rules now, but King Dafydd waits," said Magain, sitting on Brenda's unmade pallet. "Prince Howell's horse will be killed in the center of Aberffraw, by a spear going through its neck. Villagers hearing the horse's neighings will come outdoors and watch the sword fight between half-brothers. Dafydd will cut Howell's head off."

Mona gave a little squeal and put her hands over her mouth.

"Do not be eaten up by grief," said Magain. " 'Tis in the hands of the gods. Bound to happen. And do not believe those who will say no villagers witnessed the murder. There will be a big group gapin' at the crime being done. Some will say his head was cremated in a druidic ritual, but my heart does not tell me where Howell's ashes are, so I do not think there will be a cremation. Howell's head will be found on the railing of the Church-with-the-White-Porch." Her eyes squinted, then opened wide, shone bright, and she whispered, "The little mother carries someone's ashes. The four of ye have wandered round about like gypsies. 'Tis no way to live. And ye"—she pointed to Llorfa—"are a First Order druidess, same as I." She spread her tattooed hands for all to see. She leaned over and took Mona's hand. "Ye will hear things here that ye must not repeat. We have to trust each other with our lives."

"You can trust me," said Mona.

"The gods give us life," said Magain, "but they leave it short as a *pennillion*, a very short verse. A few of us are given something extra, such as the Gift. Once when the northern lights turned red, a child was conceived and the gods made him special. Not many have heard of this. I have seen the baby and be brushed with luck. He is a shipmaster now. His name is Madoc."

Magain saw that Brenda was uncomfortable and said, "I tell no secrets ye have not told."

Annesta could not hide her curiosity. "You mean my Madoc is truly special?" she asked. "He is a nice lad—but special?"

Llorfa and Mona wondered if the old woman was a bit barmy and rolled their eyes toward the ceiling.

Magain laughed and said, "Last night I saw saw a falling star, which means unexpected company, so I was not surprised to see ye. Yur husband's specialness was given to him by the gods and is revealed to those who believe." She put her knotted hand around baby Gwenllian and lifted the corner of Annesta's petticoat. She saw the same blue eyes and light hair-fuzz as on the other baby whose name she chose years ago. She asked Annesta if this was a fairy child that never grew old.

Annesta looked puzzled until Magain said that the wee lassie looked like wee Madoc.

"Gwenllian," said Magain, "has the blood of the special one."

Annesta was baffled about how the mysterious old woman knew her daughter's name. She bit her lip thinking about the "special" talk.

Baby Gwenllian, the innocent one, grabbed Magain's thumb in her tiny pink fist and held fast.

Magain whispered a lullaby and her eyes glistened with tears when she looked at Annesta. She hummed an ancient song made up of only three notes, then said, "Wise ye shall be, Gwenllian. But not overwise, for an overwise woman's heart is seldom glad." She turned the baby over nine times,

closed her eyes, chanted singsong words under her breath so
that no one could hear, popped her eyes open and said,
"Gwenllian shall marry the gentle son of a lord. That is my
gift to her."

Annesta was frightened when her baby, never waking, was
turned topsy-turvy nine times in those wrinkled clawlike
hands. She gathered Gwenllian back into her own arms and
said, "*Diolch yn fawr*, thank you for the gift."

Magain's eyes became hooded and her voice trembled.
"Little mother, yur hands be deathly cold."

Annesta felt a chill, an unknown anxiety. She frowned and
held her baby close.

Magain saw her fear and quickly added that Gwenllian, the
wise one, would live long and happily on Mon, Anglesey Isle.

Llorfa left, thinking maybe Magain's reasoning was under
a dark cloud, and found a kettle of burgoo warming over coals,
and bowls to put on the table. She called the women, saying
it was time to break their fast. They dipped bread into the pot
of hot burgoo, which was made of spiced lamb, barley and
beans, and spoke little. They ate their fill leisurely, enjoying
each mouthful and thinking about what Magain had said.

"I do not measure gratitude by bulk, but 'tis nice to have
everyone pleased with my burgoo," said Magain. "Faith! This
day I feel rich for having friends about me. We shield each
other from life's hurts. A few more such pleasures and the
God of gods will call my name. I be ready."

"Do not speak of Death," said Brenda, "which will come
soon enough to each of us." She asked Magain if she would
like to go to the royal court with them to talk to Lord Iorwerth
about the shipmaster.

"The last time I was there was right after the shipmaster
hired my grandson as a sailor. Do you know that the shipmaster wears an Augustinian's gown and lets people call him
priest, and he with fresh woad honor markings? You will
know him when you see his blue eyes and blond hair—the
one I named Madoc." She smiled at Annesta and watched
Brenda from the corner of her eye.

" 'Twas not more than a week ago that he ate my laverbread. Handsome, Madoc is!" Her eyes twinkled.

"Where is he?" asked Annesta.

Magain hesitated, closed her eyes and said her heart told her that he lived in the ancient abbey, near Abergele at Afon Ganol's quay. She said her heart was never wrong and often knew more than her brain. "Gods forgive me! My brain's knowledge flickers like a flame and goes out. I have become forgetful. I used to believe knowledge was power. Now I believe power is overrated and knowledge is simply knowing things. In that case, knowledge is simply impossible to overrate." She opened her eyes.

Brenda asked if Lord Iorwerth knew Madoc.

Magain replied that Lord Iorwerth told her the shipmaster-priest might be a spy from King Dafydd's or Lord Rhodri's court and deserved a scout to track him. She said she had the strongest feeling that Madoc was above espying, that he was against war. Then her face became pale and her hands shook. "My heart says we must see Lord Iorwerth!"

"This scout, surely, would not bring Madoc to the wrong court as a slave or—you know, annihilate him?" asked Annesta. "I know hardly a thing about my husband. Who were his folks? They drowned, he said." Her face was cold and white, her heart pounded and she shivered so hard her hands trembled. She could hardly believe anyone would hurt Madoc, yet she knew Dafydd and Rhodri, and the times were such that anything was possible.

Magain jumped to her feet, spry as a sixteen-year-old, spry as a *geneth*. She went back into her closed room and brought out a red wool bratt for herself and a small quilt to wrap around baby Gwenllian. "Put on yur underskirt. No wonder ye shiver," she said to Annesta. "The gods' secret is locked in only a few hearts. 'Tis not the right time to break that lock, even though Prince Owain and yur *tad-cu*, grandfather, are on the Otherside sharing their stories with my Doconn."

XXVII
Iorwerth

Owen Gwynedd ap Griffith succeeded his father as Prince of North Wales [in 1137]. His death in [December] 1169 plunged his country into civil war.

He had made no plans for the succession, although as the descendent of a long line of kings and princes, he must have realized the uncertainty of life in regal circles and, as the father of many sons, he might also have anticipated family complications after his passing. . . .

Of the sons of Gwynedd, the eldest, Iowerth, was judged ineligible for the throne because of a "maime" upon his face. He was called Iowerth of the Broken Nose. Iowerth's right was not otherwise disputed as is proved by the fact that later when his son, Llewellyn, was of age he was chosen Prince of North Wales [1194].

Immediately after Gwynedd's death Howell seized the throne and, according to some Welsh historians, reigned two years.

Prince David, gathering friends and some of his kinsmen, made war upon Howell, killed him in battle and succeeded him as Prince of North Wales.

Zella Armstrong, *Who Discovered America?*

The women went out of the village to a wide lane beside a runnel of water that led to the ramp in front of the court.

Lord Iorwerth's court occupied two large gray-blue, stony outcrops, which were close together and formed a hill covered with gorse and whin. The larger, outer outcrop, with its wood palisade behind a mound of earth, guarded a large round tower made of adzed oak baulks. A double line of palisades joined the smaller outcrop, on which stood another tower connected to the first by a rectangular mud-and-withie structure that was the great hall, the main kitchen and several chambers. A double-doored wooden gate gave entrance through the palisades.

The royal gate guard held an irregular piece of milky glass under his chin to reflect the sun's rays onto his tanned face. He lowered the reflector. "Good day, ladies," he said. "Ye have a purpose coming to Degannwy court?"

Margain stepped up close. "Gwylan, ye know me," she said. "My friends and I have come to see the lord and his lady."

Gwylan, who looked like a young Celtic god with laughing eyes, stepped back to study Magain's friends. They looked harmless. He tickled baby Gwenllian under the chin and said, "Forsooth! 'E likes me—see 'im smile!"

"He be a girl," said Annesta.

Magain raised her weathered face to the clear blue sky. "This is the sunniest place on the northern coast. Say, have ye heard when the shipmaster-priest is due back?"

"Nay, 'e comes and goes." His eyes twinkled as he pointed his reflector toward Annesta. "I hope ye do not wish to arrange a marriage between the girl in yur arms and our lord's son, because the lord does not yet have a son! Nor daughter! But 'e is partial to weeans. Lady Marared is expected at the court tonight with another fosterling. Ye will find the lord playing catch-ball inside the inner bailey with 'is fosterlings."

Magain smiled and herded the women inside, where they found a carelessly groomed, lanky blond-haired man tossing a leathern ball to a group of laughing children. His eyes were green as peas. His nose was slightly misshapen, as though it had been broken and poorly set. His bare arms and legs were sun-browned. A large fish had been tattooed on the right front calf. Brenda recognized him right away, "*Dydd da*, Lord Iorwerth, good day," she said. "I be Brenda, Owain Gwynedd's friend. This is Mona, who was my maid, and Annesta, who was Lady Christiannt's maid. Baby Gwenllian is Annesta's daughter." Then she pointed to Llorfa. "This lass was a fosterling studying medicine with the Prydians until your father died. She is Llorfa."

Iorwerth smiled and stared at Llorfa's balled fists.

"To protect all of us, she hides her honor marks when she is with strangers," said Brenda.

Iorwerth told Llorfa she did not have to worry about him, because he knew and loved the Prydian druids well. "New Religionists and their priests do not come here. Once I heard the priest in Aberffraw say the Lord God speaks to him in a loud voice. There is no worse sin than endowing human perceptions with divine certitude. I be happy this is small and out of the way for priests and strangers." He winked at Magain as if they were old friends. "Good day, ladies. I welcome all of you."

Llorfa relaxed and smiled at the children waiting behind Lord Iorwerth to be excused from the ball game.

Magain raised her right arm and extended her fingers. Lord Iorwerth placed the first two fingers of his right hand below her elbow, enfolded her in his arms and kissed her on both cheeks. "You look younger today than the last time I saw you, Grandmother. Would you like some water?"

"No, thank ye," said Magain. "We came to talk. Iorwerth *Drwyndwr*, Crooked Nose, these are friends who spent the winter near Holyhead waiting for a ship to Dubh Linn. They need yur help."

Llorfa held her hands out so he could see the honor marks on her thumbs and asked a bold question. "If you are a proper druid, as your handshake with Magain indicates, why do you not have first honor marks around your thumbs or fingernails?"

"Look closely," he said, and held out his large hands so she could see that the markings were nearly invisible. "Archdruid Llieu made the dye weak so that the marks would heal without festering. The gods approved of his caution and smiled on me, because when I travel today's Christians do not suspect I be not one of them. Thus, I am not harassed, nor are those in my court."

Llorfa's question and the frank answer emboldened Annesta. "We heard you have a scout watching a certain shipmaster—a priest. Where?"

He looked away for an instant, then said, "Aye, I did, until this wise grandmother"—he nodded toward Magain—"told me the trader was not a real Christian priest. I should have noticed that the man has a sense of limitation, eschews begging and does not use his religion to promote his own agenda or inflate his ego. He lives in the old abbey, near Abergele at the mouth of the Afon Ganol's quay, with four others, who are men of the Old Religion. They built a fleet of ships from the meanest, sorriest bunch of wrecks I have ever seen. The 'shipmaster-priest' is sailing a clinker called the *Gwennan Gorn* from north to south. We have become friends—good friends."

"Humpf!" said Magain. "Ye know he is a pagan, same as ye and me."

Annesta's heart raced. A smile tugged at her mouth. She wanted to shout, "Where is Madoc now, today?" but instead she hid her face in the baby's quilt so the others would not see the sudden rush of tears.

"Annesta is the shipmaster's wife," said Brenda. "He has not seen his baby daughter."

Iorwerth took Brenda's hand and said, "I heard that four women stole four horses from the Aberffraw royal court and were being sought by Lord Dafydd." He told them there had been an unbelievable exodus from Gwynedd after Owain died and another great exodus ready to go if Lord Dafydd went to war with Prince Howell. "Lord Dafydd tried to stop the first getaway by declaring that he would behead anyone leaving the province. He swore to find and execute druids, former mistresses and maids of his late father no matter where they hide, because it is what he says the Lord God asked him to do."

Brenda's heart thumped against her chest. They were in deeper trouble than she had realized. "I be exhausted," she said, "even after a night's rest at Magain's inn. I need a place to sit."

Iorwerth took her elbow and walked her to a bench. "Did you know that before my father died, he went to see Thomas of London on more than one occasion?"

She nodded. "And Thomas came to the royal court once to see your father."

"The last time my father saw Thomas he went out of his way to come here and ask me to look after his beloved Brenda in case anything should happen to him. He had some kind of dream, a premonition, that he was going to be killed. When I heard he was on the Otherside I had scouts follow you."

"You did?" She swallowed hard. "Once I saw footprints in the snow and once I spied two men. Llorfa thought they were Dafydd's dragons. Mayhap they were your retainers. I would like that water now. 'Tis awfully warm." She leaned down so that her head touched the cool stone, closed her eyes and hoped she could calm her pounding heart. A breeze kissed the back of her neck and she shivered and realized her palms were wet. She could hear the others talking and laughing with Magain. After a while Iorwerth came out of the great hall carrying a tray with beakers and a pitcher of water.

"Llywarch told me about the lad Madoc a few weeks after Lady Gladys died," said Iorwerth.

"Llywarch was Annesta's grandfather," said Brenda. "He is on the Otherside."

"I heard," said Iorwerth. "What a terrible loss. He was one of the finest men I have known. He saved my life."

"He saved mine. . . ." Brenda said, feeling the tears well up in her eyes.

"I did not protect Llywarch and I shall never forgive myself."

She brushed her fingers across the back of Iorwerth's hand. " 'Tis done. Do not be so hard on yourself."

"I expected you to come here as soon as you found you could not leave Holyhead. Garth did not tell you?"

"Nay, not in words we understood. But Hyfra said something and I ignored her. I believed she was just thinking out loud. It took us a couple of days to realize that we could come here."

"Crooked Nose, I wish ye were king!" called Magain. "Are these friends safe? Ye see with yur own eyes there are no horses, only a baban."

Lord Iorwerth said he would do his best to protect Magain's

friends, and said he did not wish to be king of Gwynedd even though he wished his nose was straight. "Same as the ship-master, I do not believe in fighting. That does not mean I would not fight if pushed against a cold stone with nowhere to go. I suspect Madoc would say the same."

"Has Lord Dafydd ever come to your court?" asked Annesta. "He collects Gwynedd's taxes and sends a ransom to England."

"Degannwy is not wealthy," said Iorwerth. "Her taxes are collected by a retainer once a year and sent to Gwynedd's court. Madoc finds ways to have his trade goods inspected and his taxes paid at the Aberffraw court so Dafydd does not have to send someone to collect them. Dafydd cannot understand a man who would ride a ship rather than a horse. He cannot believe Madoc means no harm. He thinks of traders as swindlers and advised King Henry to send freebooters to take over the *Gwennan Gorn*, even though 'tis a disreputable clinker."

"King Henry cannot take something that does not belong to him!" said Annesta. "Madoc has broken no law." Her heart fell to the ground and baby Gwenllian whimpered.

"He will if he can, but it may not be so bad," said Iorwerth. "Dafydd is hot-headed and unsure of himself. He listens to rumors, lashes out at unseen ghosts. Invisible angels coax him into purgatory. He believes that his father's spirit has come to deliver a tidal wave somewhere along the coast of Gwynedd. If it does not wash away everything, 'tis a sign for him to declare war on Prince Howell. He keeps no friend unless the friend makes his beliefs the mirror of his beliefs. 'Tis a crazy time in Gwynedd." Iorwerth gestured for the women to follow him into the hall, where a meal was waiting.

The women were seated along the left side of the table, and Iorwerth sat in the carved oak chair at the table's head. They were served salmon and buttermilk and barley bread. A jug of sweet mead was placed beside the huge platter of salmon.

Magain smacked her lips, filled her beaker with mead, took a drink and leaned forward. "Have any of ye ever seen a corpse-candle?" she asked.

"Nay, and I have never seen wee folk called fairies," said Iorwerth. The corners of his mouth turned up in an amused smile. His green eyes sparkled like emeralds. "Have you?"

Magain took another drink. "I tell ye for troth I saw the candle just twice in my life, once the night before yur father died. I remember clearly because 'twas the night before the sun hid its face in shame. And last night—I saw the candle-light plain as I see ye. I was comin' back from the market in a hurry so my little maid could go on home. The light flickered in front of my path all the way to the inn. There it stood at the door-sill until I came close and it disappeared. I tell ye 'tis a warning. If 'tis for me, ye will know when it happens. I will be thinkin' of ye until the last. I have things arranged. I shall be cremated in the druid way and the ashes put beside Do-conn's under the rock pile near the old standing stone beside the holy spring. Ye know where 'tis, in the oak grove west of Degannwy. 'Tis a pity Doconn is not here to advise us how to read the corpse-candle. To let a warning, good or bad, go unheeded is a pity."

Iorwerth reached out to break a piece of bread. "Let us figure how we can get our friends safely to Ireland. Could you be disguised as messboys on the trading ship? Could the babe be wrapped as a loaf of bread? I know not what hour Madoc will be here, but he promised to bring sacks of grain for my hungry crofter families."

Magain said, "Until the sail enters the bay, keep our friends here. 'Tis safer than my inn. Mayhap that is the warning! Aye! The light stopped at my front door! I be known as an Old Religionist not by honor marks, but by what I say and how I live. *Bobol annwyl!* Good gracious! I heard Lord Dafydd and Lord Rhodri are both looking for provisions as well as pagans. 'Twas their foolish soldiers who burned all the grain fields and slaughtered the cows, pigs, sheep, goats, horses and chickens. They ought to be hanged in a withie basket and torched. One of those soldiers could ask me when the trader's ship is due. If I do not know I cannot tell him, even if he cuts my throat. Look here, I carry a polished amethyst to ward off evil. Evil takes a strong, cold stone to neutralize. Mercy Anna, I know the gods deplore fear. So today I be brave because I use a little magic folk remedy to kill fear and give me courage." She took another drink of mead. "I looked in the reflection pool and did not recognize myself. I tell you the pool does not show people like it used to! Everyone is like the dew on the meadow-rue, like the foam on the sea's comb. Here today. Poof! Gone tomorrow."

"Grandmother, I have told you many times that you may stay here and be safe," said Iorwerth. "Let the boy, Thurs, run the inn. He can wash sheets and cook burgoo."

"There be more than sheets and burgoo to running an inn. Besides, my grandson, Thurs, is a seaman on the *Gwennan Gorn*. I told ye, I have my magic protection and will stay with my inn." She refilled her beaker. "Fine batch of mead."

Baby Gwenllian whimpered again and Annesta took her outside to the split-log bench to nurse. Overhead the clouds were piled high against the sun and the air was cooler. It seemed best to stay close to Lord Iorwerth, but because the hope of seeing Madoc anytime soon was uncertain, tears ran down her cheeks. She wiped her eyes on the back of her hand and looked up to see Iorwerth sitting beside her.

He took baby Gwenllian and put her over his shoulder as though it were the most natural thing for a man to do. "Before many morrows we will know where your husband is. I augur well he is on his way to Degannwy Estuary. The last time I saw him we talked about men using integrity, generosity, good will, courage, even in minuscule amounts, to grow in wisdom. I told him when I have a son, I will teach him wisdom."

She liked Lord Iorwerth more and more, and told him that Magain had predicted that Gwenllian would grow to be a Wise Woman.

"Gwenllian may influence our people in ways you do not dream of," said Iorwerth. "She will be wise if Magain says so."

He patted the baby's back to ease a gas pain. "My wife would love holding her," he said, and put the baby into Annesta's arms. "*Nos da*. Good night. I shall walk Magain to her inn." He summoned a dark-haired maid called Brigid to show his guests a chamber with four sleeping pallets.

Brigid took the women to the large room, brought warm water and clean cloths for bathing, found a woven truckle with a feather mattress, some wool squares for diapers and rocked baby Gwenllian to sleep.

Brenda recognized Brigid from years ago. She was the maid who had tended her when she left Ireland and almost made trouble for her with Owain. She hoped that Brigid did not recognize her. However, what did it matter now? she thought.

Annesta spoke of Lord Iorwerth's kindness and the fact that he did not put on airs. She asked Brigid what she thought of him.

Brigid said that he ran foot races with his crofters, sat at their table from time to time and wiped their children's noses on the hem of his tunic. She said Marared, his wife, wanted more than anything to have a child, but so far was barren. "A few years ago they announced that they would foster all children that the crofters or villagers would send. At present they have seven children whose parents cannot feed them because their livestock and crops were burned. Marared invites the families of the children to visit. She knows how much they miss each other."

In the morning, instead of Brigid, tall, dark-haired, fair-skinned Marared came to see how they had slept. She brought news of the shipmaster-priest, who had left the Isle of Man and was expected in Colwyn Bay any day. "I think his ship is carrying grain from Ireland. He will land where 'tis safe and we will bring the grain back here for storage, then divide it among those who need it most. 'Tis also said that Lord Dafydd and his brother, Lord Rhodri, want to keep Iorwerth from buying the grain."

"Huzza," said Brenda, feeling the news was good. Iorwerth could surely outsmart Dafydd and Rhodri in a grain deal.

Marared grinned at Brenda. "Hear this," she said. "Iorwerth has a plan to get you on the priest's ship before she sails back to Ireland. Be ready anytime."

Three days of talking, storytelling and eating passed and still there was no word about Madoc or the *Gwennan Gorn*. Annesta imagined the worst. "Mayhap English freebooters have Madoc and his ship," she said.

"Do not worry until there is reason," said Mona, putting an arm around her.

"By now I think your husband knows how to sail sideways and backwards," said Brenda.

On the fifth day, hours after supper, there was a pounding on the door. Marared bolted into the chamber with her dark hair flying and her arms loaded with soldiers' gear, loose-necked mail hauberks, quilted jerkins, chain-mail leg and arm wrappings, round helms. "Off with the nightdresses, ladies! I will help you into this gear. Madoc is bringing his ship in at Colwyn Bay near the quay at Rhos on Sea to unload the grain at daybreak. The messenger said Madoc will not sell nor give grain to armed soldiers, no matter whose retainers they be. He will sell only to Iorwerth to be divided among the needy families in this cantref.

"You are to board the ship as seamen, after the grain has been unloaded. For safety you will wear hauberks that are covered and out of sight by tunics and bratts. Iorwerth is calling in crofters and others to also wear this garb and act as our bodyguards. The servants and handmaids like Brigid, even myself will be peaceful Degannwy retainers in a neutral trading area. I must warn you: There is potential for a battle. Lord Dafydd and Lord Rhodri are desperate for grain to keep their starving dragons awarring. I be so put-out with those two. I want to starve them so they know how the crofters feel. Magain, may the gods bless her, would tell me to 'overcome evil with goodness.'" She lit a torch from the iron wall-scone, which crackled and smelled of resin.

"I be so cold the heat of three torches could not quell my shivering," said Llorfa.

"This hauberk will warm you," said Marared.

Llorfa examined a short hauberk of scale armor and said, "Why this protection?"

"For the trouble you are in," said Marared. She turned away for a moment and drew a deep breath, then she faced the women. "This is so hard to talk about—to think about. It is so—awful. Magain is like a beloved grandmother to our foster children—to all of us. I—I tried not to alarm you, but you ought to know what has happened."

Brenda sighed and said, "Tell us."

"Dafydd's soldiers are in Degannwy not only to buy grain. They are armed with spears and looking for Mistress Brenda, who Dafydd claims poisoned Prince Owain."

"Dafydd poisoned his own father," said Llorfa. "I was there!" Her cheeks flushed. "He hopes to hide his sins by blaming innocents. A mace in his face!" She paced from one end of the room to the other. Finally she stopped, let Mona fasten hooks and tie on metal leg-hauberks.

"Overcome anger with goodness," repeated Marared. "Surround Magain's spirit with love."

"Her spirit!" cried Brenda, raising her brows.

"Aye. Brigid and I went to her this morning for last-minute advice on our plan to get you out of here, but—Dafydd's soldiers were there first. Oh, Lord's heart, our sweet, wonderful Magain—we saw the bloody mess! They mangled her face, cut her throat and ripped open her stomach!" Marared's mouth was crooked and tears spilled down her cheeks. "Brigid wanted to find Dafydd and cut off his hands with a butcher knife. She was so devastated she ran."

"Why run away?" asked Brenda, dropping the pair of gloves Marared handed her.

"She was scared to death," said Marared.

"And where is she now?" Brenda trusted no one and thought mayhap Brigid had run to tell Dafydd what was happening.

"I do not know. She disappeared."

"Is she a spy for Dafydd?" asked Brenda. "I could have been hanged for something she told Prince Owain years ago. I do not trust her."

"No, no! You imagine the worst, and I cannot fault you." Marared wiped the back of her hand over her mouth to straighten it. "Years ago Brigid told me she told Owain something that could mean trouble for you. She never said what, but she was truly sorry she talked to him, and she disliked him for his cajolery. He was known to charm a maid so that she would tell him whatever he wished to know. Brigid was angry with Owain, but she is deathly afraid of Dafydd, because he killed her brother who was a druid. Mayhap she went to warn her family, who are Old Religionists. These are bad times!"

"The white-livered coistrel! Lord Dafydd, a curse on thee!" said Brenda. "I shall find thee and scratch thine eyes out!" She waved her gloved hands and squirmed from Marared, who tried to slip a hauberk over her head. Her mouth was dry as fine flour, her hands covered her face and she broke into a sweat. Her arms and legs were like goose flesh. She felt beaten. "What is the use? 'Tis so hard to change things. We should give up and run away. Instead we will stay together and make things right!" she said, thinking of Ailin, who would not want her to give up. Mayhap the lad was speaking to her from his world of spirits, giving her courage. "What else happened this morning?"

"The inn was set afire," said Marared. "A tub of water in the loft spilled when the supports burned, so Magain's body was only singed. She still held her amethyst crystal. It was supposed to bring luck and protect her from evil." Her voice dropped to a whisper, "I took it from her bloody hand before the gravediggers came for her." She reached into her apron pocket and held the crystal in the torchlight. " 'Tis all the luck that is left of a dear friend."

"I cannot believe anyone would harm that dearest old woman," said Mona. "The world is upside down."

"Magain made the quilt that covers my baby," said Annesta, "She knew her name was Gwenllian without any of us telling it. This is the same tyranny that beheaded my grandfather, who would never hurt anyone. What is the Lord God thinking when He sees the tide of vice that is loose?"

"Greed," said Brenda. "Lord Dafydd's pleasures are his laws. In youth he was taught gentle breeding, logic and figuring but it became his practice to bear a grudge, to mutiny and to rise against authority. His mother and father and nursemaid are to blame because they cherished him as something precious and indulged him to ride far too long upon his own tide." She held out her arms and let Mona tie leather wrappings around them, then around her legs. She pulled breeks over the leg wrappings and said, "Annesta, put this jerkin on over your hauberk for warmth. Let me pin up your hair. You want to look like a sailor?"

The echo of Brenda's voice thrummed in Annesta's mind, softer and softer, like a vibrating harp string. "How can I carry a baby when I be so heavily dressed?" she said.

"Worry not. I will take care of baby Gwenllian," said Marared, fastening the metal breastplate, which could ward off flying arrows.

"Her father has not yet seen her," said Annesta. "Naught must happen to her."

Marared's gentle brown eyes flashed. "Listen, here is the plan: I be going with you to the ship. Baby Gwenllian will sleep while carried upright on the side of a horse, protected by a shield with wicker backing. She will be warm and safe. Once you, looking like ordinary seamen, board ship, I shall hand the shield up as if it were part of the ship's equipment."

Annesta drew in her breath.

"Sshh, hear it all. She will be given a gentle sleeping liquid made from crushed poppy seeds. One drop on her tongue will put her to sleep for most of a day. She will feel no ill effects when she wakes. I give you the vial in case you need to give her more when she is on the ship, but remember only one drop a day or a night."

"My babe in a shield?" Annesta was bewildered. "When is Madoc coming?"

"In a shield, safe as in her mother's arms," said Marared. "We had word from a man who rides the bay in a coracle that the shipmaster-priest is due in the Conwy's mouth at high tide."

Annesta's tear-wet face glowed in the torchlight. She folded her hands together in her lap and thought, My love is near; the day is clear. If Madoc is close there is hope. Reluctantly she handed Gwenllian to Marared, who put her in the truckle and carried her out. Annesta patted the leather pouch that held her grandfather's precious ashes, pressed her head against the wall and wondered if she could pull the heavy shield over a ship's gunwale.

"No one will suspect we are women," said Mona. "Look at us! We are well-fed seamen, fat as butterballs in all these layers of clothes. I be ready!" She marched about the room brandishing a pair of sewing shears.

The women were led out to the inner ward, where there were house- and kitchen maids in loose chain mail and leather lamellar armor, all hidden under wool tunics. The only protective weapons Brenda could see were kitchen knives and scissors, which would be hidden under clothing. Men were in leather tunics, or bare-chested; some had brass helms on their heads. If they carried knives or daggers, they were well hidden. No bows, arrows or swords were in sight. They looked like ordinary retainers who came with their lord for the bargaining of a shipload of goods, grain in this case. There were whispers and quiet chanting among little groups. Marared reassured each one that all would be well.

XXVIII
Annesta

Many legends from the Middle Ages refer to circles that formed in the fields overnight. Back then, pundits talked of fairies dancing through the corn, or of mowing devils who came in the night and cut the crops in rings. . . . The circles are caused by whirlwinds. Terence Meaden [an atmospheric physicist] envisions the summer air hanging motionless over these hills during the night, until the first stirring of wind toward morning starts to pick up near the level of the crops. When these winds strike the hillsides, they ricochet back, forming spinning columns of air. . . . Often air continues to pour into the vortex from all directions, spiraling inward and upward. Then a bulge may develop partway up the spinning column, where the air is rushing in and rotating rapidly. The bulge then "relieves itself," Meaden says, by breaking down—namely, bursting and falling to the ground, where it leaves its telltale mark on the cornfields.

As the vortex sucks in air, it strips electrons off the molecules, turning them into ions that glow in the dark. Airborne particles of pollen, dust, and sea salt hovering over the fields accelerate the buildup of electric charge inside the whirlwind, making it hum and shimmer with orange, yellow, or red light. From a distance, the bulge in the whirlwind may look like ball of lightning, and its noise may sound similar to humming, buzzing, or even a siren's wail.

Dava Sobel, "Field of Dreams?" in *Omni* Magazine

Lord Iorwerth's retinue stood in the inner courtyard stamping their feet to keep warm. Their breath left little white clouds in front of their faces. Iorwerth raised his hand and said, "Word is that Lord Dafydd and Lord Rhodri and their dragons are on their way to meet the grain ship. I want no fighting. Ladies, no screaming. We carry a few shields only to show we are from the House of Gwynedd. We go peacefully to purchase Isle of Man grain by proper, lawful ceremony. Let us go before the dragons arrive and daylight betrays us." He brought his raised right hand down fast.

Two lines were formed, walkers and horsebackers, who led packhorses to carry the grain. Iorwerth, leading a packhorse, took his retinue past the guards, out of the courtyard, down the ramp, through the sleeping village, past the desolate, black shell of the Seaside Inn, to the narrow path that hugged the shore.

Annesta had no trouble keeping up with the fast pace set by the walkers. Her anticipation of seeing Madoc was barely clouded with the sad thoughts of Magain's brutal murder and the smell of smoke and ash emanating from the fire-gutted inn.

Brenda felt guilt about Magain's killing. She could have persuaded her to stay the night with them. She began to worry where danger would come next, and looked here and there through the darkness at the tall grasses along the rocky shore. She shivered and prayed the trading would be quick and peaceful. Once she stopped, put her arms around the trunk of a huge oak. She patted the trunk, as if permitting it to give her some sort of blessing. She had seen Llieu do the same when he was anxious about the future. The oak's upper branches were covered with mistletoe, leaving only the highest spindly ends to reach out in the moisture-laden night air and, she supposed, the daylight's sunshine, as if ultimately seeking to reach the gates of Heaven.

Annesta said the oak's upper branches looked like huge birds or flying horses.

They came down a rocky hill covered with yellow whitlow grass. The headlands reflected onto the starlit black seawater.

From the top of the hill they saw large concentric circles of flattened oats and speculated as to their cause. Some crofters, looking thick-chested with hauberks under their bratts, talked about occasional whirlwinds accompanied by an eerie, moving orange light in their fields. Others said they had heard the whistling sound that came with the whirling winds and said that the next morning they always saw the rings, each perfectly drawn and the grain bent but not broken. Iorwerth's flag-bearer said he was certain the small forest creatures danced by the light of the orange glow on certain nights, trampling the crop down into a perfect ring and their little feet went this way and that way as they danced. Then stalks were swept into a matted pinwheel pattern turning clockwise and then counterclockwise. The horsebackers talked about the times they heard the strange warbling sound. Mona, wearing a bowl-like helm, said it was the animals and wee folk singing as they danced.

Brenda thought of the childhood stories she had heard of the little people or a warren of rabbits flattening the growing crops as they danced hand-in-hand on a starlit night. The crop circles beckoned to her as a safe, snug mat for sleeping. She pulled a tender green blade from the trail's side and cupped her tongue to catch the dew. The cold dew was better than the warm water in the skin bottle that hung around her neck. She quenched her thirst by sucking dew from more than a dozen tender blades, then chewed two or three blades of grass, savoring the fresh, green taste. She kept looking at the circles, hoping that she would see tiny dancing figures. But when she saw that the last walker was far ahead of her, she ran to catch up and said to Llorfa, "What do you think? Will there be a fight?"

"Would cats hunt mice if the mice be dressed like cats?" said Llorfa. "I hope and pray we see no soldiers, but if we do, I pray they never discover half of Lord Iorwerth's retainers are women dressed like men."

Their path crossed a second path and there was a satisfied murmur when Iorwerth said that two intersecting lines were a sign of protection. The main path disappeared in a place where one side went up the cliffs and the other down to the estuary. They followed the rock-strewn lower path as if they had done this every morning. No one complained about the cold, damp wind, but there were murmurings when a polecat, on its nocturnal hunt for food, became frightened and left its powerful smell behind.

Brenda felt Annesta clasp her hand. "You are going to let a skunk frighten you?" teased Brenda.

"Will you recommend my soul to Heaven?" asked Annesta in a small, dry voice.

"Certes, but hush, you are not ready for death."

"We are moving so fast. I feel like a sheep being led by its horns to slaughter."

"Pin your mind on the morrow's joys," said Brenda. "Madoc will be so happy to have you in his sight that you could convince him the moon is the sun."

The words mollified Annesta for a moment, then she wondered if Madoc would recognize her in a hauberk and padded jerkin.

"He will know you even if you look like a round hedgehog," said Brenda. "Tuck your dreams in your shoes and hurry up." A cold shiver ran up Brenda's spine as they passed a silvered withie hut that was green-splashed with lichen. She thought she heard a rustling in the grass or the gurgling of a small creek, but could see nothing in the dim gray light of a new day.

Annesta whispered, "What if I cannot find my baby! Marared's maid, Brigid, does not carry a shield!"

"Marared has your babe in a safe place," said Brenda, inhaling the brisk salt air. She moved off the shingly path to walk more easily on the damp sand. Suddenly she imagined that the air had a fleeting smell of woodsmoke. Humming the lullaby the others sang, she looked here and there, trying to make her eyes pierce the dark shadows.

Annesta sniffed. "We are watched! I feel it! Over there, look!"

Three hundred ells away there was a brief, flickering light no larger than a pinprick. It came and was gone. Brenda half expected to see the cotoneaster shrubs with their red and white flowers caught up in a roaring flame, but there was nothing. She nodded, hung tight to Annesta's hand, but did not stop humming. It gave her courage. If I hum loud enough Annesta cannot hear my heart beat against my ribs or know that there is an acid taste of fear in my mouth, she thought. "The light is some kind of reflection, mayhap a sign to someone at the quay," she said aloud.

They walked steadily until slowed by the sight of an owl rising from a black grove of trees and vanishing into the wispy fog. Brenda saw four cowled monks rise up from the grass and join the marchers behind Iorwerth. No one else near her seemed to have seen them. Mayhap fatigue was playing tricks with her eyesight or she was the target of gullery by little people, small as shrews but strong on spells.

In the pearled, swirling mist, Brenda saw a ship that carried the name *Gwennan Gorn* on her prow. She stopped, took a deep breath. It was almost beyond comprehension that this beautiful, buoyant monster was something Madoc had rebuilt and mastered. I will get to know about it on the way to Dubh Linn, she promised herself. Dubh Linn and Sein. I have thought about him for so long, I wonder if my thoughts are true. Has he long ago forgotten me? He said he would love me no matter what happened, but I never promised him a thing. How will I act when I see him? Oh Lord God, do not let me be foolish.

She stood on her toes to look up at the faces leaning over the side of the ship. She could not tell one face from another. For a moment she thought that perhaps Madoc was not among them. She bit her tongue so that she would not call and be disappointed if he did not answer. She eased herself back on her heels and let out her breath.

"Do you see him?" asked Annesta.

"Nay, not yet."

Iorwerth led the horsebackers and walkers to the willows and water-reeds alongside four cowled men, looking like out-of-place monks with sun-darkened faces, listening to the pre-dawn cries of the seabirds. Like druids, they were going to divine the message given by the birds' chatter. Brenda smiled at the four monks and knew her eyesight did not deceive her. Had not Iorwerth said Madoc lived in an old abbey with four others? So here they were, four druids dressed like monks.

She moved closer to hear the prophesy for the day's outcome.

One of the monkish men pushed his cowl back, exposing black hair and bright blue eyes. He waited for Iorwerth to dismount, then they shook hands with two fingers laid below each other's right elbow, in druidic manner. He spoke in a deep, musical voice that carried up and down the quay. "The signs are worthy. The omen is favorable for buying and selling grain. Only time is short. When the stars fade and the silver-white dawn turns to gold, look out for trouble."

Brenda drew in a sharp breath, and felt Annesta's hand tighten.

There was a whir, sparks and a burst of orange flame. One monkish man held up a torch. More were lighted from it, making a bright, smoky line along the quay to the foot of the wharf.

Iorwerth told the horsebackers to position themselves in a semicircle in front of the torches as proper for a large sale. He told the foot-marchers to stand behind the horsebackers so that they were between the torchlight and the quay. He stood by his flag-bearer, watching the red flag with three golden lions ripple in the breeze. Words were spoken in whispers, "Hurry!" "Coming through!" "Make room!" "Grain sacks here!"

Thumps and curses came from the ship's deck. Flickering torches showed that a rope ladder had been dropped from the gunwale and made firm on the wharf by a wooden brace. Seamen scrambled down, each gripping a coarse linen sack over his shoulder.

The grain sacks were longer than the usual and not filled right up, so that a man could hold one by its neck. They were dropped onto the sand just behind the torches and a half dozen seamen stayed to guard them.

"Is that Troyes?" Mona whispered, pointing to one of the guards who had a definite limp. But no one could say for certain.

"They have smeared something on their faces," said Annesta.

"They all look alike," said Mona.

Llorfa watched a dark-haired seaman touch each sack as he counted fifty knots tied on a long string. Iorwerth took off a money pouch that was tied to his belt, took it under a torch-light and let the man with the knotted string look inside. The man smiled, nodded, opened and closed both hands five times. " 'Tis Conlaf counting fifty sacks," whispered Llorfa. "Lugh's liver, I know him even with a dirty face. He will be on the ship! I would fain like to hold his hand right now!"

"Ha, I be looking for Troyes," said Mona. "He is my Adonis."

"Do you see Madoc?" asked Annesta. "Where is our baby? Is everything all right?" She sounded as if she were rubbing sadness into happiness.

"Everything is fine," said Brenda.

Iorwerth inspected the grain sacks at random. He lifted one, then another, testing their weight. When he was close to the four women he said, "Board after the sale, while my men load the packhorses." His voice was low and he was all smiles. Everything was going quickly and well.

Brenda crossed her arms across her breast to hold herself steady. Iorwerth was talking to a man in a black robe similar to the ones worn by the four monks, who stood in plain sight on the wharf, on either side of the ship's ladder. She guessed that this fifth monk, with a parchment tablet fastened firmly inside his belt, had come to complete the purchase ceremony. The monk saw her, rubbed his rough, dark face and grinned. In the torchlight she saw that he was blond and—gloryoso!— had a space between his top front teeth. "Madoc!" The taste of the word was sweet on her tongue. She could not have held it back. Her heart pounded and a frisson ran down her back-bone. She touched Annesta's shoulder.

Annesta stared and spoke in a whisper that sang like thin crystal, "Madoc! Thank God, 'tis you, the light in my soul!"

"Sshh," warned Brenda, giddy with joy. She squeezed An-nesta's arm so that she would not run to him and break the ritual of trade.

Iorwerth put his arm around Madoc, said something close to his ear, pointed in the direction of the four women and, without looking back, they joined the men who were tying sacks onto the backs of packhorses.

Each sack had a blue-woad half-moon under a parallelogram dyed on the loose end. The half-moon was a ship and the parallelogram was the full sail, with a Roman numeral dyed in the center—Madoc's trading mark. A hundred sacks were counted and loaded onto the packhorses. Brenda saw that Madoc wrote on his tablet, cut the written parchment in half, rolled it and gave the bottom half to Iorwerth, who wrote something on the top half and gave it to Madoc. Iorwerth then gave Madoc his money pouch and smiled as they again laid two fingers below each other's right elbow.

Brenda said, "Trading is over. Time to go."

Annesta hung back and said she did not know if she could climb the perpendicular, swinging ladder. "If I look down, I will be dizzy."

"Oh posh, Annesta, just go!" said Brenda. "You get to the top and I promise Madoc will be there." Brenda looked at the water, which was the color of quicksilver, then she turned and her eyes met Annesta's. She was startled to see something different from fear, something more like despair.

"What is it?" asked Brenda.

"I have a dreadful foreboding. The day is unlucky."

"You heard the druid prophesy; the omens are favorable," said Brenda.

"What if—Brenda, I want you to look after Gwenllian."

"You have my word," said Brenda, "but you worry too much."

Llorfa said, "Annesta, you have to live above the dizziness."

" 'Tis not really the dizziness. 'Tis that I cannot climb and hold Grandfather's ashes. I have broken the thong so that it cannot go around my neck. The pouch does not fit in my pocket. I cannot hold the ladder with it in my hands. I have not found a suitable cave to leave it in. I cannot leave it behind. I just cannot! Someone like Lord Dafydd could find it and desecrate Grandfather's ashes."

"Fie! This is no time to look for a hallowed cave. What is the matter with you?" said Mona.

"Naught. I need a moment to think." She closed her eyes and tapped her foot.

Llorfa and Mona thought Annesta was overdramatic. They

forgave her, and whispered between themselves that she was
nervous with the thought of seeing Madoc after so many
months. They wore smug smiles, ignored Annesta and looked
at the big ship.

Brenda looked beyond Annesta and saw that some of the
packhorses were being led away. Joy flared in her chest like
brushfire. "In a few moments we will be aboard ship and on
our way to Ireland," she said. "Each one of us has to make
do the best we can with what we have. The gods ask nothing
else of us. Annesta, here, slip the cord of the water bottle
around your neck and let me take Llywarch's ashes."

Annesta opened her eyes, took the bottle and sat on the
sand like a child reluctant to leave the seashore.

"What are you doing?" asked Brenda, her voice showing
agitation.

"I be making do," said Annesta. A tiny smile pushed up
the corners of her mouth. She took the plug out of the water
bottle, dumped in Iorwerth's ashes, shook it, lifted it to her
lips and drank without stopping for a breath. Afterward she
made a face, laughed, ran her tongue around her mouth and
said, " 'Tis done."

"Annesta!" Brenda was horrified.

"Grandfather is gritty, but safe, in a dark and sacred place.
No one can take him, nor make me throw his spirit away."
Her eyes shone with triumph.

Brenda picked up the sooty leather pouch and held it to her
breast, then rolled it up and put it inside her hauberk. She took
the muddied water bottle from Annesta and hung it around her
neck, thinking it was a shame to waste anything that could be
used again. "I be ready," she said.

Suddenly there were vibrations under their feet and a deep-
throated chant beyond the rise of the hill. Atop the rise a line
of horsebackers in black tunics arose with the morning light.

"Get down!" hollered Iorwerth.

"Out of sight!" yelled Madoc.

The women crouched together close to the rock quay.

A gathering of blue butterflies rose over the green turf like
a nervous eisteddfod chorus. Behind them limed-headed riders
swayed as the horses, with feathers attached to their manes,

came galloping down the hill. Foot soldiers, with unsheathed broadswords that reflected the glint of light, followed. They stopped on the flowery meadow and swatted at the annoying clouds of fluttering, speckled butterflies. Their eyes scoured the smoky shore as if trying to count the number of house-holders in the trade ceremony.

Iorwerth's voice boomed across the meadow. "Hark! You dragons know Lord Iorwerth has never gone awarring against his brethern! Why do you unsheathe your swords in a neutral trading area?"

Brenda's fear sharpened. She clasped Annesta's hand. "Come! Be quick!"

The two of them ran to a niche in the quay where several stones had broken away. Brenda looked through the broken stone to the road along the shore where the only movement was men in black tunics leading away Iorwerth's packhorses, loaded with sacks of grain. The torches roared in a gust of wind. In the meadow, beyond the torches, there was movement in the ranks of the black dragons. There was a sharp whis-pering of commands, which Brenda could not make out, and some of Iorwerth's people crouched behind clumps of willows. Probably women like us, thought Brenda.

Annesta asked if one of the women behind the willows was Lady Marared carrying the shield with baby Gwenllian.

Brenda squirmed around trying to see. She saw seamen from the ship standing beside Iorwerth, still as trees. A spotted stallion came forward with a thick-chested, bull-necked rider. " 'Tis Dafydd," whispered Brenda. The fear in her midsection was nearly impossible to keep down. Stay above it, she said to herself. Once inside the ship we are safe. Oh, Lord God, hear me—safe!

The rising sun thrust long yellow fingers above the hill. Brenda could feel its warmth on her face and shoulders. The molten, metallic-looking quay turned soapy pink and blue as the wind riffled it into froth.

Dafydd faced Iorwerth. "The most powerful lord and next king of Gwynedd bestows Heaven's blessing upon you, Brother Crooked Nose," he said in a loud, gruff voice. " 'Tis my right, as the foremost lord, to claim both grain and ship. They are mine if I say so—and I do."

Brenda shielded her eyes from the sun and saw Dafydd's lips pull thin. A black band kept his hair in place and she was sure that he wore a vestlike hauberk under his black tunic.

Iorwerth sat silent atop his horse. His blackened bare shoulders looked like polished iron under the morning sunlight.

Dafydd pushed his headband higher on his forehead, and his walrus mustache rose in a mocking grin. "I be asking you if four runaway women are hidden at Degannwy Court? These harpies, Brenda, Annesta, Mona and Llorfa, are my prisoners. When troth is uncovered, as the Lord God is my witness, 'twill be known the last three I named gave aid to Brenda, our father's mistress, when she poisoned him with a pagan's deadly potion. Do you hear me? Mistress Brenda murdered our father!"

"That is not troth!" shouted Iorwerth. "I see you ride the back of one of those hungry lions pictured on the arms of Gwynedd and you dare not dismount for fear of being chewed to death."

"What will happen to my baby if Dafydd finds us?" Annesta whispered, blinded by tears.

"Sshh," said Brenda, going numb. Her sight and hearing were tuned more delicately than ever before. She heard the women in the willows whisper until it grew to a buzz.

Lord Iorwerth looked in their direction and slashed the air with his hand. "Brother Dafydd," he said, "there are no women hidden in my court. I invite you to have a look when I am finished here. The grain has been paid for and the packhorses are mine. I work within the laws of Prince Howell. If you wish to buy from me, we can talk about it. My retainers are unarmed and we wish to part in peace."

Once again the earth vibrated, and the air carried a sound like the rustling of leaves. At first Brenda thought it was Iorwerth's men leading the loaded packhorses out of sight down the shore of the estuary before doubling back to Degannwy Court. But those men had not moved. Instead, peeking above the hill's brow, there were more nodding horse heads. The picture changed to include riders in yellow tunics, erect and swaying. Behind them ran yellow dragons, or foot soldiers.

Annesta's eyes turned dark and she said, "Rhodri followed Dafydd here!" Her arms folded against her midsection as if she were protecting her grandfather's spirit. "There *is* going to be a fight."

"Why?" asked Brenda. "The grain is no longer in Iorwerth's hands."

"Rhodri believes he is greater than Dafydd and will try to take the grain from him," said Annesta.

At that moment, Brenda saw one of Dafydd's foot soldiers creep between two horsebackers toward Lord Iorwerth. The moist air was so thick with torch smoke she could hardly breathe. Dafydd's soldier stood with his legs apart, ready to throw his lance at Iorwerth's chest.

At the instant the soldier moved his throwing hand, a deep-throated cry, like a feral growl, escaped Brenda's lips. "No! No, no!"

Iorwerth's horse danced sideways and the lance struck a stone with a clang that might have deafened for life any fairy-folk living underneath.

Iorwerth's eyes flashed fire and Brenda saw his head dip in disapproval, toward her hiding place. She felt the heat in her neck rise to her face and she hunkered closer to the ground.

"You were not supposed to scream," whispered Annesta.

"I could not help it," said Brenda. "Did I frighten Iorwerth's horse?"

"It saved him," said Annesta with awe in her voice.

Iorwerth's voice boomed through the morning air, "Dafydd, when was the last time I threw a lance at thee? What is my kill-count against thee? The answers are never and naught. It beseems thee to seek an excuse to do battle and mayhap thine chance is nigh. Look behind. 'Tis Rhodri, not me, who seeks to unhorse thee."

From the yellow line of dragons came an ululation louder than a thousand hornets leaving a smoke-filled nest. The dragons were led by a horsebacker whose dark hair was cut in a straight line below his ears. He scowled and became pinch-lipped when he espied Dafydd on horseback close to Lord Iorwerth. He let his horse prance this way and that, then raised his hands and shouted orders to his men to go after the pack-horses carrying the grain.

Brenda recognized Lord Rhodri's voice and in the sunshine saw his pudgy baby-face as he sat atop a large black stallion.

Dafydd whistled once and ordered his soldiers to surround the horses on the roadway. Rhodri's horsebackers held their spears high and went dashing after the packhorses.

Iorwerth saw his own horsebackers move away from the packhorses. Some of them scuffled with Dafydd's men, but they were unarmed and no match for the spears and daggers. They trotted back beside Iorwerth, as if to protect him.

A trumpet blasted the air and more of Rhodri's horsebackers came up over the hill and halted in the bright sunlight.

There were fist shakings and high-pitched hollerings among Iorwerth's horsebackers like the rattled spiel of traders.

Iorwerth's foot-marchers surreptitiously pocketed stones as they doused the torches in the estuary. They pelted the men wearing black tunics, then stealthily moved around clumps of willows near the quay and threw stones at the men in yellow tunics. Some of the women hiding in the willows began to collect stones for them. The two armies believed the stones came from each other. Now they shook their fists and cater-wauled at each other.

The morning sun became a burning disk.

A trumpet sounded again and Rhodri's foot soldiers let out a blood-chilling whoop that caused a flock of seabirds to rise screeching from the willows on the far side of the estuary. The dragons ran forward, trusting in their own agility and speed to strike blows at Dafydd's men, who milled around the pack-horses. Dafydd's horsemen held up lances ready to hurl and moved into two straight lines.

Rhodri's dragons moved back, leered, pulled their bows taut and let a barrage of arrows fly. Screams rent the air. The packhorses reared, pawed the air and snorted.

Only two of Dafydd's men fell from their horses.

Rhodri's dragons fired another round of arrows and moved back, letting their horsemen approach in a straight line with spears and lances held high.

Suddenly Dafydd's close-ordered ranks opened, stood still to take in as many enemy soldiers as possible and make sure they never drew off an arrow.

Rhodri's enthusiastic but poorly trained horsemen were unable to temper their speed, and were caught in a web of black horsebackers who hacked them with swords and ran them through with lances.

The foot soldiers in yellow tunics were not an easy mark for a barrage of arrows from Dafydd's bowmen, because they ran off in all directions. Showing contempt for the scattered men in yellow, Dafydd's men slung their bows over their shoulders and pulled axes and daggers out of their waistbands for hand-to-hand scuffling in the meadow grass. Some of Dafydd's soldiers tried to pull frightened, rearing packhorses away from the fighting.

Iorwerth saw this as his chance to send most of his retainers back to Degannwy. He waved his hands to let his people know they were free to leave.

At the same time Brenda heard Marared speak to Annesta from a clump of willows. "Go aboard! Your babe is safe." Then she told each of the women hiding with her to take a sack of grain from the packhorses to the old lichen-covered withie hut. "Hide as much as possible there. Hurry before the soldiers notice. Then go back to the castle. I shall scatter the packhorses so that neither Dafydd nor Rhodri will relish looking for them. 'Twill be a hellish round-up. The gods be with you! Hurry!"

Brenda watched the women slowly taking away the grain. She wondered where the four monkish men who lived in the hut were now. Next she saw Rhodri waving his sword only thirty or forty ells away. He rode his horse around Iorwerth, shouting gibes and taunting him with the point of his sword. "Do not worry, brother, we shall make good use of your grain and mayhap even eat your packhorses."

Iorwerth held out his hands so Rhodri could see he had no weapons, and without warning grabbed Rhodri's wrist so hard his sword clattered to the ground. Iorwerth leaned down, picked up the sword and swung it around his head and let it

fly high in the air and splash in the estuary. Rhodri was wea-
ponless.

An ax struck a rock close to Brenda and she hunkered
closer to the ground. Annesta put an arm around her and they
crawled into the tall reeds. They heard screams, the swish of
lances that slashed the air, and the ring of metal shields that
were pelted with stones. Under cover of reeds Iorwerth's men
threw the stones.

Brenda inched up to see better, and felt a hand cover her
mouth and shove her down against Annesta. She felt herself
sink down into black depths and thought of the people she
loved. Her life hung over the very edge of the world and she
forced herself to open her eyes to look Death in the face. Out
of a dreamlike calm the apparition came slowly: slender, lithe
and bright as sunlight. Golden ringlets hung over his eyes; his
face was dark, smeared with mud and ash stripes. He smelled
like woodsmoke, and with a shake of his head, she saw his
deep blue eyes and the wide smile that revealed dazzling white
teeth with a notch between the top front two. His soft, whispered voice was like a Welsh bard singing to a frightened
child. The strong, warm hand fell away and his dark face was
somber, but his blue eyes twinkled. "I look for Monà and
Llorfa," Madoc said.

"They must be close," said Brenda.

He touched Annesta's cheek. "I have missed thee."

Brenda saw the tears spring out of Annesta's eyes and held
hers back as Madoc left ever so silently, like an animal hunted,
like he was avoiding being stalked. When he was out of sight,
Brenda put her arms around Annesta and told her to dry her
tears. "If 'tis the gods' will, all will be well. You shall see."

"I never saw him with his face painted for war," sobbed
Annesta.

"I think 'tis more a disguise," said Brenda. "Most of the
sailors had their faces greased or painted." She admitted that
she had been terrified when Madoc's hand went over her
mouth. "I was of a mind to bite a hunk from it. 'Twas the
thought of all that blood that stopped me." She asked Annesta
when she had last seen Llorfa and Mona.

Annesta shook her head back and forth.

Brenda stood to look around and for an instant wondered where the four monkish men were. "Lugh's legs!" She pointed. "Look there! Llorfa is scrambling up the rope ladder. We had better go too!"

"Nay, Madoc will tell us when," Annesta said, staying in the cover of reeds and putting a finger to her lips. A string of guttural curses sounded close by as two soldiers in black tunics, one with a limp, tried to calm a single packhorse that had begun snorting and rearing in an attempt to throw off its heavy sacks of grain. "I swear there are other women hidden in these weeds," said one of the men, who had blood-spattered leather brogues.

"Tcha," said a disgusted hoarse voice. The owner of the voice limped when he tried to grab the lead rope from the rearing horse. "You see a woman behind every tree. I told you to keep the packhorses surrounded. First you let Rhodri's dragons get to them. Then you frightened them and they ran in all directions! Damn, I should run this sword through your skinny belly out your backside. I do not want to hear about imaginary women! They sound like the invisible Irish Dananns! Lord, a man gets hard just thinking about a woman he can feel but not see."

"But, but you said we can take any woman we find," said the man with the bloody brogues. " 'Tis a soldier's reward. This one fought like a Celtic Fir Bolg, with her fingernails—and shears. Look! See what she did! I swear I be not imagining!"

"You fornicated yourself while dreaming of a wild damsel. Warring does that to a hungry dumbhead like you. I see naught. So close your bloody mouth or I will cut off your lips!"

Brenda thought she recognized the limper and ducked deeper into the boggy reed bed. She saw that Dumbhead's thigh-high black stockings were snagged and torn. The right stocking had been badly ripped by something sharp. His leg was slashed and covered with blood and shallow puncture wounds, as if a pointed knife or scissors had jabbed him.

She peeked from the reeds and was close enough to look under Dafydd's tunic. There was a large, ugly puckered white scar high on his thigh. It was as recognizable as if it were her own. She gasped and let the air out slowly. She looked up to his face, saw angry-yellow eyes, grabbed Annesta's hand and whispered, " 'Tis Dafydd." Together they crawled sideways, like twin crabs, out of the way of the two soldiers and the rearing horse.

No more than a dozen spears' length from where the two women had been, Dafydd stood bewildered, listening. He blinked red-rimmed, half-blind eyes at a bloodied broadsword Dumbhead held out to him, then he let out a piping screech that could wake the sleepers in Sid. "Someone is hiding in these reeds! Stand up so I can see thee!"

Brenda and Annesta crawled through grass and reeds toward a gully. Annesta slid over the edge and whispered, "Destiny no one escapes."

Before Brenda found the gully's edge she bumped into two long, round, cool things. She turned to look, and saw a pair of bare legs stretched out, side by side. They were bloodied at the top where they came to a V. There was blood on the leather tunic and brass helmet. She eased off the helmet and dark, sweat-soaked hair tumbled out. She looked into Mona's dead-fish eyes. She smelled blood mixed with decaying vegetation and something else, thick, whitish fluid mixed with the blood of torn flesh. Rape was on the top of Mona's legs. It smelled earthy and acidic. "Oh, Lord God," said a voice inside her head.

She stared at Mona's right shoulder, a quivering scarlet mass swarming with bloated black flies. The cut-off arm lay alone, stone cold, in the sticky, reddish grass; the red fingers were curled into a tight fist that gripped a pair of sewing scissors. Brenda pulled off her gloves, loosened her hauberk and vomited green, bitter bile while tears streamed down her face. She stayed crouched and put her hands over her ears and closed out the terrible battle noises. She was horrified at the blackness that grew in men's souls. She tried to wipe Dafydd's angry-yellow eyes out of her mind and remembered how Madoc's wide blue eyes had sparkled when he found Annesta. She prayed the sparkle was because he had found his wife, oh please God, not because he took pleasure from this terrible killing.

She laid her cheek against Mona's cold white face. "Your skin fits you well, your heart and mind are just right, and you are a person of great worth," she whispered.

She heard nothing but cicadas high in the trees along the quay, mixed with blowing and wheezing of horses, and pulled herself inch by inch through the grass toward the gully. The angry voices split the air again—a hand came down on her shoulder. She blinked and the fear in her belly turned to a hard knot. "Dafydd!" she mouthed.

Dafydd's partially blind *wylit* eyes darted here and there as if he were lost and trying to find his way. "Aye! I cannot trust my dragons! See there, that is not my father's mistress, Brenda. The dummy hacked the arm off the wrong maid!" He held up Mona's thin arm and let it drop like a chunk of rotten, termite-infested wood. "Prithee, point me toward my army before my wretched brother, Rhodri, kills me. The *truan*! Damn the bad luck, I have to fight two wretches, Lord Rhodri and Prince Howell, to become king of this bloody land."

Brenda backed away, wishing she had her gloves and hoping he could not see that she was not a soldier. He pounced, twisted her arm so hard that it was all she could do to keep from passing out. "Where is Brenda?" he screeched like a cat at rutting time. "Whose soldier are you? Iorwerth's? Aha, one of mine!" He blinked and squinted to see her face better. She kept her head down. "When I was a lad, this Brenda preached respect and honesty and love. Ha! Pray pardon, that stuff is out of date." His voice became low and gravelly, "*She* poisoned my father. Fie upon her!"

He pummelled her shoulder with bony fists and she gathered all the strength she could muster to push him away. He fell on the ground and swore at the stone that tripped him. He was on his feet in a moment. "I shall kill Brenda ever so slowly, which will give me more pleasure than anything I can think of."

Brenda fought the wave of panic that slammed against her chest, making it hard to breathe, and moved away from his line of sight, scuttling backward as quietly as possible.

He raised his voice. "The priest's ship is mine to carry English grain and meat. King Henry promised to open his larder to me when he is convinced I have cleansed Gwynedd of pagans. He likes me because I saved his ugly sister, Emma, from being an old maid. I like him because he promised to keep me and my men fed. Hungry men cannot sleep. There is no bread, no mead in the Aberffraw keep. All the previous retainers have fled." He lowered his head and looked at her sideways with a rapscallion's leer.

Food, thought Brenda, is why Dafydd is here. He and his men have burned and pillaged the land barren. He is starving. His men are starving. He dreams of food onboard Madoc's ship. She rose up, kicked his shin, and he staggered. "Beshrew you!" she said. "For besmirching the names of decent women who left Gwynedd's court. I pray God's breath plants a putrid plague on you." Before he found his balance, she kicked his other shin. "I bemoan the fate of your wife."

Dafydd staggered; his greasy brown curls rolled on his shoulders as his black head-binding came loose. He found his balance, shrugged, rubbed his shins and drew his sword. His voice was insolent. "Shut your maw. I be the next king, not some lad you can push around. You are nobody, just a lousy soldier that I no longer need in my army." He aimed the sword at her throat.

She planted her feet firm on the rock-strewn sand and pulled the water bottle from around her neck. She grimaced, held her hand up ready to swing with all her might.

A strong, hot hand clamped down on her shoulder. She jumped when she heard a calm voice say, "Thank Lugh I have found you!" It was Madoc in his long black gown. He looked Dafydd square in the eye and said, " 'Tis my luck to meet the notorious future king of all Gwynedd and 'tis my happiness to find him concerned with the weak and wounded. God's greeting to you."

Brenda's eyes grew large and she clapped a hand over her mouth in surprise.

Dafydd made the sign of the cross and blinked, trying to clear his eyes to see Madoc's features in the bright sunlight. His teeth chattered and his outstretched hand shook in Madoc's face. "The sun is not as warm as it used to be. I mistook this soldier for one of my own. You see he wears a dark helm, hauberk and boots. But he is a *buwch* and has the temper of a berserker. He is yours, trader-priest! Your sailing ship is mine!"

Madoc only nodded toward Mona's bloody corpse and said, "Pray tell what happened here?"

"Well, could be that this here soldier fancied the female dragon, but quickly tired of her. The dead creature will be a great flesh-feast for wolves." He put the toe of his brogue against Mona's side. " 'Tis pitiful that women serve with Lord Rhodri's troops because he cannot get enough men to follow him."

"Your Highness." Brenda's lips pressed tight against her teeth, and she tried to make her voice low and husky. "You know full well that this is what is left of Brenda's maid, Mona, who is not a soldier but who must have come to buy a few sacks of grain. In years past, when you were a wee lad, Mona cleaned your room and bedclothes. And this is how you treat her now? For shame!" Dafydd lifted his sword. Brenda wanted to spit at him for calling her a cow, but her mouth was dry as summer grass. She raised the hard-leather water bottle and imagined smashing his nose flat against his smirking face.

Behind her back, Madoc told her to hush and stepped on Dafydd's foot, pretending it was an accident.

Dafydd yipped like a stepped-on cat, waved his sword as if he were after a bouncing ghost. "You goddamned hell-hound!" He pulled his foot away with a jerk, lost his balance, dropped the bloody sword and fell on his knees in a fit of coughing.

Brenda put the water bottle back over her head and pointed to the gully, where Annesta was waiting.

Madoc moved toward Mona.

"No, no!" said Brenda. "We can do her no good. She is beyond hurt. A horsebacker will take her to Degannwy court. Come, before Dafydd's coughing stops!"

Madoc picked up the bloody sword, drew back his arm, and threw it far into the estuary.

Together they pulled Annesta from the swampy gully and ran headlong toward the *Gwennan Gorn.*

A sulfur stinkball thrown from the ship dropped into the meadow. Brenda's eyes burned and watered, but she did not mind, if the acrid fumes kept soldiers from coming too close to the ship. She ran wildly for the ladder.

At the top, Troyes grabbed Brenda's arms and said, "Pull your leg up, over, and you are home!"

With her feet steady on the deck she leaned against the gunwale, trying to will her hammering heart still and her throbbing knees to stiffen. She heard Madoc yell, "Climb! I be right behind you!"

Annesta was not moving, but clinging to the rope with a white-knuckled grip while she loosened the lacing of her hauberk. Then she scampered up as though she had the fleet feet of a squirrel. Llorfa and Conlaf pulled her onto the deck and enfolded her in a tender embrace.

Madoc jumped onto the deck and took her into his arms. She pulled away. "Where is our baby?"

Madoc was puzzled. "Baby?"

"Yours. Ours. Oh, Lord! Marared took her for safekeeping." Her knees wobbled like mush. "She sleeps—" A cold bite sank deep into her neck where the protective hauberk had been. She cried out, reached up and felt the shaft of an arrow. Her knees gave way, and she fell against Madoc.

He held her close, thinking she had fainted. Then he saw that an arrow had plunged into the back of his beloved's neck, pierced through the windpipe, and come out through the skin in the front. He threw off her helmet and let it fall into the water. Her thick auburn braids fell out and brushed his hand. "I love you," he said. "I be with you."

Annesta's eyes closed. "We are together, my love," she said. "Everything is all right."

A burning torch fell onto the ship's deck. Troyes threw it back into the grass, where it sizzled and crackled like hot mutton in a fry pan.

For Brenda things moved in slow motion. She saw Madoc lean against the gunwale and cradle his wife's head on his shoulder. She saw Dafydd again, this time on horseback next to the quay. He screamed, "Lord Rhodri is trying to kill me!" Stones flew out of the reeds. Dafydd dismounted holding an arrow in an arbalest. He kneeled, pulled back and let the arrow fly. It penetrated the flank of a horse hiding in the reeds.

The horse whinnied, reared, thrashed and threw its rider into the water. The rider crawled onto the sandy bank on leather-padded knees, held his hands up as if he meant to surrender. His face was round and pink. There was no doubt he was Rhodri.

Dafydd shook his fist at his young brother and yelled at his own dragons standing in a line behind him armed with arbalests. "You careless bloody toads! I hit the horse! Now you shoot the bloody rider!" He ordered the thrashing horse run through with lances and left as host food for red kites.

Onboard ship, Conlaf was in charge of stinkballs, made of sulfur and iron filings held together with pitch. He ignited one and threw it into the reeds, making some of Dafydd's men stand up and reveal their hiding place. They rubbed their eyes, coughed, cursed stinging epithets, held rags to their faces and scattered far away from the quay.

Rhodri dodged an arrow and called to his sputtering troops, who had forgotten any of the battle plans they had practiced, to retreat.

Brenda watched another stinkball fall among Dafydd's milling arbalests. The choking sulfurous fumes engulfed them. Their throats stung as if they had swallowed a dozen scorpions, and they staggered away even though Dafydd called them back to take the ship for him. Dafydd rubbed his eyes, coughed and scratched at his burning skin. He mounted his horse and joined his lingering dragons, who hastily tied dead and wounded companions behind their horsebackers.

Madoc shifted Annesta to his other shoulder and let out a groan like a wounded animal. He tried to pull the arrow all the way through, but the haft was caught. He moved it gently, trying to shake it loose.

Brenda grabbed the spear point, pushed and pulled until it came out spraying blood. She threw it into the water and said, "Annesta did not feel a thing, my son."

Blood gushed like a fountain from the front and back of

that awful, gaping hole and also from Annesta's nose and open mouth. Red bubbles tumbled over Madoc's arm. The deck under his feet became red as madder-root dye. His feet slid in a macabre dance. He laid Annesta's body on the deck and went to see if Troyes was holding the steering oar.

Llorfa knelt beside the body and chanted a druid prayer to send Annesta's freed spirit on its journey to the Great Mystery, a place called Sid, on the Otherside. Brenda wiped blood from Annesta's unblemished face and pushed back her hair.

Madoc returned, told Brenda to move out of his way and Llorfa to be still. He pushed them roughly against the opposite gunwale and let his gown drag through the blood until he sat cross-legged with Annesta's head gently cradled in his arms. His face was ashen.

Brenda could not bear to look at him and bent her head over the gunwale. She saw a commotion at the bottom of the ladder. The four black-gowned men, like out-of-place monks, were filling slingshots with stones. They appeared ready for anyone who now dared to throw a spear or fire an arrow toward the soldier, who scrambled up the ship's ladder. A young man Brenda had never seen pushed a pike over the gunwale's edge. He was ready to push the soldier off at the top of the ladder, but there was no sign of a sword or other weapon on the soldier coming up, only a bulky, wicker-covered leather shield that was thrust against the young man's chest. On the shore the four monkish men cheered.

Suddenly Brenda recognized the soldier who carried the shield and gave a little cry. "Marared! Marared!"

Marared nodded and spoke quickly to the young man, who was so embarrassed he set the pike aside and said he was sorry he had not recognized her right away.

She took hold of his arm and said, "Thurs, this whole day is mixed up with yesterday and I do not have time to make this easy. Your grandmother, Magain, is dead. I am sorry." Still holding on to him, she pointed to a little group of dragons in black tunics, "They will say 'twas done by looters, who burned the inn, but 'twas done by Lord Dafydd himself."

Thurs laid down the shield and slumped against the gunwale, feeling rage creep into every hollow in his body. How could the king of a Welsh province do such an unredeemable act? There was no one kinder, more gentle than his grandmother. She was not rich enough for robbers or looters who wanted coins or material goods, even though she was Degannwy's richest in wisdom and humility. He howled like an animal that was trapped and could not get out unless it gnawed its own leg off. It was a sound that could harrow up the souls of the dead.

Marared started down the ladder, then stopped and looked up with tear-filled eyes. "Brenda!" she said, "Mona's body is on its way to Degannwy. Lugh and Lord God be with you." Then she slid down as if on bears' grease. There was no time for Brenda to tell her about Annesta taking Dafydd's arrow. Maybe she had seen it for herself.

Thurs picked up the shield, hardly looked at it, and laid it near the oak block that closed the slot in the mast partner. He went to the gunwale and looked across the flat meadow to the little rise at the foot of the hill. The air was filled with the smoke and dust of fighting. A lord of his beloved Gwynedd had not only killed his grandmother and burned her inn, but he had also killed the wife of his shipmaster. "How can any man of honor live under such a tyrant's rule?" he asked out loud.

"Amen," whispered Madoc.

"Mona!" said Troyes in his French accent. He left the steering oar, dragged his bad foot and stood beside Llorfa. "She was my sweetheart."

Llorfa, her face sallow as unbleached linen, said, "I thought Mona was right behind me when I ran for the ship. When I got my feet planted on deck, I saw naught but commotion where I had been with her. I decided she had stayed behind with Brenda. I should have gone back for her. 'Tis my fault she was killed!"

"There is no time for blame," said Madoc. He nodded at Thurs, who had no time to dry his eyes before he pulled the ladder off the gunwale hooks, rolled it, laid it on the deck and hauled on the anchor's warp.

There was a thump of stone on wood and Madoc called out, "Man the oars! Be quick. No one follows! We are gone!"

He stood, raised his right hand to his forehead in a salute. The four black-gowned men waved their slingshots from behind a clump of willows.

"What was that for?" asked Brenda.

" 'Tis done," said Thurs. "No skulking dragon will board the *Gwennan Gorn*."

A lone horsebacker in a black tunic followed along the shore. He cupped his hands around his mouth and called, "You bloody pagan, 'tis my ship you sail! I shall kill you!"

A rising wind mocked him, feeding tiny blue flames of burning sulfur and pitch to become hungry orange fingers caressing the brittle, dry grass until it became a black, amorphous carpet. With oars out, dipping, the ship creaked, swayed and heeled to one side, then the other. Water swirled and gurgled past the ship.

Brenda pulled the water bottle over her head, planted her feet apart firmly, said a prayer for strength and good aim. She squinted and threw the bottle at Dafydd as hard as she could. It had a long way to go, and she was surprised when he slumped over his horse and cried in pain. She smiled, knowing that he, half-blind, had not seen what hit him or whence it came. She laughed. It sounded shrill and hysterical. When the laughing was spent, she looked at Llorfa with forgiveness in her eyes. " 'Twas in no way you, but Dafydd's dragon, who brought on Mona's fate," she said. "Not your fault. Mona was in a bad place at a bad time." The two women embraced.

Conlaf threw a final stinkball onto the shore, where the blue flame gave off more devilish stink and choking smoke, making the lone horsebacker, who kept one hand on his injured shoulder, bend double with a rasping cough.

Thurs chanted, "*Hynd! Hynd!* Go! Go! Run for yur life! Run, ye devil!" He kept time with one waving hand for the rowers. Once he kicked the strange shield, mumbled something about keeping a clear deck and propped it against the water barrel.

Brenda brought the shield to her lap and sat with it, rocking to and fro. The day was too heavy to do more. She felt a hundred years old. She wanted to reject all the tragedy; instead her thoughts were tangled with love for Annesta, Mona, Magain, Llywarch and Owain, and knotted with bitter hate for Dafydd. She wanted to squash the bloody life force out of him with her fists. She wanted to plunge a dagger into his heart not once, but until her arm ached with fatigue. She wanted to hear the crack of his neck as it broke between the crush of her hands. For the first time in her life, she understood why men went to war and killed one another.

XXIX
Gwennan Gorn

He [Madoc] had married and had a daughter, Gwynllian.
. . . Gwynllian remained in Wales, married and left descendants. It is possible that Madoc lost his young wife
during or about the time of the war between [Lord] David and Prince Howell and that therefore he desired to
leave his home.

Zella Armstrong, *Who Discovered America?*

Brenda held the wicker-backed shield and watched Madoc
rock Annesta's body. He shivered, looked up. The sun was
covered by black clouds. The wind blew across the gray water,
making it riffle. The wind ruffled the hair on the back of his
head.

For a moment he imagined it was Annesta's strong fingers
in his hair. She was playful that way. Suddenly he was angry
with Brenda for not using her knowledge of medicine to stop
the great gushing of blood from Annesta's neck. He was angry
at Llorfa for not bringing Annesta with her when she came
aboard. He was angry at the gods for permitting the arrow of
his half-brother to spill the living red fluid from the light of
his life, the person who was most precious to him. He was
angry at himself for not seeing the arrow arc against the sky
and not moving away from its flight.

He stood up, contemptuously smoothed his soiled gown,
went to the opposite gunwale, where Llorfa and Brenda huddled together, and said, "I expect you to make my wife presentable to be among friends by the time we are in Dubh
Linn!" He walked to the steering oar, waved the Frenchman,
Troyes, away and said, "I will take over." He was numb and

had no more feeling than a cold stone. He kept his eyes on the rudder and the sea. His anger grew larger than the grief so that he saw nothing wrong in planning something he had always said he was against.

He fantasized running a longsword through Dafydd from front to back. He planned how he would take on any one of Dafydd's dragons and cuff him around until he was lying on the sand unconscious and stinking. The avenging thoughts swelled, multiplied, until it seemed his head could not hold them. But he could not let these tumbling thoughts go outside his head. He could not speak of Dafydd as his half-brother. Inside his head he questioned the druidic wisdom that was against warring with a mortal enemy. Druidic law forbade the taking of a life, unless that life was found by a druidic court of a dozen lawmakers incorrigible, too corrupt to live. He held his tear-wet face to the sky and wailed, "No man has naught but misery, let him be never so sick, oh Lugh."

"Oh, alas, this cruel day!" cried Brenda. "The babe shall be our heart's ease." She started to open up the wicker covering.

Madoc yelled, "Nay! Nay! Lugh's legs, do not touch that! It might be some kind of weapon—a trap, a trick put on this ship by Gwynedd's mad lord!"

Brenda said, " 'Tis not. This is—"

"Hush, madam," he said. "I know what I be saying. Get out of the way!" He told Troyes to stand by the rudder and pushed aside the curious who had gathered around the shield. He took it astern and opened it carefully.

Brenda prayed Gwenllian was all right, not suffocated. She held her breath as she watched Madoc study the small wool blanket that was under the wicker. He pulled up a short knife from a loop tied to his belt, cut through the wicker and felt something move. "What is this? A young lamb or piglet?" he said. He was on his feet, about to take the thing to the mess-mates to see if it was fit for supper. He thought again and said, "Have to make certain 'tis not something poison, a coiled snake, a huge, hairy spider, or a nest of honey bees."

Llorfa and Brenda looked at one another.

He laid down the shield, pulled off the wicker and lifted the blanket. "Lugh's liver!" he said.

Inside was baby Gwenllian, wrapped in a little quilt, sound asleep. She was bald as an old man except for fine, pale gold fuzz.

Madoc shielded her from the wind and misty rain with his arm and watched the rhythm of her heart beat in the top of her head. He picked her up and let her diapered bottom lie in the palm of one hand while her head lay in the palm of the other. For several minutes he looked at her belly, watching the quick breaths she took. Then he laid her back in the padding of the curved shield and carried her to the women. "What is this that was so rudely shoved aboard my ship? An elfin child?"

" 'Tis your child," said Brenda.

"Mine! You dare to jest on this day of all days?"

"In the depth of our grief we forgot to tell you. The Lord, Chief of all gods, has left this little bit of hope. She is Gwenllian, your daughter. Annesta, the gods bless her soul, could hardly wait to show you." Tears mingled with mist and ran down Brenda's face.

Madoc looked around at the crowd of seamen and waved his arm for them to go back to their work. He shook his fist toward the breaking rain clouds, handed the baby in the shield to Brenda and turned back to the rudder without a word. Now he remembered Annesta had asked about a baby.

Brenda held her hand above Gwenllian's face; even though the drizzly rain stopped, the wind continued.

Thurs pointed to the shield and said, "Is he going to sleep all day?"

"*She* was given something," said Brenda. " 'Twas your grandmother's idea to get her safely onboard. When she wakes, she will cry like a wildcat." She rewrapped the baby, covered her with the blanket and put her shield near the steering oar, where Madoc could easily see her.

Brenda thought he would at least pick up his daughter, but he carefully stepped around the shield. She thought perhaps he was afraid of infants, until she saw that he glanced into the shield from time to time. Gwenllian's hands, curled into tiny pink fists like delicate, spiraled seashells, jerked here and there once in a while. She woke all of a sudden with such a wail that Madoc called Brenda.

"Do something to stop that," he said, pointing his toe toward the tiny thrashing arms and legs.

When the baby was warm and dry, Brenda made soft gurgling sounds, patted her back and walked the creaking, groaning deck. The crying continued and Madoc put his hands over his ears. Brenda pulled on his sleeve and said, "What can I do? There is no milk."

"Lugh, god of water, what have you done to me?" he said. "You watched the spilling of my wife's blood. Then you left me this tiny bit of life. Is that the wind in the sail or do I hear you laugh above the infant's caterwauling? I thank you for not leaving me completely destitute. But I tell you I be sick of death and warring!" He crashed his fist against the gunwale, turned to face Brenda and said, "*You*, a mother and physician, ask *me* what to do? Well, try a sailor's trick. Find some clean wool, wadmal. Stuff it in the mouth of a bottle holding watery gruel. If she is hungry she will suck it dry."

"Oh Lugh's legs—I did the same for a wee lad with kinepox a long time ago," said Brenda with a chortle.

The crew marveled how Gwenllian sucked gruel through the twisted wool, then soaked her diaper's wadmal, while Madoc fussed over the rudder and acted as though it was nothing to get excited about.

With heavy hearts, Brenda and Llorfa managed a kind of screen with their underskirts strung on flax rope so they could undress Annesta's corpse, cleanse it with seawater and pat it dry with wadmal. Tears spilled down their cheeks. They scrubbed the ship's bloody deck with seawater but a huge rust-brown stain was there to stay.

Brenda went to one of the messmates for a clay pot of cooking oil and a needle. She oiled some linen thread and had Llorfa pinch the neck wound tight over the severed windpipe and esophagus as she sewed it closed. Once she felt faint and closed her eyes. She washed Annesta's clothes in seawater, rinsed them in fresh water and hung them on another rope line. She found the leather pouch that had once held Llywarch's ashes and a linen purse that was pinned inside Annesta's chemise. She thought the purse held ear ornaments and was surprised to find silver coins. She asked Madoc if he knew Annesta wanted to be cremated. He said she and her grandfather were close and he understood that she did. Then she gave him the empty leather pouch and told him about the incident with Llywarch's ashes and how brave Annesta was to swallow them for safekeeping, " 'Twas an uncommon act of enormous love and commitment," she said. He folded the pouch and slipped it in his tunic pocket, saying he would replace the broken cord one day. She gave him the coin purse.

He smelled it and was instantly reminded of the clean, heathery smell of Annesta. He held it for several moments before he whispered that it was a purse with coins he had given her when he left for Afon Ganol. He paused for breath and his words were choked. "She packed my heart full of joy. Now my heart is broken, empty and cold. My life is without song or dance, without color or sweet smells, a life that is tepid, flat and pointless."

"Life is a gift and can change from day to day. Your dear wife was a gift of love given to you to cherish. She was a gift of friendship given to the rest of us to treasure. The gods of life take back their gifts from time to time," said Brenda.

The rest of the day stayed overcast and smelled of rain. Neither Brenda nor Llorfa thought of sleeping, although they had been awake the night before. When the ship was well out of Colwyn Bay and into the Irish Sea, they were still in a flurry of activity behind the underskirt curtain. They washed Annesta's hair and combed the auburn ringlets against white shoulders that had been rubbed with oil.

When the wind made the water boil with rolling waves, Troyes ordered the sail hoisted. It groaned with the strain of the wind. He too thought of the needless waste of human life, especially the death of the little maid, Mona, who had enchanted him.

For most of the early morning a great faraway roaring filled Brenda's head. Finally she said to Llorfa, "Annesta asked me to promise to care for Gwenllian. She had a premonition about dying."

" 'Tis possible," said Llorfa, "even though she was not druid, she was close to Llywarch, who was. Some say if a person sees a forest move, that person is on the line between being and nonbeing. Did she see a forest that was not a forest?"

"She saw strange shapes, like horses with wings, in the oaks. She talked to her grandfather's spirit in that little bag of ashes," said Brenda.

The wind dried the wash and Brenda pulled it off to dress Annesta. Her own gray tunic looked good under Annesta's blue jerkin. Brenda shivered and pulled her bratt around her shoulders.

She was pleased with the way Annesta looked and tried to show Madoc. He shook his head and kept his eyes on the roiling sea.

Llorfa took the underskirts off the line so that if he glanced across the deck he could see that Annesta looked nice.

The night was as black as a sleeping bear's den when Madoc, with the help of Troyes, had the *Gwennan Gorn* beached on a mud bank in Dubh Linn Bay. Annesta's body lay astern on a pallet under a little canvas awning that flapped in the wind.

Gwalchmai and Llieu came aboard, followed by a crowd of other druids, many from Wales whom Brenda recognized.

Madoc and Conlaf took the finely groomed corpse to the caves where the druids hid for safety. Brenda tucked the quilt inside the shield and carried the cooing baby off the ship. She was met by Molly, Eira and Vivian, with whom she exchanged hugs and murmured words of sympathy.

Molly took her to the sleeping cottage and brought her a bowl of gruel and told her to sleep. Molly and Eira promised to look after Gwenllian. Brenda was grateful and did not argue.

Before morning Brenda woke, went outside and found a pile of newly cut oak logs. She could not help but think of the time baby Madoc had kinefever and she witnessed a heartbreaking funeral pyre of her wee friend Ailin in this same place. She sat a moment on one of the funeral logs and thought of Annesta.

Later, during the ceremony that preceded the cremation, she exchanged quiet hugs with Eira's father, Gorlyn, with Maud, Conn, Finn, Sigurd and Archdruid Llieu. She put her arms around Gwalchmai, whose cheeks were tear-wet, and despaired that this was not a joyful welcoming.

Llieu pulled her aside and told her he had some folk he wanted her to see. His face was solemn, but his eyes sparkled. He dived into the crowd of mourners and brought back two dark-eyed lads and a vibrant, blue-eyed, blond lass who seemed unable to keep her feet still. Brenda's heart thumped as she studied the misty blue-green eyes and the thick golden curls that tumbled and bounced on the lass's shoulders. In the sunlight, she looked no older than a twelve-year-old fosterling, except that she had blue fretting around her fingernails.

"Goeral!" cried Brenda, and gathered her daughter into a tight circle with her arms.

"This handsome lad is my husband, Willem ap Eber," said Goeral as she pulled away. "We did not know when you could get across the Irish Sea. I think Archdruid Llieu believed Willem would ravish me before we were husband and wife, so he married us when he got here." She giggled, and dark-haired Willem's face turned red, but his gray eyes crinkled merrily. "Grandfather Howyl came for the ceremony."

Brenda felt overwhelmed. Her only daughter was grown, not the wee lass she had imagined. Her father was here for his granddaughter's wedding. She had a son-in-law.

Willem took her hands and said he had looked forward to this day for months. His hands were honor-marked. "We came with the intention of going to Wales to help the Welsh trader build ships, you know, the shipmaster-priest. We have not met him, but he is going to be surprised at the following he has. We heard him talk to a crowd about an Irish monk, Brendan, and a Norseman, *Eric y' Coch*, Eric the Red, who found land never before visited by men. I want to be a part of his crew when he sails for our unproved land."

"This shipbuilder, trader, gathers people like an Irish piper gathers children," she said slyly. "What do you know about him?"

"This Welsh trader has the voice of an orator," said Riryd, the black Welsh lad with snappy dark eyes. "Some say he is a chosen one, chosen by the gods to take the druids through storm and hardship to another land where 'tis peaceful, fertile and safe." Riryd moved up and stood before her. "Mam, you look like I remember." His hair was black and straight. His face and arms were tanned as if he spent time outdoors. "I shall sail with the trader."

She put her arms around him and grinned, because soon they would find they were kin to this mythical shipmaster.

" 'Twas centuries ago when Moses led his people to a better land by passing through the Sea of Reeds, the hot, dry wilderness, then to the fertile, peaceful land promised by the Lord God," said Willem. "The trader is like a new Welsh Moses."

"Willem said it right!" said Riryd. "Mam, you cannot know half the stories we have heard about him."

Brenda smiled a secret, knowing smile. Riryd was a grown-up version of the laddie she remembered, wiry as a rabbit, attractive and high-spirited.

He walked around her, noting that she had no gray hairs, that her shoulders were not stooped. He looked relieved and thankful. "What do you do now that Prince Owain is dead?"

"Is that a polite question?" she asked. "I be a healer, a physician. I studied with Archdruid Llieu."

"Is my mam a pagan healer?" He examined her short fingernails and work-roughened, suntanned hands.

"I have great admiration for pagans and if I stay with this group of Taliesin and Prydian druids I will have no choice," she said with a glint in her dark eyes, "but to become one of you."

Riryd did not stop grinning but stuck his hand out in front of her eyes so she could admire the intricate blue-woad honor marks.

"I be so glad to be here with my children," she said. "We have been apart too long. I pray we shall spend many days together. This day, even though sad, marks the end of my howling anguish for all things terrible in Gwynedd. I cannot live there and now I do not have to. I shall stay where my children are." She kissed Riryd, Goeral and her new son-in-law, Willem. She excused herself to check on baby Gwenllian and felt her heart sing with hope above the sadness.

When she looked up, Sein was smiling at her. She did not know what to say. For the moment it was enough just to look at him, to be aware of his clean, woodsy smell. He was no stranger, but someone she had known and dreamed about for years. His rich, red-gold hair was a halo of fire and sunshine. There were fine laugh lines at the corners of his blue eyes and sober mouth. His face was tanned with a scattering of freckles. His body was slim, compact, and his long, bare legs ended in brogues shiny with fresh lard rubbed into the leather. Brenda was sure she saw a new honor mark above his right knee. She supposed he would be equally at ease in a royal court or in the hut of a shepherd. She felt a shiver run down her backbone and a surge of pure joy that this man could put himself any-place on earth, be content with what he was doing and others would accept him with respect.

He stood quietly and looked at her. Then he led her to the oak logs and together they put fern and heather on them. To be next to him gave Brenda a soothing feeling that things would be all right. Finally, when he did not speak, she thought perhaps he had taken a wife. She was flustered, confused, blushed a fiery red and stepped away heavy-hearted.

"Brenda, where are you going?" he said softly. "We have not even said hello."

Brenda looked up into his face and felt her legs turn to mush.

"The Lord God and all the lesser gods know that I have waited a long time for this day, when I could be with you again," he said in a mellow voice that was like mead being poured into gold goblets.

"Aye, me too," she said, and the heaviness of her heart lifted.

He gathered her around the waist and pulled her close. At the same time someone set the oak logs on fire and for a wild moment she thought all that heat came from the kiss Sein planted on her forehead. "I love you and I will always love you no matter what happens," he said softly.

"I know," said Brenda. "I love you, no matter what." She had not planned to say that, but she knew it was true and had been true for a long time.

There was much to talk about. So much to tell each other about the years they had been apart. But today was the day to honor Annesta's short life, and today they were both tongue-tied and shy. They stood side by side holding hands, feeling the heat of the flames that consumed Annesta's earthly remains until there was no form, nothing but the lightest, softest gray ash that could fly away on a gust of wind. Brenda wept.

When the fire cooled, Gwalchmai made a speech saying that Annesta's spirit was with her grandfather's. "Some say life is preordained. I do not know, though I have thought about it many years." He said that there were countless others who also had been murdered and they were equally as important to their families. "This is a time *Y Cymry* cannot be proud of themselves. Annesta's spirit is free to wander again. It comes here, now there, and occupies whatever frame the gods decide. From beasts it passes into humans, and from humans into beasts. In the end some say the spirit goes on to Heaven or Hell but never perishes. I cannot say much about this because I do not yet know."

Sein stepped away from Brenda, stood with Gwalchmai before the crowd and said, "I be not going to tell Annesta's husband a handful of platitudes, such as his grief will heal in time or that he needs to find something useful to fill his time. In his heart he knows this." He put his arm across Gwalchmai's stooped shoulders and said, "I cannot believe the gods determine eternal life for some in Heaven, and for others who have not earned salvation, everlasting Hell. I believe naught happens without cause. The chief cause of this young woman's senseless death was power. 'Twas ambition for domination and amassing land by Lord Dafydd of Gwynedd, a New Religionist and King Henry's puppet. In my mind a person's destiny is not always his choice, but still that person can bring good to himself and others. 'Tis an accomplishment. There are times when one person's destiny destroys others. If 'tis not

accidental, that destruction is wrong. But people do not always
have control to stop the wrong. Control and destiny begin with
ourselves.

"Today we honor Annesta, granddaughter of the bard,
Llwyarch, mother of Gwenllian, wife of the trader, called the
shipmaster-priest, who is my most beloved fosterling."

Brenda told herself that she knew Annesta better than anyone, except perhaps Madoc, and it was right for her to tell the
gathering about Annesta's courage. She moved to the front
and stood with her back straight and her eyes on the crowd.
"Today I be not a druid," she said, "but I notice that tomor-
rows bring inexorable things." Then she told the story of Annesta swallowing her grandfather's ashes because she could
find no suitable place to house them and could not bear to
have Lord Dafydd or his dragons discover them. She told how
she and Annesta ran through stinkball smoke toward the
Gwennan Gorn before another barrage of rocks, battle-axes
and spears began flying over their heads. It was a glorious
feeling to feel safe on the ship's deck, but a terrible irony took
place because of the path of an arcing arrow that found Annesta's throat instead of her own. "Dafydd told an untroth, that
I poisoned Prince Owain and for that he means to kill me."
She told them that she believed the same energy behind that
arrow was organized to wipe out all druids and it could be
stopped only if druids left this land. "Annesta wished to be
cremated, and as she was in life close to her grandfather, so
shall she be close to him in death. Their ashes together in one
jar will rest on a shelf in the sacred cromlech. I believe their
spirits have come to visit us today."

There were murmured verilies, like amens, and wet eyes
when she finished. Llieu put his hand on Brenda's shoulder
and pointed to Madoc, who was sitting near the front of the
crowd. His unshaved face was drawn, with dark circles under
his eyes. A smile of extraordinary, heart-rending gratitude
curved his pale lips.

Brenda went to him and sat down.

Llieu stepped to the front of the crowd. " 'Tis yonder trader
that we console," he said. "He is the druids' future, our destiny. Last night when most of you slept, he walked the shore

with Sigurd, Caradoc and me. We watched the sky and talked of the men and women who came before us and how they also knew the placement of the stars and the movement of the moon and sun. We talked about the spear of sunlight that touches that white stone inside the small cave once a year. He asked questions about the smallest details of the earth and the sea. Sigurd told him that the position of stars change when one sails either far north or far south from our homeland. Caradoc said that the evening star cannot be used for navigation because it disappears and a few days later becomes the morning star.

"When we were finished answering his questions he said, 'Before more hearts are broken, more corpses are counted, I have a dream of filling ten sails with druids and going west to unproved lands.' This man knows more than most shipmasters about Brendan's voyages and the Norsemen's manner of building ships. Before becoming a trader he was a Gwynedd emissary to France and a sailor on a trading ship that went as far north as Iceland. For a long time he has dreamed of sailing to lands where no man has set foot. 'Tis said that druidic knowledge will never die, but flourish in another place. This is the man to fulfill that prediction. He is one of us, a druid."

Finn came forward, stood beside Llieu and said, "Today this Welshman is comforted by Gwenllian, a wee lass, who shall keep the spirit of Annesta, her mother, alive. For us the trader, called Madoc, is willing to trade the known for the unknown. I say, wrap him in friendship; the tiniest moments of love are precious."

Madoc stood up and walked to the front of the assembly. "My beloved wife and I thank you." His voice rang out like the crackle of lightning. "I say to all of you who will follow me to a new, unproved place. 'Tis time to be ready to leave the familiar for the unfamiliar. I be not your protector and I do not have a wife to keep me home. But I be of sound mind and willing to help you save yourselves and the knowledge gleaned throughout nine times nine times nine generations of Old Religionists. 'Tis only my wife's—Annesta's—terrible death that makes this mystery of destiny possible." He had to think consciously of speaking Annesta's name out loud, to push it out into air waves that touched the ears of others.

There was stunned silence and wonderment among the people. This was far more than the usual eulogy. There were whispered questions about this unproved place and no real answers.

Later that day, the second part of the ceremony took place. At the ring of stones Sein, head of the Irish druids, led them in songs, and the fosterlings played harps. The songs were meant to help Annesta on the final leg of her spirit journey to the Otherside. Gwalchmai strummed his favorite crwth and sang poems about how beautiful Gwynedd was in the old times.

Madoc imagined he could feel the presence of Annesta all around him, even though he was sure, in life, that she had never been to this place. He closed his eyes and heard her singing and saw her smile as she ran toward him with arms outstretched, auburn hair flying and eyes bluer than the sea on a summer day.

Later, when the sun was gone, a small bonfire was built between the king stone and heel stone. Vivian and Eira brought out bread, cheese and mead. The people spoke quietly among themselves as they ate. Some came to say a few words to Madoc, who sat with Brenda and Sein.

Brenda, her chestnut hair in braids to her waist, felt herself drawn to Sein as though she were made of bits of dark iron and he were a magnet. She looked around and wondered out loud why Riryd and Goeral and Willem were absent.

"Sshh!" Sein whispered. "They have gone across the Irish Sea in a curragh, to work on the ships."

"I wanted Madoc to meet them and know he truly had a brother and sister," Brenda whispered back.

" 'Tis better for him to meet them later, when he is himself."

Sein cleared his throat. "I intend to tell you that I welcome you and ask that you stay with us—with me."

"I will not soon go back to Gwynedd," she said. "I want to be useful here."

Eimher, a dark Irish lass, brought a crying Gwenllian to Brenda, who put the infant against her shoulder and patted her until the crying stopped. Tentatively Brenda offered the baby to Madoc, who first looked away, then after a long moment, smiled at his daughter. The vast emptiness that was in the middle of him, that would never completely go away, began to shrink and he thought, Anger and warring have naught to do with this wee one. Such a small thing should not suffer because her mother is gone. My own mother and my foster father, Sein, are the best any child could ask for. He thought of his childhood with Sein. "You had better behave, my wee Gwenllian, or you will find that Sein can be like a brown wolf and his disapproving growl hurts worse than a dozen strikes on the backside," he said.

The next morning Brenda went with her son to the ancient cromlech where seven-year-old Madoc had taken the ashes of his first foster family. As before, Madoc carried a white clay jar of ashes. Brenda carried something hidden under her bratt. They sang Welsh songs to cheer both Annesta's and Llywarch's spirits. The singing made them feel less sad.

Brenda stood on her toes to place her silver hair clasp on the cromlech's whitewashed shelf beside the clay jar and said, " 'Twould have looked pretty in Annesta's auburn hair." Then she pulled out a crwth from under her bratt and put it on the shelf beside the jar. " 'Tis a gift to Llywarch from Gwalch-mai," she said. "If I stay here, will you let Gwenllian stay with me, while you work on your ships? *Os gwelwch chi'n dda.* I will continue the practice of healing arts, become a druidess, possibly a Wise Woman. This is my trail as far as my eyes can see."

"Aye, my daughter could have no better care, but I want you to think about something else," said Madoc. He wondered if he was going over the line to ask what was on his mind. Then quickly he said, "Sein? What do you think of him?"

Brenda's eyes showed surprise at Madoc's boldness. At first she wanted to tell him it was not his business, so she hesitated. After some thought she said, "You know I have always believed Sein is one of those grand men who come once in nine generations."

"Would you be his mate?"

"What?" Brenda eyed Madoc with suspicion, wondering if

Sein had asked him to see what she would say.

"He loves you."

"Well, what do you think?" she asked.

"I think you should—together, you could be the best medicine team on proven land, mayhap unproven land. The two
of you would give Gwenllian a wonderful life. You would be
a family."

"I will think about it. Now, hush," she said, when he tried
to interrupt. " 'Tis my desire and responsibility to care for your
wee one. If I ever mate, Sein will be my choice. Likewise,
'tis your responsibility to go back to Wales, repair those
wretched ships and figure out how to sail the druids to a land
of peace. The gods give us hope to replace sadness, but we
are left with the work. Llywarch used to say that crisis is
opportunity. I know now what he meant."

Madoc's heart felt a surge of love for his mother. He gave
her a quick hug and was back in a few minutes with a handful
of small white quartz stones and half a dozen bright bluebells.
He put the stones in a ring around the white jar and poked the little
bluebells into the gray ash. In his hand, he rolled the little
quartz crystal Annesta had given him the day they had married
themselves. He put it back in his pocket and from under his
tunic pulled out a round rim from the wickerwork of Gwenllian's shield. He placed it behind the jar, giving the bluebells
a kind of halo. For a moment he could not speak. He wiped
his eyes before the tears spilled and looked here and there on
the shelves. He found three small dusty bowls, their ash hard
with age. He laid a bluebell in each bowl. Around the three
bowls lay an elliptical hoop made of thin pieces of dusty, dried
gray wood. It was the rim of a cradle or tiny coracle. He
picked it up, wiped it clean and whispered, "I be still outside
the loops." He reached into his tunic pocket and took out the
old pouch with the broken cord. Inside was his silver bratt-
brooch embossed with the three lions. The same brooch had
once held his diaper cloth together and showed that he was
related to the royal court of Gwynedd. "This belongs to Gwenllian. Mayhap 'twill help you tell her who she is, give her life
meaning and purpose."

Brenda put the brooch in her pocket. "You know I shall

tell her about her mother and father every day."

"Take this to help care for you and Gwenllian." He gave her the linen purse Annesta had kept full of coins.

"Aye. Your wee Gwenllian shall be safe with Sein and me in Erin."

After the midday meal Brenda went out with Conlaf to comb the fields for wild clover and flaxseed.

"Sein called a council meeting for tonight," he said. "I would slay a dragon to be a physician on one of Madoc's westward-sailing ships. I may go back to Wales with him."

Brenda's heart skipped a beat and she said to herself, Young men are carefree but reckless. They are the ones who take the big chance and make the big change. What happens if Madoc finds new land? Or will he be drowned at sea? Will he return for his daughter? Will Sein want to go with him? Things are moving faster than I dreamed. "What about Llorfa?" she asked aloud. "She loves you."

"Brenda, you are a healer and I thought you knew that a man's love is a thing apart from his life. 'Tis a woman's love that is her whole life. Madoc controls his thoughts and emotions while he builds a wall around Annesta's memory. He bites on tough meat and will use all his intelligence and energy to find this new land where no man in druid memory has gone. He will plant crops, build cottages—mayhap on the other side of the earth—then return for others, like horses, sheep, cattle and women. Madoc anticipates his life being hard. He does not now need another woman to make life soft. I too be such a man.

"Llorfa and I will always be friends; we cherish each other. I love her as much as I can love any woman, but our work is our first love. We both understand that. When Madoc and I return, I shall ask Llorfa to come back with me, but I will not force her. Madoc will want you and Gwenllian to return with him, but he will not force you."

The council was held at sundown, outside the caves under a ring of nine oaks. The archdruids, in their gray gowns, stood inside the ring, as silent as the old sacred oaks. The moment

the sun streaked its final day-path across the center of the ring
and sank below the horizon, Archdruid Llieu praised the gods
for protecting Lord Iorwerth and most of his people during
the battle of Afon Ganol. He added a thanks to the gods for
hiding the unfinished ships from the eyes of Lord Dafydd, near
the tiny village of Abergele. He pointed to Madoc in his black
Augustinian gown and cowl, standing in the center of the ring.

Madoc pushed back his cowl and said simply that he was
going to sail to the other side of the earth. He paused long
enough for the words to soak in.

"There are those who believe the earth is flat and the sea
falls over the edge into darkness ad infinitum," he began. "We
know that wise men from early times made measurements
from one side of the horizon to another and said the earth is
round. The earth travels around the sun. I be asking permission
to build ten sails and man them with druids. I want to start a
colony in a new land, where people of the Old Religion are
safe to gather in one place or to separate to their own crofts.
A land where brother does not slay brother, no druid is beheaded out of jealousy and no one covets the land of another.
I look for a place where druidic knowledge is not feared. I
shall find a place where carefully placed stone circles and astronomical markings will not be disturbed. Where men can
study the movement of the sun, moon and stars, the winds,
plants and animals without fear of being gutted or beheaded.
I will take two hundred men, mostly druids, who keep the old
knowledge and wisdom alive while learning new. I will sail
south, not north to the Northmen's western colony, where cold
pillars of crystal float nine months out of the year. I will go
past Portugal to the Fortunate Islands, then west across the
Great Western Sea to a warm, fertile land. I must know by
tomorrow morning what you decide." He stopped to let the
council think on his words. Then, before anyone could raise
an eyebrow, he said, "If you grant me permission to rebuild
the rest of my ships and a colony on unknown land, I will
fetch the valuables that are hidden in the Aberffraw Prydian
camp, if they are not already looted."

Llieu smiled and was pleased that Madoc had used the suggestion to show good faith. If the druids did one thing for him,

he would do another for them that they had not been able to do, because Dafydd's soldiers skulked around the Aberffraw camp day and night. Madoc was just.

Brenda nudged Molly and said, "I do not think he should make such a fetching, 'tis too dangerous. I know what is happening around Aberffraw!"

"You sound like a mother," said Molly, patting her hand.

Madoc walked away so the council could go to the caves and debate in secret, but Conlaf called him back. "Why must you know so soon?"

"If building is delayed and word gets out that a Welshman is sailing to the other side of the earth, there are those who will sink my ships before they leave port. If 'tis rumored that I sincerely believe the earth is round and travels 'round the sun, the New Religion priests will have my head lopped off for blasphemy. They *know*, from no study, but from stories of superstitious sailors, that the world is flat and the seas, which have never run out of water, pour over the side into darkness, forever. These New Religionists also *know* the earth is the center of the universe and does not move, but 'tis perched on a mystical scepter, while the sun and moon and stars circle it. We know for troth that the moon travels in a wobbly, round path, and only returns to the same position every eighteen and a half years. We know from hundreds of years of study at the stone circles that the earth is not the center. But troth cannot be forced on those who close their eyes and minds. Only time will open them, and I do not have that much time.

"The men who volunteer to be my seamen or whom I choose to sail my ships will be sorely harassed if their names be told. Their lives will be in danger. I believe we ought to leave before word gets around and fall rains begin. Think about it. Tell me your decision at sunrise." Madoc left.

"It makes me proud just to know that lad, who was chosen by the gods to protect us druids," said Molly. "I learned about Madoc from Llieu when I was given honor marks." She held out her hands, dry and brown as seaweed, with blue fretwork around each fingernail.

"He is a secret between druids and me," said Brenda.

"So, I be a druid," said Molly. "Let me tell you, I be a

mother with a heavy heart, but I be ready to let my older boys go. If I were a lad, I would go in a minute, no matter what my mother said."

"You are a saucy minx," said Brenda. "My firstborn, Riryd, and my new son-in-law, Willem, are going. Oh, Molly, our world is changing. I do not know whether to cheer, laugh or cry. I feel half hysterical, and half in awe at what is taking place."

"We had better stick together," said Molly. "You talk to me. I will talk to you."

Brenda watched from the doorway as the dawn came and went, but still the archdruids had not emerged from the cave. She paced and fretted and finally pulled a blanket around her shoulders and went outside to wait.

Someone came from behind and sat beside her. She thought it was Molly and whispered, "By the gods 'tis hard on a mother waiting for an answer."

An arm went around her shoulders and Sein's voice said, "The council gave its permission, but first Madoc must go to Aberffraw."

"Why did it take so long to decide?" asked Brenda.

"Well, Gwalchmai sang, we argued and said some secret chants and prayers for advice. I tried to convince those old men that Madoc was the only man who had taken matters into his own hands to save the Old Religion from oblivion. I told them that if druids did not find a peaceful place to study and teach and take their women, they would all be wiped out or die in secret hidey-holes, leaving little to remind generations to come of their existence as surely as the monks who moved to the Faeroes with no women. Finn said that if Madoc and his ten sails full of druids were lost in a storm, future generations would never know of them. Sigurd said, 'If Madoc finds unproved land, how long will it take before he comes back to Wales or Ireland?' Someone else asked, 'Will he come back or will his ships be lost on the return trip?' Then Gorlyn topped all by asking, 'Will he bring back minerals, stones, plants and animals and beautiful women never seen before, unknown to us?' No one could answer any of those questions and it was decided to call Madoc back."

"Whatever for?" asked Brenda, feeling a catch in her throat. "Did they want to change his mind?"

"Llieu cleared his throat several times and said that he had something that belonged more to Madoc than to him and he held out his fist, and gave a little speech. This is what he said, almost word for word:

" 'Remember how long we kept Lord Howell in camp before his tongue healed? He was grateful that he could talk. He gave me this to show his appreciation for the good nursing care you and Conlaf gave him. I did not have the heart to say that if he referred only to your care, Madoc, his tongue would have fallen off.'

"The old druids chortled, remembering how clumsy Madoc was with sewing wounds. When they were quiet Llieu opened his hand. There was a gold ring with an onyx stone on which had been carved the arms of the house of Gwynedd, three lions, one under the other, on a shield."

Her eyes filled with tears. "I have known this all my life. 'Tis predestination. You do not believe in predestination. You believe a man makes his own destiny. But I am telling you, the gods have a reason for everything and they are getting their way. Madoc is going to be a leader of men. The gods must have slept well last night. I be glad and I be sad. If Madoc were to ask me what he ought to do, I would tell him to go, but my heart would shout, Stay here with your daughter and your mother! Stay and promote peace and prosperity in this unhappy province!"

"And if he took your heart's advice, how many more druids would lose their lives?" said Sein.

She thought awhile and said, "Are you going with him?"

"Nay, by the time he leaves I will have a wife and child to look after. My wife and I shall be known as the best healers around Dubh Linn. If the Welsh bring their warring here, you and I will care for the wounded and the orphans. In our own way we shall promote peace."

A tingle ran down Brenda's back and her throat tightened. She put her arms around Sein's neck and kissed him on one cheek then the other, and when he did not say anything she kissed him hard on the mouth. "Riryd and Willem are going with Madoc," she finally said. "Until they return, you, Goeral, and I shall make a fine family for Gwenllian."

"Goeral shall look after Gwenllian while you and I take long walks in the woods," he said, his eyes shining. "Let me tell you the rest of Llieu's speech before I forget. Do not turn around, but everyone inside is watching us."

Brenda turned and saw Molly's laughing face peeking out from the shutter. She blinked and saw more faces. Even old Finn was there!

"Ignore them. They are just busybodies. Sit still and listen. Llieu said on account of Madoc belonging to the House of Gwynedd, he might do more to put North Wales on the map than any of her other rulers. He said Madoc was entitled to wear the ring whenever and slipped it on his left middle finger. Madoc just stared at it, then said, 'I thank you. I shall claim any unproved land, by authority of this ring, for the province of Gwynedd. I want you to be on one of my ships.'

"Llieu looked at him with the tiniest of smiles curling his lips and he said, 'Lugh knows I would like naught better than to see unmapped land, study new sights and be a real part of forming the laws of a new settlement as long as I do not lose all of my teeth and die of the black rot while sailing in one of your ships, my foster son. If you promise not to chain me like a slave to the oarlocks and the gods permit, I shall come.' Llieu took Madoc's hand and pressed the ring to his cheek. He had tears in his eyes when he said, 'I will not tell you this often, but you are like a true son to me, even though Sein also calls you son and Llywarch called you grandson.' "

"What did Madoc say?" breathed Brenda.

"In the torchlight I saw his sea-blue eyes meet Llieu's green ones and he said, 'I have had more than my fair share of fathers and the amazing thing is I cannot complain about any of them. I not only love but truly like all of them.' He laid two fingers below Llieu's elbow in the druid handshake and came over to do the same to me. And said close to my ear, 'I have a brave and beautiful mam that I want you to cherish forever.' "

"So will you?" said Brenda, wiping her eyes to see better the first long rays of sunlight turn orange and pink over the hills in the west.

"Aye," said Sein. "Madoc promised to have the druids settled and be back for their women and children in not more than two years. He goes with ten seaworthy sails before the year is out. Tomorrow he leaves for Wales on the *Gwennan Gorn*, with half a dozen of our people, to finish repairing his ships."

"So soon! I would have suggested he ask Llieu where he thinks all the coins to get the necessary work done on those ships are going to come from."

Sein laughed and kissed Brenda long and hard so everyone watching could see. Afterward he put his mouth close to her ear and said, "I have word that during the grain sale you saved Lord Iorwerth's life. You have proven yourself eligible to be a druidic Wise Woman. I be pleased to invite you to become a druidess—a Wise Woman—this night before the moon is at apogee. I mixed the woad solution and will tattoo your honor marks myself. What do you say?"

"I accept the honor," she said without hesitation. "I have studied long to reach this goal."

"One more thing," said Sein. His eyes sparkled plain as a fish in a shallow pond. "I have something to teach you about grown sons. Have you noticed that lads, especially shipmasters, no matter what is said, do not take kindly to suggestions from their mother?"

"Aye," she said, smiling. "Have you noticed, no matter what, I love you?"

Afterword
Brenda's Legacy

He [Madoc] was an expert mariner and he determined according to the story to sail away from his native land, to find a country where he could know peace and quiet, if such a country existed.

Zella Armstrong, *Who Discovered America?*

The Mandans, whom I found with so many peculiarities in looks and customs . . . might possibly be the remains of this [Madoc's] lost colony, amalgamated with a tribe, or part of a tribe, of the natives, which would account for the . . . changed character and customs of the Welsh Colonists.

George Catlin, *Letters and Notes on the Manners, Customs, and Conditions of North American Indians*

The exploits of Brenda's son, Madoc, in Wales, France and Iceland are another story. The migration of the Welsh up the Missouri River and into Central America followed Madoc's second voyage to bring Welshwomen and fresh horses to his new colony. Centuries later, this odyssey terminated with an unusual North American tribe of people first recorded in 1738 by the French explorer, Sieur de la Vérendrye. He believed that tribe, called the Mandans, had European ancestry. A hundred years later George Catlin, artist and author, painted pictures and wrote about the blue-eyed, blond and red-haired Mandan Indians, who used bowllike fishing craft astonishingly similar to the Welsh coracle. Other early explorers in North Dakota's Knife River region reported that the language, winter tales, motte-and-bailey shelters and palisaded walls of the Mandans appeared to be Welsh.

Two intriguing questions are not answered in bardic poems or in our present history books: Was Brenda, the heroic Irish-Welsh maiden, the ancestral mother of the North American Mandan Indians and were the Mandans the New World connection to Old World druidism?

Circle of Stones is the first in a series of historical novels based on these provocative questions. I hope Brenda's story and those that follow, leading up to the end of the Mandan civilization in the nineteenth century, not only entertain you but leave you fascinated with history you may not know.

—Anna Lee Waldo

Acknowledgments

I thank my husband, Bill, for his support. He went to Wales with me in May 1980. Enthusiastic but with concentrated care, he drove on the left side of the road in a car with the steering wheel and gear shift on the "wrong side." We went to museums, libraries and historical sites all over the Welsh landscape, where there was perpetual variety. Wales has a never-ending green beauty, mountains, rock walls, sheep and slate in the north; pine trees and coal mines in the south. The people are a delight: lustily friendly, mysterious, stubborn, evasive, romantic and intelligent.

I express my appreciation, from the bottom of my heart, to *Y Cymry* whose names follow, for their help and advice in my investigation of the old Madoc legend:

Librarian R. Geraint Gruffydd, Archives Assistant Catherine Hughes, and Senior Assistant Archivist Ann Thomas at the National Library of Wales, Aberystwyth; Architect Vernon Hughes, specializing in conservation and Welsh architectural history; Trefor M. Owen, Welsh Folk Museum Director, University College of North Wales, Bangor; Iorwerth Peate, Welsh Folk Museum Curator, St. Fagan's Castle, Cardiff; Richard White, Gwynedd Archaeological Trust Director, University College of North Wales, Bangor.

I thank the women, who would not give me their names, at the County Offices, Archives Services, Caernarfon, where I obtained one of the genealogies of "the Tribe of Owen Gwynedd," which listed Madoc as one of Prince Owain's fourteen illegitimate children; Madoc's mother, Brenda, as Owain's mistress, the daughter of the Irish Lord, Howyl of Carno, and a permanent resident of Gwynedd's royal court in North

Wales. Before Madoc was born Brenda gave birth to Riryd and Goeral, who were fostered by her father in Ireland.

Geographer Michael Ratcliffe was a great help on the coinage of twelfth-century Wales.

I am immensely grateful to Oscar Collier and Susan Spano for the time they spent reading and commenting on my original manuscript.

My agent, Jean Naggar, suggested I cut the weighty, thousand-plus-page original manuscript into two parts. "Separate Brenda's story from Madoc's story," she said. I confess that it took months before I appreciated her suggestion. Now I applaud Jean and her staff for their intelligence and patience.

I praise the *rhyfedd*, editorial expertise of Jean Brody, for knowing exactly which "thrilling" dramas to slash.

Hope Dellon and Regan Graves, and everyone in the Editorial Division of St. Martin's Press, deserve gold stars for their enthusiastic work to bring the finishing sparkle to Brenda's story. I am truly grateful for the copyeditor, Karen P. Thompson.

I thank all the copyright owners, authors, publishers, and people who so generously gave me their permission to use quotations from their books, magazines, pamphlets or journals.

Finally, I am thankful for Richard Deacon and Zella Armstrong for their diligent research and George Catlin for his writings and paintings of the Mandan Indians. The three of them inspired me to go ahead with this whole big project.

Bibliography

ASTRONOMY

Jastrow, Robert and Malcolm H. Thompson, *Astronomy: Fundamentals and Frontiers.* New York: John Wiley and Sons, 1977.

Lerner, Eric J., "Space Weather," *Discover*, Vol. 16, No. 8: August, 1995.

BRENDA AND MADOC

Armstrong, Zella, *Who Discovered America?* Chattanooga, Tenn.: The Lookout Publishing Company, 1950. Interesting material about Brenda and her son Madoc and Prince Owain's family.

Bowen, Benjamin F., *America Discovered by the Welsh.* Philadelphia: J. B. Lippincott and Co., 1876.

Dane, Joan, *Prince Madoq: Discoverer of America.* London: Elliot and Stock, 1909. A romantic novel.

Deacon, Richard, *Madoc and the Discovery of America.* New York: Braziller, 1966. Contains much well-researched historical material.

Iomaire, Liam Mac Con, *Ireland of the Proverb.* Grand Rapids, Mich.: Masters Press, 1988.

Rhys, Aurther, "Did Prince Madoc Discover America?" Chicago: A pamphlet by A. Rhys, 1938.

Williams, Gwyn A., *Madoc, The Making of a Myth.* London: Eyre Methuen, 1979.

CELTS

Markale, Jean, *Women of the Celts*, translated by Mygind, Hauch and Henry. Rochester, Vermont: Inner Traditions International, Ltd., 1986.

Rees, Alwyn and Brinley Rees, *Celtic Heritage*. New York: Thames and Hudson, 1978. Good for Celtic traditions, holidays and mindset.

DRUIDS

Bonwick, James, *Irish Druids and Old Irish Religions*. London: Sampson Lae, Marston, 1894.

Ellis, Peter Berresford, *The Druids*. Grand Rapids, Michigan: Willian B. Eerdmans Publishing Company, 1994.

Elder, Isabel (Hill), *Celt, Druid and Caldes*. London: Covenant, 1938.

Frazer, Sir James George, *The Golden Bough*. New York: Macmillan, 1951.

Piggott, Stuart, *The Druids*. New York: Thames and Hudson, 1985.

Wright, Dudley, *Druidism, The Ancient Faith of Britain*. London: E. J. Burrow, 1924. Today we know little about the religion, orders and life-style of druids, who were intellectuals, law givers, physicians and teachers. Julius Caesar left us the best, but sketchy description of druids.

GENEALOGY

Dictionary of Welsh Biography, Down to 1940. London: Printed under the auspices of the Honourable Society of Cymmradarion, 1940.

Griffith, John Edwards, FLS, FRAS, England, "Pedigrees of the Kings and Princes of Wales," *Pedigrees of Anglesey and Carnarvonshire Families with Their Collated Branches in Debighshire, Merionthshire and Other Parts, Compiled from Authentic and Reliable Sources*, p. 393. Printed by W. K. Norton and Sons, Ltd., 27 High Street, Horncastle, Lincolnshire, County Archives, Caernarfon, 1914.

O'Laughlin, Kathleen, *A Few Notes on Madoc ap Owen Gwynedd Including His Genealogy*. Ontario, Canada: St. Catherine's, 1947.

MEDIEVAL MEDICINE

Magner, Lois N., *A History of Medicine*. New York: Marcel Dekker, Inc., 1992.

Thorwalk, Jurgen, *Science and Secrets of Early Medicine*, translated by Richard and Clara Winston. New York: Harcourt, Brace and World, Inc., 1962.

Wellcome, Sir H. S., "Ancient Cymric Medicine," Swansea: *Meeting of British Medical Association*. B. Wellcome and Co., 1903.

MEDIEVAL SHIPS

Buechner, Frederick, *Brendan*. San Francisco: Harper and Row, 1988. This story was well written, like Irish poetry.

Freuchen, Peter, with David Loth, *Book of the Seven Seas*. New York: Julian Messner, Inc., 1967.

Severin, Tim, *The Brendan Voyage*. New York: Avon, 1978. Severin made the voyages of Brendan come to life.

Tryckare, Tre, *The Viking*. New York: Crescent Books, a Division of Crown Publications, Inc., 1986. Excellent descriptions, photographs and drawings.

Tword, Rolf, *Ships Through History*. New York: Bobbs Merrill Company, Inc., 1973.

PLANTAGENET ENGLAND

Barlow, Frank, *Thomas Becket*. Berkeley: University of California Press, 1986.

Collis, Louise, *Memoirs of a Medieval Woman*. New York: Harper and Row, 1964.

Oman, C. W. C., *The Art of War in the Middle Ages*. Ithaca, New York: Cornell University Press, 1986.

Rembar, Charles, *The Law of the Land*. New York: Simon and Schuster, 1980.

Strayer, Joseph R., ed., *Dictionary of the Middle Ages*, Vol. 4, New York: Charles Scribner's Sons, 1989.

Winston, Clara and Richard, *Daily Life in the Middle Ages*. New York: American Heritage Publishing Company, Inc., 1975.

WALES

Arnold, Ralph, *A Social History of England from 55 B.C. to 1215 A.D.* London: Constable Young Books, Ltd., 1967.

Barbier, Professor, *The Age of Owain Gwynedd*. London: Nutt and Company, 1908.

Beach, Russell, ed., Bassingstoke, Hampshire: *AA Touring Guide of Wales*. The Automobile Association, Fanun House, 1975. Excellent descriptions of Wales.

Craster, O. E., *Ancient Monuments in Anglesey*. London: Her Majesty's Stationery Office, 1977.

Dodd, A. H., *A Short History of Wales*. London: Granada Publishing, 1976.

Davies, V. Eirwen, *Gruffudd ap Cynan, 1055–1137*. Cardiff: University of Wales Press, 1959. Written for competition at the Ebbw Vale National Eisteddfod, 1958.

Gants, Jeffrey, translator, *The Mabinoqion*. New York: Dorsett Press, 1976.

Hartley, Dorothy, *Lost Country Life*. New York: Pantheon Books, 1979. Excellent information on the life of crofters.

Llewellyn, Sian, *The Welsh Kitchen*. Swansea: Celtic Educational Services, Ltd., 1977.

Macaulay, David, *Castle*. Boston: Houghton Mifflin Co., 1977.

Morris, Jan, *The Matter of Wales*. New York: Oxford University Press, 1984. Well-written description of the Welsh character and interesting, little-known bits of information.

Rein, Alan, *The Castles of Wales*. London: Letts Guides, 1973.

Smith, D. J., *Discovering Country Crafts*. Aylesbury, Bucks: Shire Publications Ltd., 1980.

Sobel, Dava, "Field of Dreams?" *Omni*, Vol. 3, No. 3, Dec., 1990.

Tomes, John, editor, *Blue Guide Wales and the Marches*. London: Ernest Benn Ltd., 1979.

White, Richard, *Early Christian Gwynedd*. Gwynedd: Snowdonia Press, 1975.

Willis, Michael J., *Discovering the Great Orme*. Aberconwy: Leisure and Amenities Department of Aberconwy Borough Council, 1977.

Woodward, B. B., *The History of Wales*. London: Virtue and Co., 1953.